ANCIENT LIGHT

By the same author:

A HAWK IN SILVER

GOLDEN WITCHBREED

ANCIENT LIGHT

MARY GENTLE

NAL BOOKS

NEW AMERICAN LIBRARY

NEW YORK
PUBLISHED IN CANADA BY
PENGUIN BOOKS CANADA LIMITED, MARKHAM, ONTARIO

NAL TRADEMARK REG. U.S. PAT. OFF. AND FOREIGN COUNTRIES
REGISTERED TRADEMARK—MARCA REGISTRADA
HECHO EN DRESDEN, TN

SIGNET, SIGNET CLASSIC, MENTOR, ONYX, PLUME, MERIDIAN and NAL BOOKS are published by NAL PENGUIN INC., 1633 Broadway, New York, New York 10019

Library of Congress Cataloging-in-Publication Data

Gentle, Mary.
  Ancient light.

  I. Title.
PR6057.E525A84   1989   823'.914   88-28904
ISBN 0-453-00644-2

First Printing NAL BOOKS, March, 1989

1 2 3 4 5 6 7 8 9

PRINTED IN THE UNITED STATES OF AMERICA

Acknowledgements

Many people have contributed to the writing of this novel, but I would like to thank, individually, the following, without whom *Ancient Light* would not exist:

David V. Barrett, who provided the music (especially *Redgum*) and much else besides;

Eda Field, who sent me a portrait of the Orhlandis, from Australia, and who asked the right questions;

Liz Foulger, for allowing me the benefit of her extensive medical knowledge;

Daphne Watson and Tony Warren, for the inspiration of the chapel at Milton Abbas;

Sarah Watson, who read the earlier part of the novel aloud, and commented honestly;

Sylvia Witherington, for her friendship and support.

Contents

Principal Characters

Lynne de Lisle Christie, special advisor to the PanOceania Company
Douglas Clifford, Earth envoy on Carrick V
Molly Rachel, PanOceania's Company Representative
David Osaka, Company Commercial Liaison officer
Pramila Ishida, Company Administrative officer
Rashid Akida, Head of the PanOceania research team
Dinu Machida, climatology
Chandra Hainzell, xeno-biology
Jan Yusuf, xeno-demography
Joan Kennaway, medic
Ravi Singh, xeno-physicist
Corazon Mendez, Commander of the Company Peace Force
Ottoway ⎰
           ⎱ lieutenants, her *aides*
Jamison ⎱
Stephen Perrault, acting head of the PanOceania Liaison Office on
   Earth

Dannor bel-Kurick, Emperor-in-Exile at Kel Harantish
Calil bel-Rioch, the Voice of the Emperor-in-Exile
Pathrey Shanataru, *aide* to Calil

Sethri-safere, of the *hiyek*-family Anzhadi, a leader of mercenaries
Jadur ⎰
Wyrrin-hael ⎱ members of Sethri's *raiku*
Charazir-hael ⎱
Hildrindi, of the *hiyek*-family Anzhadi, a *keretne* mystic
Feriksushar, of Hildrindi's *raiku*

the Hexenmeister, of the Brown Tower of Kasabaarde
Tethmet Fenborn, of the Tower
Annekt, a Kasabaarde trader

Haldin Damory, a mercenary of the Medued Guildhouse
Branic, her *aide*

9

Haltern n'ri n'suth Beth'ru-elen, a politician of the Hundred Thousand
Blaize n'ri n'suth Meduenin, an ex-mercenary
Nelum Santhil Rimnith, *T'An* of Melkathi province
Cethelen Khassiye Reihalyn, the Andrethe of Peir-Dadeni
Howice Talkul, *T'An* of Roehmonde province
Bethan n'ri n'suth Ivris, *T'An* of Kyre province
Geren Hanathra, *T'An* of Ymir province

Bekily Cassirur Almadhera, an Earthspeaker
Achil, an Earthspeaker
Jaharien Rakviri, *s'an* of Rakviri *telestre*
Haden Barris Rakviri, his *arykei*

Roxana Visconti, WEBcaster for the Trismegistus WEB
Mehmet Lutaya, WEBcaster for the Ariadne WEB

PART ONE

CHAPTER 1

Rooms Without Doors

The alien settlement merged with the desolate earth on which it stood, half a mile away. As I stepped down from the shuttle's ramp, I couldn't help thinking: *Is this the great discovery?*

Nothing but cleft and gully and hillock surrounding me; rock and stone and dust. To the south were cliffs, and a hint of mountains in the haze. And to the north, the Inner Sea.

The hot, bright winter light washed over me, shattering into dazzles on the sea. Too sharp and subtle, this white sun, Carrick's Star – and the pressure of the world underfoot, gravity slightly different. . . . All but imperceptible in these equatorial regions, Orthe's daystars shone. Orthe: Carrick V, whose sky is full of the Heart Stars, that cluster at the galaxy's core.

Then the smell hit me: an odour of heat and rock and rank water. That is the most ancient sense, and it bypasses rationality. For one second I felt hollow in the chest, as if I had been punched under the ribs, and I thought, *Orthe, this is Orthe, I remember* –

And then, like seeing a face once so familiar, that now you can't name, ten long years reasserted themselves and I thought, *I don't know this world at all.*

Which is unfortunate, girl, because that's what they've brought you back here for.

As if she were a mind-reader, the representative of the PanOceania multicorporate Company said, "You were never on this southern continent, were you, Lynne?"

"Once," I said. "Briefly. But that was a good few hundred miles west along the Coast from here. At least there they could scratch a living out of the dirt." And, looking round, I thought, *No species should be able to survive here, this land is sterile as a moon – !*

On other continents of this world, things are different.

The Pacifican woman left the shuttle-ramp and walked over to join me. The scrape of her boots on rock was louder than the lapping waves.

"The Earth-station on the northern continent must have more extensive records." She glanced across at me. "Do you want to stay in the ship? You look as if the heat's too much for you."

I glared at her. Molly Rachel's total lack of tact is something I find

13

disconcerting and pleasing in about equal measures. Only the young can be so honest.

"Molly, you think this is bad? You want to be here in the *hot* season. And shall we assume that a few years' difference in our ages doesn't make me either decrepit or mentally deficient?"

"Or even bad-tempered?"

"Oh, very witty."

I don't know why I like this woman when she irritates me so much. No, that's a lie. What I do know is that I have to dislike her, because I dislike what her people are going to do. And – God help me, being special advisor to her Company – her people are my people too.

Molly Rachel craned her neck, looking at the nearest settlement-structures. "I still find it difficult to believe we've found any kind of alien technology here. Either relics, or functional."

"*I* don't believe it's functional – "

Orthe's technological past is dead. The Golden Witchbreed are a dead race, perhaps as alien to this world then as we are now . . . and the high-level technology they had was destroyed, millennia past. Not without consequences: witness this desolate land.

" – but I know what you mean, Molly. This is a post-technological world, and pre-tech and post-tech societies don't look that different on the surface. Primitive. The difference – "

"Maybe there isn't much difference anyway. If the Ortheans allowed the necessary infrastructure for technology to decay, it's no wonder they're reduced to *this*."

I winced. She didn't notice. Orthe is more than this, I silently protested. Much more. But do I want the Company to realize that?

"Maybe things have gone too far," I said, "and then it won't matter if we *do* find a few artifacts that still function. Unless we're very lucky, that won't tell us the nature of the alien technology that built them."

And what if the artifacts that the xeno-archeology team found, so recently, tell you no more than the shells of ancient Orthean cities, that Earth has had ten years now to study? Or the ruins of the Rasrhe-y-Meluur, dead these three thousand years? What then?

"Maybe the Company needn't have come here," I suggested, but she shook her head, negating that.

She stood silhouetted against Orthe's pale blue sky: Molly Rachel, tall, angular and black, with a mass of fine-curled hair, and the flattened features of her Aborigine mother. Like most people from Earth's Pacific Basin area – Asia, India, South America, Australasia – she is possessed of a certain impenetrable self-confidence. It comes from knowing that

14

history is on your side. And since Earth's economic centre shifted there, we all take good care to be on the Pacifican side.

Dear God, I thought, was I ever that young? But come to think of it, she's thirty, and I was four years younger than that when I first set foot on Orthe.

A world must be vast, one thinks, taking in cities and mountains, ancient civilizations, strange skies and suns. But it shrinks. The whole bright gaudy carnival shrinks to a coloured dot in the night sky. And feels to me now like an achievement of youth, recognized and remembered, but put aside for other things.

A warm wind blew off the sea: sparky, salty, electric. Carrick's Star dazzled. The world touched me, alien and unfathomable, too real to be safely locked in a memory.

"One of us should stay here with the shuttle," Molly said. "David Osaka, or you?"

"David. The multicorporate's seconded me here to be advisor. Let's say I need a refresher on some points of alien culture."

The woman gave me a shrewd look. "I've studied your old reports. Let's say wild horses couldn't keep you out of.*that* settlement."

I laughed, but it was wry humour. Here, in the early light of the sun, the native settlement towered above us.

It is a settlement without streets or city walls.

Flat-roofed stone buildings clung together. Five- and six-sided, like the cells of a beehive; three storeys tall. All faced us at ground level with blank white walls; windows were fifty feet above us, black slots. Squinting up, I could see where wooden steps led from one roof level to another, and from there two or three different stairways led to different roofs, and in turn from them to others. . . .

Long shadows fell towards the west. I saw no movement on those roofs. Multiple layers of a celled alien city, a city like a scatter of sun-bleached dice.

The first exultation of arrival faded. This is not the same world and I am not the same person – and the reason I'm here is not the reason for which I would have chosen to return.

"Shall we go?" Molly Rachel said.

"Sure."

The morning sun glittered on the sea, and the white buildings shone, embedded in the rocky coast, and I took a sudden sharp breath.

Once I might, just *might*, have believed I would come to Orthe again. But I should never have believed this – that I would come to this backwater settlement on the shores of the Inner Sea, to the rumoured and disputed last stronghold on Orthe of the race called Golden Witch-breed . . . to the city of Kel Harantish.

A metallic note rang out. Flying rock-splinters stung my ankle.
I exclaimed sharply; simultaneously Molly said, "*Wait –* "
Nothing but silence and sun.
"That's close enough," she observed. "We'll consider ourselves warned."
A white chip scarred a boulder just ahead, and the sun picked out a metal dart that lay in the rubble. My heart hammered. I felt foolish, tricked. And at the same time irritated by the young woman's confidence.
"Some of the xeno-archeological teams have had this problem," she said.
"I've read the same reports that you have."
She gave me a very straight look.
Heat made movement an effort, slowed thought. The half-mile walk from the shuttle exhausted me. Now I looked up from the broken ground to the blank walls of the city that rose up like cliffs. I tasted dust on my lips. Walls and rock seemed all one colour, as if the sun had bleached them together for uncounted thousands of years; vertical slabs that leaned over us.
A foot scuffed rock.
"Lynne – "
Movement drew my eye: a humanoid figure that bent to pick up the fallen dart. Swift and economical action – but disorientating: the human eye reads alien musculature as *wrong*. As the figure turned, I saw the crest-like mane growing long on the narrow head and down the spine. Skylined, the proportions of his limbs subtly different from the human. I saw bleached skin with an almost imperceptible scale-pattern, as six-fingered hands gripped a crossbow-like weapon.
For a moment his glance caught mine, an almost triangular face, wide at the brow, narrow at the chin. His whiteless eyes blurred now with the movement of the nictitating membrane, that third eyelid of the Orthean race. A glance unfathomable and clear: ophidian.
Without the slightest forethought, I said, "*Kethrial-shamaz shan'tai.*"
A greeting and offer of hospitality, in a northern dialect of the language of the Desert Coast. And it was nothing to do with thirty-four days shiptime spent revising Orthean culture, but with that overpowering shock of familiarity.
The Orthean male didn't speak, but wound and reloaded the bow. A small group of Orthean natives appeared from the deceptive gullies. Molly Rachel walked forward until she could talk without raising her

voice, and in a southern Coast dialect said, "Give you greeting. You need not fire on us, we're not armed. Our weapons are in our ship."

That's a nice blend of conciliation and threat, I thought. Now why not try the Orthean for 'take me to your leader'?

Despite the heat, I felt cold. In the northern continent's settlements, I might know what to expect. But even there, time has passed. Here . . .

Orthean faces turned first towards the harbour, and then to the shore where the shuttle was visible, regarding it without detectable change of expression. There was a silence that made my mouth dry. They stood each a little distance from the next, and, as far as it is possible to read the signs, were both alert and afraid.

"There are just the two of us, at present," Molly Rachel added.

I saw two Orthean males and three females, with dyed-white manes that lay lank over tunics, and what looked to be a brown metal scale-mail. These carried winchbows. A fair-maned female leaned on a thin spear, her exposed lower torso showing the paired nipples of vestigial second breasts.

If I could read their faces, I would be terrified, I thought.

"Give you greeting, *shan'tai.*" A sleek, plump male stepped forward. Light glinted from his brown skin. His mane was braided elaborately, and chains and belts wound round his tunic-robe, but for all that, there was something indefinably seedy about him. Like the others, he stood a good handspan shorter than Earth-standard.

More comfortable now, I stepped up beside Molly. "*Shan'tai,* this is the representative of the Earth multinational corporate Company Pan-Oceania – " at least half of that had to be in Sino-Anglic and not Coast dialect " – who is called Molly Rachel. Our people have visited your city, a half-year ago."

The Orthean male seemed confused. I put it down to my imperfect memory of tenses.

"Our people came to study the ruins of the ancient Witchbreed civilization," Molly Rachel said. "*Shan'tai,* I believe we have business with the authorities in your settlement. We have come entirely without threat, and dependent on your goodwill. When will it be possible to discuss these matters?"

I mentally crossed 'assistant interpreter' off my list of duties. While the plump Harantish male spoke to his companions, I said: "You're fluent enough, aren't you? Hypno-tapes?"

"No. Hard work," the young woman said, without taking her eyes off the Ortheans. "Hypno-tapes scramble the brains."

There are times when I wish they'd known that ten years ago; it would have saved a lot of us time, trouble, and subsequent analysis. But I forbore to mention that. What she didn't say was, *Am I doing this right?* and what I didn't say was *Jesus Christ I hope so.*

The Orthean male turned back to us and said, "I believe you should speak with the Voice of the Emperor-in-Exile. These guards will see that you truly have no weapons. Then you may enter the lower city."

Molly Rachel let out a breath, momentarily relaxing; then she craned her neck to look up at the pale walls. The tension returned. Half of me thought, We've got closer than even the xeno-archeology team, they didn't get into the city itself. And the other half thought, This is Kel Harantish and I don't want any part of it! But that was the half that could remember the rumours and superstitions of an alien race.

"Do you want to go back to the ship?" the Pacifican woman asked.

It seems to me – though no doubt it's an illusion – that kids her age get through because they don't know enough to fear. And because they don't believe in luck.

"I'll come," I said. "The sooner this is proved a wild-goose chase, the sooner I can go home."

"You've *seen* the artifacts the team brought back. I don't believe the Company is wasting its time trying to analyse this technology – there must be some profit – " she broke off the long-standing argument, frustrated, as two of the Ortheans came to body-search for weapons.

Orthean skin is fine-textured, dry, warm; the beat of a different pulse beneath the surface. That brief touch brought back, shockingly abruptly, how it feels to dig fingers into the depths of a rooted mane. . . .

Dislocation of reality paralysed me for a moment. Air pressure and sunlight: *wrong.* The air rasped drily in my lungs. Daystars were pinpricks in the arch of the sky. But more – this heatstricken moonscape is not the Orthe of my memories, not this barren rock and sterile sea, without even the sound of an insect. I felt twice-exiled from expectation.

"This is a weapon," the plump brown-skinned male said, holding Molly's belt-communicator in his delicate hands.

"It's not a weapon, it enables me to speak with my ship."

The nictitating membrane slid over his dark eyes, and flicked back. He said, "I could imagine circumstances, *shan'tai,* in which that would prove as deadly as a winchbow. But keep it, if you will."

I had walked perhaps fifty yards closer to the city before I identified that gesture and tone as amusement.

Here the ground was smoother. I looked up, dazed with heat, to see the outcrops of buildings recede away and back, like chalk headlands. At the base of the nearest sheer wall, wooden platforms were being winched down on ropes.

Molly said, "There isn't *any* native vegetation or forestry. God, you don't realize what that means . . . didn't you say in your old reports that this place survives entirely on imported goods? What's funny?"

"You remind me of me," I said. "It's the sort of thing I used to notice. Generally when about to embark on something horrifically dangerous. . . . At the moment I'm just worrying about whether those rope and pulley contraptions are as unsafe as they look."

The young woman sighed, a little self-consciously long-suffering.

I saw how the nearest buildings stood separate, roofs on a lower level than the main mass. Rope-bridges, just visible, were slung across the narrow crevasse between this cluster and the city proper.

With a scrape of rock, the wooden platform grounded. We stepped on. The ropes creaked, and I caught Molly's arm to steady myself. The dark Orthean male got on with us. I reached out to touch the sheer city wall, and it was smooth under my palm, not yet fully warmed by the morning sun. Then the platform lifted and swung free.

"Pardon?" Molly Rachel said.

"Don't mind me – I can throw up quietly."

As we inched higher, I saw how ancient bedrock cropped out on this coast, worn down to this Harantish peninsula and a crescent scatter of islands that the sea could not erode. Far out on the water were sails, lost in the molten white glare.

"You come in trade-season," the dark male said. "Ships commonly come in Wintersun – if not commonly such ships as yours."

"*Shan'tai* . . ." Molly left a demanding gap.

"Pathrey Shanataru," he supplied.

"*Shan'tai* Pathrey, our archeological team didn't report any contact with the city authorities here."

"The Emperor-in-Exile has no love for your people," Pathrey Shanataru said. "He did not see them. He will not see you. You will meet his Voice."

"Who is Emperor-in-Exile now?" That alien title comes to me with no hiatus of memory: *K'Ai Kezrian-kezriakor*, the supposed lineal descendant of the rulers of the Golden Witchbreed.

Pathrey Shanataru said formally, "The present heir of the bloodline of Santhendor'lin-sandru is Dannor bel-Kurick."

"I think – I've met him?"

Pale sea and sky blotted out: for a second I felt dizzy and half blind – *some subterranean room, a chamber lit by candles set on rough iron stands. Candlelight and . . . the ruins of technology? He is bending over a panel or cube of some material. And then he lifts his head . . .*

That face that is half child and half old male: Dannor bel-Kurick. Wideset eyes veiled by nictitating membrane, white mane rooting down his spine;

and faded skin whose reptilian texture has in it a hint of dusty gold . . .

"How could you meet him?" Molly asked me in Sino-Anglic. "The archeological team said the local ruler doesn't leave this settlement."

The Emperor-in-Exile leave this paranoid fortress? No. But –

"I . . . may have seen a picture, I suppose."

She nodded, minimal curiosity satisfied.

I was suddenly uncomfortable, and pushed the thought away. That is ten years ago. Still, such a clear mental image of that face, and something *almost* there –

The wooden platform lurched to a halt, level with the flat roof. I stepped unsteadily on to plaster-roughened stone.

Surrounded again by guards, we were ushered across one roof and up a flight of wooden steps. Square penthouse-structures stood on each roof. As I stepped inside, under the low arch of the nearest, the sudden shadow blinded me. When I could see again, the plump male was already descending a rope-web that led down through a great open trap door. Molly Rachel followed him. I paused.

Ropes are easily cut, trap doors easily barred.

But I hesitated because of a much more mundane fear. I may have grown less agile than I once was; I have grown no greater liking for looking a fool.

Those Ortheans that carried winchbows remained on the roof. I climbed cautiously down, and found myself in a spacious room. Pale light slotted in through narrow windows. With some relief, I saw that a further trap door opened on descending stone steps. By the time our party had gone down two more floors, I realized something else: there were no interconnecting doors between individual buildings.

"Given the level of technology here," Molly Rachel observed, "this place must be impregnable."

Paranoia, I thought. To take Kel Harantish, you would have to take each building, individually, and from the top down. That partly solved a question long on my mind: how a settlement so hated and feared could remain undestroyed.

The male, Pathrey Shanataru, paused at the foot of the next steps. "*Shan'tai*, here you will meet the Voice of the Emperor-in-Exile."

Molly nodded, walking in front of me as we entered. This room was windowless, a silvery light reflected in by concealed mirrors; the air was hot and still. I heard someone move.

An Orthean woman rose from where she sat cross-legged on a mat by a low stone table. She was tall for a Coast Orthean: some five foot and an inch.

"*Kethrial-shamaz shan'tai*," she said, her voice oddly accented.

20

I could only stare.

This world's rumour says that the Kel Harantish Ortheans claim Golden Witchbreed blood. My memory, prompted by shiptime study, said, *But that race is extinct – surely? And Kel Harantish's claim, propaganda?*

Small, thin, electric: her skin was pale as stone-dust, in the room's dim light holding a faint glimmer of gold. Her white mane seemed so fine as to float on air, a breath of fire. I looked into her narrow-chinned face. Her eyes were yellow – buttercup-yellow, capriped-yellow, unnatural as flowers. She wore a white tunic girdled with thin gold chains, the tunic badly stained at the hem with spilt herb-*arniac*.

– stone arches that open upon depths, and that narrow face with coin-gold eyes, and the scent of charnel-halls –

With an effort, I shut the mental image out. Hypno-tape data thrown up by the chance firing of synapses, that's all; fragmented and confused by hypno-erasure and the passing of ten years. Maybe after a while I'll get used to it.

Molly Rachel said, "Thank you for consenting to see us, *shan'tai.*"

Orthean ages are difficult to judge: this women seemed younger even than Molly, but that might be deceptive.

"Pathrey told me that an offworlder ship had come. And that you would speak of what your people found in the Elansiir mountains." She seated herself again, and gestured for us to do the same. There was a stone table beside her that stood only a few inches above the floor, and on it were ceramic bowls containing a hot liquid. Droplets of steam coiled in the air, and there was a sharp strong scent: *arniac*-herb tea.

"The Company's archeological team brought several interesting artifacts to light in this area." Molly cupped one of the bowls in her pale palms. "Unfortunately it was at the end of their projected stay, so they couldn't complete their work."

"Complete?" queried the young Harantish woman.

"Establish if the artifacts were from the old technological culture, the Witchbreed."

I saw Pathrey Shanataru, who was kneeling down beside the Voice of the Emperor-in-Exile, hesitate momentarily at that word.

The woman linked claw-nailed hands. "Pardon, *shan'tai*, but that is the name that superstitious barbarians give us. We are the Golden."

Molly Rachel passed a ceramic bowl over to me. I was vaguely aware of her covert scan, and her nod that it was not poisoned. Crimson liquid steamed: the bitter *arniac*-herb tea of the Desert Coast. Taste and odour were utterly familiar. That hot drink scalded my mouth, brought back names and faces – memories of what this Harantish woman would designate the 'superstitious barbarian' northern continent, and that long year when Kel Harantish and the Emperor-in-Exile had seemed as much Earth's enemy as enemy of the Hundred Thousand.

"Earth may at some time in the future be interested in Golden science – "

The Orthean woman interrupted Molly: "More 'archeology'?"

"A more complete investigation."

The nictitating membrane veiled those chrome-yellow eyes. "Well now, *shan'tai*, do you know what that might mean?"

"I'm aware that certain cultures on this world are technophobic. Earth has no intention of importing technological knowledge. This is still classified as a Restricted world."

"What I meant, *shan'tai* Rachel, is that there have always been those who, since the Golden Empire fell, desired to build it anew. If they could not find the key to the lost science of those 'artifacts', how will you do so?"

'Artifact' is an interesting word. It doesn't have the implications of dysfunction that 'relic' does. I thought it time to interrupt, and disabuse the Voice of the Emperor-in-Exile of her ideas of ignorant offworlders.

"I understand that not *all* knowledge of Witchbreed technology is lost. Doesn't Kel Harantish maintain the canal system on the Desert Coast, keep it functioning?"

Molly Rachel said, "The Company is also very interested in the canals. We understand their construction dates from the time of the Golden Empire."

The Harantish woman shrugged. The humanoid frame admits of many variations. I watched the movements of alien musculature: the sharp-hulled ribs, thin limbs, the long-fingered hands and high-arched feet. Those signals that stance and gesture send are oddly muffled, uninterpretable. She looked at me: "You are not new to this world, *shan'tai*. What is your *hiyek* – your name?"

"Lynne de Lisle Christie," I said. "New to the Coast, *shan'tai*."

Molly leaned forward. As she spoke, she unconsciously hunched down, and I realized that with her height – she topped the two Ortheans by a good ten inches – she must feel giant-like.

"Naturally there would be the necessity for discussing trade privileges." She slightly stressed the final word.

The brown-skinned male, Pathrey, leaned over and muttered something inaudible to all but the Harantish woman; she, for the first time, smiled, and briefly touched his arm.

"Why, yes," she said; and then to Molly: "It seems you offworlders

22

have new ways of negotiating. You've quarantined us for ten years, and now this?"

Molly smiled. "What I say is of course subject to an Earth government's approval."

No kidding? They *will* be pleased to hear that. . . .

And then I thought, Sarcasm would become you better, Lynne, if you weren't Company-employed yourself.

Pathrey Shanataru said, "The northerners have been content with quarantine. What will you say to them, *shan'tai* Rachel?"

"That depends on how it concerns them." Molly, without a word, implied the addition *If it ever does*. . . .

Old habits die hard. With the Pacifican woman playing conciliator, it left me the perfect opportunity to ask awkward questions.

"If the Emperor-in-Exile has no intention of negotiating with us, is there any point to this?"

Pathrey Shanataru leaned forward as if to speak, and a mere gesture of the nameless woman's hand silenced him. Beginning to interpret Orthean expressions, I thought there was real fear on his face. For an instant it became real to me, this position of power: the Voice of the Emperor-in-Exile.

The young Orthean female rose and for a time walked back and forth, without looking at anyone.

Dropping back into Sino-Anglic I said to Molly, "Are you going to push this much further now?"

"I'll push as hard as I have to."

Pathrey Shanataru was kneeling beside the stone table, his gaze fixed on the Orthean woman. I wished desperately that I were reaccustomed to Orthean expressions.

I said to Molly, "I don't think you realize what a destabilizing factor Earth is."

The Harantish woman stopped, and then turned with a dancer's grace and balance. She spoke rapidly: "I'll see others close to the Emperor, later today. Pathrey, convey these *s'aranthi* to a place where they may rest until then – "

Her bare feet scuffed the stone steps, and she was gone.

"What – ?" Molly stood.

Pathrey Shanataru looked apologetic, almost embarrassed. He rose to his feet. "Pardon, *shan'tai*. I will show you to more comfortable quarters."

Molly looked at me, and I shrugged.

The dim silver twilight and heat were oppressive; to climb the steps –

23

even if only towards the scorching sun of the Coast in winter – felt like liberation.

As we stepped out on to the flat roof again, Molly said, in Sino-Anglic, "Do you think they know we've got Witchbreed artifacts that may well turn out to be functional?"

Before I could answer, Pathrey Shanataru spoke. In badly-accented Sino-Anglic he said, "Do you know who put them there for you to find?"

Stunned, I made to frame a question, but the Orthean male stepped aside and gestured for us to precede him down rope-webbing, into the entrance of the next building. Molly swung down, I climbed more slowly, and then I turned to Pathrey Shanataru.

We were alone.

The trap door fell shut above us. I heard the click of lockbars sliding into place.

CHAPTER 2

The Spoils of Kel Harantish

At midday everything stopped except the fighting.

Running footsteps sounded on the roof. The trap door vibrated, but stayed closed. I felt each sound, deep inside; a physical ache. There was a distant clash of metal.

"What the hell was that?"

Molly Rachel, from where she clung to the rope-webbing, leaned across to the narrow window. Her arms shook with the strain.

"No," she said at last, dropping lightly down. "I can't see anything but the sky."

The light of Carrick's Star slotted down from the high windows like bars of white-hot iron. Outside, it would be unbearable for human eyes without protective gear. Inside, the heat robbed any desire for movement.

I sat with the small comlink in my lap, the case open, trying to manipulate the receiver-amplifier. Static crackled in the hot twilight. My fingers were clumsy. That ache of tension settled in my gut.

Molly squatted down on her haunches. "I don't think it's the comlink. It's the atmospheric interference. Communications are hell on this world."

"After ten years, I'd've thought you'd've solved that one."

"Talk to the Company about my shoestring budget, why don't you."

The heat made me dizzy, made all movement exhaustion. I wiped sweat from my face. From outside came a cry that might have been pain or triumph or something quite other.

The comlink's static resolved into a voice.

"Here."

Molly took it. Her tone was sharp. "David? What's the situation there?"

". . . shuttle's secure. A few . . . groups from the settlement. You want me to take any action on that?"

"Negative. Not yet. Stay secure."

David's voice suddenly came through loud, Sino-Anglic accent plain. "Are you going to put in an official complaint to the native authorities?"

Molly looked at me, and then up at the trap door, and for the first time smiled. "I don't know if the 'authorities' now are the same ones that existed this morning. Why we had to arrive here just in time for a palace revolution. . . . Can you contact the orbital ship?"

"Negative. But we expected that."

"Sure. Contact me again if the situation changes."

She flipped the comlink case shut. One dark hand rested on it for a moment, as she stared blankly into the middle distance.

I said acidly, "As for being 'just in time' for a palace revolution – I doubt there would have been one at all if we hadn't arrived. Whichever faction supports contact with Earth, we've made it worth their trying to take control here. . . . I thought that was likely, when we were kept away from the Emperor-in-Exile."

The air was hot, stifling. The trap door that led down into the lower building was also locked. Claustrophobia ran a close second to hunger and thirst.

"It's like you said, Lynne, we're a destabilizing factor," the Pacifican woman agreed, "but that's inevitable."

"Is it? – No, *is* it? Molly, you tell me. PanOceania doesn't *need* to be here –"

She stood, rising to her full height, took a few steps and then swung round: "Tell me what *you* know about it. You were envoy here for eighteen months, and that was ten years ago! For God's sake stop acting as if you owned the place. And if you'd like to get off my back for five minutes, I'd feel a whole lot better! I don't hear anything from you except criticism. And if I want advice, which is what you're here for, all I get is –"

"Is what?"

" – is you acting like a sulky three-year-old. You're paid to do a job here. For God's sake, Lynne!"

"Shit," I said.

I thought, Dear God I'm too old for this, what am I doing here, I don't have to take this –

Midday silence is oppressive; the ear needs birdsong or human voices. There was not even alien sound. Two of us, in the heart of a violent city. Sometimes it's safer for one to come alone, one is easily missed. With two . . . well, then, an example can be made of one of them, the least valuable. What price a Company representative here? I thought. What price a special advisor?

"This place unsettles me," I said.

The young woman still stood looking down at me, with fading anger. I felt ashamed of half-hearted apologies.

I said, "You're doing what I used to do here, as envoy. And maybe doing it rather better. So."

"So tell me something I don't know." She gave me a brat's grin, and sat down again, long legs folding under her.

"Sorry. It's because of having been First Contact with this world. I know that if it hadn't been me, it would have been someone else, but . . . there's a responsibility. Maybe a guilt."

The white square of sunlight had moved on the dusty floor, falling now to illumine the corner of a low stone table. Molly leaned back against the wall. She watched the narrow slot of sky. Then she turned her dark, dazzled face towards me.

"Not guilt. A world's too big for one person's responsibility."

I've lost the ability to balance fear against result, and gamble. This angular young woman has it still.

"It's . . ." I searched for words. "It's as if I'd stepped back into the past, to my year on Orthe, and it was being repeated in a minor key. The same theme, but somehow darker."

"Ah, but those days, the Dispersal – it was a bit unreal. You could touch worlds and hardly change them. It isn't like that now."

Her tone carried the conviction that her present time and 'the real world' are identical.

A shadow flicked across the falling sunlight, and another, and another; perhaps a dozen Ortheans passing the window-slot, unseen but for that. Voices on the roof above us were muffled.

That accented voice sounded again in my mind: *Do you know who put them there.* . . . No! I thought, we have to hear more from Pathrey Shanataru. Who is it wants the Company here that badly?

Is it those people who are fighting now; is it that woman, the Voice, who's in favour of Earth? Or was she bluffing? I don't know. I don't know. We're blind, here.

I said, "I feel as if there's something important that I ought to remember."

Molly's expression changed, so that I recalled she was the Company representative of PanOceania; a thing I have difficulty always keeping in mind.

"Something that could help us now?"

I shrugged.

She said, "There are gaps in your old reports."

"How do you mean, gaps?"

"When they've been on alien worlds, there are always things that people don't say. You don't say more than most. I know you had a very bad reaction to hypno-tapes. I wondered if it affected your memory."

That directness hurt.

For an unguarded moment, all the self-doubt and fear that made up

27

that 'bad reaction' hit me again. Memory *is* identity: lose the one and you lose the other.

"It's possible," I said. "I don't know. Okay, no more three-year-old stuff. But I do find this world more disturbing than I thought I would, when I agreed to come back."

From somewhere above came a scream, choked-off; and footsteps that ran into silence.

Molly laughed, wryly. "I don't find it all that reassuring myself."

White light hardly shifted on the dusty floor. Orthe's day is 27 hours, E-standard; a slow time passing – but even fear rests. Not so long after that, I looked across and saw that the Pacifican woman had slumped into the obtuse angle of two walls, and was soundly asleep.

They won't take one of us, I thought.

But it's been done before.

Sudden light, the grating of stone: the trap door flung back. Many harsh voices resolved into one: "*Shan'tai* – come from there."

Molly started up. The pattern of the fibre-mat had imprinted on her arm, and she blinked and rubbed at cramped shoulders and neck. To give her time to collect her thoughts, I climbed with some difficulty up the rope-web, and stepped out on to the roof.

White fire dazzled. I fumbled shields over my eyes and the world turned sepia. Voices were loud. I blinked away after-images, and at last began to see through blood-haze to the afternoon light of Carrick's Star.

Molly appeared beside me. "*Shan'tai*, you owe us an explanation."

Five or six young Ortheans jostled us. All were armed – spear or winchbow or curved hand-blade – and tension was plain in every glance over the shoulder, every sudden movement. Is that residual? I thought. Or is fighting still going on?

One male had an arm bandaged, and the blood that seeped through was black.

"Come with us, *shan'tai*," he ordered.

"But the Voice of – "

"Move!"

I stumbled after the Pacifican woman, herded across that roof. We were enclosed in the group. The male followed. His face was masked against the glare, and I thought, Yes, I've seen those masks on another part of the Coast; north, in Kasabaarde –

Molly gripped my elbow. "Problem?"

"No, I – it's the heat, I think. I'm okay."

I barely noticed as they escorted us across the fibre-rope bridges to the main city. Like the vibration from a bell struck long ago, the name repeated in my mind: *Kasabaarde, Kasabaarde.*

And I wasn't even there that long, though God knows they helped me when I needed it – Kasabaarde: that city that is toll-gatherer of all trade between the two continents (standing far to the west, where the Archipelago meets the last habitable strip of the Desert Coast); that has, besides, an inner city of mystics and madmen; that has also, at its heart, the Brown Tower of the Hexenmeister. . . .

Molly sucked in her breath. I followed her gaze.

This wider roof was bleached by the alien sun. A scent came off it. Not unpleasant, a little sour; but I suddenly realized it came from liquid that soaked the rough plaster surface, two great stains that were dark, dark-red, black.

"Is ship-contact a possibility for us now?" Molly said.

"I'd give it a fifty-fifty chance."

"Okay. If that's as good as it gets." She unconsciously straightened, towering over the Harantish Ortheans.

They took us into the warm shadow of a larger roof-house, and we descended through another trap door, down into a twilight that smelled of dust and herb-*arniac.* Without pause, they took us down steps; one flight, two; down into lower levels, three and four and more, and the mirror-directed light brightened. I tried consciously to deepen shallow breathing. My legs were beginning to ache badly.

On the next floor down, the pale sandstone gave way to blue-grey walls. A semi-translucent substance as cold to the touch as metal or stone.

"In the northern continent there's a wasteland called the Barrens – " Momentarily I was far from these silver-dim warrens, in winter air and desolate tundra. "There are ruins of ancient Witchbreed cities. They're built of this, *chiruzeth.*"

"I've read the same reports you have," Molly echoed, smiling without malice.

"They were my reports," I said; and then, "Jesus Christ!"

This level was spacious, one vast subterranean hall that stretched out in perspective, lit with the sheen of reflectors from the roofs high above. To me, the ceiling felt low; Molly actually had to stoop. Water-channels ran beside the nearer wall, and the air was cool and sweet.

"This place is a junk-heap," Molly whispered, sounding momentarily closer to thirteen than thirty.

Mirror-light is deceptive, distances blur. The hall's long perspectives were tenebrous with glints of silver. Bright tapestries hung against the *chiruzeth*, between the great low arches groining the walls; tapestries that hung four and five layers deep, but still showed great rents and patches of decay. Threadbare embroidered cloths were scattered underfoot. Metal gleamed in the shadows.

The spaces between the arches were so cluttered that one could only walk down the centre of the hall. The guards escorted us there, between two rows of iron candletrees, sparsely furnished with tallow candles. Junk had spilled from the arch-spaces. Carved stone chairs, swords; great bales of metal-cloth, the links now frail with rust; broken fountains, crystal tanks starred with shatter-lines, and mirrors set in *chiruzeth* frames, and old discarded implements of crafts and warfare. . . . I had a sudden image, totally incongruous, of a child's rocking horse abandoned in some dusty attic; the children long since dead and turned to dust.

"There could be *anything* in here. . . ."

I said, "You expect to reconstruct Golden technology from *this*?"

Molly looked at the Ortheans at the further end of the hall. "At the moment, that's the last thing I'm worried about."

The guards pushed a way through the crowd. Ortheans: lithe, quick-limbed, ophidian-eyed. Their close scent surrounded me. We drew stares and whispered comments. A female half turned, hand on knife; a male spoke softly over the shoulder of another; one pulled bright robes aside as we passed. With sudden memories of the north, I thought, But there are no children present.

With the presence of children there is, sometimes, more safety.

"Can you see Pathrey Shanataru or that woman, the Voice?" Molly asked quietly. Even Sino-Anglic might not be a refuge here.

"Not a sign of either." That made me certain: whichever faction they were, the opposition is in power now.

We found ourselves isolated in the space between the crowd and the arched end of the hall. The guards took up station behind us. The great archway-space made a frame, deliberately dramatic, for the Orthean who sat there in a tall carved *chiruzeth* chair.

"Give you greeting, *shan'tai*," Molly Rachel said.

Above the Orthean male's head, spheres of light clung to the *chiruzeth*. As I watched, one drifted a few inches lower. It glowed . . . a shadowless light, the colour of lilac and lightning.

Dannor bel-Kurick. Something in the light keyed memory. When this thin, tense-looking male had a child's face, hardly more than a boy; I *did* see him – but not in person. I saw him through a viewscreen.

"I did not command *s'aranthi*-offworlders into my city," he said.

For a moment, metal-gilt and gems confused the eye; then it became clear that the jewels were polished pebbles; the gilt, green verdigris.

There was an underlying scent of decay. Molly's gaze went continually to the one genuine treasure in that heap of trash, the light-spheres, globes no larger than a child's fist. I recalled one, identical and soon dysfunctional, in the research labs of PanOceania.

She said, "My people will demand explanations, *shan'tai*. The imprisonment of Earth personnel – "

He blinked, a slow veiling of citrine eyes. They were so pale they seemed to have a light behind them. There was little of that boy-Emperor in this haggard man.

An elderly male, standing beside the carved chair, spoke smoothly: "*Shan'tai* Rachel, what else could we do? You were in danger from the fighting. Not intentionally – but accidents happen. This was for your protection."

"We would have been equally well protected on our ship."

"You could have stayed with your ship and not entered the city," Dannor bel-Kurick snapped. Then he said, "What other Coast cities have you been to?"

"None as yet, *K'Ai Kezrian-kezriakor*." She stumbled, giving him his title.

"Not to Quarth or Reshebet or Maherwa?" His tone, that had been hectoring, became quiet. "Or Kasabaarde?"

A pulse of adrenalin hit me. To recall Kasabaarde now is to recall shelter, the Brown Tower there a refuge from a hostile world – and to recall that Kel Harantish is Kasabaarde's traditional enemy. I must have had some expression intelligible to alien eyes, because Dannor bel-Kurick looked straight past Molly Rachel to me.

"You are not a stranger to Kasabaarde, *shan'tai*."

"I've been there. Many years ago."

"Those who have been there bear always a mark."

A certain tension was plain among those in earshot. The Emperor-in-Exile made an irritable gesture, and the men and women round him drew back instantly.

To my surprise, he turned back to Molly. "What do you know of Kasabaarde, *shan'tai* Rachel?"

The Pacifican woman shifted her stance, still slouched down to avoid hitting her head on the archways. I caught a quizzical expression on her face.

"I know it's a small settlement with a reputation for being a centre of religion and trade."

"And otherwise?" He looked at me.

"A centre of – news." I chose the word carefully. "The Archives of the Brown Tower there are said to go back over many years. I always understood them to be equally interested in present-day history. Which they collect from many sources."

"*S'aranthi*, I think you have forgotten much. The Tower has a hand in all conspiracy, plot, and cabal on the Coast; and in the barbarian north, also. Now I wonder if they draw offworlders into their plans? I wonder, *shan'tai*, if you have not come from them to us."

Tension stopped breath. That's the only question he wants answered, that's the reason nothing's been done to us –

"We haven't been to Kasabaarde; we don't have plans to, at the moment," Molly said. "All our business has been with this settlement, *shan'tai*; I'd hoped to continue that."

She was young enough for the truth to be plainly discernible in her voice, and I was glad of it; I've dealt with too many equivocations ever to be that honest in appearance.

Dannor bel-Kurick leaned back in the carved chair. That strange lilac-blue light fell on his face, casting violet shadows on his pale mane. His thin six-fingered hands picked at the folds of his tunic. When he spoke, he sounded infinitely weary.

"You know we have long had Kasabaarde for our enemy. I do not know you, *shan'tai*. But if you know that city, you will have heard the Tower disseminate lies about us. If you have only heard of Kel Harantish from them, you have heard little truth."

The Pacifican woman said, "Our business is with you."

Her face was guarded, but she couldn't keep from looking at that treasure-junkheap that cluttered the length and breadth of the hall. I think she looked right past the faces of the Ortheans who watched us.

"You have no business here now." He smiled, sudden and unwilling, and for a moment I saw Dannor bel-Kurick young again: mercurial, cruel, unpredictable.

"*Shan'tai* – "

"I have ordered a guard to take you to your ship," he said. I went cold. Caution and hatred contended in his voice: I couldn't tell which would win. Then he said, "I will give you a message to take to the rest of your people. Kel Harantish is closed to you now. If one of you *s'aranthi*-offworlders enters the city, now or ever, I will have you instantly killed."

CHAPTER 3

An Echo of the Lightning

"I call it fucking incompetent!" David Osaka shouted. "The stuff's *in* there, and you get us banned from the settlement – !"

"If I hadn't got in, you wouldn't know for sure that it was there!" Molly Rachel slapped the palmlock as she passed, and the port irised shut. "There are still the canals. And the northern continent."

Inside the shuttle, light was a soothing green. There was the subliminal hum of systems on stand-by. I dropped into a reclining seat beside David Osaka, feeling the padded comfort enwomb me.

He stood, now coldly angry. "That stuff is the only reason we're here. The Company – "

Molly Rachel rubbed her temples. "You didn't expect to walk out of there today with it, I hope? There have to be preliminaries. Remember, this is a technophobic culture."

David Osaka leaned over to adjust a scan-screen, kneeling on a seat. His fair hair had grown long enough to fall into his eyes, and now he tucked it back behind an ear with a characteristic gesture. Then he looked over his shoulder at her.

"Molly, it was a stupid thing to do, going in under those conditions. The risk . . . You think the Company's name is enough to protect you? This is some backwater world that's hardly heard of Earth, never mind the multicorporates."

I said, "That's something of an exaggeration, David," and they both ignored me.

"It's going on report," he said. "It's not just yourself you're risking, it's the Company's future here."

"Unless we come up with something concrete, the Company won't *have* a future here. I didn't bust a gut getting a team together just to look at some post-holocaust agricultural muck-heap – if it wasn't for the chance there's something *real* here – "

She broke off, and took the navigation-comlink seat, fitting her long legs in with some care. Shuttles are too cramped to quarrel in, we are all within each other's space. She tapped desultorily at touch-controls. "Communications systems out again?"

David grunted, leaning over the console. "About sixty per cent of the time. As far as I can make out, it's the background interference again."

I said, "We always put it down to some quirk in the solar radiation here. It could be looked into, when you – when we – take time off from the commercial interests."

"If it weren't for the commercial interests, PanOceania wouldn't be on this world."

David brushed fair hair back again. A slight, wiry man, with a smooth-skinned face, and folds of skin at the corner of dark eyes; I would have put him around eighteen, I knew him to be a decade older. He had that kind of sexual attractiveness that becomes plain in movement. When not angry, he can be both charming and amusing.

He touched the console, converting one of the screens to 3D-cartographic. "Carrick V."

A globe formed, turning slowly. Figures superimposed over it: mass 0.93465 E-standard, gravity 0.9482745 E-s, atmosphere . . .

Travelling against the sun: a scatter of islands showed up, and then the slow revolution brought continents over the slope of the world.

"You really think there's something here?" His voice lost its sharpness. "You know the odds against it?"

Northern and southern continents connected by an island archipelago, all but enclosing an equatorial sea.

Molly Rachel said, "There's evidence, here. It's not been possible to investigate fully *all* the worlds the Dispersal found – "

"Wouldn't be possible even if every woman, child, and man on Earth took a world each," I put in.

" – why shouldn't something be tucked away in a dirt-poor settlement on a post-holocaust world? Why shouldn't it be here?"

" 'It'?" I queried.

David added, "And even then, it has to be something we haven't found on half a hundred other worlds."

Molly leaned forward, watching the map's population-indicators fill in: round the shores of that Inner Sea, and further inland on the northern continent. She touched a key.

"Desert Coast," she ordered; and then, "I don't mean artifacts. That's toy stuff. I mean some science based on a totally alien perception of the universe, something we couldn't create on our own. . . ."

"And what d'you think you'll do with it when – if – you find it?" I asked.

The light from the screen shone on her blunt features, gleamed in her hair. I recognized a hard ambition in her.

"Maybe there's – I don't know. Simultaneous communication, so we don't have to spend days waiting for FTL-drones between worlds. Trans-galactic stardrives, cures for mortality, who knows?" She grinned.

34

"Whatever it is, better we should have it than NuAsia or any of the other Companies!"

"And you personally would settle for a fat promotion?"

"Be ungrateful to refuse, right?"

In the screen, webs of lines shifted. A perfect illusion: the God's-eye view of this world. It zoomed in to the southern continent, cutting out all but its northern coast, that strip of barely habitable land some few hundred miles long, bordering the Inner Sea. . . . West to east, names came back: L'Dui and Lu'Nathe, Kasabaarde, Quarth, Psamnol, Reshebet. And here, on the hook of the easternmost peninsula, farthest from the trade-routes, Kel Harantish. The backwater settlement of a backwater world.

I said, "I've a feeling that Kel Harantish would have found something, if there was anything to find. They're the only ones here that would go looking for it."

Memories of that treasure-junkheap were plain in her face.

"And just maybe they *have* found something. God, I wish I could get back in there with a full research team!"

Her intensity bothered me. It didn't seem to worry David. But he's Company, himself.

Molly sent the narrow-view north from the Desert Coast, over the representation of the Inner Sea, and even to scale it was long minutes before the sea gave way, first to the Eastern Isles, and then to Lone Isle. And then, long moments after, to the coast of the northern continent.

"I want to get in touch with the Earth representative before we make another attempt here. There was something in his report about political negotiations in progress now, between the Desert Coast and the northern continent – " She touched other keys, frowned. "Navigation back-up out as well?"

David said, "I've made contact, but not reliably. I wouldn't advise night-flying without it. Not in an old model like the QKN-40."

I think it's standard practice these days for an orbital ship to broadcast a complex system of navigation aids over any non-tech world; it makes piloting a shuttle no more difficult than piloting a groundcar. It also means you don't have the on-board equipment necessary to do without it.

The woman studied figures. "It's much faster, but it's a waste of fuel to go back up to the orbiter. . . . If we stay on-world, we'll have to do a night stop-over on one of those groups of islands. Dave, can you punch a transmission through and let the others know?"

"I'll get on to it now."

I said, "I'd stay on-world, if it was me."

35

"Mmm. There's something to be said for that, psychologically." She rested her chin on the heel of her hand, gazing at the screen.

I tried to see it just as that – lines and beads of light, neatly-scripted Sino-Anglic names, figures, latitudes. . . .

"I've notified them," David said.

"Okay. Lynne, what's the settlement the British government envoy will be in? Didn't they change it from the original first contact?"

"Northern continent." I indicated a point about midway along the coast of the Inner Sea, a river-port in temperate, fertile latitudes. "That was my original base, Tathcaer. The records say there's been a move west along that coast, here, to Morvren Freeport."

She nodded. "The government envoy, Clifford. From what he reports, over the last decade there have been considerable changes in the northern continental culture."

No cold recitation of names can hide them: Tathcaer, the city where first I came to negotiate with the Hundred Thousand – with Dalzielle Kerys-Andrethe, and Haltern, and the Orhlandis woman. And Morvren Freeport, a city seen once, ten years ago, on the run for a murder I didn't commit. . . .

Changes. Reports are sketchy, don't see what I would see. *What* changes? The Desert Coast is nothing to me, I hardly know it, but I know the Hundred Thousand *telestres* of the northern continent, I've been over them on foot or by riderbeast, honoured or hunted, I know the Ortheans of the Hundred Thousand –

Fierce impatience fired me. To have come so far, to be so close; no room now for other considerations, nothing now but urgency – how have you changed since I've been gone?

David began routine flight preparations. Molly flicked the screen back to exterior-view.

The winter sun's dry heat gone, temperatures plummeted. The Coast's rocky landscape glittered now, thickly furred with frost.

Once, in a room where alien sunlight shone upon the still surface of a well, an Orthean woman marked me with light and sacred water, for her Goddess. I thought it then either a charming irrelevance, or some obscure privilege. I know now it is neither. It is a responsibility. For all the years gone by, this alien world and I still have business with each other.

Luck held. Flying north and west across the Inner Sea, late afternoon of the next day brought the shuttle away from unbroken cloud-cover, into clear weather over the coast of the northern continent.

Land shone grey and blue in the viewscreen, furred with a moss of forests; silver-thread rivers thirty thousand feet below. Nothing showed it to be inhabited country. And yet every acre down there is accounted for, I thought. A great jigsaw of interlocking territories – the *telestres* that are (in human terms) estates, farms, communes, communities. . . . And are in Orthean terms the heart and centre of kinship, and love of the Goddess's earth. They have been so for two thousand years. What changes might there be?

"I've got an intermittent signal," David Osaka reported. "Standard code. Must be a landing beacon – hell, we must be right on top of them!"

"I thought this world was Restricted, no hi-tech?"

He shrugged. "Don't ask me. Ask your government's envoy."

Did I imagine an emphasis on *your*?

"One has to be reasonable," Molly added. "Is it enough to bring us in, Dave?"

"It's as good as we're going to get. Activate crash-straps."

Linking the web across myself, I saw land swelling from a blue bowl to a misty plain, indistinguishable from the sea. The shuttle thrummed and lurched, losing height rapidly.

I felt new enthusiasm. Kel Harantish and that room without doors: I could put that behind me now. Let me get back on firm ground, with the Company administration and the government envoy. That's a system I know how to work. I can *do* something there.

The shuttle levelled out, and then switched into hover-mode. I watched a sea too pale for Earth, and white stars in the daytime sky. For the first time since my return, I felt confidence.

The port irised open. A blast of cold air and rain rushed in. A break in the mist showed water, the estuary shore, and blue-grey mossgrass uprooted by the landing. We disembarked. Rain drizzled, warm and sparky, leaving a tang on the tongue. Clouds shifted, bright, echoing Carrick's Star beyond. Wind drummed in the ears.

"I'm not landing blind again," David swore.

"We were coded to this area, but I don't see – " Molly Rachel turned her collar up against the drizzle. " – where . . . ah."

Morvren Freeport is built upon islands, across the massive estuary of the Ai River. Walking round to the other side of the shuttle showed us a dock-shed, and ferry, and a figure who left that shelter and walked towards us. It was human, and I let him speak to the Pacifican woman, and then: "Douggie!"

We embraced, and then stood back to look at each other. I thought, How dare you look this young?

"It must be, what, five years?"

"Six," Douglas Clifford said. "I heard about Max. I'm sorry, Christie."

I've never managed to answer that one satisfactorily. 'So am I' seems flippant, though it's true; 'thank you' is no acknowledgement of grief.

"Yes," I said. "You're looking well, Doug. Offworld agrees with you. And you're the government's – "

"Peripatetic representative," he said, relishing every syllable. Douglas Clifford: a short, slightly-built man in his mid-fifties, with bright eyes and grizzled red hair; dapper even in these conditions. "I've got a six-world circuit, two months on each. It's good to see you again. You should have come back to the Service to visit us."

"With this?" I touched the PanOceania logo on my shoulder. "I'd have been as welcome as the plague."

"Can we get out of this weather?" David Osaka protested.

"I have quarters in the city." Clifford indicated a nearby island. When the shuttle was secured, we walked down to the water. Spongy mossgrass gave way to mud, and an uncertain footing, and the rain-haze quickly cleared. Across the narrow strip of water, I saw pale walls, long low buildings. Like shadows, tri-vaned sails of windmills stood locked and still.

I smiled at a memory. "Do you still have to pay to get in and out of the city?"

For answer, Clifford slid metal beads from a thong, handing them to an Orthean in the ferry-shed; a cloaked and hooded figure.

The ferry was a wooden platform with canvas stretched over wicker hoops; I walked uncertainly down the floating jetty and on to it, gripping the near rail. The two young people huddled under the canvas, Molly with her head ducked down; and after a word with the Orthean male, Clifford joined us. A cold day. I tried to place the season – Orventa Eleventhweek? Twelfthweek? Late winter, anyway.

"How many Earth personnel on-world at the moment?" Molly asked.

"None, I think, not since the Richards brothers left. They had an archeological dig up in the Barrens," Clifford said.

"We paid a visit to a Company archeological site on the way here – Kel Harantish."

Douglas Clifford looked at her with a certain stillness. Yes, I thought. Circuit world or not, you know Orthe. . . .

"You went to Kel Harantish?"

"That's right."

He let the challenge in her voice pass. Chains clanked as the wooden platform pulled away from the jetty. Choppy water tugged us seaward. I held the rail tightly, looking out across that level expanse of water; and it seemed odd, in that flat country, to look *up* at the Freeport's walls.

David Osaka, glancing back at the small island we'd left, asked, "Is that the only available landing site?"

"The locals are touchy about land. So yes," Clifford said, raising his voice over the sound of the sea. The fresh wind blew in his face and made him squint. He watched Molly, not the boy.

"I'm beginning to wonder if your Earth-base is in the most advantageous position," she said. "The Desert Coast has more to offer."

"That depends on what you're looking for. The Hundred Thousand is the largest political entity – "

"I'm looking for Witchbreed technology. Not agricultural societies in cultural decay. I need somewhere for my research team to set up a base – I've got to get the demographic people down soon, and the basic equipment."

Wind whipped hair, drove cold spray into cloth. The ferry platform shuddered as it was winched into the quayside; I saw the turnpike-winch was powered by squat reptilian quadrupeds, copper-coloured beasts with cropped horns. *Skurrai.* The sour smell of their dung was overpowering.

"If I may say so, this world is still nominally under the guidance of the British government. Restrictions are still in force as regards the importing of technology."

She watched Clifford, and there was no compromise in her expression. "I have authorization for what I'm doing. You can rely on the Company's being responsible – "

"Of course," he said mildly. I winced.

"I need results," she said. "I need them fast, if I'm to get the funding to stay here – and I need to stay, because I'm certain there's something here for the Company. More likely on the Desert Coast, but possibly here. So if you'll set up a meeting for Lynne and me with the local *T'An* or *T'An Suthai-Telestre* or whoever – "

He said, "There is no *T'An Suthai-Telestre.* Nor is there a *T'An* of Morvren Freeport."

"There isn't *what?*" I demanded loudly.

The platform grated against stone steps, and I followed David up to the quay, treading somewhat unsteadily; then I swung round on Doug, as we stood among deserted, canvas-covered bales of cargo.

"Douggie, what the hell are you talking about?"

"The *telestres* don't have a central authority now. Or local leaders. It's a little difficult to explain. The system of administration has been in abeyance for some years."

"Cultural decay," the Pacifican woman repeated.

I thought, Christ, you've been quiet enough about that in your reports. And I guess her kind of comment is the reason why.

39

The rain passed, and every moment the other Freeport islands grew more distinct: Northfast, Little Morvren, Southernmost. Daystars made brilliant points of light in a silk-blue sky. One sound underlay all conversation: the ceaseless beat of the waves, driving back sand into the estuary. There was a smell of rotting vegetation, *siir* and *hanelys* that, having died upriver, was now swept down on rain-fed winter floods.

I thought of that small, pale-maned Orthean woman, Dalzielle Kerys-Andrethe: *T'An Suthai-Telestre* in the white city of Tathcaer. If those days are gone . . . what could have caused it?

Not cultural decay. Orthe is never so simple to comprehend.

I heard David Osaka's sharp exclamation, and looked up to find him staring south across the estuary. He said "*That* . . . ?"

"That," I said, "is the Rasrhe-y-Meluur."

Chill wind made my eyes water, squinting south across the islands and multiple channels of the Ai river estuary. And there, six or seven miles away, on the last outcrop of the mainland. . . .

The winter air is pearl-blue and grey, so close in colour that the massive *chiruzeth* structure hardly shows against the sky. A great spire, or pylon, its sides reflecting silver light; so vast that the passing clouds cast shadows on its surface. I had forgotten the sheer size of it, greater than PanOceania's hiveblocks back on Earth.

It is a hollow ruin. A *chiruzeth* shell.

The simplicity of its line is broken once only, where a thin bridge-structure juts out, soaring straight across the Inner Sea to where (dimly visible in haze) there is another spire, and then another. . . .

One should see it so. I was grateful to the cloud-cover, because for some odd reason I hadn't wanted to look down on this from the air. Bridging the waters on which its shadow falls, this that was once both highway and air-hung city of the Golden Witchbreed. . . .

And once, on a sailing ship, I travelled beside it for the full length of the Archipelago, from Morvren across the Inner Sea to Kasabaarde – two hundred miles and more. Just to look was to feel the sheer weight, the massiveness of these ruins.

"The satellites picked that up on low-orbit." Molly sounded stunned.

"That was the level of technology here," I said, still looking at that shell. "Five, maybe ten thousand years of it."

As if by common consent, we turned away. Paradoxical as it may seem, the Rasrhe-y-Meluur is somehow too *big* to be seen. The mind rejects it.

Molly Rachel, as she turned to the first buildings of the Freeport, said, "Isn't it tragic that these people should have lost all that?"

I said, "That's a matter of opinion."

CHAPTER 4

Old Friends

We entered Morvren Freeport by a side gate.

"There must be *somebody* I can speak to," Molly protested in exasperation. "Lynne, what would you advise?"

That hour called second twilight was on the city, when the light of Carrick's Star fades, and the stars have not yet their full strength. I turned my collar up against the cold as we walked through muddy alleys, away from the docks.

"It's difficult. When I was here, the *telestres* named a *T'An* – an administrator, of sorts – for each of the seven provinces. It cut the legwork down."

The provinces are more language-divisions than political territory.

I saw Molly blink, apprehending the sheer size of the Hundred Thousand: a hundred thousand communities, autonomous units, communes, nation-states – whatever label you care to put on them. I have known them be of as few as fifty, as many as five thousand Ortheans.

"Someone here once said to me, 'If you attack us, you have not one enemy but one hundred thousand'." I put out of my mind the Orthean woman who had said it, and added, "If that applies equally to negotiations – God knows how you're going to speak with each individual *telestre!*"

"With difficulty," she said: a flash of mordant humour. "I don't have several centuries to spare."

The alleyways opened out to avenues. Molly spoke in Sino-Anglic, not especially quietly, and heads turned as Ortheans recognized offworlders.

With a sensation of shock, I met the eyes of a dark male, then two young females, and then an elderly woman in a slit-backed robe, mane braided down her spine. That Orthean stare – clear as ice. Outrageously egotistic, the thought went across my mind: *Do you remember me?* I smiled at that.

Ortheans of the Hundred Thousand are taller and stockier than Coast Ortheans, and these wore *harur*-blades glittering at the belt or slung across the back. They turned away. I heard talk begin behind us, in the soft Morvrenni language.

Molly said to Clifford, "Is there *no* part of the administrative system still working?"

"If you give me time – I've just come in from Thierry's World; you'll appreciate that I've hardly had a week here myself – "

"I want to speak to someone now. Not tomorrow morning. Tonight."

One elegant brow went up in one of Douglas Clifford's more theatrical mannerisms. He has his own brand of self-mockery, does Doug.

"While my government is more than willing to give the Company every assistance – "

The Pacifican woman said, "Tonight would be convenient; I've other business for tomorrow."

He looked up at her, blandly unhelpful, and then he smiled.

"In that case, you'd better see – hmm – the Almadhera. Now."

David Osaka caught my eye, and I believe I had a very similar expression to his. Visions of a warm Residence and food vanished from my mind as Clifford glanced round, and then led off up a wider avenue. The mud was pale, crunching underfoot where river gravel had been thrown down to help traction. Here in the shadow of the blank-walled buildings the wind was bitter cold, and I looked through gateways into courtyards, seeing the yellow glow of lamps being lit, and smelling the cooking-fires for the evening meal. This hour left us all but alone on the streets.

I said, "If there's no local authority, who or what is the Almadhera?"

Clifford's gaze slid across to me. Diffidently, he said, "There is no official *takshiriye* – not without a *T'An Suthai-Telestre* to lead it – but the Freeport's the only place now that trades outside the Hundred Thousand, so it does have a kind of unofficial *takshiriye*. The Almadhera is one of its members."

He used the southern term for the Court of the *T'An Suthai-Telestre*, that I have so often used in Tathcaer.

Now we were coming to buildings three and four storeys high, with slot-windows lining the top floors. The land was flat. With no view of anything beyond, the city seemed tall, overwhelming.

"Can this person speak with any authority?" Molly sounded bewildered.

"She's one of – well, I call them 'the Morvren triumvirate'." Clifford's brown eyes twinkled. "She's all the authority you're liable to get."

Multicorporates and national governments agree as well together as cat and dog. Without any surprise, I thought, It's going to be a rough night. . . .

"Here we are," Clifford said. "If I might offer one word of advice: the Almadhera's political status may be slightly dubious, but she *is* an Earthspeaker in the church of the Goddess."

As he went up to the closed gates of a courtyard, Molly dropped back a pace.

"I think he's giving us the runaround. What do you make of this?"

"He's no more anxious to help the Company than any government envoy – but I wouldn't underestimate this person. Not if she's an Earthspeaker. I used to convince myself that I understood the political system here. I never *did* convince myself I understood the church of the Goddess."

The gates swung open, disclosing a small lantern-lit courtyard. Dusk had fallen without my noticing. Now the stars were coming to full strength: the billion stars that make up the galaxy's core, flowering in Orthe's night sky. By that hard light, I saw a child at the gate. It was no more than five or six years old; unsexed, as all the young of the species are, being *ashiren*, genderless, until their fourteenth year.

"Give you greeting," it said. "Enter and be welcome."

Frost was beginning to glitter on the flagstones as the child led us across the courtyard, which was surrounded on three sides by inward-facing rooms, and up an outside staircase to an entrance on the first floor. A coin-bead curtain swung back in my face; I pushed it aside, and stepped into a wall of heat and noise.

The room was wide, low-ceilinged, with shallow curved ribs supporting the roof; and it was full to the roof with clutter. I thought, But the place is full of *children* –

Silence spread out from where we stood.

As they stopped what they were doing and turned to stare, I counted seven *ashiren*. In that ill-lit room there was something disturbing about their sharp gestures and rapid speech. They could be human, until an opaque glance or clawed hand became briefly visible. Manes clinked and glittered, woven with crystal and ceramic beads.

"What's all the fuss – " An Orthean female entered, from where the room continued round the L-shape of the building. Her arms were full of scrolls, books, and papers. She walked between the braziers that were set on the stone floor, dumped the armful on one of the many couch-chairs (dust flew: a stream of papers slid to the floor), and came to meet us, smiling broadly.

"*T'an* Clifford – and more of you? What are you here for? – Cethelen, put the *siir*-wine on to heat! All right, the rest of you, that's *enough*."

They ran. Bare feet scuffed the stone floor, there was the susurrus of flowing robes. Two *ashiren* brought out cushion-mats, dragging them close to one of the braziers; and I saw that the couch-chairs – as well as the tables, and most of the floor space – were piled with scrolls, papers,

43

and maps. An older *ashiren* looked round the corner of the room at us, and scuttled back.

The Orthean woman whacked at her crimson robe, raising a cloud of scroll-dust. She grinned. I put her in her sixties; a short, brown-skinned female with a tumbling scarlet mane.

As Clifford introduced us, she said, "I take it you arrived on that ship we heard? And came straight here? What's so urgent, *t'ans*?"

She used the word with the inflection that can mean either 'strangers' or 'guests'. Molly Rachel gave me a look that said *Earn your keep*. Better the special advisor should look a fool than the Company representative.

"Goddess give you greeting and fortune, *t'an* Earthspeaker." I spoke in Morvrenni.

She responded automatically: "And to your mother's daughter." The dark eyes clouded and cleared, this time showing humour. "So you know how to talk to Earthspeakers, do you, *t'an*? That's not as common as it might be among *s'aranthi*."

We followed her example, sitting on the cushions by the brazier.

"I used to know some of your church, *t'an*, and some of the *takshiriye* – but that was many years ago. That's also part of the problem. We're from the multicorporate Company PanOceania. If I didn't know better, I'd say we needed to talk to somebody in authority. This being the Hundred Thousand, what I will say is that we need to talk to people who can get word out to other *telestres*. We have questions to ask."

It was quite a bravura performance, considering the circumstances, and I saw Molly Rachel look chagrined, and Doug grin to himself.

"When were you here before?"

"About ten of our years ago – that would be, what, just over eight years by your reckoning."

"I . . . see. Yes. It's true there have been changes." Her six-fingered hands glinted as she reached up to take a goblet, and I saw there were gold studs set in the webs of skin between those narrow fingers.

Clifford said, "I thought it best to see you, *t'an* Almadhera, since news has a way of coming to the Church before the rest of the Freeport. I thought it might work the other way about. Communication appears to be essential."

A small *ashiren* handed me a goblet that spilled a hot green liquid, and I surreptitiously wiped my cuff. It was disconcerting to find a half-dozen children curling up on the mats round us, watching us intently. Molly Rachel drew more attention than anyone. It was her height.

"What is it you want to ask the *telestres*?" the Almadhera said.

I let Molly field that one.

"We're here for trade," she said, partly uncertain, partly challenging.

44

"Naturally, since this is a Restricted world, regulations still apply. However, our Company has been given a licence to import a certain amount of non-technological goods."

The Orthean woman tucked her feet up under her. Then she sat still. In that stillness I began to recall the church and its priests – who are mystics and craftsmen, warriors and philosophers, farmers and poets.

"No," she said.

Molly, startled, said, "What?"

"*T'an s'aranthi*, if you trade with us, what's the price you're asking? I've spoken with Clifford here often enough to know something of your world – and besides, I know our history. All you *s'aranthi* are ever interested in are the abominations of the Golden Witchbreed – am I right?" The woman paused just long enough for Molly to fumble and stutter, and then said, "Yes, I am. *T'an*, there's nothing of that Empire left in the Hundred Thousand. We ceased to need such things long ago."

The oldest-looking *ashiren*, a black-maned child of ten or eleven, spoke. "That's the first time I ever heard *you* say what the Wellkeepers tell us to say."

The Almadhera protested, "I'm not just giving you the Wellhouse orthodoxy. I believe it's true."

"Just because there are *s'aranthi* here, you don't have to suddenly like everything the Wellhouses say." The child stared up at Molly Rachel. "I'm Cethelen. I think we ought to let you trade with the Freeport. Everyone else does, why not you?"

Molly opened her mouth and then shut it again. I caught Doug's eye at just the wrong moment, and he and I and David desperately failed not to laugh. The *ashiren* looked at us in some bewilderment.

The Almadhera chuckled. "You should talk to some more of us. I'll send these out with messages, it won't take long. We'll heat some more *siir*-wine, too. Have you eaten?"

David's heartfelt negative prompted a scuffle of action among the younger children, who fled down inner stairs to the kitchens. I saw him and Molly put their heads together, and I didn't have to overhear them to know what they were saying – *these Ortheans are crazy*. . . .

"You must have been one of the first *s'aranthi* we saw." The Orthean woman stopped, an almost comical surprise on her face. "Grief of the Goddess! You're that Lynne Christie, Christie *S'aranth*? The Kerys-Andrethe's friend?"

And it was not until then that I made the connection: the nickname *S'aranth* become the generic term *s'aranthi*, 'offworlder'. . . . I shivered. And then grinned at the black irony. When I first came here I was called *S'aranth*, 'weaponless', because I didn't carry the *harur*-blades that

45

Ortheans do. To have that become the name for hi-tech humanity – !

"Christie *S'aranth*," I confirmed bleakly. Did I avoid the realization?

"Dalzielle Kerys-Andrethe called you that?"

"No, it was Ruric Orhlandis – "

She and I looked at each other. The scarlet mane fell forward, masking that narrow-chinned alien face. She stared down at her claw-nailed hands, and then back at me.

The gaze was as cold and clear as water: that mark of the Earthspeaker, their difference from other Ortheans.

"There is no Orhlandis *telestre*. There was no Ruric Orhlandis, only a woman branded traitor and land-waster and exile."

I wanted to say *Yes, I know*. Who knows it better than me? I forgot that I shouldn't mention –

But my face was burning red, and I couldn't speak for embarrassment. A fair-maned *ashiren* refilled my cup, and the clear green liquid was hot to taste, and spicy: fermented juice of the *siir*-plant.

"I'm sorry," I said. "I knew her very well, and it isn't easy to remember now what I should and shouldn't say."

"No. . . ." The Almadhera was thoughtful. "*T'an* Christie. *S'aranthi*. That's very strange. For you, too?"

"Very strange, for me."

I found that I liked this untidy, forthright Orthean woman, while still being aware that there were intonations and expressions in her that I was blind to.

"There'll be others here soon," she said. "Still, there's someone here you ought to see. Round that way – I'll keep your colleagues entertained."

You want to even up the odds, I thought. Since Douggie's half on your side – if 'sides' are what we're talking about here.

"Sure," I said, and left them talking, as I made my way to the end of the room and round the 'elbow' of the L-shape. An *ashiren* who lay asleep on a couch-chair (sharing it with a pile of maps and books) flicked one membraned eye open as I passed.

Small-paned windows shone with starlight. This part of the room was darker, the light coming from a great fireplace; and there were deep chairs there, in the shadows and embers.

A low table held a carved hexagonal board, cut by triangular divisions, on which scattered groupings of triangular counters lay.

"He's beating you," I said to the *ashiren* Cethelen, who was seated on one side of the *ochmir* board.

"He cheats."

"He always did. Hello, Hal."

46

Cethelen stood to move a lamp closer, and I stopped. Ortheans live longer than we do, and stay longer in their young and mature phases; old age is a swift and ravaging decay.

"I thought I recognized your voice," said Haltern n'ri n'suth Beth'ru-elen.

I saw a fair-skinned male, plump, dressed in the plain robes of the church. He was all but lost in the cushioned chair. The yellow-white mane was a mere crest, the eyes in that triangular face permanently half webbed over with nictitating membrane.

"Hal, I'd expect to find you round corners, listening to other people's conversations."

"While you try and bully poor Cassirur Almadhera?"

His hand was dry and hot, the grip not strong. I kept hold of that six-fingered hand as I sat down by him in another chair. For a time, nothing was said. There was a brilliance in that half-blind gaze.

"It *is* you. You look well." He chuckled, a fat and healthy sound. "And young. Though I'd wager you're not. Are you surprised at the way I look?"

That mixture of slyness and honesty is essentially Orthean. It brought back so many memories.

"Yes, I am."

"Nothing but time, *t'an S'aranth*, and age – all the Beth'ru-elen age early. It's in our family."

To shut my eyes was to bring him back: Haltern, fair-maned, harassed, sweating; a deceptively competent man, no older – then – than Doug Clifford now.

That voice, no less strong, said, "You've proved me wrong. I always said you wouldn't come back. And now you come in company with traders?"

"I did intend to return. I got posted away. Maybe I didn't try as hard as I might to prevent that. There was a lot to come to terms with, afterwards, and then – well, then there were other people."

He nodded, slowly. The firelight shone on his skin, the faintest scale-pattern visible; on whiteless blue eyes. For all his frailty, that intelligence was undimmed.

"I'm glad you came back," he said.

"Hal . . ."

Deliberately picking up on other matters, he said, "Are you really with a Company? From what Clifford's said of them in the past, I find that difficult to believe. And a Company that's chasing Witchbreed technology?"

47

"It's a long story, but 'yes' and 'yes' are the answers to that. And if it comes to it, what are *you* doing here?"

"I like the company of Earthspeakers. I was always of a contemplative frame of mind, given to meditation – ah. Now *that's* Christie." He grinned, and deep lines shifted in his face.

Having snorted incredulously, all I could say was, "This place is as peaceful as a madhouse, and you're about as 'contemplative' as – " Similes eluded me.

He took a goblet of *siir*-wine from Cethelen, reached over to move an *ochmir*-counter, and under cover of getting the child to stir the fire, switched another two counters to show a colour favourable to him.

What did Clifford call it – the 'Morvren triumvirate'? Now I wonder . . . "You associate with this Almadhera a lot, do you, Hal?"

"Associate?"

"I'm told there's no *takshiriye*. No official *takshiriye*."

He slid gracefully over that, saying thoughtfully, "It was about six years ago; none of the *T'Ans* could name themselves *T'An Suthai-Telestre* after Dalzielle Kerys-Andrethe died."

Reading that in records, I had been sad, a little shocked: she wasn't old. And when she was (to use the common tongue) Crown, Hal was a Crown Messenger; the first of those intelligencers that I ever met.

"After that, the provinces rubbed along well enough; and the *T'Ans* mostly returned to their own *telestres*." He set his goblet down carefully. "That's not to say they won't name a new Crown, if they see the need for one."

"The lack of one is confusing someone I know," I said, thinking of Molly, and the likely reaction of the other Pacificans.

"I can see that we have to talk – or is it still Douglas Clifford that I should speak with?"

Noise came from the other part of the room. I guessed there were people coming in.

"I haven't had time to talk with Doug myself. . . . He and I know each other from way back. And every time he's looked at me since I got off the ship, I've seen him thinking the same thing – what the hell's she doing with a multicorporate?"

'What *are* you doing?" Haltern asked waspishly. "More to the point, what are you doing with them on Orthe?"

"Minimizing damage," I said. "Or at least, I hope to."

"Is Witchbreed technology the only interest they have in us?"

"As far as I can make out." You can't expect a Pacifican Company to learn from a 'post-holocaust' world.

There was a pause. I thought I ought to go and greet the newcomers, but he stopped me with a word: "I can't help but think back. Christie, do you remember what Ruric Orhlandis once said? 'You are utterly unlike us, and when you come here we can't help but alter. And if we're ever found to have something that Earth requires – ' "

" ' – why then Goddess help us, because no one else will!' Oh yes. It's something I've never forgotten. That's why I'm here. That's why I *had* to come."

He blinked, that old male, in the fire's yellow light; and as I stood to go, touched my arm. With that I knew we had – somehow – resumed an old friendship; not unchanged, no, but still there.

"Hal, what happened to Ruric?"

"She died, on the Coast. It was many years ago."

I'd heard, by Service rumour, but I wanted him to say it. Records can be wrong and she was only one woman in what was – for those not involved – only a very minor political incident, on a primitive world. The record might have been wrong.

"Are you sure?"

His gaze, alert, was that of an old spymaster. There was the automatic, professional pause before he spoke.

"I made certain to enquire. And I had word, also, from the servants of the Hexenmeister – *you* have good cause to remember the Tower's veracity."

Ten years ago I met that 'serially immortal' (as the Ortheans term it) custodian of the Tower and the Tower's Archives, the Hexenmeister of Kasabaarde; an ancient male whose investigations cleared me of the accusation of murder. Hal and I, we were deep in that together.

"Will you . . ." I offered him my arm, to rise, but he shook his head.

"Later." He had a covert smile, that meant there were other conversations he wanted to overhear. "Yes, we must talk later. Go and meet the others now."

I left him playing *ochmir* with Cethelen (unsurprisingly, he was winning) and walked back round into the main part of the room. If anything there were more *ashiren* present than before, older children who'd act as messengers.

Molly, rising to stand beside me, said confidentially, "Things are moving fast. Some of these people are just opportunists, they want a piece of what the Company has to offer, but there are a few that are genuine. One in particular. See that one there, by David?"

The other Pacifican was talking with a group of male and female Ortheans, seated beside a brazier with the Almadhera and Doug Clifford. One youngish, dark-maned male had winterscale skin splotched with

49

those mottled patches that Ortheans call 'marshflower'. It made his features seem large, crammed into a small face.

"Don't be so sure these people want what the Company can offer. What about him?"

"His name is Rakviri. He's prepared to take us out to his *telestre*, tomorrow. And by the description he's given me, there's something there worth investigation."

"Christ, things *are* moving."

She said, "They've had ten years to think about it, Lynne."

The room was crowded now, but I detected an air of expectancy, as if not all the unofficial *takshiriye* were yet present. That was confirmed when the cords of the bead-curtain swung apart, and an Orthean male walked in. He pulled off his cloak, under which he wore the britches and slit-backed shirt of Rimon province. Two *harur*-blades – the *harur-nilgiri*, that is too short for a sword; and *harur-nazari*, too long for a knife – were slung from his belt, the hilts worn with use.

"You know him?' Molly said.

"Oh yes." I shook my head in wonder. "Lord, two old friends in one evening? First Hal, and now – "

I took an instinctive step forward. It seemed at first that he stood half in shadow, this stocky male with the cropped yellow mane, but the shadow that lay over half his face was a scar. A burn. I saw a whiteless blue eye, bright in ruined flesh; and as he turned, his other profile was a lined face, looking not a day more than forty.

"Blaize n'ri n'suth Meduenin," the Almadhera said.

"Blaize!" I held out both hands. I couldn't keep the grin off my face.

His expression changed. I thought, Good God, have I altered so much, don't you recognize me?

Without taking his eyes from me, he spoke to the Almadhera: "Your *ashiren* brought me the name. I thought it might not be true, but I see that it is. I shall have to leave."

One hand rested on the hilt of a *harur*-blade, that gesture so familiar; and all I could think was, After all these years he still speaks Morvrenni with a Rimon accent.

And not believe that cold tone.

"Blaize – " I took my hands back, colouring like an adolescent.

The Orthean woman spoke to Blaize, Doug Clifford to the Pacificans; I attended to neither:

"We really need you to talk to these *s'aranthi* – "

" – highly advisable to speak with the Meduenin – "

It might have been a smile that made something grotesque out of his scarred face, or some quite alien emotion. There was an authority about him that was new, and plain in the way he spoke to the other Ortheans, and I felt cold, faced by that impenetrable anger.

"How *you* can come back here – " Blaize Meduenin turned to the others. "Cassirur Almadhera, *t'an* Clifford; I'm sorry. I refuse to engage in any discussions while this woman is present."

CHAPTER 5

The Customs of Orventa

A morning wind blew across the flat roofs of the city, fluttering cloth-robes hung out to dry. Windvanes rumbled, ceaselessly turning. Few Ortheans were out in the wide avenues, but I could see bright dots moving down on the quay, where (far off and silent) the sails of a *jath-rai* flapped, the crew hurrying to catch low tide.

I leaned on the rim of the brick parapet, on the flat roof of the Residence. My only clear view – since all the buildings are on a level – was seaward, through a gap between them. I saw the outlines of two other Freeport islands, Little Morvren and Southernmost one behind the other, each with their windvanes and Watchtower and low Wellhouse dome; clear as glass images. The top of the Rasrhe-y-Meluur was hidden in cloud.

"I'll be glad when I get adjusted to local time," Molly Rachel called, coming up the steps that led from the Residence's inner courtyard to the roof. She was kneading the back of her neck with strong fingers.

"You do adjust – sleep a couple of hours midday."

She yawned, wide-mouthed as a cat. "Lynne . . . is Douglas Clifford as much of a fool as he likes to make out?"

I chuckled. "Not by any means." And when she looked enquiringly, added, "I used to know him well. And also, he and Max were colleagues, when they were both groundsiders – sorry: both in the home Service, I should say. Of course, I didn't see Doug as often as I might; I was offworld a lot of the time."

If I hadn't been offworld then Max –

Such pain is unexpected. I thought I'd given up that false guilt long ago, knowing that accidents don't fail to happen just because people stay on one world together. It would have made no difference if I'd been on Earth.

News had to come to me on Parmiter's Moon, six weeks after the event. When everything else is gone, that fact remains: I wasn't there. I wasn't even there to see him buried.

Molly Rachel leaned on the brick parapet beside me and looked down. I could smell the morning meal cooking, down in the ground-floor kitchens.

"You can see what's happening here, Lynne. For all that Clifford says, it's obvious. This culture's falling apart. When the lines of administration and authority go down, what's left?"

Local Residence reports mention Watchtowers that stand empty; the Seamarshal's palace boarded up. Now the sound of dawn gongs came across the roof-tops. How do I tell her? It isn't the cities that are important, it never was.

"I've *got* to justify being here, Lynne."

"How long will home office let you carry on without results?"

She squinted up at the high dome of the sky, and the daystars that lay thick as frost. Crowsfeet laced the corners of her eyes. Because she's Pacifican and young, I tend to think she's uncomplicated. That's always an error.

"It isn't home office. If *I* think the outlay isn't justified . . . I can't bleed resources for no return, it's got to benefit us all; that's the way the Company works. I *know* there's something here. All the hard evidence points to it. But if there's functional Witchbreed technology, we ought to be picking up readings from power-sources – "

Was that a turning-point, could I have pushed her to a negative decision then? Smaller things have discontinued missions. But all I did was suggest, "Perhaps we do pick up readings, and can't recognize them. Maybe it's something we can't program the analysers to recognize."

"Just possible," she conceded. "Then the Company really would be on to something. When you were here – but that's ten years ago. With the speed of cultural decay here, they might have lost even the few artifacts that *do* exist, by now. Wouldn't that be ironic? Two or three thousand years since the Witchbreed culture fell, and we arrive ten years too late. . . ."

"Molly, you do say the damnedest things!"

She had to laugh at that. She raised her head, looking towards the estuary and the sea; taking stock.

"And now?" I said.

The wind drummed in my ears, cold, but with the promise of thaws. Morvren Freeport lies in more southerly latitudes than Tathcaer. Spring will come sooner.

"I'm going along the coast, inland, to that *telestre*. Rakviri, the name is. That's what happens now."

"We've only been here yesterday and today!"

"There's no point in wasting time," Molly said. "Unless the *telestres* are different from this technophobic city, the Company won't be interested in the Hundred Thousand. But in any case, I don't want anyone getting in ahead of us. We're not the only multicorporate that could find Carrick V attractive."

The Pacifican woman turned, looking at me speculatively. I must be slow this morning, I thought, what's she leading up to? The light was behind her, and full in my face; deliberately so. I'm too old to be foxed by tactics like that.

"I think I have to ask," she said, "since these people have influence with the *telestres*, and we need access to the *telestres*. . . . What was all that with Blaize Meduenin?"

"Molly, you needn't feel any concern. It won't affect PanOceania's relations with the Hundred Thousand."

"Don't patronize me," she said amiably, "and don't be so bloody pompous, Lynne. I'm head of mission; I need to know. What's the explanation?"

"I don't see why I should be expected to understand the Orthean mind when I don't even know how the human mind works."

"Lynne – "

If ten years age-seniority gives nothing else, it gives an ability to shut kids up. I stopped her mid-sentence with a look.

"I'll get it sorted out," I said, and crossed the roof, went down the steps, and never heard a sound from her.

That determination carried me out into the chill of the street, and across the city, walking briskly from the Residence to where Cassirur Almadhera had her quarters. I found no adult Ortheans there, but an older *ashiren* directed me down towards the quay.

The sky was hazed, a high milky blue, and the air had a thin clarity. The human body senses difference: sunlight too thin, wind too cold – still, this day felt like the beginning of Spring season. I walked down between biscuit-coloured walls, remembering how late Hanys in Morvren Freeport is hot and glaring and harsh, and how *jath-rai* from this port sail out to all the coasts of both continents.

The wind whipped the estuary into choppy waves. I felt the spray, shivered; looking up the quay and down. A few coastal *jath-rai* were moored down towards the Portmaster's office, and there were more across the channel in the docks of another Freeport island. Ten years ago I stood here and saw Kel Harantish traders leave (but Morvren Freeport has always had an odd reputation). Ten years ago I was running blindly south, in good company, to what I didn't then know would prove a refuge and a sanctuary: Kasabaarde's Tower. . . .

I turned to walk along beside tall warehouse frontages, and stopped.

He stood in the open arched entrance of a warehouse, one thin, strong finger jabbing at the Orthean male he spoke to. The other claw-nailed hand rested back on the hilt of *harur-nilgiri*. Sun illuminated his yellow mane. I noticed that he now habitually stood so as to put his half-scarred face in shadow.

Blaize you bastard –

Anger made me hot and cold. The thought of our last meeting was like a slap across the face.

The younger male saw me. "*T'an s'aranthi*, give you greeting! Have you come to speak with the *takshiriye*? This is Blaize n'ri n'suth Meduenin, if you don't know him."

"I do have a passing acquaintance. Two assassination attempts on my life, wasn't it? And an occasion when you gave false evidence at a trial?"

A brazier burned in the warehouse entrance, and I stepped up to warm my hands at it, giving him back stare for stare, not displeased to have said that in front of witnesses. The young male inclined his head, and precipitately left.

"I won't speak with you." Blaize Meduenin turned to follow.

"You *will*." I put myself between him and the quay outside, too furious to consider danger. As I have cause to know, Ortheans have no scruples about violence. "I won't be treated like this. None of us can afford personal quarrels. I . . . can be professional enough to forget your behaviour last night."

He stopped. That pale gaze raked me up and down. What does he see now – an alien: a tall woman, blonde hair flecked white, thinner than health demands? I never could read mirrors truly. And I was so much younger when we crossed the Barrens. . . .

The wind blew his mane across his eyes, that yellow mane cropped in the Rimon style, that grows out silver where the burn-scar is. Plain slit-backed shirt, boots, britches; all dusty with warehouse chaff. And *harur*-blades at his belt. Still a fighter. And swordfighters in their middle years are dangerous: experience replacing strength, doubt replacing confidence.

He met my eyes and smiled, quite deliberately. And said, "I'd thought there could be no worse betrayer of the Hundred Thousand than Ruric Orhlandis. But what would even she say now, that kinsister of yours, if she were living? To see you as you are?"

Using the dead woman's name was such deliberate malice that I could escape the hurt of it. Only to fall prey to memory: *You* used to call me your kinsister, Blaize Meduenin.

Cold air cut through warmth, and the smell of burning *lapuur*-wood in the brazier. Ortheans shifted crates in the interior of the warehouse, and *ashiren* outside the nearby companion-house chanted an atonal rhyme, but it felt as though we two were alone.

"I don't understand you." Frustration choked me. "And what I do

55

understand, I don't like. I was prepared to be reasonable, *more* than reasonable – you humiliated me – "

He took a few steps towards the entrance, looking out at the docks and bare masts of *jath-rai* ships. Then he turned to lean up against the mud-brick arch, with that automatic gesture that swept *harur* blades out of his way. His pale eyes cleared. A stocky Orthean male, fair-maned, ageing; still carrying himself with a fighter's grace. Age, as it does with some, made him more solid, more himself.

"Are you so certain you're right, to be afraid of Earth?" I meant it to sting. He shrugged.

"I know what the Witchbreed were. How their engines devastated this world. And I know how like them you offworlders seem – " He broke off. Then: "I'll negotiate with Clifford. With the Company, if the *takshiriye* must. I've had to negotiate with all kinds of people, here, over the years – even Dannor bel-Kurick's Harantish Witchbreed. But *not* with you."

"Because I'm doing what I'm paid to do? Be reasonable – "

"*I* took Guildhouse oaths, and served who paid me! I never pretended moral necessity to mask it." His voice was loud with disgust. Someone in the warehouse called his name. He ignored it. Carrick's Star brightened, casting the shadow of the archway at my feet, striking fire from the harbour beyond.

"I remember your mercenary 'ethics'! How ethical was it when you abandoned me in the wilderness at Broken Stair? And Maric with me, and *ke* no more than a child – I thought then, you're nothing but a paid killer. As if what happened before we were hunted out of Roehmonde hadn't told me that!" Anger left me breathless: "Don't play soldier-turned-statesman with *me*. You may be in the *takshiriye*, but you still don't have any conception of the wider issues over the personal – "

He shrugged, almost sullen. "SuBannasen *telestre* paid me and I made two attempts to kill you. And it might have been better for Orthe if one of them had succeeded. Is that view wide enough for you? Impersonal?"

"This is pointless. Just pointless."

He didn't shout. Razors hurt no less if gently applied. I wanted to sit down, I was shaking; there was nowhere in the dusty warehouse entrance to sit.

"And childish. What do you want me to say? That I should have left *you* to die, when we were being hunted through the Fens? Blaize, for God's sake!" My voice echoed in the vaulted roof. I tried to speak with more restraint. "I'm here because there have to be negotiations between the Company and the Hundred Thousand. The Company would have come here with or without me, so don't blame me for it!"

He pushed himself away from the wall, stepped in front of me. Automatically, I tensed; aware of physical power. That silver-seamed burn made something unreadable of his face.

"Does the Company trust you – *S'aranth*?"

"Why the hell do you think I'm here?"

He picked up the less obvious implication. "I know why you *think* you're here."

" 'Think'?"

Sardonic, he said, "You think you can play both hands in the game. Be a friend, while being an enemy. Mercenary ethics, *S'aranth*? You report to the Company on *t'an* Clifford. Advise the *t'an* Rachel. The *takshiriye* hears these things. With your experience of us – the Company must find you very useful. If not trustworthy."

His feet scuffed the stone flags. I felt his presence; the warmth of the brazier. Caught off-guard and all the more angry because of it, I said, "What else can I do?"

His reply was instant, and bitter. "Go back eight years. Tell me *then* that restricted contact means restricted as long as it pleases Earth, and then no longer. Tell me then what your coming here meant!"

He reached out, rested one claw-nailed finger on the PanOceania logo on my shoulder; a heavy pressure. I wanted to grip that hand, impress on alien skin some vestige of my pain. I couldn't speak.

Blaize said, "I've been offworld. I've seen what the Companies do on other worlds. I've seen what they've done to *Earth*, grief of the Goddess!"

"That's what I'm trying to prevent, you stupid bastard – "

"You're Company," he said, implacable. "While you're in the Company, you'll do what they tell you."

Ten years ago I would have been with you, and with Hal; discussing government and Company and what we might be able to do to cushion culture shock. And now I'm not. It hurts.

I said, "The only way I can act as some kind of restraining influence on the Company is to stay *in* the Company. The governments can't do a thing. And maybe that means I have to do some things that aren't wholly defensible, but that's the way things are – there isn't any other way. Don't tell me you're part of the *takshiriye* and never do anything you can't justify!"

He let his hand drop back to his side. My shoulder ached.

"*S'aranth*, I've heard that from mercenaries – 'my Guildhouse ordered me to do this'." Blaize rested a hand on the hilt of *harur-nilgiri*. "The answer's easy: leave that Guildhouse. Don't say your hands are dirty but it isn't your fault! You like to think you're playing both sides – *S'aranth*.

57

You're not. Like goes to like. You're offworlder. You're Company. And I was a fool, eight years ago, to think different!"

"You don't have the right to say that to me!" Then I stopped, and turned away. I stretched my hands out again to warm them at the brazier. *Don't take the past away from me as well.*

Why can't we all of us get back to the way we were? That's the perennial vain regret. The last time I came to the Freeport I was on the run, but at least I knew I was innocent of the accusation against me.

"There isn't anything else I can do!"

Somewhere voices shouted, and winches creaked; and the smell of cooking came sourly from the companion-house a few yards away. Stone was cold underfoot. I tucked my hands up under my arms and shivered.

"It's a fine profession," Blaize Meduenin said. "You can leave your mistakes behind you when you leave a world. No one can tie you to the reparation of error. *We can't leave.*"

I couldn't look him in the face and that made me furious.

"You're not my conscience. You don't know the world I live in, but I do, and I know how to handle it, and I don't need facile, simplistic judgements!'

His voice came quietly from the interior of the warehouse behind me. "Christie, *you* can't use ignorance as an excuse. Not you. Goddess, I was with you from Corbek to Shiriya-Shenin; I know that you know Orthe! I'm not Haltern, I don't understand doing what's wrong for the right reasons. When you were here before – "

"You speak as though it was yesterday."

"Yes, I do." I heard him sigh heavily. There was the quiet rasp of metal, as he shifted his stance, from the harness of *harur*-blades. "Grief of the Goddess, Christie, why come back? With a Company like this one? If you could stay away eight years, you should have stayed away for good."

It was as if he spoke his thoughts aloud. Very Orthean, that merciless honesty – and I call myself human. When I put that mental distance between us, I could turn and face him: "What you say is unforgivable – "

One word from him and I would have lashed out, but he only looked at me, that half-scarred face with a kind of innocent gravity in it. And pain. I sighed.

"I usually handle matters better than this. . . . Do you remember when we found each other, here, the first time I ever came to the Freeport? You were hiring out your services from the Mercenaries Guildhouse. I've – grown used to thinking of you as the one in a morally indefensible position."

"Do you seriously think I'm not?" He grinned, twistedly, and stepped out on to the quay. And then looked back at me. "Because I tell you not to bring Earth technology here, not its harm, nor its benefits. I can say that for the *telestres*, the Hundred Thousand. We don't need you. I can't say it for all of Orthe – but I do, *S'aranth*, I do."

He turned away, squinting up at the buildings and the pale daystarred sky. Because there was nothing I could say to that, because I saw no hope of response or resolution, I walked away into the cold Freeport morning; walking to find Molly Rachel where she was negotiating a journey to Rakviri *telestre*.

Two hours and ten miles later, on the dirt-tracks of the Hundred Thousand, the *skurrai-jasin* swung eastwards, and I rested my arm on the carriage rail and shielded my eyes with my hand.

"That Rakviri male wouldn't say much about the old technology last night – " Molly Rachel was thoughtful " – because Cassirur Almadhera is in this church of theirs. This technophobic church. I wonder, will that matter less on a *telestre*, or more?"

"More," I said.

The reptilian quadruped *skurrai* hissed, raising their narrow muzzles and pointed lips. Winter sun gleamed on their harness and metal-capped horns. The wooden *jasin*-carriage rocked and jolted. Open carriages are cold, the driver had bundled us in the black-and-white featherfur pelts of the *zilmei* carnivore. I fastened my coverall tighter at the throat, and flicked the temperature-control in the weave.

Molly huddled in the pelts. "There's a point on any Restricted world, when I'd swap all my principles about cultural contamination by hi-tech for a warm seat in a groundcar. . . ." And she grinned, exhilarated by the thought of possible discoveries ahead.

We drove past grey boles of *siir*-vine, thick as a man's thigh, that hugged the earth. Ahead, shapes resolved out of haze and glare. Grey stone, white stone; buildings with flat façades, and windows that – though copiously ornamented – are no wider than slots: difficult targets for winchbow bolts. Many buildings, all linked. I looked ahead, down through long colonnades, seeing how each block was joined to the next. Rooms, halls, courtyards; pens for *marhaz* and *skurrai* . . . an interconnected warren of buildings, the whole thing the size of a village.

The *jasin* rattled into the courtyard. A great number of Ortheans were passing in and out of the buildings and yards, so we were partly concealed by the crowd. I glanced up, seeing a sky that glowed pale blue, freckled with daystars. As we dismounted from the carriage, a flock of *rashaku-bazur* rose up from the cornices of the surrounding halls, the scales on

59

their breasts glinting, the beat of their wings like gunshots. They wheeled and flew seaward. Their cries were metallic, out-of-tune bells.

An *ashiren* came to lead the *skurrai*-carriage away. Molly turned, boots crunching on the sea-gravel that floored the yard. "Now where – ah. That's him."

A dark male pushed his way through the bustle. I recognized the patchmarked face of the night before.

"Haden Barris Rakviri." He bowed. Barris, the child of Haden, of Rakviri *telestre*: so names go in the Hundred Thousand.

"*T'an* Barris," the Pacifican woman acknowledged. Then: "I understood you to say there was a Witchbreed-technology artifact here that we can see."

His dark gaze flicked sideways at me, and I saw humour there. Her directness made me wince. It made him amused.

"Several artifacts," Barris Rakviri said, "but I doubt that I can bring you to more than one. Still, that should be sufficient to begin with, I hope?"

As a comment, it silenced Molly Rachel completely. He beckoned, and we walked towards a near entrance of the main building; walking briskly, because of the cold. Cages hung from the round-arched entrances, and in them squat lizardbeasts gripped the bars with spatulate fingers, and whistled a shrill alarm. The male Orthean glanced up, and silenced the alarm with a gesture.

"You must meet the *s'an* Rakviri," Barris said. "It is tradition."

"And then – "

"And then," he confirmed. I saw what I hadn't noticed in Morvren, that he dragged one foot; it had a slight deformity. He was not as young as I'd thought him. His mane was fine and dark, braided down the spine, where his slit-backed coat showed crystal beads in the braiding; and he carried a stick of *hanelys* wood, partly for ornament, partly (I thought) for support.

As we came to the entrance, I said, "What's all the rush and bother here? Isn't it a bit early in Orventa to begin trade-voyages?"

"We're shipping food east to Ales-Kadareth; it's urgent, there's famine in Melkathi province."

"Who ordered the *telestre* to do that?" Molly asked. I could see her thinking of authority-channels.

Barris halted momentarily, leaning on his stick and looking up at her. "The Kadareth *telestre* asked us. Would your Company have to be forced to do such a thing?"

You can't translate 'order' into Morvrenni without it having that

60

implication of force. Nor, indeed, into any other Orthean language with which I'm familiar.

We passed a group of five or six Ortheans standing in an antechamber, and entered a long hall. Barris Rakviri glanced round.

"Wait here. I'll find the *s'an* Jaharien."

Molly opened her mouth to comment, and then her attention was caught by the hall. It had the air of a place hastily abandoned; I guessed all but a few Ortheans were helping with the food-ships. A few *ashiren* were still present. They glanced up with no great curiosity.

"Lynne – "

"*Don't* say 'this *telestre* is about to have an industrial revolution'. Please."

She stepped forward, feet planted squarely on the wood-tiled floor, raising her head to gaze round. Light shone on her dark features, in the silver-dusty air. She had almost the expression she'd worn in Kel Harantish.

Books, scrolls, and manuscripts lined the walls. There were low work-tables and benches the length of the hall. And there, tossed down carelessly on a hand-drawn map: an astrolabe. Next to it stood an orrery, finely made, planetary circuits corresponding to no known solar system. One low table held what might have been a powered loom, a length of *chirith-goyen* cloth spilling from it. I saw one *ashiren*, fair mane falling about its face, engaged in some machinery with cogs and pendulum; the other group of older *ashiren* had lenses mounted in a frame and were trying to focus the light from one window to burn a scrap of paper.

Molly Rachel reached out to a table, and with one finger spun a wheel: pistons moved smoothly. A spirit-powered engine, no larger than a child could carry. . . . She stared up and down that winter-lit hall, and then she nodded.

"You reported something like this. That winter you spent in Shiriya-Shenin, in the north. This is their custom when travelling isn't possible."

"For Orventa, winter season. They do this – and they fight, and make poems, and plays, and have *arykei*, lovers – " Which are old memories. "The first time I saw it, I thought 'industrial revolution'. And then at the end of Orventa, the spring Thaw Festival, I saw every last machine broken up, melted down. . . . It's their amusement, this."

"And the Wellhouses police it?"

You want to believe that, I thought. Because that will mean you'll be able to bribe the *telestres* with Earth tech – oh, Molly! "The Wellkeepers couldn't make them do it if they didn't already desire to."

Barris Rakviri reappeared, his halting footsteps easily recognizable. "I can't find Jaharien, he may be down at the bay."

"Then perhaps you yourself could show us the Witchbreed artifacts," Molly Rachel said.

And in case you're wondering, t'an Barris, that wasn't a suggestion. . . . I wanted to throw my hands up; monomaniac determination is one thing, discourtesy quite another. But Barris inclined his head urbanely, and greeted one of the younger *ashiren*, asking for *siir*-wine.

"*T'an*, I have to be a little careful. For you to see such artifacts. . . . The *s'an* would not object. But to think of trading them to offworlders – " Barris gestured with his stick at the remaining Rakviri Ortheans. "Were I Jaharien in such a case, I should fear the *telestre* naming a new *s'an*. So you see, we must be circumspect."

"And the church?" I said.

He smiled wryly. "Ah – the eminent Wellkeepers, the worthy Earth-speakers. . . . *T'an*, they fail sometimes to perceive necessity. To learn, one must give up something. I would be willing to give, or rather trade, what Rakviri has."

Molly frowned. I could see it puzzled her, this attitude of *telestre* Ortheans: neither technophobe nor technophile.

Some memory stirring – perhaps the implicit comparison with the Desert Coast – I said, "And the Hexenmeister in Kasabaarde? It always seemed to me there was some influence on the Wellhouses from there."

The 'marshflower' that dappled his skin made his expression difficult to decipher. He said, "They say the Hexenmeister lives out the world from age to age, there in the Tower. What can he say to us, who live, and pass, and live to meet again?"

It was that effortless Orthean transition from material to mystic. Many things are spoken in the *telestre* that you won't hear said in the cities.

As if fumbling for a landmark, Molly Rachel said, "Could you call the Kasabaarde settlement a political force here, as it is on the Coast?"

"No. . . ." He turned as the fair-maned *ashiren* tugged at his sleeve, the child holding bowls of *siir*-wine. It spoke quietly to him: something I couldn't catch.

"Is he? I'll go, then. *T'ans*, please wait; Cerielle will bring you anything you need." He went towards another exit, a narrow curtained archway; dragging footsteps fading. The *ashiren* remained staring up at us for a moment, and then in a comically adult manner shook its head and walked away to the group at the further table. This is the generation that has grown up with knowledge of offworlders: obviously we are no major sensation.

"What the hell – !" Molly Rachel frowned. "Well, I suppose you did warn me. Barris . . . His attitude seems to be that what we're doing is halfway between heresy and, oh, stealing a museum exhibit. . . . These people! This might be a major commercial proposition. Can't they take it seriously?"

Having drunk the hot *siir*-wine, I put the bowl on a nearby table; and we walked the length of the hall, and turned to walk back. Winter light fell through slot-windows, the pale brick walls here showing three foot thick. There were *becamil* cloth-hangings; *zilmei* pelts on the wood floor. Sounds echoed. I kept my voice low.

"There always were a few Witchbreed relics in the Hundred Thousand. But I'll tell you now, Molly, you're not going to deduce the ontological basis of Golden science from a handful of defunct toys."

"If this is a blind alley, I still have to check it out. I know I shouldn't have got us thrown out of Kel Harantish." Self-condemnation roughened her voice. "That was our first chance and I handled it badly – too eager to get in. We'll have to get back there, Lynne. But, with respect, you don't know what we might find in the Hundred Thousand, with a full research team. It may not all be defunct."

Being true, that irritated me.

"While we've got a minute," she added, "you've had a chance now to sound Douglas Clifford out. What can we expect from him?"

"Firm support of the status quo: keep Carrick V a Restricted world. He doesn't like multicorporates."

"Jesus, the Service! – but I can short-circuit that, we're not obliged to have him present on all occasions."

"It might be politic if we did. Why cause friction – until it's necessary?"

She stopped, resting her hands on the back of a couch-chair lined with the grey-and-white featherpelt of the *zilmei*. I waited.

"I'm not going to have time to attend to all the little details," she said. "Suppose you handle liaison between the Company and the Service, Lynne?"

Good grief, I thought. "You know I was Service myself, once."

"Then you'll know how their minds work."

There was a challenge in her sudden, direct gaze. I don't appreciate amateur manipulations of my loyalty. But nor do I turn down an advantageous position when it's offered.

"Why not?" I said. "In a strange way, it's what I've been doing, groundside, for the past four years."

The light in that hall shone silver against black shadows, glinted on metal in one corner where a complex structure of mirrors, prisms, and lenses projected up to a skylight-dome. Scrolls lay at its foot, scribbled over with notations of star positions: the milliard stars of day and night sky.

Frustration exploded in the young woman's voice. "How can they live like this! Like primitives!"

The Hexenmeister of Kasabaarde once said to me, *I don't wish to take away machines, only take away the desire to use them so badly.* I said, "The *telestres* have had two and a half thousand years to think differently about technology."

"It's ludicrous!" Caught in this momentary lull, she seethed with impatience. "And I intend – *there* he is; at last. Lynne – "

From the far end of the hall, Barris Rakviri entered; a short male beside him; in green and white robes, that I thought must be the *s'an* Jaharien. With them –

I put a restraining hand on Molly's arm. With the two Rakviri males walked a middle-aged female Orthean, short and brown-skinned and with a curling scarlet mane: the Earthspeaker Cassirur Almadhera. The three of them slowed their pace, suiting it to the halting steps of an elderly figure, all but smothered in *zilmei* travelling coats, who walked with his arm through Cassirur's. Haltern n'ri n'suth Beth'ru-elen.

And with these two of the Morvren triumvirate walked six Ortheans in the plain robes of Wellkeepers and Earthspeakers.

CHAPTER 6

A Far-Off Cloud

A terrace, covered in with sheets of clear glass, faced southwards. Musicians played the complicated music of south Morvren, as chill and intricate as frost on a window. Noon lay white on the flat land beyond, scoured down by coastal storms to a tangled network of *siir*-vine and scrub-*hanelys*, under a powder-blue daystarred sky. The mossgrass was losing its winter brown, growing through a pale azure. Carrick's Star was warm through the glass. And the glass held also the reflection of the Orthean female who walked beside me as we leisurely paced the length of the terrace.

"You should, after all, take time to breathe," Cassirur Almadhera said. "None of you offworlders will do that."

"I didn't expect to see you again so soon after last night, *t'an* Cassirur."

Urbane as that was, I saw it provoke a flicker of humour in her; but when I glanced from her reflection to her face, it was gone.

She said, "I hear that you offworlders have been to Kel Harantish."

Hardly necessary to ask where she'd heard it: Douglas Clifford.

"That's no secret, *t'an*; we deal with Orthe as one world – "

"We won't trade with you."

At that interruption, I stopped. We looked at each other. She was a flare of colour on that pale terrace: scarlet mane braided down her spine with crystal beads, green-and-gold slit-backed robe, gold studs set in the skin-webs between fingers and high-arched toes. Age hardly touched that sleek brown face, those whiteless eyes.

Dropping civility and diplomacy together (because I judged it safe to do so), I said, "For God's sake let's sit down and talk this over. You don't strike me as someone to do the Wellhouses' dirty work for them, but I can't think why else you're here."

"I suppose I am here for God's sake, though She'd say it was for mine. . . ." Cassirur Almadhera inclined her head, and moved towards one of the long tables on the terrace, where a spirit lamp stood ready to heat *siir*-wine. Her hands were steady as she lit the flame. "We won't trade with you for the same reason that we won't trade with the Desert Coast or the Rainbow Cities – "

"You do trade with them."

"Nothing of *this*." Her emphasis took in all the customs of Orventa;

65

the group at the far end of the terrace engaged in constructing a complex mechanism that might (I thought) be a water-clock.

"I know the Hundred Thousand are under the impression only they can be trusted with even this much technology. Cassirur, tell the Wellhouses you can't use the same techniques to deal with multicorporate Companies."

In a measured tone, she remarked, "You don't strike me as someone to do the Company's dirty work for them, but I can't think why else you're here."

That touched me on the raw. I'm here to act as a brake, I thought. A shock-absorber.

"Seems to me we're in a similar position."

She did grin at that. "Hal told me you weren't like the young one there." She waved a hand vaguely down the terrace at another table, where Molly Rachel sat with Barris Rakviri and the *s'an* Jaharien.

"Cassirur, I'm probably more like her than I am like you. And it's her generation that represents PanOceania here on Carrick V. Co-operate a little?"

She shook her head, not in negation but in wonder; a gesture at once weary and graceful. "But that's strange, to have one generation so different from the last."

We're not Ortheans – who will tell you (if they speak of it) that they are born remembering all their past lives upon this Goddess's earth. I said, "We have no past-memories, *t'an* Earthspeaker."

Speaking her title reminded me of how unlike other Earthspeakers this woman seems. Yet as we sat on the *zilmei* pelts that covered the stone bench, breath smoking on the chill air, scenting the tubs of indoor *kazsis*-vine, I began to sense something of that odd perception that belongs with Earthspeakers and Wellkeepers.

She said, "But you *have* past-memories, Christie. I know the look of one haunted by them, and you are."

She was grave, leaning forward to warm her fingers at the spirit lamp; dark eyes holding a brilliant clarity.

"I . . ." Not memories of past lives, I thought wryly. Fragments of old hypno-data, possibly. "When I was here last, we used to say that you have past-memories of past lives, and we have *dreams* – " there was no term for it in Morvrenni " – visions of sleep. Yes, I dream. But not – haunted."

The soft hissing of *siir*-wine as it boiled recalled me to that cold noon, and I took the metal jug and tipped hot wine into ceramic bowls. The Almadhera cupped her six-fingered hands round the bowl: that immemorial gesture of seeking warmth.

I said, "The Wellhouses won't trade with Earth. What about the *telestres*? Will they?"

She was not to be caught by such tricks. "All hundred thousand of them? Christie, how could I know? Still, we've had eight years' knowledge of Earth, and seen no great necessity to trade with you before."

"That was then. This may be different."

She leaned back against one of the metal struts that supported the terrace's glass cover. Then she trailed one claw-nailed finger down the condensation on the surface, which rang thin, high, and clear.

"Considering you're no stranger to Wellhouses, Christie, you haven't asked a question I'd expected."

Siir-wine's heat was welcome. The pepperspice taste carries fewer memories for me, it wasn't in season the last time I was in Morvren. And the last time I was in Morvren . . .

"I know your Wellhouses have contacts outside the Hundred Thousand, if that's what you mean. Dalzielle Kerys-Andrethe, when she was Crown, had a link – albeit tenuous – with Kasabaarde." I tried to judge from her expression whether I was on the right track. "How far will the church follow the Tower's advice? And how far will the *telestres* follow the church?"

Her face showed that paradoxical mixture of awe and friendly contempt that the *telestre*-Ortheans have for Kasabaarde. "Don't speak of the church in one breath and the *telestres* in another, we're the same. We've gone our own way, always, in the Hundred Thousand."

Somehow the discussion had got away from me, out of my control; and that rarely happens. Cassirur Almadhera was tough, but that's my job. I thought, It shouldn't faze me like this.

"When I was in the Tower – " I broke off, meeting her eyes.

"Haltern said something of that. Few have ever been further than the inner city of Kasabaarde, but he, also, entered past that and into the Brown Tower. . . . I wonder your Company doesn't go to Kasabaarde. Although you would find it no different from us," Cassirur said thoughtfully, "with some few relics of the Empire, but no great desire to use them. We've moved beyond the days when there could be an Empire – "

"There's no Witchbreed technology in the Tower; none, none at all!"

Her startled expression told me that I'd interrupted. There was a cold silence. I tried desperately to think of a way to smooth it over, regain that rapport struck up between us, but I couldn't formulate explanation or apology.

"You and Haltern Beth'ru-elen will know more of the Tower than I," she said, retreating into Morvrenni's formal inflection.

I sat dumb, watching her.

I didn't know, then, what it meant, that blank confusion in my mind. I only sensed trouble, like a far-off cloud. And I didn't know that I would be diverted from simple ambition to ease culture shock on Orthe, into something far more complex and momentous. I could only look into her cool and whiteless eyes.

Distant gongs clashed. A general movement began among the Ortheans on the terrace, summoned to the kitchen-halls for the midday meal. Cassirur Almadhera nodded, and excused herself, and went to join them. I still sat, until Molly Rachel's voice recalled me; and then I rose, a little stiff with the cold, to walk towards the kitchens with her and Barris and the *s'an* Jaharien Rakviri.

Lamps hung suspended from ornamental brickwork. The kitchens were vast warrens, round-roofed brick halls warmed from the open doors of ovens, and smelling of cooking – the last dried provisions of Orventa, the first sea-harvest of spring. Several dozen Ortheans settled into this hall alone. We got curious glances, a few friendly comments, but I took no notice.

I know what's next on the agenda, I thought.

And sure enough, as that *zilmei*-swathed figure ensconced himself in a couch-chair, the half-blind bright gaze of Haltern n'ri n'suth Beth'ru-elen found me. He beckoned me across to his alcove. Even if he hadn't planned to have the Almadhera soften me up, he was much too old a hand to see me shaken and miss the opportunity to question me.

"Give you greeting," I said, a little sardonically, and pulled the end of a bench across so that I could sit down beside him. "Cold for travelling, isn't it? And ten miles in a *skurrai-jasin* is wonderfully bracing. . . ."

He smiled, leaning back, basking in the warmth of an oven door six yards away. The windows here were roundly arched, and set with an amber glass, so that winter's pale glare was transmuted to warmth, and the light fell on his lined skin and crest-mane like a benediction. A faint and permanent tremor showed in those six-fingered hands.

He let the talk from the other tables mask his voice. "Journeys end in – "

"Diplomat's meeting?" I suggested.

"I was about to say, in hot food and good company." The nictitating membrane slid across his eyes, still pale and clear blue. "Such concern with motives! Such suspicion . . . I like to travel in the company of Earthspeakers, especially when of so liberal a mind as Cassirur; and since she'd determined on visiting her Rakviri friends . . ."

"Give it a rest," I advised. "I may be getting old, but I *do* remember your profession in Tathcaer."

"There's no office of Crown Messenger now; nor will be, until we've named a Crown again."

"You haven't arrived at Midsummer-Tenyear. But you'll tell me that ceremony won't stand in your way?"

Some of the younger Rakviri brought food: *rukshi*, and breadfungus, and the early shoots of the *hanelys*. His fingers shredded a piece of breadfungus, crumbling it to release the sharp lemony smell.

"I confess I don't clearly see how we shall deal with PanOceania," he said. "Christie, don't take it amiss if I heartily wish you gone – all of you."

I made an attempt to look mortally offended, and he chuckled; a thin, asthmatic sound. Then, more seriously, he said, "I do conceive of a future when, since we can't be manipulated, the Company may leave us. To do anything else under present circumstances, you would have to use force. And if young Rachel is a reliable clue, that would require some very concrete evidence before PanOceania would risk it."

"And perhaps not even then." I took some of the breadfungus. "Which presupposes we won't find concrete evidence."

"Indeed it does. You presuppose, however, that there's something to find."

"Indeed I do. . . ."

Such half-humorous, half-bitter fencing is what I miss among ground-siders, on Earth; to come back to it now is to enter the element natural to me. But like any *ochmir* player, one can prize the game more than the conclusion. That's always a mistake.

"Well, we have our own business," the old male said philosophically. "The Coast is troublesome again, and, having no *T'Ans* nor *takshiriye*, we must make the best of that and send some of our Freeporters to talk with them. In the spring, to Kasabaarde."

"There's been fighting with the Coast?"

"The last few years have seen sea-raids on the Melkathi *telestres*, and the city Ales-Kadareth, and on trading ships on the Inner Sea."

His bird-bright eyes flicked up; the glance aware of names from the past: Ales-Kadareth, Melkathi. . . .

Now I could look across and see Molly Rachel talking with Cassirur Almadhera. The red-maned Orthean's head went back, an unrestrained laugh sounding above the general noise; Molly addressed some remark to the *s'an* Jaharien, and she and both of them laughed again.

"Hal, if we're talking about wishes, I'd wish to have the situation as it was ten years ago: nothing demanded of Orthe, nothing we wanted."

Some sudden perception made me see this for what it was, a lull, paradisiacal by its very ordinariness. We won't talk so easily again, I

69

thought. What I do here, now, supersedes what I did then. And so I tried to imprint on memory those Orthean faces, the bright robes, the rich food; Molly Rachel the centre of attention, all wit and good humour; and the old male with me, Haltern Beth'ru-elen, decade-old memories round us like a benevolent haunting.

"It troubles you to be here," he said.

"I'm here because you need someone who can see your interests as well as ours."

"Which, of course, you don't trust any but Lynne de Lisle Christie to perceive. . . ."

That was so like Molly Rachel's opinion, and so accurate, that I winced. It may be vanity, I thought; does that make it any the less true?

"I'll tell you something, Hal. Molly Rachel doesn't know how to deal with the Hundred Thousand – but she doesn't *have* to know. The Companies aren't under any necessity to understand alien worlds. They don't need to. Come a little way to meet us. Or you'll get steamrollered."

The metaphor I used was not quite that one, but the inference was equally plain. Haltern rubbed at his half-covered eyes; and blinked.

"Threats?"

"Hal, if in your advanced state of wisdom and contemplation, you fail to recognize a friendly warning – "

He spluttered a little, that old male; and the light shifted on his winterscale skin as he smiled. The great arches here were open to the cloisters outside, so we sat between oven-heat and frost-sharp air; and the scent drifted in of *hanelys* and *siir* and the warm musk of *skurrai*.

"Rakviri is a beautiful *telestre*," Haltern said. "My eyes aren't good enough now, but you may have noticed: from the south terrace you can see the beginning of the Rasrhe-y-Meluur."

That great pylon, soft blue against a pale blue sky, almost lost. Bridging two continents: ghost-image of that past Empire.

"We're not the Coast," he added, following the connection. "We don't scratch out a living between rock and bitter sea. You have no – what's a suitably technological metaphor? No lever, to move us all with. Now on the Coast it's the water of the canals, and that lever's been held for two thousand years by the Harantish Witchbreed; do you contemplate taking it from them? I confess I would, were I PanOceania, which the Goddess forbid."

The entertainment value of seeing Haltern n'ri n'suth Beth'ru-elen play at devout old alien, laboriously reinventing the metaphors of a technological society, is high. If entirely unconvincing. I heard what he said: *Go away*, and *We have negotiations in progress with the Coast, do what*

70

you like with Kel Harantish. And I wished that I had access to his memory, instead of PanOceania's data-nets.

"You could make an argument for there being a lever to the Hundred Thousand," I said. "The anti-technology ethic. And the Wellhouses being in control of it. For example, *you* know the *T'An Suthai-Telestre* spoke to us of them and Kasabaarde – "

What curiosity can gnaw a man, even (or especially) a man like Haltern, so long used to knowing the secret side of all events? He said, "You know more of Kasabaarde's influence than I do – and you an offworlder. You know more of the Tower."

"The Tower had enough influence to contact me, sight unseen, that winter in Shiriya-Shenin – "

It's slipping, I thought; I'm losing it again: why?

A smell issued from one of the nearby alcoves, where slaughtered carcasses were hung up to drain. Until now mere sensory background, now with that thought, that blood, memory within an instant became concrete –

Spring twilight fills the Crystal Hall in Shiriya-Shenin, the quartz windows gleaming. The Andrethe of Peir-Dadeni has her back to me, sitting in a chair facing one of the dying fires.

"Excuse me, Excellence. . . ."

She is leaning back, one fat arm over the side of the chair. Asleep. As I step round her, over the dappled furs, the spring light shines on her dark face and red-and-white robe. Her fingers hold reflected red firelight, streaming on the furs and stone floor.

The smell –

Not a red robe. A white robe, sopping red from shoulder to lap to hem. The stink of blood and faeces. Blood dripping from her curved fingers. Her open unveiled eyes stare at me. Jammed under her chin, amid rolls of flesh, a knife-handle keeps her head back –

Nausea: more acute than I thought memory could cause.

You should thank God for Kasabaarde, I thought; Lynne, if the Tower hadn't cleared you of the Andrethe's murder . . . Dear God: old memories!

As if his memory paralleled mine, Haltern reached across to rest a hand on my arm. "That was a bad time for us all."

"Are you certain Kasabaarde isn't a lever? Don't forget, I've proof of how highly the Hundred Thousand regards the Hexenmeister's information. *You* believed it instantly when he told you I hadn't killed Kanta Andrethe."

"To begin with, I know Lynne Christie." His warmth metamorphosed into curiosity. "And I have often wished I had all the Kasabaarde traders

71

to bring *me* intelligence of what passes in the world, as the Tower has. That's not all the story, though, is it? The Hexenmeister spoke as if – "

"As if he was there," I said.

"And yet there's no memory or past-memory of the Hexenmeister ever leaving the Tower."

"That's the truth," I said. "And very wise: if I had what's in there, *I'd* stay in the Tower. It must be the most securely defended structure on two continents – "

" 'What's in there'?"

"What?"

"I have often wondered," he said.

"I don't understand."

If he laughed, it was at himself. "Because you and I have both faced that serially-immortal Hexenmeister . . . and while Hexenmeisters live and die, there's but one same Hexenmeister in the tower; my memory – " he gave it the inflection that included memory of past lives " – tells me this is so. But not why. Christie, you know my curiosity!"

"Hal, I really don't understand what you're talking about."

He frowned, and his claw-nailed hand closed over mine as if he were trying to reassure or comfort me.

"If it troubles you so much, I'll say no more. I'd thought, since you spent time within the Tower, and left it so changed, that you might have spoken often enough with the Hexenmeister to gain some knowledge I don't have. Don't be distressed."

"I don't know what you mean."

"Christie – "

I stood and walked across to where Molly Rachel sat among the uncleared bowls and platters, temporarily separated from Cassirur and the Rakviri. She looked up as I approached. A comlink was open in her palm.

"What have you been saying to the Beth'ru-elen?" Molly asked, glancing across at the place I'd just left. "He's not too happy about it."

When I concentrated, I could stop that fine perceptible shake in my hands. I looked back at Hal. No memory of a farewell – did I really do that? I thought. Did I just stand up and *go*?

I would have returned, but Cassirur Almadhera slipped into that seat and began talking quietly with the Beth'ru-elen.

"I've been trying to get through to Morvren Freeport," Molly said, replacing the comlink at her belt. "Communications are going to be erratic here, to say the least of it. . . . David Osaka says the shuttles are coming down from the orbiter."

Whatever reaction I have to being back on Orthe, whatever version of hypno-psychosis or offworld syndrome this is, it shouldn't be allowed to affect my job. With that thought, it was as if my mind returned to a sharp focus. I thought, I'll make an appointment to see the Psych people sometime this week. Until then, I'll manage.

"What about the Witchbreed artifact here?"

Molly nodded. "That's priority. Sometime over the next couple of hours, we *must* find a way to talk to Barris Rakviri on his own."

CHAPTER 7

Heirs of an Empire Long Passed Away

With that new mental clarity came an appreciation: *we're close to being out-manoeuvred here*. With no *T'An Suthai-Telestre* or *T'Ans* now, it's the Wellhouses that watch offworlders – and they don't want Earth tech at all. And the *rashaku*-relay will have taken the news out. . . .

"How does this sound? I'll talk to *s'an* Jaharien," I said. "For one thing, it might give you a chance to get to Barris.'

"And?" the Pacifican woman prompted.

The kitchen-halls began to smell stale with old cooking. Light fell through amber glass on to the few Ortheans left drinking *siir*-wine and talking. Not that they ignore offworlders, precisely; it's a kind of self-sufficiency they possess.

"And – I might be able to persuade Jaharien. I don't know. Because my name carries weight here?" I shrugged. "Molly, understand me. I want you to see, as soon as possible, that nothing here in the Hundred Thousand is useful to the Company."

The black woman rose from the chair in one smooth movement. Something tireless in her, both physical and mental.

"You'll help because that's your job. If that means using the *S'aranth* name, then do it." Her gaze was not on me, but searching for Barris. She said, "You're as much a part of the Company as I am."

Kites flew on the cold wind; yellow, scarlet, and viridian against the daystarred sky. Streamers fluttered. The glittering curves of the glass terrace formed a looming backdrop to all these small courtyards. I walked with the *s'an* Jaharien beside white walls, hearing the hiss of penned *skurrai* and the larger *marhaz*. The cold kept me alert – it was that hour in early afternoon when I needed sleep. Even in spring, Orthe has too many daylight hours for human comfort.

"*S'an* Jaharien . . . your *telestre* isn't much impressed by offworlders, is it? But then, I suppose you've had time to get used to us."

"Ask instead, how many of us are capable of seeing what it means to have offworlders here." He spoke sardonically, with the slurred Morvrenni river-dialect. I guessed from his broad shoulders and rope-scarred hands that he sailed either Ai River ships or coastal *jath-rai*.

"Perhaps you underestimate the people here."

74

"*T'an*, perhaps I do." The wind blew his short, unbraided mane forward, and he put it back with one claw-nailed hand. "Barris tells me – he is my *arykei*, and should know – he tells me I think no other but myself capable. And that's why I am *s'an*. And that's why I see *s'aranthi* here, and doubt our wisdom. Your *t'an* Molly Rachel, she sees nothing but her desire."

"That I'll admit is true."

Sea gravel crunched underfoot as we walked down the colonnade, and the kites made bright curves in the alien sunlight. Frost still lay in the shadow of the gate-arch, where we passed through into another court-yard. I shivered. And wondered what angle of attack to try next.

"The Beth'ru-elen speaks of you," Jaharien said suddenly. "Is it true – *are* you that Christie, Christie *S'aranth*?"

His voice was wiped momentarily clear of the cynicism that seemed his natural idiom.

"I'm Christie," I said.

His head turned towards me. I saw the slow glide of nictitating membrane: a gaze darker (and somehow deeper) in those unveiled, alien eyes. The edge of his robe hissed on the gravel path as we walked.

"When Barris told me, I called him a liar; the *S'aranth* – " Jaharien stopped abruptly. One six-fingered hand sought the hilt of *harur-nilgiri*, as if for comfort. Now, on those alien features, I could recognize a kind of awe. Even though I'd been counting on something like it, it disturbed me.

Words came from him in a spate: "So many Orventa tales of you! – that year, that first year; the Crown, Suthafiori; Kanta Andrethe, and Wellkeeper Arad, and Sulis SuBannasen – "

Even in that unguarded enthusiasm, he left out the name of Orhlandis.

" – and the first meeting with offworlders; you and your kin in Tathcaer – !" He shook his dark-maned head, laughed at his own capacity for being impressed. "Pardon, *t'an*. You must have heard this often since you came back to us."

Enough to conceive of it as an influence, that *S'aranth* name. Nonetheless, I felt embarrassed. "There were a lot of us on that first contact team, not just me."

"But you were the first to come to the *telestres*."

We walked on. It was too cold to stand and talk. There was a soft discordancy: the clash of bright *harur*-blades belted at his hip.

"I went to *telestres* and Wellhouses," I carefully reminded him.

"Corbek-in-Roehmonde. The tale is that the Wellkeeper there had you imprisoned, but you escaped to Shiriya-Shenin and had him brought to trial."

I heard no resentment in Jaharien's voice. No indication that he would support church against offworlders, regardless.

"And does Cassirur Almadhera talk about the *S'aranth*, too?" I asked. "I don't have to wonder why an Earthspeaker's in Rakviri, do I? Jaharien, I'll say something I shouldn't, but it's for my peace of mind . . . what *will* it do to the Hundred Thousand if we trade with you for Witchbreed technology?"

Jaharien Rakviri had an expression almost of delight. This dark male, a handful of years younger than I; looking at me wide-eyed as any *ashiren*.

"I'd always thought Christie *S'aranth* would ask such a question. *T'an*, pardon me; you don't need to ask that, you know already. It won't do anything to the Hundred Thousand. No more than burning Orventa's machines at Spring Thaw Festival, and building them again next winter."

His voice had triumph in it. With some self-disgust at the manipulation, I thought, I've obviously lived up to the public image. Does the mask of Christie *S'aranth* still fit? What have they made my name into while I've been away?

Jaharien went on impetuously: "Earthspeakers, even Cassirur; they're overcautious. You and *t'an* Rachel . . . I think you understand us. Barris was right. There can be no great harm in this. If I allowed it, and didn't believe it safe – I should deserve to have the *telestre* name another *s'an* in place of me."

I glanced across at his unguarded expression. It's a little late to feel – what? Ashamed? *Don't make me into something I'm not.* Don't let me persuade you against your judgement. I feel as though I'm here on false pretences.

"You know the telestres," Jaharien added. "I have some confidence in my powers of judgement, *t'an*. And in yours."

We turned a corner, passing under another arch, returning towards the crystal façade of the great terrace. My fingers were white with the cold. Carrick's Star blazed.

Against all professional instinct, knowing it might lose me what I'd just gained, I had to protest. "For all you've heard about the *S'aranth*, I . . . oh, I'd have made a better anthropologist than diplomat; I did better work up in the Barrens than I ever did in the Hundred Thousand *telestres*. In Melkathi I failed – but if you know that story, *s'an* Jaharien, you know how it ended."

"*S'aranth*, Rakviri isn't Orhlandis."

He pronounced the name of that Melkathi *telestre* with a kind of arrogant condescension. What I meant for honesty, he took as self-deprecation. No way to get rid of that *S'aranth* name.

76

As we came under the bright reflections of the terrace, I thought, I've made you trust me. All the easier because you're arrogant, and being impressed catches you off-guard. Christie *S'aranth*.

For a long, vertiginous moment, I wanted to turn him against me. If *S'aranth* is the key to the lock, I don't want to go through the door.

Molly Rachel said, *You're as much a part of the Company as I am.*

"Come with me," Jaharien said. "We'll find Barris, and your *t'an* Rachel. I'll take you to where we keep the relics of the Golden Witchbreed."

I said nothing. I followed him inside.

Somehow, although I know the Orthean mind, I expected more conceal-ment. But Jaharien led us through the sprawling *telestre*-house to the unguarded entrance of a small hall, the ground floor of an octagonal tower.

"Here?" I said.

Jaharien pushed the bead-curtain aside. Barris Rakviri's cane tapped on the echoing stone floor as he went in. Molly Rachel followed, gazing up at the glass mosaic ceiling, in this room where the air smelled of dust and the light is always pale.

"What about the Earthspeaker Cassirur?" I asked, letting the curtain fall back into place behind me.

The Pacifican woman gave neither of them the chance to reply. "*S'an*, you said – functional relics."

A look went between the two Orthean males, the opaque glance of some shared past-memory. Barris small and thin, leaning on the *hanelys* stick; and the burly Jaharien at his shoulder. Both dark-maned, pale-skinned; in heavy Morvrenni robes.

"How long has Rakviri kept Witchbreed relics?" I asked.

"There was a lost time after the Empire fell. Out of it came the *telestres*. Since then, *t'an S'aranth*." Jaharien's membraned gaze was blind with two millennia.

In this octagonal room, one wall held the entrance, another an embrasured window; and all the others deep alcoves, set back into the masonry. I could hear the voices of *ashiren* in the courtyard outside.

Molly, impatient, said, "Then can we *see* – "

Jaharien's gaze cleared. Our eyes met. I saw in him the first intimations of doubt. He put one claw-nailed hand on Barris's shoulder; spoke equally to the younger Orthean male and to Molly Rachel: "This isn't to be done lightly. The *telestres* . . . offworlder, we don't forget. In four days, at the Festival of the Wells, we'll burn the devices created through Orventa. *This is why.*"

Barris moved away, rejecting the older male's urgency. The marsh-flower dapples made a sneer of his expression. He leaned the *hanelys* stick against the wall, and went to the nearest alcove, which stood some three feet above floor level. I saw how he tugged his dark *becamil* over-robe about himself, as if he felt cold.

Without looking back at us, he said, "We're free of the Empire. There are none of the Golden Witchbreed now but in past-memory. Nor will we ever become as they."

For all her mask of professionalism, Molly Rachel's long-fingered hands were trembling. I thought I felt something of the cold that touched the Rakviri.

Since the Witchbreed Empire fell . . .

We are not Witchbreed, said that nameless Voice in Kel Harantish. *That is what superstitious northern barbarians call us. We are the Golden.*

Since the Golden Empire fell, and all its cities: Simmerath, aKirrik, Archonys (that brilliant beating heart of Empire); since that great alien culture fell, and all its works. . . .

"I have no memory to help me in this," Barris said. There was something bitter in his tone. "The Empire didn't allow its slave races such knowledge." The alcove held copper and glass, woven into a fine mesh cage; and the patchmarked Orthean reached into small ceramic pots, touching the metal with several substances.

"*Ashiren.*" Barris turned his head; that dark gaze like a blow. "We're *ashiren*, playing in the ruins. The Witchbreed could do this merely by bending their will to it, and I . . . *S'aranth*, I play *ashiren*-games with herbs and metal ore."

He stepped aside, and I saw that the glass and copper mesh cage enclosed a globe of *chiruzeth*. Was it a trick of light, or was that blue-grey substance faintly luminous?

No illusion. A faint light, the blue-pink colour of lightning. Molly's hand closed over my arm.

"Bel-Kurick," she whispered. Remembering the haggard face of Dannor bel-Kurick, Emperor-in-Exile, in Kel Harantish. But this light was faint, fading . . .

cold high walls, webbed with darkness; the smell of dust, and musk, and the stale air –

"I thought, in Kel Harantish, one responds to it with more than just visual perception." She spoke in Sino-Anglic, in a tone of suppressed excitement. "Did you feel it? Like a touch, a smell. It's some pan-spectrum broadcast, not just visible light."

Revulsion touched me. "If we can perceive it, it might damage us."

She was oblivious. If we can perceive it, we might be able to understand it. Lynne, we might!"

The *chiruzeth* globe's colour faded to an inert blue-grey. I almost wanted to touch the masonry of the alcove and feel if the light had *stained* it – absurd. But I feel what makes Ortheans fear Witchbreed relics. The echo of a dead power. And is this what I thought I could keep the Company away from?

"It's necessary!" Barris's voice rose, and he stepped back, glaring at the older male. Jaharien paused.

"If you must," he said finally. Jaharien looked at me, then. More *s'an* Rakviri than admirer of the *S'aranth*. Here where Witchbreed relics were more than a name, I could see him realize how I'd used the public legend. His expression was cold.

The next alcove held a shallow bowl, wider round than human arms could span. Roughcast iron, still jagged here and there from the forge, and with a scar of orange rust on one curve. Barris Rakviri reached up to a niche in the back of the alcove, repeating his first procedure, and another sphere-light began to glow and illuminate the cold masonry.

"Jesus!" Molly said loudly. I echoed her, involuntarily.

What I had taken to be fragments of *chiruzeth* in the iron bowl were not broken pieces. The blue-grey substance *flowed*. A viscous movement began wherever that lilac-and-blue illumination fell on the *chiruzeth*, and an answering translucent depth gleamed in that substance that moved with the tropism of plants, of living matter. The mass moved. The iron in the bowl's scarred interior flaked away, turning to brown-and-orange rust, and decaying into the very air. . . .

"Energy transfer," Molly whispered. "Christ, will you look at that!" There was no fear in her voice. Wonder, greed, joy; but no terror.

The *chiruzeth* darkened to a dull grey; began to build itself up in complex shapes. All breathing ceased, and all sound. When the device it formed stood complete, part solid, part moving to the pulse of that strange energy, only the lace-like shell of an iron bowl remained.

In Sino-Anglic Molly said, "You told us they were soft-sciencers, the Witchbreed. Look at it. . . . What would you call it? Analogue-DNA? Living crystal?"

"Gene-sculpting?" I suggested. Still lost, still awed.

"Something between living and inanimate tissue." Her eyes shone.

"If they patterned the structure – genes, viruses – and then . . ." Then some transfer of will, that Ortheans now could only mimic by chemical or biological stimulus-triggers.

Molly leaned closer to the relic. The dimensions of it twisted the eye. I saw curves and angles and solids within that polyhedral shape, but I didn't know what they *meant*. And so perhaps I didn't truly see them.

"How does it function?" she asked.

79

"You mean, will it function for *s'aranthi*?" Jaharien was leaning against the door-arch, idly keeping watch. "I do believe it might – you have a persuasive manner, you offworlders."

That casual tone held black irony. I expected it: still it made me uncomfortable.

Barris Rakviri, oblivious to what Jaharien implied, said, "It holds images of the time of the Empire."

I thought, I'm not afraid of what it could show me. Witchbreed cities: cyclopean architecture that, for all the myriad sphere-lights, was never more than one-tenth illuminated; sky-flyers, scent-fountains, metalmesh cloth. Nor do I fear the sight of the Witchbreed, those long-dead faces with coin-gold eyes. Ten years ago I looked on the millennially-old image of Santhendor'lin-sandru, called Phoenix Emperor and Last Emperor . . .

But I am afraid of what unshielded exposure to alien technology might do to me.

"We'll trade for it as it stands," Molly Rachel said. She tucked her hands under the belt of her coveralls. In Sino-Anglic she added, "I'm having nothing to do with that outside laboratory conditions."

"That's the first sensible thing you've said since we came here."

It was the alteration in her expression that warned me, an instant before all else was utterly changed.

Instead of light, the *chiruzeth* device radiated blindness; a blindness as brilliant as forked lightning. Where it fell on my skin, it had a velvet touch. A scent filled the air: nothing ever known before.

"Stop this – "

As if I could perceive with some sense that was not sight, I saw Molly Rachel, Jaharien, Barris Rakviri. We moved through a vast chamber. No knowing how great: only the age of it was a weight, a pressure. Walked at a slow pace, bearing a burden. . . .

Metalcloth robes slide with a dull hiss over a chiruzeth floor. The air is burningly chill. Sphere-lights illumine only the base of cyclopean pillars, carved with patterns that are intricate, stylized or naturalistic variations on one theme only: the death's-head. . . .

"_____ ___ _____ _____"

Molly's voice, chanting. Language incomprehensible. She walks on bare high-arched feet. Her mane is a pale cloud of flame. All the dimensions of bone and muscle subtly wrong: wrong as the skin that has the sheen and depth of gold. Her robe is patchwork enamel, black-and-white. She paces slowly. In her arms she cradles a cup, a globe, a ragged staff.

Her eyes are yellow gold.

Nightmare, this movement that cannot be stopped, as we pace towards the darkness ahead. A greater darkness, visible negation, anti-light.

"___ __ __ _____ __"

"_ _____ __ __ ___"

Jaharien paces in hooded robes all the colours of sunset. His gold-skinned hands outstretched: in one a twin-bladed sword, in the other some deadly construct of chiruzeth and onyx and gold.

Behind him, Barris moves at a slow processional pace, his arms raised to carry a bier. Whitefire mane, yellow eyes. My shoulder aches to the same burden. My mouth moves to the same incomprehensible chant.

"___ __ _____ ____"

"_____ __ _____ __"

The burden set down where a circle of thrones stand on a dais. Our chant in many voices passes from throne to throne. Over, in, around us: that brilliant blackness.

The burden set down: a slender alien body, pale as ice against the dark: a woman of the Witchbreed. Gold skin blotched with pus-yellow, blue-green: the colours of corruption. Lowering that burden, soft and heavy in my hands, to a raised slab of chiruzeth.

"___ __ _____ ___"

"_____ _____ ___"

"__ __ _____ __"

The chant continues. Celebrants, we stand. There is a knife on the chiruzeth, at the feet of the corpse. I see on alien lineaments the stirring of ritual appetites. Whose hand will lift the knife; whose hand will cut and divide the flesh?

Surrounded by these faces: faces of the imperial Golden bloodline: she who stands beside me, they who flank the body; even (discernible yet in corruption) that dead face: gold skin, white mane, and coin-gold yellow eyes.

That radiant shadow working on me, like a splinter of metal working inward to the heart: what realization might come when it pierces? Death's bright shadow –

– gone from that pale octagonal room. Sunlight shone on the human face of Molly Rachel, on the two Rakviri males. The masonry of the wall was cold under my hands, where I leaned back for support. And the most banal scent possible brought the world back to me: the pepperspice odour of *siir*-wine.

I thrust images out of my mind, and, determined to take some initiative, managed to say, "Give you greeting, *t'an* Earthspeaker," to the Orthean woman standing in the doorway. She held back the coin-curtain with one hand; in the other she carried a jug and bowls. Scarlet mane, green slit-backed robe.

"Trouble?" asked Cassirur Almadhera, letting the curtain fall behind her as she entered. She was encumbered by the jug and bowls, and put them down on a low table by the door. "Hal thought he or I could find you, and I thought you might need *siir*-wine – "

Without more than a glance, she gestured with one claw-nailed hand. The *chiruzeth* device lost energy. In moments, it was inert, blue-grey; could have been nothing more than some eye-twisting nightmare sculpture.

Earthspeaker, part of me thought; and another sceptic voice, barely recovering wit to think, said, *Showmanship*. She waited outside until it had – what? – finished its cycle, gone quiescent? And then she made an entrance.

"*S'an* Jaharien," she acknowledged. "I've just met with Mezidon, she's looking for you. Some problem with loading the food-ships, I believe."

The burly male looked across the room at me. Traces of shock and revulsion remained in his expression, but what I chiefly saw was an odd kind of satisfaction. That offworlders had been shown Witchbreed technology? That the experience had left one of us, at least, shit-scared? That experience of trauma –

Whose hand will take the knife, under that bright shadow?

When he saw me then, what did he see?

"Thank you, *t'an* Earthspeaker." Jaharien turned and left the room, his footsteps echoing. Barris looked as though he wanted to speak, but only grasped his *hanelys* cane and limped after the *s'an*.

Cassirur said quietly, "Look to your friend, Christie."

Molly Rachel still stood balanced lightly on the balls of her feet, eyes fixed on a non-existent horizon. The flat, dark features were distorted, as though she squinted against some light.

"Is that *siir*? If you give – " Finding that an insistent gentle pressure induced her to move, I steered her to the low table, and took the bowl that Cassirur held up. "Molly, can you drink? Try."

She drank quite naturally, wiped that long-angled wrist across her mouth and put the bowl down, and then caught at the edge of the table.

"Lynne – "

Cassirur, having almost to stand on tiptoe, brushed black curls aside to touch the woman's brow. Molly pushed her hand away. The Earthspeaker nodded. "You'll manage. *T'an* Christie . . ." Both her hands gripped my shoulders, fingers covering too wide a span for human body-instincts. Then the nictitating membrane slid back from her eyes.

"I see an old tale's true," she said wryly. "You have been in Her Wellhouses, and marked for Her, and She has received your name. Count yourself lucky, *S'aranth*. It could have been much worse."

Molly Rachel rubbed her hands across her face. Then she let her hands fall and I saw the quite unconscious check: comlink, CAS-IV, wristlink-medicall. "I don't like mysticism."

"I say only that Christie's been marked with the water of the Well of the Goddess."

In Sino-Anglic, the Pacifican woman said, "Superstitious barbarians!"

The Almadhera shook back the sleeves of her robe, and began to pour more *siir*-wine. I saw those whiteless brown eyes were full of laughter.

"Not barbarians, *t'an* Rachel, surely? We've treated you with all hospitality. As for superstitions . . ."

"Please." Molly Rachel shook her head. "*T'an* Cassirur, forgive me; I don't think I know what I'm saying."

"As for superstitions, to be marked for the Goddess means only that we meet, and part, and meet again; and do not forget."

Molly ignored that. "It's all mysticism. It's technology I'm concerned with."

"*T'an* Rachel, when I speak of the Goddess it embarrasses you."

"Oh, I . . ." Molly shifted her stance. "The way it is on our reports, your Kerys Founder set up the church after the Empire fell, so that no technology would ever be allowed into the *telestres*."

"And you will find it reported also, I think, how the mystic, Beth'ru-elen *Ashirenin*, came to find that lie a truth?"

I recall that Hal's *telestre* is said to have been founded by that remarkable Beth'ru-elen, who made a genuine religion from what began as a politic philosophy.

Molly Rachel crossed the room to look at the *chiruzeth* artifact: the congeries of globes, solids, lines, curves, angles. "Technology isn't good or evil. Only what it's used for can be that. And if the Witchbreed were insane enough to make a technological society into some barbaric, disgusting, cult-ridden – "

She broke off, nodded abruptly to Cassirur, and said, "I must talk to Barris and Jaharien. Excuse me."

In the silence after the curtain clashed behind her, Cassirur Almadhera said, "One forgets. At her age . . . yes, it would frighten her. We, on the other hand – "

Image: figures filled with light too bright to look on, phosphorus-brilliant; that vulture-feast and then a transformation . . .

"It frightened *me*. It still does. I don't comprehend it."

In repose, her features began to show their age. The Orthean woman said, "Don't you recognize it? Or is it too strange? They fell in love with that bright shadow, Death."

"Cassirur – "

"And it frightens me, Christie, because it is so akin to Her realm; Her fire that permeates this world like breath, Her fire made flesh in we who meet, and part, and meet again; and do not forget. But for the Golden there was nothing but this world. And so, imagining some final cessation, they worshipped it. To be out of the world, to be nothing – "

In her voice, I heard the beat of that litany of death; those untranslatable words echoed in the cadences of her speech. I took a bowl of *siir*-wine and drank, and fumbled as I set it down, spilling the green liquid as the ceramic crashed to splinters on the stone floor.

"I'm sorry; I feel – I'm not well – "

She was businesslike, abruptly all Earthspeaker. "Is it with you still? Speak it aloud, then. You need to. Those of us who remember such things, we need to speak of them."

A solid truth: might not that language, left unrecognized, control; like a dream forgotten but never resolved?

"To be out of the world. . . ."

I picked up the litany, straining for words, knowing how far I failed: "To go into that bright shadow, to seize on nothingness; willing to leap into the abyss – to love it more than life. Not to reject Her, but to love the bright annihilation *more* than Her. To be hollow with the longing for it. And burn all up in one final self-consummation. . . ."

"More," Cassirur demanded.

"The highest achievement: to reach after it, the only voice made incarnate flesh; to praise annihilation – pain that becomes joy, as cold can seem to burn. Holding it all for one instant within mortal compass, a glory of annihilation. . . . Go willingly, joyfully, to meet it; consumed in that brilliance – to choose that bright shadow Death and die, and go into utter nothing. . . ."

And it was true, to voice it was to divest it of its splendour. If only because I'm so bad at it, I thought; and then I could relax, even laugh with the Orthean woman.

"I don't have the words – I'm an empath, you need a poet."

She put back tendrils of mane from her angled brown face, the wisps scarlet against her claw-nails. Her smile faded. "That's the mere image of the Golden Witchbreed. What would you do if you had our living memory? The slavery of millennia, to *that*." Passion roughened her voice on the last word.

And strangely enough, it was that that restored the human perspective to me. There are enough problems in the present, now I know for certain there is technology here that the Company will want. I stretched, fingers in the small of my back; and then shrugged. "It's in the past, Cassirur. It *is* only an image. Will it hurt Rakviri to be rid of it? Trade with

PanOceania won't make the Hundred Thousand into another Golden Empire, I know that as well as you do."

"Do you want me to reassure you, Christie?"

"I wish *somebody* would."

She chuckled at that, some release of tension visible in the line of arm and shoulder and high-arched ribs. "Ah. . . . It's bad that these matters divide us. We could have been friends, you and I."

"Are we enemies, then?"

In the Freeport, in that room crowded with the *takshiriye*, she had seemed an Earthspeaker; here, she seemed all politician. One of those who have always to yearn towards the different parts of their divided natures.

"I *fear* the Golden Witchbreed. That Rachel-*ashiren* may be right; I'm nothing but superstitious. Christie, I fear them, whatever name they come under."

"I'll talk to you again," I offered. "If you'll speak with me. Cassirur, we need goodwill on either side. Whatever happens."

She briefly gripped my hands, her skin warm and dry. 'You have that. . . . I must go. It's not in my interests to let your Rachel talk too long alone with Barris and the *s'an* Rakviri, is it?" And she gave me a grin that dropped ten years off her age, and strode out.

Earthspeaker, *s'an*, Wellkeeper, *takshiriye* . . .

The *chiruzeth* artifact gleamed in the depths of the alcove, and for a moment I couldn't think of the manipulations of influence, or of what assistance PanOceania might need; how near or far we might be from a trade agreement. That pale octagonal room was cold, and the alcove held the only shadow.

A coldness: a bright burning shadow . . .

And Cassirur Almadhera doesn't fear it because it's repugnant to her. She fears it for the same reason that momentarily overpowered me: that the bright shadow is so easy to look upon and love.

85

PART TWO

CHAPTER 8

War Damage

Carrick's Star was setting in all the colours of frost and fire when I at last brought Barris Rakviri, alone, to the great terrace. Molly Rachel turned from staring out through the curved shells of glass. Some disquiet showed in her expression. She put it from her.

"Do we have an agreement?"

"We've got a price," I said. "Knowledge."

The Pacifican woman looked at Barris, his pale skin warm in the citrine light. Her brows raised. "What do you want to know?"

"Everything," Barris Rakviri said.

There was an intensity in his tone that shocked me. I am not used to hearing such need in any Orthean voice; it belongs to races who have no assurance of reincarnation.

Molly said, "I'm not sure I understand."

"He wants access to the data-nets. Unrestricted access."

The terrace was all but deserted now. A temporary, hard-won privacy. Somewhere towards the far end, a musician fingered some intricate, cold song. Molly Rachel's gaze returned to Barris, that small and dark-maned male, whose chemical-stained hands were clasped atop the *hanelys* stick on which he leaned.

"Good God, the things these people hear about. . . ." She went from Sino-Anglic to Morvrenni: "*T'an*, if you want to learn about the inhabited worlds, you could apply to leave Orthe."

A tone of condescension came into her voice. "Yours is one of the species that suffers offworld syndrome, I know; but you could have a short time – "

"Be fair," I said, "I've known humans have offworld syndrome too."

She looked at me thoughtfully. I put it down, then, to my being defensive about Ortheans.

The dark male said, "Does it matter what you call it, *t'an*? We live, under Her sky. We are part of Her, and we cannot live away from Her."

According to records, there have been eighty-seven Ortheans who, unofficially, and at one time or another over the past ten years, have been offworld. Of those eighty-seven, sixty-eight returned to Orthe within a half-year – the unanimity is almost frightening. But then the other nineteen . . . the other nineteen *died*. Not by illness, or accident. Not even by their own hand. But died like feral animals that can't live out of the wild.

The Pacifican woman said, "Some of your people have lived offworld."

"For a very short time, *t'an* Rachel. I need to know more than I could learn that way."

"I'd like a word," Molly said, with an apologetic glance, drawing me a few paces from Barris. Cold radiated from the glass of the terrace now, glass that darkened and distorted our reflections.

In Sino-Anglic I said, "This is a Restricted world; how can you open access to the data-bank network?"

"Is that all we can offer?"

"It's all he's interested in."

She frowned. "It's a Restricted world, it's not a Closed world."

And now we're on dubious territory. As simple as the stone that triggers an avalanche: if Rakviri is successful, then other *telestres* –

"Don't do it. Irrespective of the law, or Company policy; don't let Barris Rakviri loose on unrestricted data-networks. I don't say one person can make a great difference to anything here, but all the same. . . ." And I wonder: when the customs of Orventa demand that reinvented technology be destroyed – does Barris Rakviri regret it?

"We have to take some risks." Molly raised her voice, drawing Barris into the conversation. "*T'an* Barris, this is going to take some negotiation with my Company, but in principle it doesn't seem an impossible request."

Principles? I wondered. Maybe this is my first opportunity. If I leak the news to home office in advance, and maybe to the government, through Douggie, they'll protest – I hope. How else do I put a hold on culture shock, except by delay?

"*T'ans s'aranthi.*"

Jaharien Rakviri walked on to the terrace. His step was soundless. Several other Rakviri were with him; males and females with dark manes and opaque eyes. Not Cassirur Almadhera, though; nor Haltern n'ri n'suth Beth'ru-elen.

"*S'an* Jaharien." And I wondered how much he'd heard. This one we'd better take with dignity, I thought. Since I judge dignity is about all we're going to be left with. . . .

He looked at Molly first, and then at me, not hiding his satisfaction.

"It seems I was wrong." There was a kind of joy in his abnegation. He stood brushing shoulders with the younger males and females, and they crowded close. "Wrong to let you come to this *telestre*. *T'ans*, I gave you guest-right. I revoke it. Leave Rakviri. That's all I have to say."

At this hour? How are we supposed to travel to Morvren? Skurrai-jasin across desolate heathland by night – impossible!

I was proud of Molly Rachel. She made none of those protests, only inclined her head slightly, after the Orthean manner, and said, "We'll leave now, *s'an* Jaharien."

The discordant music from the end of the terrace rang in the cold air. There was a smell of cooking, at this hour of second twilight. Frost formed on the glass. Jaharien tugged his dark robe more closely round his burly shoulders.

"You'll leave in the morning," he said.

Judging by Molly Rachel's face, she didn't like that humiliating charity any more than I did. She said, "Thank you, *s'an*."

"In the morning," Jaharien said, "because I won't ask any of this *telestre* to put themselves in danger by taking *skurrai-jasin* to Morvren at night. No other reason than that."

He turned his back on us and walked away, the other Rakviri Ortheans walking with him; and the hiss of their bright robes on the stone floor died away into silence.

We left when Carrick's Star was a searing white line along the eastern horizon. I saw Molly exchange a few words with a sullen Barris Rakviri. When she climbed into the *skurrai*-carriage beside me, she was too preoccupied to talk. I didn't see Cassirur or Haltern – And that's probably just as well, I thought. It would strain my professional courtesy, to say the very least.

As the *skurrai-jasin* jolted down the rough track, Molly Rachel swore. She sat for a moment with head bowed, arms resting on her knees, skin dark against beige coveralls; and then she straightened, sighing.

"God*dammit* – " And glanced sideways at me, and shrugged. "That's two. Two chances gone: Kel Harantish settlement and this *telestre*. How many more chances am I going to get?"

Two unsuccessful attempts at getting functional Witchbreed technology. . . . I can't think of it in Company terms, now.

"You talk as if it was just machinery – "

"That's *all* it is." Her face went blank. "It may be based on some alien perception of the universe, it may not; either way, *it's nothing but technology*. Get that clear."

There are unbidden memories in my mind: the dead images of a long-dead race.

Deliberately businesslike, Molly said, "We're going to have a couple of busy days. I've been in contact with Pramila Ishida: the team will be coming down from the orbiter now. And I've *got* to have something I can give them to work on."

As long as there are Ortheans blocking the Company from Witchbreed technology, I thought, I don't have to take any decisions. But what happens if – when – we find someone who'll co-operate? What do I do then?

Orventa Twelfthweek Eightday: the Freeport city streets are white with frost. Walking up from the Portmaster's office to the Residence, I smelt on the air the hot sharpness of burning *lapuur*-wood in street braziers. Four days. Four days now, and the alien beginning to be comfortable, to fit like old clothes – or is it clothes I've outgrown?

Sun shone through the *hanelys*-creeper. Its iron-black sharp stems linked the walls of *telestre*-houses, forming a canopy overhead. A few wild *becamil* had made a nest in the right-angled junctions of the plant. For a moment there was no sound but their high-pitched humming. Then, as the avenue opened out into a square, I heard a noise.

Skurrai being harnessed to stout carts stamped and hissed. The larger *marhaz* raised their snake-muzzles and cried. Ten or fifteen Ortheans, mostly young males and females, were working; strapping loads on to tri-wheeled carts with rapid efficiency. The winter sun brought steam rising from the mud, and shone on crates and *becamil*-cloth sacks. I stepped back as a cart rumbled past, and felt its heaviness in the vibration of the earth.

"Give you greeting," I said to a small, pale-maned female, as she turned from watching the cart on its way to the docks. "What's happening here, *t'an*?"

Whiteless eyes were slowly lidded. Then her gaze cleared. She nodded, and rubbed dirt from her six-fingered hands.

"*T'an s'aranthi*," she acknowledged. "I'd heard there were offworlders in the 'port again – Brovary! Tallis! *you overload that and I'll* – that's better."

A winter haze made daystars into ghost-images, blotted out by a swooping flight of *rashaku*.

"We're sending a *jath-rai* coaster along to Ales-Kadareth in Melkathi," the Orthean female went on. "Last year was a bad harvest for them. I doubt this year'll be better."

The names bring back a summer long gone, and words spoken by – Ruric Orhlandis.

"Someone said to me, once, that, if it wasn't against all custom, Melkathi province should be made to have half the number of *telestres* that it does have – and then it might be able to support its population."

"You know Melkathi?" She pushed a wisp of mane away from her face with the back of her wrist. "I'm Mezidon, by the way, Anrasset Mezidon Rakviri. Yes, there's some truth in what you say."

"There's no truth in it at all!" a new voice interrupted. "The *telestre* boundaries haven't changed in two thousand years, nor should they ever!"

I turned, to see a young male Orthean leaning against a crate. He wore boots, britches, and sleeveless slit-backed jacket; and *harur*-blades on shoulder-baldrics.

He demanded: "Who are you, to say what Melkathi's *telestres* should do?"

He's young, I thought. Not long out of *ashiren*. A thin, intense boy; with satin-black skin and a cropped red mane. When he shifted off the crate and walked towards us, he had the controlled grace of a *harur*-blade fighter.

"Give you greeting," I said, amused. "My name is Lynne de Lisle Christie, *t'an*."

His stunned eyes met mine. A sudden pulse of adrenalin made me cold. Even an offworlder couldn't mistake it: his face came alive with hatred.

"*T'an* Asshe is here from Melkathi to assist with the relief ships." Mezidon glanced back and forth at us both.

"Oh yes," the boy said, "this – animal – knows Melkathi. And Melkathi knows *you*, Christie *S'aranth*."

The people nearby stopped loading carts and stared, hearing his voice. Mezidon Rakviri looked embarrassed: "Asshe, I'm sure the *s'aranthi* meant no harm; and it's a thing we've often said about Melkathi ourselves."

He ignored her, his eyes fixed on me. "Shall I tell you who remembers Christie *S'aranth*? I'll tell you. Those who were there when Sulis SuBannasen died by poison, by her own hand. Those who were there when *T'An* Commander Ruric Orhlandis burned Orhlandis *telestre*. When the *T'An Suthai-Telestre* Suthafiori declared Orhlandis not to exist, and scattered its people across all the Hundred Thousand – "

"And that has what, precisely, to do with you?" I asked.

He stared at me with an adolescent defiance I was hard put not to laugh at. And then with his next words it wasn't funny at all: "My name is Pellin Asshe Kadareth – now. I was *born* Pellin Asshe Orhlandis."

But you could only have been a baby – ! when Suthafiori declared all Orhlandis children must be adopted *n'ri n'suth* into other *telestres*. You could only have been a child. But I can't comprehend the loss, for an

Orthean, of land he has lived on, in past-memory, for a hundred generations. . . .

"*T'An* Ruric burned Orhlandis," he said, anger sharpening that unlined face, "but you made her do it!"

His arrogance and ignorance caught me on the raw.

"*T'an* Asshe, let me tell *you* something. You don't have the right to hate me, or to say one word about Ruric Orhlandis. You never knew her. *I did*."

"You made her betray the Hundred Thousand!"

I have memories of her, that dead woman; she with her black skin and mane and yellow Witchbreed eyes. That narrow, merry face . . . *T'An* Commander and travelling companion, friend to the envoy; she who had Shiriya-Shenin's ruler killed and the envoy disgraced for it. And I see her trapped and filthy in the burning Melkathi heathland, remember her branded exile in the prison in Tathcaer, and even I cannot say, that was not justice.

"*T'an* Asshe . . . she could do nothing but what she did, believing as she did. It could have been any *telestre* that happened to. Yes, and it could have been any offworlder."

Twenty or so people were listening now, others having come out of the Rakviri city-house; Mezidon Rakviri winced whenever Orhlandis was openly mentioned, and the others grinned broadly at scandal.

"You were the first," Asshe said. "Well, I will revenge Orhlandis on you, *t'an S'aranth*, if I do nothing else with my life. It's a gift of the Goddess; who could have thought you'd return?"

The sun cast his shadow on the cold earth, that thin dark boy. Violence was in him, savage and ridiculous and entirely pragmatic. To be hated so bitterly hurts. I wanted to laugh, to cry. Empathy rose strongly in me: looking into unveiled eyes I could feel the heft of sharp metal, feel how hard this frost-bitten earth would be to fall on; taste blood. . . . At the same time anticipated how these Rakviri would disarm him before he could attack; and, standing in that winter light, I wanted to put my arms round him and hug him like the boy he was, say *It isn't her fault, she hurt you as badly as she hurt me, she's dead now, it was all ten years ago*. The empath's sense of multiple possibilities. As so often, it left me incapable of any action.

"It's not advisable to make threats, *t'an* Kadareth."

The voice startled me out of immobility. I looked round, amazed, at the stocky figure of Blaize Meduenin. And belatedly thought, That's the connection between four days ago and now: he must be the one of the Morvren triumvirate responsible for getting Rakviri's ships to Melkathi. . . .

"I knew Sulis SuBannasen when she was *T'An* Melkathi." Blaize's mouth twisted in wry humour. "She hired me to kill the Earth envoy – the *S'aranth*. And it was her choice, when her plotting with Kel Harantish was found out, to go to the Goddess as she did. As for the *T'An* Commander Ruric – boy, you know nothing of that year."

Pellin Asshe said sulkily, "If not for the *S'aranth*, *T'An* Commander Ruric wouldn't also have turned spy for Kel Harantish; I'd still live with the earth I loved."

The fair-maned male frowned, his scarred face bewildered, surprised into defending me: "It was not done at the *S'aranth*'s direction."

"She was the cause!"

"We were all the cause." Nictitating membrane slid down over the Meduenin's eyes. "Don't waste your blame on that, boy, when it's now you should worry. Work to see it doesn't happen again."

Pellin Asshe never took his eyes from my face. "I spoke in anger, *t'an* Christie, forgive me. I mean you no harm."

My legs felt momentarily unsteady, and I reached to grip Blaize's arm; hard and muscled. His eyes cleared, watching the boy walk off between the carts. Loading resumed. I looked at Asshe's retreating back and thought, *I wasn't afraid – until you apologized.*

"I'll see he goes back with the *jath-rai* to Kadareth." Blaize looked at me, all but shuffled his feet, and then unwillingly smiled. There was an ironic awareness of our last meeting. "What else was I to say – *S'aranth*?"

The years have deepened the creases in that scale-patterned skin, have faded the blue-purple burn scar; but there is still the same Blaize Meduenin who hunted the envoy, helped her across the Wall of the World, abandoned her in the wilderness, and became in later days kinbrother to her kinsister.

Caught between then and now, I felt the knot of acrimony inside me loosen a little. If I were to talk to you now, what could we say to each other?

He turned back to the loading; and I left, feeling relief and resentment in about equal measure.

I walked on into the city-island's interior, to the Residence; passing through that small *telestre*-house's courtyard, and up steps to the first floor. Inside, lozenge-shaped windows cast patches of sunlight on the walls. The light emphasized the dust, and the air of a place that is shut up ten months out of the twelve. David Osaka was sitting at a table on which stood an old model data-net, tinkering with the display in the holotank, and studying the offprints pinned on the wall above. I paused beside him.

95

"Is the comlink with the orbital ship working now?"

He shrugged. "We're having to use a heavy-duty infrared laser system for ground-to-orbit, and put the ship in geosynchronous orbit."

"Dear good God! Use industrial lasers for comlinks?"

He leaned back, brushing the fair hair out of his eyes. He has the impatience of the young, I thought. Or is it that he picks up my dissatisfaction here?

He said, "We're having comlink problems all over – on-world and ship-to-ship. Can't bypass the background interference except under the most local conditions. But all this government equipment is outdated. We could end up using *shuttles* for communications."

The coin-cords rattled as Molly Rachel pushed through the curtain in the door-arch. She nodded a greeting to me; picked up on his remark: "We don't have that big an energy-reserve; the situation is ridiculous. Dave, see if you can find Doug Clifford, will you? I want to know if government records can shed any light on the problem."

"Sure."

As he left, she padded across to the window and stood gazing out. "Clifford's spending far too much time over at the Almadhera's quarters." She ticked off names on her long dark fingers: "Bekily Cassirur Almadhera. Haltern n'ri n'suth Beth'ru-elen. Blaize Meduenin. I know he claims they're influential people here. . . . I don't think the Company can rely on him at all."

I said nothing. The daystarred sky shone beyond the thick glass. Distantly came the rumble of *skurrai*-carts, voices calling, the metallic tones of *rashaku*. Now on the verge of spring season, Hanys, when *jath* and *jath-rai* are fitted out for trade-voyages. . . .

"Any word from Rakviri?" I thought, She won't have given up on Barris that easily.

"Nothing. And no approaches from other *telestres*." The Pacifican woman turned, hearing human voices, and footsteps coming up from the lower rooms. "You're only just in time for the meeting."

The Residence's upper rooms began to fill. Faces I'd become familiar with on the ship out from Earth, the Company's research scientists – and now, as I took my place round the table with them, they seemed curiously stolid, graceless; eyes forever wide and staring, thick-fingered hands, manes shaven . . . that double image that comes with being an empath, and seeing through eyes that are never entirely your own. . . .

And then they came back into focus. Pramila Ishida, the Representative's *aide*, quiet-voiced and round-faced; and beside that young Asiatic-featured Pacifican woman was a tall black medic, Joan Kennaway. An older, sharp-faced Pacifican woman, Chandra Hainzell, seated herself on

96

a couch-chair with two more men from Research: Dinu Machida and Jan Yusuf. Beside them, stiff-spined and looking as though he hated every minute of this, I saw the head of the team, Rashid Akida.

"I realize this face-to-face meeting is unusual," Molly Rachel began, "and that none of us have comlink-access to the resources of our departments right now. That's the first point I want to raise – have we got anywhere analysing the communications interference?"

A sea mist was pressing against the windows, and the damp air was not warmed by *lapuur* and *ziku*-wood braziers. I could see on the faces round me the longing for a Pacifican environment: heat, light, technology. I wouldn't have turned it down myself.

David Osaka came in at that moment, Doug Clifford following; and there was a small disturbance while other tables were shoved together, and people's seats rearranged. Two or three of the younger team members sat cramped in window embrasures. It's a far cry from an all-screen holo-image conference.

"We're discussing comlink problems," Molly said. "Dinu?"

Dinu Machida, a stocky Sino-Indian, spread a printout across the two tables. "First, I'll have to deal with weather patterns. You can see the problems we're having with satellite surveys. The interior of the southern continental landmass is more or less permanently covered with cloud. Also, considerable areas on the northern continent: here, and here. . . ."

Far north of us. Into the Barrens, and beyond, where I've never travelled.

"You've tried infrared," Molly prompted.

"Naturally. Comes up featureless. It's – " He looked round, obviously itching for a holodisplay-tank. "Can I explain the seasonal climate pattern? Take this 'Coast' area on the southern continent. A steady influx of winds from the sea, bringing a corresponding monsoon season, then a steady outflow of air from the centre of the continent, and consequently a very long dry season – "

"Hold on," I interrupted. "Dinu, I can see a few other people as bemused as I am. For the non-specialist – what are you saying about the climate? And what does it have to do with communications?"

He brushed black hair out of his eyes, and sighed. "The Coast area is an example. It's too hot for its latitude. There's a climate anomaly, and it's far from being the only one."

I caught Doug Clifford's eye then, and began to think: I know what this is leading towards. . . .

"At a guess," Dinu continued, "I'd say the land surface of the interior has to have an extremely high albedo, to reflect back that amount of solar radiation; hence the greenhouse effect and the cloud-cover. . . . There

97

are only two geological areas that have that high an albedo – a reflective surface. Deserts and ice fields."

Molly Rachel said, "You don't get that many ice fields on the equator. . . ."

When the general laugh died down, and she'd grinned appreciatively, she said, "Desert, then. How does that tie in with the atmospheric disturbances in communications? Doug, is there anything in your records that illuminates this?"

Doug Clifford let the silence grow. A small, neat man; his hands clasped in front of him and resting on the table. All that self-mocking theatre was curbed now; I saw no humour on his face.

"Not desert, in either case," he stated; and with a nod of acknowledgement to me, said, "You'll have seen reports on an area north of here, that Ortheans call the Glittering Plain. You forget that this isn't a 'primitive' world. It's a post-technological world. Post-holocaust, to be accurate. I suspect that what they call the Elansiir, in the centre of the southern continent, and the areas north of the Barrens, are fused bedrock. War damage. Plain and simple devastation. You will, I think, find that there is more than one contributory factor to the communications interference, but that the root cause of it is that damage, done in a war that destroyed this civilization's high technology. Three thousand years ago."

Ten years ago I stood on a scarp, north and west of the Freeport –

The sun reflects off something in the western distance. At first I take it for water, but it doesn't end as water does. Where it touches the brown heathland, it ends in streaks. Sharp edges, like cat-ice on a puddle, like splinters. With the sheen of volcanic glass. Then Carrick's Star clears the haze, and all that horizon blazes with unbearable light.

– overlooking what Ortheans call the Glittering Plain.

The silence that ensued in that upper room had a curious quality, because when someone from the Old World says that to a group of Pacificans, it inevitably raises certain historical tensions. And because the thought of damage great enough to change world climate on Orthe is awesome.

The discussion shifted, moving on to the first results from the demographic team's surveys, and it wasn't at all subtle how Douglas Clifford was excluded – Doug and, to a degree, myself. Inevitable. But none the less, it disgusts me.

When I could slip out (a short absence being advisable) I went down to the kitchens to boil *siir*-wine, and taste the acrid hot liquid. Clifford's *l'ri-an* – Ortheans apprenticed by their *telestres* to this temporary duty – clustered round the ovens, cooking, talking, playing *ochmir*. I heard the midday gongs sound while I was there, and stayed to eat, and to play three-handed *ochmir* with a young male and an *ashiren*.

"Need any help up there?" the young Orthean male said, as I conceded the game and stood to leave.

I smiled at that. "All I can get."

He scooped triangular counters back into the *becamil*-cloth bag. "I hear you may be getting a message from Rakviri *telestre* soon."

Chilled, I thought: Jaharien wouldn't change his attitude – would he?

"And where did you hear that, *t'an*?"

"I heard it in a game." His inflection could have applied to *ochmir*, but it had all the Orthean connotations of intrigue, cabal, challenge, and art.

When I came back into the upstairs chamber, the thin-faced Rashid Akida was on his feet.

"You're giving us the go-ahead on Carrick V?" he asked Molly. "Good. How soon will we have an on-world base?"

Pramila Ishida leaned forward. A slight woman, much the same age as Molly, and with an air of deference – she glanced at the Company Representative before she spoke: "The local humanoids seem reluctant to lease any territory to us, even on a short-term basis. This is a problem area. It's riddled with traditional and religious prohibitions."

Molly nodded. I thought she might bring me in on this, my knowledge being intended to cover such gaps in this ill-documented culture, but she ignored me. She put her long fingers through her hair, pushing it back from her face, and glanced round at the assembled team.

"I may be able to solve that one, if I can swing a small addition to budget. We could bring in one of the unit-construct bases the Company uses on water- or foul-atmosphere worlds. With a sealed-environment base, we can anchor offshore in the river estuary here. End of problem."

You have to admire the thinking behind that. Even if the casual 'small addition to budget' is a chilling reminder of PanOceania's financial power.

Rashid Akida's chin lifted. In his thirties, he spoke with the gravitas of a man twice his age. "If I may suggest . . . all things considered . . . looked at fairly . . . is this where you ought to base the team? If we could return to the Kel Harantish settlement – "

Molly cut him off. "That's not possible."

And then I knew what she would say next. It's the obvious move for anyone looking at Witchbreed artifacts – even if they are defunct. The canals. The canal system on the Coast, that Kel Harantish controls.

"The Desert Coast canal system is an example of Witchbreed science."

"The evidence is ambiguous," Rashid Akida protested. "Are you certain this isn't just a charming irrelevance?"

He indicated a data-tank offprint.

99

"From what I gather, the canals were built *after* the war, and the damage that occurred then. A brave attempt to set up irrigation after the climate changed. But the system is unfinished; it trails off *here*, to the west . . . and in the east it comes within forty miles of the Kel Harantish settlement and – stops."

Molly leaned back. Her long fingers moved, rubbing against the grain of the *tukinna*-wood table. "The archeological team reported the canals were Witchbreed constructs, and that should be enough to make us investigate."

Time to be obstructive under the guise of being helpful, I thought. "I know why you haven't suggested it before, Molly. Primarily because it may or may not be functional in any sense that we can understand. And, secondarily, because there are local political difficulties."

Pramila Ishida spread out a demographic survey. As always, her eyes were lowered. She said quietly, "The Coast area is a poverty-line culture. They have a long history of raiding this more prosperous northern continent. My local contact here says this has reached such a point that negotiatory talks are being set up in a Coast settlement. The Company naturally wants to avoid on-world political conflicts."

And who's been talking with the *takshiriye*, then? I thought sardonically. With Douggie and the Morvren triumvirate. . . .

The aquiline Chandra Hainzell said, "Isn't the northern continent a more likely place to find functional technology? If this poverty-line Coast *had* tech, they'd be using it now."

The sea mist began to clear, a watery sunlight shining through the lozenge-crystal windows.

"It isn't that simple," I said. "You've heard about the areas of war damage – I know we can't survey them accurately because of the interference, but I'm of Doug's opinion – and you must remember: these people have a very clear memory of where technology can lead. Where it did lead, in their case."

Molly nodded. "Lynne's right. These people . . . they're not technophobic, as such. There are Witchbreed artifacts in the *telestres*. It isn't that they can't use technology. They *won't*. I've a strong feeling they could build up a hi-tech civilization in a couple of generations, if they wanted to, but they won't do it."

Frustration showed on her dark, smooth features. Then she shrugged: "The reason's obvious. Pramila says this northern continent is prosperous. Fertile. There's a low population, too; they don't need hi-tech. Or, I should say, they don't need it with the urgency that these Coast Ortheans obviously do – if that's a poverty-line culture, the Company's got things to offer them, and that's where we come in. We trade with them."

For Witchbreed technology?

Oh yes, that's PanOceania; and I'd wondered how long it would take the Rachel woman to put that at the top of her list of priorities.

"I've got continuing investigations here," Molly concluded. "Either way, whichever continent we concentrate on, I want results. I want to get an FTL-drone off through Thierry's World *soon*. The quicker reports start getting back to home office on Earth, showing progress, the sooner we'll be officially established here."

Jan Yusuf, a wiry and suntanned man of indeterminate age, said, "The fact that there's alien technology still extant here *doesn't* necessarily mean we'll be able to analyse it."

Rashid Akida verbally leapt on him. I stayed for a while, listening to conversations as the meeting broke up – listening, I suppose, for something more than blinkered interest. I didn't hear any. When I saw Molly go out, I followed her down the outer stairs and into the courtyard. The sea mist clung, pearl-pale, to the roofs. The *kazsis*-vines that clung to walls were beginning to bud, and to bear the nodules that incubate *kekri*-flies. After the talk and claustrophobia of that upstairs room, it made me want to run and shout like a child.

"Shit!" Molly Rachel said. She put her hands in the small of her back and stretched, arching; and then pushed her fingers through that mass of dark frizzy hair. She squinted up at the mist-blurred roofs of the Freeport. "For God's sake, can't you keep Clifford under control?"

"You didn't go out of your way to conciliate him."

"No. . . ." She took a breath: *kazsis*, the dung of *kuru* rooting in the mud beyond the archway gate, the brackish dockside water. I looked past her to where a Pacifican – I recognized David Osaka – stood in the street with one of the kitchen's *ochmir* players. Was that the *l'ri-an* I spoke with earlier?

"You had a quarrel with Blaize Meduenin," she said. It wasn't a question. She tucked her hands under her belt, an oddly Orthean gesture. "Lynne, you understand these people. You know what makes them angry, what makes them laugh . . . I think I'm beginning to see it myself."

"No one ever fully understands the alien. It's not possible. That's a hard saying, but it's true."

With a startling perception, she said, "But no one ever fails to understand a part."

I looked up at the young woman beside me; her black angular height, that direct gaze.

She said, "All we're going to take from them here is something they don't use, don't want – that they're afraid of. They don't need Witch-breed technology."

I don't agree with why you're saying it, but . . . "That last is certainly true."

David Osaka walked into the courtyard, glancing back over his shoulder. He said something to the Pacifican woman.

Molly frowned. "I can't see everyone who just walks in off the street."

"He mentioned the name of Rakviri *telestre*."

"Send him in. You go upstairs and keep the meeting going."

I sat back on the wall of the cistern, waiting; but the Orthean who entered the courtyard was not what I expected.

"Achil," the Orthean male said. "Earthspeaker. Give you greeting, *t'an s'aranthi*."

He stood barefoot in the muddy courtyard, looking at Molly, and finally at me. He was thin – almost as thin as a Desert Coast Orthean – and dark-skinned, and his mane was shaven down to gold fur. Impossible to tell his age. Brown cloth was knotted at the hip, a garment that didn't cover his back, where the shaven mane went down to a vee at mid-spine; nor the sharp-angled ribs and paired dark nipples. *Harur*-blades hung from a plain belt. His eyes were wide-set in that narrow-chinned face.

"What can I do for you, *t'an* Achil?" Molly asked.

It was a shock to meet those unveiled eyes: clear as water. His expression changed, but whether it was amusement or disquiet, I couldn't tell.

"I have spoken before with *s'aranthi*," he said. His high-arched feet were bare; he seemed oblivious of the cold wind.

The Pacifican woman waited.

"*T'an* Rachel, you have visited the Desert Coast?"

Her gaze flicked across to me, an exasperated look that plainly said: *Is there* anything *they don't find out?*

"Briefly," she confirmed. "*T'an*, I understand that you've come from Rakviri *telestre*; if there's a communication – "

"I have also spoken with the Earthspeaker Cassirur Almadhera, and with Barris Rakviri."

Now the Pacifican woman was quite still. "Yes?"

"You must understand, *t'an*, our place is with the land. With the earth. We are born of it, care for it, return on it. Protect it."

Return on it. . . . Sharp and real, I saw again the ruined city of the Barrens: heard that scarred mercenary talk of past-memories, of once-lived lives. Except in extremity, or among Earthspeakers, it is rarely spoken of.

"'Protect'," the Pacifican woman echoed. There was a hardness in her tone. "What does this have to do with Rakviri and my Company?"

Something in her voice crystallized a realization. You don't like the

Ortheans of the Hundred Thousand, I thought. Just don't like the culture. I wonder if you know that?

Achil said, "We have – long memories, I believe your people would say. And we know why we mistrust all Witchbreed science."

"Meaning?"

"To be plain, *t'an* – our history is not your business."

I looked over at that slight figure, standing in the mist-filtered sunlight; caught a glimpse of some private, tragic humour . . . and decided the pun was both bilingual and deliberate.

"And Rakviri?" I said.

"I have been travelling down the Ai River, from Wellhouse to Wellhouse, and came to visit Rakviri some few days past."

"That isn't what I asked, *t'an* Earthspeaker."

For all efforts to anchor discussion in the practical, I could feel the atmosphere change. One forgets – because inexplicable – the very real effect of an Earthspeaker's presence. Now I felt the cold wind, heard the creak of windvanes and *skurrai*-drivers shouting in the street outside; all with a sharp intensity. At the arch of the sky the mist was gone. Daystars shone like a scatter of flour. Carrick's Star was bright. A *rashaku* called.

The Orthean male stepped forward and touched claw-nailed fingers to Molly Rachel's forehead. She flinched. He stared into her face.

"*T'an s'aranthi*, there are those who say time is not the same for us as it is for you. It may be that we remember our future, not relive our past. Seeing what you bring to Orthe, I have thought, perhaps, that there never was such a race as the Golden Witchbreed – until now. That you, in our future, are the Golden Empire that we foresaw. . . ."

Molly stared back at him, silenced.

"Then who left all those ruins laying around?" I asked, acidly.

The Earthspeaker Achil laughed. Head thrown back, delight in the sound of it, but still a certain bitterness there. "*T'an* Christie, give you greeting; the Almadhera said that I should like you."

Molly Rachel said flatly, "Why have you come here, *t'an* Achil?"

His head went up as he heard human voices from the first-floor windows. The light made the planes of his face harsh, animal, alien.

"Why, to tell you this, *t'an* Rachel. Barris Rakviri is come into Shalmanzar Wellhouse for a time, as our custom is. And certain things that he kept with him in the Rakviri *telestre*-house have also come into Shalmanzar's keeping. And will stay there. And I think that the Wellhouses will not, at this time, willingly admit *s'aranthi*."

"Damn them!" the Pacifican woman said, as soon as he had passed the archway gate. "If there's one thing I don't need, it's alien cult-religions –"

She slammed both hands palm down on the rim of the cistern, the noise of flesh on brick like a gunshot in that small courtyard. A *rashaku*, startled into flight from the roof, swooped into the watery-blue sky.

I quoted an old Service cliché. "When diplomacy meets religion – diplomacy doesn't stand a chance."

"It's a pity you couldn't charm that Earthspeaker with the *S'aranth* name, the way you did Jaharien Rakviri – " Some remnant of shadow left her eyes. She made no mention of Barris, or that pale octagonal hall. "Lynne, I'm sorry."

"I suppose the *S'aranth* name is as much a liability as an asset, now," I said. "And . . . Earthspeakers aren't like other Ortheans."

For a second it's as if the sun-warmed stone of yard and buildings encloses me; as if I stand at the bottom of a well.

Molly Rachel raised her head, shutting her eyes briefly, and then gazed at the clearing sky. "I need to be here myself and push for access to *telestres*. But we also need to open up the Coast area on the southern continent. I can send someone down ahead of me – "

"I'll go."

I can't stay here in the Freeport. I have been trying to say that Orthe is strange to me but it isn't. It's as if I'd never been away – and I have, I'm not Christie *S'aranth* now, to think so is dangerous.

And then there is Blaize Meduenin . . . I need time to think it through.

Molly narrowed her eyes, studying me. "You don't really know the Coast. Still, none of us do. It's not a well-documented area. And you *can* handle Ortheans."

Not 'well-documented', no. Carrick V is a neglected world. . . . Above me now in this pale stone courtyard are daystars. The sky is full of the Heart Stars that lie on the edge of the galaxy's core. Look up: it is a crowded sky. Each world of those millions is crowded with life, and we, humanity, we cling to those Home Stars nearest Earth, and can't pay attention to every backwater world that falls within our domain. . . .

Until something unique is discovered.

The Pacifican woman turned towards the steps, going to the upper floor. The shadow of the house wall was cold.

As I climbed the steps with her, she said, "I want to get a foothold on the southern continent. Before things get complicated there. There are these talks coming up between the Freeport *takshiriye* and the Coast settlements. . . . I've got one of the canal settlements in mind for contact – remind me: you haven't seen the latest data on that."

She paused, then: "Yes, you go down ahead of me. We've had two chances at viable Witchbreed science, we can't afford now to miss the third. Lynne, I'll be relying on you."

CHAPTER 9

Canals

When I was in the Service, it used to strike me how closely our missions approximate the shapes of our lives: born out of the ship-womb into a world full of incomprehensible experience, no sooner gaining a kind of competence than called out of that world again. Flying down to the Coast held something of that feeling – cold ice-thin air outside the ports, the blue-purple of the stratosphere, and Orthe an ochre shadow thirty thousand feet below.

I flicked the holotank-image from exterior-view to Records, and then had to lean forward while Pramila Ishida went past to take the pilot's console with David Osaka.

And I could do without having Pramila along, she's a direct conduit of information back to the team –

How can I hope to cushion culture shock, faced with something like *this*?

The departed archeological team left a message-capsule in orbit, and it was only days after landfall that the team had got round to deciphering its last image. I leaned on the rim of the holotank, studying it – a close shot of an inland Coast city. It was ill-resolved, taken from a shuttle overflight. Satellite surveys are no better, the area being comparatively close (in continental terms) to the southern continent's war devastation. I wondered briefly how the research team were doing with their plans to override the atmospheric interference.

And if Molly hadn't been determined on the canals already, this would have brought her running! Jesus, I thought. If I do my job, I'm helping the Company to move in on Orthe. If I *don't* do it, I'll be out myself. And if this fulfils its implications. . . .

Three-dimensional and miniature, the holotank held a barren landscape. Five canals cut straight lines through the desert. The shot had been taken towards dusk: Carrick's Star reflected back amber from the water surfaces. And where the canals would have intersected, a great cylindrical pit gaped in the desert, a pit big enough to land a starcruiser in; and in its terraced walls, tiny humanoid figures moved . . . the city, Maherwa, according to the archeologists' report. To whet the Company's appetite still further, it lies thirty miles inland from the Inner Sea, and only sixty miles to the west of Kel Harantish.

Doug Clifford, emerging from the shuttle's rear compartments, came and sat in the holotank's other viewseat. He smiled.

"Out of communication range with young Molly? She'll miss hearing how obstructive a government envoy I am."

"I'd like to have read your last FTL transmission to Earth," I retorted. "Especially what went in under 'Christie, L. D.'."

"Ah, well – one has to say certain things."

"Doesn't one. . . ."

He leaned back, looking at me over steepled fingers. There was a certain affectionate mockery there that I would have missed, badly, had it been absent.

"I find it interesting that a government representative is permitted to come on this mission . . ."

He left that invitingly open, but I declined to comment. 'Special advisor' is a flexible designation; the duties of 'liaison' are not always specified; and if I choose to let Douggie Clifford take a close look at the Company's *modus operandi* – that's my responsibility. The multicorporate's presence has to be counter-balanced somehow.

A little sourly, he said, "Why should a multicorporate Company worry about a national government, after all? Britain's nothing more than a client state to PanOceania."

"That's an exaggeration."

"I believe you've been out of the Service too long. If I were to call you a groundsider – "

"You could end up walking back to Morvren Freeport." I gave due consideration to the Inner Sea. "Or swimming."

He chuckled at that one, eyes bright. "I must say, I do prefer offworld service to my groundside days." His gaze flickered, going round the small cabin, passing over David and Pramila at the pilot's console. "Lynne, just what *is* it you do with the Company, now?"

"You mean when I'm not being hauled out of my Company department and booted off to the further reaches of the galaxy as a special advisor?"

"Something like that."

"I'm a groundsider. No – quite genuinely, Douggie. On Earth, I run the department that liaises between PanOceania and the British government. After all, if you want to regulate the relations between a multicorporate and its 'client state', that's best done from the inside, wouldn't you say?"

"Which side of the inside?" He grimaced, primly displeased by his own phraseology.

"Sometimes even I'm not sure."

He twinkled. The irony doesn't escape me – I balance affairs between

PanOceania and the government much as I once did between Earth and Carrick V. It's the same job.

The shuttle thrummed, wallowing in the thin air. Clifford leaned back. "I thought you seemed a little confused. Now let's see – PanOceania won't entirely trust you because you're British-born, and we won't entirely trust you because you're contracted to PanOceania. I don't envy you your position, Lynne."

"I'm a professional outsider. I'm used to it."

I keyed the holotank to images of the Desert Coast. Lines, contours, symbols. But I watched that bland, round face.

"Of course, Orthe won't ever have major trade status, even with the Company's presence here." His tone was deliberately dismissive. "We've run several Health and Agriculture Aid programmes here, but for no return. The place is unco-operative as well as uneconomic."

"True enough." I noted he couched it in terms that would appeal to the Pacifican woman. Aiming to have it get back to her. "It's not me you have to persuade, Douggie. By the way – Molly Rachel is of the opinion you spend too much time with the Freeport Ortheans. She thinks you're unreliable."

"I do hope so." He was almost demure. Then: " 'Unreliable'?"

"They used always to say Service people were prone to going native," I said. "Which, being empaths by profession, isn't too surprising."

"You know as well as I do, we're trained to put Earth's interests first."

"Which I suppose accounts for Service tendencies to emotional confusion. And our – your – reputation for instability, unreliability, and hypocrisy – "

He straightened, met my gaze. "I don't know that you're entitled to say those things now."

"Since I left the Service? Possibly not." Still testing the water, I said, "You don't think I mean you? Two months out of twelve on-world, that isn't long enough to go native."

"Nor is eighteen months, ten years ago?"

"Thank you, Douglas."

Neither of us was entirely unserious. That's a kind of barbed joking that the Pacificans wouldn't understand. I thought I'd better pay some attention to the record-abstracts on the holo, and so watched the tank for some minutes. Clifford went back to making notes on his personal memlink.

The holotank showed networks of canals, some mine-workings, and seaports; all in that narrow ribbon of land between the Inner Sea and the first mountain range of the Elansiir. There was no data for the Elansiir wasteland itself, under permanent cloud-cover; and precious little detail for anything else. I went back to the archeology team's report, running the image-loop of Maherwa over and over, concentrating on the 'floor' of the pit. Small, badly-resolved, there was none the less a structure of some sort there – it stood out by its size and isolation.

And it might be purely ornamental, and it might be anything, but it *might* be what the archeologists suggested: an entrance to the canals' maintenance system. . . . I went back to the government archives. And came up with nothing.

"You haven't been exactly extensive in these reports." I glanced up at Clifford. "Most of them are second-hand sources. As far as the south-east Coast's concerned, you might just as well have said 'Here Be Tygers' and 'Terra Incognita'."

He protested, "There's a lot on the languages."

"That's no help, without knowing the context they're used in."

Doug Clifford frowned. "You seem to have forgotten a great deal. The social context is well sketched-in, at least in these areas here – "

Pramila Ishida leaned back and interrupted: "We're coming up on the selected landing site. Can I put us down close to the settlement?"

Tactile memory washes over me: the hammerblows of heat on the roofs of Kel Harantish, only ten days ago. Spring season here, but so great a change from spring in the Freeport. Climate anomalies. . . .

"Yes, take us in," I directed. "Coast Ortheans don't have the taboo on land. Put us down a tactful distance from the settlement itself."

She nodded, almost absently, and I saw her lean over to speak to David. He frowned, and they remained with their heads together for some moments.

The vibration of the flight changed subtly.

"Nobody's paid that much attention to the Coast until now," I said.

"The Coast Ortheans didn't have anything that anyone wanted." Doug raised his eyebrows: a self-mocking play to the gallery. It occurs to me that, without the nihilistic sense of humour that he often displays, D. Clifford might not be on what is, after all, considered a fifth-rate Diplomatic posting.

He said, "I did go to the northern areas of the Coast a few years back. Round Kasabaarde and the islands. Lynne, you may contemplate, at your leisure, what it's like trying to cover something the size of the Hundred Thousand when there's no central authority. I've had to spend a considerable amount of my time there."

"Mmm; sorry – "

The typical fate of backwater worlds: under-staffing, lack of interest, neglect.

" – but I still wish there was more in records."

He scratched at his grizzled hair, that was turning quite grey over the ears, and looked at me quizzically. Douggie's always been prone to capitalizing on that fifteen years' difference in our ages.

"I'll tell you something, Lynne. *You* want to treat this trip as a First Contact. A fact-finding mission. Things aren't like that any more. There aren't any purely academic questions, or answers of purely hypothetical interest. Where you go, the Company follows."

The shuttle thrummed throughout its length, and for a split second lights and holo-images dimmed.

"Go for the crash-straps," Ishida said, "we're coming in." She hooked a viewscreen down to helmet her eyes; flicking switches, bringing David in as pilot-standby.

Exterior-view in the holotank: the horizon a haze, where an immense plain of land at last loses itself; the sky luminous, pale blue; Carrick's Star diamond-brilliant. Fifteen hundred feet, rapidly descending, and everything unreal: perfect scale-miniatures – ridged brown land; that multitude of browns, oranges, ochre, white. Hummocks of wrinkled earth beginning to rise: the foothills of the Elansiir mountains. Beyond them, splintered silver in the cloud haze. And the shuttle a tin box. How does it shut out the world so well? The world so real . . . Aware of being held, suspended, from some mythical skyhook-point. . . .

Thirty miles distant, the glimmer of the sea. A wonder: this country, that was irrevocably 'inland', is from this height coastal. Canals are thin ribbons, every curve distinct as map contours. No sight of any city, but I know how easy it is to lose that on aerial-view.

I fastened the crash-straps across me, turned to speak to Doug. The shuttle swung down into a landing-pattern, curving off to the left. A long and gradual curve, a tightening curve –

I didn't shout. Conventions hold, even on such occasions, perhaps because such occasions aren't easy to recognize as they happen. I glanced at the land below, at Ishida, at the girl again; and the shuttle wasn't slowing, was speeding up.

Her fingers moved rapidly over the controls. "We're coming in too fast," I warned, levelly as possible; she shouldn't have her attention distracted now, and I wanted to scream, *Pull out! Get us out of here!*

A slow turn, pushing me hard into the seat; insistent pressure throwing me away from the direction of the curve. Why did I think, before I ever flew, that I wouldn't feel that downward pull? *Nothing* between me and the earth. Empty air. Most of the human body is water: as the shuttle banked, I felt it answering gravity, surging like the tide.

Made speechless; thinking, *Stop this fucking thing* –

The shuttle plunged down, still on the curving trajectory, and the image in the holotank abruptly cut out. Fast; faster. Acceleration pushing me back into the seat; a hot fear swelling in my head, feeling as if my skin enclosed an infinite pressure. At one and the same time thinking *we're crashing this is it* and *I always knew this would happen* and *but I'm not really afraid – why aren't I?* Gravity pressed me back, pinned me down. The shuttle bucked and rumbled underfoot; a terrible grinding sound; I couldn't breathe.

The slide, that uncontrolled plunge –

Something hit the underside of the floor. The cabin jolted violently. I heard a crash, only felt the skidding sideways – both hands gripping the seat – and violent braking threw me forward, back. And then a juddering halt.

"*Christ!*" Douglas Clifford said.

As if that were a signal, everybody began to move and speak. I wrenched at the straps, forced co-ordination, and stood up. The exit irised open. I stumbled out, on the heels of David Osaka.

" – what – "

" – we're down, we're – "

"*Jesus* Christ!"

Silence, then realization, then speech.

A hot wind hit my face, and I stumbled over shale underfoot; slippery, dry, and treacherous. Open air; sky above. My hands were shaking, but only slightly. The white dolphin-shape of the craft. . . .

"You wouldn't know we'd hit a thing!" David: amazed, exultant. "You wouldn't know – "

"What – "

Standing safe, I can look, can ask: where did we cross that momentous barrier between safety and danger? When did a normal day become abnormal?

There's where we hit, jolting over a shale slope, rutted and grooved with crevasses (*if we'd hit there*) and a stone tor (*did we come that close to – ?*) and the shuttle, there, drunkenly slewed at the foot of the shallow rise.

David and Pramila clung together, each pounding the other's back, panic and rapture indistinguishable on their faces. Doug said again, "What – ?"

An expected sharp panic wasn't there. I shook a little, soon stopped; felt a kind of floaty sensation, and then an acute nausea.

They fell in love with that bright shadow, Death –

Cassirur, we can understand them better than you ever will.

Only for an instant, then natural human fear reasserted itself. And shock: I shouldn't be able to feel such alien emotion.

Empathy is no prized gift.

"Lynne!"

"Uh – "

"All navigation systems cut out!" Pramila Ishida said, at last moving from David's embrace. "Total freak conditions – we were flying *blind* the last few seconds."

She grinned, all deference and all quietness gone. Her sallow face was shining with sweat. She made no attempt at self-justification, very sure of herself. In these situations, even the guiltless protest their innocence.

A hot silence, nothing but sun blazing on the earth. My eyes stung, the alien light too harsh for unprotected human vision. Through tears I saw our four black shadows on the shale. Brown shale, specked with orange; prism-shaped pebbles, flat leaves of rock . . . sharp focus. Pinned sweating under that incandescent dome of the sky, dry-mouthed, hollow, I felt a change: *Orthe* for a moment become only *Carrick V*. A separation, a betrayal.

"Christ!" Doug repeated, his face grey.

That second when the shuttle sank away from under me, that long dive, like a hawk's stoop, is sensation imprinted into cells, not conscious memory. I remembered, as it happened, a feeling almost of satisfaction: 'This is the worst that can ever happen, and it's happening; nothing in the future can be as bad as this.' And, paradoxically, *knowing* I wouldn't die.

Static electricity sparked from clothing, from hair. Round the rim of the horizon, heat-lightning flickered continuously. I turned to speak to Doug and I couldn't; throat muscles paralysed, tongue thick in the mouth. That *knowing* is only the refusal of something living to believe that it can die.

And we get from here to Maherwa – to anywhere – *how*? This shuttle's grounded.

Between fear and self-pity I thought, It was going to be so simple. Fly a shuttle down to the canal junction nearest Kel Harantish, visit the settlement, ask questions –

Now we're stopped before we've begun.

Impossible to stay outside, unprotected, in the heat; but the shuttle's cabin was claustrophobic. I sipped flat liquid from a water-bulb, and leaned up against the frame of the open exit-port. Hours had passed. It felt as though it should be midnight, but Carrick's Star was only declining into late afternoon, light still harsh. I ran a finger under eyeshields to clear dust, and looked out at a sepia landscape.

The earth was golden. Not a thing moved on the wide plain, no animal, no insect. There was no cultivated land. Nothing but dry earth.

Only in the north-west, round Kasabaarde, are there ridge-backed lizards, and the packbeasts called *brennior*, and fields of *arniac* and *del'ri*.

"Here," Doug said, passing a belt-holster across. I fastened it round my waist, and drew the CAS-IV sonic stunner – it's one of the few handguns that look impressive on pre-tech worlds. And, being keyed to human biopatterns for use, is not often a two-edged sword.

"The orbiter got us located yet?"

He shrugged. "Not yet. Pramila says she can get through to them about thirty per cent of the time."

I rested a hand on the butt of the CAS-IV – Coherent Amplified Sound was originally developed to be a communications device, not a weapon. Technology is mutable.

When I glanced behind me, I saw Pramila Ishida still leaning over the comlink; David with both hands on the back of her chair, talking loudly. Such self-possession.

"It's a miracle there are settlements here at all." Doug surveyed the landscape. The neck of his coverall was unfastened and he picked at it with oblivious obsession. "We didn't by any chance cross the mountains, get into the wasteland beyond? It's hardly believable that there are cities here."

I said, "We ought to move."

"We're not in any immediate danger."

"That's what's so misleading, Doug. We can talk to the orbiter – some of the time – but that's a fragile link. Think of them trying to locate us without it. In the middle of all this. We've got food and water here, no problem; but look out there. How far away is the nearest settlement?"

He rested his hand on my arm for a moment.

"Douggie, it's okay, I know what this is. Because of what happened, it – well – "

"Makes one aware of how much depends on chance?"

"*Everything*. . . . Dave and Ishida, they don't believe in luck. When you've lived long enough to know how much is . . . is dependent on . . . what happens, outside your control, in a few seconds."

"I'll tell you this, Lynne." The level sun made him squint, even with eyeshields, as he stared out at the plain. "I'll tell you. I've finished with weighing-up and judging and – the rest of it. From now on I'll do whatever comes along, to get PanOceania off this world. And off any world in my circuit. But *you* know that already."

With the last words, he looked at me; that small, bright gaze serious. The implied invitation was plain, and I was within an ace of taking it up. . . . And knew, as I felt that infinitesimal hesitation, that it meant I wouldn't. "If I did that, I'd be useless here. You can't stop a thing like this, not once it's been put in motion, but the effect can be cushioned. The way things are, that's what we have to settle for. Reachable goals."

Doug, unusually direct, said, "But when young Rachel tells you to go to the Coast and find a foothold for the Company, you do it."

Pramila Ishida called out. At the same moment that Ishida exclaimed, David pointed.

"There – what is it?"

The level plain was made sharp and clear by the westering sun, behind the shuttle. A flake of brighter gold moved, changing its shape. And by some sudden comprehension that changing shape became a wide triangle, not altering itself, but emerging from behind what must (the eye now saw) be a ridge in the plain. It rippled, taking the wind. A hundred yards distant? A mile? Still partly obscured by the ground –

"It's a sail," I said. "It must – a canal. . . ."

"I'm getting heat-sensor readings," Pramila Ishida called. "At last. Lynne, there's life out there."

A figure moved at the base of the sail. All things to its scale: now I saw the craft was some two or three hundred yards distant, still partially concealed by a ridge of earth.

"David, you come with me; Pramila, keep the shuttle secure." I didn't give Douggie the option. I walked down the ramp, hesitated, drew the CAS-IV and then reholstered it. I don't like to carry even stun-weapons.

"They might have scouts," David Osaka said, catching me up. "The reports say the Desert Coast *hiyeks* are hostile to each other."

Hiyek translates literally as 'bloodline'. It carries all the implications of family, lineage, inheritance.

"From what I used to hear at Mercenaries Guildhouses, the Coast *hiyeks* are almost permanently involved in some petty war. . . ." Treat it as familiar and maybe the boy will forget the hair-trigger violence in Kel Harantish. The rest of the Coast is no safer.

Our footsteps were loud on the shale, soft on the earth. The heat leached all strength, muscles ached; and I paused for a moment to look round. The shuttle was a white humpbacked shape behind me. The sail glided slowly north. Now we were climbing a long shallow slope, losing sight of all but that and the daystarred sky.

"Hail them, David, will you?"

The Pacifican broke into a trot. A few moments later, I reached the top of the ridge. So deceptive: it was no more than a fold in the landscape. A scant few feet below me, a stone wall marked the rim of a canal. The water was pale azure, reflecting sky and shoals of daystars, in a channel some thirty yards across, and travelling north in a curve so gradual it appeared straight.

David shouted again.

"They've seen us," I said. I watched the sail altering, sending the low flat barge in towards the bank near us, and realized, They've had time to prepare to stop. That means they do have scouts – and where are *they*, now?

Deceptive land. Memory of Kel Harantish: the whiplash sound of winchbow bolts. I took a step towards the approaching barge. What do we have to protect us? Not weaponry: that's just a sign for them to read, since we're so few. . . .

Our difference. Earth's name. Apart from that, only wit and words.

"*Kethrial-shamaz shan'tai*," I called, as if there was nothing more to be thought of than courtesy. "Give you greeting."

CHAPTER 10

Upon Such Fragile Links

Two young Ortheans leaped from the deck to the paved walkway, fending the barge with ropes and hooks. They were armed. Hooked knives hung from their belts, winchbows were slung across their backs. They went barefoot, in much-mended britches; pale manes braided into protective mats on head and spine. One of them kept her gaze on me, eyes permanently veiled against the glare.

A young male Orthean stepped to the ship's rail, looking down. "Are you what they call *s'aranthi*? Offworlders?"

I stepped down on to the walkway, on to pale, dusty, hard-packed earth. At close hand I saw the barge wasn't made of timber but of riveted metal plates. Sails hung from between metal hoops shaped like wishbones.

"Yes, we're offworlders. Is this near Maherwa?"

The dialect of the south-east Coast is not so different from other Coast dialects, a little easier to follow, if anything. I was aware of David Osaka close behind me, with drawn CAS-IV handgun; of the mixture of languages in which comments were being made on deck. I hazarded a guess, before the young male could answer: "Are you mercenaries?"

He nodded. "Under command of one from *hiyek*-Anzhadi."

"Then tell your commander I want to talk."

Another Orthean male, this one seemingly in his thirties, left the group and came down to the rail. Unlike the others, he had the bleached skin of the Desert Coast. Dust patterned in the creases of the *meshabi*-robe belted round his narrow hips; his mane – cropped at the front, braided down the spine – was yellow. As he turned to shout an order back at the crew, I saw the vee of his mane, the arched ribs and paired nipples. Then he moved with a loose-boned ease, vaulting the rail and dropping down to the walkway.

"I heard there'd been *s'aranthi* on the Coast, but not here. What do you want?"

"How far is the city?"

He didn't answer. He stood lightly, relaxed, as if capable of instant action. His white robe was torn, patched in several places, and belted with a length of chain, from which hung a hook-bladed knife. Seen close, he had a thin, almost gaunt face; wide-set eyes and a fox-jaw. And then the nictitating membrane slid back, disclosing eyes the colour of wet sand, and for one second he looked at me with a wickedly amused and conspiratorial grin.

"More than a day's journey, *shan'tai*, but that shouldn't trouble you with the 'ship' you have."

"What's your name, *shan'tai*?" I had to ask something to gain me time to think.

"Sethri-safere of *hiyek*-Anzhadi."

In the *hiyek* nomenclature that translates as 'firstborn of a triple birth, child of firstborn of twins'; which shows the priorities of the Coast, if nothing else.

"I'm Lynne de Lisle Christie, this is David Osaka."

"Give you greeting. And the other offworlders with you, the female and the old male?"

I looked at him for a while.

He said quietly, "There is a war just finished, *shan'tai*, between *hiyek*-Anzhadi and *hiyek*-Rythana; and so I do not travel without knowing what lies before me."

I said, "I want to talk to some of the Coast *hiyeks*, Sethri-safere. I'll talk with yours, provided it's understood that we come peacefully, and intend to have it stay that way."

"Talk of what?"

"Trade?"

Again that movement of the nictitating membrane; and he put his head a little to one side, gaze going beyond me to the Pacifican. He said absently, "So I address you as – ?"

"Christie."

"*Shan'tai* Christie." He returned the full force of that brilliant gaze to me. "To be truthful, Christie, the city is probably less than a few hours' journey north. You could reach it tonight, but I doubt that you want the city just yet. There's a *siiran* of *hiyek*-Anzhadi that we'll reach very soon. Why don't you come there, with us?"

"What's happening?" David said in Sino-Anglic. "Lynne, I can't follow half of what he's saying."

Impolite, but it did at least inform me – if I read him rightly – that Sethri-safere had little understanding of Sino-Anglic.

We couldn't reach the city tonight, not with a temporarily grounded shuttle. . . . A small part of me noted that the literal translation of *siiran* is 'enclosed garden' or 'shelter'. We need shelter on this hostile Coast. The orbiter can track us, but we don't have supplies for a long wait.

I briefly repeated the conversation to David Osaka.

He said, "What will happen if we refuse?"

116

Light caught the burnished hull of the canal ship, and I squinted up against the glare. The sails had metal slats, capable of being turned to catch or release the wind, and lithe figures swarmed to alter them. Faces lined the rail, watching us. Young, armed Ortheans; eyes veiled, cautious. I looked back at Sethri-safere.

And he also is in hostile territory, the territory of a just-fought war. I wish I knew, are offworlders a liability or a prize on the Coast?

"They'll keep us under surveillance," David guessed. Involuntarily, he glanced back towards the shuttle. "If they wanted to take us for interrogation . . ."

"On the other hand," I said, "an ally would be very useful in the city."

As David Osaka keyed a channel on his wristlink, I turned back to the yellow-maned Coast Orthean.

"*Shan'tai* Sethri, it would be helpful if you could wait a few minutes. One other person will be joining us. And I must talk to my own people, through my ship." Which I don't want to risk trying to move, but I'd as soon you didn't know that.

The yellow-maned Orthean smiled, with a look that said *consider me warned*, and I thought, It's good to talk to someone who understands a precaution without having to have it explained.

In the formal mode, I added, "We're pleased to accept your invitiation, *shan'tai*."

"And even more pleased not to spend the night in a wasteland full of wild mercenaries. . . ." Sethri grinned. His tone made it collusive, a joke shared only by the two of us, and I thought, Yes, you're one to watch – and don't you know it.

I turned to go back to the shuttle, and found David Osaka leaning on the low wall that rimmed the canal, absently digging at the stone-plaster surface.

"Something interesting here," he said in a casual tone, putting the fair hair back from his eyes. Equally casually, I stopped beside him.

Where he had chipped away the pale plaster, and where he had dug with his boot-heel in the packed earth of the walkway, there shone the unmistakable blue-grey opalescence of *chiruzeth*.

It was not a long journey.

The Coast is a different Orthe. Brazen sky, daystars hardly visible; air like the breath of a furnace. Chains ratchetted loudly as the barge's sail collapsed. I saw David take the opportunity to speak into his wrist comlink, look both pleased and startled, and not in my direction. So Pramila Ishida's still in range on the shuttle? That's mildly reassuring, I thought, wonder how long it'll last?

Doug Clifford joined me at the barge's rail. "Is this a way-station of some kind, do you think?"

A cluster of low, flat-roofed buildings stood back from the canal. They were small huts, all but indistinguishable from the surrounding hillocks and ridges. As we came closer, I saw Ortheans. All carried blades, winchbows. Like the mercenaries, they were ill-dressed; the metal the only thing pristine. The place had the air of an armed camp.

"Maybe we should have tried to make the city," I said.

We docked, and the barge's holds were opened; anonymous bundles were unloaded, with much shouting from the Guildhouse mercenaries. By the languages, most were from the northern continent: Melkathi and Rimon by my guess. Some wore that dress, and some the same metal-belted *meshabi*-robes as the Coast Ortheans. There were some languages I couldn't quite place . . . the Rainbow Cities? The Storm Coast?

I walked down the gangplank, the others behind me. Sethri reappeared on deck, hailed us cheerfully, and jumped down to join us on the dock. He looked around and then shouted, "Jadur, you idle sack of guts!"

Another male ambled across the quay, taking a drink from a water-can, which he tucked back under his arm. He looked to be much of an age with Sethri, and had a tan skin and copper-coloured mane, what could be discerned of it under a layer of dust. *Kekri*-flies settled on his eyes. He blinked both membranes to dislodge them.

"Everything's under control – " He saw David Osaka, and gaped, and then visibly realized that there were three of us. "Sunmother's tits!"

With some satisfaction, Sethri announced, "This is Jadur, he's one of my *raiku*. The barge can handle itself; I'll take you in. The rest of Ninth *raiku* should be here too."

Live contact is preferable to hologram records. I want to hear someone who lives in it define it, I thought, and queried, " '*Raiku*'?"

"'Bonded group' – ?" Jadur-safere frowned, and tried for Old Anglo terms that must have come to the Coast with the first demographic teams: " 'Wives'? 'Husbands'? 'Families'?"

"In the north they would say '*arykei*', bed-friend," Sethri added.

In the data-net they say group-marriage. But that is what it is, not how it feels. We walked on. Jadur held out his flask to me: "*Kethrial-shamaz*, offworlder."

The phrase snapped into focus – 'share our life'. As I walked, I looked at the arid rock, the canal's water under the pitiless sky. Stepping outside the formal role, I said, "*Shan'tai* Jadur, can you afford to share it?"

Jadur glanced over at me. The hot breeze lifted his coppery mane, and his dark eyes veiled whitely against the dust. With too-casual bravado, he said, "Share. It's *hiyek*-Rythana's water. My brother-in-*raiku* Sethri has made certain many of them have no use for it."

And then he grinned, piratical, and slapped the hook-knife where it hung at his chain-belt. "By next season we'll be at war again, for water or *siiran*, but don't let that concern you – what's one mouth more amongst so many of us? You drink, *shan'tai-s'aranthi*."

The water tasted tepid, from having been in a metal flask in that sun. Not until I had drunk did I realize that I was also passionately hungry.

The earth was trodden down here between the dock and the small buildings, and the heat of it struck up through the soles of my boots. A chain-line of mercenaries were passing the cargo towards the huts, they and the place looking about equally shabby. As we approached, I saw a middle-aged Orthean woman supervising: small, with beige skin and a gold mane, and wearing the hook-bladed knife of the Coast. She shouted at the mercenaries with an authority very like Sethri's, hailed him without levity, and her expression went a degree or two further towards severity when she saw Jadur.

"*You're* here, are you?"

Jadur caught one of her six-fingered hands and touched it to his forehead, a gesture I hadn't seen among Ortheans before.

"*Hiyannek*, beautiful one, when will you let me be one of your *raiku*?" He stepped back as she swatted him.

"When the Sunmother brings harvest twice a year – !"

Sethri pushed the copper-maned Jadur aside. "Feriksushar, here are offworlders come to talk with the *hiyek*."

The female's gaze went from him to us, and back to him. There was almost contempt on those blunt features. "I'd sooner they'd met with those of the *hiyek* who are respectable, not one who commands mercenaries. Still, it can't be helped."

Sethri avoided my eyes.

"Sunmother be your friend," the woman said formally to me, and added in atrociously accented Sino-Anglic, "We are welcome you to us."

"I'm Company representative for a group of Earth traders," I simplified; giving our names.

Feriksushar looked from me to David Osaka and Doug Clifford, and still in Sino-Anglic said, "And these are your . . . your husbands?"

"Er – regretfully, no. . . ."

Doug grinned and put his arm round my shoulder. David Osaka looked rather more worried than I thought quite tactful. In fact, considering a brief but interesting episode on the ship out from Earth, less tactful than he had any right to be.

"I'm so sorry," the woman, Feriksushar, said politely. 'I was *kei-raiku* myself for some while. Please, come inside."

As we walked up to the nearest hut, Sethri-safere recovered himself enough to ask her, "Which *raiku* are running trade this season?"

"Twenty-Eighth, Third, Seventeenth, as well as Twenty-First." She glanced over at me. "Sethri is Ninth *raiku*. I'm Twenty-First. Arastari and the rest of my *raiku* are in Maherwa now."

The hut's entrance was low and narrow. I added the number of Ortheans visible, the apparent housing-room, and concluded that, like Kel Harantish, there would be underground installations. Which accounts for why satellites have never told us much that's useful about the Coast, I thought.

"Do you want anyone to stay outside?" David asked quietly. "I could ask to be shown the docks."

"Yes. That might keep us in comlink-range of the shuttle for longer. I'll go down in. Doug, what about you?" And when I caught Doug's mandarin stare, added, "You're not Company, I can't give you orders."

"I believe I'll see what the inside of a *siiran* looks like." He switched to what would be unintelligible to David Osaka: Oldworld Anglo: "If you tell these people about the grand and glorious benefits to be had from trading with PanOceania, I'll tell them the other side of the story."

"Douggie, don't let me offend you, but there are times when you're a liability . . . ."

I followed Feriksushar and Sethri under the arched entrance, seeing inside (as I pulled off the eyeshields) a flight of steps spiralling down below ground level. Doug muttered, rubbing his eyes. I felt muscles relaxing, knew I'd unconsciously been hunched up against the impact of Carrick's Star.

We descended the steps, going deep underground. The air became warmer, but not with the parching dry heat of the land above. This was humid, and smelled of dank earth. Sunlight began to be replaced by reflected mirror-light. Bare feet scuffed the stone steps. Going down, still: sweat sprang out, and I wiped my face. The light from below brightened. Sethri looked back and smiled. The steps made a right angle and ended abruptly, and the passage opened out.

For a moment we jostled together. Total confusion swept round me: Ortheans milling near other entrances; shrieking *ashiren*; mercenaries stacking cargo. It took a long second to absorb the impact of what I was actually seeing.

The eye was taken up immediately to the bright roof of this under-ground chamber, thirty feet above our heads. A long, flat expanse of semi-translucent substance, shimmering with rainbow lights; and from it fine streams of water ran in channels, down into tanks of earth. Walls, ceiling, floor: all cold and seamless *chiruzeth*. Garden-sized tanks flanked pathways, vanishing into distant perspective. Tall knobbed *del'ri*-stems rose two metres high, near to harvest; and the crimson leaves of *arniac* grew in profusion.

"*Shit!*"

Doug, at my elbow, murmured, "I couldn't agree more. . . ." in a casual tone at odds with his blank, amazed expression.

There were two levels of chambers set back into the *chiruzeth* walls. Looking carefully, I could see where wall corners were rounded instead of sharp, but not by design – by erosion. Two and a half thousand years after the Golden Empire's fall. . . . And I looked up into that opaquely-lit space, smelling the stink of used air, and realized that the roof of this vast structure must somehow be underneath, and a part of, the *chiruzeth* base-channel of the canal.

As my eyes grew accustomed to the rippling light, I saw how the water for the tanks ran sometimes in open channels, and ran sometimes within the substance of the *chiruzeth* itself, moving back *up* into the main channel of the canal. I thought, This is seawater, something must purify it before it reaches the earth-tanks and the plants, something must make it circulate . . . functional *chiruzeth*.

"This wasn't our *siiran* until Wintersun-10. Sethri and the mercenaries took it from *hiyek*-Rythana in the war," Jadur said. He and the older woman, Feriksushar, went to clear away the crowd. I saw them answering excited questions.

Doug Clifford walked forward to the edge of the nearest *chiruzeth* tank and buried his hands in the earth. It was as if he needed that touch to convince him of reality. I followed, splashing through mud and water that pooled on the *chiruzeth* floor.

"How . . . how many of these *siiran* are there?"

When I looked for Sethri, the shabby yellow-maned male was leaning against the wall. He met my gaze. There was something almost protective in the way that he watched us – seeing us as naïve aliens? As prospective allies? Enemies? That maturity that he had seemed to lose under Feriksushar's contempt returned to him.

"Too few for all the *hiyeks*, *shan'tai* Christie."

Still stunned, I walked to stand beside Doug, oblivious to the curious stares from the crowd.

"Ten years' contact with Carrick V, and no word about this?" Douggie shook his head, incredulous. "I had imagined the canals to be like the Rasrhe-y-Meluur, only a *chiruzeth* shell. This. . . ."

"You're right. The silence is positively deafening."

I touched the cold *chiruzeth* tank, aware of the smell of warm, wet earth, of *del'ri* growing, and scrub-*arniac*. The contrast made me dizzy. That gleaming blue-grey material, eroded by time; force-grown vegetation; and the shabby, malnourished Ortheans of the Coast. . . .

"Who would conceal this?" Doug asked, and then answered his own question: "the Kel Harantish Ortheans, of course. They maintain the canals, they have the monopoly of technology. Earth science might upset the balance of power."

Pathrey Shanataru wants it upset, I thought. And so does the Voice. Kel Harantish is divided, there's a faction that wants contact with Earth. . . . "Dear God, what got started when someone managed to plant one Witchbreed artifact where an archeological team could find it!"

Clifford brushed earth fastidiously from his fingers. "Undoubtedly. And how many times has that been tried and prevented, I wonder, in the past ten years?"

I felt curious glances from the *hiyek*-Ortheans; was aware of Sethri-safere's hawk-poised patience. What might these people want from us . . . ?

Sethri put one six-fingered hand to the *chiruzeth*: "Do offworlders recognize this? A 'Witchbreed abomination', some call it. We could not live without it." He smiled, briefly. "That, and Kel Harantish, who keep it living. *Shan'tai* Christie, all the great *hiyeks* exist between Kel Harantish's power – and the power of Kasabaarde."

The light shone from the ceiling, from the walls; made his young face angled and alien. Dust in that yellow mane, *meshabi*-robe stained with travel; a beggarly commander of mercenaries. And yet he's testing the extent of our knowledge, I thought, and he isn't slow to do it, either.

Deliberately bland, Doug said, "You have the crops and water that Kel Harantish must have to survive. Some might call it a fair exchange, *shan'tai*. And then, on the other hand, Kasabaarde is only a small settlement, primarily interested in regulating trade between the two continents. Why should the *hiyeks* fear Kasabaarde?"

The young Orthean male laughed. He stood lightly, one hand on the hilt of a hook-bladed knife; and self-confidence came off him like a glow. "Say 'this *hiyek*' or 'that *hiyek*', the *hiyeks* have no unity! We have been fighting each other since the Empire fell, and left us in this wilderness."

He sobered, and the nictitating membrane slid back from those tawny eyes. The humid heat made me dizzy, and slightly sick; symptoms that are often indistinguishable from fear.

I said, "It's true the Tower has some authority on the Coast. I saw that last time I came to this world. Ten years ago, the Hexenmeister stopped a war between Kel Harantish and the Hundred Thousand, by threatening to close the Coast seaports to their ships. But what does that have to do with these *siiran*?"

"Without *siiran*, this land would be empty."

Sethri reached across the *chiruzeth* rim of the tank, squeezed earth in one claw-nailed hand, and let it drop. Behind him, tanks of green *del'ri* stretched in diminishing perspective.

"We live in the ruins of what is past, here. Live and starve! Even for that we depend upon Kel Harantish – depend upon their knowledge of the past, and those whose mere shadow the Harantish Witchbreed are: the Golden. And Kasabaarde *condemns* us for it – "

He spoke with such passion and speed that Douggie looked bewildered, losing track of what he said; and I had no time to analyse a moment's fear: *I remember this too well.* Put that aside, face it later.

Sethri took hold of my arm above the elbow, a strong and painful grip.

"If you know the Tower, *shan'tai*, you already know how they hate the Witchbreed abomination above all things. The Tower won't let the *hiyeks* build again – we're barely suffered to live as we do! The Hexenmeister of Kasabaarde keeps us as we are!" He visibly recovered the self-possession he'd lost. "You offworlders, you'd call it a . . . a spiritual authority that the Tower has. Speak to my brother-in-*raiku* Jadur, or to Feriksushar, and they'll tell you we can live no other way. We have been born to no other way for two millennia."

I looked at him until he loosed his grip on my arm. There was no apology in his face. Young, violent, impulsive . . . Some touch of the old professional empathy made me think, There's more to you than that.

"I've waited for offworlders to come to the Coast," Sethri said. There was an arrogance about him that was entirely unconscious. "I know other *raiku* in *hiyek*-Anzhadi who are of my mind. I don't speak for *hiyek*-Anzhadi alone. There's a double stranglehold on us, Kel Harantish and Kasabaarde, and we have to break it."

"That's plain speaking," I said.

He grinned, with all the Orthean addiction to open conspiracy and cautious foolhardiness. "It's more than that, it's rash. But now you offworlders have come to the Coast, matters will move with speed. As they should."

When the filtered light ceased to dazzle, other things beside *chiruzeth* became visible in the *siiran*. I looked down at *ashiren*, their faces thin, all eyes; and saw how half the garden-tanks were barren, not sown with any crop. The unloaded cargo now proved to be *del'ri*-grain, and was being doled out by Feriksushar in scant handfuls. It's not merely human prejudice, I thought, this is a place that's badly overcrowded.

I thought of Molly Rachel, back in the Freeport; tasting the sharp irony that it should be me to find exactly what PanOceania is looking for. Functional Witchbreed technology.

Doug, white about the mouth, said, "From the point of view of personal safety, don't you think our position is a little exposed?"

The palms of my hands were wet. I heard the clatter of blades, where mercenaries unloaded cargo: armed mercenaries in a *siiran*. Orthean factions – those who want to use human technology, and those who want to keep it off Orthe at any cost. Those who abominate Witchbreed science, and those who want to revive it, or to keep its remnants to themselves. . . . Few friends to Earth, and many enemies. And at Kel Harantish, ten days ago, there was the ricochet of a winchbow-bolt. . . .

I raised my wristlink, keyed for open-channel.

The Company can't know what effect it might have here, won't see anything but the canals. It's true that Witchbreed science doesn't affect the Hundred Thousand, but here – here it's life. And subsistence-level life, at that. Oh, I can see why the Brown Tower is (like the Wellhouses) against the old technology; it's the ruin of this continent in old wars that has made the Coast so barren. I can see why the Hexenmeister is determined there should never be another Golden Empire. But what about this shit-poor, fight-against-starvation *hiyek* –

"If we'd known the poverty was this bad . . ." Doug glanced at me. "You're calling the Company."

"They'll come, irrespective of what I do. And if I don't report, Pramila or David will."

It will have to be a relay: to David outside the *siiran*, to Pramila in the grounded shuttle, to the orbital ship and then to Morvren Freeport. Upon such fragile links, we depend.

"Look at it from the practical point of view," I said sardonically. "The more widespread the knowledge, the less personal danger to those of us who are here first."

I didn't hesitate. I saw Jadur returning, with the woman Feriksushar and other Ortheans; and despite his stare, despite being watched with keen intensity by Sethri-safere, there in the chaos of *del'ri*-grain distribution and children shrieking, I opened the comlink channel and sent out the alert.

Sethri waited until I finished.

"I'll take ship for Maherwa soon," he said. "Come with me, *shan'tai*. Word will have gone out. You offworlders may find it safer, now, to be moving targets."

CHAPTER 11

The Legacy of Kasabaarde

Activity on the Coast is impossible for several hours around midday, and so extends well into second twilight and the night. A few hours later, the metal barge sailed north under a sky blazing with the Heart Stars, on a cold canal that reflected back the silver brilliance.

"Cities are supposedly neutral territory," Doug offered. We shared a *del'ri*-fibre blanket, huddled on the deckhouse bench. I nodded.

"I hope you're right. . . ."

Sethri crossed the deck, leaving David Osaka talking with the copper-maned Jadur of Ninth *raiku*. An older male walked beside Sethri. Although he had the pale skin and mane of the Desert Coast, I was somehow reminded of the Earthspeaker Achil.

"This is Hildrindi-*keretne*," Sethri said.

The elderly male had a thin face, the skin about his pinched mouth shadowed with illness. I said, "*Kethrial-shamaz keretne*. Give you greeting, Eldest."

Doug Clifford shot me a puzzled look. I couldn't account for it – wrong dialect? If I could remember which language I'm speaking, I thought, things would go better. Coast speech is beginning to seem like second nature. . . . My vocabulary translated *keretne* as 'eldest', but that doesn't refer to biological age. It's wordplay: *keret* can mean 'truth' or 'memory'.

"You know *keretne*?" Sethri frowned.

"I know that you – " I bowed to the faded, elderly male " – carry the remembered history of your people, as Earthspeakers and Wellkeepers do in the Hundred Thousand."

"Their memory is of the mind," Hildrindi said, "ours is of the blood. Give you greeting, *s'aranthi*. You will meet other *keret* in the city. We will have much to say to you."

He inclined his head, and walked on across the deck, bare high-arched feet soundless on the metal. There was a pause. Then Sethri took his gaze from the distant *keretne*, and rested one hand on my shoulder. I felt the indentation of claw-nails through the cloth.

"I came to give you some advice, *shan'tai* Christie, if I may. There'll be mercenary companies in Maherwa, now the fighting with Rythana is done. Why not hire one for your protection?"

125

"Oh my God." Doug shut his eyes for a moment, and then smiled with an unshakeable public face. "Indeed. Thank you. . . . Lynne, if there's a company from a Guildhouse, one could do worse. I've learned to trust their code, over the years."

"It could serve as a visible warning," I speculated. Also, paid mercenaries hear (and repeat) things that wouldn't be said in front of offworlders.

There is a time to dispense with subtlety. It would be ridiculous, if I didn't have the whole weight of Earth's name behind me, and if we weren't stuck in a hostile wilderness; and as I did it, I thought, It may be ridiculous anyway . . . but I don't underestimate the Orthean capacity for violence.

I stood, letting Sethri see the holstered CAS-IV, letting that remind him by implication of the shuttle, and Earth. "We're not entirely defenceless," I said.

Thinking, *Douggie don't laugh.* A pair of middle-aged adventurers, both of us would be better with desk jobs; I can be excused for attempting the bravado of the young, can't I?

I saw, by starlight, Doug Clifford look up, and give me an anxious and encouraging nod.

Six hours later we docked at Maherwa.

Water lapped at the *chiruzeth* steps, where the canal came to an apparent dead end. Stepping from the deck, my legs felt unsteady. Doug joined me, and we followed Sethri-safere, walking towards a sheer edge and a void.

Above, the dome of the sky was half pearl, half indigo; stars temporarily hidden. Dawn on the Coast is rapid. Already there was enough light to see the city.

The *chiruzeth* fell away vertically at our feet. I stopped, catching hold of Doug's arm. Across a space of air, shimmering with the beginning day's heat, the far edge was visible: a cliff-face, curving round. To look down into that vast circular pit made my head swim. The emptiness pulls . . . I dragged my gaze back.

Ten yards to my left, the cliff-edge split, a paved road going down; spiralling on a long curve to the flat canyon floor. As it descended, it ran beneath overhangs until it became a part of the cliff-wall. Set further back into the sides of the pit were the arched entrances to *chiruzeth* rooms . . . the eye following that curve down and away. Vast as a meteor-crater, but with the shaped edges of Witchbreed construction, this pit-city of the wasteland.

126

Dawn became a brazen flare in the east, flooding the world with white light.

"Come down," the yellow-maned Orthean said.

I felt a slight breeze, and smelled cooking-fires, as we set foot on the paved way. Walking down, heat sucked all energy away, put a rim of perspiration under collar and cuffs, even with the temperature-weave adjusted. Then we passed into the shadow of the overhang. The tunnels and archways were crowded with Ortheans: small, slightly-built, with bleached skins and pale manes, and the *meshabi*-robes belted at the hip, woven with metal-fibre patterns. They stared. I smelled the musty-spicy odour of the crowded city, tasted the gritty dust. All the time I was aware of the yawning emptiness at my right-hand side.

Douggie glanced back; I caught a glimpse of David Osaka, and the *keretne*-Orthean following.

"Satellite images give no idea, do they? This is . . . impressive."

I bit back a comment, seeing Doug Clifford's face. It showed that fear of isolation that makes the mouth go dry.

Young *ashiren* crowded closer now. Dirty lengths of cloth veiled the rooms set into the cliff-wall; beyond them were cluttered chambers. Babies whined. A child ran past me, limping, and I glimpsed ulcers on the stick-thin limbs. An anonymous voice hissed *"Witchbreed!"*, and a group of young males laughed and fell silent as we went by.

None of us spoke. It was a long walk. I said nothing until we had come nearly to ground level, on the opposite side of the pit to the dock. Dawn put a curved shadow across half the flat expanse of the pit-floor.

"Is that – ?" And then I couldn't finish the question.

The shadow fell short of the only structure to break that flat expanse. Holo-images had given no clue to its size – it was as large as the grounded shuttle.

A dome or half-globe rested on a tier of circular steps, and where the edge of the dome met the steps, I could make out the deeper darkness of an entrance. A carved archway. Three squat pillars were set at equidistant points round the dome, and set back into the steps, so that they touched the dome-wall. The top of the pillar nearest to me was broken. There were carved statues on the other two, but erosion and dawn light left no detail – only a hint of claws, wings, scales. At one time, quite plainly, all the surfaces had been painted: scarlet, yellow, and blue. Now the paint was chipped and peeling, *chiruzeth* showing underneath it.

On the facing edges of the steps, on the door-arch, and round the base of the pillars, are carved stylized and alien representations of death's-heads. I stood in the dawn light and was chilled. The Golden Empire, worn down by time and wasteland erosion, still incarnate among its poor and shabby inheritors.

There was light enough now to see that all around that enigmatic structure there were guards armed with spear and winchbow. And they wore the brown scale-mail of Kel Harantish.

"Surely this has to be the Company's primary objective," Pramila Ishida said, as we turned into the entrances of the lower level rooms. "These people must want to trade. They're so poor."

Evening of the next day: I'd decided to risk lifting the grounded shuttle the short distance to Maherwa. Now I had Pramila here, and better comlink equipment. I led the young Asian-Pacifican woman towards the inner chambers, where Douggie and David Osaka were eating with the Ortheans, an evening meal of *del'ri*-bread and *arniac*-tea.

"You go through." I stopped in the outer room. "I've something to do. I'll join you."

The low-ceilinged room was partially lit by mirror-reflected light. The walls were plaster-covered, stained in bright patterns with metal oxides. This room was full of outlanders, some in Melkathi robes, some – despite the heat – in Rimon boots and britches; out of place among the *hiyek*-Ortheans. All of these northern continent Ortheans wore *harur-nilgiri* and *harur-nazari*; and were mostly stretched out on the padded benches, drinking fermented *del'ri*-grain and playing *ochmir*, and talking in a patois of Rimon, Melkathi, Morvrenni, and four or five different Coast languages.

I halted beside a female Orthean. "*T'an* Haldin, isn't it?"

She was lying on a bench, legs up on a table, booted ankles crossed. "Haldin Damory, of the Medued Guildhouse. Have you made your mind up yet, *s'aranthi*?"

"A contract," I said. "Guard duty. And no other contracts taken on while you do it."

She grinned lazily. "That costs more."

So Blaize Meduenin once told me. When I think of him, I wonder that I trust mercenaries at all.

"I'll pay."

Whoops, yells, appreciative comments and a few raucous jeers – her fellow mercenaries approved. They were all young, not one over twenty-five; and all had that savage, laconic, and utterly careless attitude towards violence.

Haldin, hands resting on the hilts of *harur* blades, said, "Guard duty . . . does that apply to *all* you offworlders here?"

I made a mental note to repeat that question to Doug, he has the sense

128

of humour to appreciate it. "All," I said firmly, and we closed the contract. I thought, I'm not sorry to be doing this where *hiyek*-Ortheans can see and know. Another precaution.

I walked through into the inner chambers, pushing past Ortheans, most of whom had *hiyek*-Anzhadi patterns woven into belt or headband or *meshabi*-robe. Some light still entered the unshuttered windows. The last evening breeze brought the smell of dried-dung fires. Clusters of glass bells hung from every window and door-arch, chiming softly. I sat down between Doug and Pramila, on one of the fine metalwork benches, padded with *del'ri*-fibre matting; and drank the acrid *arniac* while Doug and David talked with Ninth *raiku*, and imagined schemes of advantage behind every friendly, curious, or indifferent Orthean face.

I should steer this in the right direction, I thought. *Can you help us with access to the technology here? If not, are you useful as a way back into Kel Harantish?* That's all the Company needs to know. But . . . But?

The young Asian-Pacifican woman beside me stirred, restless. Then she raised her head, looking me right in the eye. "Lynne, these people are *starving*. The children show all the signs of chronic malnutrition. I've been talking to some of them – there hasn't been a *siiran*-harvest brought in without a war for the last nine years. Lynne, these people *need* a Trade&Aid programme!"

The outburst surprised me; not something I expected from this small, sallow-faced girl. No, I realized guiltily, and you didn't expect her to object to this, because she's Company. As if being in a multicorporate made you blind. . . .

"It isn't that simple," I said.

"Isn't it?"

"You set up Trade&Aid, feed these people, and you'll send the birth-rate up," I said. "The *siirans* will be even more overcrowded, they'll overflow. Instead of harvest-wars, you'll have fighting all year round. Soon the cities won't be neutral territory, and the *ashiren* won't come in to them, to group into *raiku*."

I sipped at the *arniac*, cupping the metal bowl between my hands. "Then there'll be dozens, hundreds of *kei-raiku* people here. Do you have any idea how that will unbalance this culture? The *raiku* are self-supporting groups, everything – trade, crafts, ships, the *hiyek*-bloodline itself – is based on that group. Break that up and you'll have changed these people out of all recognition!"

Pramila, looking stunned, said, "Did the Ortheans here tell you that?"

"No, I – "

am under the starry sky of Dustsun, standing with my four companions, before the keretne of the hiyek.

129

'By this blood –'

The metal knives cut. I put my gashed hands in turn to those of my brothers and sisters in raiku, feeling the flow of memory between us.

' – rediscovered, bind us together –'

The rock cold under bare, high-arched feet; meshabi-robe a scant protection; but joy warms me, I have found my other sharers in truth –

"Lynne?"

What the – ?

I shut down the flood of vision, concentrated on Pramila's face. "I'm saying that leaving these people to starve is cruel, and changing their world out of recognition would be cruel; what kind of cruelty should we prefer?"

Voices interrupted as the small room began to fill up with *hiyek*-Ortheans. Sethri, with Jadur and the others of Ninth *raiku*: the twin sisters Wyrrin-hael and Charazir-hael . . . Feriksushar and a crowd of others, and the *keretne* male Hildrindi. . . .

What happened? Is it so easy to think like a hiyek-Orthean?

Frighteningly easy.

"Bad news?" Doug Clifford asked, as Pramila moved over to talk with David Osaka.

"What? – No, sorry; I was thinking of something else."

"You've surprised me," he said, under cover of the general noise. "I don't have anything like your grasp of the Coast culture, and I've been here – well, the Hundred Thousand – "

"The Hundred Thousand isn't the Coast."

That round face was bland. "Lynne, there's no need to bite my head off. There would be much on hypno-tapes, I suppose, that never got transcribed into data-net holo-records. It's a pity, in some ways, that we can't use hypno-tapes now."

"If you'd been through the Psych programmes that I have, to undo the damage – "

"Oh yes. Quite. Not a serious suggestion."

If I could talk to anyone, it would be to Douggie . . . but I held off. Held off and thought, *Am I ill?* If it's a recurrence of that trouble I had after the hypno-tapes . . . but it isn't like that. In Morvren I thought, *It's as if I'd never been away from the Hundred Thousand.* And I have the same feeling here. I know how the *hiyeks* function, what life is like in the *siiran*; every language falls familiar on my ears. But I *can't* know. Ten years ago, I never even came near the *hiyeks* of the Desert Coast. . . .

David Osaka, leaning forward intently, finished giving the standard advantages-of-Trade&Aid speech. He glanced over at me. *Yes it's my job* and yes, it'll get back to Molly Rachel that I'm not displaying proper enthusiasm on behalf of the Company. Too bad.

An *ashiren* stood, slender and pale-maned, and reached up to close the metal window-shutters, excluding the night air. Another child brought fresh *arniac*. There were a dozen or so Ortheans here I could put names to, far more that I couldn't. Now the mirrors began to reflect starlight into the chamber, bright enough to read expressions on alien features. Sethri-safere pulled a metal lattice shutter across the door-arch. Through it, I saw Haldin Damory and her troop still in the outer rooms.

". . . and if we do go to war with *hiyek*-Nadrasiir, the fighting will end when the rains come. *If* the rains come." The woman Feriksushar glanced up from her conversation with David Osaka. She looked at me. "Your *shan'tai* Clifford has said we will not benefit from trade. That it would change us. That we would become like Earth."

Pramila frowned. When I caught Doug's eye, he was entirely unrepentant. I thought, The Coast is not the Hundred Thousand . . . and we sit here and drink *arniac*, eat *del'ri*-bread; relying on hospitality that *hiyek*-Anzhadi may not be able to afford.

As much to myself as to Feriksushar, I said, "If you have Trade&Aid here, it *will* change your lives. I don't know. Before, I was in the Hundred Thousand, and to them one can say 'stay free of Earth' because they don't need help. I don't know if we can say that to you."

Glancing past the gold-maned female, I saw the pinched face of Hildrindi-*keretne*. When I mentioned the Hundred Thousand, I saw a hatred as brief as it was impersonal.

"That said – I have to be honest. All PanOceania's help will come with a price-tag attached. This time it's access to the Witchbreed technology, the canals. You'll have to decide whether or not you can pay that price."

A heated discussion broke out. Jadur, seated on the floor, leaning back between Sethri's legs, looked up and caught the arm of his brother-in-*raiku*, speaking urgently. Wyrrin-hael leaned across to speak to her twin, white mane falling across her eyes. Each of the *hiyek*-Ortheans in the room seemed determined to out-shout the others. I saw Pramila lean forward to speak to David, and Feriksushar (in a gesture that passed unnoticed) take Hildrindi's *arniac* bowl from his hand that shook with weakness.

"We can't trade in Witchbreed abominations!" the *keretne* said.

Jadur lurched to his feet. "*Shan'tai* Christie, we fight our wars with mercenary troops and weapons. Weapons from offworld would aid us. Will your Company trade for them?"

Shit, I thought. That's a question I hoped I wouldn't hear.

In the days when my government controlled relations with Restricted worlds, I could quite genuinely have said, We have a policy forbidding that. Now the multicorporates have the same policy, but I fear how flexible it might prove to be.

Before David or Pramila could express an opinion either way, I cut in: "I'm not convinced that you *can* offer access to the canals, *shan'tai* Jadur."

He scratched awkwardly at his mane, and sat down again beside Feriksushar. "It would have to be secretly . . . with danger . . . perhaps not even then." Forced to that honesty, he looked away, discomfited.

When Hildrindi spoke, it was with an effort. The nictitating membrane opaqued his pale eyes. "The *keretne* will not agree to this. We listen to the Brown Tower, and to the Hexenmeister; and the Tower will not have *s'aranthi* weapons or *s'aranthi* engines on the Coast!"

"There is this," Sethri-safere interrupted. "While we live in this arid land, we will always be in debt to someone. We have merely a choice of creditors. Kel Harantish, or Kasabaarde, or – *s'aranthi* offworlders."

Voices were raised again, and I leaned back against the cool wall, watching. Sethri made himself heard: "Listen to me! War between *all* the Coast *hiyeks* is coming. It can't be avoided now. We'll be fighting before the end of Wintersun. The only choice is whether to have war to our advantage, or to our enemies'."

Claw-nailed hands gestured, one of the males I didn't know stood up, shouting; Charazir-hael drew the hook-bladed knife from her belt, but Jadur restrained her. The stocky Feriksushar was on her feet. A tall male, blustering, shouted, "Give us weapons, we'll free ourselves of the Harantish Witchbreed!"

Another male looked up lazily and said, "There are no pure-blooded Witchbreed now. Our *ashiren* have gone to Kel Harantish, their *ashiren* have come into our *raiku* – "

"If you have 'Breed blood in your *hiyek*, no need to accuse us of the same filth!"

Sethri-safere came and sat down on the bench beside me. I saw Doug had gone – and then saw him talking with Pramila. The yellow-maned Orthean grinned at the violent reaction.

"That's stirred them up. They don't trust me, because I've commanded mercenaries, and that's a dirty job. But it does mean I know what I'm talking about."

War between the *hiyeks*? "Who are your enemies, Sethri?"

Nictitating membrane slid over his tawny eyes. He said, "When your Company comes offering to trade, all the Coast *hiyeks* became each other's enemies."

Some cold professionalism in me ignored the implications of what he was saying; merely thought, Thank God for someone who understands the problem.

"Suppose I tell you – and it's true – that there's a strict prohibition on our bringing in Earth weapons technology?"

No matter what we might be offered in exchange?

He looked down at strong, narrow fingers, spread on the weave of dirty *meshabi*-cloth; the claws trimmed back on all but the sixth finger.

"Christie, anything is a weapon. Say you trade us a cure for crop-blight – there's a *hiyek* that will grow strong, have many *ashiren*. A *hiyek* that will be able to pay to send mercenaries against other *hiyeks*, to seize what *siiran* it needs to feed that number." He shrugged. "Which means that the three or four most powerful *hiyeks* at the time will band together to fight that one, and then fall out among themselves when the war's over. . . ."

Sethri-safere. An attractive face, with a deceptively open look that owed much to fair mane and brows and nothing at all, I guessed, to temperament.

"You have an answer?"

He turned his head slightly so that no one should see what he said, and it was an automatic gesture: he was more than used to concealment, he revelled in it. I thought, You should have been born in the Hundred Thousand, a player of the game.

"There aren't answers. Maybe we can adapt. If *raiku* can be allies, then why not *hiyek*?" The skin round his eyes crinkled, bare evidence of amusement. "I've little talent for sowing or harvest in the *siiran*, the city trade bores me, commanding mercenaries is a regrettable necessity – but I *can* persuade *raiku* into seeing things my way."

His hand was cool on my arm, dry, with the swift Orthean heartbeat felt through fingertips on my skin. I thought, I trust self-interest even more than expediency – you want to break the stasis the *hiyeks* are held in, but even more, you want it to be *you* that does it. . . .

"Christie, you see, I'm honest with you. Who else is to help me to that leadership, if not *s'aranthi*? And who else but me would be willing to help *s'aranthi* get what they want from the ruins of the Golden Empire?" His smile was warm, mocking, collusive. "I mean to make a friend of you, Lynne Christie."

An hour later I left the crowded chamber, going out to stand in the cool night. A boot-heel clicked. I glanced down the paved way, under the overhang – the mercenary, Haldin Damory, lifted a hand in reassurance, and stepped back into the shadows.

I looked out across the pit-floor of Maherwa. The Heart Stars shone

133

bright enough to cast shadows from the dome-structure and pillars, and illumine the distant figures of Harantish guards.

And word will have gone back to Kel Harantish. That's the obstacle – or should I be grateful that there is an obstacle?

All the Coast hiyeks exist between the power of Kel Harantish and Kasabaarde, Kasabaarde –

I swung round, and hit the *chiruzeth* wall hard with the heel of my hand. Vision trembled at the edge of consciousness. A tide of memory that will flood over me, sweep away all that is Lynne Christie –

What *is* it? What's happening to me?

"Lynne." Doug Clifford's face was in the shadow, but concern was plain in his voice. "If there's anything I can do . . ."

"Let's leave Pramila and David to it," I said. "The mercenary troop have a few bottles of *siir*-wine; let's have a drink, and catch up on what we've been doing since – where was it? – Melhuish's World."

And Doug Clifford, with urbane tact, agreed.

Four days later, Wintersun-28, word came through on the comlink of Molly Rachel's imminent arrival.

All through the intervening days, *raiku* from Anzhadi and other *hiyeks* poured into the city: groups of three, four, or five Coast Ortheans; some elderly, some still *ashiren*. The speed of communication amazed me, until I saw the heliographs flash across the flat, barren landscape; and as for their mobility – travel along the waterways is, like sea travel, faster than most forms of land travel in low-tech cultures. By Wintersun-28 there were Ortheans in Maherwa from as far up the Coast as Quarth, all of two hundred and fifty miles away.

And by Wintersun-28 I had grown used to sleeping three hours at midday, and six at night, to fit into *hiyek* life; and to carrying on PanOceania's business while armed mercenaries guarded the door.

"We'll go up and meet the shuttle," I said. Haldin Damory stood, and joined me at the door. The dirty *del'ri*-cloth curtain had been looped back, to let in morning light, and the noise of squabbling *ashiren* on the paved way outside.

"Are you interested in a warning?" the young female swordfighter said as we left the inner chambers.

Nights in Wintersun have still a bitter cold, but the frosts were passing. Now first twilight had gone, and Carrick's Star as it rose left half the city in deep shadow. Haldin paced beside me, alert; dark curled mane carelessly braided up. She wore a horn-mail coat, and one six-fingered hand rested lightly on the hilt of *harur-nazari*.

134

Four days is long enough to hear rumour, gossip, intrigue. I slowed as we passed an area where the overhang was deeper, going further back into the cliff-face, where the stalls of a market were being set up.

"Warning?" I said.

"I'll tell you a fable, *t'an*, and you draw the moral." She glanced at me. "Meeting you isn't the first time I've heard the name of *S'aranth*. When I first came to the Coast as a mercenary – oh, I was an *ashiren*, no more – there was a Commander, a woman of the Hundred Thousand. An exile. She was crippled, she'd lost an arm."

The young female's face was serious. Is she old enough to remember that long-ago summer in Melkathi?

"I'd heard, yes. Ruric Orhlandis died, in exile." I don't think my voice was quite controlled.

Haldin Damory said, "Ah, but that's it, *t'an*, she didn't die – she was killed. An assassin killed her, in the trade-quarter of Kasabaarde. And now draw the moral: I hear talk in this Goddess-abandoned hole, and I hear there are still people who'd willingly see offworlders, *and* friends of offworlders, killed. That death was a long time ago, but things aren't different now."

Shall I ask what she said about the *S'aranth*, those many years ago? Ask: was she bitter, driven into exile from her beloved Hundred Thousand, did she hate me for the part I played in that? No. Whatever was said, I can't change it now.

"There," Haldin Damory said. She dropped back a pace, and I saw her check by line of sight that two of the other mercenaries were not far from us; and then I saw what she'd seen. A head taller than any of the Coast Ortheans, walking where the sun cast a shadow on to the paved way from the overhang, and entirely alone – Molly Rachel.

"Lynne!" she called. She looked past me. "Are Pramila and David here? Has Rashid arrived yet?"

"No. I wasn't told he was coming." I stood and waited for her. "How were the Barrens?"

"We kept to high-level aerial survey. The readings didn't tell us much. Then I got your transmission. Lynne – "

Of all the tribal Ortheans I met in the Barrens, I can remember only O'he-Oramu-te, the Woman Who Walks Far. In that place of tundra and Witchbreed ruins, will she even be alive now?

" – this place!" Molly scratched through loops of her tangled black hair, and slowed that long-legged stride. She stared out across the pit, at the opposite cliff-wall honeycombed with chambers. She pulled down eyeshields, blinked. An *ashiren*, two or three years old, stopped and stared up at this dark giant; and then ran when Molly smiled at *kir*.

135

"I must say, we've been marking time," I said. Thinking, Don't ask me why, Molly, please.

She stepped close to the edge of the walkway. At her feet, a sheer drop; empty air, and then – isolated in the centre of the pit-floor – that *chiruzeth* dome and pillars.

"It was the last act of Empire," I said, unwillingly sharing her fascination. "The generation that saw the Elansiir destroyed, built this. But they destroyed themselves, fighting; left only the Ortheans. . . ."

"That's it, that's what we've got to have."

We turned to go back down the walkway, Molly ducking to avoid catching her head on the *del'ri*-cloth awnings of the market stalls. Ortheans pointed as we went by, commenting in a variety of Coast languages. There was the ring of hammers from a metalworker's stall nearby.

"Can the *hiyeks* help us get into that?"

I glanced up at her. "It's the incredible balance – Kel Harantish with the technical knowledge, the *siiran* with the food and water. I honestly don't know whether you'll get the *hiyeks* to risk it."

"It all comes back to Kel Harantish," the Pacifican woman said.

"And I don't think you'll get back on negotiating terms with them in a hurry." That pleased me: the thought that I don't have to block the Company here, circumstances will do it.

"Lynne, whose side are you on?"

"Ah, now, if I knew that. . . ."

"Joking aside. I know Doug Clifford's against ninety per cent of what we're doing here. It's you I can't make out."

"You've been talking to young Pramila."

"I've been talking to *you*."

Sunlight dazzled me, shining into the walkway. I put my eyeshields back on. The market stalls wouldn't stay open long, it was rapidly becoming too hot. I looked out at a steel-blue sky peppered with daystars.

Deliberately putting her off, I said, "It's a barter economy here. They exchange promissory notes on the next *siiran*-harvest. Taking into consideration they pay mercenaries too, it's no surprise there isn't a *hiyek* on the Coast not chronically in debt. Of course, Kel Harantish uses that to stir up dissent. The last thing they want is for the Coast families to unite. . . ."

Molly looked down, shook her head, watching me. The light made silver curves of her round features. She walked with one hand always near the CAS-IV holster.

"They use mercenaries because there's a taboo on personally attacking the bloodline, and all the *hiyeks* are more or less inter-related." Which the Pacifican woman would know; but it was only an attempt at distraction.

The crowd was thicker here, and we were stopped at the edge of a group of *ashiren* watching glass-blowers at work. Molly and I stood for a moment looking over their heads. Groupings of *ashiren* that would, when their city time was over, become *raiku*.

"*How* do I get into that?" Molly gazed out at the *chiruzeth* dome and pillars, and the guards. Then she looked down at me, and with an abrupt change of tone, said, "My father was of the Masai. My mother was Aruna. *She* had a choice. She could die alcoholic, because the old life couldn't be lived, or she could take. She *took*. She went to the University of Melbourne, and then to Tokyo. Lynne, sometimes cultures change. It's that simple."

I listened hard, and I heard nothing at all defensive in her tone. I said, "Change imposed from outside."

"It comes to the same thing." She squinted up at the brilliant sky, and fingered the eyeshields that hung round her neck. "My mother taught me what she learned when she was a *burri* – a baby. Sooner or later one culture goes under, so you don't give up, you take. These people here, the *hiyeks*, they're capable of learning that."

The crowd thinned a little, and I walked on. Aware of Haldin Damory and the two mercenaries, never far away. That honeycombed cliff towered above. I walked slowly towards the Pacifican quarters further round the curve of the wall. After a few seconds, Molly Rachel's long stride caught up. She walked beside me.

"You're looking tired." Concern in her voice, and something else; something inflexible. She said, "Lynne, if you want to go back up to the orbiter, not just back to Morvren-base, that'll be all right. I'm certain that you've found what we want, here – if I can get to it. And I won't need you in the negotiations. This isn't your specialist area."

I can't believe that I didn't see this one coming.

"There's no necessity for me to return – "

" – immediately. No, of course not. You could just as well go in a day or two, Lynne. Go with Clifford, when he goes back. That'll be in the very near future."

The sun was a brilliant glare, drowning daystars. I stopped to wipe my forehead, and try to control uneven breath. I ached. Angry with myself: I won't let myself be used and thrown out!

"Molly, I think you'd benefit, still, from having the advice of someone with experience of the area – "

"But you haven't. Not of the Coast."

Worn flagstones were hot underfoot, too hot to stand still for long, and

137

so I walked on, thinking, Douggie isn't going to like the news of his imminent departure, and I –

I can't be a restraining influence on the Company if I'm not involved in Company negotiations.

A wind stirred the dust on the city floor. It rattled against the *del'ri* awnings. Three young *ashiren* pushed between Molly and me, running; thin limbs and ragged *meshabi*-robes.

Morvren Freeport, the orbiter, and then what? A ship back to Earth? Because there's no need for a special advisor if you know as much – or as little – as she does about the Desert coast and Kel Harantish. . . .

I licked my lips, tasting dust. On an optimistic estimate, two days, to save my position here?

"*T'an* Christie."

Both of us turned. It was Haldin with one of her mercenaries, a crop-maned male. The male said in accented Rimon, "I have a message, *t'an*, passed to me to give to the *s'aranthi*. There are people here who wish to speak with you."

Molly frowned. "From other *hiyeks*?"

Haldin Damory snorted. The mercenary spoke with the sardonic humour of the young: "They *say* they're from Quarth, come down the Coast by *jath-rai*. *T'ans*, if you were to ask me, I'd say they come from a different port – from Kasabaarde. Or if they don't, that's where their report will go back to. Kasabaarde, and the Brown Tower."

CHAPTER 12

Dreams of Gold and Silver

What I'm doing here sickens me.

That thought came quite suddenly, following the Pacifican woman under the *chiruzeth* overhang, back along the walkway. It felt cooler. I pulled off the eyeshields.

No, I thought. It's the self-deception that sickens me. While I stay here, I have to act for the Company. What good am I doing Orthe? What good am I doing myself?

Molly Rachel's stride took her ahead, and I followed, climbing the gradual incline. The mercenaries checked doorways to inner rooms. I stopped for a moment, short of breath. White sun glared from the city's far wall, where figures moved like flies, and I trudged on again, higher up, further round the pit-wall.

If it wasn't me it would be someone else –

That's no excuse. It never was.

And I had to smile, thinking, These qualms of conscience have come only when I'm on the verge of losing my post here anyway.

Shadow lay under the *chiruzeth* overhang in a black curve. My lungs burned with the effort of climbing. Haldin Damory glanced back, with a look of concern. At intervals the overhang widens out – or rather, goes back deeper into the rock cliff itself. The Pacifican woman stopped in that shadowy, low-roofed space; staring round at the featureless archways. No wind stirred those ragged *del'ri* curtains.

"*Shan'tai* Haldin."

Haldin approached her. I stopped, gratefully, a few paces away. Young *ashiren* playing pebble-games scattered as they saw us. I caught sight of one child's thin cheek marred with a raw ulcer, another with suppurating membraned eyes.

Just maybe I'm right about the Hundred Thousand; we could trade with the *telestres* for Witchbreed technology and it wouldn't change their lives. But here – how can we *not* trade, not change? Knowing what culture shock, what disruption; still . . .

The close heat and shadowed twilight made me dizzy. Aching, hot; all the discomfort of alien air, protein, gravity. And ten years less resilient now.

Molly Rachel said, "One of you fetch Pramila Ishida, I want her here for this, and – "

"Doug Clifford," I put in, saw her hesitate, then accept.

When I came to Orthe I thought I knew what I had to do, if not how to do it. Now I don't even know what I should be trying to do.

The Pacifican woman said speculatively, "Traders from Kasabaarde?"

"From the Hexenmeister," Haldin said. " – S'aranth?"

In the dream, a woman stood before me. She had the bleached skin of the Coast, and a rough dark mane coming down from complex braids. In her forties (and I younger, then). And held between brown-robed servants, her shirt torn, her eyes unveiled and so wide that the whites were visible.

I spoke to that ancient Orthean male, the Hexenmeister, who stood beside me: "I have heard that those whom you – question – are not unchanged by it. Some say it's possible to recognize them forever after, because of what they become."

"T'an, you can hurt her greatly and she will perhaps tell you the truth, and perhaps a lie. I will hurt her not at all, and to me she will tell only the truth. But – "

"But?"

"But it is true she will be changed."

That subliminal hum that underlies the Brown Tower intensified the silence. Aphasia, amnesia, blackouts, idiocy; all the possible symptoms of brain-damage – oh yes: changed.

The woman looked at me with a desperate appeal. I couldn't even recall her name.

"Yes," I consented. "Question her, master."

The Hexenmeister of Kasabaarde watched me with black, bright eyes. And I dreamed that we went down into the maze of the Brown Tower, among the masked and brown-robed servants, to a cool dry hall lit with faintly blue iridescence, and sarcophagus-machines.

"Havoth-jair!" I cried as I woke, stumbled; Molly Rachel caught my arm, and Haldin's mercenary turned swiftly to survey the low-roofed space. The sky beyond the overhang was molten brass. The air stifled. Loud voices echoed back from the walkway.

Not dreaming (but it has, I remember, been a recurring dream for many years); not dreaming, but caught between one step and the next into memory –

False memory.

"It wasn't me! I didn't give him permission to question her." Bewildered, I found the young woman's arm round my shoulder, half supporting me. "Her name. Her name was Havoth-jair."

Rachel looked down at me, frowning. "Are you all right? Can you stand? Good. Lynne . . . you're not going to like me saying this, but I've seen this coming on."

I pushed her hand aside, still unsteady. Her skin was slick with sweat. Details of the dream were already fading.

"Lynne, it's on your record. You had an extremely bad reaction to hypno-tape implants. Now you're where everything triggers off those old implant-data memories. I think you'd better go back up to the orbiter. The help you've given has been invaluable, but I won't make you stay here and crack up."

Her words had a slight reverberation: sounds echo between these *chiruzeth* walls. *Chiruzeth*: cloudy blue-grey. I want to sit down, I need a drink – I'd even drink their fermented *del'ri*-grain. I need to know what's happening to me.

When I rubbed my forehead my hair was plastered down with sweat. Pulse hammering: rapid and unsteady. I walked a few steps, hearing the echo of my boot-heels. The vast emptiness beyond the edge of the walkway shone bright: sun and dust and air. I turned, facing – as I must – that young woman.

What hurts most is that her concern is genuine.

"It isn't that – "

Suddenly and simply, I knew two things. The first and more obvious: it was no use remonstrating, I would condemn myself out of my own mouth. And the second was that this was *not* hypno-tape psychosis.

I've been through that, I thought. I'd recognize it again. I'm in a mess, sure, but that isn't the reason – thank God

A laugh bubbled up, uncomplicatedly cheerful. Unreasonable to be so happy, knowing that – but I do know; I've had long enough to know how I function. With a macabre humour, I thought, I may be having hallucinations, blackouts, false memories, and paranoia, but it's okay. If it isn't that identity-destroying reaction to hypno-implants (I dread that above all things) then it's *okay*. . . .

Something of that must have come through in the way I laughed. Molly Rachel looked at me dubiously and said, "I could be wrong."

"Believe me, you are." That irrational joy was still with me. I saw, further down the walkway slope, the approaching figures of Doug Clifford, Pramila Ishida, and David Osaka, with one of Haldin's mercenaries. "We seem to be all here. Shall we go and talk to these traders from 'Quarth'?"

Haldin Damory indicated one of the curtained archways. Molly blinked.

"I . . . er . . . well – "

I beamed, walked past her into the inner room close by, so dazzling her with bonhomie that she didn't tell this troublesome woman she had no right, officially, to be present. There are advantages to being thirty-eight and in one's right mind.

Inside, in mirror-light that cast strange shadows, a group of five Ortheans were seated round one of the low metal tables. I let the Pacificans crowd in behind me, and Molly do the standard introductions. Five of them, four males and one female: none of them old.

A thin Orthean male rose to his feet. He wore a plain brown *meshabi*-robe, and carried no weapon; what was visible of his pale mane was shaven down to white fluff. And he wore a mask. A half-face mask, with some translucent glass or crystal in the eyeholes. Such masks are common on the Coast in summer – and in Kasabaarde all year round.

When he had introduced himself as Annekt, I said, "Quarth? Give you greeting, *shan'tai* Annekt; I think you're out of your way. I think you mean Kasabaarde."

Molly Rachel winced at that high-handedness. The Pacificans froze in the action of seating themselves round the low table. Doug Clifford coughed.

Only that curved pale mouth visible: the thin male's face was unreadable.

"We've sailed by way of Kasabaarde's trade-quarter. Many do." Annekt's voice was husky, with an indeterminate Coast accent.

"And when you sail back, what will you say to the Hexenmeister of Kasabaarde about Company offworlders?"

Molly seized my elbow. "Sit down!" she hissed. I had little option, and half fell on to one of the padded metal benches.

The Orthean remained standing for a moment. I saw that his long six-fingered hands moved nervously. And then I saw answering small gestures from the seated traders. Communication.

"You're quite right," Annekt said mildly, "that all the traders of the Coast commonly bring news and rumour to the Tower in Kasabaarde. I shouldn't wonder but that the Hexenmeister knows of your arrival here."

Molly glanced round, momentarily helpless. Pramila settled in next to her, and David Osaka seated himself awkwardly on the end of another bench. It was a shabby room, the painted images on the plaster chipped and fading. I saw Doug Clifford exchange a greeting with the other traders and sit down.

The lattice grid of the inner doorway opened, and Haldin Damory re-emerged. She gestured. One of the young mercenaries served *arniac*-tea, handing the bowls to us, but placing them on the table before the Kasabaardean traders. Molly passed her wristlink over her bowl, and I saw Haldin stiffen – an insult to a mercenary's efficiency, to check for poison.

I pitched in again: "No doubt the Hexenmeister recalls offworlders from when I visited him before – unless there's a new holder of the title. Ah, I forgot. That wouldn't make any difference, would it?"

I wanted this faceless young Kasabaardean male to respond to that needling tone, but only Molly Rachel got irritated.

"Lynne, if you don't mind!"

Annekt said, "No, shan'tai, the Hexenmeister will still remember offworlders. Memory dies not, though we are mortal, and there is always a Hexenmeister in the Tower."

There was a loud crash. Haldin Damory threw down a ceramic bowl. In a high, tight voice she said, "No! The Hexenmeister has no past-memory, no *true* past-memory, only some heresy brought about by Witchbreed engines and devices – "

My stomach went tight at the tension of the silence that followed. For a mercenary to lose control – she and the masked young trader stared at each other, poles of power and tension, until at last she turned, spat, and walked out, her boots loud on the *chiruzeth* floor. She curtly directed one of her mercenaries to guard the outer door, and strode off out of sight.

"*Shan'tai* Annekt, I can only apologize." Molly passed a hand through her tangled black hair, and glanced at Pramila and David. "If we could perhaps continue this discussion in a calmer frame of mind . . ."

"Of course," the Kasabaardean male said. He reseated himself. One of the other traders signed something on claw-nailed fingers that made him smile.

How far can I push this? I thought. Ah, since Molly's trying to get me out anyway, I doubt it matters what I say now.

"*Shan'tai* Annekt." I got his attention. "What does the Hexenmeister want with us? Is it merely curiosity?"

The male didn't answer for a moment. Then he reached up with both six-fingered hands and undid the lacings of the mask. He put it on the table, and wiped his face – a thin-featured face, under that shaven white mane, with green eyes brilliant against the pallor of his skin. He smiled.

"*Shan'tai*, if you're so well informed, tell me why it should be anything else except simple curiosity."

Doug Clifford leaned forward, resting his clasped hands on his knees, unexpectedly coming to my rescue. "It's in our Service records that the Tower's influence stopped a war, once. As I understand it, the Tower threatened to use its influence and cut Kel Harantish off from trade with the rest of the Coast – starve them, in fact. Kasabaarde seems well placed to control the flow of trade."

The green-eyed male blinked. That shaven mane accentuated the alien proportions of his face: broad forehead, narrow jaw. He said, "Stopped a war? An exaggeration, *shan'tai.*"

I said, "If not a war, certainly a very nasty hostile incident." And why not mention it all? I thought. There's no one in this room now who'll be offended. "You may not recall, Annekt. It was some eight years ago. The Harantish Witchbreed were financing rebellious factions in the Hundred Thousand *telestres* – SuBannasen, Charain. Orhlandis."

The male shrugged thin shoulders, looked at me helplessly. *"Shan'tai,* I'm only a trader. If I carry word to the Hexenmeister's brown-robes . . . well, all Coast traders do that. I know little. There will be word sent to you, I doubt not, if the Hexenmeister of Kasabaarde would hear more of you."

David and Pramila had their heads together, muttering. Doug Clifford appeared to be examining, with absent-minded interest, the patterns of reflected mirror-light on the shabby walls.

Molly Rachel, in Sino-Anglic, said, "Lynne, we can do without mentioning spies and informers from some cult-ridden settlement in the north. I think we'll consider the subject closed."

The talks went on after that in much the usual Pacifican manner. Molly conducted affairs, bringing in Pramila and David for logistic and technical support; and the five Orthean traders asked the standard questions about the standard Trade&Aid speeches. Only the unmasked male looked at me, from time to time, and then the nictitating membrane slid back from those apple-green eyes.

The room grew hotter, the air more close; and about the time I judged there'd be a mid-morning break, I edged round until I could speak to Doug Clifford.

"What's all this about, Lynne?"

"Did you know you were leaving for the Freeport today or tomorrow?"

Not what he expected: at first bewildered, then that affable public expression vanished. "I'm still government representative here!"

"I know."

Molly said something I didn't catch, there was a scuffle of people rising to their feet: the time well judged. As we went out I said, "Douggie, we should talk."

A square of sky was visible through this outer room's window, daystars obscured by a haze. Anzhadi-*hiyek* had given Clifford rooms high up on the city wall. The air was hot and heavy with the promise of rain. The end of Wintersun. I collapsed into one of the padded *del'ri*-fibre chairs, wiping my forehead. Doug crossed to where he kept a flask of the fermented *del'ri*-grain spirit on a low table, poured two bowls, and lifted one in silent acknowledgement of exhaustion.

"Jesus Christ, Douggie, I'm getting too *old* for this!"

He seated himself in a chair beside me, smiling with squirrel-cheeked bonhomie. "You're not fifty, my girl. Just wait. You don't know what being tired is."

"What a pair of old wrecks we are – eh?"

Humour faded. The light beat in and hurt my eyes. There was the constant stickiness of sweat, and that undefined irritation that is the precursor of many minor ills. A few months on the Coast, I thought, and what little stamina I have left will be gone.

"I mean, too old for offworld service. Douggie, I swear I don't know how you do it."

He sipped the acrid *del'ri*-spirit. "I do it – used to do it – by never getting involved beyond professional limits. Lynne . . . but if I'm being shipped back to the Freeport, it's academic. Thank you for the warning, by the way."

"Probably the last time I'll be in a position to give one."

Noise filtered in from the walkway outside, and the shadows of passing *hiyek*-Ortheans fell briefly on the *del'ri* curtain of the archway. There was a smell of cooking, and dung-fires; a last burst of activity before the midday cessation.

I said, "It's all falling down behind us like dominoes – a palace revolution in Kel Harantish, the *telestres*, the Wellhouses, the *hiyek*-wars . . ."

Doug said grimly, "Reports *are* going back to Earth."

I thought, I came here to talk; how do I raise the matter that's important? That sudden influx of confidence, of energy, now gone. I don't have the reserves of strength I had at thirty. Eroded by heat, by exhaustion, by the sheer pressure of demand.

"I thought, when I came here with the Company, that I could *do* something. I really thought that, you know?"

"You've kept the Company's policy within restricted limits." Doug raised a thoughtful eyebrow. "Very restricted, if one were to consider, say, Melhuish's World – or the European Enclaves."

He smiled. It warmed me. He's the only one here with the same knowledge of the Company that I have, the same objections to their methods.

"All the same, the problem isn't that simple." I wiped sweat off neck and forehead. "Life here – this is subsistence-level, here on the Coast. Sometimes not even that. Is it right for us to be isolationist?"

He shrugged, a gesture that meant he wouldn't consider arguments. "It's the life they've chosen."

"Chosen? What choice?"

I pushed myself up out of the chair and went to loop back the *del'ri* curtain, hoping to coax some movement of air through the door-arch. There was none. This room was small, like all Maherwa's rooms. I looked across the narrow walkway at sunlit space.

"Maybe I can persuade Molly I'm still useful," I said, a little whimsically. "If I say I'll go to Kasabaarde, perhaps, with the traders? But she doesn't need that if she's got the Witchbreed technology she's looking for."

He crossed one leg elegantly over the other. "Lynne, as an old friend, let me ask you something. How long are you going to keep running?"

"Until I know what I'm running from, what I'm running to, and *why*."

"I'm worried about you. I've been worried about you for some time."

The low ceiling of the room was claustrophobic. I moved to stand by the window, and felt a feather-breeze of humid air. You want my help against PanOceania, I thought; Jesus, Douggie, that isn't it, that isn't what's important now!

"It's like this," I said carefully. "I've admitted to myself that there's a problem. I've got some sort of balance back, but I can't hold it, I'm up one minute and down the next. I get . . . wiped out, by memories. If I don't go on and find out what this is, I'll lose that balance, and that's the finish. But if I *do* find out the cause . . ."

Doug put his bowl of *del'ri*-spirit down on the low table. "Find out what, precisely?"

"Everything I see now triggers off memories. I think that something was done to me, a long time ago. There's something about it that I can't remember, but I'm afraid to, because if I do remember, then I'll . . . well, make myself a target."

He looked startled. "Target for whom?"

"I don't know!"

Doug came and stood beside me at the window, and looked out at the Ortheans on the walkway. Without turning his head to face me, he said, "Lynne, this is classic hypno-tape paranoia. You think you have knowledge acquired by some arcane method, but it all comes out of old research data. You know what this is! And as for laying yourself open to attack – "

"It isn't just me. It's all the offworlders here. I *know* that sounds paranoid, but . . . and you never saw Havoth-jair."

"Who?"

"She was a Harantish woman who spied on us in Kasabaarde, when

Blaize and Hal and Evalen Kerys-Andrethe were there with me. She was behind an attempt to assassinate us. We let the Hexenmeister's people question her – break her."

Why can't I get her out of my mind? I look in this old city's polished metal mirrors and I see her face.

"Douggie, don't tell me to go and see the Psych people."

He looked at me, indecision in every line of his face. "I may have to. I know – "

"Know what?"

"What happened to you after Max died."

The wall was cool against my back: *chiruzeth* under the painted plaster. I looked at Doug; could still see from the corner of my eye the city outside.

"I fell apart. Some of it was Max's death and, yes, some of it was reaction to hypno-implants. I see that now. At the time I thought it was all Max. All right, Doug, I was out for a year, hospitalized. But I do still know what I'm talking about!"

Sincerity isn't always an advantage. I saw how the effort I put into convincing him was making him doubt still further.

"Let's leave it at that," I said. "It isn't something I can prove. Not yet. This isn't just some ex-Service woman going crazy. There's something behind it that's going to affect us all."

I pushed through the *del'ri*-cloth curtain, and went out on to the walkway. Slow anger began to burn, and I strode down that long curve, heading toward the city-floor; not looking back to see if Doug called me. I will not be doubted! I thought. If *I* think I don't know what I'm doing, that's one thing; but I won't have anyone else saying it!

The ridiculousness of that dawned on me as I came to the foot of the walkway. I couldn't help chuckling, but I didn't know whether to laugh or cry. . . .

Five or six Ortheans pushed past me. As they went into the cliff-wall chambers, I saw they wore brown scale-mail and carried winchbows, and so must be the Harantish guardians of the dome – I stopped dead and stared. A small, dark-skinned male was last in the group; a plump Orthean male who wore armour uneasily, as if it were the last thing he was used to. He had a cropped black mane. It was as he vanished into the inner rooms, and I realized that I had last seen that mane elaborately braided, that I thought in shock *Pathrey Shanataru!*

I took a step in that direction, and then hesitated. Pathrey Shanataru, and the nameless woman who had been Voice of the Emperor-in-Exile, had vanished in Kel Harantish's 'palace revolution'. To see him here,

147

now, and obviously in disguise . . .

No, I thought. This wants thinking out.

I entered my quarters, to find Haldin Damory sitting on the bed. She stood, with that apparently effortless movement of the swordfighter. *Harur*-blades clashed. She wiped six-fingered hands on the thighs of her britches. Embarrassment brought the nictitating membrane down to cover those brown eyes.

"*T'an*, I – I'll understand if you want to call our contract void."

"What?" Then I realized: the incident with the Kasabaarde traders. "Oh, no; no, I don't." I sank down on the nearest metal bench and pulled off my boots. Then I glanced up, surprising a look of gratitude on the young Orthean female's face, and recalled that all her troop depended on the contract too.

"You've been in a Wellhouse, *t'an* Haldin," I guessed.

She stood with her booted feet a little apart, balanced lightly: swordfighter's stance. That tangled dark mane was falling from its braids. Shabby, stubborn, a hired killer; and yet . . .

"The Hexenmeister mocks us," she said, almost sulkily. "I shouldn't speak of it outside a Wellhouse."

"I was once marked for Her, in a Wellhouse."

If I keep saying that, some manic hilarity assured me, someone someday will tell me what it means.

She said, "He mocks us. If his memories are nothing but Witchbreed trickery, passed down from one Hexenmeister to another, then our past-memories . . ." She paused, the nictitating membrane sliding back from her dark gaze. "As I grow older, I remember more. *T'an*, I don't truly believe our past-memories are deceptive. We have lived before, under Her sky, and we return; we meet, and part, and meet again, and do not forget."

That change from doubt to certainty would be inexplicable if she were not Orthean.

"I don't want to cancel the contract," I said finally. "There is something I want you and your people to do. Before mid-afternoon if you can. Certainly before tonight . . . ."

The sky clouded over. The drop in ambient temperature was amazing. I could sleep now, I thought; at last, sleep through midday. But I don't dare sleep.

Feriksushar had said, *When the rains come*, and the rains would be a monsoon, I guessed, and not far off now.

Two hours passed before I heard Haldin Damory's cheerful voice ring through the outer room. I turned away from the window as she entered, pushing the *del'ri* curtain aside.

"I've found him," she announced. "What's more, *t'an*, no one else knows I found him; not *hiyek* nor *s'aranthi*."

"Ah, good. Is he amenable to a meeting, here?"

"He – they – they're here now, *t'an* Christie."

They? I wondered, and followed her back into the outer room. "Give you greeting. . . ."

"*Shan'tai* Christie."

The sleek, plump male bowed, his brown face beaming. He looked little different from when I'd seen him in Kel Harantish; only that cropped mane, and his face slightly thinner.

"Pathrey Shanataru," I acknowledged. Then I turned to his companion. "I'm sorry, *shan'tai*, I never did learn your name."

That whitefire mane was dyed sepia now, and some brown stain had been used on her gold-dust skin. She was in a plain ragged *meshabi*-robe. Still she gazed at me with luminous yellow eyes, this small Orthean woman who had been Voice of the Emperor-in-Exile in Kel Harantish.

"My name is Calil bel-Rioch," she said softly. "I'm glad you came looking for my Pathrey Shanataru. I want to talk with *s'aranthi*-offworlders."

A kind of silence surrounded her, that made the noise and jostle of the mercenaries outside these rooms meaningless. Meeting that yellow gaze, I shivered. *A wordless chant, a ritual feast . . .* And then she smiled, and was only a young Orthean woman, stripped of the pomp of Kel Harantish.

"If you didn't recognize me," Calil bel-Rioch said, "that's because I have no wish to be killed by the Emperor-in-Exile's spies. I've come here to find allies. I want to talk to you and *shan'tai* Rachel and *shan'tai* Clifford."

Names, too? Now that's interesting.

I said, "I need to know something. Have you come here with the intention of trading with the Company?"

Calil looked at me thoughtfully. "I may no longer be Voice, but there are still those of a like mind with me in Kel Harantish. I understand your Company is anxious to trade with the Harantish 'Witchbreed'."

The last word had a very curious intonation, part mockery, part self-contempt. The small woman gazed out of the window, at that enigmatic structure of dome and pillars, black in the sunlight on the floor of the Maherwa pit.

"I once served my years among the guards," Calil bel-Rioch said, "and

I have friends, still, amongst them. Friends who are all the closer since I rose to be Voice – "

"But you're not the Emperor's Voice now."

She turned to face me. Nictitating membrane slid down over those yellow eyes.

"*Shan'tai s'aranthi*, they know *me*, whether I am Voice or not. What you offer me, I can guarantee to them. I have friends who, when their turn comes to guard Maherwa, will open doors to me; and to PanOceania too, if I so desire."

Pathrey Shanataru added, "Some say we have in Calil bel-Rioch a closer bloodline to the Last Emperor Santhendor'lin-sandru. . . . There are those of us who follow bel-Rioch, not bel-Kurick."

"We'll trade," Calil said.

And just that simply and undramatically, it became clear to me. This is the final point at which I have the chance to make a decision. All the time Kel Harantish was hostile, the likelihood of getting into the canal system was small. With renegade Harantish, though –

Up until now, circumstances have acted to slow the Company down. Now I either take Calil bel-Rioch along to Molly, like a good Company employee, and let it all go on from there, or I. . . .

What?

And if I don't, if I take *that* path, then maybe I'm stopping any chance of Trade&Aid to the Coast, help that the *hiyeks* desperately need.

That simple: in a small, shabby room overlooking the cylindrical pit that is Maherwa; among mercenaries and *hiyek*-Ortheans, a little after the furnace-hours of midday. That simple: what do I *do*?

Calil, with a pure and pitiless curiosity, said, "*Shan'tai*, I think you not unfamiliar with my city. Why fear to deal with us? You have had dealings with Kel Harantish before."

Did she mean that visit with Molly Rachel? Her words keyed memory, took me back to heat and dust and how, as I stood by that city, I heard from Pathrey, for the first time in ten years, the name of Dannor bel-Kurick, then and now Emperor-in-Exile –

I am standing beside a great block of some translucent substance. The Hexenmeister lays his palm flat on its surface. It clears from the centre, as if viscous compartments become transparent.

"*Where –*" *My voice is husky.*

That old male, the Hexenmeister, his face is shadowed, the eye-sockets full of darkness. "*There are no other devices like these left but here, and in that ancient city, Kel Harantish.*"

The image forming in the block is clear now, and through it I see a room.

In that other room are geometrically-patterned carpets, and candlestands whose holders are shaped like beasts' skulls. Candlelight and the ruins of technology.

And an Orthean – his face framed by a bleached mane: narrow chin, broad forehead, and half-veiled eyes the colour of wet sand. And he is no more than nineteen or twenty.

Dannor bel-Kurick.

I recall the face of Santhendor'lin-sandru, Phoenix Emperor, when the Golden woman brought the Empire down. Dannor bel-Kurick is a poor second to that, though he might pass, now that the Last Emperor is forgotten.

This halfBreed, this Halfgold, this Witchbreed boy –

"I make no quarrel with the Emperor-in-Exile," the old male says. "But I remind him that his city is a city of exile, and survives on trade. Can you eat rocks and sand?"

A communications device. A viewscreen. This degree of power – whatever the energy source – ought to show up like a beacon on satellite surveys of Carrick V. Did they miss it, skimp the survey, have a transmission failure?

"Your assassin, Havoth-jair," says the old male. "She spoke of ships that went north to the Hundred Thousand, ships that carry gold, to subvert telestres. . . ."

"What of it?" the boy asks tiredly.

"Nothing. But if I hear of any more ships of Kel Harantish in Tathcaer, then something."

Defeat visible on that young face.

"I am Golden!" He stares at the Hexenmeister. "I am Emperor! How many lies have you fed me, old man, telling me I'm nothing but a hollow man ruling a dying city? There's a price paid for power here that you never paid, never in your lives!"

The image fades to clarity.

"Let him have his temper," the Hexenmeister says, "he's cruel and wilful and cunning, but I could find it in my heart to be sorry for him."

One thing bothers me (and it doesn't bother me as much as it should). In my reports to the government on Witchbreed technology, I went fully into their past history, mentioned the ruined cities in the Barrens. I never mentioned the communications devices used by the Hexenmeister of Kasabaarde.

It's unimportant, not worth mentioning, it doesn't worry me.

And it should.

It should!

Sweat sprang out on neck, brows, palms. I met the gaze of the young Harantish female. Nictitating membrane slid back from eyes as yellow and clear as honey, with pit-black pupils that reflect a star of white light.

A friend's eyes in a stranger's face. . . . In desperate pain, memory overwhelmed my sight. The dark face of the dead woman Ruric

Orhlandis. Yellow eyes that laugh in that thin face, raven's wing of mane falling over the high forehead; she astride *marhaz*, *harur*-blade slung for lefthand use, right sleeve empty and pinned up – *amari* Ruric.

Ah, Ruric, why is it that you're dead and your betrayal isn't?

Memory threatens again, the tide of the past, and if giving in to it is desertion –

We'll trade.

That simple: what do I do?

If it's desertion, then I can't help it. Ten years vanish as if they were so many minutes –

It is night, in the Citadel, in Tathcaer. The small room is candlelit, and crowded. Here are Haltern n'ri n'suth Beth'ru-elen, Crown Messenger; and the Crown herself, Dalzielle Kerys-Andrethe; and others, too. And Ruric.

Our eyes meet, and I look away. She stands, in blue and silver, the candlelight like honey on her black skin. Tall, gaunt, carrying herself with a crook-shouldered balance.

"My intention was to discredit the Earth envoy, and so also that world."

I ask bleakly, "Why not kill me?"

"What use would that be? They'd send others. I wanted us rid of you and your world."

And Dalzielle Kerys-Andrethe, called Suthafiori, Crown of the Hundred Thousand; slow and amazed: "You never agreed with me on that, but I didn't imagine you traitor because of it."

"I'm no traitor! All I've done, even to murder, I've done for the Hundred Thousand."

Haltern (young, then): "Even to taking Harantish gold?"

"I see no reason not to take my enemies' gold, if I can use it for my friends' good."

Ruric within a foot of me, the vibrant breathing warmth of her body, the energy of her eyes. Keeping her hand flat on the table, making no move towards harur-nilgiri. The calm of the professional soldier: T'An Commander, T'An Melkathi.

"If you'll have reasons," *she says simply,* "they are these. Earth will destroy us. Either it will change us out of all recognition, or it will destroy the land itself. As I love the Hundred Thousand – I love it more than life – so I have tried to protect it."

I say, "We'd never do it."

"Never is a long time," *she says,* 'and while we're a backwater world with nothing desired from us, perhaps we're safe from war. But even then, not from change. You are utterly unlike us, and when you come here we can't help but alter. And if we're ever found to have something that Earth requires – why then Goddess help us, Christie, because no one else will!"

Ten years dead, that voice; and she lived on a little longer, branded exile. Ah, that's no life.

"I knew – " My voice was thick. "Knew a woman who had Golden blood, and dealings with your city, Calil – what did it do to *her*? What will it do to me?"

Haldin Damory's voice said sharply, "Christie!"

Images faded, like water soaking away into sand. I saw the tan face and dark mane of Haldin Damory. No sign of Calil's yellow gaze. . . . I was sitting on one of the *del'ri*-padded benches, without any idea of how I got there. One of Haldin's mercenaries stood at the door, *harur*-blade drawn.

"Ahhh – " I stood, swayed. If it were a physical pain I could bear it, could cry out, scream; but not this, this *fear*, this void that suddenly opens underfoot, that –

"*T'an*, please, be quiet!" Haldin Damory caught hold of both my arms. Her grip was strong. Her dark eyes veiled. "What is it? Are you poisoned? What?"

My throat felt sore, I must have cried out. When I could focus, I saw no one but Haldin and those half-dozen other young males and females, her mercenaries.

"I said you were ill. I got the Harantish Witchbreed out, in case they . . ." She let go of my arms. "Was it them?"

All I could say, stupidly, was, "Havoth-jair." The words that Haltern Beth'ru-elen spoke to me in Rakviri *telestre* came back with preternatural clarity –

' – *since you spent time within the Tower, and left it so changed –* '

So changed.

What is it I can't remember?

I dreamed that we went down into the maze of levels under the Brown Tower, to a cool dry hall lit with a faint blue iridescence, a light the colour of lilac and lightning; and there, there were alien machines that had the shape of sarcophagi. . . .

And when she left the Tower in Kasabaarde, to come with us and give evidence in Tathcaer, she was little more than a zombie; Havoth-jair, whom the Hexenmeister put to the question –

I knew, with a cold certainty, exactly what I had to do. I fumbled in a belt-pouch for coins valuable in the Hundred Thousand. That cold metal touch threatened to overwhelm me with memory, memory of once sending Blaize Meduenin on a mercenary errand. Hadn't I said, days ago, *As if it were my year on Orthe repeated, in a darker key?*

Haldin Damory took the coins doubtfully. "*T'an* . . ."

"You're still under contract to me. Leave half your troop here in

Maherwa – I want that woman, Calil bel-Rioch, I want her kept away from the Company people here. Don't kill her, mind. I never said murder. Keep her away."

A fair-maned Medued mercenary said, "We'll try, *t'an*."

"And you, Haldin." I held down the tide of synaesthesia, the visible and sensory memory that threatened to flood my mind. "You bring the rest of your troop. You're my escort."

"But, *t'an*, where?"

I had no guard on my tongue, thoughts spoken aloud: "If I let Molly put me on a shuttle, I'll be back on the orbiter, on my way back to Earth – no! I can't leave now. Not like this, not without knowing *why*. . . . There are canals, boats, *jath-rai*. I've travelled Orthe before. Haldin, you keep me alive, you hear? That's your contract. Asking questions isn't your business. And I'm leaving Maherwa *now*."

PART THREE

CHAPTER 13

Violence and Vision

I woke from a deep sleep, thirsty and hot. Light shone in through a round-arched window. The air smelled damp. Voices sounded in distant rooms. A *del'ri* pallet on which I lay scratched against my skin. I stared up at the ceiling: the white plaster and hairline cracks.

Something flopped down on the *del'ri* mattress.

"Max?" I said sleepily.

When I turned my head I saw a tiny face, narrow-chinned, with a short pale mane. A child, no more than two or three seasons old. *Ke* yawned, showing teeth; then lay down on the pallet, curled up against my back; a small lump of heat, breathing with a rhythm that is not human.

I should know something from this, I thought. A child so trusting, the air that smells of rain. Before I could work it out, I fell into sleep like a stone falling down a well.

Waking clear-headed, as from long convalescence.

First one note, then two or three more, then a chorus: the thin tintinnabulation of *rashaku* lizardbirds. The air felt wet and mild, and somehow full of energy; sparky wth ozone and the smell of the sea. The window was a hoop-arch in a curving white wall. Morning put soft blue shadows across the ceiling of the dome, ten or twelve feet above my head. I rolled over on the *del'ri* pallet, and saw a young Orthean male sitting on a bench by the doorway.

His dark crop-maned head was bowed. He sat with booted feet splayed apart, leaning forward, with his six-fingered hands clasped together between his knees. Sleeveless slit-backed jacket showed his bony torso. He wore straps for *harur*-blades, but no blades.

"God give me strength!" I said, sitting up. "Should I know you, *shan'tai?*"

The air was warm on my skin – I realized I was naked: coverall, CAS-IV, wristlink; all gone. A dirty *meshabi*-robe was my blanket. I pulled it over my head, tied the belt slowly.

"Sent t'check," the young male said. His dark mane stood in a cut crest. No more than sixteen, seventeen? Barely out of *ashiren*. His surprisingly deep voice slurred a Morvrenni dialect difficult to understand.

"What?"

"T'check on you. 'S difficult, *t'an*. You keep moving round the Order Houses." He stood. "I'll get Damory."

Order Houses?

I stretched, feeling the *meshabi*-robe slide across my skin. Aches slid awake as I rubbed the last sleep from my eyes. I looked up at the boy: "I think the traditional question is 'where am I?' – but I know *where* I am. Try: how the hell did I get here, and *why*?"

He muttered something inaudible and, when I queried, repeated, "You ordered it, *t'an*. I heard you."

"Who are you?"

He had dark eyes, far apart and slightly slanted: nictitating membrane slid down to cover them. "I'm Branic. Haldin Damory's troop."

The tiled floor was warm underfoot. I stood, walked to the window, leaned on the wide sill. The sky was a pale blue, in this dawn hour still freckled with daystars. A haze silvered the high arch of the sky. Damp shadows fell towards the west, lying on the white earth, the white dust. *Rashaku* called.

Pale, rounded domes rose up from the earth, here with scarcely an alley's space between them, and some doors were shaded by awnings on rickety poles, and some had only a flight of low steps and an archway. A group of four or five Ortheans sat on the steps of this dome. There was no talk among them. One rocked back and forth, back and forth. Three had their faces masked. As I watched, another Orthean male came out on to the steps and began to brush away the dust with a broom. His *meshabi*-robe was clean, the rope-belt woven with coloured thread.

"The inner city . . ."

I have known this, even in my sleep. Kasabaarde's inner city, that breeds within its walls philosophical violence and brutal vision. Why did I think I needed to come here, of all places on Orthe?

"The Order Houses of the inner city. . . . And this is Wintersun what?"

The boy grunted. "Not Wintersun. Wintersun's over. It's Stormsun-18."

"Shit!"

"I'll fetch Haldin – "

"I'm coming with you." I glanced round the small chamber again. It was bare. Through the arched exit, I could see the steps that went down into the underground rooms – but that would be equally fruitless. "They didn't even have the decency to leave my boots, the little thieves – "

No translation for that last word in his language. The boy, as we walked through to the outer chamber, said, "I 'spect someone's using 'em, *t'an*."

I almost laughed; held it back. The Orthean male sweeping the outer steps stood aside to let us pass, and bowed slightly. I hesitated, turned to Branic, and held out a hand for his cord of coins.

The Order House male smiled. Standing on the top step, his head was just level with my shoulder. He looked at the coins I offered.

"You do forget," he said coolly, "though we told you when you came here. This is the inner city. By ancient custom, here you may eat and drink freely, and freely be sheltered. The Order Houses will clothe you," he said, and I smoothed down the wrinkled *meshabi*-robe. "This is not the gift: the gift of the inner city is time. And that breeds violence and vision, idleness or wisdom."

Yes, I remember. . . .

Branic looped the cord of coins back over his neck, and signed himself on the breast with the circle of the Goddess. He turned away without a word. I followed. The customs of the inner city are difficult to follow: my instincts screamed *criminal*!

Earth was damp under my bare feet, and the dawn wind mild. I briefly worried about mundane things: sickness, infection. And then thought, *Stormsun-18!* with utter incredulity. The boy began to walk down winding alleyways, going towards the dawn, and I followed him, hard put to keep up with his pace.

As we came out into an open space, and saw a high wall before us, I said, "Branic, where is Haldin?"

"Trade-quarter. All of us."

I stopped. The wall in front of me was high, as high as the dome-roofs, and built of massive sandstone blocks. About thirty yards away, it widened. A low gatehouse was set into its twelve-foot thickness. Most of the Order Houses here looked deserted.

"No. Tell Haldin to come into the inner city, to me."

He scratched at his cropped mane, and his hand automatically fell to where the hilt of *harur-nilgiri* would have been, at his hip. "I can't – she won't – they make you leave weapons at the gatehouse! She won't come in unarmed."

"She has no business to be outside, she's still under contract to me."

The boy's eyes cleared, then veiled. "Are you well? Then you're well enough to pay us."

I did laugh then; stood in the dawn sun with the scent of *kazsis*-vines in the air, and laughed until I was weak and breathless, and had to grab hold of the boy's shoulder to keep my balance. He looked affronted. I clapped him on the shoulder, sniffed, and managed not to laugh again.

"I don't know why they send idiots like me to places like this. . . . Branic, please don't agree with me." That got a flicker of humour from the boy. "Tell Haldin Damory she must come in and see me, now. I'll be at – " I dredged memory for decade-old names ' – at the Order House Su'niar. That's near the Seagate. Tell her that I can't leave the inner city now. It's the only place where I'm safe."

He left, but for that moment I hardly noticed he had gone.

There. All other problems set aside, Company and government, Coast and Hundred Thousand; all else secondary now, because there – I see it clearly. Between the low white domes, over the stunted fronds of *lapuur*, in the heart of the inner city. That small and squat building, surrounded by gardens, built of dark bricks and no more than two storeys high: the Brown Tower.

A bowl hit the wall: ceramic splinters flew. I ducked down. The tall female still stood with her arm upraised. A dark-maned *ashiren* shouted something unintelligible. Then both turned and fled up the steps from this underground hall, one maybe in pursuit, maybe not; and quiet fell again. A fair-maned male on the next bench drew a splinter of clay from his hand, and stared with fascination at the trickle of blood. Mirror-reflected light shone on the benches, on the now almost empty hall.

"Goddess!" Haldin Damory came down the steps from the entrance-dome. Her claw-nailed hands clenched, went to her empty belt. She grunted, and all but fell on to the bench beside me. "Goddess, it's hot up there! So you can talk sense again, can you, *t'an*? I thought Branic was joking."

A young female with Su'niar Order House's colours woven into her rope-belt brought over a jug of *arniac* and more ceramic bowls. With no expression of surprise or distaste, she then fetched a broom to sweep up the broken bowl. She paid no attention to the fair-maned male's injury.

"How long is it since we left Maherwa?" I asked. "It must be more than two weeks."

"Twenty-five days," Haldin Damory said; sipped the *arniac*, and made a face. "What I wouldn't give for good Morvrenni *siir*-wine. . . . Yes, you look well. As far as I can tell, with *s'aranthi*." And she grinned.

"I am 'well'," I said. Knowing as I spoke that it was true, that somehow – at some level below the conscious – I could hold it all in balance: memory, vision and the past. I haven't resolved the problem, but I've learned to live with uncertainty.

"You picked the right time," Haldin said approvingly, as she leaned back against the wall, and put her booted feet up on another bench.

"Our contract runs out in two days. I'd thought of just taking you up the Archipelago, to Morvren Freeport, whether you liked the idea or not – your people in the Freeport might have given my Guildhouse a reward!"

She chuckled. She would have done it: bundled me on to one of the coast *jath-rai*, like any other piece of cargo.

"But I don't want to leave the Coast right now," she added. "There's going to be a *beautiful* fight, *t'an*."

Her enthusiasm was unselfconscious, unashamed.

"There were going to be talks. . . ." That memory came clear, unbidden. I blinked in the soft mirror-light. Why, it's gone, I thought. That fog in the head, synaesthesia; gone. I am I, and I know what I know, and the rest is – under my control. . . .

I smiled at Haldin. "Talks between some of the Coast *hiyeks* and the Hundred Thousand, I remember it being talked about back when I was in the Freeport. Has that happened yet? Or is it over? Or what?"

She put the curled black mane back from her eyes with one sword-calloused hand, and her dark gaze cleared. "Now that's sensible, *t'an*, that's knowledgeable. That isn't the puling babe I've had to nurse from Maherwa to Kasabaarde."

Her words hurt. I stood, and walked a few paces to where the underground hall's ornamental pool lay still and gleaming. Under water, the soft gleam of *chiruzeth*. The water's surface showed me a thin face, with dirt ingrained in the tanned skin; hair bleached by the Coast sun. I dipped my fingers in the water and rubbed at my skin, but the paleness round my eyes remained. Of course: I would have been wearing a mask to travel. . . .

Clear, now, these memories: the metal decks of *jath-rai* and canal ships, too hot to walk on in the noon sun. Flat land where only the water moves: no *rashaku* fly, there are no clouds. Only heat-stricken earth. Brown and umber, ochre and black, white and grey. A sea as bright as broken glass. Descending into *siiran*: the curiosity on pale-maned faces. Midday rests and midnight travel, and I do not recall ever speaking; not to Haldin, not to the *telestre* mercenaries, not to the Coast Ortheans, whose bright robes are worn and patched, who live crowded under the earth, hiding from that inhuman heat.

Twenty-five days, heat building to monsoon; all the thousand *hiyeks* between Maherwa and Kasabaarde; north and west, four hundred miles. *And for the last twenty-five days, I've walked in a dream.*

Now I'm free of it, I must act.

"So many *jath-rai* in the harbour settlements." I turned to sit on the rim of the pool, facing Haldin. "Stormsun isn't the best season for trade. Why so many ships?"

161

Haldin stretched her lean arms restlessly. Her six-fingered hands moved to the *harur*-blade harness. Ten years ago, when I first came to Kasabaarde's inner city, they took my belt-knife at the gatehouse. I had been living an Orthean life long enough to feel the lack of it.

"I'm not a Crown Messenger," she said dourly. "Not even a *S'aranth*'s Messenger, if there was such a thing. I fight, I don't spy or collect intelligence. But it's simple enough. Those *jath-rai* are warships. The *hiyek*-families are going to massacre each other, just for a favourable glance from your Company."

That thought seemed to cheer her.

"They mustn't fight. Jesus wept! Molly will have the Company's Peace Force in to protect our interests – "

No longer 'our' interests. Not any more.

Haldin said, "The great *hiyek*-families are in Kasabaarde now, talking with us, and with each other. You wait. They've been here all of Stormsun. I give it nine days, outside, before they fall out. Then I'll pick a likely side for my troop, and . . ."

Again, that grin. Difficult to hold the thought: what this woman looks forward to with such enthusiasm is *harur*-blades and winchbows and – for all the bloodless chessboard strategy of mercenary wars on the Coast – inevitable casualties.

"In Morvren Freeport . . ." It seems longer than a month ago. "It isn't just the *hiyeks*, is it? I've heard talk. What will you do, Haldin, if the Coast *hiyeks* attack the Hundred Thousand?"

Haldin hooked one booted foot up on to the opposite knee, gripping her ankle with thin six-fingered hands. She shook her head with lazy cheerfulness.

"You mean invasion, instead of just raids? Ah, it'll never come to that. There's no chance of it. The *hiyeks* can't be allies for long enough. They never have. Cuirduzh is going to fall out with Thelshan, and Pelatha with Anzhadi, and . . . you take my word on it, *t'an S'aranth*. We've only got to keep them talking for a few more days. Then it'll all fall apart."

"And if it doesn't?"

Haldin put long fingers through her tangled mane, and looked at me with good-natured superiority. "*T'an*, it will." She paused. "Is there anything else, before we end the contract?"

There were footsteps and voices in the dome above, but no one came down the steps. I dabbled one hand in the pool and watched the ripples, and then glanced at Haldin. At least part of her expression was contempt. But she's seen me all those days between Maherwa and here, I thought, and so there'll always be that certain amount of contempt. When I think back to then, I could agree with her.

"Two things you can tell me, *t'an* Haldin. I seem to remember . . . did I ask some of your mercenaries to stay behind in Maherwa?"

"To discourage the Harantish exiles. Shanataru and bel-Rioch." She shrugged. "You wouldn't have them killed. They didn't frighten. Don't you remember Ty and Gabril caught up with us at Quarth? Said the two Harantish had at last got speech with your *t'an* Rachel."

When each visual image, each sound, each smell, plunges you into a flood of memory – no, one can't tell what is happening from what has happened.

"How long have I been here in Kasabaarde?"

"Two days."

She grew more tense moment by moment, it was visible in the taut line of her back. I have known Ortheans who refuse to enter the inner city of Kasabaarde at all. There is no place on Orthe remotely like it – not even Kasabaarde's Tower.

"Let's go outside, shall we?" I led the way up the steps, out of the dome, and into the air.

The noon air felt hot and heavy with storms. We stood under the *del'ri*-cloth awning. The haze thickened to cloud. Heat-lightning flickered over the dome-roofs, and as we watched, raindrops fell like metal bullets to spatter in the dust. Within thirty heartbeats the dust was mud, rain falling in rods, and springing up again a foot high in spray.

I asked, "Do you know where the envoy Clifford is now?"

"He's here." The female raised her voice a little, to be heard over the drumming rain.

I smiled ruefully. "I've been something of an idiot. . . . I thought I had to do it all on my own. Someone once said to me: a world is too big for one person's responsibility. Or even many people. But we're all there is. I *do* have friends. We'll have to see what we can do."

Haldin frowned. "*T'an*, I don't know what you're talking about."

"Just thinking aloud, that's all."

The rain eased quickly. Rings spread and faded on the alley puddles, where the last drops struck. Haldin peered out at the sky, moved down the shallow steps; and then spun round as the Su'niar female came to the archway behind her.

In accented north-west Coast dialect, Haldin muttered, "Your pardon, *shan'tai*; here, take this – "

The Order House female shook her head, smiling a gentle refusal of the coins offered. Haldin turned abruptly and strode away. As I caught up with her, she glanced back at the Ortheans who sprawled by the

Order House, and as if she spoke to herself protested, "But people can't just do nothing!"

That was my instinctive reaction when I came here, ten years ago. I let her walk a little further and then said, "Where's *t'an* Clifford now?"

"One of the Order Houses near Westgate; Cir-nanth, Gethfirle; I don't know." Membrane veiled her eyes, though the clouded sky was not bright. "*T'an*, you don't need mercenaries here!"

"Medued Guildhouse can owe me the two days' service," I said. "Leave when you need to, *t'an* Haldin."

She walked away, with no other farewell, heedless of the rain's last drops that soaked her mane and tunic, hurrying back towards the inner city's wall and gatehouse, where she had left *harur-nilgiri* and *harur-nazari*. Going back to where people can't just do nothing. What she hadn't said, but what had been plain in her face from the moment she entered the inner city, was, *This place is a mad-house!* Certainly it's inexplicable, I thought. What will PanOceania make of it?

I turned and began walking briskly through the muddy alleys, going towards Cir-nanth and Gethfirle and the other Westgate Order House. I passed several Ortheans gathered under one of the *del'ri*-cloth awnings. One called out, accent thick, hostility apparent. I walked on, heart hammering.

The alleys widened into avenues, still lined with low white domes. *Kazsis*-vine budded on the curving walls, and an ash-blue plant grew along the base of the domes. *Rashaku* called. Despite the cloud and heat, the ground under my bare feet was cold, and when I looked down I saw the scratched translucent surface of *chiruzeth*, the underground canal waters dimly visible beneath.

And this too was a city of the Golden Witchbreed.

At the end of that long avenue I stopped a young, white-maned Orthean female. "Are there *s'aranthi* here?"

She looked up with veiled eyes. "Oh yes, *shan'tai*. And some of them wear Orthean faces."

She walked a few yards and then knelt down, and began to wipe the mud from the steps of the nearest Order House with bare six-fingered hands.

"Lynne? *Lynne!*"

Bemused, I swung round; and before I knew it, Doug Clifford gripped my hands and then hugged me (which seemed to surprise him rather more than it did me). The twenty-five days since I'd seen him had wrought changes; Carrick's Star had tanned that lined skin, begun to bleach the sandy-red hair. To Service coveralls he had added Orthean boots and a belt-knife. Now he stepped back a pace and looked me up and down, still the same small, neat man.

"Lynne, is that you?"

"Ah, I see – the difficult questions first, eh?"

He snorted, shook his head, regarding me with wonder. I thought, This is one of the few times I've ever seen you speechless.

"Haldin Damory told me you were in Kasabaarde," I remarked. "Why the inner city, though? Or is that because of these talks between the *hiyeks* and the Hundred Thousand – "

"Jesus Christ, woman! You've been gone for a month, the Company's got you on the missing persons list, and now you come back and ask *me* questions!"

The livid sky shed a few drops of rain, but he took no notice. Faces appeared at Order House entrances, made curious by the sound of a foreign language, and this man so plainly *s'aranthi*. He frowned. Then he shook his head again, helplessly.

"I don't believe it! The difference between the way you were then and the way you are now – Lynne, why didn't you let me know where you were? Of all the irresponsible, *stupid* actions. . . ." He paused, recovering a little of his natural reserve. Then he added: "You have no idea what I've been afraid of for you. Which is somewhat imperceptive of me, I don't doubt; I seem to recall that in your Service days you made a habit of going walkabout."

"It was stupid," I said meekly. "It's nice to see you too, Douggie."

He fixed his mouth in a prim line, then laughed. "Why do I even try?"

"Let's take it that was a rhetorical question." I linked my arm through his. "Can we talk inside? I think it's going to rain again."

Doug Clifford looked appealingly at the heavens. "She vanishes for a month, and then she turns up out of nowhere and talks about the weather. Why me? What did *I* do to deserve her?"

I could do nothing but laugh, still knowing he used that humour to distance himself from some very real emotion. We walked a few yards to an Order House, and entered the dome. The rain-twilight gave an odd luminous glow to the walls inside. In the underground chambers there would be no mirror-reflected light now, and so we sat in the ground-level chamber. An Order-robed *ashiren* brought *arniac*.

Clifford walked to the window, and looked out. That self-observing theatricalism vanished.

"David Osaka and the Ishida girl are here. Or do you know that? Have you seen them? I wasn't aware that you would attend these talks."

"Or that I'd been in any condition to do so." I side-stepped the questions: "I could say the same thing to you."

His face was turned away, I couldn't see his expression.

"The Rachel woman gave me a choice. Stay out of the Company's dealings in Maherwa, or find myself recalled to the next world on this circuit. So I came here, to Kasabaarde. I should have had to attend these talks in any case. Or so I tell myself. The Company's busy in Maherwa. You know the Harantish have let Rachel put a research team into the canal system?"

Fear at last realized into reality: it made me go cold. I had a vision of that dome and pillars, of Calil bel-Rioch's golden-eyed face. No need to ask which Harantish. Does she want the Company as an ally, or is she just hitting back at the Emperor in Kel Harantish?

"Have they come up with an analysis?"

"Lynne, I'd be the last to hear."

A flash of lightning illuminated the low dome, and a moment after, thunder crackled. The warm spring air blew chill. Another of the north Coast's brief tempests. Clifford walked back to the low table. I saw him scrutinize my face.

"Are you sure that you're all right?"

"If you mean, do I still have someone else's memories in my head, the answer is yes. What I've done by going walkabout, as you call it, is learn to control them. Instead of having them control me."

I expected disbelief, was braced to see that look on his face. Instead, he nodded slowly. Those bird-bright eyes were thoughtful.

"I've had a scan through your old reports. Lynne, I still think you're misinterpreting something that happened to you, but – I could be convinced otherwise." Doug smiled. "One sees much, in the Service. Don't underestimate my ability to comprehend the alien. But I need to know what did happen to you. And then I need more evidence than – forgive me, Lynne – merely your unsupported word."

Warmth and relief swept through me. I wiped my hands on the dirty *meshabi*-robe; I hadn't realized my palms were sweating. Searching for words, in the instant between intention and speech, I made a controlled recollection of memory; held down sound and vision until it was mine to use.

"Douggie, I'll tell you how it was. It begins with the Hexenmeister, in the Brown Tower – "

There is a room lined with shelves, on which rest scrolls and parchments. Evening light falls on woven del'ri mats, on a table, and chairs. A library? Yes, this could be any library-room on Orthe; and the summer breeze that drifts in is soothing – but through the window-arch I see the last spire of the Rasrhe-y-Meluur, that stands outside Kasabaarde, that is a millennially-old reminder of the Golden Witchbreed.

There is a room in the Brown Tower that is like a library because it is a room (the only one) that is sometimes seen by outsiders. It is designed to reassure, to allay fears of long-dead technology. I stand in that room. Before me, in a chair by the cold hearth, is the Hexenmeister of Kasabaarde.

Like most Kasabaardeans he is a head smaller than me, and bent with age besides. His hands are bird-claws, his skin a diamond-pattern of wrinkles, and his mane gone except for a crest from forehead to spine. A brown sleeveless robe covers his tunic.

"What do you know of me?" he asks.

I say, "I know that you dream no past-dreams because you're immortal, that you see all that passes in the world, and that the Archives of the Brown Tower hold all knowledge."

These are all stories Ortheans have told me.

"Such superstition!" he says mildly, amused. "Well, you and I have much to speak of, envoy, and I will tell you why. I know much of what passes in the known lands – because most news comes either here to this city, or is heard by my people who travel. And it has been the custom, since before Tathcaer was a city, that they bring such news to me. The Archives hold much knowledge – but not all. No, not all. And for the other, that is answered more simply – yes, I am immortal."

"I'm sorry, I don't believe that. I can't."

"You must believe, envoy. Or else you'll believe nothing I tell you, and that could affect the relations between two worlds."

He eases forward in the chair, lifting himself with the weight on his wrists, as the old do. I automatically move to help him. His warm hand closes over mine, a frail, many-fingered grip. He stands.

"I think I must prove to you what I am."

We walk along a diffusely-lit passage, slow, at an old man's speed. His weight on my arm is considerable. We pass a door that opens, slides shut behind us as we step into a small chamber. There is pressure underfoot, a sickness in the stomach. We are descending. Then it stops, the door opens. A great hall. The light changes quality; the air is cool, dry.

"That causes you no fear," the old male says. "Well, it is not to be wondered at, you come from the stars."

Disbelief that paralyses. I think, Kirriach was awesome, that city in the Barrens, but Kirriach's safely dead; and this. . . .

"The Brown Tower has stood for ten thousand years," he says softly, "and hasn't been above borrowing Golden technology when needed. Machines fail, you see. Even these. Though not for a time yet, I think." He takes a few unsupported steps into the hall, resting his hands on the edge of metal casings. "These are precious to me beyond all price, their like is not to be found in the world today."

167

An underground hall, banks of machinery, screens and cubicles like sarcophagi. Quiet, chill; a subliminal hum.

"You have heard," he says, "of those of us who possess a perfect memory?"

"Yes. Some humans have that."

"These transcribe, store, and transfer such a person's memory intact to another person."

Is my disbelief so apparent? The hypno-implants might pass as a primitive prototype – but no, such a thing isn't possible!

"And that person, also, to another and another." He smiles. "With no loss of detail, down through the generations." And touches his thin chest. "I am not immortal, but the Hexenmeister is. In a few years, when I die, there will still be a Hexenmeister. Who'll remember speaking with you, Christie, remember this moment as I do. Who will be me – as I am all who went before me."

"It's incredible!" I realize I'm pacing; come to a halt in front of the old Orthean male. "What real proof do you have?"

"If it were proved to your satisfaction that these machines act as I claim?"

"I don't have the technical training to prove or disprove that."

"And language is inadequate. Perhaps we misunderstand each other more than we know." He reaches out, grasping my arm for support. "It will be obvious to you, I suppose. I wish to record your memories, Christie, so that I will know your world. And as trade is the mark of Kasabaarde, I am prepared to offer you access to some of my own memories of Orthe. I know this world. Perhaps I am the only person who truly does. So when Orthe comes to deal with other worlds – I am the only one qualified to speak for us."

Assuming it's true, I think, and assuming alien technology can be adapted for human use as well as Orthean – how dangerous will it be? Physically, mentally, politically? I'd be a fool to do it. And a fool not to.

And then there is a memory of days spent in Kasabaarde, that long-ago spring. Dry, dusty days. Held back by fear: it's beyond my brief as envoy, have I the right to pass on information about Earth? And pushed forward by knowledge: if Earth deals with this world, it must know this world. It must. I must.

Daystars, half-invisible points of light over the domed roofs, the glare of Carrick's Star drowning them. White dust, and heat. And I was alone, and not yet thirty, and I did it anyway.

'Have you rested?" the Hexenmeister asks, some days later. "That's well. We can begin. First, though, I ask you to undertake never to speak of what you see or hear."

"That's not something I can promise. As envoy, I have to report fully."

Now I can hear the irony in his tone, that I never heard then. You knew, old man. Of course you knew.

"Well then, envoy, say that you will report it only to your own people, and then only if you believe it to be necessary. . . ."

The cubicle is slick under me, with a sensation unlike metal or stone. I know it now – chiruzeth. There is a hum that might be sound or vibration. I close my eyes, sick with panic. Closed in alien science like a sarcophagus, a tomb.

I feel a sensation that – if it lasted more than a microsecond – would be intolerable agony. No way to describe how it feels: as if the closed confines of the self fragmented into pieces in an ever-expanding maze.

Total fear: and I struggle, his memory happening to me with all the force of synaesthesia, entangling, inescapable.

Pain, memory, memory not mine: and I am a mirror shattered into a million pieces, a million lives.

CHAPTER 14

Exiles

Outside the window-arch, rain slants across a slate-blue sky. A sky that seems too bright to human eyes. Carrick's Star glares whitely beyond the clouds.

"It wasn't that I couldn't talk about it," I finished. "It was almost that I couldn't *think* about it – even to myself. I knew I'd been in the Tower, but my mind kept telling me it was unimportant, trivial, to be forgotten. . . . I couldn't even think in terms of being mentally blocked, let alone blocked by something someone had done to me. All I could do was remember someone else whose mind had been tampered with by the Hexenmeister. Havoth-jair."

Doug Clifford drank from his bowl of *arniac*, grimaced, and paused to pick a fallen *kazsis*-bud out of the scarlet liquid.

"Lynne, I find myself somewhat at a loss. . . . I might go to the Tower, myself, I suppose. Send a message in to the Hexenmeister's people. I *am* still government envoy to Carrick V."

Qualified support, but support none the less. I would have thanked him, but tension made my mouth dry. I stood to pace the Order House's confined floorspace, too restless to sit still.

"Douggie, assume for the moment that I'm right, what will the Hexenmeister do when he knows I'm here?"

Doug said lightly, "If you had to choose a place to be, you've picked the right one. I dare say even the Tower won't be too eager to interfere in the Order Houses."

The inner city is separated from the trade-quarter of Kasabaarde by a wall and a millennially-old rule of amnesty; and from the Tower that lies at its heart by a few strips of garden land and a vast gulf of philosophy.

". . . which, I suspect, is why the *hiyeks* are holding their peace conference in here. That reminds me, Lynne. While I'm busy, you'd better contact David Osaka or Pramila Ishida, hadn't you?"

A touch of malice in those last words. I am still Company-employed. And besides, you don't have dealings with Ortheans for long without picking up the respect they have for the Tower. Clifford, I thought, you're rattled. And who can blame you?

"You're right," I said mildly. "I'll find them. Douggie, when you speak with the Tower, remember one thing. It's what I told you at

Maherwa. You're not doing this to help one person who's been badly affected by some kind of alien technology. The Hexenmeister told me once that he was the only person with the knowledge to speak for all of Orthe – and if I'm right, and he is, then with a situation as precarious as this one, we're going to *need* someone with that knowledge."

Walking through the inner city towards Westgate, I came, between one Order House and the next, to the edge of a crowd. I pushed between male and female Ortheans, in brightly-coloured *meshabi*-robes. Some sat on steps, on benches under awnings, or on woven *del'ri* mats. The scarlet, blue, and emerald-dyed *meshabi*-cloth was patchily coloured, often frayed. A deafening hum of talk beat against me – *hiyek*-Ortheans gesturing unrestrainedly, heads together, gathering in groups. I passed some that clustered round a spirit lamp, boiling *arniac*, while an old male in Order House robes looked on worriedly.

It was difficult to pick a way between the seated groups. Heads turned as I passed. Manes braided with crystal beads flashed in the sun. Being a head taller than most *hiyek*-Ortheans, I drew the eye; and some called comments, and I answered noncommittally and walked on.

A few desiccated *lapuur* trees occupied the wide empty space near the Westgate's gatehouse, their ash-grey fronds uncurling by reflex under the heat of Carrick's Star. Pramila Ishida was standing under one *lapuur*. An Orthean stood with her.

Two together: a contrast of fair and dark. The dusty yellow mane of Sethri-safere was thrown back as he laughed – no way would *you* miss being here, I realized – and there was an answering smile on the sallow, round face of Pramila. She wasn't speaking to him, but into her wristlink. Then she saw me, and stared in complete amazement.

The young male followed her gaze. His tawny eyes opaqued, then cleared, and a smile twitched one corner of that wolverine mouth. His white *meshabi*-robe was dusty, and (this being the inner city) no hook-bladed knife hung at his belt.

"How's Molly and the Company these days?" I asked. He had the grace to look disconcerted.

"*Shan'tai*, I haven't seen her – I'm here with the south-Coast *hiyeks*, for the talks. I've got them together without slitting each other's throats, that's an achievement, wouldn't you say?"

We spoke the Maherwa dialect with a fluency that I saw Pramila couldn't follow. I met Sethri's gaze. His insouciant humour had an edge. *I mean to make a friend of you*, he had said, and proceeded to ingratiate himself with Molly instead. When I spoke, it was with malice.

"Some advice, Sethri, if you like. When you're on your way up the ladder, don't kick the rungs away behind you. You're going to need them, coming down."

He placed one hand on his breast, bowed slightly, with a rueful amusement. "Forgive me if I underestimated you in Maherwa, *shan'tai*. I have much to learn."

"Not that much." I switched to Sino-Anglic, and to Pramila, who still held up her wristlink, mouth open in silent bewilderment. Before she could speak, I said, "Is that Molly on the comlink? Tell her I apologize for my unavoidable absence. I was taking advantage of an opportunity that arose."

Pramila made as if to speak, stopped, stared at me with total incredulity, and then said, " 'Opportunity'?"

"To investigate the political climate among the influential *hiyek*-families on the Coast – "

I always say, if you're going to tell a big lie, do it with style and a smile.

" – I knew the *hiyeks* would be meeting the Hundred Thousand here, for talks. I thought Molly might want a wider view of the Coast culture than just the area around Maherwa. There is over four hundred miles of inhabited land, you know." I paused, and stepped into the scant shadow that the *lapuur* provided. "*Is* that Molly you're talking to?"

Pramila Ishida stared at me for a full thirty seconds. Then she said absently, "No, it's David, we've grounded the shuttle outside this settlement. 'Opportunity' . . . but there was no report! We haven't known where you were, what you were doing – "

"I see. . . ."

When I like, I can use all the old Service noncommittal urbanity.

"That's most irregular. . . . Yes. I'll have to have words with certain people when I get back, I can see that. If you weren't aware – good grief, Molly must think I've gone completely insane! I must get on the comlink to her. Perhaps I'll come out to the shuttle with you. I need to use a shuttle's resources in any case, pick up a supply of protein and vitamin supplements. . . ."

"I can't go yet. I have to help Sethri-safere set up additional venues for the talks." She rubbed a hand across her forehead, tucked a strand of black hair behind her ear. She was sweating. And not greatly fooled, I thought, by a more than threadbare excuse.

"Molly *will* want to speak to you," she said. "She may think it better if you return to Maherwa, or the Freeport."

She wore a CAS-IV holster on her belt, the comlink connected her to the shuttle: this small and somehow compact figure standing in the noon heat. It was an odd contrast with the stunted *lapuur*, the white mud that was cracked and drying, with Sethri and the Ortheans at the nearby Order Houses.

"Maybe you'd better patch me through the shuttle and the orbiter," I said. "I'll stay in the city for the talks. Who's here?"

I could see her internal debate: how much to tell this unreliable, eccentric woman – who is, however, still special advisor to PanOceania on Orthean affairs.

"*Hiyek*-Anzhadi, Pelatha, Thelshan." She paused. "The Freeporters, the *takshiriye*. I think there are some Ortheans from the Kerys-Andrethe *telestre*, and the Telmenar Wellhouse. And Meduenin; there are Meduenin here."

There would be. A knot of tension began to form in my stomach. For a moment I fiercely resented that. Don't I have enough to concern me, without having Blaize Meduenin continually on my mind? The tension remained, no effort of will able to dismiss it. And we shall meet, I thought. It's inevitable, both of us here. God damn it. Some part of me was outraged that my peace of mind should depend on anyone but myself.

And then with resignation I thought, That settles it, girl. When your sense of humour vanishes, you *have* got it bad. . . .

Pramila Ishida said uncertainly, "We're acting as neutral arbitrators. With all the Coast people and the Freeporters here, some of the Houses are saying they can't provide food for them."

The inner city's Order Houses finance themselves from the tolls and taxes all traders pay to enter and leave Kasabaarde's trade-quarter. It gives the inner city a deceptive appearance of inexhaustible wealth. Looking at the crowds round us, I thought, But it wasn't designed to cope with *this*.

"You'll want to talk with the heads of the Order Houses, and the *hiyek-keretne*."

So easy, to slip back into the Company frame of mind. But half the memories I call up about the inner city are not mine. And all I can think now is, *How long until Douggie's message to the Tower gets an answer?*

"I'll give you a hand here," I said. "Let me talk to Molly first, though."

Pramila keyed in a contact through the wristlink. I wished briefly that I could get out to the shuttle. YV9s may be old models, they do at least contain clean-up facilities and spare uniforms. Then Molly Rachel would see in her comlink a neat, middle-aged woman, smart in PanOceania coveralls and logo; hair bleached, skin tanned, otherwise no trace of that month's journeying from Maherwa. . . .

Who are you fooling, girl? I came out of the daydream: dirt-stained, hair straggling, barefoot, with only a threadbare *meshabi*-robe to keep off the sun – but still, I thought, I have the presence now to convince Pramila I'm in authority, and *that* didn't happen before.

"Here." The Asian-Pacifican girl handed me her wristlink, and stepped aside out of earshot, conferring with Sethri and – Jadur, is it? – of *hiyek*-Anzhadi.

The 'link cleared, showing in miniature the interior of a grounded shuttle, and the Aboriginal woman's face. Stark light from an open port made her squint, put specks of brilliance in that black hair. Her coveralls were stained with dust. There was a rim of dirt on her face, marking the edges of just-discarded eyeshields.

"It *is* you," she said grimly.

I said, "I must apologize for being out of contact for so long. Quite inadvertently, you understand – "

"Bullshit!" Molly Rachel interrupted. "If I had a spare hour out of the twenty-seven, I'd shuttle up to Kasabaarde and find out what the hell you've been doing. You're advisor to PanOceania, Lynne. The Company's interests are your interests. And your tin-pot government's, tell Clifford!"

She took a breath.

"I ought to have you shipped back to Earth on the first ship out of Thierry's World!"

" 'Ought to'?"

She glared, and then wiped her forehead, and looked absently at the pale dust on her dark fingers.

"I ought to bust your ass, Lynne. *You* know that. Just be grateful I don't have the time. Things are happening here."

The tiny image of her face showed exhaustion, and a febrile excitement that might mean success. But now is not the time to question her.

"Lynne, are you all right? Pramila said you seemed . . ."

"In my right mind? Yes. I intend to check with the Psych people on the orbiter later on, but yes."

"So it was offworld syndrome. I'm relieved. There's enough going on here."

I could glimpse, through the open port of her shuttle, the bleached moonscape of the south-east Coast. I faced that Pacifican smugness, hating for a moment that all their answers are (for them) easy.

She sighed, shook her head. "Lynne, *why* are you so bloody unreliable? I can have you offworld tomorrow – I was going to, I still can; but I could use your help, with Pramila and David, on condition that I know where you really stand on Carrick V."

"Were you ever in any doubt?"

"*You* were," Molly said. "Now you know, and we both know, that you want the Company off Carrick V. Fine. Work for that. Just tell me if you're still willing to give specialist advice. And if I listen to it, I'll bear the rest in mind."

Why do I underestimate her? God knows it doesn't pay.

Then she laughed. I had to laugh, too. We'd be watching each other. Watching ourselves. But maybe we have a *modus operandi.*

"Call me again later today," Molly said, "and we'll talk it through. There isn't time now. We'll talk. Lynne, it's good to have you back."

The wristlink image blinked out. For a moment I was shamed by her honesty. And then I thought of the Tower, of memories that are not mine, and of Havoth-jair.

How many hours now until there is an answer from the Hexenmeister?

Stormsun-18 wore away to evening, and a hot and humid twilight. I slept a few of the afternoon hours at the Order House Thelmithar, and then came out to sit on their shallow steps, and drink one of the last flasks of *del'ri*-spirit that the House had.

Evening's citrine light shone on a group of us. A tan-skinned female from a mid-Coast *hiyek*, two thin and languid males who claimed origin in the Rainbow Cities, and an older male who didn't speak.

– *that same citrine light, a Coast evening ten years gone: I see an Orthean girl sitting on the rim of a fountain, in gardens of stunted arniac and lapuur, her arms cradling a child perhaps a year old. She is pale-skinned, tan mane braided with beads, wearing the brown meshabi-robes and rope-belt of the Brown Tower. Just past ashiren, not more than sixteen. Her face is unsmiling, bent in concentration over the child that plays with her six-fingered hand.*

"There is one of this generation's apprentices," says that old male, the Hexenmeister. "She has many of the memories stored in her mind. Another few years – when I die – and she may be Hexenmeister. And she'll remember speaking with you, Christie, remember this moment as I do. And she will be me. As I am all who went before me." –

The memory is small and hard and clear, like a brightly-coloured pebble that I can take out and examine, and now put away. Because I have learned that it is only memory, not madness. I wondered if Doug will hear that an Orthean female is Hexenmeister now. Could the old male still be alive, after all this time?

When Doug came to Thelmithar an hour or so later, the Rainbow City Ortheans had left the steps, and I sat alone. Second twilight gloomed: Carrick's Star set, the Heart Stars not yet visible. I poured a bowl of *del'ri*-spirit for Doug. The act needed concentration.

"I've seen the Tower servants, the brown-robes. They listened politely

175

enough." He sat down beside me, loosening the neck of his coveralls, and wiping sweat from his forehead. "Then they talked for some while, without actually saying anything. I'm told the Hexenmeister will consider an answer. . . . Are you going to suggest to the Company that there may be alien technology in Kasabaarde?"

I sipped more *del'ri*-spirit. The effect on human biology is slightly hallucinogenic.

"The Tower must be wondering the same thing." I grinned crookedly at him.

And the Tower has nothing to protect itself except secrecy – and reputation. No weapons, no troops, only a few defences within the actual walls. Nothing to protect that fragile, ageing machinery that he said cannot be replaced. Except Kasabaarde's reputation. Have I made myself a target?

"Douggie, I wanted to talk to you. Wanted to say this at Maherwa, but I didn't have it straight in my mind. I ought to hand in my resignation to PanOceania," I said, "but I won't. Not yet. Not until I've got everything useful out of them that I *can* get out of them."

Twilight blurred the dome-roofs of the inner city. To the north, just visible, the tip of the last spire of the Rashre-y-Meluur was illuminated by the vanished sun.

"I hope you meant what you've said," I added. "Or I'm going out on a limb for nothing. But I'm still going. I can't condone what the Company's doing on Orthe. I'll act as a source of inside information as long as I can – which won't be long, if I know Molly Rachel – and then I'll quit, and carry on here, outside the Company. God knows what I can do, but I'm going to try."

Doug leaned back against the dome-wall, and took a long drink of the fermented *del'ri*-spirit. He said shrewdly, "And then you want a bolt-hole to run to. Government Service."

"If I don't get that, PanOceania can deport me off Orthe. I'd find ways to stay, but I need a position of influence."

He chuckled wryly. "You're joining me."

"A little late in the day. Believe me, Douggie, I know that."

"And I don't know all of your reasons, do I? No, and you don't know all of mine." He raised the ceramic bowl in a salute half ironic, half sincere. "Welcome to the conspiracy."

I shifted over to sit beside him, sharing the flask of *del'ri*. The last light faded from the Rasrhe-y-Meluur. We talked for a while, quietly. Lamplight spilled from the arch of an Order House further down the alley, and voices were raised inside; the thin wail of a metal flute rising over the din. A humid, sweaty evening. Above, the Heart Stars began to blaze like silver fur.

We sat side by side, he with the collar of his coveralls unfastened, that grizzled red hair slicked up as close as it ever comes to disarray. Behind me, an Order House male lit lamps. Yellow light shone from the door-arch, limning the edges of the steps, and the alley dust rough with the print of bare feet. It shone on Douggie's bowed shoulders, and the small curls of hair at the nape of his neck. I thought, I want to touch that soft, creased skin – here, where air and twilight and gravity are not Earth's. Here, a very long way from home.

I said, "I took a look in records, back in the Freeport. Sophie's where, now? Arminel-III?"

"On Thierry's World. She's doing xeno-biology research there."

He got up slowly, heavily. And then remained on his feet for a while, looking up at the Heart Stars. *You're warned: I mentioned her name.* I saw his profile silhouetted against the brilliance. He hesitated and then seated himself again, on the step beside me. The place where he had been half leaning against my shoulder felt cold and unprotected.

I put the bowl of *del'ri*-spirit down in shadows cast by starlight. The Order House's arch is open, leading to domed rooms and *del'ri*-fibre pallets, and to *chiruzeth* chambers below us, where hidden canal waters flow. Doug Clifford sat, hands linked, staring at the ground between his boots. Then he turned his head fractionally, caught my eye, and gave me a deliberately theatrical version of his mandarin noncommittal stare.

I reached down and took his hand, risking the rejection of that touch, not knowing – when he returned the grip – if it would be to move my hand aside. But his fingers closed over mine with such force that his knuckles stood out white. And I love the breathing warmth of him, human warmth not felt for so long a time, and his smile –

Later, in terrible clarity, I thought, *But it should have been Blaize Meduenin.*

The dawn was hazy, heavy with a sea wind; and I stood with Doug outside the Order House. Morning, and an odd mixture of satisfaction and regret. *Now I'll feel awkward in the future, meeting Sophie Clifford again* – and some self-disgust, at self-interest so nakedly displayed.

"I wouldn't want you to think that . . ." Doug's worried expression faded into a smile. "We understand each other, Lynne, don't we?"

Only powerful embarrassment could provoke such a cliché out of Douggie. I smiled reassurance, hoping for that slight barrier to vanish, for him to be what he was before. I thought, I wish I could walk down through Harbourgate and stand on the docks, and see the wide horizon, and the long morning shadow of the Rasrhe-y-Meluur on the waves, and the first islands of the Kasabaarde Archipelago . . .

A voice from the alley said, "*Shan'tai* Clifford. *T'an* Christie."

I looked down the steps. A slight figure stepped out of the dawn shadows – masked, and barefoot, and wearing a brown *meshabi*-robe. And it was an *ashiren*, a child.

"I have a message," *ke* said, in a pure, archaic form of Coast dialect. "From the Tower. The Hexenmeister says that you may come there and speak with her, *t'an* Christie."

Doug glanced at me, shaking his head.

"I know," I said. "I'm not twenty-six any more. This time I'm not going to enter the Tower just because I've been invited. Not with what I know. Without some better reason, I won't enter it at all."

Doug turned up his collar against the sea wind. "I'll go. It's envoy's business. I'll speak with them again."

The *meshabi*-robe felt too thin for the dawn chill. I'm too old to go barefoot, I'd found a pair of the *del'ri*-fibre sandals that Kasabaardeans wear. An Order House's gift. That niggled. The inner city can't afford gifts now.

"Doug, has it occurred to you – it's all very well to condemn PanOceania and loudly support Orthe. We've still got to work out what we can *do*."

That lined, round face held a determination unlike his usual urbanity. "Get Carrick V declared a Protected world. If the Company research in Maherwa is successful, that won't be easy."

"Nothing's easy. If the Company goes, the Coast's left to starve. If the Company stays, everything changes out of all recognition. Where's the easy answer, Doug?"

Knowing that in Maherwa, facing Calil bel-Rioch – was it blocked Tower-memories that sent me over the edge, then, or the simple impossibility of taking that decision for Orthe? It's not a decision anyone should be called on to take, and we so often are.

He squeezed my arm reassuringly, and, as he followed the brown-robe, called, "I have every confidence, Lynne. Wait here for me. I'll have an answer as soon as possible."

A cool wind blew, flapping the *del'ri*-cloth awning.

I waited in that bright dawn – knowing nothing of what Molly Rachel and Calil bel-Rioch were doing, four hundred miles south and east of Kasabaarde; nothing of what was said and thought that same hour by the Hexenmeister. The wave that had been gathering momentum since PanOceania came to Carrick V was about to break, and I didn't know what rough water I would have to ride.

I don't know what I'll do, I thought, I only know that, for better or worse, I've come home to Orthe at last.

Midday in the crowded city, and I saw among the *hiyek*-Ortheans the uniform of a government envoy. Doug and I met at the edge of a stretch of bare earth that lies between the Order Houses and the Tower gardens. He shrugged.

"Lynne, I've talked to the brown-robes again. They say the Hexenmeister won't speak with any offworlder in person except Lynne de Lisle Christie. I don't know what you want to do about this. I believe I would think very carefully – "

– three of us running through the dusty city, under the molten-metal sun. My lungs ache, and my head; adrenalin from the attack of Havoth-jair's assassins. Blaize Meduenin moves cat-silent, alert, glancing rapidly from side to side.

Are there more of them? In alley-entrances, in doorways; the assassin's knife, that sound – like ripped silk – of a blade being torn from its scabbard. Are there more, near us, now?

My heart hammers.

And the third one of us, that slender white-maned woman, stumbles as she runs. Black blood wells out from between her fingers gripping her arm. No more than a child, Ruric's child: Rodion Orhlandis. Who stumbles against me as we cross that stretch of bare earth between Order Houses and the gardens surrounding the Tower.

"There." No other sanctuary. And as the girl falters, I pick her up, and stagger the last few yards into that one refuge from all attack: the Brown Tower. . . .

The light of Carrick's Star is still as acid-white, and I saw Doug squint against it. He fumbled for eyeshields. I put that decade-old memory back into my mind. Adrenalin still made my heart pound. The effects of memory? Or this, now?

"Doug, the Tower depends on secrecy. I'm the only one they're likely to let in, because I already know . . . and you're right, it needs thinking about; that's no good reason for going, is it?"

Light glinted off the glass shields covering his eyes. He said, "It may well be considered unwise of me to pass this on, but I suppose it would come to you in any case. I have a message I was directed to give to you – a *verbatim* message, if the Ortheans who serve in the Tower are telling the truth. From the Hexenmeister. I understand from reading your old reports that you've received such messages before."

"Douggie, for Christ's sake, *what did they say?*"

"The message is 'Come because you remember there was a room in the Citadel, in the island-city of Tathcaer'."

Deliberately I cut off all thought, all feeling, all speculation. The sun beat down like white-hot iron; somewhere a *rashaku* called. The air was loud with the murmur of the *hiyek*-Ortheans a dozen yards away.

"Doug, walk with me as far as the Tower."

Two pale-skinned and tan-maned Ortheans in brown *meshabi*-robes stood at the entrance. I was conscious of the warm dust, almost ankle-deep here; and the smell of the *lapuur*, and the *kazsis* that spidered its crimson way up the brown brick wall in front of me.

"Give you greeting," said the male. His shadow pooled at his feet, black as a pit.

The female stood with her back to the slab of metal, ten feet high and seven feet wide, that was the only break in the brickwork. Set back into a plain brick arch, the colour of silt.

Doug touched his wristlink. "I'll call you at five-minute intervals. Let them know this is patched up to the orbiter, through the shuttle. Lynne, I wish you wouldn't do this."

His spare comlink was fixed round my left wrist; a permanent discomfort. I put my hand on his arm for a moment, then walked forward. The metal slab slid up, disclosing a smooth-walled corridor beyond. I didn't look back as I entered.

Something in the dry air hushed speech. There was a soft noise as the metal slab sank back down, cutting off the heat and white sunlight. The two brown-robes stood beside me. I put out a hand and brushed fingers across the wall. Dry stone, pale and seamless. Yes. There are certain places in the Tower that Ortheans sometimes see. And nothing visible there to disturb them.

"Come, *shan'tai*," the female said. Both of them seemed young, no more than early twenties.

As I followed them, I was conscious of a subliminal hum, just below the threshold of perception. I thought, Have I ever been away from here? The last ten years could be a dream. Oh but this body is not a young woman's body, and as for me. . . .

We came at last to a room once familiar. One of the few with windows, and the light of Carrick's Star slanting whitely in to bleach the already pale walls. The room was small, darkened by the shelves that stood in almost every free spot; and the shelves were piled with scrolls, bound books, papers, maps. I moved forward, wondering if there would still be the great table standing before the hearth.

"You don't have to cater to my tender sensibilities," I said, "I know there's more technology in the Tower's Archives than pen and ink – "

The world went away. The mind refused belief but the body reacted: dizzy, cold, stunned.

A lean Orthean woman sat writing at the table. She wore a white shirt and black britches, and her high-arched feet were bare. She turned as she glanced up, leaning one arm on the back of the chair. That sleeve was rolled up casually, showing the dusty anthracite skin of her forearm, the long fingers that held a writing-stick. The other sleeve was empty and the cloth tied in a rough knot below the shoulder.

I don't believe –

Her mane fell like a raven's wing across her forehead where (half hidden) the black skin puckered with the scar of an old brand. The mark of an exile. Put on her in a room under the Citadel in the island-city Tathcaer. In her forties now, by that face; that high-boned face. Proportions just slightly wrong: cheekbones that make the face too wide, jaw that makes it too narrow. She brushed the back of her wrist across nose and lips, and her eyes cleared as the nictitating membranes slid back. Sad, unshocked eyes as yellow as sunlight; in that shade almost luminous. This lean and ageing woman; casual, competent, silent.

She threw the writing-stick down on the table and stood up, the chair scraping back, all in one movement. And stood with a crook-shouldered balance, and looked.

"Ruric," I said. Could only say. *Amari* Ruric Orhlandis. Older; and I would have known her out of ten thousand.

And because I needed to be certain this was no memory, I took a step forward and reached out and gripped that six-fingered hand; dry, hot skin.

"'Ruric' . . ." The Orthean woman shook her head, then. "Christie, I wish I was – I wish that I were all Ruric, all Orhlandis, but I'm not. I'm Hexenmeister, now."

CHAPTER 15

A Mirror Seen in Mist and Pearl

There was a plain wooden bench set where Carrick's Star shone whitely in through the window. I sat there. Motes in the sunlight were bright, distinct. The Orthean woman stood beside me, the long fingers of her hand resting on my shoulder, kneading a part of the shock away.

You can't be anyone else and therefore you must be –

"Ruric?"

She moved to the table, hitching one hip up to sit on the corner there and pour the ubiquitous *arniac*-tea with that long-practised and crippled dexterity.

"I'll have to ask you to keep this one of the Tower secrets. It shouldn't be known in the Hundred Thousand who the Hexenmeister is." The woman put down her bowl, brushed back her mane. The brand was a jagged line from brow to temple, pale brown against her black skin; a raised ridge of flesh. The brand of the exile. For a second the fine web of lines round the yellow eyes smoothed out: she could have been the young Ruric, *T'An* Commander of the army, *T'An* Melkathi.

"You're *supposed* to be dead."

It sounded querulous. The woman grinned.

"Sorry I can't oblige you. You wouldn't be the only one to feel disappointed."

"I didn't mean that."

"Didn't you? You might feel that way yet."

Noon light made her a shadow, black on black. This lean, forty-year-old Orthean woman, with the youthful grin. How do I know if what's different about her is being Hexenmeister, or being ten years older?

"If you're Hexenmeister – " Then I'm speaking to that old male that I met in the Tower, when Ruric Orhlandis was plotting and intriguing in Tathcaer. . . . I remember his voice: *And when she speaks with you, she'll remember this, as I do now, and she will be me.*

The woman came to hunker down on her haunches before the bench, and I met that yellow gaze. "Yes, I am Hexenmeister. Christie, you think you understand what I mean by that. You don't."

"How can you say that? You know what I know!"

She grimaced, stood, stretched her back. The white slit-backed shirt was open, showing her small high breasts, and the second pair of rudimentary nipples on the lower ribs. She turned, and I saw how that black mane grew in a vee down her spine to the small of her back.

"No *harur-nilgiri*," I said, surprised. "You might convince me yet. A *telestre*-Orthean without a *harur*-blade, and especially Ruric Orhlandis – "

She swung round, eyes blazing. "They exiled me, that doesn't mean I'm not of the land!"

In a room in the Citadel in Tathcaer – "*Ruric Orhlandis, once T'An Commander and now T'An Melkathi, first named Onehand and Yelloweyes, and now and for ever after to be named murderer, conspirator, and paid traitor to the Hundred Thousand.*" – And those words themselves written by a traitor.

I stood, unsteadily, and went to get a bowl of *arniac*. She watched me. The crimson liquid was only lukewarm, and I drank it down in a draught.

"I wanted to speak with you first." She glanced down. "I've sent my brown-robes to invite the government envoy here, and the two offworlders from PanOceania."

"You'll let them come *inside* the Tower?"

"The Tower needs to consult with Earth. I've been planning for that. The problem is you, Christie – " The Orthean woman hesitated, and said wryly, "That's a name I thought I'd never use again. You're the problem. You're muddying the water. And I can't see any way to solve matters, except by doing this."

A breath of dry air blew in the open window, rustled the papers on the shelves, set the *kazsis*-vine tapping against the brick arch. Ruric Orhlandis reached out and weighted down the papers on the table with her ceramic bowl.

"And just how am I supposed to be muddying the water?"

"By making known something that my predecessor let you believe – no, I won't lie. Something he made you believe. It was done deliberately."

All the fear and insecurity that I felt in Maherwa returned in a moment, doubled and tripled; and then slowly began to ebb. I studied her face intently.

"Perhaps I've got stupid as I've got older. Ruric, you're going to have to spell it out."

I saw her take a breath. It is not a human movement, that sharp intake of arched ribs. Nictitating membrane slid down over her eyes.

"It wasn't my responsibility. I wasn't even here. Christie, I feel ashamed." She rubbed at her forehead. The claws on that six-fingered hand were neatly trimmed. Then she flicked a sharp, hard glance at me. "Sunmother! You don't make it easy. This, then. The Hexenmeister who held the title before me . . . Well, there are drugs, as you'd call them. And techniques that sometimes come out of the inner city, that make one see or hear unrealities. Christie, trust nothing of what you thought happened to you when you were here before! He told you the lie that the Tower always tells, about memory; but he made you believe it."

Ruric paused, then at last added, "How can I say I'm sorry? I wasn't even here then. I don't know what made him do it, nor whether he knew that it would damage an offworlder as it's damaged you. It's an evil thing to have done."

I stared at her. "No. No, I know. I *remember.* . . ."

Again, that crooked smile. "I don't expect you to believe what I say, what anyone in the Tower says. That's another reason why I'm bringing other offworlders in. They'll need proof, too. Proof that you're – misinformed. You've half convinced that man Clifford."

"For God's sake, I didn't go through the last month just to – I *know* what I know! Ruric, it's been hard enough to work it through. I know; I'm certain."

And then I thought again of that dark-maned Coast woman, Havoth-jair. Damaged. And my memory of how it happened is sharp and clear – and inaccurate. It *wasn't* I who condemned her to that, it was Evalen Kerys-Andrethe (though I could have stopped it). If that memory is no memory at all . . .

There was no time to think. Ruric turned as a brown-robed servitor came to the door of the room, exchanged a brief word, and nodded.

"I'm told the government envoy is here."

In total disbelief and confusion, all I could manage to say was, 'How can you let outsiders into the Tower?"

"Because they are outsiders. I couldn't allow my people in. There are things in the Tower, even if they're not what you think is here. And Earth and I have to talk," Ruric said quietly. "If I've learned nothing else in eight years, I've learned the nature of the problem. I won't try to solve it with fire or *harur*-blades this time. Christie, it's been a long time, but believe this: I still won't stand by and see your people ruin Orthe."

It's impossible to take it in, I thought. *He told you the lie that the Tower always tells, about memory, but he* made *you believe it.*

". . . assure you this is a great privilege," Doug Clifford said smoothly, as brown-robed Ortheans ushered him into the small library-room. He frowned, then concealed it.

"Give you greeting," the Orhlandis woman said. "Strange to meet, *t'an* Clifford, at last. I've had indirect dealings with you and your government for six years now."

"Hexenmeister." Barely a question in his voice. Is he familiar enough with my old reports to realize who she must be? Then I saw the curiosity even his diplomacy couldn't hide, and realized *yes, he knows.*

Ruric moved aside to talk to a fair-maned male in the Tower's brown robes. While she talked, her gold-yellow eyes sought mine; veiled and cleared.

Doug muttered, "Lynne, are you all right?"

"No, but give me time."

"I wasn't expecting this," he said. "I've linked a time-alarm through the shuttle to the orbiter. If we're not out of here within a reasonable time – "

"Warning people we're in here is one thing. Getting out may be another." Part of me observed that that was a sensible comment, considering the state of mind I was in. The rest was panic.

The brown-robe left, and Ruric turned to face us.

"The two offworlders from the PanOceania Company will be here soon. I've got things to say to you before they get here. *T'an* Clifford, you and Lynne Christie have influence so far as Orthe's concerned; you want a policy of non-interference – "

"May I ask how you come to that conclusion?" Doug's politeness was marked.

"I hear things. The inner city." She looked at me. " 'I'll act as a source of inside information.' And the rest."

I watched her, waited. She walked across to the window, and reached up to slide a fretwork metal shutter halfway across the arch. Noon glare diminished. The shadow dappled the white *del'ri*-cloth of her shirt. Skin and mane vanished, blended with darkness.

"I know what Christie's told you. It's important we start clean," Ruric said, "not believing lies and half-truths. *T'an* Clifford, there *is* Witch-breed science in the Tower. It's *not* what Christie's told you. We have to deal together, for Orthe. We have to believe each other. And so I'll have to show you what the Tower's Archives really are."

One step took her across the line the shutter cast, into the light of Carrick's Star. Her face showed age in that white glare.

"Whatever I choose, there's a risk. To bring offworlders inside the Tower, tell them truths that my people don't know – it's dangerous. Letting you believe the lie is more dangerous. Especially since we may need Earth's help." Her face changed when she looked at me. "I didn't have to have you here, now. I owe it to you. For what the last Hexenmeister did. And for a lie I once told you."

All I could say, out of ten-year-old memories, was "How can we trust anything you say!"

Her eyes shone clear and dark as amber resin. "I don't expect belief from anyone."

Was it unspoken: *except from you?*

"Come," she said decisively. "I'll leave it to you what report you make, *t'an* Clifford. Just don't talk to *my* people."

Clifford sniffed, raised an eyebrow. "My government favours non-interference with alien cultures. It therefore follows one wouldn't, shall we say, implement the dissemination of internal information. . . ."

I got up off the bench, finding my legs unsteady. The smell of old paper and parchment was momentarily so strong as to make me dizzy. Clifford took my elbow. For all his screen of verbiage, he was nervous; his hand trembled. The two of us followed the Orthean woman out into the corridor. I thought, I know the way. . . .

Here there was no sun, only a dim reflected mirror-light. Deeper into the interior of the Tower now, and the colour and texture of the walls changed, to a slick brown substance. I thought it all seemed smaller than ten years ago. But memory plays such tricks. At a dead-end corridor the Orthean woman and I halted simultaneously, only Doug Clifford caught off guard.

He glanced at me, at the Orthean woman, and back to me. There was reassurance in his expression. For a moment, he would rather believe the impossibility: my story.

What can she show us to change that? I wondered. And was so lost in thought that I barely registered the familiar repetition of entrance to the lower levels: the wall that split and slid aside, the small chamber that we stepped into, the pressure underfoot as it descended. Not until it halted, and the wall again parted to let us out, did I concentrate. *Here*, memory told me.

I walked past them, out into a cool high-roofed hall. There was faint light the colour of lilac and lightning. The walls were blue-grey *chiruzeth*. And not six yards from where I stood was the first of a row of tomb-shaped objects. *Chiruzeth* sarcophagi. Large enough so that an Orthean or an offworlder might lie there enclosed. . . .

"Douggie, isn't this what I said I saw?"

The small man came to stand at my shoulder. The blue-pink light made his complexion look unhealthy. There were beads of sweat on his forehead.

"Yes. Somewhat reminiscent of a *siiran*. I imagine about the same level and development of civilization could produce this." He glanced back. "How can you take the risk of letting anyone inside this installation, Hexenmeister?"

"*T'an* Clifford, I don't want the Tower ripped apart by offworlders looking for Old Technology. I know what PanOceania's doing with the canals round Maherwa. It's necessary they should know there's nothing here useful to them."

The dark Orthean woman walked past us, to the nearest tomb-like object. The fingers of her single hand moved delicately on its carved rim. A faint iridescence glowed within the *chiruzeth* tank.

But that's not what happened when I –

A voice whispered almost inaudibly in the sarcophagus-tank, and an image grew. Faint, immobile. A still image.

"Welcome to the Tower Archives," Ruric said sardonically. She again hitched herself up to sit on one corner of the *chiruzeth* device, and glanced round the distant reaches of the hall. "Not as impressive as it might be, is it? But precious. These devices can't be replaced. Not now."

Archives?

Clifford moved closer to the *chiruzeth* tank. "Hexenmeister, I have to confess that I don't quite see the implications of what you're telling us."

Ruric caught my eye, grinned. Her dark hand moved on the *chiruzeth* surface. The still image changed. The voice whispered.

Without meaning to speak, I said, "That isn't what these devices do!"

Her head bowed over the tank, black mane falling forward. The image was of *ziku* and mossgrass. They grow in the Hundred Thousand. Unbidden, her hand came up to rub at the stump of her right arm.

"He didn't lie to you in everything." She raised her head. "That's why you believe. You can take evidence two ways. The Tower does have Witchbreed technology. The Hexenmeister – anyone who holds the title Hexenmeister – has a more-than-mortal memory. It's stored in these devices. The Tower's been adding to the knowledge held here for sixty generations."

Doug Clifford stared at the image in the tank. "Data storage and retrieval."

"The Witchbreed Empire – " She made a grimace, her distaste plain. "Now they're gone, these devices can't be replaced."

She slid down, stood with that swordfighter's balance; and her head came up, and for a moment it was Ruric Orhlandis, the Crown's Ruric, Melkathi's Ruric, the Ruric I mourned as dead.

"*T'ans*, this doesn't change anything. The Tower is still the guard against the rise of another Golden Empire. Our hands aren't clean. What of it? Whose are? All the Hexenmeisters have used every method in their power to keep us from becoming what the Golden Witchbreed became – what your people are. Forgive me, it's true. We have information and secrecy and not much else." She smiled wryly. "But I knew that when I agreed to become Hexenmeister."

187

Clifford's face was intent, his eyes fixed on that *chiruzeth* tank. Data storage and retrieval. Without looking at her, he said, "If you were to have contact with a pro-isolationist group, one that has some influence with Earth governments and multicorporates – "

"*No.*" Both their heads turned towards me. I took a breath. "I need things explained. What are you telling me? That I was – what? – hypnotized, drugged into believing that memory-transfers are possible? And they're not?"

The Orhlandis woman said, "The last Hexenmeister was very practised in making people believe they hadn't spoken with the Tower. Or that he had powers that do not exist. Christie, he couldn't have known it would damage an offworlder as it's damaged you."

Too stunned to think, I could only stare at her.

"It wasn't a right thing to do." She sighed. Then a hardness came into her face. "But the Tower has only secrecy to protect it and the Tower *must* survive."

I walked forward and put both hands on the rim of the *chiruzeth* tank. No more than a data-link, a holotank? Remembering how I lay down in one of these slick coffins, and the stab of a mental violation.

Shattered into a million pieces, a million lives –

The air cool, the light a frozen instant of lightning; and cool blue-grey walls . . . and that all but imperceptible hum. A sudden image came to me of the white hall in Rakviri *telestre*, the intent faces of Barris and Jaharien, the iron bowl eaten away in energy-change to *chiruzeth*. The effect that just one relic of the Empire could have. Can I have built up a whole delusional system, just based on alien data-storage archives?

I swung round and faced them, the human male and the Orthean woman.

"What right – how the fuck did he dare do that to me!"

As I spoke, I knew: There is still a doubt. That younger Christie who first came here, she would have voiced her doubts. I looked at Douggie's bland expression, and the ageing features of the alien woman, and I kept silent. Desperate to get out of the Tower and think this through alone.

"Does that satisfy you now?" Ruric asked Clifford. "Questions later. I'll take you back now. I must talk to the PanOceania offworlders. *T'ans*, you see the risks I take. I can't prevent you spreading this knowledge on the Coast and in the Hundred Thousand. I can only ask you to wait."

"That would seem to be acceptable."

Looking at Clifford as he spoke, I couldn't tell what he was thinking. Which means that I know exactly what he thought.

★

All children who go to the sea pick up pebbles, shining black and red and white from the water. Nothing left later but a handful of dry and salt-encrusted stones. Pyrites; fool's gold.

Memories hard and solid and bright: should they be colourless now?

"Explain the languages," I said, as we left the desiccated Tower gardens and walked down between Order House domes. "That's just *one* of the things I know. Explain how I can be fluent in most of the languages of the Coast and the Hundred Thousand."

Clifford shrugged off the challenge. "Lynne, for all I know you've spent the last ten years studying Orthe. Don't be angry – I'm saying what others will say. I have to keep an open mind until I'm presented with proof."

How could you . . . ? Douggie!

Real worlds and hard facts, they tip the balance. I nodded, let him walk on towards the Westgate. Cold bites deep to the bone, and fear is cold. Though Carrick's Star radiates fiercely, and the hot Coast gales blow, and the dust is warm underfoot: such a chill . . .

A six-fingered hand touched my arm. I looked down, saw a thin-faced male in a faded *meshabi*-robe. The nictitating membrane slid back from his eyes so far that a rim of white was visible round the green iris.

"Who cut off your mane and hurt your eyes?" His interest was childlike.

"I'm not Orthean, *shan'tai*, I'm offworlder."

His head cocked sideways, like a bird's. "You wear the mask of the Tower. How many masks do you wear?"

Not now, I thought, and rubbed a hand across my bare face. At this precise moment I don't need the inner city and its madmen.

He added, "I used to have a name and that was a mask."

I shook his hand off, walked rapidly away. He called something unintelligible. Winding alleys put distance between us, and I made my way between the curving white walls of domes; and the heat of the sun at last made me slow and seek shelter. There was a glimpse of sandstone blocks between white domes, the wall of the inner city; and a massive low arch: Harbourgate.

Some instinct said: In the mental state you're in now, they'll talk to you. All of those who are outsiders, and have no other world to go to. All of those who come here to heal themselves, before they go back and change this world. All those who will never leave, because for them there's no world at all. . . .

"Show me your hands."

A shadow fell across me. I glanced up, saw a woman on the low step of an Order House. Half a dozen Ortheans sprawled there. She had an accent I couldn't place. A mane bleached to colourlessness, a skin like coal; wearing nothing but cords on which pierced stones were strung.

"Show me your hands!" she repeated. "They're gloved with blood to the elbows."

She stepped down on to the dry earth. I said, "I can still defend myself – "

"You are alone, but there's a multitude with you. You think defeat, but victory is only a thought away. I can see you where you stand. Your robe is dirty and your eyes are veiled." Her dark face shone with a smile, too febrile for comfort. She stepped nearer. "Let me be your mirror. I show you – "

"What you see."

"What you think I see."

Adrenalin hammered. No control in her. The sun's heat made me dizzy.

Do I mirror you? I know how it feels to be you, how you carry yourself; fear raising hackles of mane down your spine, eyes veiled against the white sunlight.

When she spoke again, her voice was soft. "Why did you come here?"

Was my smile as crazy as hers? I grinned, reckless. "I came here because I thought I might find – I was about to say, find asylum. Now I think about that, it's been one, the inner city, and it is one, in quite a different sense!"

The corded pebbles slid against her dark skin. She was a head shorter than I, and that made her look up, and veil her eyes against the light. A gust of warm air caught her mane and wrapped it across the sharp ribs: white on black.

She said, "Your hands are empty and your eyes weep blood."

"*Shan'tai*, I don't think you any more reliable than – than any other mirror."

After a long moment, she turned away. I walked away from the Order House steps, crossing the open ground between there and the city wall. Thinking, Will I become like her?

After Max died, I found that I could believe exactly what I wanted to believe – until the distance between that and the truth widened so far that I fell down the gap, ended up on the floor of hell in a hospital bed. Could I have built up a delusional system here? Alien interference an irritant grit: the Tower-myth the pearl that builds up around it? Surely not –

Not all monsters are of the mind. Not all delusions are totally detached from the truth.

The shadow of the sandstone wall fell cool on my skin. I stood in the

arch of Harbourgate, staring out at brightness. Carrick's Star shone on
the ceaselessly-moving water of the harbour. The hoop-masts of *jath-rai*
flashed in the sun. I put both palms flat on the sandstone surface, rough
and dry against my skin. The Order-robed male in the gatehouse looked
curiously at me. He wouldn't act unless I showed I wanted to leave the
inner city. . . .

Where would I go?

I blinked, blinked again at the harsh light. Wanting to do what human
bodies can't: bring down a third eyelid to cut the glare. Do I only think
I know how that feels?

Now I don't know: did I come to the inner city to learn to control
these visions, or did I come because I had learned to control them – to
accept them as memories? They still wash over me. Take over. All I've
learned is to stop fearing that. And if they're delusions, not memories,
does the fear return?

I rubbed my hands against the sandstone, anchoring myself in physical
sensation. Stone, and bright light.

Those lost days, I became not just the person to whom the alien
memory happened, but Christie-experiencing-the-memory. As one sometimes clearly thinks in a dream, *I am dreaming.* Two simultaneous levels
of awareness.

Is that delusional too?

Okay, girl, now you do what you did in those twenty-five lost days –
call it up deliberately, and go into it. Only this time, watch. Judge. Does
it feel fake? *Does it?*

The reflected sunlight from the water dimmed. I let the sensation carry
me. Feeling that deep difference, a self that is not mine, is alien, and is
yet utterly familiar.

*Dim light, grey and shifting, which I see now is fog. Swirls of mist that
move above me, around me. I move six-fingered hands, drawing a robe closer
about myself. The cold bites bone deep.*

That bright shadow.

*And underfoot is broken ground. Shattered slabs. The mist puts beads of
water on the blue-grey surface. Bending to touch it, I find the chiruzeth not
broken but distorted, melted, warped.*

A brilliant blackness.

*Without volition, I am moving, scrambling across the tilted slabs. It is 'I'
who moves, and Lynne who has no control over it. Breath harsh in the throat.
The drag at muscles climbing a slope, where the mist thickens to fog again,
and so I move in a grey sphere continually shifting, myself at its centre.*

A brightness that ends in splinters like crystal, or the edge of cat-ice
on a puddle –

191

A silver glow in the mist. Moving on up the slope towards it. Does the sun, hidden now, cast light enough to shine on something beyond the ridge? Only the fog clings close, dark grey and heavy, smelling stagnant as the floor of the sea.

A wall grows out of the fog, massive chiruzeth blocks; a wall that as I follow it, one hand trailing along the cold, wet substance, ends suddenly. The surface is rounded, ridged like candle-wax. Beyond are the regular lines of halls, chambers, towers. I climb over the low part of the wall. Walk the chiruzeth floor that I have never seen (but I recall Kirriach, over the Wall of the World; great ruined city of that barren land). . . .

Carrick's Star shines on the Glittering Plain, and a flare of light flashes out even to the western horizon –

I stop, crouch down, touch the mist-damp floor. And something else. It could almost be an inlaid line of glass or silver, this streak in the chiruzeth paving. But as I follow it with my eye, I see how it widens. Grows. Splinters of silver-glass following the contours of broken walls. See how, beyond the next broken arch, that sky-exposed floor is all silver; pure and bright as the surface of a mirror.

The infinite sun of Golden rule. The brilliant beating heart of Empire; Archonys, that great city –

Cold makes me shiver uncontrollably; I can hardly walk. The muscles of my legs are weak. To step through that arch takes long minutes. Fog mats damply in mane and robe. Each sound, each footfall, is muffled.

Some trick of air shifts layers of cloud, somewhere in the thousands of feet of space above. The mist begins to turn from grey to white. To the heart of pearl: sea-cold, iridescent.

Walls of mirror rise up round me. Broken silver towers, lost in the earth-touching clouds. Arches clear and brilliant as glass with the sun on it. And I see through those arches distant landscapes of silver; walls, paving, bridges. . . .

Remember that what you see is not a primitive but a post-holocaust world. What you see is plain and simple war damage –

White mist swirls and shines. The cold works its way into my body. I reach out and touch the silver-glass wall. Claws slide from its diamond surface.

That touch is obscene, as if I touched fossil-flesh.

An iron bowl transformed to a lacework of rust. And in it, *chiruzeth* grows.

What made this a living city – is dead. Pearls of water hang on the surface of dead mirrors. As I turn, the cloud-cover for one freak moment thins. I am standing at the top of a hill. Below, and stretching out for miles to east and west and south, the broken city lies. Broken, dead, fossilized: turned to glass and silver, mist and pearl. That in an instant, then the light reflected sears into eyes that are agonizingly, irrevocably blind –

– light from the lapping waves of the harbour of Kasabaarde.

For some minutes I could only lean against the hot sandstone wall. At last lifted a hand to wipe the tears away, and stepped out of the arch's shadow. The sun's heat soaked into me.

Is that what lies under the cloud-cover of the Elansiir, the Barrens, the Glittering Plain? Or have I built it up from surmise, words overheard, that brief sunset glimpse off the hills that look west to Eriel? *Is* that what causes climate anomalies, changes a world's weather? I have reason to think it could be exactly what that war damage looks like.

Is it memory, is it delusion?

A gust of wind whisked a dust-devil towards Harbourgate. Masts and sails creaked in the harbour itself. There was the smell of stagnant water.

And there's my answer.

There is the source of that vision's blinding light – the sun on the surface of the harbour. There is the smell of the mist – that stagnant smell of the sea. And I have seen the war damage on the Glittering Plain, and seen the ruins of Golden cities in the Barrens; what easier than to put the two together?

And how could 'I' come, blind and lost, at last to the Tower, to give my memories up to the Hexenmeister's Witchbreed devices? The 'I' in that vision was close to death, and far from Kasabaarde. . . . Except that, since it's delusion, there is no 'I'. Only me.

Voices came distantly from the Order Houses, and I walked a few steps in the hot sun, away from the gate and the harbour. Our concern now is that threat of war, not one woman whose mind has been messed about by alien science –

And is that all there is? some child-part of me wailed. I miss the myth of the immortal being in his Tower, holding the living memories of a hundred generations behind membrane-veiled eyes. Mechanically-stored archives are no substitute. But this is the real world, I thought. If there's no immortal Hexenmeister, still, there *are* records of the past.

I do at least know why Ruric Orhlandis says the Tower must survive. Even if my visions of it were false, there *was* a weapon that could turn the very earth on which that city stood to crystalline stasis. The unknown weapon that made those dead wastelands is gone now, gone with the Witchbreed Empire, but there must be no chance of Ortheans ever creating or acquiring such a weapon again. The Tower must stand, and guard against the rise of another Empire – Orthean or *s'aranthi*.

"Doug Clifford said I'd find you here."

The voice interrupted thoughts that were light-years away. I blinked,

193

realizing David Osaka was standing in front of me. He wiped sweat-sodden blond hair back from his forehead, squinting against the brilliance of Carrick's Star.

"We need your advice," he said. "All hell's breaking out in the Order Houses."

CHAPTER 16

Domino

A storm passed, rapidly, and spring sunlight fell on the inner city with noon brightness. I thought, I didn't realize so much time went by while I was at Harbourgate. . . . The shadows of domes seemed black pits on the white earth. Now no breath of air stirred. Coast cities usually cease activity over the hours of noon, but as I walked with David Osaka, we pushed through crowds of *hiyek*-Ortheans in the alleyways.

"Where's the *shan'tai* Rachel?" an Anzhadi male called out.

"Trade for weapons, *s'aranthi*, we'll buy!"

"Feed us, or war – " A tan-maned female's comment was cut short as she tripped over someone's outstretched legs and cursed.

David gave a genial wave, a smile, and kept walking. I sweated, the dry heat making moisture instantly vanish. An iron-blue sky promised heat and tempest. How long now until the monsoon?

"There isn't anyone to negotiate with!" David said, frustrated. He glanced at the plentiful crowds, and I saw no humour on his face. "No one we can persuade, who'll then tell the rest what to do."

The old problem with Orthe: no hierarchy. Everybody is talking to everybody, and some decision will arise out of it, but as for what, and when . . .

"Lynne, I'm thinking of advising Molly to let the fighting break out."

"*What?*"

"Then, whichever *hiyek*-family emerges as victor will be in a position to dictate to the others. They can help us bring in T&A to the Coast cities, without other *hiyeks* being able to object."

I looked at him, the frown of concentration on that old-young face. "What about the suffering a war will cause?"

Self-righteous, David said quickly, "I'm not suggesting it's the *best* way."

We turned into a wide, *chiruzeth*-floored avenue, between large Order House domes. The avenue was crowded wall to wall. Voices were raised in a dozen Coast dialects. That and the sun began to make my head ache. I shouldered my way through, behind David Osaka, elbows digging into my ribs, mouth dry, gazing over the heads of the Coast Ortheans.

"Wait – " I heard a familiar voice, searched; then saw faces I knew, under the awning of a dome. David stopped, looking where I pointed.

195

Hildrindi-*keretne* was on his feet, facing a group who sat on benches under the awning. Sunlight threw the planes of the elderly male's face into sharp relief, cast shadows in deep-set alien eyes, so that for a moment it was a skull I saw. Only a month since I saw him in Maherwa, but illness had ravaged him.

"Answer me, *shan'tai* Meduenin!"

Blaize Meduenin sat resting back against the Order House wall. I saw that dusty mane, that scarred face; heard his sardonic answer.

"I know the Coast. I've been here as a mercenary in your bloodline wars. And I've been there when your ships raided the Melkathi and Rimon coast *telestres*."

A red-maned woman sitting beside Blaize leaned forward, and I saw it was the Earthspeaker Cassirur Almadhera. "It isn't Anzhadi-*hiyek* that we blame, *shan'tai* Hildrindi, or any other *hiyek*. If the Coast was prosperous, there'd be no cause for raids. Still . . ."

What a music-hall double act, I thought. Carrot and stick, conciliatory and tough. And for a moment, as David and I stood unnoticed at the edge of the crowd on the steps, I hated the red-maned female simply for being able to be where she was. And despised myself, as one does, for feeling so.

The elderly *keretne* leaned on the arm of a stocky gold-maned female – Feriksushar. He raised his thin voice to be heard by all around: "We live in a wasteland. Tell us about your *telestre*, Meduenin. Tell us about the river Medued, and the *marhaz* and *skurrai* that graze on its banks. Tell us of *ziku* forests, of *rashaku* that nest there, and *hura* in the river whose flesh is sweet, and the *makre*-grain that grows on the face of the earth that She does not burn!"

Blaize stood. The scar that half masked his face was a livid ruin. Roughly, he said, "Tell *me* what we can do about it! Not *ashiren*-tales, not fantasies – tell me! We can send food-ships to our own *telestres* when there's famine, but not to all the *hiyeks* of the Coast!"

I was about to move on, to get to the shuttle and use the comlink, when Hildrindi said, "You have the land."

A silence fell. Cassirur raised her head, eyes veiled, face white and stark against her red mane. She said, "We hold the land for Her, live under Her sky and return. We care for it and it for us. The land is not ours to give!"

The Coast, to whom location doesn't matter, so long as the *hiyek*-family is together . . . and the Hundred Thousand, to whom the land is a part of themselves, is the *telestre*, is the root from which they draw their source of self.

Blaize shifted his booted feet, balanced as a swordfighter is. He glanced around, alertly scanning the alleys and domes; he did not (ten years ago) like or trust the inner city. "*T'ans*, I'm neither Earthspeaker nor *keretne*. I'm a plain man. I know the *telestres* have been as they are for sixty generations. They're what we return to, when we return from Her. We can't change. That's all."

A voice from the other side of the steps called, "What if we act as one, *shan'tai*? What if you don't face *hiyek*-Anzhadi and *hiyek*-Pelatha and *hiyek*-Cuirduzh but *the Coast*?"

David Osaka said in my ear: "That's what I wanted you to see. They're threatening invasion!"

Dominoes. One goes, and the next, and who can see where it ends? Not the Company, with its data-net predictions of possible cultural change. Not me, with a head full of Orthean memories that are neither mine nor memories. If ever we had need of the Hexenmeister of legend – ! Well, there is no omnipotence in the Tower.

I said, "Dave, you stay here and monitor the crisis level."

"Where will you be?"

No reason, if I'm not a target, to stay within the dubious protection of the inner city. . . . "Out in the shuttle. I'm going to contact Molly."

But there is somewhere else I'll go first.

The Tower entrance remained firmly closed. Eventually I persuaded the brown-robed servants into an exchange of notes: 'The situation between the Coast families and the Hundred Thousand is deteriorating – can't you take action to stop it?'

I waited in the heat and dust, by the brown brick wall, until a male brought me a folded parchment: 'The Tower does not interfere in local squabbles.'

Ruric, for God's sake – !

Then I turned the paper over, seeing what that dark hand had written on the fold: '*S'aranth*, will the Hundred Thousand heed the Tower if they know an Orhlandis is Hexenmeister? I must be secret. And only secrecy protects what is stored here; we cannot risk being attacked. You see I have no choice. But the Tower has its friends on the Coast. What we can do, secretly, we will.'

The YV9 shuttle rested outside Kasabaarde's walls, in a rock gully between the city and the last spire of the Rasrhe-y-Meluur. A gleaming white dolphin-shape. . . . I plodded up the shuttle-ramp, grateful for the shade inside, flopped down beside the holotank, keyed the dispenser for a drink, and glanced over at Pramila Ishida.

"I'd like to talk to Molly privately."

The Pacifican girl shrugged. She walked down the ramp, to stand outside in the shadow of the hull. The hot Coast sun blazed in at the entrance-port. I tasted dust, then nutrient-drink.

The rim of the holotank was hard under my palms. It cleared to show the pale moonscape of the south-east Coast, the time there early afternoon. A wristlink contact. And there – I peered into the 'tank. When I spoke to her yesterday did I ask. . . .

"Molly, what's your location? Are you still at Maherwa?"

The Pacifican woman's face came into focus as she adjusted her wristlink with her free hand. I got a clear view of the settlement behind her. A scatter of sun-bleached dice: white walls, spiderthread rope-bridges, roof-houses and steps. . . .

"I'm at Kel Harantish now," Molly Rachel said. "We haven't got back inside the place yet."

The ground behind her was full of activity. Massive F90 shuttles come down from the orbiter, hulls gleaming palely in the light of Stormsun – six, no, seven of them – and crews unloading cargo. Men and women in Trade&Aid Corps uniform drove cargolifters and groundcars over the rocky earth, shifting terra-forming equipment. And among the Corps people I glimpsed Ortheans with white manes, in the brown scale-mail of the Harantish guard.

"The Emperor-in-Exile did a *volte face* ten days ago." Molly Rachel's voice crackled, the 'tank snowed for a moment. "He decided to experiment with Earth tech. Or, I should imagine, his advisors decided for him. The ex-Voice, Calil bel-Rioch, seems to have friends highly placed in the Harantish caste system." She grinned. "You should have seen the reaction when we set up the water-purifiers at the edge of the harbour! I've seen it on other worlds. Crop-improvers take time, but drinkable water – that's instant, and it hooks them every time!"

It took me a second to adjust. I said, "What the hell are you doing?"

"I'm grabbing a chance. Maybe, just maybe, this will lead to us getting back inside the Harantish settlement."

You still want the Witchbreed artifacts that are in there, I thought. "Isn't Rashid Akida getting anywhere with the research team in Maherwa?"

Molly scratched absently at the back of her neck with her free hand. Patches of sweat darkened her coverall. She wore a CAS-IV in a belt-holster, and I saw that she had that look we all have after a few weeks on-world, with no trips to the orbiter or FTL. In the Service we called it 'grounding in'. Gravity has a grip on the body, the sky becomes an impossible high ceiling.

198

"Rashid's people have had no success at all. He keeps *telling* me they're on the verge of a breakthrough."

Molly squinted – against the Harantish sunlight, but it took me back to a room on the northern continent, how she stared as if into bright light, unseeing.

"Perhaps," I said, suddenly short of breath, "it isn't possible to comprehend Golden science without having their world-view. That we caught a glimpse of in Rakviri *telestre*."

If the Pacifican woman had been an Orthean, her eyes would have veiled over at that moment. She said, "No. I think that's false reasoning. It's just a matter of time before Rashid comes through. I'd hoped it would be in less than a year, his team have got the whole resources of Earth's data-nets at their disposal – but I'll be happy if we get a result in under two years."

She shrugged, then, and added, "If you want to look at the interior of that dome in Maherwa, the maintenance-entrance, I've put it on the shuttle data-net. Oh yes, before I forget, call the orbiter. They've got a blip for you, from your department on Earth. Lynne, about these talks in Kasabaarde – "

"Have you got any idea what's going on here? If we're not careful, it won't be *hiyek* fighting *hiyek*, it'll be the south continent fighting the north!"

The woman shifted, stretching her shoulders that were hunched against the heat. A voice hailed her from the T&A site, and she called something over her shoulder to them, and then turned back to me.

"Lynne, please. Stop panicking. David and Pramila are keeping me advised. No Orthean is going to risk a major war with an Earth presence on-world, and if there are a few minor incidents – well, they'll defuse tension."

We're talking about casualties here! I opened my mouth to protest, but Molly got in before me: "I grant you it's not ideal, but I'm taking the long view. If we can keep hostilities to a minimum until harvest season, then we'll have won. Lynne, when these people see what T&A can do to their crop-yield, they're not going to *need* to fight."

Anything can be a weapon. Isn't that what Sethri-safere told me?

"I've had David's report on the Tower and the Hexenmeister," Molly added. "I'm glad we've got that sorted out. That place might be a very useful source of information. Lynne, I want you to shuttle down here to me. If the talks are breaking up, I could do with an update on that; and I could use your advice on dealing with the Harantish caste-system. How soon can you get down here?"

It is four hundred miles and I'm tired – with a weariness not purely physical. I feel overwhelmed by the Pacifican view of this situation. I thought, But there are more *hiyek*-families on the Coast than are present in Kasabaarde now – suppose I were to speak with them? Sethri said also, *the hiyeks have no unity*. It takes a lot of organization to fight a war, and if that could be undermined somehow . . . Get the south-east Coast *hiyeks* to back out of this . . .

Girl, you sound like Kasabaarde. And Kel Harantish. Isn't that the principle they've used to control the Coast *hiyeks*, these two thousand years?

"Not tomorrow," I said. "I'll come down to you the day after, Stormsun-20."

The holotank faded to clear.

I sat back in the seat, the padding coolly enclosing me. Pramila's restless footsteps were loud outside the port. I leaned over to key in the orbiter-comlink, and record hi-speed transmission of the message-blip that Molly mentioned. The systems took so long to mesh that I thought the Freeport infrared must be out – at last I banked it in the shuttle's data-net.

"All right?" Pramila Ishida queried, wiping her forehead as she walked through the shuttle-port.

"Yes. Sorry. I didn't intend to keep you waiting." I put my version of a security seal on the banked message-blip, and keyed out.

Pramila leaned on the back of the bucket seat. Because I've seen that demure face almost always turned aside, refusing eye-contact, I think of her as a subdued person. Now she raised her head, green eyes direct.

"Lynne, I need you to answer a question. I can't ask Molly or David or – I need to ask *you*."

Do I want to learn what's preoccupying this young Pacifican woman? I've never seen myself as the maternal, confidential type. I managed, "What do you want to ask me? Does it have to be now?"

"This is private. The opportunity might not . . ." Determination was plain on her face. "Your old reports. Your First Contact with Orthe. It's in the records. In north Roehmonde, in a city called Corbek. There was an Orthean male, called Falkyr – "

"Sethin Falkyr Talkul!"

I haven't thought of that name in years. But if I recall anything, it's that panic moment when I first realized: I can't remember his face. Can recall detail, those whiteless and slanted brown eyes, and the texture of bitter-dark mane, but not his face.

And how often over the last two days have I seen Pramila in the company of Sethri-safere? Falkyr . . . too long ago to think about, he and I were *arykei*, in a far northern province of the Hundred Thousand.

"Pramila . . . We used to say, in the Service, that it was better for such things to happen with one of the truly alien species. Hominids are too close, too nearly the same, and not quite ever alike. Like monkeys, a caricature of humanity."

"He's not a caricature!" She scowled.

"That's you," I said as I got up from the bucket seat, and stretched. "And that's partly because you're an empath: offworld personnel are. Nine out of ten alien hominid races will look at you and me and feel – revulsion. Pure and simple. No matter what you feel for them."

She smiled to herself, and then at me. "Revulsion isn't what I feel."

She surprises me, this small Pacifican woman. No protests about it being unnatural, in any sense.

Pramila said, "I just wanted to know that I, that I'm not a freak. That I'm not the only one ever to have felt . . ."

"No," I said, "you're not the only one to feel that way."

Don't look so pleased, don't look as if it were some great adventure; it's no less troubling than human emotion. And much, much stranger. Or do I mean, as strange, no less and no more?

"But when you – "

The holo-signal cut across her question. She reached down and keyed in reception. The signal was blurred, coming in weakly, and half-drowned by crowd-noise; and I could hardly make out the flustered voice of David Osaka: "You'd better get back fast!" he repeated. "I'm in the middle of a riot here – "

The trouble with kids is that they panic. David's too inexperienced, I thought. And found my mouth was dry.

The old, low masonry buildings of the trade-quarter were surrounded by chaos. Bodies pressed against me from all sides. I shoved a way through the crowd by force. *Hiyek*-Ortheans staggered past, loaded with baggage – or is it looting? – and heavy reptilian *brennior*-packbeasts hissed in protest. A riot? Or are they evacuating the city? Or already fighting – ?

I caught Pramila's arm, pulling her under the arch of the Westgate entrance to the inner city. Male and female Ortheans shouted, calling across the alleys in a babel of noise. I saw some in the robes of Order Houses at the gate, standing back in despair from the mob.

" – David be at Su'niar – ?" Pramila, her mouth close to my ear, warm breath feathering the skin. I nodded, pushed between a Rainbow Cities male (his fox-face painted with a scarlet and blue mask) and a group of south-Coast *hiyek*. Pramila followed. The shadow of Westgate's arch fell across us.

The press of bodies moved me forward, and I staggered; caught an arm to stay upright, and looked into a white face under a wire-tangle black mane. *The Barrens!* I thought, but the nomad male was gone. I pushed through into the inner city. For the first time since its founding, there was no taking of weapons, no ritual of entry.

Silence. . . .

White dust in the alley round Su'niar House was trodden down to packed earth. The awnings that had shaded the steps hung in tatters. Rubbish was scattered on the ground. Storm-light shone on two lone figures, David Osaka and Doug Clifford, emerging from the entrance to the underground chambers.

"What happened?" I looked from one to the other. David shook his head. His fair hair was grimy, lines of strain showing on that Pacifican face.

"The *hiyeks* . . . they wouldn't let the Order House ration out food any longer. They just took it. They rioted – "

Doug walked down the steps. As David moved aside with Pramila, Doug said, "It's likely that messages arrived from down-Coast cities. To say that the *jath* and *jath-rai* ships are prepared for war. The *hiyek*-families are leaving."

The storm-light brightened, easing to the haze of late afternoon. Our shadows were watery on the white earth. Douggie's eyes were dark with exhaustion, and he swayed slightly where he stood.

"I'm talked out, Lynne. I've said it every way it can be said – the only way my government can get Orthe declared a Protected world is if the Aid situation is taken care of internally. In plain terms, the Hundred Thousand will have to feed the Coast – they won't listen." His voice wavered on the last word. "Is it so difficult to understand? This is the perfect excuse for PanOceania to move a peace-keeping force in!"

So it is, I thought. Movement caught my eye. A young male sat in the dust at the side of the Order House steps. Fragments of blue ceramic bowl surrounded him, and with total concentration his six-fingered hands fitted shards together. The complex braiding of his mane was coming unbound. And then I saw that he didn't wear the rags of the inner city's mystics, but the *meshabi*-robe and woven rope-belt of the Order Houses.

Faint daystars littered the sky over the white domes. A thread of smoke rose, growing blacker.

I said, "Where are the *telestre*-Ortheans now?"

Shouts and calls came from the quayside, echoing under the sandstone arch of Harbourgate. I led the way through the gate. Dazzled for a second by bright lapping waves, the swaying masts of *jath* ships. Beyond the harbour arm, a faint olive-coloured mass was the first island of the Kasabaarde Archipelago. And, blue on blue, the immense pylons of the Rasrhe-y-Meluur faded into haze.

"There's the Meduenin," Doug said, pointing into the crowd round the nearest ship.

Voices were raised at the foot of the *jath*'s gangway. As I approached, I saw Cassirur Almadhera gesture extravagantly; her back to me, that crimson mane tumbling from its braids. And there, Blaize Meduenin, looking like some shabby captain of mercenaries grown old in service, instead of one of the Morvren *takshiriye*. The warm wind lifted that fair mane. His head was lowered: I recognized that bullish look.

" – according to your experience, the 'alliance' wouldn't last," Cassirur burst out. "But there'll be no war between *hiyeks*, now they've turned on us instead!"

She was careless of age, or Earthspeaker's dignity.

"And the church offers nothing at all!" Blaize said. "Tell me, *Earthspeaker*, what wisdom has the Tower given you, to take home to the Wellhouses? What will the Tower say when the *hiyeks* burn the land around us? You and the Hexenmeister, we'll have no help from either of you!"

"That's not important. What matters now is that the *hiyeks* have offworlders as their allies. And where are those offworlders now? Kel Harantish, with the Witchbreed! I tell you we're fighting the same war that Kerys Founder fought, to keep the land-wasters from the Hundred Thousand, to keep the *telestres* alive!"

The middle-aged Orthean woman's voice attracted stares. Now some of the Morvren people had seen us, and were beginning to look in our direction. I would have faded into the sandstone-wall background if I could. Blaize at that moment looked up and saw me. Nictitating membrane slid down over his pale eyes, flicked back; and that burn-scar twisted a smile into something monstrous, anger replaced by ironic amusement.

Cassirur spoke, a warning note in her voice. Pramila Ishida reached out and gripped my arm. Her fingers tightened. A group of *hiyek*-Ortheans watched us from the side of a *jath-rai*, moored a few yards further down the quay. A yellow-maned male was walking down the gangway.

"Leave while you can," Sethri-safere advised, speaking so as to be heard over the bustle and noise of departure. "The truce is ended. Even the inner city is unsafe now. Outlanders, your people won't thank you for what you've done here, but they sent you to do the impossible, and now they'll have someone they can blame."

His Morvrenni accent was atrocious. Are you baiting them, I wondered, or is that genuine sympathy? In an Orthean it wouldn't surprise me.

Without warning, a young male (whom I have seen with Cassirur, I realized) stepped out of the crowd. He swung clumsily. I flinched. It seemed he only struck Sethri a glancing blow, open-handed. The Desert Coast male looked round absently, tried to take a step back, and his legs folded and he fell. Pramila swore. A shout came from the *jath-rai* – one of the *hiyek* males. Jadur? Sandstone chippings flew past me, Sethri called something, and the Ortheans on the ship lowered winchbows. In a dead silence, Sethri got to his feet. I wanted to laugh at this playground violence – laughter choked in my throat, held back by a hammering pulse.

Dazed, I looked for the winchbow-bolt on the quayside, but it was trodden underfoot. The metal dart had scarred the sandstone wall two yards from my side. And then I looked up to see the yellow mane of Sethri on the *jath-rai*'s deck, Jadur complaining volubly to him.

Did we think we could restart the peace talks? Folly. And I thought, God forbid, how can we choose sides between them?

The Freeporters gathered round Doug, and I saw David Osaka speak to Cassirur. Pramila, silent, gazed down the dock at the Coast *jath-rai*. I shook my head. For the moment this is familiar, I stand with Ortheans who have faces I know – from the *telestres* of Kerys-Andrethe and Beth'ru-elen and Meduenin. . . .

A hand gripped my arm, a hand calloused with swordfighter's hardened skin.

Mind still running on the past, and forgotten faces, I said, "Is Rodion here? Or back on Meduenin *telestre*?"

When I turned to him, his half-ruined face had an expression I couldn't identify. He was still breathing rapidly, from the argument and from that swift, anonymous violence.

"I thought you'd know – *S'aranth*. Rodion's dead. She died in her year of exile."

A decade ago? Rodion, whom I knew as an *ashiren*, called Halfgold for her pale skin and mane and yellow eyes – Ruric's child. Rodion Orhlandis, carrying Blaize's children, condemned to a year's exile after that Melkathi summer . . . Rodion, in my mind always a young woman, as I last saw her. No need now to try to imagine what she might be like in her twenties, no need at all.

God prevent me being – is it glad? – over the death of my friend, Blaize's *arykei*.

Blaize Meduenin, in a quite different tone, said, "I thought you knew. I would have told you. You and she were close."

That shaggy yellow mane of his is beginning to grow too long; the whiteless blue eyes are veiled against the dust of the inner city. He wore empty *harur*-harness – and moved as if that left him half complete. And once you came to me, called me kinsister, and asked if I thought the Orhlandis child, Rodion, would ever look at a shabby, out-at-elbows mercenary. . . .

I said, "I'm sorry."

He frowned, the scar turning into something fierce. "She died here, in Kasabaarde. She was a mercenary with my troop. Wounded in a *hiyek*-war we had, a few miles east of the city."

Words desert me: I want to say, I'm sorry you had to come here, to remember, how it must hurt. . . . And I would like to know how soon after that it was that Blaize Meduenin left the Meduel Guildhouse, and entered Haltern Beth'ru-elen's service. Oh I would like to know.

The acid brilliance of the sun stung my eyes.

"It's ironic," I said. "Isn't her mother supposed to have died in this very city?"

Thus I approach, sideways and quietly, the subject of *amari* Ruric Orhlandis. How can I tell the Hundred Thousand that their 'traitor' is Hexenmeister? How can I *not* tell Blaize and Hal that Ruric is alive?

"Hal – I – " Scar tissue made a sardonic curve at one corner of his mouth. It was not a smile. We stood there in the late sun, and he looked dazzled. His voice was unsteady. "*S'aranth*, shall I tell you something about that? The Orhlandis woman didn't die, she was assassinated. Because she might have been a danger to the Hundred Thousand, alive. Hal had her killed. Haltern n'ri n'suth Beth'ru-elen."

He hit every syllable of the name with a kind of dreamy precision.

"Took him time to tell me about that. Can't trust an exile, you see. She could have raised an army against us. And now it isn't her, it's those Shadow-begotten Anzhadi. . . . Hal won't like hearing that."

He looked at me, and his face twisted. Alien and unreadable, somewhere between grief and laughter. I have not thought, had time to think, what hopes have been destroyed here today for him, and for the other Freeporters.

"What will you do now?"

"I don't know." And then he did smile: humour and defiance in it.

"Don't tell me you've been in the Freeport *takshiriye* all these years, and don't have any ideas what to do."

"For a copper coin I'd leave it all. Turn mercenary again. I understand that, Christie."

He sat down on the quay wall, heavily, and squinted up at the hazy sky. I stood beside him, staring down into the black and green depths of the harbour. The heat kept even the *rashaku* in their burrows. Voices rang, and *jath* creaked, and there was the smell of the sea.

"We should have done better, here." He looked up. "Christie. Eight years gone. . . . Why did you never come back? That was the last word I had from you, when you left. That you'd return."

Because it is this man, his face vulnerable, because for some strange reason I have always felt I owed Blaize Meduenin honesty, I tried to find a truth for him.

"There was another life to go to. And – no, I know what it was. I knew that, if I came back to Orthe, I wouldn't leave it again." Surprised, I added, "I don't think I realized that until a few days ago."

He stood, resting his arm round my shoulders. I turned to fit into the shape of him, conscious of how natural it seemed; of his warmth, of the arhythmic pulse of his blood.

"I've thought of you," he said, "kinsister."

That isn't the word I want to hear – but it'll do to be going on with. I smiled to myself, caught an answering humour in his face. A gust of warm air blew along the quay. *Del'ri*-cloth cracked, tied loosely over stacked cargo. Late afternoon light turned the world sepia, as shadows took on an evening slant. I rested back against Blaize's arm and shoulder. Heat sapped strength. Just for a minute, to let someone else carry the weight. . . . Yesterday morning, Stormsun-18; this evening, Stormsun-19; fifty hours, give or take a few, and so much has happened –

I straightened, moved away slightly, and nodded to Cassirur Almadhera as she approached.

"It's simple," Blaize said. "We can't feed the Coast families. We can't give up *telestre* land. We can't stop the *hiyeks* attacking us. Give it three or four weeks – the beginning of Merrum – we'll see *hiyek* ships off the Melkathi or the Rimon coast. And what will the *s'aranthi* do about that?"

"That's what I'm going to find out from Molly Rachel," I said, "as soon as I can shuttle down to where she is."

Cassirur said, "What else, *t'an* Meduenin?"

He eyed the ageing, red-maned woman; hid humour at her formality. As if she had never raised her voice a few minutes before, he said politely, "Six years ago, the *s'an* Dalzielle Kerys-Andrethe died, and not one of us found it necessary to step forward and take up the Crown of the Hundred Thousand. Isn't that necessary now, *t'an* Earthspeaker?"

Before Cassirur could answer, a young male with Kerys-Andrethe features protested: "This Midsummer isn't Midsummer-Tenyear."

Blaize's smile was sardonic. "The Kerys-Andrethe have always liked formality. The rest of us know necessity when we see it. We need a new *T'An Suthai-Telestre*. And there are a hundred thousand *telestres* a Crown might come from."

Cassirur chuckled, then nodded decisively. "As soon as I'm back in the Freeport, I'll get the Wellkeepers to send word out through all the provinces, tell the *s'an telestres* to come to – "

"Tathcaer," Blaize said.

"The city's empty," she protested. "I doubt there's been fifty people in Tathcaer these past five years!"

"It's where the *T'Ans* have always come, when it was necessary for there to be a *T'An Suthai-Telestre*."

The two of them spoke of *rashaku* message-carriers; but I was taken back in an instant to my last midsummer in Tathcaer, that white city that lies at the mouth of the Oranon River, that has been called (in jest) the eighth province – and that has stood deserted since the plague raged there one summer. . . .

"Come to Tathcaer," Blaize broke in on my memories. "You, the *t'an* Clifford, any other offworlders. We're running out of time."

"Midsummer is at the end of Durestha, isn't it?" I touched his hand, the sword-callouses; looked up to meet that pale blue gaze. "I've got work to put in with the Company. So has Doug. I'll meet you in Tathcaer before midsummer. There ought to be time."

Time enough to stop the avalanche? Time enough to stop the dominoes tumbling down? Ortheans jostled me, the crowd moving. An elbow caught me in the ribs and I winced, rubbing shoulders with bright robes. Faces were excited. I braced myself to peer over their heads, and heard Blaize call out to Cassirur, and then I realized what was happening.

Two pale-maned Ortheans in Order House robes came from the gatehouse, carrying a *del'ri*-fibre basket between them. They set it down on the quay with a clash of metal, and began handing back to each *telestre* male and female their *harur-nilgiri* and *harur-nazari* blades.

CHAPTER 17

In a Bright Day, In a Time Of War

Company regulations state that shuttles must not fly with only one pilot aboard. Looking at the back of David Osaka's head where he sat at the pilot's console, I thought, Yes, but that leaves me with nothing to do for the next few hours. . . .

Which is an opportunity to read that message-blip from Earth.

I keyed the holotank to exterior-view while I waited for the blip to decode. Kasabaarde was a brown stain on the earth, already fading into distance. Pramila elected to remain there, to continue observation. Not that there will be much to see, except *hiyek*-families leaving the city.

This morning of Stormsun-20 shone sepia; and flashes of heat-lightning walked along the southern sky. We flew east over acres of stony ground. The few strip-fields were soon gone, giving way to ridges of rock, and to the angular network of canals. Land flicked past below like stills from a film – wide canals, small buildings that are entrances to *siiran*, infrequent 'pits' that are cities at canal junctions, the seaports that lie where canals run out to the Inner Sea. . . .

It'll take the *hiyeks* a week or more to get back to their home cities and *siiran*. It took Haldin and her people a month to bring me from Maherwa to Kasabaarde. And when it takes me only hours to fly back across this barren country – why then, in a very real sense, we don't inhabit the same world, they and I.

The 'tank chimed, cut exterior-view, and began to run the message-blip from my department.

An image formed of a young man, leaning back in his desk-console. He had his feet up, and as the holo-record clicked on, raised a mug of coffee in casual salute. Acting departmental head Stephen Perrault of the Liaison Office. In the window behind him the sun shone, deep yellow in a dark blue sky.

". . . I've commented on the section-heads' reports, this is an unofficial summary, right?" He smiled. It aged him, made this bearded young man into something piratical. Which is not as fanciful as it might seem, considering Perrault's character; and I can be forgiven for hoping he wasn't coping *too* well in my absence, since I may need a job to go back to.

His recorded image continued: "As far as summaries go, I can give it

208

to you in a sentence, Lynne. While the cat's away, the rats are at play. Nothing personal."

"Miaow." Perrault shares my sense of humour.

"The north European Enclave project has had its completion date put back six months, that's because PanOceania's finance department is hooking us about. So the new housing camps aren't going to be occupiable before next spring. I'm negotiating to get the section of the population that's involved into temporary accommodation – but if we *had* any, we wouldn't need the housing camps."

"Don't let them screw you," I muttered. No matter that he couldn't hear.

"I'm also putting out feelers to NuAsia and ChinaCo," Stephen Perrault's image continued. "I know that technically this office is part of PanOceania, but Liaison has a legally neutral status, and we're European-staffed."

Meaning that if you threaten to bring in other multicorporates, it may bring PanOceania through with the finance? That's not a safe game to play.

"We got the tariff question settled in the last parliament, pushed the Bill through; so provided none of the other Enclaves reneges, we should have grain prices down by next July. Or October, if we're lucky.

"Nothing new on the fuel situation.

"PanOceania's taking out its linkman with us here in London. Replacing Singh with some kid who's got no track record, so he's somebody's protégé. God help us.

"One problem that's come up after you left. The British government and PanOceania are squabbling over the demarcation lines of this department – "

Damn it, I knew it; it's *not* safe to push!

" – want to put us firmly under Company control. I know this one comes up regularly, but it looks sticky. Hence the rush report. If we're not careful, we'll be eased out of our status as neutral arbitrators."

Stephen Perrault paused, drank from the coffee cup. By his grimace, it was cold. He scratched through fair hair and beard.

"Sorry about this – late hours for a few nights. We're fighting on two fronts, and if I have to come down temporarily on one side, it'll be the government's. Unless I hear different from you. I ought to redo this tape, I'm too tired to think. . . . No time, if I'm going to get it on the FTL-drone. Listen, you notice they waited until you went offworld? They're going to find out they underestimated the rest of us."

"The last thing you want to do is antagonize the Company," I said.

The department's status is ambiguous enough as it is – and it's useful that way.

Message-blips travel on unmanned drones that aren't restrained by the limits of living flesh. Stephen would have sent this off ten or twelve days ago. I thought, I wonder how he's holding out? Shit, they need me there!

As he reached across to cut off the holo-record, Perrault added, "I'll send reports regularly, as we arranged. Contact me when you can. Oh – word here is, PanOceania might have found something startling on Carrick V; true? Message ends."

That other life presses in on me. Memories of blue sky and cold wind and half-derelict office blocks in the London Enclave, and Perrault and the rest of my team; of days on the holo-link to governments in Westminster and York and Edinburgh, and to PanOceania in Melbourne and Tokyo. Does that put what I do here in perspective? Orthe, only a distant world in the Heart Stars, only Carrick V. . . .

I got up from the 'tank, blinking against the shuttle's pale-green interior lighting. I have a responsibility here, put on me in a Wellhouse by a woman called renegade and traitor; put on me by my own actions, when I set foot on this world as First Contact. For the moment, Perrault will have to manage on his own.

"Halfway mark," David Osaka announced. "Want to take over, Lynne?"

"Yes, I'll take it."

"There's an anti-error repeat loop on the navigation systems," he added. "We're still getting interference on location signals, but as far as I can make out, *that's* where we'll rendezvous with Molly."

I took over the console. Aware that, however unreal it seems to my imagination now, fifteen thousand feet below us there are *jath-rai* sailing east to Quarth and Reshebet and Nadrasiir, and the other Coast ports; crewed by Orthean men and women who look north across the Inner Sea with ever-hungrier faces.

"The question is, what is the Company going to *do* about this situation?"

Molly ignored the query, steering the groundcar over rough terrain. Balloon-tyres crunched on shale. Here the pale earth fell away in scree-slopes, and Carrick's Star cast our shadows blue-black on the ground, and the mid-afternoon sky held only a handful of daystars at the horizon.

"I don't understand – why Tathcaer?" she said at last. "That settlement's been deserted for years. So have all the cities of the Hundred Thousand, except for Morvren Freeport. Logistically it would make more sense if they chose a *T'An Suthai-Telestre* in Morvren."

I leaned forward to key a control, and a panel in the dome of the groundcar retracted. Smell of sun on hot earth, and silence: the silence of a sterile land. . . . "In Tathcaer, there's a *telestre*-house for each one of the Hundred Thousand *telestres*. And there's the great Wellhouse of Kerys Founder; and the Crown's Citadel. That's why they'll go back there. Molly, I want to know what the Company's going to do about the *hiyeks*."

"This is Reshebet," the Pacifican woman said. "This is what I wanted you to see, Lynne."

The groundcar slowed. Groups of young males and females were squatting outside low-roofed buildings. The wickedly sharp hook-bladed knives that hung at their belts were *del'ri*-harvest tools. Turned to butchery now? As we drove between the groups I thought, They're farmers. That's all. And so are the Hundred Thousand; this isn't a war of *armies* –

Reshebet swarmed like a hive of *kekri*-flies. Molly let the groundcar nose gently through the crowds of *hiyek*-Ortheans. Some took off their masks to stare at us, and younger *ashiren* hung over the rails of the *jath*-ships that choked the canal here and called out to offworlders. Storm clouds massed on the northern horizon, and the sea beneath shone like gunmetal.

Narrow hoop-masted *jath-rai* and *jath* were jammed so tightly together that I couldn't see canal water, only the decks; vessels sheltering behind the sea-lock wall from the coming storm. Shouts drifted up from the canal where it went inland, and I stood up in the groundcar, and saw great dun-coloured *brennior* on the walkways. The packbeasts were harnessed by cables to *jath*-ships, straining with all their reptilian bulk to drag the craft northwards. I looked to the south and saw an endless train of hoop-masts and metal-weave sails glittering in the sun.

"The *hiyeks* have been coming from inland for a week now," Molly Rachel said. "Same goes for all the coastal harbours. You can see I didn't have any alternative."

"Alternative?"

"I've sent a request through the orbiter's comlink, asking that the nearest detachment of the Company's Peace Force be seconded to Orthe."

She keyed power, and swung the groundcar away from the buildings, out on to rough earth again. No roads here, not even a footpath. All travel is by water. The 'car jolted, and a stab of nausea went through me.

"Jesus Christ, Molly, you're bringing *troops* in!"

She frowned, concentrating on driving. "It's a police action. Nothing more. They happen every day. You don't think the Ortheans will fight each other with the potential threat of military technology hanging over them?"

Carrot and stick. How many worlds have the Companies done this on? And on how many has it worked? And some small voice inside me said, *An enforced peace is better than a freely-chosen war – isn't it?*

Cool air circulated under the groundcar-dome. The exterior temperature reading was something unbelievable. I leaned back in the padded seat, squinting through the polarized plastic. Saw shale and rock, and the dust-plume of our arrival not yet settled. In the distance, moonscape mountains mark the beginning of the Elansiir. I have lived Orthean for too many days to be sped from shuttle-landing, across country to Reshebet, and now back to Kel Harantish in an hour – I haven't adjusted.

"What about Rashid's people, in Maherwa?"

Molly shook her head. Permanent lines marked her face now, incised deeply round her eyes. That black-wire hair was growing shaggy, and I saw she had pinned it down with two of the fragile *del'ri*-wood combs that Coast Ortheans use. Is Orthe beginning to touch her, or is that just for convenience?

"Nothing!" One dark fist hit the console: the groundcar swerved. "It *is* something we've never met before, some completely alien way of perceiving the universe – if we can't understand Golden science, we should at least be able to reproduce it blindly! But all I get from Rashid is *no*. And none of these natives understand the concepts their ancestors used."

Now we drove parallel to a ridge, running into a brief strip of shadow, and emerged into level wasteland. The horizon shimmered, wavered, dissolved. Streaks of mirage-water receded ahead of us. The white mesa of Kel Harantish hung in the heat, pulled out of shape like toffee; pocked with black windows like onyx eyes.

"Lynne, do *you* understand Witchbreed science?"

I turned my head, startled. "Me?"

"If you were to tell me that somewhere in those fake memories that Pramila reported on, you had the slightest idea of how it functioned – I'd listen."

An octagonal hall in Rakviri: *Whose hand will take the knife, under that radiant shadow?*

"I don't know," I said. "Even if these delusions were the implanted memories I thought they were, or even if they're based on data in the Tower Archives; then either way, the Hexenmeister wouldn't pass on any knowledge of Witchbreed science. I don't want to discuss it. I feel incredibly stupid to have let myself be tricked that way."

"Sorry. Lynne, I apologize; that was unfair."

The towering heights of Kel Harantish solidified from heat haze. The F90 shuttles grounded on the wasteland before it were dwarfed by the sheer massiveness of the walls. I saw movement: winches hauling rope-platforms up to the city roofs.

"We might have time on our side," Molly Rachel said. "I've got the orbiter keeping a close eye on climate changes. It's not long until the monsoon season. Ships won't cross the Inner Sea in that. If that happens, and we sell T&A to the *hiyeks*, and with the Peace Force here . . ."

The groundcar swung to halt by the nearest shuttle in a spray of shale and wheelspin. She grinned at me.

"You're so anxious to get PanOceania off this world. What I've done here will change your mind. I've got some things to see to – I'll want your advice later. Pathrey Shanataru will show you what we've set up here."

She was out of the groundcar while the dome was still retracting, running up the F90's ramp, hailing the humans and Ortheans there. I got out of the 'car more slowly. Rock was hot underfoot. I stepped into the shadow of the F90's hull. Voices are the only sound here: no wind through *ziku* or *lapuur* trees, no cry of *rashaku*. . . .

"*Kethrial-shamaz*, Christie."

A plump, brown-skinned Orthean left the group near the shuttle. Pathrey Shanataru. He bowed. His ragged *meshabi*-robe had gone, and so had the scale-mail, replaced by swathes of black cloth woven with myriad tiny gold threads. Amused despite myself, I thought, Not only seedy, but flashy too.

Temporary T&A bases were set up here on the rocky earth. Standard issue, featureless metal and plastiglas domes, hardly larger than the shuttles that brought them. I could see, between them, the harbour: its surface like broken mirrors. And hear the lapping of the waves. I turned and walked as Pathrey led me, past the domes to the harbour. The pumps and sealed units of the desalination plants stood black against the glare. A linked series of them ran from the edge of the harbour nearest us, out along the harbour arm to the open sea.

"Congratulations," I said. "The last time I saw you, you were in hiding. You and the *shan'tai* Calil bel-Rioch – is she here, too?"

The plump male smiled. His six-fingered hands flashed with jewelled rings.

"The *shan'tai* bel-Rioch has friends." His shrewd brown eyes cleared. "All the friendlier now, since she could promise to bring back to the city all the engines and advantages of *s'aranthi*-offworlders. . . ."

It came to me that this middle-aged Orthean male was as excited as an

213

ashiren, hugging to himself the triumph of their return, his and Calil's. Does that mean an unguarded tongue?

"The Emperor Dannor *agreed* to all this?" I was incredulous.

"Not precisely," Pathrey Shanataru said. "But there are those in the city who see the Coast families moving out of our control – their taking *s'aranthi* gifts is inevitable – and think we should seize advantage while we still can. Before we're left a small city and powerless."

Heat made pale rock waver, and the horizon ran like water, I halted, panting, then trudged on up the rough slope at the edge of the T&A excavations. Dust buried my feet and ankles, chips of stone lodged inside my boots. Pathrey gripped my shoulder, six-fingered hand warm through coverall-fabric to flesh, and helped me to the top of the ridge. From here out to the harbour arm, the excavators had ripped up Coast rock to a depth of fifty feet. Looking between the gleaming machinery, I saw tanks of pulverized rock, the beginning of a system of interconnected chambers.

"They're modelling it on *siiran*," I realized, wondering if that were one of Molly's more sensitive notions. "You realize the Company want something in return. Witchbreed artifacts. And Dannor bel-Kurick isn't going to let offworlders back inside the city, is he?"

"He may," Pathrey said. "His advisors put it to him most strongly. I have every confidence in his wit, *shan'tai*. He can see advantage, even when it is Calil bel-Rioch who brings it to his attention."

I peered across at channels, chambers and tunnels, seeing the sites for the hydroponic systems; the connections to the desalination plants. Basic T&A: extract trace elements from the seawater during the desalination process, introduce them back into the soil to grow crops. Companies have terra-formed inhospitable worlds with larger versions of this process. As for long-term effect on climate and environment – has the Company run a prediction-pattern? I wondered.

"If the Company trades these to the Coast *hiyeks*, then that'll be the end of Kel Harantish's controlling monopoly of the canals. It'll leave the Emperor with no power. Just this tiny settlement, and – starvation."

Pathrey Shanataru scowled. Then he glanced past me, back the way we'd come.

An Orthean female climbed the slope. Her skin with that white-metal sheen, fox-face and yellow eyes; dressed now in Harantish mail, and all the sepia dye washed from her mane, that had disguised her in Maherwa.

"*Shan'tai* Calil," I said. Seen first here, then in Maherwa, now here again: how the wheel turns, and takes us with it. . . .

The white-maned woman halted, looked at me with a certain humour in those yellow eyes. Then her expression changed. She spoke:

"———— —— ———— ——— ————"
"—— ———— ——— —— ———"

My response was automatic, was natural; and then as I slurred and stuttered, I realized it was in a language that no human should know, that no human tongue should be able to form. *Celebrants, we stand. The ritual chant* —

Calil bel-Rioch smiled.

"Give you greeting, exile," she said. "How is my sister in the Tower?"

Bile surged hotly in my throat. I coughed, pulled out a rag into which I could spit, and waved aside Pathrey Shanataru's hesitant offer of assistance.

"Sorry – must be the heat – "

I shuddered, almost grateful for the body's revolt. The first time I've seen her since that clouded time in Maherwa, and again . . . Obviously she planned to unnerve me, *has* unnerved me; this gives a respite.

Pathrey's plump brown face showed concern. He offered a flask. I drank and found it tepid water, water with that taste peculiar to desalination. My eyes ran, Calil was a blurred image of white and gold. And then I saw that Pathrey's eyes showed a thin rim of white round them: wide open with apprehension at hearing that tongue spoken.

"Life on the Coast is hard," Calil said urbanely. "The heat – that hammer forges us all."

Do I want to be alone with her questions? Compared to false memories in my head, the Kel Harantish Witchbreed are degenerate stock, interbred with Orthean bloodlines. If I were to think as a *keretne*, I would wonder if some freak of ancestry could, after sixty generations, produce a true Golden. This woman facing me, membrane sliding back from those chrome-yellow eyes, as much Witchbreed as Santhendor'lin-sandru, called Phoenix Emperor and Last Emperor – No: that's Orthean thinking, not human.

Fighting for self-possession, I smiled. "Kel Harantish gives an interesting welcome each time I arrive, *shan'tai* Calil. *Shan'tai* Pathrey, thank you for the drink."

Evening began to put long shadows blackly on the broken earth. Daystars clustered at the horizon.

"As for the Tower, which you mentioned – I'd be interested to know which the Hexenmeister hates more: seeing the Coast *hiyeks* slavishly dependent on your maintenance of the canals, or seeing them abandon you to begin using Earth technology. It's a difficult question, isn't it?"

She sucked in a breath. I thought, Why, I've offended you. Good. A little more of that and I might know what sort of person we're dealing with here.

215

"My people tell me you were in the Tower," she said. "Where else could you get that look of Empire? That's why I spoke as I did. That's why you could answer."

But the Tower's memory is only historical archives. . . . I rubbed the back of my neck, where the evening sun shone heavy on me. *Jath* sails were visible beyond the harbour arm, losing themselves in the glitter of that Stormsun sea. Footsteps were loud on rock, human voices called from the shuttle landing site, and the blank cliff-face of Kel Harantish reflected back the day's heat. I was covered with a thin sheen of sweat.

"The Emperor could stop the *hiyeks* now," I said, struggling for balance, "if he threatened to let the canals rot, and the *siiran* harvests fail."

She shrugged. "What would that do except make the *hiyeks* turn even more swiftly to Earth? And why should we care for them, or for the *telestres*? They're nothing but thieves. That land is ours, a part of the old Empire – we're only in exile, here."

Her tone held some intense, all-consuming emotion. Curiosity? Nostalgia? I thought, There's something in your voice when you say *Empire* that even Dannor bel-Kurick doesn't have, and he is Emperor-in-Exile. . . .

"That's the past," I said.

Her chin came up, and she looked me in the eye. "Is it?"

Her sun-whitened mane blew across her face in the first soft wind of evening. She glanced over her shoulder at the blank wall of Kel Harantish. She looked older now than a bare month ago, when she had been Voice of the Emperor.

I smiled, in recognition. "Is that what you do – pretend omnipotence, knowledge of the past? You look more of a Witchbreed than even Dannor bel-Kurick, I imagine they fear you for that, even your own people. Don't try it with me. The Empire fell long ago. And it doesn't surprise me that you know there's a female Hexenmeister. How much careful spying does it take, to keep up that 'omniscience'?"

"It's true. I do that." Calil faced me. A young Orthean woman in dusty scale-mail, standing barefoot in the rubble; and then she raised her head again, with such a sudden and total grace that I could only think *Witchbreed!* Her husky voice went on: "*Shan'tai*, don't they say always that the Golden Witchbreed have no past-memories, that that is what marks our race off from the slave race and their 'Goddess'?"

She stepped forward until we were almost touching.

"Offworlders have no past-memories either, but you do, I see it in you. And I – I *remember*. I don't know how or why. I only know I see that millennial time, see that great Empire, and the cities that were

216

greater in size than all this Desert Coast! I've seen aKirrik and Archonys of the Six Lakes. And I have seen that disease that the slave races created to be our downfall, so that we bore no more children, and our last generation turned in their fury against each other, and brought those great cities down. Now tell me *you* have not seen this also, in the Tower!"

For a moment I felt only the dislocation of shock, and then I came back to harsh sunlight, and to Calil's dazzled face.

"Or is it a delusion," the Harantish woman said, "built up out of scraps and hearsay, and tales told to a child?"

I have thought that the light of logic, harsh as Carrick's Star, illuminated one thing: Whoever witnessed those ancient scenes of terror could never have come living to the Tower, could never have become Hexenmeister, and passed on their memories to others. And so the whole edifice collapses, the 'memories' are fakes. And now I know I'm still ignorant – I don't know if what I experience is based on Tower Archive data, given to me by the Hexenmeister ten years ago; or whether it's gossip, history, speculation; made up by willpower into some synaesthetic vision.

Looking into Calil's yellow eyes, I see that same desperate *don't know*.

Calil switched again to a Coast dialect and said urgently, "The woman in the Tower. Who is she? What is she? I must talk to you again. I'll send my Pathrey to you, when it's safe for you to enter the city."

I watched her walk away across broken rock. Company domes and shuttle dwarfed by Kel Harantish's walls, and Calil bel-Rioch a small pale figure, merging into pale earth. . . .

Just when I thought I had all the facts (even if I didn't like the answers), I find out there are still things unaccounted for.

Some change in the light made me look westwards. Steel-grey clouds were beginning to rise where Carrick's Star was setting. Cargolifters rolled; T&A personnel shouted. Excavation here will proceed rapidly, now that the day's heat is fading. Sixty miles away the *hiyek*-families are moving – how long, now, until the rains come?

Second twilight, shifting into night: a shuttle dropped down as I walked beside the walls of Kel Harantish. The roar of its landing hardly penetrated my thoughts, though I registered a night-landing as unusual here. I didn't want to go back to the shuttle-HQ just yet.

The rocky earth was warm, radiating back the day's heat. I stopped and looked up at the stars. The early summer sky of Orthe, so full of stars that they run together in blazes of silver, in great flowers of light. When I looked down, black dazzles floated in my vision.

In that second it flooded back into my mind: *T'An* Commander Ruric,

Suthafiori crowned in Tathcaer, Haltern meeting me at the docks that long-ago spring; all the long journey north into forest and the Lesser Fens and those mountains called the Wall of the World. If I were free now, what would I do? If I did nothing but follow my instincts –

I took a microcorder out of my belt-pouch and flicked it on: "Lynne de Lisle Christie to Company Representative Molly Rachel, dated – " I couldn't remember a non-Orthean date " – Stormsun 20, local time. Molly, this is my formal and official resignation from the post of special advisor to the PanOceania multicorporate Company, to take effect immediately. From tomorrow, Stormsun-21 local time, my rank will be advisor to the government envoy; which Douglas Clifford will confirm. Message ends – "

My hand shook as I clicked the microcorder off. *Dive back into your bolthole, girl!* Back to the Hundred Thousand, who know you; back to government Service. Doug will confirm my position. Then –

Lynne, I thought, how long before you're handing in a resignation to the government, too? Because all you want to do is go back to the Hundred Thousand, back home. Inaccurate as that may be, with all the reservations about being an alien in this culture, and ten years a long time. And why do that?

Because it means I don't have to think if Molly's right to do what she's doing here. And because it means, above all else, that I don't have to think about Calil bel-Rioch and that dead Empire.

Sorry, girl, escape isn't that easy.

I stood in that starlit darkness, and on impulse keyed my wristlink into records I'd studied earlier in the holotank. The preliminary reports from Ashida's research people in Maherwa.

I studied the image: small in the wristlink. An identification-grid covered the film, but I cut that out, wanting to see unbiased by Rashid's preconceptions.

That dome, with the pillars set back into the steps, casting a sharp-edged shadow. . . .

Then the viewpoint approached the black entrance, cut out for a second, adjusted to the lack of light, and showed a bare *chiruzeth* chamber. Vision improved. Serpentine curves decorated the walls. Carved vines, that seem to form features in peripheral vision. The viewpoint joggled, continuing across the chamber and down a flight of steps leading underground. So like those underground halls in Kel Harantish. . . . I scrolled forward, to the point where the steps opened out into a network of low tunnels.

Tunnels with curved walls, and oval openings into yet more tunnels, so that one saw receding perspectives framed by irregular arches. These curves and supports are less like the architecture of men, and more like organic patterns of hive and vine. A maze, below the city.

All the research team's explorations so far have recorded are tunnels like these. With one exception: an underground location that must, by measurement, be under the actual honeycombed wall of the cylindrical pit that is Maherwa. Here the confined and constricted tunnels open into vast spaces. Walls soar up to meet in gothic arches, seventy feet overhead. Squat pillars jut from a floor that, though it has no pattern to the eye, is to the hand's touch carved with vines and skulls and shells. And there are other pillars that seem, from their translucent interiors, to contain a flow of water; but as to how or why . . . the team can speculate about pumps and water-purifiers, but can't be certain. And can't attempt to dismantle, or sample; not with the Harantish guard always there. But that will come. . . .

I keyed the wristlink off. Half dazzled and waiting for night vision, I began to pick my way towards the trackways that the excavators had already worn into the rock, going back towards the shuttles. It must have been close on an hour I wasted, walking round the edges of the site and watching the excavators at work. When at last I came back to the shuttle that Molly had designated her HQ, I thought there was an unusual amount of activity inside.

David Osaka passed me as I walked up the shuttle-ramp.

"What's going on?" I called after him.

He tossed words over his shoulder, still moving. "It's the detachment of the Peace Force – they're here."

CHAPTER 18

The Heartland of Corruption

Which means that Molly put in the request some time back. It takes time to get here from Thierry's World. Did the Company *expect* to have to do this – or is that question naïve?

I entered the shuttle and walked down the cabin to the rear compartments. I found I was gripping my belt-pouch that held the microcorder, knuckles white.

" – only way I can see to keep the invasion fleet from sailing." Molly stopped as I entered the rear cabin, looking up from where she and a Peace Force officer sat over the remains of a meal. "Ah, Lynne. I don't think you'll know Commander Mendez. Commander Mendez, this is our special advisor, Lynne de Lisle Christie."

"Hello, Lynne."

"Hello, Cory." I briefly enjoyed the pleasure of scoring off Molly Rachel. "Must be, what, six years?"

"Must be." The woman nodded thoughtfully. Commander Corazon Mendez: a tall, thin woman with cotton-white hair; now in her mid or late fifties. Not looking any different: the same beak-nosed, gaunt face; the white hair cut sleekly round at neck length. She wore a black coverall with the Peace Force logo.

"Does Doug know you're on-world?" I asked.

"Doug? Not Doug Clifford?"

I explained to Molly. "Cory was seconded to the Service some years back, as military advisor, round about the time that Doug and I were there."

"Ah. Yes. The envoy's in Tathcaer, I think." Molly looked blank. "I was saying to Commander Mendez, the only way I can see to keep the invasion fleet from sailing is to turn the *hiyek*-families' attention to T&A. Once they see what desalination and hydroponics plants can do – but it's going to take them until next harvest to be convinced, and we don't have that much time. The monsoon will only last two or three weeks. Then there's nothing to stop ships crossing the Inner Sea."

The Pacifican woman was seated on one side of the table, Cory Mendez on the other. I sank down into the seat beside Cory, willing neither of them to see that my hands were trembling. The older woman smiled. She has one of those dark-complexioned hawklike faces you often see in the old Anglo-Argentinian families, and at the moment I could see on it a contempt for Pacificans that is not uncommon among Anglo-Argentinians; and a contempt for the commercial side of the Company, not uncommon among the police corps.

"What about the other side of the conflict?" she asked.

"That's a reasonable point. Molly, if I can sit in on this, I think it might be helpful." Thinking, It is ironic. What I do now will take me where I wanted to go, without the abdication that would have been involved. Without anyone seeing, I reached a finger into a belt-pouch and keyed *erase* on the microcorder. A superstitious impulse.

"I think I can see an interim solution," I said. "As Cory mentions, there are two sides to the conflict. We ought to talk to the northern continent. Not to the *telestre*-Ortheans – that's where the Kasabaarde talks broke down – but to the Wellkeepers and Earthspeakers. They're the only people that just might let Coast Ortheans share some land, on the northern continent – "

"Land-*sharing*?" Molly said, incredulous. "Lynne, you know the *telestre* system better than anybody; they'd never – "

"Share *telestre* land, no, I grant you. But there's land north of the Inner Sea that isn't occupied by *telestres*." I paused. "Sure, that's because it's wilderness; but even a wilderness there is paradise compared to farming the Coast."

Cory Mendez nodded. "You could make what you're doing there well known here. If you can get a result that's halfway positive, it may delay the invasion, or fragment it; either way, it's easier to contain and control."

Molly Rachel stirred uncomfortably. The Argentinian woman caught my eye, with a smile that never reached her lips. Yes, I thought, I feel sorry for the girl too. Technically she's superior to both of us, as Company representative – age and experience give us a very unfair advantage. And knowing Molly's resilience, I'd better take advantage of her being off balance to get what I want.

"The Company needs to know what's happening in the Hundred Thousand, in any case." I turned to Mendez. "Cory, have your people grounded yet?"

She stroked the rings on her bony fingers. "I've come in advance. An observer. I'm old-fashioned, I like to see things for myself, not send my junior officers."

"Then, if Molly has no objections, you could observe first hand in Tathcaer – I say Tathcaer, because it'll be awkward to ground a shuttle on the mainland, and that city has different rules. We can go oversea, stop over on Lone Isle rather than go back up to the orbiter."

Anything to defuse hostilities here.

Molly Rachel looked at us. Her long fingers clenched into a fist, and then relaxed. While I watched tensely, she keyed a comlink contact to David Osaka, to Pramila in Kasabaarde, and – after some problems – to Clifford in Tathcaer itself.

"Yes," she said finally. "The *takshiriye* are moving back into Tathcaer. As soon as they're established, use that settlement as a base. Take a comlink-booster. I want eight-hourly reports. And I want results. The climate's unpredictable here, the monsoon may not arrive, or it may end before we expect it to – so the data-profile says. Commander Mendez, I hope your troopships are here by then."

The comlink chimed. She answered it, and then said, "For you, Lynne."

David Osaka's voice came through. "One of the locals is here, asking for you. Pathrey Shanataru. Says it's about a meeting the bel-Rioch woman arranged to have with you – inside the city. What shall I tell him?"

I keyed hold and looked questioningly at Molly.

"It's a foot in the door," she said enthusiastically. "Even if nothing comes of this meeting, it sets a precedent. And I don't think you have to be too concerned about your personal safety, Lynne, with half the Company on Kel Harantish's doorstep – "

"Okay, okay, I get the message." And to David: "Tell him I'll be there in ten minutes."

Molly nodded approval. I can't very well avoid doing this, even if it does get the Company back inside the city; and besides, it's something to do while we're preparing to go to Tathcaer –

And that is all rationalization. I *must* see Calil bel-Rioch again. To ask her how she can speak a tongue I have only heard spoken in a vision, in a northern land. Ask how she knows a forgotten language. And ask: how is it that I know it, too?

Cory Mendez said, "How's the research progressing? Are my people likely to face anything more than primitive weaponry here – any kind of alien tech?"

Molly Rachel shook her head. "This is a used-up world. There aren't the resources for the natives to make Golden technology viable again, even if the knowledge of it had been preserved. I know Lynne doubts the technology can be reconstructed, even with Earth tech. From your viewpoint, I think there's no need for concern."

"You don't credit the rumours, then?"

Molly stared. "Rumours?"

"I stopped over several hours on the orbiter," Cory Mendez said.

222

"Sometimes it pays to listen to mess gossip. It's unsubstantiated, but I hear that there's now a trade in more than agricultural equipment going on here. That sonic stunners, CAS-IVs, small handguns, are turning up in Orthean hands in some of the Coast seaports. That there's a black-market arms trade on Carrick V."

"No." Molly shook her head firmly. "Nothing comes on-world that isn't checked by my people on the orbiter. If there is any small amount of Earth tech here, it's come in illegally some time in the past ten years."

Fear distracted me: the thought of Pathrey, waiting. And Calil bel-Rioch. And then I thought, No, not even she would abduct a Company employee at this juncture. . . .

"I'll be back in an hour or two," I said. And left the shuttle, walking out to where the dark night was broken by strings of radiant lights rigged up across the hydroponic site excavations; and by the sound of seawater pumps, and the rumble of rock being pulverized. The earth was rough underfoot. Thunder scraped and rumbled along the northern horizon. I stopped, sweating, and looked up. The monolithic dark of Kel Harantish blocked out all the southern sky. Silhouetted against the Heart Stars, I could see the ropes and hanging platforms necessary for entry to the city.

David was waiting, and Pathrey Shanataru with him. I walked on to meet them.

Pathrey showed me to the city rooms occupied by the Harantish woman. He oozed obsequiousness, standing aside to let me walk down the steps inside the roof-house; and then as I reached the lower rooms, smiled and made as if to efface himself.

"And this time *go*."

The woman stood with her back to a narrow window. Pathrey spread plump-fingered hands in protest: "But, Calil – "

"Listen to my conversations again and they'll be the last things you do hear."

She smiled. It was a threat: blatant, brutal. The plump dark male bowed, and his eyes flicked once to my face. I caught a look in which there was not just fear, but puzzled hurt.

Calil waited until he climbed the steps, and the roof trap door slammed shut behind him. Then she said, "Come here, Christie."

I walked across a floor of varnished *del'ri*-wood. Floor, walls and ceiling; all panelled in that pale wood. In this stone and metal culture, wood is opulence. Ceramic pots held oil-lights, and their light glimmered on the *del'ri*-fibre mats and the window-arch. My boots scraped grit on the polished floor as I came to stand beside the white-maned woman and look out of the window. Warm wind blew in a gulf of darkness.

Immeasurably far below, I saw the glare of the T&A site.

"I have been thinking about truth." She smiled again. Some quality in her voice was hypnotic, at once amused and detached.

Double image: she is only a small Harantish woman, in a white *meshabi*-robe. No taller than my shoulder; thin, barefoot. And she is Golden. I thought, When I look at you I see another face, satin-black skin and mane, but the same Witchbreed-yellow eyes.

"One of the great lies they tell," Calil said, "is that truth is simple, and is easy to understand. But truth is complex, with hidden inner workings, and outside masks; and understanding it is difficult, or impossible, and most of the world is condemned to dying without ever understanding a smallest part of it."

She padded across to the low metal-lattice table and sat cross-legged, and began to pour *arniac* into bowls. I could only stare. As if pursuing some thought, she added, "I have no right to the bel-Rioch name. I assumed it. It's useful to me."

I must have looked bewildered. She laughed. It was a short, smothered noise. As if in some past-memory or vision, I came to sit down by her on the *del'ri* mat. The *arniac* tasted peppery. The Coast poison *ruesse* has no scent to Ortheans, but to human senses it is obvious. No taste of it here – do I expect it? I wondered. I don't know *what* to expect.

"Have you been made Voice of the Emperor again?"

She grinned. Her features, seen close, are uneven: the corner of her left eye droops slightly.

"I don't need to be. Didn't you tell me, Christie, that I assume a mantle of mystic infallibility? And if people don't quite believe, at least they don't disbelieve; and I have my own 'Voices' to keep me informed."

I thought, If it comes to pretending infallibility, you're not the expert. That sounded bitter. It's the Tower you want to know about. What can I say to you about Ruric Hexenmeister that Ruric would want known outside the Tower?

Chiming in with my thought, Calil asked, "Christie, it's always been said there's but one Hexenmeister in the Tower, through all the years; is that merely something they'd have us believe, or is it true?"

"I want to know: why must you know that?"

She held her *arniac* bowl cupped in hands that are white, with a gold-dust glimmer in the skin. The surface of the crimson liquid shivered. When she looked up her yellow eyes were clear.

"I have had visions all my life. Only the Hexenmeister could tell me if they are true past-memories – *if* the Hexenmeister is what the Tower claims."

"Does it matter?" I protested. "Listen. That's the Company's excavators you can hear. Earth technology here on Orthe. What does the past matter, compared to that?"

She shook the white mane back from her face, watching me.

Fighting not to be indiscreet, I said, "And what does the Tower matter, really? We have no way of telling if their knowledge is immortal memory, or only archives; and whichever it is, we still wouldn't have any way of knowing if it were *true*. Three thousand years is a long time. Memories distort, and archives get corrupted – "

Calil, trying the thought out to see how it fitted, said, "Could it be that's all there is? The great Tower no more than a collection of weevil-eaten parchments, and her spies and agents no less fallible than Harantish's. . . . Is that what I can believe, now?"

Argue round it how you can. The 'parchments' are Golden tech data-storage, but it comes to the same thing. In that flickering lamplight I was suddenly tired of deception. It surprised me how bitter I felt against the old man, the old Hexenmeister. All that talk of remembered lives. And I *believed* it. So much grief for so many years.

The Harantish woman said cynically, "It makes little difference to my city. The Hundred Thousand would hate us still, for what they remember of the Empire, and that even without the Tower to tell the Wellhouses how evil we are." Now Calil sounded bitter. "If the past didn't hang upon us like stones, why, we'd not be shut up in a city of traps in the middle of a wasteland. They call us 'halfbreed Golden'. They fear us, that land to the north. And the Coast fears us, also. Christie, I have had visions that show them not so innocent. They claim they were a slave race of the Golden, bred up from fenborn aboriginals – but there were those who were not slave, and who built up the Empire hand in hand with the Golden Witchbreed."

"No one's innocent," I said. Hearing her *I have had visions*. And I couldn't stop myself asking, "How do you know that language, *shan'tai* Calil?"

"Perhaps it's still spoken in my city. Perhaps I learned it in the Tower. Perhaps – "

Cutting across her provocation, I said, "We've no records of it anywhere. I've looked. Nothing, in ten years on this world; if it was known, I think we'd have heard it somewhere. As for the Tower . . ." Intent on explanation, I said, "There's always a Hexenmeister. There are always others who could pick up the role and continue it word-perfect. But as for it being one and the same Hexenmeister, over millennia – "

I broke off, regretting it the instant the words were out of my mouth. My tone would have told her, if nothing else. Haven't I just told this consummate Harantish politician the truth about her traditional enemy?

Indiscreet. Perhaps more than indiscreet. . . . But traditions count for nothing now. What does that rivalry between Kel Harantish and Kasabaarde's Tower matter when the Coast is attacking the Hundred Thousand, and Earth is bringing technology and troops here? And won't it make Ruric safer if they know she's only one of many, and not an all-knowing authority? Won't it? A little more and I might convince myself, make good excuses for that one unwise word –

All I could think was: *Now I owe a debt to her: to Ruric, and to Orthe.*

The *arniac* had grown cold, and Calil bent forward to adjust the spirit lamp that heated it. These walls muffle sound. Nothing could be heard from the other cell-hive rooms below and either side of us. Calil bel-Rioch sat back.

"Well," she said, "then there's no one to judge the truth of my visions of the Empire – except myself."

I made an inarticulate protest. She didn't hear. There was a look on that cold Golden face, so that I thought, This is a turning point for her, but how? *Why?* What has she just chosen to do? Could I have stopped her?

Calil, almost under her breath, added, "And I have nothing to fear from *her.*"

Nothing to fear – and nothing to gain. If I didn't have it implanted in my memory by the Tower, where did that Rakviri vision come from? If Molly experienced it too, was it exterior to us? I don't know. Oh, you can say that when the Hexenmeister messed up my mind, he used data from the Tower Archives –

That is perfectly rational as an explanation: *why can't I believe it?*

I sat sweating, dry-mouthed.

Calil, still with that new deliberation in her face, turned her head for a moment towards the window; looking towards the dark heat-soaked landscape, the bitter sterile sea.

"Have I seen the Golden?" My voice cracked. "Have you? I don't know."

Calil bel-Rioch said, "I have seen. I do see."

She reached, without looking at me, and her six-fingered hand closed over mine. Scale-dry and warm, and I felt as if that touch went beneath my skin and marked me clear down to the bone.

"When the Elansiir was a garden land, and not a desert. . . . I see the City Over The Inland Sea, in a bright day, in a time of war – "

Between one word and the next, vision flooded up; and then I didn't know whether she spoke, or I, or both of us:

"The City Over The Inland Sea . . . ."

"*Chiruzeth,* shining . . . ."

★

226

The sound of the sea, lapping at cyclopean wharfs. . . .

Light blooms into colours. There is a sudden scent on the air, heavy, sweet, an odour of summer. Humid heat. The light, that strange radiance, comes from chiruzeth: chiruzeth that shines with living light.

Above me, the suspended city blocks out the sun.

Under the gigantic pillars of chiruzeth that support the city, dark green shadows hang in the sea depths. Great soaring spans, curving over and up and across, their shadow falling on the Inland Sea. And in infinite distance I see a rim of clear water, shining gold: the distant skyline, between the city and the sea.

The towers of that incredibly-supported cityscape merge with the pale-blue sky, and with daystars that shine in constellations wholly unrecognizable. Small figures move on the towers, thin and intensely bright.

And chiruzeth shines: blue, blue-white, diamond-brilliant. That light touches deep instincts: a longing for gardens, for isles where darkness never comes; a world quite other than this, shot through with fire and light unbearable.

And one of us says, "There is the city of our enemies. Have you the heart to do this?", *and the other answers,* "I can, and I do, and I will."

We stand long enough to see the sunlight fade on the city, and the twilight come and go. The light of the sun shines level under the city, in the air between it and the sea. Above, mile upon mile of towers, bridges, streets, battlements, cupolas, fountains. Now the City Over The Inland Sea lies like a dream of stone, under stars so brilliant they fuse together, burn in a sky like white phosphorus. A few sphere-lights cluster under eaves, or gleam as signals for flyers to land. At the foot of one of the great spans, that is also a bridge-way up into the city, we stand: and a faint and living luminescence clings to the chiruzeth.

"Because we have entered the city, a wasteland will grow here. Because we have entered the city, great ones will go to corruption, their flesh will lie unconsumed – "

" – because we have entered the city. We are the bringers of death. How shall we enter?"

And I see her with starlight on her face, that gold-dust skin, that whitefire mane: see her eyes that are yellow as childhood innocence and flowers. She kneels down on the cold earth. The span and the bridge-arch are before her.

"Go and cry: Zilkezra is dead, Zilkezra of the High Lands is dead and come to corruption, and her flesh must not lie unconsumed. And when you come to the first gate, cry this cry, and they will send out the people of Santhendor'lin-sandru to carry me home, and commit my flesh to their bodies. And cry this cry at the second gate, and they will send word into the city that all may see me pass, and all the slave race and beastmen shall be shut within walls, and so I shall pass into the city. And when you have passed the third gate, cry this cry, and Santhendor'lin-sandru, Phoenix Emperor, he himself shall come to do that which is necessary for one of his blood, and so I shall pass into the city, and so the city shall pass away."

I say, "Are you determined on this?"

"I am as we all are: I have no kin, and none to follow me. I am determined on the death of my enemies. Will you do this?"

"I can, I do, I will."

And I walk up the slope of that chiruzeth span, one of the supports of the city. Nothing beneath me but stone and air. And there are none but slaves at the great arch, that race we bred up from our blood and from night-hunters in the northern fens: claw-handed, rough-maned, with translucent skin across their eyes. They cover their faces, seeing one of the Golden blood. I speak:

"Zilkezra is dead, Zilkezra of the High Lands is dead and come to corruption, and her flesh must not lie unconsumed."

In this time of war the gates are shut, no flyers scour the night sky. The wind off the sea is cold. At last comes the guard of the first gate, a woman of Golden blood:

"Enter the city, blood-kin of Santhendor'lin-sandru. Bring that dead flesh into the city, and there shall be done what must be done. Only forgive us that we take from you robes and weapons."

She calls our people (slave races must not touch flesh of us) and six of them bring a bier, and set upon it the naked body of Zilkezra, that does not move nor breathe nor speak. And I walk naked beside it as they carry it into the city, and to the second gate.

Here there are few sphere-lights, and so massive are the buildings round us, blocking out the sky, that I know I see scarcely a tenth of their bulk.

"Zilkezra is dead, Zilkezra of the High Lands is dead and come to corruption, and her flesh must not lie unconsumed. Let the people of our blood come and see her brought home to the halls of Santhendor'lin-sandru."

The commander of the second gate is a young man, who speaks to his guards. I see them go forth into the dark streets. Their footsteps call out the echo of an echo: dim memory of that space that lies below us, between the city and the sea. The commander speaks:

"Enter the city, blood-kin of Santhendor'lin-sandru. Bring that dead flesh into the city, and he will do what must be done. Only forgive us that we bind your hands and shackle your feet: the living and the dead."

And so we pass on into the City Over The Inland Sea: six of Golden blood who carry her bier, Zilkezra who does not move nor breathe nor speak; and her hands and feet are tied with silken cords, and my hands and feet are

228

shackled with iron, in this time of war. And as I follow, I see how on great terraces, and flights of steps, and in entrances to wide avenues, and on seven-span bridges, the people come out to watch the procession pass. And these are true Golden, white manes like fire in the night's chill, eyes gold and cold with the sight of death.

At the third gate I cry the cry:

"Zilkezra is dead, Zilkezra of the High Lands is dead and come to corruption, and her flesh must not lie unconsumed. Let Santhendor'lin-sandru, Phoenix Emperor, come to do what must be done."

And the third gate opens, admitting us to that city-within-a-city where scarcely a light shows, the spider-heart and lair of the Emperor. I follow the bier up a wide and great flight of steps, to a terrace that lies before carved doors and pillars and an entrance all in darkness. There they lay down the bier, and she lies without motion or breath or speech: the colours of corruption already gleaming under the surface of her skin.

"_____ ___ _____ __ _____"

"___ _____ ___"

"_____ __ _____ ___ _____"

An echo comes back from those gleaming blue-grey walls of chiruzeth. The ancient tongue of the bloodline of the Golden Empire. I see how the guards step back from the bier, and she lies with her face to the cold stars: Zilkezra of the High Lands, sister to Santhendor'lin-sandru.

"_____ ___ _____"

"__ _____ _ ___"

Unwillingly our tongues echo his, compelled to it. And he, Santhendor'lin-sandru: tall and thin and bright, whitefire, and his eyes as yellow as summer, as yellow as the sun on the Inland Sea. He stands in the shadow of the pillars.

I raise the cry:

"Zilkezra is dead, Zilkezra of the High Lands is dead and come to corruption, and her flesh must not lie unconsumed."

And Santhendor'lin-sandru laughs. He holds up slender hands, gloved in some substance light and impenetrable. That laughter is soft acid.

"O brave, sister! What, have you swallowed poison for my sake? And am I to forget our long enmity, and shroud your poison corpse in my own body? Will you have me go into nothingness, as you have gone? O, sister, no! For I will not do it. Not a drop of your blood, not a morsel of your flesh will I eat – "

Shock radiates out from that focal point, his voice. I hear the crowd cry at this sacrilege, and I hear him laugh again. He holds up one gloved hand, and in it the knife shines: gleams once against the dark.

" – but I will scatter you, blood and body! See, here, what I do now. And you have killed yourself for nothing!"

*My hands and feet are shackled, I can only shuffle forward; and she – she!
– is shackled and bound before him. I protest:*

"She lives! She yet lives – "

*Before I can speak again, Santhendor'lin-sandru throws himself down full-
length on her body and slashes wildly. She cries out, face streaming blood, a
cry that thrills through the stone city. His knife slashes the cord that binds her
hands, half severs her wrist. Zilkezra throws wide her arms and scatters blood-
drops. Santhendor'lin-sandru springs back, face wet with her blood. The
guards run; the crowd seethes in panic, and she – on her feet, face slashed
open, laughing – she gives me one look of pure triumph:*

"So: my revenge. So: my love. *So.*"

*And then, almost tenderly, to Santhendor'lin-sandru; who stares in frozen
panic at her blood on his hands:*

"That will not hurt you, lover, brother. My poison is not for you. Not
yet for you. Zilkezra is dead, Zilkezra of the High Lands is dead and
come to corruption, and here her body will lie, unconsumed."

*She stoops and picks up the knife, and draws the blade across her throat.
The skin puckers as the metal draws it, and then parts: raw flesh pushes up
and out; blood rills down her breast as she falls.*

And he looks up at me in bewilderment, Santhendor'lin-sandru.

"*What revenge is it – for her to come here and make herself dead meat, and
harm no one else?*"

I kneel down beside him, and wipe a little of her blood from the chiruzeth.

"Not all poisons are for us, you who shall be called Santhendor'lin-
sandru, Phoenix Emperor and – Last Emperor."

*Her blood, warm and rich, can incubate the virus, the death she and others
have created. Could not the slave races create that bloodborne sterility that
makes ours the last generation? Well and so: she has made a death that,
cancerous, turns things to feed on their own substance and transform
themselves. . . .*

"See."

*Already, the faint shine of the living chiruzeth has dimmed. He reaches out
to touch a mark, a lichen, a flower: chiruzeth is turning under his hand to
dead crystal. Spreading as rapidly as ice forms on water, as swiftly as a crack
in a mirror – spreading to the nearer pillars, the terrace, the towers of this
chiruzeth city – spreading unstoppably now, until even this earth, even this sea
itself, are turned to crystalline death –*

"She brought it. She freed it. She has given you a great gift, brother
of Zilkezra. She has given you the death of all cities, the death of the
Empire."

*The night air begins to shimmer. As that genetically-engineered virus
spreads, multiplying as it causes chiruzeth to transform to dead matter, the*

energies it releases will kill almost as many as this plague of stone itself.

The City Over The Inland Sea will shine, a beacon, a brilliance. Shine as other cities in the Elansiir and the north will shine also – others have their vengeances, too.

"__ _____ _____"

I can't name it, human tongues can't speak so; and Calil bel-Rioch, her eyes full still with vision, can only stumble for the name the Last Emperor (his face filled with love of his sister) gave to that weapon, and in poor translation say at last, " 'Ancient light'."

PART FOUR

CHAPTER 19

Recognizable Strangers

How could I have told her?

Ten days later and a weary monologue of self-justification is still playing in my head: sooner or later Calil would have heard, her people listen to Company gossip, they'd hear, 'the first envoy was tricked into believing one of these natives is immortal' . . . oh, she would have heard without me to tell her!

The shuttle grounded. Tact took me out of it ahead of Cory Mendez – a small figure waved a greeting, and even in the dimness of first twilight I could see it was Doug, leaving his own grounded shuttle to meet us.

First twilight smelt of rain recently fallen, the flagstones underfoot slick with damp. Mist began to rise. Light grew swiftly, the east a magnesium flare; and I smelt the wind and rubbed cold hands together and, as Carrick's Star cleared the horizon, began to walk away from the foot of the shuttle-ramp. A full minute later, the echo of my footsteps came back from distant walls.

"Good timing," Doug greeted me. "The first *takshiriye* came in on the ships from Kasabaarde yesterday."

Then his gaze went past me to the shuttle, that was marked with a Peace Force logo.

"Molly's going ahead with this? Without consultation?"

The light grew stronger. I walked on a few paces across the square, seeing the city take shape round me. Mossgrass rooted in the crevices of the paving underfoot, blue-grey fronds tightly curled. The arch of the sky was milky, freckled with daystars, and I could taste on my lips the sweet salt of Orthean waters; could hear the sound of the sea.

"Douggie, come on; it was obvious after the talks in Kasabaarde broke down, the Company would have to do something."

"You *approve* of this?"

The first time I came to Tathcaer, I came aboard a *jath*-ship, a ship that catches the dawn tide as it sails the barren sandy coast of Melkathi, and comes to where river meadows of mossgrass are blue and grey, mist still curling where *marhaz* and *skurrai* graze. And there, held between the two arms of the Oranon River, is the island-city of Tathcaer. . . .

The air above was cold and vast now; and I wondered, Are there ships up there already? Cory Mendez' Peace Force ships, docked in the

Company orbital station? Are they landing on the Coast now? And when they see that threat, what will Sethri and the Anzhadi do?

I said, "Storms won't keep those ships in harbour forever. What do you plan to do when the *hiyek* fleets sail north to the Hundred Thousand?"

There was a high flush of anger on his round face.

"This is an internal matter. Internal hostilities. The Company has no right to bring its own forces in!" He took a breath. "I'll see how home office reacts to this. And how people in general like the idea – I don't think PanOceania is going to find itself very popular back on Earth."

Now the day shone clear, the white gold of early morning, and I stand in the great Square below the Citadel, in the heart of the white city, Tathcaer.

That walkway that zigzags up the sheer cliff-face behind me, up to the top of the Citadel crag, that's where I went with Haltern Beth'ru-elen when he took me to my first audience with the *T'An Suthai-Telestre* – light shines on the rock now, and on the masses of blue vines that have overgrown all the cliff-walk, choking it, that hang out questing tendrils on the morning air; vines that spill down to cover the deserted gatehouse and archway where the Crown Guard stood.

"Douggie, if you're thinking of starting a media propaganda campaign . . . just be sure you're right."

"I am. I am," he said, "and I'm amazed that you can't see it."

He broke off then, as Cory Mendez left the shuttle and came to join us, be-ringed hands behind her back. Her rings clinked. "If we're going to go down into the city – "

Doug said, "I'll do my best to lead you, Commander. I'm afraid it isn't easy to get around in the city yet. Lynne – Lynne?"

Only the deserted Citadel stands unchanged, each tower and balcony and cupola and terrace clear in the light that puts precise shadows on luminous grey masonry.

"I didn't think I'd see the day. Douggie, I didn't ever think I'd see the day."

I turn one way, and there on the east side of the Square are high walls, and beyond them the dome of the great Wellhouse that imprisoned us when we returned from Kasabaarde: Blaize, Rodion, Havoth-jair and me. The gates hang askew in the wall's archway, and through the gap can be glimpsed a courtyard, and fountains that are now dry.

Cory Mendez tapped her fingers impatiently together. There was a CAS-IV in her belt-holster.

"Are we likely to find native authorities here?"

"They won't be happy about the shuttle landing," I realized.

Doug said, "This is the only open space on the island of sufficient size for a shuttle to land. But, as you imply, we're stretching *telestre* custom to have it here at all. If I might suggest a course of action, we should attempt to get down to the harbour on foot. One of the old Dominion consulates used to be there, on Westhill."

The silence was broken by the raw, metallic cry of a *rashaku*-lizardbird. It was enough: suddenly there was a catch in my throat, water in my eyes. Once I saw a *rashaku* cling to an awning-pole here, the sun bright through its spread pinions, and that on a day when the whole Square was full of *telestre*-Ortheans – *s'ans* in robes and bright tunics, gems and *harur*-blades shining, some with young *ashiren* sat up on their shoulders; city tradesmen and merchants and young Ortheans from the Artisans Quarter, and those in Mercenaries Guild leathers, and Peir-Dadeni riders with their plumed manes. . . . And we sat the whole day here and played *ochmir*, Haltern and Blaize and I, at Midsummer-Tenyear, when the new *T'An Suthai-Telestre* was to be named.

Emotion is never less than ambiguous. I am hurt by the desolation of this city, so there is some love for it in me; but this, now, is a city of strangers. Those were the last few days before the treachery of Ruric Orhlandis was made known. I think of her now, in the Tower, perpetrating that massive necessary fraud –

There is a link between vision and memory and the Tower, and I don't know what it is.

". . . something on her mind," Cory Mendez was saying. "For a few days now. Lynne, shall we go?"

"What? Yes, of course."

We began to walk across the Square, leaving the shuttle secure behind us; moving away from Citadel crag, that is the point of this arrowhead-shaped river-island. It seemed we hardly moved, so large a space the Square is, and so empty. No crowds, no *skurrai-jasin* carriages.

"Who drove these people out of this settlement?" Mendez asked Doug Clifford, as we walked.

"No one. They decided they didn't need it."

"And now they do?"

"Haven't you realized, Commander? They're coming here to make a new *T'An Suthai-Telestre*, a new Crown."

Corazon Mendez, all Peace Force, said, "It doesn't do to allow political unrest when a war-sequence is in operation. We could stop that."

Seeing Doug's face, I hastily cut in with, "That might be unwise."

"It would be an unjustifiable intervention," Doug said.

Cory smiled. "Still trying diplomacy, Douglas? Good. Just remember, I have to cope with what happens when diplomacy breaks down."

I let them argue, and walked ahead. The remaining sides of the Square are taken up with the white façades of low-roofed blocks of buildings. We were coming to the gap between them, that marks the beginning of the one named, paved road in all the city, that runs from here clear down to the harbour: Crown Way.

There is a link between vision and memory –

I should go to the Company, to Molly; but Molly thinks of that experience in Rakviri as a 'side-effect' of alien technology. Who else can I go to? When I am desperately, steadfastly trying not to think of a room in Kel Harantish, and the face of Calil bel-Rioch. Who?

At the top of Crown Way, I stopped.

Tathcaer lay sprawled below me in the early-morning sun. The light made a clarity of the air. I looked down the hill at the pale-plaster *telestre*-houses, with their blank outside walls and inner courtyards, and their cisterns now standing dry. I saw no smoke rising anywhere. Only a sprawling confusion of white and sand-coloured buildings, with narrow unnamed alleys between them; and now as my eye grew keener I could pick out landmarks: the Guild-Ring, Wellhouse domes, the barracks on that prestigious district known as The Hill, home of the *T'An* Commander. . . .

Silence. No dawn bells. All the alleys are choked with the feather-fronds of *lapuur*, growing unchecked, and the sporeborne red-and-black branches of *ziku*.

Melkathi summer: the smoke from brush-fires obscuring the sun. Orhlandis telestre, burning. And she, cornered, ash-stained; only the harur-nilgiri bright in her hand. She who had been T'An Commander and T'An Melkathi; and there is no one now who will not willingly see her exiled – I wanted, suddenly and desperately, to hear her tell me how she'd survived from then till now; what had happened, what the truth is.

And will that tell me what really happened between Calil and myself?

Looking east, I see the wider and more shallow branch of the Oranon River, sparkling under ten or twelve bridges; and beyond it, blue meadows fading away into the hills of Ymir. And, looking west, there is a deep and narrow channel, once crossed by the Salathiel ferry; and in the distance, mudflats, and the chalk headlands of the Rimon coast. Not an acre of this land but I have memories of it.

As Doug and Cory came up with me, Doug said, "It will be difficult crossing the city, I'm afraid. I've only just got here myself; I didn't realize quite how bad it is."

I gazed south, across the dips and hollows of the city and its clustered buildings. Two hills rose up. On them are squat brown forts, pocked with the black shadows of window-arches. On Easthill I once had a *telestre*-house, Easthill-Malkys; but now at four or five miles' distance I can't make out individual buildings. The Westhill *telestre*-houses I didn't often visit.

Invisible from here, over the saddle between those two hills, lies Tathcaer's harbour. The two branches of the Oranon rejoin there at the estuary. It was the harbour I first saw, under a daystarred sky, crowded with all the ships of a trading port, and the young Haltern there to meet the Earth envoy. I don't know if I can stand to see that harbour silted up, deserted. . . .

I wonder if, when Ortheans return on Her earth, they feel the same: neither the place nor the person are the same?

"Where now?" Cory Mendez asked.

I put all doubts and problems into that corner of my mind reserved for procrastination. In that moment of searching, I caught sight of what I'd been looking for: "There." I pointed to where *telestre*-houses, blurred by distance, went down a long slope to the place where the Salathiel ferry used to run.

A thread of smoke rose up into the bright morning air.

"Mother of God!" Cory Mendez swore, stopping to push away pale green fronds of *lapuur*. Heat-sensitive, the feathery plants coiled with vegetable slowness around her bony wrists. She added, "Damn all technology embargoes – what I'd give now for a laser-cutter!"

"Depends how badly you want to be in the middle of a forest fire," I observed. "Looks like it's been a dry summer."

The walls of this choked alley were carpeted with bronze foliage of *kazsis*-nightvine; sapling *lapuur* rooted in the earth. A ribbon of blue sky overhead showed noontide stars. I picked black spines of *ziku* out of my sleeve, and was showered with that tree's red spore cases. Two- or three-year growth, most of this; equally hard to push through or walk over. Stems of *kazsis* gave soggily underfoot. Doug Clifford emerged from the next alley-entrance, beating away swarms of *chirith-goyen* and *kekri*-flies that shone like mica in the hot sun. He wiped sweat from his red face.

"I can't see a thing," he confessed. "We'll have to try getting up to a roof-top again to get our bearings."

How can I cross half the Hundred Thousand and then get lost crossing half a city? I grinned, thinking how I'd asked that question in exasperation ten years ago. Tathcaer has a way of doing that to me.

"Four hours," Doug added gloomily. His coverall was dusty with *ziku* spores, his boots snagged with the thorn of *hanelys*-tanglebush; he looked as uncomfortable as a ruffled cat. "I despair of reporting to Molly Rachel that we've spent *four hours* trying to cross a native settlement. . . ."

"Douggie, you're cute when you're angry," I said, quiet so that the

Mendez didn't hear; and decided to ignore the explosively obscene comment that D. Clifford made in reply.

Corazon checked her wristlink. "I'll call in at the end of the hour. The satellites – "

I held up a hand for silence. They waited.

"There," I said. *Kazsis*-stems crunched as I climbed through to the blocked end of the alley.

The sound of voices grew more distinct.

Two spindle-trunked *ziku* grew up at the alley's end. Their scarlet foliage cast shadows on the sandstone masonry of the *telestre*-house walls, that here stood twenty-five or thirty feet high. I stepped between them, feeling they made a natural entrance to this unnatural clearing. A fire had burned here, perhaps last summer – young *ziku* and *lapuur* sprouted in the blackened earth, mossgrass began to cover the tumbled masonry. Five or six Ortheans were sitting on fallen stones, boots stretched out idly on the flagstone floor, now open to the sky. There was a low Wellhouse dome beyond. Then a young male looked lazily up at the *telestre*-wall above my head.

"Right, Hana, they're here. You can go back on watch."

A lithe, yellow-maned male dropped from sound to broken wall, sure-footed, and from that masonry to the earth. "Shadow take it! Send someone else. I'm tired of baking in that sun."

There was laughter: the others glanced up from where broken walls and seedling *lapuur* protected them from the heat. Mercenaries, by their dress; by the *nilgiri*-blades and *nazari*-knives, and the *ochmir* board that lay between them on the rubble.

A dark-maned female raised her head. She lay on her back, face in the shade, eyes veiled with translucent membrane. "I'll go on watch – if you go to the Wellhouse, Hana." She got to her feet, turning casually to me; "You *s'aranthi* want the Wellhouse, yes?"

Doug emerged from the tangle of vegetation at the alley-mouth, followed by Cory Mendez, her hand resting on the CAS-IV holster.

"Yes," I said.

The city had a quiet so intense that, when no one spoke, you could hear the shifting of warm summer air; could almost hear the sunlight falling on the stones. Each small sound was magnified: the creak of leather boots, jingle of *harur*-blade harness as the woman walked across the burnt earth. I heard some heavy animal shift padded feet, and saw the shaggy bronze coats of *marhaz* in the shadow of a wall.

"Who's *T'An* in the city?" I asked a male with braided mane, and northern province dress, whose belt-badges proclaimed him captain. "Can you tell me who has your contract?"

240

"I won't answer your questions," the male said, and his gaze went to each of us in turn. *Three offworlders, all armed, one plainly from the paramilitary forces* – not in those words, but I saw the thought in his face. And something I'd never seen in an Orthean before: that half-ashamed and half-defiant ignoring of hi-tech weaponry. He said, "Hana, take them to the Wellhouse."

I saw, across that stretch of rubble and sunlight, the low dome of a Wellhouse. An Orthean stood at the door. The scarlet mane was a flare against the brown brickwork, and she lifted a hand in casual salute, and I recognized the Earthspeaker Cassirur Almadhera.

"One thing occurs to me," Commander Cory Mendez said. "The Company must station a detachment here, as well as on the southern continent." She paused, then lifted her wrist to key in the comlink transmitter. "I'll relay through to the orbiter and check – my squads should be making hi-orbital docking about now."

Doug Clifford blinked. "Out of interest, what size force did the Company assign here?"

"A small force," the white-haired woman said, "three squads in fifteen F9os; that's two hundred men. If it wasn't for the ban on anything except medium-tech, I could handle these assignments with a tenth of the manpower. PanOceania abides by home regulations, of course. . . ." Here her smile became cynical.

"You don't change, Cory," Doug said. He couldn't hide his distaste. Corazon Mendez shrugged.

"You and the groundsiders who make 'humane' legislation ought to try it, Douglas. Try forcing a cease-fire when you can hardly do more than bluff. These beings here are alien, they don't think like we do, but they'd understand a seismic-nuclear missile if they saw one demonstrated!"

"*Cory* –"

She glanced at me as we began to walk towards the Wellhouse. "That would put a stop to your 'farmers' war', Lynne. As it is, all I can do is threaten – and a little more."

Inside the Wellhouse, Cassirur Almadhera didn't seem at all surprised to see us. I assumed she'd had word of the shuttle's landing earlier on.

"I'll take you down into the city to meet with the others who are here," she said, with a slight inclination of the head that acknowledged both Doug and Cory Mendez. "You must eat first, I think. The *ashiren* will fetch food. Christie, Blaize Meduenin gave me your greeting when he returned from Kasabaarde. I didn't expect to see you again in the Hundred Thousand so soon."

"You've heard what's happening on the Coast, of course? Yes. We have to talk. Earth and your new *T'An Suthai Telestre*, when you have one."

"Soon. Soon now."

Cassirur's children ushered Doug and Cory through into the Wellhouse dining-chamber. I followed. Heat had robbed me of hunger. When I came to the central part of the dome I went on and into it, hardly aware that Cassirur Almadhera followed me.

Midday sun slanted through the roof-slot of the low dome. Where it fell on the mouth of the Well, bright coruscations danced from the water's surface and cast mutable shadows of light on the white walls.

Here is Your daughter from a far world. Receive her name. Words spoken by the Earthspeaker Theluk in a northern Wellhouse, with Ruric as my second; none of us knowing then that one would die and the other be proven traitor, and I – I would forget that naming ceremony, because I never knew what it meant.

"Who's here from the Freeport?"

She said, "Haltern Beth'ru-elen. Blaize Meduenin. I've had word on the *rashaku*-relay that the *T'Ans* of Melkathi, Rimon, and Roehmonde will be here soon; and even that the Andrethe will leave Peir-Dadeni to come here."

"To an abandoned city," I said, still half in the past.

"Ah, that was Suthafiori's death, and the summer of the white plague." She smoothed her green *chirith-goyen* robe with brown six-fingered hands, and then wiped tendrils of red mane from her forehead; squinting up at the inner curve of the dome with unveiled eyes. "Tathcaer was never abandoned, Christie. Without Wellkeepers, summer lightning would have razed it. Now we need it again, we come back to it." She paused, looked at me. "Different from our meeting in the Freeport, this."

Just a few months have put us here, I thought. The Company arrives, the Coast goes to war, the Hundred Thousand fears Witchbreed technology, others crave it – and then the Tower. . . .

"I said in Morvren that you had the look of one named for the Goddess," Cassirur said. "One sick with past-memories. You've lost that – or it's changed. Does She still know your name?"

That abrupt, natural change from politician to Earthspeaker. I smiled to take the irreverence out of what I said: "Probably not."

Her dark eyes went cloudy, membrane sliding across them. "If I were a superstitious woman, I'd wonder if that wasn't because you've been to that abomination, Kel Harantish."

"You trust one Desert Coast city, you Earthspeakers – but do you know as much about Kasabaarde as you do about Kel Harantish?"

She laughed, a short bark that sent her head back. Then she shrugged. "Perhaps the Hundred Thousand doesn't listen as closely to the Tower as you believe. We trust ourselves only. Not outlanders. And not *s'aranthi*."

She knelt, one knee on the rim of the circular Well, trailing a claw-nailed hand in the water. Her slit-backed robe pulled aside to show the complex braids of her mane, rooting down her spine.

"And when it comes to war, Cassirur?"

Without turning round, she said, "Many will go to the Goddess. But we meet, and part, and meet again, and we do not forget. And the earth is always here for us again."

A steep western scarp falls several hundred feet to a plain, desolate as these hills, that stretches out to the horizon. Sun reflects off something – water? snow? No: it ends in sharp edges, splinters. . . . I kneel under a daystarred sky, feeling dirt and grit beneath my hands, and there the earth itself changes. Crystalline mirror: each shard of stone or frond of mossgrass transmuted to a fragile, sterile petrification –

I made the hard-learned effort and pulled free. Cassirur looked up at me as I said harshly, "*Is* the earth always there? You ask the Coast families. They'd use Witchbreed weapons if they could, or Earth technology; and you're going to find your only way out is that technology – improve food production here and share land with those who are starving – "

The scarlet-maned Orthean woman got to her feet. Her expression told me I'd miscalculated, broached the subject too soon and too baldly.

"We're not *hiyeks*, Christie. We won't take offworlder science. We won't take that path that leads to a new Golden Empire and a new destruction!"

This untidy, middle-aged Orthean female, with little of the Earthspeaker about her; she spoke now with a hard anger in her voice. It was automatic (but I disliked myself for doing it) to go straight for the weak point and attack: "Has Barris Rakviri come to Tathcaer?" I asked. "Or is he still back on Rakviri *telestre*, making Witchbreed relics into functioning technology?"

The Almadhera held my gaze for a long moment. "Barris Rakviri is dead."

"What? *How?* When did it happen?"

"A month ago. We gave him *saryl-kabriz* in his food," the Earthspeaker said. She spoke quite calmly. "He died. Jaharien Rakviri chose to follow him, and he took the *saryl-kabriz* poison also. And that is an end to Witchbreed science in Rakviri *telestre*."

Light from the Well rippled across her pale features and green robe, and in the silence I heard *ashiren* in the dining-hall, and Doug and Cory's voices raised in argument, and I could only stare at this Orthean woman that I had thought I might be coming to know. What's more appalling? I wondered. What she says or how she said it?

"You killed him?"

Cassirur Almadhera inclined her head. "I killed him. I suppose by that I'm the cause of Jaharien's death also, and for that I'm sorry."

"How can you stand there and say that!"

"I sent him to a joy," she said, "that *I* would sooner have than any of the shadows it casts on earth, which are love and ecstasy. I gave him *saryl-kabriz* poison to close his eyes, and death to open them in that bright realm; poison to close his mouth, and death to open it to breathe in the fire of Her world."

We meet, and part, and meet again, and we do not forget.

I stared at her, and she smiled. It was warm and friendly, and a little humorous. She made a gesture to follow her into the dining-hall, and walked through the archway.

Pain made me aware that I was digging my nails into my palms. What I feel is shock, I thought. Is outrage. It is *not* familiarity, there's no way I can have Orthean memories of what it feels like to have past-lives, no way I can be thinking how different it is from how the Witchbreed glutted on death, fed on cessation, worshipped extinction, but Ortheans love the cycle of turn and return *because that is a delusion.*

I thought *I am human, there's no part of me that's Orthean, much as I want that* and the light of Carrick's Star sent ripples across the curve of that radiant dome.

It was some while later that the silence was broken by footsteps, and Doug Clifford entered the dome, glancing up at it as he came in.

"I'm going to open up the old government quarters on Westhill," he said. "There's hi-tech equipment under store there, we ought to be able to contact the Company and the orbiter. I want to know how they're reacting to Orthe at home."

I said, "The people here aren't going to be co-operative. We'll have our work cut out. And it won't be long now before Coast warships can cross the Inner Sea."

That day was Durestha Seventhweek Nineday, a Fast-day; the next, Durestha Eighthweek Firstday, a Feast-day. It dawned with the clarity of summer, drowned daystars in a mid-morning heat haze, shone warm on the neglected stonework of the Dominion government quarters.

". . . the department has had to come down on the government's side," Stephen Perrault's image told me from the holotank. I didn't turn to watch, but stayed looking out of the window. His message-blip continued: "That means the multicorporates want to close us down now, and open up a new Liaison Department. One that they can control. I can stall them for a few more weeks, but we need you here to fight for us!"

That's my career, I thought. It seemed faint, far away, drowned in the blaze of colour that is Tathcaer: the white city in summer. This was a small *telestre*-house, Westhill-Ahrentine, and from its first-floor windows I could see the ferry and the western end of the harbour. Ships jostled, moored at the docks, and brightly-robed crowds seethed round them. A constant influx of Ortheans and *marhaz*-riderbeasts streamed from the Salathiel ferry. Once on the island, they vanished into tangled alleyways that were rapidly becoming cleared. The city was coming alive again.

And I just want to bask in it, I thought, that long and golden summer of Tathcaer. . . . All the while, urgency nagged me. Beacon-forts were manned all along the coast, the *rashaku*-relay and heliographs brought nothing but warnings to watch the sea. . . .

Stephen Perrault's voice ceased. I realized I'd paid him no attention, would have to replay the blip. And then as I turned away from the window, for the first time since my return, I heard the harsh carillon of the city's noon bells.

Doug came through from the next room. "The comlink's out again." He frowned. "I haven't heard anything about reaction at home yet. Which indicates either a superfluity of apathy on their part, or that my esteemed masters are failing to authorize media coverage."

Something of the Cliffordian humour in that, for all that his was a genuine concern. I said, "Could be they're keeping their heads down. My deputy, Perrault, says the Companies are on the warpath again."

"I have to confess, if I were a national government, *I* wouldn't quarrel with a multicorporate Company whose GNP exceeds mine by several orders of magnitude. . . ."

He moved to the window, looking down at the bustle on the quay.

"The Almadhera tells me the church is reopening the big Wellhouse up by the Citadel. You said we should be talking to Earthspeakers and Wellkeepers, Lynne, are you coming up there with me?"

"I'll come," I said. "Where's Cory?"

"Our esteemed Corazon. Now that," Douggie said, "I would very much like to know. She's Company, not government. I have no authority over her."

Do I? I wondered. As special advisor? Dubious. Only Molly has that authority; and Molly, damn her, doesn't care one jot about the low-tech Hundred Thousand.

"If we can take a *skurrai*-carriage across the city – "

"You go," I interrupted him. I leaned both hands on the sill of the window-arch, looking down into the street. "I'll join you in an hour or two. It was about time some of them started coming to us, instead of us running after them."

Two Orthean males were plodding up the steep alley to the entrance of Westhill-Ahrentine. One, dark and in middle years, I had a feeling I ought to recognize from somewhere. The other, supporting himself with a staff and his companion's arm, but gazing round with a bright-eyed curiosity, was Haltern n'ri n'suth Beth'ru-elen.

CHAPTER 20

A Visitor to Westhill-Ahrentine

"Give you greeting," the dark male said. "We have met, *t'an* Christie. You may not recall. I'm Nelum Santhil, of Rimnith *telestre*."

Dear God, Nelum Santhil! I covered shock. Haltern was regarding me with covert amusement. I stared at the dark male, with his thin Melkathi robes, and short-cropped mane, and I would not have recognized the man who, ten years ago, had been Portmaster of Ales-Kadareth in Melkathi – who allowed SuBannasen and later Orhlandis *telestres* to ship in illegal gold from Kel Harantish, who then betrayed both SuBannasen and Orhlandis. . . .

Haltern's staff tapped on the floorboards as he crossed the room, and sat in one of the couch-chairs by the window. The sun gleamed on his fine, white mane. With deliberate casualness, he said, "Give you greeting, Christie. Nelum Santhil's newly arrived from Ales-Kadareth, where they named him *T'An* Melkathi."

It was a major effort to keep still. *T'An Melkathi?* But that's Orthean politics. I offered herb-tea to both of them, and Nelum Santhil accepted, and as I poured it from a stone jug I thought, *Hal, you're a wicked old man!* And you've never given up your ambition of having the edge over *s'aranthi*.

"And what can I do for you and the *T'An* Melkathi?" I asked, sitting down beside Hal on the couch-chair, proud of my self-possession.

"As representatives of two provinces – ah," Hal interrupted himself. With a charming air of apology, he went on: "That's something else I should perhaps have mentioned. Morvren Freeport has been foolhardy enough to name a Beth'ru-elen as their Seamarshal – that is, myself."

I looked at him. Lines puckered the reptilian skin round that neat mouth; unveiled eyes were brilliant, pale, and lively.

"Got any more like that?" I slipped automatically into colloquial Peir-Dadeni, that Santhil wouldn't know. "Don't think I can take too many shocks to the system – very funny, Hal."

He gave way and chuckled, resting a claw-hand on my arm. It wouldn't be so bad if I wasn't glad to see the old rogue, I thought, quelling exasperation. There was laughter in his eyes, and that paradoxical Orthean combination of humour and utter seriousness.

"What can we do for you?" I repeated.

"You can help make certain that the right man has a chance to become *T'An Suthai-Telestre*."

I must have glanced at Nelum Santhil because the dark male shook his head. "Not myself, *t'an S'aranth*. I only support this."

It's the *s'ans* who name one of their number to become *T'An* of a province, but to take the Crown one must – in the great Wellhouse below the Citadel, under the eyes of all gathered there – name oneself. So at the heart of all *telestre* politics and intrigue there is this final, public honesty.

"Who? Not you, Hal?" It would be like him to ask.

"Blaize n'ri n'suth Meduenin," the old male said. "The Rimon *s'ans* want to name him *T'An* Rimon and he won't hear of it; if he's not *T'An*, he can't take the Crown, and I think – Christie, disagree with me if you can – I think Blaize Meduenin is the best *T'An Suthai-Telestre* we could have now. Christie, we want you to talk to him!"

It stopped me dead. "Why him? And why me?"

"He's been a mercenary," Nelum Santhil said. "We need a Crown who knows how to fight, and who knows how to avoid fighting. All Howice *T'An*-Roehmonde knows is how to keep himself *T'An*; Geren *T'an* Ymir isn't trusted, he's been out of the Hundred Thousand too often; and The Kyre's too remote a province for people to know Bethan *T'An* Kyre – "

"Romare Kerys-Andrethe will be *T'An* Rimon if Blaize won't, and Romare is a fool," Hal said. He clasped six-fingered hands on the top of his staff, and stared down at the dusty floorboards. When he raised his head, his gaze had all the intensity of a younger man's. "Why you? Christie, you know him. You crossed the Wall of the World in his company. He'll listen to you because . . ."

"Well?" I prompted.

The old male said thoughtfully, "Because you and he should have been *arykei*, and he let the time go past. I don't say it lightly, but you're one of the few people that he trusts. If you tell him he should be *T'An* Rimon he'll believe you."

Hal, you don't change. Always manipulating people, always working behind the scenes. . . .

"He'd make a good *T'An Suthai-Telestre*, and perhaps it would be a good thing for the Coast if he were. I'm not convinced it would be the best thing for us."

Hal looked at me shrewdly. "'Us'?" Now is that the Company, or your government, or some other faction on Earth that we know nothing of?"

Voices from the street echoed in the silence, and *rashaku* cried. *Kekri*-flies danced in the window-arch, glittering blue and green. There was the scent, faint now, of *kazsis*-nightflower.

248

"Talk with him," the old male said, in his own Peir-Dadeni tongue. "Talk to him, and make up your own mind. . . ."

I looked at him. "Three words occur to me."

" 'I'll do it'?" Haltern suggested hopefully.

" 'Devious old bastard. . . .' " I managed to translate the sense of the expression. He laughed. Nelum Santhil looked at us both in bewilderment.

"I'm a little worried about something else at this moment," I said, "as I haven't seen Corazon Mendez today – "

"Commander Mendez is with Romare Kerys-Andrethe, in the barracks at Hill-Damarie. Now if that eases your mind," Hal said drily, "you can answer my question."

I said, "Where will we find Blaize Meduenin?"

Skurrai-jasin jolted across the Square, the squat reptilian beasts treading down mossgrass that had rooted between the paving-stones. Their shaggy coats and cropped, metal-capped horns gleamed in the sun. Like the others, our driver avoided the shuttles that stood locked and silent at the south end of the Square. Across at the cliff-walk, twenty or so young Ortheans with curved knives were hacking back the vines and creepers. Above, the Citadel merged with the cream-blue sky. A warm haze put blurred shadows on the stone.

Haltern signalled the *skurrai*-carriage to pause, spoke to a male leading a *marhaz*, and several yards further on did the same thing, this time talking to a young female who led one of the beasts of burden. As the *skurrai-jasin* halted before the gates of the great Wellhouse he said, "A week to the naming. We'll be ready. Ah, yes . . . you'll find Blaize in the Wellhouse here."

I got down from the carriage and then paused, resting one hand on the brightly-painted wood. I studied the unremarkable face of Nelum Santhil.

"The *T'Ans* Melkathi had bad luck when you were their Portmaster, *t'an* Santhil, I wish you better luck with yours."

The dark male winced. "*T'An* Haltern said you had a sharp wit. Are you still so bitter for your Orhlandis *arykei*?"

Haltern eased himself down from the carriage-step, clattering his staff. He made a gesture to the driver and the *skurrai-jasin* jolted away. Carrying Nelum Santhil to whatever other business a *T'An* Melkathi might now have.

"My Orhlandis . . . *arykei*?"

"The tale's told that way." Haltern smiled. "If it doesn't have you and Blaize *arykei*. Or you and Howice *T'An* Roehmonde."

Ortheans must have a very curious idea of human sexual appetite. *Howice?*

"Ruric Orhlandis won't come back to the Hundred Thousand, Christie, if that's what you're thinking."

He took my arm, leaning heavily on it. We walked up the steps and into the courtyard, where a crowd was in evidence; some talking, some cleaning, some eating. Many hailed the new Seamarshal of the Freeport with respect.

"Hal, about Ruric."

He paused, leaning on his staff. The sun gleamed on that wispy, cropped mane. I saw he still wore a *harur-nazari* blade at the belt of his white, slit-backed robe. Haltern Beth'ru-elen: come off the sidelines at last, come out of the political shadows to be recognized as Seamarshal *T'An* Morvren.

"Blaize told you I made her exile . . . permanent." Those pale eyes were less harassed, more adamantine. Then he said quietly, "I tell myself she was traitor, land-waster, exile; she would become a leader for our enemies, there was nothing else I could do, and still I don't believe it." He paused. "She dreamed no other lives. I often wonder now, will she return from the Goddess's realm? Or had she so much Golden blood that she died as they did, with no rebirth?"

It was a physical pain not to say 'she's alive!' I have risked her secrecy once, I can't do it again.

I let the silence stretch out. The old male at last began to walk on, turning his steps towards the Wellhouse entrance on the far side of the courtyard. I held his arm.

"There," Haltern said.

Blaize Meduenin stood outside the arched entrance with a group of dark-maned Ortheans. Five or six young males and females, with chain-girdled tunics, and faces masked in scarlet, ochre, and indigo paint. From the Rainbow Cities, the subtropic lands of the far south. With them was a thin male, mane a black barbed-wire tangle, tanned skin marked at ribs and hip with old white scars. Untanned leather garments marked him as being from one of the nomad tribes that live in the dead cities over the Wall of the World.

Haltern walked through the entrance into the dome-hall, beckoning for Blaize to follow. The fair-maned male excused himself from his companions. As we met, I had time to think how small the dome seemed, how shabby the tiers of stone seats leading down to the Wellmouth, and then the smell of the *becamil*-wax candles hit me; the candles they always used to illumine this dim amphitheatre. I felt as if someone had scooped my chest cavity out hollow.

"*T'An* Morvren, *t'an* Meduenin, give you greeting." A dark-maned Wellkeeper bowed as he passed us, hurrying down the tiers towards a group of other Wellkeepers and Earthspeakers. Young *ashiren* in Wellhouse robes came respectfully to offer herb-tea. Hal waved them away. Blaize's eyes met mine. He smiled. And then must turn aside to answer a query from a *s'an* in Ymirian dress; reassure him and send him away.

And here we are, I thought. Hal, frail and silver-maned, but with all the dignity of the Seamarshal about him; Blaize, whose Rimon boots and britches and sleeveless jacket were all fine; *chirith-goyen* cloth and *marhaz* leather. Here we stand, deferred to, respected; where Suthafiori and SuBannasen and Orhlandis once stood, when Blaize was a shabby mercenary, and Hal a spy, and I nothing but wide eyes and youthful enthusiasm.

"Would you have believed this?" the stocky male said, and that half-scarred face twisted into the old smile.

Hal eased himself down on to the stone tier. "Not when you hunted us at Oeth, into the Great Fens."

"Not in Corbek," I said, "when you gave false evidence against me in a Wellhouse trial."

Blaize grinned at that. Then he stood looking down at Hal, and his expression became serious. "I was a mercenary then. I was under contract, following orders. That's the way I like it. You must know that through the years I served you in Morvren, I never wanted to be *T'An*."

Haltern cupped his six-fingered hands over the top of his staff. He sighed, that frail body sagging. "We've been friends for too many years to talk of 'service' – or am I wrong in that?"

"No," Blaize protested. He looked helplessly at me. "Tell him, *S'aranth*. Why not leave the *telestres* to deal with the Coast, as they've always done?"

Haltern put in sharply, "You're a soldier. You know the difference between raiding ships and an invasion."

"And there's Earth technology to be taken into account," I said. "Earth weapons. You've – we've – got to make peace with the Coast. Or else the Company's going to let Cory's troops loose, and their stopping a war can be as nasty as others starting one. Blaize, you're trusted, the *s'ans* listen to you, for God's sake realize you have to take a stand. Be *T'An* Rimon. Be whatever else you have to."

He looked at me consideringly. Aware of falling into rhetoric, I thought, How do I say what I mean?

"And if what the Hundred Thousand decides doesn't please Earth?" he said.

"I don't give a shit about Earth – "

They both turned startled eyes on me. I felt unprotected. The one still young, the other old: soldier and politician. . . . In my panic I looked round to see if I'd been overheard. Doug Clifford was down in the group of Earthspeakers. Cory Mendez came in by the other entrance on the far side, without Romare Kerys-Andrethe. And then I saw Blaize smile, saw a silky humour in Hal's eyes.

"That's a dangerous fence to step over," Hal said quietly. "No going back. Your people, if they know, wouldn't let you."

Blaize cut in with, "Does it matter?" and embraced me; and then stepped back, and said to Haltern, "You, Beth'ru-elen. Will *you* name yourself *T'An Suthai-Telestre* when Midsummer comes?"

Those pale eyes veiled. Candlelight and light from the roof-slot put shadows on his face; Hal's face, that I never could read easily. He said, "If I were a younger man."

And Blaize, very soberly, said, "I can't carry the weight of it. I'm a fighter, not a politician. All I've learned from the years in Morvren is that no one knows enough to give orders to all the Hundred Thousand."

I said, "No one ever knows, but someone has to take the decisions all the same."

His scarred face was shrewd. "You push us into your patterns."

"Either you're being cowardly," I said, and saw the flare of anger on his face, that twisted the scar into something monstrous, "either that, or you know your own limitations. I don't know. You'd better find out soon."

"Yes," Haltern said, "we don't have much time."

We both push you unfairly, I thought. From our assumed positions of superiority, trying to force you into something we won't or can't do.

And if I were *T'An Suthai-Telestre*? In this my city of Tathcaer, a charmed midsummer circle, and outside it the warships of the Coast, Sethri's hungry face, the dream of Empire in Kel Harantish, and the offworlders who began by bringing knowledge and end by bringing guns –

"Yes," Blaize's voice interrupted, and I looked up to meet his gaze: he spoke as if he could read my thoughts.

I said, "I'm sorry we ever came here. To Carrick V."

He stood with his chin a little raised, claw-nailed hands resting on *harur*-blades. His gaze travelled round the hall – to the men and women in all the different fashions of Melkathi, Rimon, Roehmonde, Morvren, The Kyre . . . to the plain brown brick of the dome, and the shaft of light that plunged from the roof-slot to the black mouth of the shaft of the Well. The hum of voices rose and fell. *Becamil*-wax candles sputtered. A warm breeze drifted in from the courtyard, bringing the scent of *kazsis* and *marhaz* dung and cooking-fires.

He said, "Kerys Founder marked out the *telestre* boundaries. That was after the Empire fell, when there was chaos. And I love the land. I'm an outsider, I hardly see Meduenin, but it has all my memories, I'd sooner cut off this hand than see it destroyed by outlanders. To change is to destroy." Then he shrugged, and with all the mercenary's assurance, said, "Sometimes change *has* to happen."

Haltern caught my eye. And I thought, Yes, I know, only outsiders have the capacity to see such things. Outsiders like you and I and Blaize Meduenin.

"Be *T'An* Rimon," I said. "For no other reason than that I can't imagine Romare Kerys-Andrethe saying what you've just said."

Blaize broke into laughter that turned heads clear across the dome. For that moment we were as we had been: mercenary, intelligencer, envoy. Hal's wheezy chuckles racked him. I grinned.

"Let's talk more of this later," Haltern said. "Come down and speak with the Wellkeeper now. There are Earthspeakers here from all the seven provinces. I want to talk with them, hear what they say about the most distant *telestres*. They've heard of my time in Morvren. I want to know if they'll call it just another Freeport madness – the thought that men and women of the Coast could come here, and share wilderness land."

I followed him down the step to the next tier. Blaize remained standing, and I looked back and up at him.

The ex-mercenary said, "When the *s'ans* ask me again – I'll be named *T'An* Rimon."

Two twenty-seven-hour days lost themselves in a marathon of talk. Every Orthean in the city (and they continued to come in by the hundreds) heard of 'land-sharing', and wanted to talk about it with the *T'Ans*, the *takshiriye*, and the offworlders. Especially with the offworlders. Their objections were many and violent. Some time towards the late afternoon of Durestha Eighthweek Threeday I staggered back to Westhill-Ahrentine, exhausted. And stopped in the *telestre*-house's inner courtyard to look up at a blue sky brilliant with daystars and think, *Do we have a chance?*

These things have their momentum. Endless pressure, seemingly with no result, and then all in a minute it'll go. We only need the smallest toehold, I thought. If we can get some people from the *hiyeks* to talk here in Tathcaer. But how?

Cory Mendez walked out from the ground-floor rooms. She also glanced skyward. "Lynne. Will you be travelling back to the southern continent with me?"

"When?"

"Today. Half the force are grounded there. My second in command is sending a shuttle down from the orbiter." The hawk-faced woman paused. The warm wind scattered *ziku* spores crimson on her black coveralls, and as she brushed herself she said, "Your association with the government envoy isn't wise. Under the circumstances I'd take the opportunity to put some distance there, were I in your position."

And this is Company loyalty? Well, yes, I suppose it is. . . . I changed the subject: "What's your assessment of the situation here, Cory?"

"My assessment is that home office will let me down again and insist on 'negotiations', until the situation's past repair. Whereas a quick surgical strike . . ." She pushed ornate silver rings up her thin fingers. "You mean the *native* situation? An outbreak of hostilities. Within a very short time."

Turning to leave, she added, "I have no confidence of getting it – that would be *too* sensible for the Company's marketing side – but I've requested from Representative Rachel the free use of coercive power."

I watched her walk out through the archway and into the city. What chills me is that it's just possible she has a point. If that aborted the Coast's invasion . . .

Here I stand with the hard stones of Tathcaer underfoot, hearing the distant voices of *ashiren*. Under the weight of such normality, I can hardly conceive the reality of what I'm trying to prevent.

"Lynne," Doug Clifford called from one of the upper-storey windows. "The comlink's functioning again. Come and give me the benefit of your opinion on this."

The holotank-image was intermittent, but recognizable as twelve-year-old stock-footage: the first satellite surveys of Carrick V.

"Which news-WEB put this out?"

"A small company," Douggie said. "They're syndicated to most of the inner worlds and, were I to hazard a guess, I'd say that most of their finance originates with the NuAsiaCo."

"Your people at home know who to talk to, don't they."

The voice-over fuzzed, then cleared. ' – *Carrick V, one of the low-tech, sparsely-inhabited worlds near the Heart Stars. When asked about rumours that a form of alien technology has been discovered on Carrick V, a spokesman refused to comment. He also denied accusations that severe cultural disruption is being caused by the PanOceania multicorporate. The Enclave government with technical jurisdiction over Carrick V also refuses to comment.*' The image altered to the face of a brown-haired young woman, with slanting brows and direct green eyes. '*Roxana Visconti, for the Trismegistus WEB.*'

"That's an end-of-broadcast filler if I ever saw one," I mused. "Wonder if there's been anything since that?"

Doug keyed the holotank to Clear.

"If NuAsiaCo can put PanOceania in any kind of commercial difficulties, there's every likelihood that they will indeed do so."

I went to the table and poured bowls of herb-tea from the half-empty jug, and took one back to Douggie. He put it down absent-mindedly on the edge of the holotank.

"Lynne, one of us will have to talk to Anzhadi-*hiyek*."

I cupped the bowl, sipping the citrine liquid. "Yes. At the moment, though, can *you* find anyone willing to let an outsider on to this continent?"

He rubbed at his lined forehead. "No. You don't change two millennia of history in half a year. Lynne, the Orhlandis woman, I can appreciate she can't have her identity known; but surely she could exert some form of pressure on the Wellhouses?"

"She may be. I have to be so careful asking."

Late afternoon sun slanted through the window-arches, patching the floorboards. The rooms still seemed disused. Covers remained on half the equipment. The shifting warm air brought the scent of *ziku* spores in, and rustled through old printouts and map-images still pinned to the walls. A rhythmic hollow clop came from the alley where *marhaz* and *skurrai* passed by.

"Call Molly Rachel," Douggie said. "You still have a technical right to be kept informed by the Company. I want to know – "

"What the storms are like on the Coast right now?"

He took from the holotank the tab that contained the Trismegistus broadcast, tucking it into his breast pocket. "Pray for bad weather. We need the time."

By the time the systems linked up to give me access to Molly, afternoon had passed into second twilight, and mist from the rivers muffled all the city's sounds. The upper-storey room was hot. I welcomed the cool night air.

The holotank began to image Molly Rachel. Her skin seemed blue-black in the interior lights of the shuttle. A soft sound ran in the background, a hissing that, before she could speak, broke into a crackle that split the image. The sound that followed I recognized as distant thunder.

I keyed in a climate profile, superimposed mid-image, and the Pacifican woman smiled a crooked smile when she saw it.

"I was going to ask how weather conditions were in your area," I said. "And the rest of the Coast?"

"Same as this morning, and the last three mornings." Those long black fingers keyed an inset-image. The metal hulls of F90 shuttles shone wetly, rain drumming back inches with the force of its landing; the earth was a morass. Lightning spiked a barren horizon, and the shuttle's exterior sensor momentarily went black. Molly said, "Storms in a holding-pattern from here, three hundred miles up the Coast. Climatology put it down to the Elansiir range. And the central-continent war damage."

"What about the *hiyek* ships in the harbours?"

Molly shook her head. The tangled black hair, shaggy now, was pinned back with *del'ri*-wood combs; her coverall was crumpled. She looked as though she hadn't slept.

"The storms block surveillance," she said. "That and whatever atmospheric effect it is that the war devastation makes. At least the native ships can't slip away now. I'd hesitate to send one of the Company's amphibious craft out; *jath* and *jath-rai* are helpless." She sighed. Her brown eyes were keen, but the rims were reddened. "I seriously think we made a mistake in coming here. The natives are interested in settling old grievances, not in the benefits of technology."

"Molly – "

"Calil bel-Rioch tells me that the 'Emperor' here is threatening to forbid the T&A station, and it isn't half finished yet. She says he doesn't want the Coast families independent."

Is that what Calil's aiming for, to be Emperor-in-Exile herself? I hate to say it but we could do worse than have a pro-technology leader in Kel Harantish. . . . And then I thought of those yellow eyes, that slight droop of the lid; her smile at the imagined death of Santhendor'lin-sandru, who was also an Emperor.

"This isn't a scheduled call," Molly Rachel reminded me. "What do you want?"

"I want to talk to the Anzhadi. If I can get some of them over here and talking, other *hiyeks* will follow their lead."

She said sourly, "If you can find them. What do you think I've been trying to do? The Anzhadi are mingling in with the other *hiyeks* and keeping under cover. You can look for Sethri-safere in any of the eighty small ports between here and Quarth – my people have."

I thought, Yes, Sethri doesn't want to fight the Emperor *and* attack the Hundred Thousand and nor do any of the other Anzhadi, they're not stupid. Only they've spent too many years knowing of the Hundred Thousand, looking at them with hungry eyes.

"You've heard from Cory Mendez?" I asked.

"Commander Mendez is on her way here." Molly's noncommittal expression slid into weariness. She rubbed at her eyes. "I've told her cultural taboos are too strong for her to station a detachment of the Peace Force with you right now. Lynne, we'd better come up with something soon – "

Because actual bloodshed will make you look bad on Company reports? Or is that too cynical?

" – because I'm running out of options," Molly Rachel said. "I can't play soft arbitrator if hostilities break out."

CHAPTER 21

Midsummer-Eightyear

The next morning, six days before the solstice, they opened up the halls of the Citadel, that great sprawl of stone on its high crag. I took a *skurrai-jasin* up to the Square. Sea mist curled round the white roofs of Tathcaer, and held close to the ground the reptilian scent of the *skurrai*, the slightly overripe odour of the food-collection points. A little after first twilight and already the city alleys are crowded.

I found the Earthspeaker Cassirur Almadhera in the Stone Garden, up on Citadel crag.

"There was a question I learned to ask when I was on Orthe before," I said. "Have the Wellhouses had any communication from the Hexenmeister of Kasabaarde?"

She straightened. The green and scarlet slit-backed robes were gone, replaced by undyed *becamil*-cloth. Her skin and robe were smeared with ochre, and she held a clump of mossgrass in one dirty six-fingered hand. Her eyes cleared.

"Christie. Have you forgiven me Barris Rakviri's death, then?"

I felt uncomfortable. "That's no business of mine."

"You judge the action."

"I haven't the right to judge."

She smiled the protest away. Morning sun gleamed on the Stone Garden's miniature cliffs and crags, on the smooth and carved rock-beds covered with scarlet, yellow, viridian and blue mossgrass. Dew collected in shallow pools, shadowed pools. Thousandflower moss tumbled down a flight of steps that ended at Cassirur's feet.

"This could be rerooted," she said absently, looking down at the moss on the choked stairway. The shadow of the Citadel slanted across this garden that lies between the sprawling building and the river cliff. A sheer hundred feet below the Oranon roared, dividing to pass the island-city. The smell of the river was rank in the air.

"About the Hexenmeister – "

Cassirur settled the clump of mossgrass in a dew-wet crevice. She wiped her hands on her robe, and brushed the mass of red mane away from her face. Clear light showed the lines in that reptilian skin.

Irrelevantly she said, "Have you heard from the Tower that the Goddess was an invention of Kerys Founder, and Her Wellhouses set up only to put use of the Old Science under ban? That's untrue. She is older. When we lived in those great Golden cities we joined with Her in secret. She is older than the Tower knows."

"Cassirur, I wish you'd answer a simple question!"

The scarlet-maned woman laughed. She moved away from the thousandflower-shrouded steps, and on a sudden turned her face up to the sky. The nictitating membrane flicked back from her eyes and she gazed straight into the sun. Then she lowered that gaze to me. Such a radiant shadow I have seen in other eyes, long ago; Orhlandis eyes.

I said, "What happens when men and women of the Coast land here and burn the *telestres*, kill you? Will you fight and die, or just die?"

"The *s'ans* say we should fight first, and then, if the men and women of the *hiyeks* do not return to their canals, give them what space here that we can." She paused. Her tone was prosaic. "We must see if they can be discouraged. The fighting will mean less of us, more food, so we can take them in. And if, as I think, they prove to be land-destroyers – why, then, we can kill them later, when they're divided amongst the Hundred Thousand. And having sent them to the Goddess, hope She brings them back to fertile lands."

I stared.

"Don't take me for *s'aranthi*," Cassirur Almadhera said. "We don't need to hear from the Hexenmeister. We have always planned this, in the Wellhouses, if a numerous enemy should come against us."

There in the early sun, this Orthean woman; standing in her dirty robe, bare high-arched feet planted foursquare on the rock.

"Don't take me for an idiot," I said. "That might be the way to deal with an Orthean war. It revolts me, but it might be. These are Ortheans with human weapons. Yes, and who knows, maybe with Witchbreed devices of their own – will you give *saryl-kabriz* to *them*?"

White sun reflected back from the rock, drew curls of mist from wet mossgrass; dazzled me when I turned to walk back into the Citadel, away from that woman silhouetted against a daystarred sky. Cassirur's thoughtful voice came clearly to me:

"Perhaps yes. And perhaps not fight at all. Let them come freely amongst us, and then send them to Her bright realm with poison or with hidden knives. If you will hear it, *that* is what the sole message from the Tower these past six years has said. That old man the Hexenmeister would sooner pretend a belief in our Goddess than see a war fought with Witchbreed or Earth weapons."

I kept on walking. Was it shock, that clarity in my mind, or familiarity, or both? So very Orthean, what Cassirur said, and I remember –

Memories that are the constructs of delusion.

259

Somewhere inside the interlocking halls of the Citadel I found Doug Clifford, after wandering through silent, dusty rooms, and halls where *ashiren* were setting out braziers to combat the chill in the air. He listened, in the long gallery, while I repeated Cassirur's words of an hour before.

"*No*," he said. "I'm fully aware of the principle of cultural toleration, but it does have inherent limitations." Then, with a bright-eyed anger, "Haven't they the plain common sense to avoid a massacre!"

"Ortheans look on death differently. As something they'll survive."

"Corazon Mendez won't see it that way." Doug halted by one of the slot-windows. "*I* don't see it that way."

"Neither do I. But I'm not Orthean."

Something in me wanted to protest that. I didn't let it. Doug and I walked on down the gallery, on the floor newly spread with *zilmei* pelts and matting. Voices called back and forth. There was the sound of heavy objects being moved.

"At least we'll know in advance when the invasion is going to happen," I said. "Molly will warn me when any *jath*-ships leave the southern continent. Doug, how can I report back to her on Cassirur? It was bad enough before this happened. Now what are we going to do?"

"Endeavour to ascertain whether it's what one might call a general conviction, or merely the prerogative of Earthspeakers and Wellkeepers."

Here the long gallery opened into an octagonal hall, without the benefit of a connecting corridor. Other halls were visible through archways. Sun put blue shadows on white stone. No Witchbreed thing, this low-roofed warren. I could see through into a larger hall, where two pale-maned females were putting up hangings and ribbon-banners, and I wondered in which of these rooms I had first met that woman called Suthafiori, Dalzielle Kerys-Andrethe, Crown of the Hundred Thousand.

Doug touched my arm. "Lynne, was my impression of the Orhlandis woman wrong? Would she use her position as Hexenmeister to encourage – "

"A massacre?" I prompted. That round squirrel-face was a stranger's face, then; Douglas Clifford, who could presume to judge *amari* Ruric Orhlandis. Why should it hurt me, to think she would do that? It's the Orthean way of thinking, and she's Orthean; and yet she's an outsider too. I said, "I don't know, Douggie."

There was something of the bantam about the small man as he gazed round, getting his bearings.

"I'll talk to Romare Kerys-Andrethe," he said. "He's here, I believe. And representative of some of the *s'ans*, wouldn't you say? Lynne, you talk with the *T'An* Haltern and Blaize Meduenin. We need to know who else thinks as Cassirur does. If *telestre*-Ortheans take that kind of violent action, I'm afraid it could be seen as an excuse for Earth to take over the government of Carrick V – and God knows to what kind of action *that* might lead."

Which of the *T'Ans* first took up quarters in the Citadel I don't know, but where one went, all followed. I found the *T'An* Seamarshal's new quarters in a high tower, one of the few rooms with a slot-window. Haltern was looking down at the city.

I saw nothing but upper air, and the flick of *rashaku*-flight against a sky swimming with stars, and then coming to the stone sill, I saw what he saw. *Marhaz*-riders crossing the Rimon hills and the Ymirian meadows: groups of three and four, and *ashiren* mounted on the smaller *skurrai*, and by their dress – only spots of vermilion, green, and gold at this several miles distance – they must be from the furthest *telestres*. North Roehmonde, Peir-Dadeni, The Kyre. The wind blew warm in my face. Humid sea mist began to roll up from the harbour, gradually blotting out *telestre*-houses, blurring the white walls, turning the heat-sensitive *lapuur* from green to ash-grey. . . . Here one could look down into inner courtyards of blind-walled *telestre*-houses, see young *ashiren*, bright-clothed adults, *marhaz* in stables, and fountains playing. Roosting *rashaku* rose up in clouds, disturbed, as *telestre*-Ortheans came back to their city.

"The Andrethe of Peir-Dadeni is here," the old male said. He sank back on a couch-chair. It was piled with grey and black *zilmei* pelts, against the chill of the stone walls.

"Are there more to come?"

"The *T'An* Ymir. Geren has no love for cities."

The inner bead-curtain swung back, and a male in Morvrenni robe brought herb-tea. His brown mane was intricately braided, and there were gold studs set in the skin between his fingers; and something in the way he hovered over Haltern n'ri n'suth Beth'ru-elen made me move, turn my back to the window, so I had the old male's face under that light. His wispy silver mane seemed thin. But it was the hollows in that wrinkled face that alarmed me.

As the *l'ri-an* left, I said, "Hal, I haven't suggested this before, partly because we have comparatively little data on Orthean physiology, but one of the Company medics – "

Haltern shook his head.

I asked, "Why not?"

With no self-pity or melodrama, but with infinite regret, he said, "It would make no difference. I shall die quite soon."

Half of me was shocked, half not. Well, I have been with Ortheans long enough to know something of them; that accounts fully for the sense of familiarity. I came to sit on the couch-chair beside him.

"Soon?"

"Soon, S'aranth. No," he lifted one thin hand, and when his pale eyes met mine, they were full of a wicked humour. "I shall use this, you see. I hope to see Meduenin as *T'An Suthai-Telestre*. Midsummer falls in six days. Now if I tell the new *T'An* Rimon that I stay only to see him as Crown . . ."

A sudden lack of expression crossed his face. He lifted a hand to his mouth. I saw that he chewed *ataile* leaf, that herb that brings both pleasure and eradication of pain.

"Hal – "

"*Ataile* is a small vice. Nor I think, now, shall I be concerned over its addictive properties. No," he said, quite differently, "don't grieve, Christie."

"Hal, do you remember, in Roehmonde; that woman Sethin was ill, and she said she wouldn't stay for the pain? You stay. That's what hurts me now. I wish you'd let me call a medic in."

"If it pleases you, do."

The fire in the brazier burned low. I leaned forward to put *ziku*-wood chips on it.

"You mustn't weep," he said. "Christie, you were so young when I first saw you, so frightened and so shrewd! I have you to thank if I understand anything at all of offworlders." He rested a hand on my shoulder, and there was no weight there; bones thin and hollow as a bird's. He said, "This body pains me. Still, I would live, if I could, any way that I could – "

I looked up, startled, unguarded.

" – How can I leave young Meduenin without some guiding hand? And the *telestres*? Your people, I don't trust them, Christie; I never have. To go to Her now – " He broke off. The pale and whiteless blue eyes were veiled with membrane. In the wreckage of that face I could still see him: Crown Messenger, politician, spy, friend.

I said, "Cassirur Almadhera doesn't regret death, for herself, or for others."

"Ah." Hal nodded. "That's the church. But no matter that we return, it means losing *this* life, *these* people; and it's arrogant of me to think I can't be spared, isn't it, *S'aranth*? Arrogant and true. We have no Suthafiori, no Kanta Andrethe, now."

He leaned forward to the table to pour herb-tea. The weight of the stone jug was all but too much. I dared not help him. The cold of the stone walls must have got into my bones: somewhere deep inside I was shivering. *You mustn't grieve*, he said. Ah, Hal. That sly, quiet humour of his; now it hurts.

"Let me sit with you for a while," I said. "Hal, I don't believe what you do. We shan't meet again."

He pulled the *zilmei* furs more closely round him. "We can't afford to sit, Christie, with only six days until Midsummer – I must have people come here, if I can't go to them; you can tell me what happens in the city. I shall be in the Wellhouse on solstice day."

He paused then, and more quietly said, "You and she were alike. You and the Orhlandis. If I see her in that bright realm, will she ask me why I've abandoned the land? What will I say to her?"

I took both of those thin, six-fingered hands in mine. I felt a very Orthean humour, some emotion between wonder and melancholy; thinking, Yes, that's Hal, you'd use even your death to find out what you want to know. Isn't that just like you?

I ached to tell him the truth.

"Ruric would have approved," I said. "Of everything. Even the manner of her death, perhaps; it came out of as great a love for the Hundred Thousand as she had. Isn't it strange where that can lead. She burned Orhlandis *telestre*, and you . . ."

His hands tightened on mine, but with so little strength that they seemed boneless. "It's done. I would undo it if I could."

Droplets of sea mist sparkled on the white stone walls. For all that there was business awaiting the *T'An* Seamarshal, for all that preparations for Midsummer demanded attention, we sat there in the weak sunlight, in silence, until the harsh clangour of the city bells marked out the hour of noon.

For three of the next six days I was the only offworlder in Tathcaer. Douggie took the shuttle to the Coast to try and talk with Anzhadi-*hiyek*, but his transmissions reported only failure. Sethri and his *raiku* were missing. On the fourth day Corazon Mendez and a group of her officers overflew the land round Tathcaer, and caused problems by attempting to land in the city; a rocky islet just beyond the estuary, Kumiel, was eventually set aside by the *T'An* Ymir for this purpose. And that made me realize: Tathcaer is a city again, with inhabitants and proscriptions and *takshiriye*, it has a Court and will have a Crown, we can no longer treat it as deserted. . . .

And Tathcaer for those six days lay under a sweltering heat. *Lapuur* expanded their feather-fronds, shadowing the white walls with greenery. Passers-by hugged alley walls, where the shadows were coolest. Ortheans, still coming in from the surrounding countryside, slept outside in sun-baked courtyards; and though it was quiet from noon until second twilight, after that a hubbub of voices arose; Ortheans drinking herb-tea and *siir*-wine in brick courtyards, and even the smallest *ashiren* sitting still to listen and ask questions. On long walks from Westhill-Ahrentine to the Citadel and back I heard two topics of conversation. Overt: who is most suited to be Crown? Covert: are the Wellhouses right when they say what we should do when the invaders come?

I talked with them, and with the *T'Ans* of Rimon, Ymir, and Roehmonde; with the Andrethe of Peir-Dadeni, the *T'An* Seamarshal and *T'An* Melkathi and *T'An* Kyre.

The last day of Durestha Eighthweek: "The question is," I said, "what will the *hiyeks* do? They must know the Hundred Thousand could be planning to divide them up and then kill them."

Douggie raised his eyebrows. "Take hostages from the *telestres*? No, that only succeeds if there's that fear of death."

Heat reflected back from walls into the courtyard of the companion-house, where we sat under feather-fronded *lapuur* and the black and scarlet *ziku*. Spore cases floated down through the humid air. It was a big courtyard, several groups of Ortheans were sitting round tables talking or playing *ochmir*, and shaggy bronze *marhaz* were stabled in a pen on the far side. *Kekri*-flies hovered over heaps of dung. There was a rank smell from the harbour, visible through the archway entrance.

"My guess is that the Coast Ortheans won't split up," I said. "Would you? They'll take some land, some fertile land, and try to – well, in effect, build a Maherwa or a Reshebet. Not *hiyeks* taking control of *telestres*, but a *hiyek* province in the Hundred Thousand."

Doug, about to answer, looked past me at the archway. "Good grief."

I looked over my shoulder. A frail, silver-maned male; staff in one hand, the other resting on a younger male's shoulder – Haltern Beth'ru-elen, and the *T'An* Melkathi, Nelum Santhil. While I gaped, Hal limped up to us and sank down on a wooden couch-chair.

"*Siir*-wine, if you please," he said to Santhil, and when the dark male had gone into the companion-house, smiled at us. "I feel a little better, I think. Don't tell Blaize Meduenin. I'm still hoping to make him take the Crown." His pale eyes gleamed.

"Hal,' I said weakly; then shook my head. "I give up."

"Very wise, *s'aranth-te*."

A small child, dark-maned and some six seasons old, followed Nelum Santhil out of the companion-house; and coming up to us, said, "Will you play *ochmir*, *t'ans*?" and then fell silent, gazing at offworlders. Doug took the board and counters from *kir*. I saw a glance pass between Hal and Santhil, and the *T'An* Melkathi went off towards one of the other groups of players.

All intrigue under the surface, I thought, who knows what's happening? The *takshiriye* hear word from all the Hundred Thousand *telestres*, and not all those words are for others' ears. . . .

" – a *hiyek* province in the Hundred Thousand," Doug Clifford finished repeating our discussion as he set up a three-handed game of *ochmir*. Those small bright eyes flicked up to surprise whatever unguarded expression Haltern might have. He hadn't.

"A Witchbreed province," Hal corrected. "Listen to what's said here. The Coast *hiyeks* have the canals, that's Witchbreed science, and the *telestre* people won't see it as a 'province' but as a seed of a future Empire."

"Call it a colony," I said. "Call it what you like, I can see it being attacked. If not with *harur*-blades, then with something to starve them out of the land. Hal, could your people be brought to fire the land? Become land-destroyers, as once in Melkathi – "

"No!" His denial was too emphatic.

We played in silence for a time, making those alliances that occur in *ochmir* with three players: Hal and I, Hal and Doug, Doug and I. A shadow fell across the table. When I looked up, it was to see the clear eyes and scarlet mane of Cassirur Almadhera.

She grinned at Haltern. "Down at the harbour, listening to travellers' gossip? And you so sick you couldn't leave the Citadel! Or so the Meduenin told me. . . ."

"You've no business to follow a sick old man." Haltern, ruffled, hitched his *chirith-goyen* robe round his thin shoulders; more piqued than anything else. "It seems She spares me for a little time yet – but not for my ease. How did you find me?"

Cassirur Almadhera indicated some *ashiren* who were sweeping the courtyard free of *ziku* spore cases. Two of the children grinned, and I recognized them as hers. Haltern snorted. The light of Carrick's Star shone a pale gold here, slanting down through the feathery *lapuur*, gilding his pale mane; dazzling on Cassirur. It shone warm on the dusty flagstones, and, past the shadow of the arched entrance, on the masts of *jath*-ships moored at that dock. Not far from this companion-house at the foot of Crown Way, I had first disembarked, entering the Hundred Thousand.

"Come up to the Citadel," Cassirur said. "It's time for the *T'Ans* of the provinces to lay down their authority. Tomorrow there will be named a *T'An Suthai-Telestre*. Tonight the city is under the authority of the Wellhouses."

Haltern stood, beckoning Nelum Santhil over from one of the other tables.

"We'll come," I said. "Doug, we should speak with the *T'Ans* again before the transfer of authority happens."

Skurrai-jasin stood outside the entrance of the companion-house. The stocky, reptilian beasts nibbled at *kazsis*-vine with their pointed upper lips while they waited; and the sun shone gold on the fine-fibred shaggy pelts. A cool breeze blew off the harbour. Masts creaked. I gazed along the line of ships – fewer now than when the city was the port for all outlanders entering the Hundred Thousand – and at the cloth awnings of food-sellers' booths on the quay, and at the crowds. Haltern beckoned me to his carriage, leaving Cassirur to follow in the next with Doug and Nelum Santhil. I sat down in the *jasin*'s padded wooden seat. The flagstones jolted us. The driver leaned forward to shout at bright-robed Ortheans to move out of the way. Sun and humid heat blurred their voices, blurred the gleam of gems and *harur*-blades. When I glanced back I saw Nelum Santhil had left his *skurrai-jasin* and was walking across the quay to a Melkathi ship.

"Do you trust him?" I said.

Haltern Beth'ru-elen smiled. "No. I've known too many *T'Ans* to do that."

"Hal, you're *T'An* Seamarshal!"

"That must prove them untrustworthy. . . . *S'aranth*, he's afraid. We all are. There are rumours that the Coast Ortheans have Witchbreed weapons newly remade." Here he shrugged, and reached into the sleeves of his white robe for *ataile* leaves; and said indistinctly as he chewed them, "My *takshiriye* Messengers report that to be false, and I think it so. What may be true is that Earth technology and Earth weaponry is finding its way to the *hiyeks*."

The *skurrai* carriage wheeled as the driver shouted curses, avoiding a cart piled high with shelled edible *hura*. Then we swung away from the docks, entering the city.

I said, "Have you thought? If I were Sethri Anzhadi, I know what part of this land I'd try to take and hold . . . Tathcaer. Take this city, and the nearest farming *telestres* in Ymir and Rimon."

"It makes no difference," Haltern said. "If there's such a cancer in the Hundred Thousand we can't leave it, we must cut it away or kill it, even if it is the white city. You asked me, could we become land-destroyers . . . I fear for Tathcaer."

We jolted through the narrow alleys up to the Citadel Square. The *skurrai-jasin* often stopped, hailed by Ortheans who wanted to question the *T'An* Seamarshal. Peir-Dadeni riders with manes pulled up in plumes on the crowns of their heads, and braided intricately down their spines, leaned six-fingered hands on the sides of the carriage or gestured extravagantly. Plainly-dressed Ymirians put stolid questions, their eyes veiled against the summer sun. They walked barefoot in dusty alleys black with shadow; and in the narrow gap of sky between buildings daystars shone like a scatter of salt.

Must war come here? I thought. War with weapons that Sethri Anzhadi will call 'Witchbreed', that will be black-market Earth weapons, and really where's the difference between them? How can Tathcaer be defended against *that*?

The Square was crowded. Ortheans called comments to the *T'Ans* who passed, going up the cliff-walk to the Citadel. I gave Haltern my arm and we made slow progress up the zigzag walk.

"We shall see," he said, pausing, "if tomorrow in the Square the *s'ans* name us *T'An* again. . . . And then to see who will be *T'An Suthai-Telestre*. . . ."

I let him get his breath. The city sweltered below: Square, Wellhouse, and all. Up on the crag I saw no Crown Guard, but the brown robes of Earthspeakers and Wellkeepers were everywhere. They directed us, with Doug and Cassirur (and where, I thought, is Nelum Santhil?) to a low-roofed hall that was lit only by windows facing into an inner courtyard.

As Cassirur went to speak with an elderly male Wellkeeper, Doug Clifford moved up beside me.

"Dalzielle Kerys-Andrethe held audiences here before she died, the last time I was in Tathcaer." He kept his voice low, not to be overheard in that crowded place. "It wasn't often that she allowed offworlders to be present."

Ribbon-banners hung from the walls, muted by the crepuscular light. Both the great hearths were bare. Two or three dozen *telestre*-Ortheans clustered together in the middle of the hall, their robes and gems rich; and I saw how one fair-maned male wearing the silver circlet of a *T'An* had gold studs set between the fingers of his delicate hands – and is that Khassiye? I thought. A thin, proud face: Cethelen Khassiye Reihalyn, minister to the then Andrethe when I knew him. When he refused me entrance to the city Shiriya-Shenin, after I came down, a footsore refugee, from those mountains called the Wall of the World. . . .

"*T'An* Khassiye," I said, greeting him; and Haltern, leaning heavily on my arm, said, "*T'An* Khassiye is Andrethe of Peir-Dadeni now."

Khassiye smiled, his thin face looking little older. "*T'an* Christie. *T'An* Seamarshal. You've come to lay down that authority? It's a heavy burden for a man not well."

"Yours is the heavier," Haltern said, "since being adopted *n'ri n'suth* into the Andrethe *telestre*, I think. Reihalyn was a low-river *telestre*, wasn't it, *T'An?*"

Khassiye flushed. Debate from other groups overtook us. That needling rivalry between the *T'Ans* amused me; I didn't need to follow all its finer detail. As I stood and looked at the people gathered in the hall, I recognized many faces, pointing out to Doug those that he might not recognize:

"*T'An* Howice of Roehmonde. . . ." A plump male, swathed in *zilmei* pelts and sweating because of it: when I was in the northern province of Roehmonde, it was he who imprisoned me for a Wellhouse trial. "*T'An* Bethan; I never knew The Kyre province well, she's a stranger; that's *T'An* Geren Hanathra – "

Douggie peered at the large, fair-maned male. "Wasn't he a shipmaster? And mixed up with the Orhlandis woman?"

"He was Ruric's *arykei*. It was his ship that brought me from the Eastern Isles to Tathcaer, the first time I came to the Hundred Thousand."

That progress brought me to a position from where I could see the far end of the long, low hall. A marble block was set up there. Massive, almost translucent in the shadowy light . . . Two of those young Ortheans who act as *l'ri-an* stood by it, with a male in Earthspeaker's robes. The stone was carved in relief with *marhaz*, *zilmei*, trailing *kazsis*-vines, *hanelys*-flower. On its flat top surface were cut seven circles, Well symbols, that might hold the silver circlet of a *T'An* and were empty now; and an eighth circle cut deep into the stone, that held the plain gold circlet worn by the *T'An Suthai-Telestre*.

"The ceremony's timed for noon," a voice said behind me. I turned. It was Blaize Meduenin. The light half hid his face, but gleamed on that silver streak in his mane. He still wore plain mercenary's gear.

"Is that the way for a *T'An* Rimon to dress?" I teased.

"We need more than pretty finery now. Christie, if they name me *T'An* Rimon tomorrow, I'll raise up companies of fighters from the Rimon *telestres*. We need a *T'An* Commander of the *telestre* forces, now; the new Crown should appoint one." His hands fell automatically to the hilts of *harur-nilgiri*, *harur-nazari*.

Does that mean you'd sooner be *T'An* Commander? I wondered. Or does it sound like a *T'An Suthai-Telestre* deciding policy? Out of all these here, you're the only one that really knows the *hiyeks* and Earth. Other than Haltern; but Hal . . .

"Where's the *T'An* Melkathi?" Blaize asked, running his gaze over the group present. "If Nelum Santhil's going to be here by noon, he's leaving it late."

Now there's a man I wouldn't be sorry to see not named as *T'An* Melkathi tomorrow, I thought. Nelum Santhil Rimnith, who once took bribes from Kel Harantish – what would Ruric think if she knew? And she *does* know, I imagine; there isn't much the Hexenmeister doesn't hear.

And I wish she could be here now.

I looked round at the company, the *T'Ans* of the provinces, those who accompanied them; the shaven manes of Wellkeepers and Earthspeakers, and the lively young faces of the *l'ri-an*. All those alien faces. Wide, whiteless eyes; narrow chins. And the thin bodies in scarlet, blue and amber-coloured robes; the delicate high-arched feet and strong six-fingered hands . . . and their voices, a babel of the languages of the seven provinces. *Harur*-blades clashed gently as they moved.

None of them are Suthafiori, none of them are *T'An* Commander Ruric; but still, it's the same land, I thought. Though I saw Cassirur Almadhera talking with Doug, it didn't stop a surge of hope. There's a way through this, if we can find it. Haltern, Blaize; even Khassiye and Santhil and Howice; they're more practised at keeping the *telestres* whole than we can ever imagine, practised over long years and long lives. . . .

Because I was watching Cassirur with Doug, I saw the elder of her black-maned children enter the hall and approach her. She bent her head to listen to the *ashiren*, and her face changed. There was a commotion at the door, and then two more people entered. One offworlder – *what the hell is Cory Mendez doing here now?* And the other, half-crippled with the haste in which he'd arrived, was the dark-maned Nelum Santhil. The talking in the hall stopped. Outside, noon bells began to ring. They went unnoticed, except that Nelum Santhil raised his voice to be heard over them: "There's no time for ceremonies," he said. "Tell the *s'ans* in the city. If we're to have a Crown, we must have one *now*. There's no more time."

He reached out and gripped the arm nearest him, which was Cassirur's, and leaned on that while he struggled for breath. We stood frozen in that twilight hall, waiting. The clamour of the noon bells ceased.

Into that silence he said, "Warships from the Coast landed at Rynnal and Vincor and Rimnith this morning. They're burning the *telestres*. They're burning Melkathi."

CHAPTER 22

First Strike

"Why the *fuck* weren't we warned?" I demanded.

Cory's sharp face was livid with anger. "Surveillance showed nothing. Those vessels must have slipped out of the Coast ports under cover of hurricane conditions – damn Rachel! She should have told me primitive craft could survive that."

"Where are they now?"

The hum of voices in half a dozen languages almost drowned her out, but I heard her say: " – heat-sensors can't tell one native craft from another. I'm going to overfly the area. It's the only way. Jamison; Ottoway! *Move!*"

Two of her young officers fell in beside her as she pushed through the crowded entrance and out of the hall, head high, that sleek white hair a blazon. I forced my way through the press of bodies to Doug Clifford's side.

"The Peace Force are going to Melkathi."

"So am I," he said grimly. "This will have to be reported. I'll take the government shuttle. I'll send out tapes to every WEB in the Heart Worlds, let them *see* what the Company's doing here."

"You'll need a pilot, then – I'll come."

He nodded. The low entrance of the hall was jammed with bodies, and I shoved between Khassiye and Howice *T'an* Roehmonde, aware that Doug followed; ignored a question from Cassirur on the way out, and at last came half-walking and half-running out into the sunlight at the top of the cliff-walk. The light of Carrick's Star was momentarily blinding. I stopped. Doug pointed, and I saw far away pinpricks of light on the Ymirian hills – heliographed warnings.

"The shuttle's on Kumiel. Damn tech restrictions!" Doug's brevity and irritation were uncharacteristic.

"Look."

As we hurried down the cliff-walk, I indicated the mass of Ortheans in the Square. Nothing but a mosaic of heads and bodies: impenetrable. In fascination I saw waves of shock travel out from those nearest to the great Wellhouse entrance, heard the buzz of confusion, and realized it must mean news was coming in on the *rashaku*-relay. Then we were down in the hot, humid air at Crown Gate.

I caught a glimpse of black. *Cory?* Before I could call to her, she commandeered a *skurrai*-carriage, and her harsh authoritarian voice rang out, clearing away the nearest crowds. *And the Peace Force shuttles are on Kumiel too* – I had a blackly humorous urge to laugh. Then a pointed muzzle showed between a group of fur-clad Roehmonders. I seized Doug's arm, pulled him into the *skurrai-jasin* and caught up the harness, and as the squat beast heaved the wooden vehicle off over the flagstones a weight made it dip. Startled, I glanced round. Blaize Meduenin swung himself up on the back.

"One of the *T'ans* must see Melkathi, and quickly," he said. Doug blinked, and then muttered agreement.

We have to know what's happening, have to know if it is *an attack; how bad, what size force, what damage –*

Skurrai-jasin are not fast. As we trotted down between *telestre*-houses in that sweltering noon, I was rigid with impatience; coaxing every advantage from the beast. I caught my face growing heated, aware that we presented a ridiculous spectacle.

"I can't get a response from the Coast base," Doug said, mouth to wristlink. "Nor from the orbiter. It must be the storms."

Will it take us longer to cross the city, to come to the harbour, to be ferried out to Kumiel, than to fly the shuttle a hundred miles down the coast of Melkathi – yes, dammit, yes. *And while we're doing this, what's happening there?*

I pulled the *skurrai*'s harness and the beast shouldered its way between stalls in the Guild-Ring. Doors were shut here, entrances barricaded; and anxious Ortheans in Rimon and Ymirian dress stood by the wooden display platforms. No trade in this market now.

"They know," Blaize said softly. Membrane slid over his whiteless blue eyes. He gripped the back of the *skurrai-jasin*, boots planted firmly on the wheel-guard. When Ortheans tried to stop the carriage, he bawled at them with all the authority of a mercenary commander.

Coming down to the docks, the city was in uproar. Arguments, fights, panic-stricken barring of *telestre*-house entrances. Then suddenly it was open sunlight, salty air, as we swung on to the quay. Across the bright water, a *jath-rai* was already tacking for Kumiel. Cory Mendez? If we could only get through to Molly Rachel – *what will she order the Peace Force to do?*

"Damn all proscriptions of technology," Doug Clifford muttered.

Blaize jumped down on to the stones of the quay. *Harur*-blades jingled. He signalled to a *jath-rai* moored at steps near us, had brief words with the shipmaster. I glanced back as I got down from the *skurrai-jasin*, but the shoulder of the hill hid the Citadel now.

"This is what we get for keeping to the rules." I looked at Doug. "Cory Mendez won't put up with these restrictions now, you realize that? And if Sethri and the Anzhadi *do* have black-market Earth technology – they won't keep to the rules."

A moment of stillness. Doug squinted against the brilliance of Carrick's Star on Tathcaer harbour, scratched at his grizzled red-grey hair.

"Another boundary crossed," he said. "Another restriction removed."

There are protections that are intangible, only noticed when they're gone; and I had time to shiver, quite literally, and think, *How long before there are no rules at all?* and then Blaize called, and hurried us up the swaying plank to the *jath-rai*'s deck.

The small craft rocked in the swell. Kumiel Island hardly seemed to grow closer. The cool wind left my hair stiff with salt and lips dry, and I gratefully took the flask of *siir* that Blaize handed me, and drank as I stood at the ship's rail, and saw the Peace Force shuttle lift off from Kumiel with a hurried roar. The heat of Carrick's Star made rocks, sea and craft shimmer.

"Sunmother!" Blaize hit one stocky fist into his open hand. "For ships to cross the Inner Sea in Stormsun – " and then he grinned crookedly: "Sethri Anzhadi. He would have made a good mercenary."

"How can you say that?"

"Pride in the skills of war," Blaize Meduenin said. "You should listen to your Corazon Mendez, *S'aranth*. If this is to become an Earth war, perhaps it should be ended by Earth's ways."

That scarred face was open, honest; and he met my gaze as if this was a serious possibility he discussed. *Once a mercenary, always a mercenary?* Before I could say more, the *jath-rai* scraped Kumiel's tiny quay.

Doug Clifford spared no backwards glance for us, barely giving us time to enter the government shuttle before he palmed the exit shut. Sunlight replaced by green interior light: summer's heat by cool air, and I fell into the pilot's seat and put the console through as fast a take-off sequence as I ever hope to, and before the lurch that announced liftoff, Douggie was halfway to keying in *record* on the holotank and simultaneously opening all channels on the comlink. Blaize Meduenin leaned on the back of my chair, studying the small navigation-holo.

"I'll key us to follow the coastline east," I said.

"A hundred and fifty *seri*," Blaize directed. "Christie, use the Melkathi sandflats to place us."

Say, a hundred and eighty miles. By the time I'd keyed a recognition pattern, Doug had the comlink at last functioning:

" *– visual contact made 01.76.345/97.31.823; repeat, 01.76 – "*

" *– Ottoway, report. Report position. Where is Green Two?"*

" – *Green Two repor* – "

White noise blanked all channels, then faded intermittently.

" – *drop into low orbit from the hi-orbit station, form up on latitude 65: stabilize and observe.*"

"*Error-rate on satellite survey equipment up to 83%. Fucking hell, what kind of atmospherics does this world* – "

Doug keyed the volume low. The three of us moved to the large holotank, studying exterior-image. A haze partly obscured the land beneath us. Blue-grey sea merged with Ymir's blue-grey hills. One highlight from Carrick's Star blazed off the water, following us eastwards. At this low level of flight, no more than two thousand feet, the roads that mark *telestre*-boundaries are visible as white threads; *telestre*-houses are perfect miniatures. They were fewer and further between, now, as we began to fly over Melkathi, that sandy, barren land.

"Keep the heat-sensors trained," Doug ordered.

"It could be just a skirmish. One ship or two, or – "

"The *rashaku*-relay says fifty *jath* warships," Blaize said. "Exaggeration, of course. But by how much?"

The shuttle bucked, kicked in empty air; and I leaned back to the pilot's console, saw we were registering other air traffic – Cory's shuttle and the low-level orbital surveillance craft – and corrected for it. So long as her ships stick to surveillance. . . .

"Why don't they answer?" Douggie said, frustrated; and then made an abrupt shift to public voice as Pramila Ishida's face came on the comlink screen. "Put me in contact with Molly Rachel, please. I must speak with the Company representative."

"I don't have time for this. We have our own problems," the Pacifican girl said, her expression somewhere between exasperation and fear. "Molly Rachel is in Kel Harantish, no contact is possible, I'm afraid – "

I leaned over Douggie and said to her, "Has Cory Mendez been in touch with Molly? Does Molly know what's happening here?"

White noise cut her speech, the image fuzzed and died. I was still working out whether it was a breakdown or a deliberate cutting of the contact when Blaize stabbed one claw-nailed finger at the main holotank: "*There!*"

Flat land baked under the light of Carrick's Star. Here the coast ran down into mudflats and sandbars, fringed with white surf. Black smoke smeared the eastern horizon. I swung the shuttle seawards, then inland, dropping down below one thousand feet. The black smear became a tower of smoke, billowing up, spreading at the crown; seeping across the sky as we came closer to it, and we entered a sepia light.

"Those are Coast *jath*," Blaize said.

Hoop-masted metal ships gleamed on the sandflats, and as we came closer I saw how they listed to one side, beached; the sand churned up round them. Nothing moved.

Doug's hands were poised delicately over the sensor controls, his face showing an intent concentration, as if he were a musician or engraver. "The heat-sensors aren't picking up anything large enough to be humanoid life. . . . That fire is some thirty miles inland."

"Rimnith," Blaize said.

Even Doug looked up at that tone. I felt how earth is kin to Ortheans, that crumbling warm and fertile earth as close to them as their skin: to hurt it is to hurt them.

I swung the shuttle inland, and the smoke of the burning grew thicker. The root of that dark tower was a spot near low hills, and smoke billowed up thick and black, and at its foot there was a tiny spark of orange. White specks in the air resolved into shuttles on hover-mode: Cory Mendez and the Peace Force. I let us overshoot, skimming the edge of walls of darkness, smoke that rose up and blotted out all light. Even with air-purifiers, the smell of burning leaked through into the cabin.

"I want to go in," I said.

Doug turned from monitoring the holo-record. "That would be very unwise, Lynne."

"Look down there."

From this height they were only dots, hardly moving on a track that must be (given the speed we were moving) another ten or fifteen miles inland. But there were too many of them. Blaize said nothing, but I knew he recognized that pattern. Refugees.

"I'm taking us down. There might be something we can do." I looked at Doug. "Record it. Put it out on the WEBs; this is proof of what the Company's caused here, *it might help stop it before it goes any further*."

Blaize said nothing as I keyed in a landing-pattern, and the shuttle sank down, drifted in hover-mode to settle astride an earthtrack on a barren and sandy heath. As the power died, he touched the hilt of *harur*-blades.

"We know where the *hiyeks* were," he said then, curtly nodding at the holo-image of burning land. "We don't know where they are now."

We all have our own ghosts. I never thought that I should stand again in Melkathi and smell burning.

Even here, a dozen miles distant, the air was citrine; flecks of black ash drifting down from no detectable source. The earth felt warm underfoot. Here was little but sand, and sparse *hanelys*-tanglebush and *siir*. The heath's dips and hollows made it impossible to see far in any direction. Blaize, stepping from the shuttle-ramp, unselfconsciously bent down to touch the earth, and to sign himself on the breast with the Circle of the Goddess. Doug Clifford joined us, shutting off his wristlink.

"Cory wants to know precisely what we civilians are doing in a hostile area," he said. "I thought a communications failure might be tactful at this juncture. After I told her that we had a temporary power-fault."

"Listen – " And I realized I'd automatically stepped to one side, CAS IV loose in its holster, the old Service training surfacing after all these years. I didn't draw the stungun. Blaize looked perfectly relaxed, and I know how fast he can move.

Because the terrain was so irregular, we heard them before we saw them. The pad of *marhaz* and the jingle of their harness, loud in that noon heat and silence, and voices. . . . The first *marhaz* topped the rise, a dozen yards away. A thin beast, black-and-cream pelt eaten by parasites, horns uncropped and gleaming wickedly in the smoky light. Its rider was equally thin and shabby, a fair-skinned and dark-maned *ashiren* some fourteen seasons old.

"Give you greeting," Blaize called, "in Her name."

Two other *marhaz* joined the first. One carried its pad as if lame. A red-maned *ashiren* turned in the saddle and held up *kir* hand, but the straggling procession took no notice, and only gradually halted as they saw us. Young Ortheans, from three-births still in arms to *ashiren* old as the riders, and all ages between. Still they came over the low rise, until there were fifty or sixty of them; all with black or red manes, most with strongly similar faces – all the *ashiren* of one *telestre*? I thought, remembering Blaize's voice when he said *Rimnith*.

The Meduenin said, "Where do you travel, *ashiren-te*?"

"Keverilde *telestre*." The red-maned child's voice came harshly. "If there is Keverilde, still. *T'an*, they burned Rimnith – "

"Where are your elders?"

Ke was silent, but another of the riders, a ten- or eleven-year-old *ashiren*, said, "Gone into other *telestres* to wait."

"Wait until we can fight – "

" – they burned – "

" – burned the land – "

"We offered them guest-right," the red-maned *ashiren* cut in, over the babble of other voices. *Ke* picked absently at soot smears on *kir* thin, tawny robe. "We offered them guest-right and they burned the land, *t'an*."

No time for *saryl-kabriz* poison, I thought. Cassirur, what now?

Blaize Meduenin stared back the way they had come. Nothing was visible but that black wall of smoke in the south.

"Keverilde is too close," he said. "Eirye, or Beriah. . . . *Ashiren-te*, will you be afraid to fly, as offworlders do? We will take you all, in turns – but the beasts you must leave. Will you go, *ashiren-te*?"

"Now wait a minute – " Doug broke off. He watched the Orthean children.

All the Orthean features are delicate on a child: feathery mane rooting down the spine, slender clawed fingers and high-arched feet; the eyes that blur with translucent membrane. Alien, unsexed. The red-maned rider let *kir* beast pad closer to Blaize Meduenin, until *ke* could look down at him.

"Take the youngest of us," the rider said, with precarious adolescent dignity. "For myself, I'd sooner ride into Shadow than travel with those who are friends to the Coast."

"That's foolish. You'll be weary, and in danger," Blaize reminded *kir*.

The rider smiled, and it was adult, cynical. *Ke* said, "All of us are in danger now, *t'an*. Now that the Coast raiders have *s'aranthi* weapons."

Doug, with an exaggerated sigh, glanced from the rabble of children to the shuttle. "Three trips," he estimated, "and God knows we won't get any help from Cory Mendez. I wouldn't take the risk if these weren't children. What in God's name are their people doing sending them away alone?"

A remembered voice in my head said, *Who'd harm ashiren? Who'd dare?* When I looked across at Blaize, I knew he had no faith in that now. The restrictions have broken down.

Two hours later, back on the same spot; nothing changed but Carrick's Star declined slightly from noon.

"Link your navigation-data in," said the thin, blond man in Peace Force coveralls. His name was Ottoway, I gathered; he had prematurely creased and tanned skin, and in his eyes something of the same look as Corazon Mendez. He said, "It's funny. They seem more afraid of a ship on their soil than of the actual flight."

I watched the remaining *ashiren* and *marhaz* file up the ramp and into the F90, whose shining white bulk dwarfed the government shuttle. Blaize Meduenin stood at the top of the ramp, preparatory to going with them.

They *remember* flight, in the days of the Golden Empire . . . and it isn't to reassure them about flight that the Meduenin is going with them. They don't trust offworlders, now.

"Thank Cory when you see her," I said. "We'd have been some time taking the last group over to Beriah, and we're getting low on fuel."

"Just getting non-combatants out of a hostile area," Ottoway said.

276

"About yourself, Ms Christie, and the government envoy, Clifford – "

"Yes, of course." I smiled. And made for the government shuttle, before he should realize I'd reassured him about absolutely nothing. Away in the south there was the sound of shuttles and observer-craft, there where the horizon still was yellow with smoke. I palmed the lock shut, cutting out the faint smell of combustion on the wind.

"We're going to have to do something soon," I said, taking the seat beside Doug at the holotank.

"Mmm." He reached out to the console. "You might find this interesting. I got a signal some few minutes ago that I failed to identify immediately. Eventually I realized that it was being relayed through the Morvren communication-link from Thierry's World. . . . Listen."

" – been requesting permission from the Company to land, but they've refused. I couldn't get in contact with you, envoy Clifford – "

The replay-image showed a young woman's face. I recognized those heavy, slanting brows: the 'caster from the Trismegistus WEB. Doug ran the record forward.

" – there are 'casters from three or four other WEBs on Thierry, but transport to Carrick V is under so many Company restrictions that it's impossible to get through. Envoy, I want to 'cast from the surface of Carrick's world itself. I want to show the Home Worlds and the Heart Worlds just exactly what's happening here – "

Doug keyed out the image. "I sent her the record of the refugees here in Melkathi. I've authorized the government base on Thierry's World to finance transport for any WEBcasters travelling to Orthe." With uncharacteristic vindictiveness, he added, "It won't do Representative Rachel any harm to have WEBcasters following her every move."

"I'd sooner keep friendly relations with Cory's people. We may need them. I was talking to Ottoway," I said, as I leaned back in the bucket seat, and reached over to key a container of coffee from the supply-panel. "He says the area round Rimnith is quiet, the fires are dying down."

And was it a wet spring, a wet summer? I remember when Orhlandis burned the whole countryside was in danger –

"And they've had some success with the observer-craft. No sign of any offshore fleet." Only the normal shipping you find in summer, in the seasons of Durestha and Merrum, in those coastal waters from Ales-Kadareth to Tathcaer to Morvren Freeport and the Kasabaarde Archipelago. . . . "All they can pick up is a concentration of life forms near Rimnith, and that *must* be the Coast Ortheans. Doug, I'm willing to bet there are Anzhadi there, maybe Sethri himself – "

"For God's sake don't make the suggestion that you're going to,

Lynne. You can*not* attempt to make contact with a group of guerrilla invaders."

"Somebody has to."

The shuttle's interior was cool, illuminated with that faintly green and soothing light; and the silence was no silence, but only the hum of powered-down systems. I noticed the imprint of footsteps on the floor: the sandy earth of Melkathi trodden in. Doug leaned back and rubbed at his eyes, the light from the imageless holotank casting upward shadows on his features. He sighed.

"We're running out of time."

"I know," I said.

"I must talk with Cory Mendez. If storm conditions abate, and I can get through to Rachel at Kel Harantish, then. . . . " He looked up. "We have just enough fuel to make a landing on the way back."

For half an hour I let the shuttle stand by the ruins of the Rimnith *telestre*, partly to seem no threat, partly to see if it would provoke attack. I stayed in the shuttle, exterior-sensor and transmitter working, and didn't venture outside, because I'm not stupid. Doug Clifford stayed at the comlink, trying to contact the Coast.

The earth still smoked blackly. In the orange light, angular *hanelys* stood like iron lace. Wisps of smoke curled up from the ground. Even the stones of the sprawling complex of buildings were cracked with the heat.

"I'll move a mile or two south," I said. "I can't tell if the heat-sensors are reading body-heat, or hot spots in the earth."

The shuttle lifted heavily, wallowing south, and I set it down on bare heathland that had escaped the conflagration only because there was so little to burn. And waited. At last the sensors showed a moving body. A small figure appeared, approaching the shuttle. When he got close, I saw the filthy *meshabi*-robe that cloaked him: a male, elderly, with a brown-blond mane. At his belt hung both a hook-bladed knife and a CAS-IV holster.

"Earth tech," Doug said, leaning over to look at the holotank's exterior-image. "I want this recorded for evidence. Are there other *hiyeks* here?"

"I can't tell. The heat's still masking the sensors."

"*Kethrial-shamaz shan'tai!*" The Orthean's voice came through the transmitter pick-up. I saw how he craned his neck, looking up at the shuttle's blank walls. "Are there *s'aranthi* there?"

"What *hiyek*?" I asked. He glanced round, found no focus for the voice. His bare feet were blackened with ash, and membrane covered his eyes so that they looked blankly white. Alone. And where are the Ortheans with you, who set the fire in Rimnith's sparse fields, put the spark to the tinder-dry reed thatch of the *telestre* buildings? I repeated, "What *hiyek*? Anzhadi?"

A flicker of reaction. I keyed the image into close-up. Brown-blond mane rooted down broad shoulders; he had a square, stolid face. He said, "If there were Anzhadi here, *shan'tai*, they wouldn't come in reach of you."

"Is Sethri-safere with you? He'll talk to me. Tell him Lynne Christie – "

"You talk to me or none. What do you want with us, offworlder?"

One of the Peace Force shuttles split the sky overhead. The *hiyek* male flinched. I heard Doug talking with Cory's officers, but I concentrated on the nameless Orthean male.

"Do you want to bring *that* down on you?" I remember Cory saying: All I can do is threaten. And here am I, threatening. "It's hardly an army you've brought with you, ten or a dozen *jath*; and it wouldn't help you if all the Coast were here, would it?"

"Can you take us from among these people?"

He let the question stand. One claw-nailed hand was at his belt, close to that incongruous CAS-IV; and the rising wind blew his unbraided mane across his face, and whisked ashes into the air.

"Can you?" he repeated. "Take the *jath*. There they are. Have them. Take the empty *siiran* on the Coast, and much good may they do you; take the canals, every one of them, and the cities they flow through; take it all, we don't need it now – " His eyes unveiled, they were a striking glass-green. "But if you want us, you must pick us out from among *your friends* – and if there are few of us, there are still fewer of you *s'aranthi*!"

That clear gaze went past me, he stared only at the hull of the shuttle. In that gaze I saw *siiran*, those plant-filled underground chambers of *chiruzeth*, pictured them empty. Pictured Molly Rachel's research team in Maherwa, the canal system's controls left open to their investigation. . . . What's happening on the Coast now, under cover of hurricanes? Do all the *jath* and *jath-rai* wait there, are the men and women of the *hiyeks* beginning to drift back towards their homes, have they abandoned this crusade? Or are there other ships slipping out on to the Inner Sea, a migration rather than an invasion?

"Northerners won't have you on *telestre* land," I said.

"They will have seen this." He jerked his head in the general direction of Rimnith.

"That won't work – "

Doug leaned across and switched from outside transmitter to comlink. "Doug – "

"This is a live transmission. An observer-craft. Lynne, look."

At first it looked like a repeat image of Rimnith. Then I saw that the billowing black smoke rooted on a shallow hill, and that the burning buildings were only half consumed. No person moved, but two – no, three – bodies lay motionless in the burning *hanelys* and reedbeds.

"Keverilde *telestre*," he explained.

"Doug, that's thirty miles away from here."

Another image inset itself over the burning hillside, a close-up of a rocky gully. It was shaded over with the black rods and spines of *hanelys*, and under the vegetation was a gleam of white. Voices over the comlink went wild.

"That's a groundcar!"

"Cory's people can track groundcars, they're energy sources – when they're in use." He paused. "They say the *hiyek* people may have as many as eight or nine."

A lot went through my mind in that silent second. That Sethri must have brought them over, you could load small groundcars on *jath* ships; but what's the black-market connection for Earth technology? That the Peace Force would be able to trace where the *hiyek*-Ortheans moved in Melkathi, and what would they do about that?

I keyed back to exterior-view, but the *hiyek* male had vanished. His body-heat was lost among the deep hidden fires in the peat heathland, sensors couldn't track him now.

"Is Cory herself there? Put her on-link, Douggie, we're going to have to talk to her sometime."

"As government envoy, I have the right to know what action she plans to take – although if she has a modicum of wisdom," Clifford added, "she'll practise some masterly inactivity. . . . Lynne, you know the multicorporates, you know them better than I do: how is PanOceania going to react?"

The comlink suddenly formed a clear image. It was split: half showing Corazon Mendez in the interior of a Peace Force F90, that hawk-face and sleek hair immaculate; the other half was the unsteady image of a wristlink, showing churned earth and excavations and black cloud-cover, and then shifting to the dark face of Molly Rachel. The wind tugged at her coverall, blowing that mass of tangled hair.

" – take *no* immediate action," she was saying. Then: "Lynne? Is that you? Get out of the area. Is that Douglas there with you?" Her voice was loud, raised over the buffeting of the wind and rain.

Doug, over my shoulder, said, "I must know what action you're advising. I protest most strongly against any use of force against the local population by Commander Mendez."

Cory interrupted from the F90. "Damn all national governments! I can't even get data on the size of the invading force. This may be a raid or it may be a full-scale invasion; and until we can get surveillance working, we're as blind as the natives." Her attention shifted to Molly Rachel. "I won't engage in low-tech hostilities on those terms, Representative Rachel. Any action *must* be hi-tech, for the sake of my men."

The Pacifican woman put a hand up to hold shaggy hair out of her face. Rain starred the holo-image. She smiled, almost snorted with humour, and said, "All I want you to do is watch, for the next few hours. I need you *here*, Commander. All hell's broken loose in Kel Harantish – there's fighting inside the city. No one's attacked the T&A site yet, but I want some protection for those installations."

I cut in: "Who's fighting, Molly? Even the Coast *hiyeks* aren't crazy enough to attack the *telestres* and Kel Harantish together."

"This is something internal, some factions in the city – " She broke off. In the background, clearly heard, was the whine of CAS weaponry: the side-leakage of Coherent Amplified Sound. She said, "Some of them have CAS-III and CAS-VIII equipment. When I find out how that got imported. . . ."

"I'll send Jamison down from the orbiter with a squad of flyers," Cory Mendez said. "That should serve as a warning, to keep your installations safe, Representative."

Too much of a coincidence. Someone knew the *telestres* would be attacked, decided to take advantage and act themselves, while the Company's too busy to interfere. . . . I let Doug talk to Corazon and the Pacifican woman, and I thought of Calil bel-Rioch. Alive still, or dead; caught in the fighting, defending, or its instigator? I can't believe she has nothing to do with this.

Doug said, "What's the situation on the canals and in the Coast ports?"

"I've sent out a shuttle on visual surveillance; David Osaka – "

The split image was abruptly blank on the left-hand side, reduced to coruscating light; and Cory's image turned to bawl at her comlink officer to restore the link. Molly's face appeared for a moment, soundlessly speaking, and then again vanished.

"Get out of the area," Cory Mendez cut her link with an equally scant courtesy, and without the excuse of an equipment breakdown. I switched back to exterior-view. In the sepia haze of the sky, specks that were F90s and observation craft quartered the air above Melkathi. Not yet three hours since I'd heard the noon bells ring in the Citadel. Exhaustion had such a grip on me, I felt I could sleep where I sat. And could only then realize that this, this afternoon of Durestha Eighthweek Nineday, is the date the WEBcasters will use to mark the outbreak of war. . . .

281

And what day to mark its end?

"I'm taking us back to Tathcaer," Doug Clifford said. "I have to talk to the *T'Ans*. It's likely that they appreciate the implications, but one must be certain." And then that small-featured round face creased in a smile that held no humour. "God alone knows what they'll do about naming a new *T'An Suthai-Telestre* now."

CHAPTER 23

Night Conference at the Wellhouse

Early afternoon sun shone on the white façades of Tathcaer, on pollen-yellow air, and a harbour full of bustle as *jath-rai* put out to sea. The ferry that took us from Kumiel to the city rocked in their wake.

Riders will have gone out, I thought. And *jath-rai*. None of them can have reached the Rimnith area yet. Blaize won't be back from Eirye. And here *we* are, already back. We live in different worlds.

"It's imperative I have some contact with Molly Rachel again, and in the near future." Doug stepped on to the quay, saying over his shoulder to me: "Will you go up to the Citadel and endeavour to find out the *T'Ans'* reaction to this – " He broke off; smiled. "I'm treating you as though you were advisor to the government. Lynne, I apologize."

"This isn't the time to worry about that. Yes, I'll see the *T'Ans.*"

I stood for a moment and watched him vanish into the crowds, a small neatly-dressed man, dull among the brilliantly-robed Ortheans, intent on reaching the comlink at Westhill-Ahrentine. Faces turned as he passed. Unfriendly looks for *s'aranthi*? Perhaps. I turned to look for a *skurrai-jasin* to take me up to the Citadel, moving again at the Orthean pace.

And the Citadel, that great sprawling stone building, was empty of *T'Ans*; gone down into the city, or out towards Melkathi by whatever means they could travel; all of them gone, except one. My footsteps were loud, walking through those low-roofed halls. It wasn't until I saw his stricken, immobile face that I made the connection: *Nelum Santhil Rimnith*. Dusty sunlight shone on that sleek brown mane, on the unveiled eyes. Grief dazzled him. He no longer wore the insignia of a *T'An* Melkathi.

"Give you greeting, *t'an* Orhlandis," he said, no recognition in his eyes, "tell me how Melkathi burns."

Towards mid-afternoon I got back to Westhill-Ahrentine. The Wellhouse took in Nelum Santhil, and I could find no other *T'An*, mad or sane. Just the steps from the courtyard to the first-floor rooms of the *telestre*-house exhausted me. Twenty-seven hours: a day not to be endured without some break for sleep before evening, the human biological clock demands it.

"Get through to Molly?" I asked, looking in on Doug Clifford where he sat at the comlink.

"Her base at Kel Harantish doesn't answer. Rashid Akida and the research team are being evacuated to the orbiter. . . . " He rubbed red-rimmed eyes. "Corazon suggests that young Rachel and the other two – Pramila, is it, and David Osaka? – may be in the city itself. Some form of protective imprisonment?"

"She'd get out before that happened," I protested. "We've had that once before, she wouldn't. . . . Where the hell *is* she?"

The holotank was now showing pictures of a *telestre*-house. Low, sprawling stone buildings, with *marhaz* pens, and in the background the wind-whipped sandflats and the sea. It seemed untouched, and then the lens panned round to the north, and I saw flames, like the teeth of a comb, jagged on the heathland and sweeping towards the sea.

" – Commander Mendez will make an announcement in four hours," the WEBcaster's voice said.

"Tapping into WEB transmissions?"

"As they go from the orbiter to Thierry's World. I've given the WEBcasters on the orbital station permission to land." Doug keyed across the board, and a half-dozen other transmissions showed variant images of Melkathi. "I estimate that within twelve days every NET at home will carry these transmissions. At that point, surely, some restrictions will be imposed on PanOceania – "

"By the other multicorporates, if by no one else." I touched him lightly on the shoulder. "Leave the Citadel until evening, no one's there. Wake me for Cory's announcement, hey? If I don't sleep, I'm just plain going to fall over sideways. . . . "

He chuckled. "Lynne, you're getting old."

"And when I'm awake, *you* can sleep."

I lay down in the further room on a couch-chair piled with *zilmei* pelts, and the warm air of summer brought the scent of *kazsis*, and the voices of Ortheans in the alley below; all fragile now, all temporary and under threat.

A rough hand shook me awake. Doug's voice said, "You'd better hear this."

"What?"

"Corazon Mendez. She's broadcasting to the WEB personnel on the orbital station."

"*What?*" I sat up, swung my feet off the couch-chair, and the world swam. Light hurt my eyes. Light of early evening, not yet even second twilight. I staggered through to the comlink in the other room, still half doped with sleep.

Doug leaned over the holotank. The image split between WEBcasters, seven or eight of them, clustered in one of the orbiter's cabins, and Corazon Mendez in an F90 shuttle. Adrenalin spurred me awake.

"What has she said?"

"That she's making her announcement before the stated time – listen – "

"I repeat," Corazon's voice came thinly, "this announcement is for the benefit of the Wave-Energy Broadcaster nets. This Company has the situation on Carrick V under control. Necessary action to implement this was taken at 22.00 localworld time, when a surgical strike was made on hostile areas, using six F90 shuttles armed with mid-tech long-range weapons. The F90s used their weapons to make a high-level strike on the following Desert Coast ports: Reshebet, Nadrasiir, Mesh-lamak, Nazkali, Saransiir, Psamnol, Luzukka, Gileshta, Merari, Lakmarash, Kumek-aruk, and Quarth. . . . Satellite surveillance now shows the harbours at these locations to be blocked, and thus impassable to hostile craft intending to invade the northern continent – "

"What?" I said. "She did what?"

Doug moved his hand in an abortive gesture. "She – I don't – we – "

The WEBcasters crowded the 'link in the orbiter. I glimpsed the face of the Visconti woman, saw it stricken, some faint echo of outrage; then someone asked a question not audible on pick-up, but Corazon Mendez heard, and nodded: "Yes. Our F90s left from the government base on Thierry's World. They refuelled from the PanOceania orbiter, and left from our Company docking facilities at 21.30. They made three over-flights and three forensic strikes – "

"Forensic!" Doug spat.

" – and returned to orbital docking. I'm pleased to say all six craft returned safely."

I sank down into the comlink chair, too weary to stand. "Isn't that amazing?" I appealed to Doug. "F90 shuttles attack *jath-rai* and a population armed with knives and rakes, and the shuttles get away *unscathed* – Jesus, they were lucky!"

He gestured for silence, intently keying through the comlink channels; and I guessed he was searching for the satellite-images.

Corazon Mendez finished: "This decision was taken in view of the danger of hostilities spreading from the relatively small area of the northern continent to which they are at present confined, and in view of the possible danger to Company and government personnel stationed at present on Carrick V."

"She can't have – " I tried to key in, found the link restricted.

"What about the Company's commercial representative?" called one of the WEBcasters.

"Full consultations with Representative Rachel took place, and her agreement was given; as was that of the British government for use of refuelling and docking facilities on Thierry's World – "

Doug Clifford's hands froze on the comlink controls. He stared at the silver-haired woman's image, at her self-possessed expression. "That's a lie. That's a lie on both counts. Oh, that *stupid* woman. How could she do this? How?"

The Peace Force Commander added, "Provisional consultation took place on Earth before we left, and approval was given for this type of action."

"*Shit!*" I couldn't key in a contact. Cory wants this between herself and the WEBcasters, I thought, and none of us saying the wrong word; has she really done this without consulting Molly? Has she really done this?

The 'link babbled, WEBcasters vociferously interrupting each other to question her. Blips would already be shuttling back to Earth in FTL drones. I had to stand up, to pace across the room; and at the window I stopped and looked at the sky above the courtyard. At the blue sky and the skeins of daystars. Such a clear sky, and now so dangerous.

"If the *hiyeks* have any hi-tech weapons, they'll use them now. Any minute, any second – " I swung back to face Doug. "I want to go to the orbiter. I want to go up there and tell them *no*, the Company doesn't have our support, *no*, the government didn't agree to their using the base on Thierry's World, *no* – " Anger, shame, and such outrage it left me breathless.

"Here are the satellite transmissions."

I went to stand beside him. The WEBcasters and Mendez were tiny figures in the corner of the tank. The main holo-image shone with the acid-white light of the Coast – have the storms gone *now*, of all times? – that light that shone on ochre earth and the far-distant foothills of the Elansiir mountains.

Reshebet, is it? A curve of *chiruzeth* marks the sea wall. Now you can hardly see it for rubble, rock blasted in from the low ridges that used to line the canals; and in that rubble are the tilted hulls of *jath* ships, that metal shining, but dimmed with dust. Hoop-masts are twisted, *jath-rai* driven up one on the other by the force of the blasts. The canal that runs to the harbour is choked with wreckage and all the low shacks collapsed; the waters of the canal flooding out on to the barren land around, and sinking down and leaving no more than a shadow of water on the earth. . . . Bodies lie in the incandescent sun: Ortheans sprawled under tumbled rock, or floating face down in water; and now as the image moves a little inland there are crowds (seen from above, foreshortened), some moving, strung out along the track beside the canal; some still and silent; there a man holding an *ashiren*, there two pale-maned females, and there, and there.

"The strike was aimed at purely military targets," Corazon Mendez said, in voice-over. "Casualties have been kept to a minimum. I ordered the F90s to make a low pass over these ports at 21.40 and again at 21.50 as a signal to evacuate the local population from the harbour areas."

Doug's hand closed round mine, unconsciously gripping hard enough to hurt. His face had gone a sick colour between yellow and grey.

"The *civilians* are the only military targets on the Coast – " That from a WEBcaster, the dark-haired Roxana Visconti.

"By this action now we will have prevented greater use of force," Cory Mendez said. "Had more than a small fraction of the invasion fleet reached the northern continent, more severe action might have been necessary, which the use of punitive force at this stage has prevented."

Though I tried, I couldn't get the satellite transmission to show me more than that one image. I wanted to know if the harbours were all as devastated; wanted to know how many *jath* ships had been caught in the destruction. "How the hell could we do this! The Company *can't* just – "

"They have," Doug said. He turned away from the holotank, looking at the dusty *telestre*-house room, the brazier and couch-chair and satellite-maps pinned to the walls, and his face was blank with bewilderment. He said, "They can, because they have the power to do so. And now am I supposedly to go to the *T'Ans* here and inform them, 'my government supports what the PanOceania multicorporate has done in attacking Orthean people, and therefore *I* support it'?"

I said, "The Company's always bitching about how NuAsia grabs territory, how ChinaCo does; don't they see this makes them look like any other multicorporate?" I abandoned the holotank. "Doug, you don't have a choice; if you don't go along with the Company, they'll put pressure on at home to have you removed."

"Then I'm very much afraid that that is what they will have to do."

Too cold, too shocked, I couldn't take it all in. There is the sky over the roofs of Tathcaer, an evening sky as clean and clear as any other, and the brilliance of Carrick's Star; and now to wake up this one particular evening and find everything changed –

Doug, neatly fastening the cuffs on his coverall, said, "Some authority is going to have to inform the *T'Ans* and the *takshiriye* what's happening on the Coast now. You're the representative of PanOceania. I'm here on behalf of the government. I suspect that Commander Mendez is well aware that our duty – "

"We weren't consulted, we weren't told, we're not responsible –

Douggie, I don't believe even that *Molly* knows. I can't contact anyone on the Coast. This is Mendez acting on her own."

To outsiders, we will be called responsible. Government envoy, special advisor. . . .

"It won't be a great deal of time before *we* hear from the WEBcasters," Doug said. "Did it look as though public feeling is going to be in favour of what's happened here? I'm familiar with WEB personnel. If they're shocked, groundsiders will be appalled."

Outside, I could hear the evening bustle of Tathcaer, smell the smoke of cooking-fires; and I realized, I can't predict now what the *telestre*-Ortheans will feel about this. Which is more terrible, that an enemy burns Melkathi, or that that enemy has suffered the use of *s'aranthi* weapons?

"The government will be called responsible," Doug Clifford said. He took a breath. "I want to turn around and say I agree with all your condemnations, I am ashamed to be part of this administration. If there was anything I could do to condemn this, I would do it. All I can do is stand helplessly by and watch the mechanism grind on."

The thought of crossing six miles of Tathcaer to the Citadel was exhausting in itself, and as for what explanations would have to be made to Howice and Khassiye and Bethan, to Blaize and Hal, Cassirur, Romare Kerys-Andrethe. . . .

I said, "We've got to try and stop this here. Now. We've got to get these people and the *hiyek*-families to make peace *now*." And then, as we left the room, I said, "But Douggie, have you thought? How will we react if what Mendez has done *does* put an end to the fighting? Does that make her right?"

Starlight shone down through the slot in the roof of the great Wellhouse. That light of Orthe's summer stars, mixed with the glowing yellow of *becamil*-wax candles, shone on the braided manes of hastily-dressed Ortheans where they stood or sat on the stone tiers, shrouded the entrances to that domed, shadowed amphitheatre. Male and female voices rose in a babble; there was the wail of *ashiren*. In a moment's quiet came the whirr of *rashaku* wings and apprehension became tangible: *what message from Melkathi, now?* The clamour of discussion rose louder.

"Attacked the harbours?" Cassirur Almadhera exclaimed, outraged.

"Bombed the harbour entrances to make them impassable to shipping." Doug faced the group of *T'Ans* on the lower tiers of that stone amphitheatre. He stood with his head high; he looked beleaguered and defiant and (though no outsider would see it) ashamed. I moved to stand beside him, before that impromptu council of accusing faces – now they

288

had the news, they seemed determined on wringing us dry of facts.

The starlight robbed Cassirur's mane of scarlet, made her face an ashen mask. Her hand dropped to Hal's shoulder, where he sat below her on the next tier.

"Mother of the Wells! To fight, yes, but to destroy – " She stopped. Earthspeakers care for all land. Romare Kerys-Andrethe, dark and self-satisfied, muttered something to her, and then turned aside, speaking with the blunt and soldierly Bethan *T'An* Kyre. That Orthean woman frowned.

"How dare you act without consulting us?" Haltern made to stand and sank back, pale with anger, ill with it; and Cassirur's hand tightened on his shoulder, that Earthspeaker's sensing touch. He ignored her whispered warning. "Is that a measure of precisely how much your people take note of the Hundred Thousand?"

"Independent action – "

He overrode Doug. "Taken against *us*. Against Ortheans."

That got attention from a group of three: Howice *T'An* Roehmonde whose face held a frown of private concern (Roehmonde being far enough north not to worry just yet, but soon); the elegant and caustic Khassiye Reihalyn, *T'An* Andrethe; and Geren Hanathra, Geren Shipmaster, now *T'An* Ymir. That last looked at me with hatred.

"They're *hiyeks*," Howice *T'An* Roehmonde protested. His plump fingers wound together nervously. "*Hiyeks* and lovers of Witchbreed abominations – what does it matter if *s'aranthi* kill them?"

"Because if they can do that to the Coast," said Haltern n'ri n'suth Beth'ru-elen, "they can do it to us. Isn't that right, *t'an S'aranth*? Christie, am I correct? Pardonable violence against hostile local forces, leading to the imposition of a garrison to see that there's no fighting anywhere; Coast or Hundred Thousand; am I right?"

"Hal – "

"Am I right?" The white mane flew, his voice cracked with anger; and those small brilliant eyes veiled with membrane. "Ortheans have gone to Her at offworlder hands, that's what you've told us; how long before it happens again, in Melkathi, and how will you tell *hiyek* from *telestre*?"

I couldn't tell if he meant land or people; and language being so ambiguous, perhaps his thought was too. He sank back into the *becamil* robes protecting him against the summer night's air. Doug and I stood together on the lower tier by him, and as I looked up I saw how we were surrounded by condemnation: Cassirur and Bethan gazing down, Romare and Howice and Khassiye Reihalyn on the tier above them.

"Tomorrow's the solstice," I said. "Naming day. Midsummer-Eightyear. Tomorrow one of you will be *T'An Suthai-Telestre*. Why do

289

you think we've been so concerned to get this news to you? Nothing compels us to tell you. Listen to me – "

"Listen to the PanOceania Company," Khassiye Reihalyn said, studying the gold studs between his fingers instead of offworlders; speaking with malice.

"*No.*" I took a breath. The *becamil* candles wavered in a breeze from the upper archways, and that yellow light shone on them: picking out gems on the hilts of Khassiye's *harur*-blades, shining on Haltern's white mane, on Bethan's dark skin; making half-shadowed masks of Romare and Howice's expressions. And I remember, ten years ago, a night council in a room in the Citadel. . . .

Geren Hanathra stepped down one tier. Light shone on his yellow mane, on that hardly-aged face. He said, "If I had known what I brought from the Eastern Isles that year, I should have drowned you like vermin. Yes, stand here, *S'aranth*! Stand as she did, *amari* Ruric Orhlandis; betray us as she did – "

"Unfair."

The voice was weak, but it was Haltern's; looking up with pale and whiteless blue eyes; meeting my gaze with something of the old ironic humour.

"She has been a friend to us, Geren; and the *t'an* Clifford also. And that on occasion when it was not to their advantage, I admit it." He smiled. "Better if you hadn't, Christie. It makes it harder for us to see you offworlders as nothing but enemy, all Shadow. Or harder for some of us. . . . I am too old to lie to myself, and make anger cover what I feel, although I have tried."

In the silence that followed, the voices of the other Ortheans in the Wellhouse rang across the stone tiers; and a female in north-province Earthspeakers' gear came over to speak with Cassirur Almadhera; and a Peir-Dadeni rider took Khassiye Andrethe aside. I sat down on the lowest stone tier beside Haltern, and gazed up at the other *T'Ans*.

"You know me. You know Doug and me, and we know the Company. You won't trust offworlders now, and I don't blame you, but I'll tell you this: the only way to stop the Company getting a foothold in the Hundred Thousand is to make peace in Melkathi. Take the excuse for intervention away. You must do that."

A new voice said, "Then it's not us you should talk with, *t'an* Christie, but the Coast families that are burning Melkathi."

It was Nelum Santhil. His face showed strain, but the rationality was back in those dark eyes. He looked as though he'd slept in the crumpled Melkathi robes he wore. One six-fingered hand held a curling strip of parchment: a message from the *rashaku*-relay. Quite deliberately he walked down the stone steps and seated himself on the tier beside me.

"I'll go to Melkathi with you and the *t'an* Clifford," he said. "Christie, you don't trust me, but I care more for Melkathi province than SuBannasen or Orhlandis did. I can talk to the *hiyeks*. The Melkathi *telestres* . . . we know about poverty. About failing harvests. About famine, and plague. Help me to get to the Anzhadi and I'll talk to them about peace." He paused. "I am not to become *T'An Suthai-Telestre*, I know that, so it doesn't matter if I am absent tomorrow – "

"It's against all custom!" Romare Kerys-Andrethe protested.

Cassirur returned from talking with the northern Earthspeaker in time to say, "Custom's a guide-rope and not a chain. *T'An* Christie, will the *hiyeks* in Melkathi have heard what's happened today in Reshebet and the other harbours?"

I looked at Doug. He lifted a brow. "If they happen to have an illegal comlink. As yet I've picked up nothing in the way of unauthorized transmissions."

"If not . . ." Cassirur's eyes veiled, dark, "then they will not know until a *jath* ship reaches them, if it ever does."

"The *hiyeks* will not suddenly become our friends because of this," Romare said. "I hold with your opinion, Earthspeaker; best lull them into peace and then send them to Her. Or will that bring offworlder ships down on *us*?"

"It's a possibility," Doug conceded.

The stolid female in *zilmei* pelts and *skurrai* leather, that I knew vaguely to be Bethan Ivris *T'An* Kyre, said in heavily-accented Ymirian: "*T'Ans*, weren't there new *telestres* founded in Peir-Dadeni, some five hundred years gone? Let these others, these *hiyeks*, go north into the Barrens, over Broken Stair; or west into the wilderness. Let them make *telestres* there by Her will. The *kazsis* flowers where the vine is trained. So in ten generations they will be of the *telestre*, as we are."

Nelum Santhil looked up at her. "Is there land, or only wilderness? Can anyone live there?"

Cassirur interrupted: "The *hiyeks* have lived too long with Witchbreed science. Will you send them into the Witchbreed's ruined cities now, will you have them bring back that Empire? Who knows what lies undiscovered in the Barrens?"

Nelum Santhil and Bethan Ivris ignored her, and I looked at the two of them, this mountain woman, and this male from the arid city Ales-Kadareth. I almost wanted to laugh, seeing how the *T'Ans* of the prosperous *telestres* looked affronted. What would Suthafiori have made of these two outsiders? She might well have overruled Ymir, Rimon, Roehmonde, Peir-Dadeni, if she thought it made better sense. . . .

"Word from the *t'an* Meduenin," Nelum Santhil said, at last holding up the ribbon-message that he had been absently winding and unwinding in those dark six-fingered hands. "Blaize Meduenin sends word, he has spoken with one Jadur Anzhadi of the Coast, taken a prisoner near Keverilde *telestre*. This *shan'tai* Jadur speaks of the destruction of Reshebet."

Excitement flickered on all those Orthean faces. So the Anzhadi *do* have an illegal comlink, I thought. They know what Cory's done. Is it coincidence that Jadur is one of Sethri's *raiku*? Is he a prisoner or a would-be envoy?

Nelum handed the ribbon-message across to Hal, who peered short-sightedly at the script.

"If we can speak with the Anzhadi *now*," Nelum urged, "they and the *hiyeks* back on the Coast have suffered greatly. Let's make what offer we can, while that shock's new. *T'An* Christie's right. There must be no excuse for offworld intervention."

Geren and Howice and Khassiye broke out into protest, interrupting each other; Cassirur bent over Hal's shoulder to read the message, pointing, speaking excitedly; Nelum Santhil obdurately blocked her objections. Bethan enthusiastically spoke to other *s'ans* who, attracted by the shouting, moved down several tiers to speak with the *T'Ans*. Doug urbanely cut Howice *T'An* Roehmonde off in mid-argument. It was minutes before I realized, in the middle of it all, that my wristlink was signalling for attention.

I stepped aside from the group, on to the Wellhouse floor. A few yards from where I stood, the black Wellmouth gaped, and I felt a chill come up from the water fifty feet below.

"Christie here."

The distance-thinned voice said, "Corazon Mendez. I'm sending a shuttle to pick you up from the settlement at o8.oo localworld time."

"Now hold on just a minute – "

Corazon said, "I don't have time to argue. You're special advisor to the Company, Lynne. I have the authority to co-opt personnel."

Cory's an old hand at this, knows not to antagonize Company staff, so why – ? And then I thought, *If I didn't know Commander Mendez better, I'd say this was fear.*

The clipped tones went on: "I'm taking a squad down to the Kel Harantish settlement and I may need an expert on xeno-psychology. That's you, Lynne. Meet the shuttle on Kumiel Island at o8.oo."

The wristlink blurred: empty channel. I stood staring at the black Wellmouth, not really aware of what I saw. If Cory Mendez is this concerned . . . what has she heard from Molly Rachel in Kel Harantish? What else can happen?

"I intend to travel down to Keverilde," Doug said as he extricated himself from the crowd of Ortheans on the stone tiers. He was flushed, slightly ruffled; above all, determined. "Who was the call?"

"I may have to go down to the Coast and sort things out with Molly."

He registered my non-answer and smiled. "That information could be useful, now there's some progress here. It's a good thing that you still have access to the Company."

Starlight shifted on the floor of the Wellhouse dome. The air near the Wellmouth was cold, dark. Easy to be confident here in Tathcaer, I thought, but there are so many other factors; so many things that can still happen. . . .

More soberly, Doug said, "Ascertain, if you can, what part young Rachel played in authorizing today's attack. I need to have the full facts at my disposal when I enter the protest at home. I think that, despite current events, I shall still protest. . . . "

I couldn't hide it: I knew it then, knew it when I stood on Kumiel six hours later in the cold dawn, waiting for the Company shuttle. What drove me to leave was not a desire to find out what was happening on the Coast, urgent though that might be. I left because it would be too humiliating to have to say to Ortheans, in Tathcaer or in Keverilde, Corazon Mendez has succeeded where I have so far failed.

CHAPTER 24

A Mortal Coldness

Corazon Mendez herself led me down the shuttle's cabin to comfortable seats and flasks of coffee. That sleek white hair was immaculate, black coveralls with hardly a crease; and her face showed no strain. She said, "You're aware, no contact at all can be made now with the T&A site at Kel Harantish?"

The seats were soft. I drank, set the flask back in its socket as the F90 thrummed into flight. The angle of ascent was sharp. Rising up to hi-orbit, then dropping down to the Coast; profligate with fuel, but taking hours rather than the two days flying over the Inner Sea. PanOceania can afford it.

Cory Mendez settled seat-webs across us. Attempting humour, she said, "I'm sorry your expected disaster failed to materialize, after the strike."

"Cory, for God's sake! I warn you, I'll register the strongest possible protest at home, and I'll make it stick. When something goes wrong here the Company will want a scapegoat, and I'll do my best to make certain that it's you."

There was a smile on that lean face. To do her justice, she tried to hide it.

"It's a catastrophic failure of judgement," I said at last. "You can stop hostilities temporarily, but – Christ, I sound as though I *want* a disaster. It's not so. Cory, I'm terrified of what's going to happen on Orthe now, and that's the truth."

She nodded twice, those sharp blue eyes on me; had a smile that might be humour or sympathy. "I think you underestimate the effectiveness of being brutal. You'd let matters go on until there was no other option but a major hostile incident, and one all the worse for being delayed. I don't deny the strike resulted in casualties. That's cauterization. We can't allow what we would have had – war with an alien population who've got their hands on hi-tech weaponry." Now her smile was entirely conscious of irony. "Your Coast farmers wanted to know about CAS and projectile weaponry. Very well, we've just given them an object lesson. It's far more effective than Clifford's diplomatic bleatings. Some situations can only be resolved through fear."

294

The shuttle tilted, power roaring, reaching up towards the edge of the atmosphere. Six miles below us that blue globe turns.

"They're not children, to all be scared of fire because one burned its fingers."

"Lynne, that's exactly what they are."

As I looked round the cabin at Cory's officers at their consoles, I felt desperately isolated. "You've acted on your own authority. Will Molly Rachel back you up? If she's been in protective custody in Kel Harantish, she won't necessarily have heard what's happened. Better have a good explanation ready."

"We have to have order." Cory's face, that lined face, sharp as a bird of prey, was open and honest now. "We saw the early years of the Dispersal, Earth falling apart because suddenly there was a universe full of inhabited, reachable worlds. The Companies are the thread that ties us together now. PanOceania can't afford violence on worlds where it has an interest. Lynne, I spoke to some of your Ortheans in Tathcaer. Their attitude is the same: they'd sooner win, as I would, by the wrong means, than not win at all. Do me the credit of believing that when I say 'win' I don't refer to military battles?"

The shuttle tilted back to level, slowing, and I knew we would shortly dock and refuel at the orbiter. I didn't meet the older woman's gaze. What now? Leave Doug to mediate in the Hundred Thousand, put some Company man like David Osaka in Morvren Freeport; there's Carrick V settled as another Company market. Research into Witchbreed artifacts can go ahead unhindered. Working towards some hypothetical break-through. . . . And what happens to me? Self-pity aside, it's a good question; I've messed up at least two careers in these past few months, and it looks as though it's all been for nothing.

"Kel Harantish . . ." Cory looked thoughtful.

"I can give you a considered opinion on that," I said. "If Dannor bel-Kurick, the Emperor-in-Exile, has been fighting – it'll be over contact with Earth technology, and I think there are groups there powerful enough to overrule him. Molly won't be in any danger if, say, Calil bel-Rioch is protecting her."

"The faction in that settlement that supports the Company is strong enough?" Mendez queried.

"I wouldn't be surprised to find Calil as Voice of the Emperor again. Or, in all but name, Emperor herself. All that worries me is that Molly and the others may have been caught in the city when fighting broke out, and handled it badly."

"It may not be as straightforward as I previously indicated – " She paused. Metallic echoes thrummed through the ship as we docked. Then

295

as we waited she said, "It was unwise to risk on an open comlink, particularly when the equipment you were using is the property of the government envoy. This is another reason why I requested your presence. Your knowledge of the archeological background."

"I don't understand."

"I believe that Representative Rachel *is* in the settlement," she said. "One of her last transmissions before loss of contact had to do with the Old Technology. She indicated they might have had a conceptual breakthrough."

"Rashid's team – "

Cory linked her fingers, and the thick silver rings clinked together. "That was a deliberate lie. Rashid Akida and several of the research personnel were not among the people evacuated up to the orbital station. There's a high probability they're still with Representative Rachel."

She loosed the seat-web, preparatory to going to the comlink to authorize the refuelling. "A conceptual breakthrough on Golden science – all the more reason to protect Company personnel by keeping the peace, if Carrick V is going to be a major market for us."

I watched her walk across the cabin to speak with her officers. The level hum of power and the shuttle interior's warmth were soothing, too soothing for the couple of hours' sleep I'd had; time began to slip. Half-awake, half-asleep, I expected every chime of the comlink to announce some dream-parallel of Mendez's announcement – was that really only twelve hours ago? – from the Hundred Thousand, Doug Clifford saying how temporary this temporary peace had turned out to be. . . .

I sat up, made a mental effort to stay awake. Panic suddenly made me breathless. Is it possible to become too awake? I saw the shuttle clearly, heard the signal of completed fuelling, and at the same time felt the surge of memories – memories resisted because I knew them to be delusion – and in an instant experienced the full force of vision –

The sky is cold; palest blue. Wind cuts like ice. The light on the horizon is silver, as if Orthe's dawn came at once from all quarters of the horizon. The light is silver. Against it, silhouetted, the ramps and towers and terraces of a great city; that great city, Archonys.

"Speak," she says. "Do we have the trick of it yet; do we have the secret?"

The language of the slave race falls from those thin lips easily, and it should not, but how else could we comprehend her? And I know that thin and high-boned face, with honey-yellow eyes; that pale gold-dusted skin and floating mane: she who is given the name of Zilkezra of the High Lands, Zilkezra of the Golden, sister of Santhendor'lin-sandru.

She says, "You have laboured long and hard for it, and for us, and for love of us, and have not yet succeeded?"

"We have that knowledge," I tell her. "We have worked, we understand it, we give it to you freely. That ancient light will take Archonys, but that great city will not die alone."

Her hands on my shoulders are cold. She turns me to face those others gathered here, on the great terrace above the Six Lakes. Hawk faces and golden eyes and slender bodies in metalmesh robes, and I must lower my eyes. Their gaze upon me is a mortal coldness. And they are more beautiful than the silver dawn.

"Now you see," she says, "this that we created from the beasts of this world to be Our servant, this has served us well. This child of Orthe has given our revenge into our hands." And she says, "Let them in future time grub in the dirt, I will make death their only crop. Let this be a cold world, a sterile world, let it blaze back the sun's light like a star; let nothing move on the face of it but the cold wind, and the dust of cities, and the dust of men."

The light on the horizon is silver, older than Time; an ancient light, the brilliance of annihilation. Yet more beautiful stand Zilkezra and the Golden of Archonys; we who are but their made children, their slaves, we stand appalled at that beauty which we desire. How many of us, in other lives, will deny all but our slavery? When Orthe is a world of telestres and hiyeks, will we deny that some of us loved the Golden, worked with them, for them; and for love of them created that destruction, as some of us for hate created their sterile deaths? –

Vision gave way to an uneasy calm. I put it behind me, as I put all such experiences behind me now, and tried to think of what might be occurring below, as the Company F90 shuttle raced the dawn-line down to the surface of the Harantish peninsula. Could only think of Corazon Mendez's phrase and the Company research team: 'a conceptual breakthrough on Golden science'. And in what area of Golden science it might be.

Cory Mendez took the seat beside me. "Jamison reports dry storms in the Harantish area, suggests breathing-gear."

"What does he say about the base?"

"The excavation site is deserted. The F90s are on autolock." She steepled her fingers and rested her chin on them; silver rings dented her skin. Her gaze was abstracted. She said, "I wish communications were – more reliable."

Windlasses creaked. *Del'ri*-fibre ropes thrummed in the wind as the platform inched lower. White sky blazed over white earth; heat sucked the breath from my mouth. Dust stung the side of my face, particles sharp as glass, and I squinted up through the eyeshields at a robed figure gripping the platform's rail. As the wooden structure grounded, grating

297

on the rock at the base of Kel Harantish's walls, I saw three other figures: guards in brown scale-mail. The first figure stepped forward, peering at us through veils of white dust.

"*Kethrial-shamaz shan'tai!*" called Pathrey Shanataru. He linked six-fingered hands across his podgy belly, that was now swathed in fine-textured black-and-golden robes. He inclined his head in my direction, then included Cory and Jamison: "You are expected, which I think you may know. Come into the city."

Cory Mendez slipped the air-tube from her mouth, coughed at the dust in her throat, and said, "Is Representative Rachel in the settlement?"

Pathrey's dark eyes shifted. Veiled as they were against the dust-storms, their expression could not be easily read.

I glanced at the guards. "Is there still fighting going on?"

"No, *shan'tai* Christie." A sly smile spread over his rotund features. "I am bid, by the Empress-in-Exile, to welcome you, and bring you to her."

Cory raised white brows at *Empress*. In Sino-Anglic, she said, "We'll have to go in. It should be safe enough."

Pathrey Shanataru stood aside to let Mendez and her junior officer Jamison walk on to the lift-platform. I saw Pathrey note the presence of CAS weaponry. He made no open protest. Only, as I joined them, he stood so that his face was not visible to the Peace Force officers, and spoke quietly enough for the wind to mask his words.

"You must be cautious, *shan'tai* Christie. We Harantish are not the same now. I think sometimes – " and he stopped, and said no more.

"Is Molly Rachel in the city? Pathrey – "

'Oh yes," he said. "*Shan'tai*, it should not be I who tells you."

Corazon Mendez stood foursquare on the platform as it lifted, no thought for the gulf of air below. Dust whitened her uniform. She towered a head taller than Pathrey when she leaned over to us.

"*Shan'tai* – " the polite term came unfamiliar from her lips " – I warn you, it's ill-advised to procrastinate. The Company is in a position to demand the full facts."

It is? I thought. The small Orthean male nervously brushed away dust that the wind lodged in his robes. He gazed out at empty air. I knew in an intuitive flash what he would say.

"I am sorry for this," Pathrey Shanataru said, "and I should not tell you, *she* should, she will be angry. . . . Your Representative Molly Rachel is badly hurt."

Cory demanded, "How badly? What is the extent of her injuries? What medical care has she received?"

Fear and intuition together made me look at Pathrey, at those shifting

298

dark eyes. It came to me, that this might be bad enough to put Molly out of action for – weeks? months? *But I need her here, need her to restrain Cory's Force. Hell, I never thought I'd say that!*

"Where is she?" I asked.

"You will be brought to her, *shan'tai*."

Cory said, "Make it fast."

The wooden platform jerked to a halt, hung swaying above emptiness. The Harantish guards dismounted and steadied it as we climbed down on to the city's roofs. Pathrey hurried us without pause across the expanses of white stone, up steps, down ramps; past roof-houses first lost and then disclosed by the whirls of dust. I found the air clearer at this height, slipped the air-tube out and took a breath, smelling dry earth and sun-warmed stone, and somewhere something rank.

Pathrey dropped back a step, letting Cory and Jamison walk ahead between the guards. I said quietly, "Is it Calil bel-Rioch who's Empress-in-Exile?"

"Calil bel-Dannor." A smile vanished somewhere in that fat brown face, and his unveiled eyes were small, dark, and brilliant. "It became necessary to disclose that *shan'tai* Calil is in fact the daughter of Dannor bel-Kurick, abandoned in the lowest levels of Kel Harantish in childhood, and so," he said with a disarming satisfaction, "fully entitled to succeed him as Empress, after his unfortunate final, fatal illness."

"What a fortunate coincidence that it should be so."

He caught the dry tone, smiled; and there was something in that expression of ruefulness, of bewilderment. "She's . . . changed. Ah. *Shan'tai*, ignore what you see now. The fighting is not long over."

He spoke to the guards, and one stayed outside the small roof-house which we now entered. Corazon ducked her head to enter. I saw her speak to the burly Jamison, who checked his wristlink, and remained with the Harantish male. The other guards, pale-maned females so alike as to be a twin-birth, lifted up the heavy trap door.

I preceded Cory down the *del'ri* climbing-web into the chamber below. Despite common sense, I waited to hear the trap slam behind me – it didn't. Cory Mendez and Pathrey Shanataru climbed down. It being comparatively dark, it was not until I had stood for a moment on the stone-tiled floor that I saw the stains. Great patches of black liquid that seeped down into the gaps between the tiles and stained the plaster walls. In the dim light, the smeared print of a six-fingered hand was plain on one wall. Curving smears of black on the floor led to bundled *del'ri* mats in the far corner of the chamber. . . .

"*Shan'tai*." Pathrey Shanataru held open the trap door set in this floor, disclosing a flight of stone steps.

Corazon Mendez walked over to the heap of *del'ri* mats, boot-heels clicking on the tiles. She bent to lift one corner. I saw how her mouth quirked; expectant, sardonic. She let the corner of the matting fall back.

"Knives and swords are messier than CAS," she remarked, in Sino-Anglic.

"*Shan'tai.*" Pathrey, insistent, at the trap door. I couldn't catch his eye. I was suddenly aware of the heat, of that smell that (to human senses) is not quite rot. Disgust lodged in my throat, sour as vomit. I walked over to him and down the stone steps.

Five levels below, the stone walls changed to *chiruzeth*. My legs ached, and my eyes also, with straining against the gloom. The dust-storms outside dimmed the mirror-reflected light. Black stains spattered the stairway. I saw no more bodies.

"Pathrey . . ."

"Dannor bel-Kurick was not without friends," Pathrey said, leading us down another flight of *chiruzeth* steps. The air felt cool. The blue-grey walls held a luminosity only seen in peripheral vision. Neither Pathrey nor the guards stumbled as Cory and I did, and when he turned his face to me, I saw his dark eyes were unveiled and deep.

We went down, down steps sharp as if newly cut, for all they must date back to the days of the Empire. Through chambers whose walls were carved with bas-relief images, some glint of light striking from a curve or angle. The air seemed full of swirling, grainy particles; smelled of scorching, and that hidden corruption. Exertion left me panting for breath, heart hammering, muscles trembling.

The last flight of steps ended at the beginning of a wide, low-roofed chamber. I stepped down on to the *chiruzeth* floor. The light was dim. By chance I looked to the left. A pale-maned Harantish male lay beside the wall, face buried in the crook of his arm. The black that stained the floor was not shadow. I took a step in that direction and then stopped: what seemed like movement was the crawling of beetle-like insects on his naked back. They rustled.

"Lynne," Cory said.

I turned away. That sharp face of hers was calm. You're used to it, I thought. Then: I've seen it before. Yes. I never get used to it.

With something between black humour and hysteria, I caught the black-and-gold sleeve of Pathrey's robe. "Just how many friends did Dannor bel-Kurick have?"

"Many that one wouldn't have taken to be so," Pathrey Shanataru said. "In truth, I think some of them themselves didn't know it."

Cory raised her wristlink. In the silence, I heard Jamison answer; and after a second, an answer from the orbiter. It reassured me to hear another human voice in this charnel-house.

"Pathrey, did Calil permit this?"

He said, "You'll see the Empress-in-Exile now, *shan'tai.*"

We walked on. The two brown-mailed guards flanked us. A brighter light became visible at the arched end of the chamber, a yellow glow outlining the curve of *chiruzeth.* Our footsteps sounded loudly, but Pathrey's bare feet were silent.

"Stay here," he ordered the guards, at the arch. I saw a look of relief pass between them. Then we entered through the archway and I realized, *Dannor bel-Kurick saw us here.* This low, wide chamber; alcoves to either side still crowded with the refuse of millennia. . . . We paced down the narrow central passage between heaps of relics, towards lights and clustered groups of people. Light that came from candles on great iron stands reflected back from *chiruzeth* artifacts, from metal belts on shimmering red and blue and viridian robes, from metal combs in unbraided white manes. Heads began to turn at our approach. A young Harantish female laughed, was checked when an older woman touched her arm; three males in black robes whispered together. I looked at their narrow-chinned faces, the eyes that were whiteless brown or black, those manes dyed white; saw how they were imitations –

On the terrace that looks down on the Six Lakes, slender bodies in metalmesh robes; they who walk as dancers, white manes unbraided to the wind.

– but this is Kel Harantish, not Archonys. Kel Harantish, hard and white-shelled; inside, all the soft colours of corruption.

"The sooner we get the Representative out, the better," Cory said in an undertone. "Medical care will be on a primitive level, here, and . . ." Her voice trailed off.

Pathrey, walking with his head high, led us between towering stands of candles thick with congealed wax; between the gathered Harantish Ortheans; out into the empty floor between them and the arched end of the chamber. I felt my boot catch, glanced down, saw the *chiruzeth* floor was coated black – for a moment saw nothing else. Candlelight gave way to a light that is pale blue and lilac. The glow of sphere-lights.

"Give you greeting," said a voice, muffled; a mouth half full of food. I took a pace forward. The black bloodstains were wet on the *chiruzeth* floor. My gaze followed the liquid to where it still sluggishly flowed –

A pile of white, round objects shone in the cold light. The heap was as high as my waist. Two other heaps lay near the dais and the carved *chiruzeth* throne, that I dimly saw now was occupied. White objects, ovoid, speckled with black. Then I saw the slanting, narrow eyesockets;

the teeth in broken jaw-bones, the cranial sutures of inhuman, alien skulls. The bone before me was old, dried to yellow; but the stains were fresh, and so –

I fixed my eyes on a level, didn't (couldn't) look at the other charnel heaps, afraid (aware) that they were not old. . . .

"Give you greeting," the voice repeated. Something moved in the air. I flinched. A bitten *arniac*-fruit hit the *chiruzeth* floor and rolled to the edge of that heap of severed bone. I looked up.

She leaned back in the carved *chiruzeth* throne, chewing, and sipping from a carved bowl of *del'ri* wine. That thin face had a grin on it. Her white mane was roughly braided up, and her feet were bare and dirty. Her short white robe was stained on the breast with spilled *del'ri*. The thin copper chains that girdled her waist were green with verdigris. Sphere-lights hung in empty air above that throne, shedding light the colour of lilac and lightning.

She stood, stepped down from the throne, and kicked aside fragments of bone as she walked up to me. Her yellow eyes were sunnily cheerful. She wiped her *arniac*-stained hands down her robe. *A child*, I thought, *little and dirty and brilliant and bad. Calil bel-Rioch. Calil bel-Dannor.* Then her eyes met mine and it was a woman I saw, a Golden woman: Empress-in-Exile.

Pathrey Shanataru stepped past Cory and myself. "I told them *shan'tai* Rachel was here and injured – "

Her hand struck once, vicious and fast. The blow echoed in the low-roofed chamber. Pathrey's head rocked back, then he touched his mouth and looked at the dark blood on his fingers. Someone in the crowd behind us laughed. I glanced back. Even in that crepuscular light I could see the numbers of Harantish there were growing.

"I'm glad to see you again, *shan'tai* Christie. This will be Commander Mendez? I've heard of you, *shan'tai*; give you greeting." Calil inclined her head. Her voice held immense good humour. That studied normality chilled me.

Corazon Mendez said, "I understand you offered protective shelter to Representative Rachel and other personnel. Rashid Akida, Pramila Ishida, and David Osaka." Cory's voice stayed even, but she looked white round the eyes and mouth.

"Did we? Possibly. *Pathrey* – " This last in a very different tone. The plump dark male bobbed his head, half reached out a hand to her.

"The Representative is in the ninth level, *K'ai* Calil."

"You'd better conduct the *shan'tai s'aranthi* there." Calil turned away dismissively. She mounted the low steps to the throne.

Candles hissed, the only noise: bare feet on *chiruzeth* are silent. None of that crowd of Harantish Ortheans spoke. Light cast rounded shadows on the floor from those abattoir piles of skulls that clustered round the throne. I breathed shallowly but the stink of blood still caught in my throat; if it had been human, animal instinct would have made me vomit. Outside the circle of candle and sphere-light, eyes watched, dim figures there. Only *she* stood out clearly. That small figure, now seated on the *chiruzeth* throne, one foot tucked up under her; biting into a handful of *arniac*-fruit and dripping red juice on to the lap of her robe. She reached up to tuck a tendril of mane back behind her ear, and that claw-nailed hand left red smears on her cheek. I met her eyes. Yellow-eyed, that fox-face, bright with humour. Fear cramped in my stomach: *Here is a dream made flesh. Here is the child of Santhendor'lin-sandru and Zilkezra.*

"My Pathrey Shanataru is something of a liar," she said, still smiling. "Your Molly Rachel is not injured. She was injured. She is dead now."

CHAPTER 25

Traitor's Gate

"Don't talk to me about xeno-psychology," Cory Mendez said grimly. "That woman's a psychopath!"

She keyed her wristlink as she walked. Pathrey led us down yet more steps, into higher-roofed halls and small chambers. He glanced back at her, worried. She swore under her breath.

"Getting interference again. Lynne, I suggest we act *very* carefully from now on."

If we'd been a day sooner, half a day, could we have prevented this? I felt exhausted, afraid.

"Here, *shan'tai.*" Pathrey stopped at the arched entrance of a tiny room. He touched my arm, and said miserably, "I thought to prepare you. . . . I know *s'aranthi* are shocked by deaths. That was the reason for the lie."

His speech was slurred, his mouth swelling from Calil's blow. I pushed past him into the small room. Mirror-reflected light was dim, but bright enough to show the place was empty but for a pallet on the floor.

Molly Rachel lay there, half-curled on her left side. Her eyes were partly open, but only a line of white showed under the lids; and she was too still. I felt the cold, soft skin of her throat for a pulse; her black hair brushed my wrist, and I shivered. She had been dead long enough, I saw, for the blood to pool in those parts of her body nearest the floor. The last act of planetary gravity. A darker flush on that dark skin.

"Knife wound," Corazon Mendez said, squatting down to touch the ribcage. She picked up the unresisting hand and began to undo the wristlink. Without thought I grabbed at her arm: "Leave her!"

I stopped. "Sorry. Cory, I didn't mean – "

"It has to be a job. It's the only way to look at it. And this," Mendez said, that hawk-face with a flush of anger, "*this*, dying on some stupid backwater world, just because you're caught in the crossfire – it's tragic."

Sometimes I despise myself for the ability to become detached, but I used it now: looked down at Molly Rachel's body and allowed myself to feel nothing. I said, "We must find out about the others, Rashid and David and Pramila."

Cory bent to recover the Pacifican woman's wristlink. "Records have been made recently. Says here, they're for your eyes." She handed the

304

wristlink to me. "I have to abide by that, I suppose, but there may be data here that it's essential I have."

"You'll see it."

Cory Mendez bent over the body again, and I left the small room for the larger outer chamber. Pathrey Shanataru would have followed but I stopped him with a look. *One of these Harantish killed her, deliberately or by accident – who?*

And does it really matter now?

The wristlink's holo-image was tiny and clear: Molly Rachel's face. Brown skin, loop-tangled hair, luminous brown eyes. A squint of exhaustion drew her face into taut lines. And now she lies a few yards away, skin smoothed free of strain. . . . The dead voice came thin and clear.

"A few points, Lynne, while I'm stuck here inactive – I might as well. Have this sense of *déjà vu*. Regarding Kel Harantish, isn't this where we came in?"

Her image chuckled. Something caught my breath.

"I'm leaving the northern continent as your department, but it must be brought under control. I hesitate to say this, but make whatever deals with Clifford's government that you have to. This isn't the time for the Company to be fussy.

"I . . . might need you here for a short period of time. The Calil woman bothers me. I know it means the risk that you'll react with false memories to Witchbreed artifacts – that's why I let you go north – but I may need your help."

The dark face was illuminated with mirror-light. What I could see of the background showed a *chiruzeth*-walled room. The deep levels of this city. And is she alone?

"I'm duplicating this part of the report to home office and Cory Mendez. If it wasn't for the atmospheric interference, I'd send it through to the orbiter. . . . There'll have to be an investigation but I'm pretty certain, Lynne; the illegal CAS weapons came in on the authority of Pramila Ishida. You know she has a – connection – with *hiyek*-Anzhadi. Sethri-safere. As far as I know, she's with them now. Lynne, she's done what I, God forgive me, always expected you to do: she's gone native. I've put a stop to the illegal arms trade, but as for what's already come in under the guise of agricultural equipment . . ."

The recorded image cut out. Immediately it re-formed. Time had obviously passed. Molly's coverall was rumpled, stained on one cuff with *arniac*-juice. She spoke with strained alertness: "I've been cut off from contact with Rashid and David. If the damned comlinks would only *work*. . . . There has to be some way of overriding the radiation from the wastelands, if that's what this is. I . . . assume Rashid and David are unharmed. If I knew how the rumour got about that the Maherwa research is successful, I'd – we still don't know the first thing about Golden science, whatever Rashid says."

The image remained still for so long that I thought it might have frozen, except that the dark lashes from time to time slid down over her brown eyes. At last she drew a long breath.

"And if Rashid *is* right, that makes being caught in this settlement a catastrophic error of judgement on my part. For that reason, I've destroyed all Company records here. I don't trust Calil bel-Rioch with any technology. If you come here, Lynne, you'll hear it: she calls herself 'Empress'. Not 'Empress-in-Exile'. . . . And now I don't know if Rashid or David are still alive, or – you see, I never intended that we should break the cultural restrictions by giving Golden science to *Ortheans*, and you blame me for searching out a commercial interest for the Company but how else can we justify the aid?"

That thin recorded voice paused. I stood in the large, dimly-lit chamber. What would you feel now, Molly; what would you say, if you knew then that you were about to die?

"I can't tell what's possible," the dead woman said. "Do you know, I half hoped your crazy theory about Kasabaarde was true, if only for your sake, and then that turned out to be propaganda. How can I judge what's alien? I thought the Harantish only knew how to maintain the canals by rote, by ritual transfer of knowledge they didn't understand. Now I'm not so sure."

The image flickered again. By the wristlink's indicator, not much of the recording left to run. When the holo-image formed again, Molly Rachel looked tired and filthy, but she pushed back her tangled hair with long dark fingers, and grinned.

"Still can't get a contact out, but I can overhear transmissions. Must mean the interference is waning again. Lynne, I recorded this for you because you're next in seniority; David's here – I've just seen him. Pramila. . . . God knows what the Company's going to do about Pramila. I want you to deputize for me formally in the Hundred Thousand. Use this place as a threat, if you have to; not sure quite how, but you'll think of something! I know you. We'll have to make sure Commander Mendez doesn't overstep the mark. I believe we're nearly there, Lynne. The fighting's stopped, the Empress-in-Exile says we're released from protective imprisonment. I should see you within two or three hours – in person, or by 'link. Take care."

The record ran through to its end.

What happened in that blank time between that and her death? Silence

306

is the only reply. The *chiruzeth* hall was cold, and I shifted my weight, aware of cramp from standing so fixedly to watch the wristlink's image. When I looked up, Cory Mendez was waiting.

"Here." I handed her the wristlink.

As she activated it, I saw Pathrey Shanataru still at the entrance to that tiny room where Molly Rachel's body lay. Watching me. His black mane hung in sleek curls down his spine, but despite that and his new black-and-gold robes, he still had that indefinable air of seediness.

"*Shan'tai* Christie," he said softly, and beckoned. When I left Cory Mendez and crossed the chamber to his side, he offered me a metal flask that hung at his belt. The liquid in it had the harsh bite of *del'ri*-spirit. I drank down half of it, feeling the fire.

"How did she die?"

"I don't know. That," he said, "is true, *shan'tai*."

And if it isn't, what can I do about it? I tried again: "Where's David Osaka? And Rashid Akida?"

He wiped his forehead, looking uncomfortable. "If *K'ai* Calil says your people were never here, then believe her, *shan'tai*."

There was fear under his obsequiousness. I glanced over at Cory – lost in the wristlink's record – and then back at this sleek Harantish male. He had to look up to meet my eyes. There was something in the movement that said *Witchbreed!* even of this plump, dark male; the faintest echo of the Golden.

"Pathrey – tell me about Calil bel-Rioch. Bel-Dannor. How long have you known her?"

"All my life," Pathrey Shanataru said. "No, *shan'tai* Christie, she's twenty years younger than I, but I think I had no life until I knew her. She was a barefoot brat, then, running the roofs with the other beggars. Traders' *ashiren*, the lowest caste. I come of a science bloodline, my people know canals and *siiran*. Did that bring her to me? I don't know."

He raised the metal flask and drained it of *del'ri*, looking back at me with vulnerable eyes.

"I remember the first time I saw her. She was fighting another *ashiren* for a scrap of *del'ri* bread. Won it, too. Ate a mouthful and then stamped the rest into the dirt." Pathrey paused, embarrassed. "She speaks of you sometimes, *shan'tai* Christie. She would not like it if I spoke of her to you."

"Is she mad?"

He winced at the direct question. He brushed one claw-nailed hand over his face, an oddly ineffectual gesture.

"You can't judge her, *shan'tai*. She has always seen . . . more. She made me travel with her, we went as far as the Rainbow Cities; and everyone who set eyes on her shunned her as Golden, as Kel Harantish is shunned; and she would tell me how, one day, Kel Harantish would stand alone."

When he paused, I waited. His dark gaze was far away.

"I remember once we went to Kasabaarde, in the dress of mercenaries. She wouldn't enter the inner city. When she saw the Tower, from a distance, I remember she said to me, 'If not for that we could hold command over all the *hiyeks*.' So I asked, what about the north? And she said, 'They come of the same stock, they would follow us without thought.' I remember she looked at the spire of the Rasrhe-y-Meluur as a beggar's child looks at bread. . . . "

His soft voice raised hissing echoes, here in this *chiruzeth* chamber nine levels below ground; here in the chill that is never disturbed by the Desert Coast's heat. Mendez still watched the wristlink. Something in the line of her back told me her attention had shifted.

Pathrey's dark gaze met mine. "Do you lay blame on her? She sees our people prostitute their skills, only to keep us supplied with food and water; which elsewhere all men take for granted. . . . I saw her weep, once. The white plague took a hold on the city. It was three seasons before we could bury all the dead – bury them, because they were poison meat. All they gave her was the contempt they had for a trader's child, and yet she wept."

"That butchery in the throne-room, will she weep for that?" I grabbed his shoulders. The fine cloth robe bunched in my hands as I shook him. "That's one of my people *there*, dead, will Calil weep for *her*?"

Cory Mendez glanced up. I released Pathrey. It was an effort to unclench whitened fingers. He rubbed his shoulder with a plump hand, looking up at me reproachfully.

I said, "Pathrey, how long will you survive in Calil's court?"

That soft gaze was suddenly shrewd. The self-justification I'd identified in his tone vanished, replaced by something harder. He said, "I can talk to her. She strikes out, but – I've always had that privilege. And as she is now . . . *shan'tai* Christie, you can see it, surely? As she is now, there has to be *someone*."

Corazon put Molly Rachel's wristlink into a pocket of her coveralls. She glanced round at that ill-lit *chiruzeth* hall, and finally fixed her gaze on Pathrey.

"I'm bringing a troop in, to escort the body of Representative Rachel."

She did not add, *And for my own protection*. She didn't have to.

Pathrey looked doubtful. "*K'ai* Calil may not permit that."

"*K'ai* Calil should consider that a member of the PanOceania Company has been killed in her city," Cory said. Unconsciously she twisted the silver rings on her bony fingers. "*K'ai* Calil should also consider missing personnel. Rashid Akida and David Osaka. I want them now. Or *K'ai* Calil must consider very carefully the events at Reshebet and Quarth and the harbours in between."

The dark male made a hurried bow. I thought, Will you go running to Calil? Then Pathrey appeared to come to a decision. He muttered, "*Shan'tai*, I don't know where your people are. They said they would take one of your ships-of-the-air – " he deliberately used the Harantish paraphrase, not Sino-Anglic " – to rejoin you; but I saw no ships leave. That's all I can tell you, *shan'tai*, and that's more than I should."

He walked hurriedly and silently away towards that level's steps. I began to move in the same direction. This is too close to that small room where Molly . . . and neither Cory nor I are safe in Kel Harantish now. As I walked with the Peace Force Commander towards the stairs, I said, "You're not serious. There's a qualitative difference between a strike to block harbours and a hi-tech attack on a city."

The lilac glow of *chiruzeth* made her angular face seem old or ill.

"If I have to threaten to get Company personnel out, then I'll threaten. If I have to take further action, I'll take it. We can't afford to be seen giving in to these tactics, Lynne, we can't countenance the kidnapping of Company personnel!"

"Is it possible there is a shuttle missing? On-world transport records are pretty careless at the best of times, so – "

"It's just possible," she grudgingly conceded.

"Then there's substantial doubt. You can't take violent action."

She halted. I paused with her at the foot of the flight of stairs that led up into misty mirror-light. The hollow halls echoed to our footsteps, to our breathing. Some independent part of my mind registered the bareness, the *chiruzeth* walls carved in angles and curves; the rest of my concentration was on Corazon Mendez. I can try to talk your language, Commander. What I want to say is, You don't know what you're doing!

The white-haired woman said, "The late Representative extended privileges to you, in respect of what authority you could wield. I'm sorry that I can no longer do that. Not in the present state of hostilities."

"I don't accept that." The underground chill made me shiver. "The Company co-opted me as an expert on Carrick V. I'm best able to judge this situation. Until we find David Osaka, I'm technically head of the trade mission; I have superiority over the research grades – "

"*Not* over Security."

I know a losing battle when I fight one. If I shut my eyes, I see the light in the throne-room, see it fall blue and lilac on those empty-socketed skulls. And Calil. How she stood barefoot in those black stains, sticky on

309

the *chiruzeth* floor! Talk to me about psychopaths, Mendez.

I said, "Let's shelve that one for now, shall we? It's Rashid we need to speak with primarily, I think you know why."

That touch of authoritarianism made her respond. She nodded, and then said, "You'd better talk to whoever you can, here. We need Rashid. We need to know if there *has* been a breakthrough by his research team." And then she drew an unconsciously deep breath. "Can you imagine Golden technology here in this settlement? That woman would have control of the Coast before you could say 'Empire'."

We climbed two levels, beginning to come where Harantish people passed on unknown business, whispering as they saw offworlders. A familiar plump figure appeared. Pathrey Shanataru, returning, panting as he hurried to intercept us.

"You may bring your escort – " He turned from Cory to me. "The Empress wished you to speak with her people – fifth level is a good place – ask what you will – "

"Is there any point?"

Pathrey straightened, getting his breath back, shaking the folds from his robe. Membrane slid back from those dark eyes. "Don't think me stupid. We have one of your people here dead because we failed to keep her safe. You will hardly trust us now. And there must be trust, *K'ai* Calil needs *s'aranthi* trade, how else can we survive? So she sends you her Voice, to speak with her people."

Oh, I thought. Realizing only then that I must be speaking with the Voice of the Empress-in-Exile. He looked momentarily smug.

"I'll get Jamison down here," Corazon said.

I left her, following Pathrey up the stairs to the next level. Then without any warning, I had to stop. I felt exhausted, disorientated by the shifts in geography and time zones; and for a moment I leaned a hand against the cold *chiruzeth* wall. I squinted up the stairwell at the stronger light above and thought quite unexpectedly, *Molly's dead*.

No more of that outspoken honesty, that I've envied even when it was me she hurt. I won't see again that energy, that grin of hers, that unwarranted generosity; and why did I never tell her? To know her for so short a time, and most of that quarrelling. *The risk that you'll react with false memories to Witchbreed artifacts – that's why I let you go north – but I may need your help.* Why should she act as if I'd behaved like a friend to her?

The dark angles and dusty light of that stairwell were blurred, blind, hidden by tears.

"You have this in common with the true Witchbreed." Pathrey's voice

310

came clear, clinical almost. "Death for you is final, and no further meeting. Come, *shan'tai*."

I spent the next three hours on the fifth level of that block, speaking with Harantish Ortheans. Most of that group were science bloodlines, with some ritual knowledge of canal technology – and is it more than ritual? – and a few were traders, and one or two were of that tiny administration surrounding the Empress-in-Exile. It doesn't have to be more than a tiny administration, I thought. Because they're all of one mind. The unanimity is frightening.

A thin, elderly male voiced the general opinion: "We've been at the mercy of the *hiyeks* and the Tower for too long. *K'ai* Calil will find a way for us to stand alone, free of them. Your *s'aranthi* machines will bring us food and water, and this is all we need. *K'ai* Calil makes a friend of you offworlders where *K'ai* Dannor would not. We follow her now."

Conscious of the hours ticking away, I said, "And the *shan'tai* Akida, the *shan'tai* Osaka; what of them?"

The male looked at me with veiled eyes.

"Who?"

Pathrey Shanataru stepped forward to speak with him. I sat back on the metal bench, staring round that low-roofed chamber. Close enough to ground level for the walls to be stone, not *chiruzeth*. There were a few outside traders with this group of Harantish Ortheans – and as I thought that, I felt a touch on my arm.

"*Shan'tai* Christie, give you greeting."

I almost exclaimed aloud. A narrow face, with brilliant green eyes, and a white mane shaven down to fur; last seen in Maherwa. . . .

'*Shan'tai* Annekt," I said, very quietly.

He smiled. "So it is I who will give you the message. How strange a coincidence. No, don't look startled, be as you were. This is much safer than meeting you secretly."

"'Message'?" Thinking: I *knew* you were more than a Coast trader.

"Word has gone with all the traders out of Kasabaarde this season, which I now pass on to you, so. '*Shan'tai* Christie, because what was lost may be found, come to the Brown Tower in Kasabaarde. Come because you remember, there was a city seen in mist and pearl'."

Annekt spoke by rote: the message was not in any of the Coast dialects, but in that thick Melkathi that they speak on the heath *telestres*. *A city seen in mist and pearl* – and what was lost may be found. Rashid, what did you find in Maherwa? Will you give Witchbreed again the use of ancient light? Christ, that can't happen! Can it?

"What does the Hexenmeister want with me?"

"*Shan'tai*, it may be the Hexenmeister has need of a go-between to speak with offworlders. And I have heard rumour that you were in the Tower before?"

There was naked curiosity on his face, but I was too confused to satisfy it, even had that been wise. The Tower is only archives. Only a dead record of the past, and records may lie. And I have fought the false memories that threatened to drown me, have fought them as much as I can, but if I go to the Tower, will I 'remember' delusions too strong for a human mind to stand? And for all that she's Hexenmeister now, Ruric was once traitor to the Hundred Thousand. To us all.

Annekt's green eyes veiled. For a moment I hated him, this casual stranger. The Tower cannot be ignored, even if it is only archives; archives may tell us what we need to know, and God knows we need all the help we can get. And there is more to it than that. If I go there, I will (I know) ask her, What did I see at Rakviri *telestre*? What did I experience with Calil? And will she have an answer?

I said, "You can send word that I had the message."

Midday came and went unremarked. I felt the heat of it as I climbed back up to first level, and to the open roof, where Peace Force troops stood with the covered body of their Company Representative. As I climbed up on to the roof, I slid eyeshields into place. The dust-storms had died down. Harantish Ortheans were on the roofs, watching us curiously as we passed by; and there were others down at the harbour. I saw the whole panorama as our platform was winched down. There was no movement near the T&A excavations.

With Molly gone, the impetus of the trade mission will just . . . run down. Until the Company sends another representative. It won't be trade now, it'll be peace-keeping, and a desperate scramble after Witchbreed technology. Unless I can hang on in there and keep the T&A going?

The wooden platform grounded, scraping rock. Jamison's troops disembarked, and rested the stretcher on the earth. That dark, shrouded shape. One thinks the ridiculous: *can she breathe in there?* Dust can't hurt her now.

Cory spoke to Pathrey Shanataru again. I took the opportunity, stepped back into the shadow of Harantish's cliff-wall. Hoping that the interference had eased, I used my wristlink to call Doug Clifford.

His image appeared. After a brief greeting, it assumed that prim expression that is Doug's camouflage for self-satisfaction. "Lynne, I thought I might warn you of one thing. The WEBcasters are on their way to the Coast. They want to see the *hiyek* harbours. And Kel Harantish, I believe."

"Cory won't give them transport," I objected.

"They have shuttles through from Thierry's World that they can use. Courtesy of the government."

You have to admire Douggie. I let it pass without comment. "I've bad news," I said; and sketched in the events of the past half day, telling him of David and Rashid's disappearance, of Molly's death. I saw his shock.

"It's a bad business – " He glanced off-screen. "Lynne, I have to go. I'm taking a shuttle down to Keverilde *telestre* to talk with Jadur Anzhadi. Ah . . . it may be more urgent than even we thought. Satellites show an unusual concentration of shipping in the islands of the Kasabaarde Archipelago, and I grant you it's the summer trading season, but – "

"But we don't know how many *hiyek* ships sneaked out under cover of that storm, before Cory's strike. I'd better pass that on to her, I suppose."

The small image nodded. "I'll call you at 19.00. Let me know immediately if there are developments where you are." He paused. "Molly Rachel . . . I can't take that in. It's a bad way to go."

"Are there any good ones? I'll hear from you, Douggie."

The Peace Force troops picked up the stretcher and began to make their way cautiously across the rocky ground. Cory stood looking up, watching Pathrey's platform being winched higher, squinting through dark eyeshields.

"I've just had word from Ottoway. They've found Osaka and Akida – " She ignored my exclamation. " – in the excavation site over there. I've had both of them put in cryogenic hibernation, the orbiter medics *might* be able to save them both. Rashid Akida's in a bad way. Exposure, heat, dust . . ."

"What the hell were they doing?"

"Hiding? Running? We won't know until they can speak. Lynne, I'm going to put a permanent troop here, garrison the T&A site. Someone has to watch these psychopaths."

"Is that wise?"

Her hands, that had been twisting those silver rings, fell to her sides. Her voice went harsh. That sharp face came up: eyeshields glinted. "*You* don't have a say in the matter. Lynne, I'm sorry, I have to worry about security now. We have an invasion on the northern continent; now we have the possibility of alien technology in use here. It's a very volatile situation. The Force will have to clamp down until it settles."

And if I try to contact the Company home office, that will take twelve days. Until then . . . I can't force her to accept my authority. All I can do is continue to preserve my independent status, until I can use it.

I said, "I want the use of a YV9."

Corazon Mendez stared. "What use do you have for a shuttle?"

"We must know about Golden science." I faced away from her. The rock shimmered in the heat. The sky swam. No daystars, not even on the horizon; this land is harsh as the surface of some forsaken moon. "Is it possible Rashid's made a discovery – some synthesis of Earth and Witchbreed technology, perhaps?"

"But a shuttle – "

I don't know if that was the first time I consciously admitted it. Did I give a tacit consent by continuing to use the Tower's false memories as a guide? And now that there's Calil in Harantish, I must know from Ruric Hexenmeister how far those dreams of ancient light are to be distrusted. I must ask Ruric if she's lied to me again. Or, if not, what has reached out of the past to touch me.

I said, "I'm going to Kasabaarde. To the Brown Tower."

PART FIVE

CHAPTER 26

The Tower

I landed outside Kasabaarde, and disembarked. The spire of the Rasrhe-y-Meluur jutted into the daystarred sky, a towering blue *chiruzeth* pylon gilded on its western side by the light of Carrick's Star. Wisps of dust storms obscured its base. I stared up, craning my neck, thinking, Hard to believe it's still the same day. . . .

Midsummer. Somewhere in the hours just past, a new *T'An Suthai-Telestre* will have been named in Tathcaer. *Who?* A Crown in the Hundred Thousand, an Empress in Kel Harantish. . . . And yet it's neither of them that are controlling events now. It's the ordinary men and women of the *hiyeks* and the *telestres*. And is there still a truce in Melkathi?

Interference again made comlink contact all but impossible. I lowered my wristlink, turned to seal the shuttle and put it on auto-lock. The road here is indistinguishable from wasteland. Kasabaarde's Westgate is infrequently used, leading only to the small settlement L'Dui and the smaller Lu'Nathe. A hard, hot mile's walk to the gate; it left me sweating.

As I entered the city, I saw few people. I walked down translucent-floored avenues, hearing the rustle of canal water under my feet. Daystars paled above, in the late afternoon sky. Windvanes slowly turned. A few Ortheans in *meshabi*-robes passed. None spared a glance for a *s'aranthi*. The white dust worked down inside my ankle-boots, and the strong, beating heat of the sun made me dizzy. Easy to be lost in Kasabaarde. I walked down avenues and alleys, keeping the sun always at my back. And then I came to an open space, and a high sandstone wall.

Will there be guardians at the gate? I wondered, recalling the last time I'd been here. I had forgotten – I always do forget – that to come to the Brown Tower, one must pass through the inner city.

When I came to a sandstone arch, a white-robed male waited in the shadow of the gate. He was not long past *ashiren*, a brown-skinned boy with a white mane shaven down his spine, and a *del'ri*-fibre robe belted at his narrow hips. He stood with his bare feet slightly apart, rising up on to his toes.

"Go away," he said. "The inner city is closed."

Never in centuries – I gaped; recovered. "My business isn't with the Order Houses, it's with the Hexenmeister."

He pressed his lips together. I could see how his hands were shaking.

"Go away. No *s'aranthi* can enter here. No one. The Order Houses are abandoned, there's no *use* in going in."

"I must go to the Tower."

Oblivious, he said, "The Order Houses are all empty. The *hiyeks* rioted – " Membrane slid back from his brown eyes, leaving a rim of white all around. The wild gaze saw me. "What did the Tower do to stop it? What did the Hexenmeister do to save us? The mob stripped us of everything and what did the Tower *do*?"

"What could it have done?"

His boy's face became petulant. As his attention wandered again, he said, "The Hexenmeister could have stopped it; they would have obeyed. . . ."

He sat down in the dust, resting his back against the masonry of the arch. I saw, half-buried there, *harur*-blades. I was conscious now of the weight of the CAS-IV holster at my belt. When I was certain the young Orthean male no longer noticed my presence, I sidled under the arch and through into the inner city.

Violence and vision. The vision gone, still the violence may remain. . . .

I began to walk, as silently as possible in the dust, nerves taut; seeing no movement, hearing no voice. My mouth was dry with tension. All through the alleys, between the dome-buildings, under the awnings, lay the debris of a mob's passing. Overturned stone tables, broken *del'ri*-wood flutes, a bale of blue cloth spilling down steps like a river; broken crockery and glass. All I could hear was my pulse hammering.

I came to a dome that rose up out of the white dust, where the awning over the doorsteps was half pulled down. The late afternoon light shone in through its door, fell on rubbish, broken *arniac* bowls, a cast-off robe. Order House Su'niar. I called out but my voice fell flatly, without an echo. Deserted.

Gone, for how long? How long until they return – if they ever do? Is the inner city something we've lost forever?

At last I came to that stretch of open ground, and crossed it, and entered the gardens of the Tower. Here were stunted ash-grey *lapuur*, the earth between them trodden flat; and their fronds curled in the heat, alternately hiding and disclosing the sun-baked bricks of the Tower's west wall.

Suddenly I was overcome with a strong conviction. Everything that's important is happening away from here – four hundred miles down the

Coast, or a thousand miles away in Melkathi. Not in this backwater. I can only spare a few hours here, and even then, that's hours that are being wasted. . . .

Ah now, hold on a minute. I recognize that refusal to look at the Tower.

Deliberately I dug my nails into my palms. The pain cleared my mind. Again I felt the sharp heat of the sun. Dust caught in my throat. I looked round at the drooping *lapuur* and up at the high dome of the sky, my perception changing: it is so still here because here is the eye of the storm. . . . And something nagged at me. If I can put all the pieces of my 'memories' into one pattern, there is something I ought to see.

But those memories are false. Aren't they?

I thought on that while two brown-robed Ortheans came to lead me into the Tower; a melancholy walk through slick-walled artificially-lit corridors. They took me, not, as I had expected, to the library-room, but up through an elevator to the roof-garden. There, in the sunlight, among the stone tubs that spilled scarlet blossoms of *arniac*, a dark Orthean woman sat cross-legged at a low table.

Ruric Orhlandis glanced up as I approached. Her single hand held a bowl of *siir*-wine. The Tower roof-garden is walled, so I could see beyond her nothing of the city, only the sky and the daystars and the setting sun.

"Good," she said. "I wanted to talk to you, *S'aranth*."

I could only look at that narrow, dark face, at those sunny eyes, and hear what she said to me a month ago: *I wish that I were all Ruric, all Orhlandis, but I'm not. I'm Hexenmeister now.* I saw her smile.

How did I convince myself she meant the duties and responsibilities of the office of Hexenmeister, not that she is less – or more – now than *amari* Ruric Orhlandis?

"I came to ask about – memories? Visions? I'm not sure what they are. Came to ask you, because it seems to me that if it's only fragments of Tower Archives, it's too damn *real*." I looked at her. "And now . . . it isn't something I can prove, but I know, now, that you're not just Ruric. I can see it – sense it. But I can't explain it. You're Hexenmeister."

She said, "Yes."

"Then – I need to know why I'm not the only one to experience these memories. I could understand it, I think, if it was just me, because I've been in the Tower. But what about Rakviri, and Calil bel-Rioch?"

She inclined her head. No necessity for explanations: the Tower hears these things.

She said, "There are still dreams of ancient empires in the world, and they touch you, as if they were not quite dead. They cling to relics, and to places, and to people who desire, with desperation, the days that are past. Because you have been in the Tower, you become sensitive to this."

"'Come because you remember, there was a city seen in mist and pearl.' . . . So that was true, too?" I stood looking down at her. The Tower is the Tower, not an archive; the Hexenmeisters are one Hexenmeister; how else could she know my visions.

"Damn, you lied well! I *did* believe you. I suppose until now – " Or did I know when Calil and I together saw the City Over The Inland Sea? And couldn't consciously admit it, because that means admitting one thing more. . . . "You lied to me again, tricked me again. Except that it isn't you, is it? It's the Hexenmeister. That ought to make it different, but – "

She rose to her feet in one swift movement. All the old swordfighter's grace was there. She stood in the sunlight, in the Tower garden, and I shivered. This lean, ageing woman, skin like flaked coal; dressed in simple shirt and britches, with bare feet, and mane straggling out of a half-crop . . . is this something wearing the Orhlandis face as a mask?

"Christie. . . . " Ruric Orhlandis sighed. "Sunmother! For Her sake, don't be so stupid – it *is* me. I may have more lives in my head, but it's still me; and yes, I lied to you again, what did you expect? Do I look as though I'm playing *ashiren*-games here?" That dark, narrow face showed plain exasperation. She hooked the thumb of her single hand in her belt.

"Eight years on and you're still expecting people to act in good faith. . . . Sunmother! It's a wonder they let you out without a keeper." And she grinned, unmalicious, to take the sting out of it.

"You cynical old – " I stopped. "'Old'. Ruric, I don't have any idea, do I?"

A gleam came and went in those yellow eyes. "More than most, you do!" Ruric smiled again. "It's ironic. There was I, whining that because I'm part Witchbreed I have no past-memories, and now I've more past-lives than half the Hundred Thousand put together. Christie, I tell you, She has a very peculiar sense of humour. . . ."

"She isn't the only one."

"Ah, well. After all, this is too serious to be solemn about." Ruric turned away, prodding thoughtfully at the nearest stone tub. Then she wiped her hand free of the earth, and in quite a different tone remarked, "*Ziku* spores. A grove of *ziku* would suit the Tower gardens, but I can't get them to grow here. They're *telestre* plants. They don't thrive outside it."

Del'ri mats were thrown down round the low stone table. The Orhlandis woman sat down, folding long legs, and reached over to grab the *siir* flask, and pour the viridian liquid into her bowl. She hesitated over a second bowl, and looked up at me with only a host's curiosity.

"Ruric, Goddammit! Why am I here?"

"That's my *S'aranth*." Thin lips curved. She put down the flask, gestured at the mats beside her. I remained standing. She rested her arm across her knees.

"When he – " I hesitated. "When it was suggested I enter the Tower, eight years ago, and undergo memory-transfer, it was as proof. Proof that the Hexenmeister isn't what you claimed, a month ago – merely the keeper of archives. Now I'm so confused I don't know what I'd take as proof of anything! What you are, what happened to me. . . ."

"Same thing," Ruric said briefly. She leaned her head back for a moment against another stone tub, basking in the setting sun. The black mane fell across her forehead, hiding the scar of branding.

"It takes time to become Hexenmeister," she said. "There are always several – apprentices, shall we say? Those who've been through the first stage of memory-implant. That was what I gave you, eight years ago. It was making you unable to speak of it that damaged you, and for that I'm sorry."

"*You're* sorry?"

The response was automatic, and I saw how Ruric choked back a laugh. My legs ached with standing, so I lowered myself down to sit on the *del'ri* mats. No Tower brown-robes were visible in the gardens now, as I looked round; there was only the light of Carrick's Star falling on brown brick walls, on scarlet *arniac* and gravel paths. Familiar, why? And then I realized: This could be any roof-garden in Morvren Freeport or Tathcaer.

Ruric poured *siir*-wine into a bowl. "Do you know, I knew you'd come here if I asked? That's why I sent word out with the traders. They'd find you, and you'd come." She paused, looking at the *siir* and not at me. "Did you ever forgive me for that summer in Melkathi, and SuBannasen, and Kanta's murder? I asked you to come to me then. When they'd just done this." Long fingers brushed back that dark mane. The exile's mark: a jagged scar.

I said, "Thinking back, when you told me you were going into exile, didn't *I* say, 'Have you considered Kasabaarde?' Now *that's* ironic." But I had been thinking, then, of the inner city.

Ruric looked up.

"Now I've called you again, after I've done worse: tricked you into memory-implants, blocked off your own memories from you. Brought you here again, after eight years."

Chilling, to hear her speak. One the act of Ruric Orhlandis, the other of that old man, the Hexenmeister; she speaks as one remembering both. Like the sun on the surface of a river: one minute all brilliance, all Ruric;

321

and then the light shifts, and under that surface are depths . . . That feeling of frustration came again. On the tip of my mind, as it were: there is more to this than the accumulation of memory, and an ancient being hiding itself in an impregnable tower. . . .

Carrick's Star shone on her face, on the lines faintly incised in alien, reptilian skin. She rubbed at her nose and mouth, that gesture utterly familiar from her days as *T'An* Commander of the *telestre* army. She's tired, I thought. And if I know Ruric (*if* I do), would like nothing better than a fight. Simple action. How she must fret, as Hexenmeister. . . .

"All right," I said. "What am I doing here?"

"In plain terms, you're being kept a prisoner."

Startled, before I thought better of it, I said, "You can't hold me here."

Ruric drank from her *siir* bowl, and set it down with a clink on the stone table. Then she scratched at her mane where it rooted on the back of her neck, and shot a glance up at me from under dark brows.

"Too dangerous to let you loose, with the *s'aranthi* ripping the Coast apart in search of Witchbreed technology. I can't have them knowing what's here. As I said to you once, if you had not been desired to enter, you could not even have passed the gardens. The Tower's defences work both ways, keep people out – and in."

Not her who said that, but *him*; the old man.

"I could have made certain, early on, that no word about the Tower ever came from you. There are assassins on the Coast. I could have had you killed in Maherwa, by Annekt. Haven't I done all I could for you? But the Tower *must* survive."

I said, "Damn the Tower's survival. What use is all your Hexenmeister's knowledge if you never *do* anything with it? Have you seen what's happening in Kel Harantish? The inner city? And in the *telestres*, in your Hundred Thousand? You sit there and whine that all that matters is the Tower's survival – "

"Mine and the Tower's." She smiled: there was something of pity in it. "Christie, you do know why. Even if you don't know that you know. I'm sorry. I did you a great wrong, eight years ago, and all I do is compound it further."

The dome of the sky was ashen now; daystars fading to the Coast's swift twilight. The heat of the day became comfortable warmth. I reached for the bowl of *siir*, drinking cautiously. There was no scent of *saryl-kabriz* or *ruesse*. I looked at Ruric and, as well as human tongues can manage, stumbled out the phrase that Calil bel-Rioch had used to translate "'Ancient light'."

Membrane slid across those yellow eyes.

322

"Ruric, is that – it's what I'm afraid of. If the *hiyeks* rediscover how to use the weapon that produces ancient light; if Rashid Akida discovered something in Maherwa, or if it's possible to produce – I don't know – some synthesis of Earth and Witchbreed science."

"They don't have to," Ruric said. "That isn't necessary at all."

Heat reflected back from brown brick walls, comforting as night began to fall. Because I didn't want to think about what she'd said, I hastily asked, "And what else am I doing here, besides being a prisoner?"

"I need an offworlder." Again, that grin, white against her satin black skin; lines crinkled at the corners of her eyes. "A *tame* offworlder, shall I say? Ah, that ruffles your feathers! Christie, I want to apply to Earth, through the national governments, for Orthe to be given Protected Status. On anthropological grounds. Your WEBcasters are making us so widely known that we might have a chance, now, if we're quick. I can't leave the Tower. I need human support. That's you."

She put her hand down in a long-familiar gesture to rest it on the hilt of *harur-nilgiri*; found no blade there.

"*T'An* Commander," I said. "*T'An* Melkathi."

"I was ignorant then." She met my gaze. "One thing I did know enough to fear. That Earth would change us, destroy us. I was more right than I knew. . . . If you're to help me, Christie, you ought to remember all the reasons why. You know too much to be safe, and I should send you to Her. I could ask you for that – " she indicated my wristlink " – allow you no contact outside the Tower. But you know what I know, and I'd sooner have you as an ally."

You know what I know. Fear made my mouth go dry. I moved slightly, the weave of the *del'ri* mat had imprinted on the skin of my hands. The light of Carrick's Star as it set sent long shadows reaching for us.

"Ruric – "

"Now that I am Hexenmeister," she said, overriding what I began, "I have the memory of your coming here, eight years ago. And I have the memories the then Hexenmeister took from you. I've *been* Lynne de Lisle Christie. Can you imagine? I'd been four years in exile from the Hundred Thousand, Orhlandis was broken up, Rodion dead, Suthafiori dead. And because you were here before you went back to Tathcaer, and found out what I'd done, I saw myself through your eyes, as you saw me, a friend."

And by that time I was four years gone from Orthe, on different worlds. Different myself, because of her.

"If I know that my 'delusions' about the Tower are true," I said, "if I know that it's the Old Science that stores and transfers living memory from Hexenmeister to Hexenmeister; that that memory goes back thousands of years, to before the Golden Empire itself . . . Ruric, you *can't* let anyone who knows that leave the Tower." I challenged her: "Not if the Tower's secrecy and survival are all you care about."

She reached across, briefly resting her hand on my arm, where I had half rolled up the coverall-sleeve. Her fingers were dry, hot; the pulse of a different heartbeat felt through the skin. Then she sat back. The western light shone on her high-arched ribs, the small breasts and paired lower nipples, and then as she turned to pour more *siir*-wine, on the mane that rooted down her spine to the small of her back, showing through the slit-backed shirt.

"Christie, some people you have to trust. I *know* you. You love this world, you're *of* it. I did one thing better than I ever knew when I had you marked for the Goddess. That was a true foretelling. This is your home."

She faced me again, sipping at the bowl of *siir*, and then added, "It isn't only the Tower knowledge that matters. It never was. You know that."

"I don't know. I can't quite get there – I do know, but – "

It was suddenly as if there were three of us present: Ruric, myself, and that old male, eight years ago; who had told me what it meant to be Hexenmeister, and in face of my incredulity, said –

"'You *must* believe,'" Ruric quoted softly. "'Or else you'll believe nothing I tell you. And what I tell you may affect relations between our two worlds. . . .'"

"'Kasabaarde is the oldest city in this world, and I am the oldest person. I know this world. So when Orthe comes to deal with other worlds – I am the only one qualified to speak for us.'" I finished the quote. For a moment I was quiet, perceiving the last of the day's warmth; tasting dust on my lips, and the aftertaste of *siir* in my mouth. The *kazsis*-vines began to open their red blossoms, giving off a heavy, sweet scent.

A mile or two away to the west is the shuttle, and my 19.00 hour call from Douggie almost due, outside the city. And here there is the Tower, and all the subterranean levels of it; levels that connect with the first spire of the Rasrhe-y-Meluur, and all that great *chiruzeth* structure that bridges the Archipelago to the Hundred Thousand. I cannot ignore what I know.

"I could put a worse interpretation on it," I said. "All that concerns you is that the Tower survive. You must have defences that could make even Cory's Peace Force pause. So when do you decide to take action? When it's possible that the weapon that produces ancient light has been rediscovered. When the Tower's threatened. Am I right?"

The dark Orthean woman put her fingers to my forehead, briefly. I thought suddenly how, long ago, in the north, an Earthspeaker had done the same with water from the Goddess's well. And in that same place *amari* Ruric bears her exile's brand. And was it there that *he* put a six-fingered hand, that old man, the Hexenmeister? I met those yellow eyes that now unveiled. And thought of Calil, and how we had together called up the dead past. . . . Ruric took her hand away.

"You *know*," she insisted. "Some of the things you said in your delirium, travelling from Maherwa to Kasabaarde – oh yes, I had eyes and ears with you on that journey. That was the nearest you came to an assassin's blade, or *ruesse* in your cup, but you never spoke clearly enough to warrant it. Now I need you to speak."

I looked at her. Ruric Orhlandis; Ruric Hexenmeister.

"You are what you say you are, but that doesn't mean I can trust you."

Ruric shrugged, with that old crook-shouldered balance. "Then you'll have to do without trust."

Assassin's blade; *ruesse* in the cup. Yes, I thought. You'd do it. Even as *T'An* Commander you would have done it; it's part of the game. The Orthean game that is too serious to be solemn about. . . .

I said "I don't see *why* – "

The woman rose to her feet. She rested that one hand on the edge of a stone tub; six-fingered, claw-nailed, black against the scarlet *arniac*. She turned her head; those yellow eyes met mine.

"Why? Because there's something I plan to do, and I need your help. It's that simple. Forget that year and Melkathi if you can. Everything I did then, I'd do again. Still . . . I need your help. Christie, please."

She knows me too well, I thought, and, *I have never known Ruric Orhlandis ask anyone for help*. As simply as that, I let the world, the Tower roof-garden, the evening sky, all slip away.

Because there was a city seen in mist and silver . . .

I remember:

The darkness is profound, so great that I cannot see how high the walls are, or how far above is the ceiling of this great hall. There is only the blackness of space and the abyss. I feel its coldness on my skin. The floor beneath my feet is a mirror-blackness, made of that rare chiruzeth that only the Imperial bloodline can shape. I see my frightened face reflected: the face of an old woman of the slave race.

I raise my head. There is a little light, enough to show the bases of great pillars; yards in circumference, vanishing up into darkness. And –

He is there.

Steps rise to a dais. On it is a structure both throne and mausoleum, black chiruzeth, shaped over with vines and death's-heads. Blue-and-lilac light from one floating sphere puts a shifting blackness in empty eye-sockets. And he rests back against that tomb-throne. His pale mane shines, his hands are gold dust. I see how he stares up into that infinite darkness: the last, lost heir of glory.

Here is no echoing ritual chant, the ritual is forgotten. Here is no soft corruption waiting the knife. Here is only emptiness.

A young male steps out of the shadows by the throne. His dark skin and mane proclaim him one of the slave race, but his eyes are yellow. He gathers round himself a robe that is all the colours of sunrise, and kneels down on the dais. His sibilant voice hisses in the vast emptiness of that hall:

"Slave, come forward."

My old body aches. What shakes it is not age, but fear; and I hobble closer, and kneel down upon that mirror-darkness. I bow my head, and say no word.

"___ _____ ___ _____"

The gold-dust hands clench; his head comes up in one animal-swift movement, and this is He: Santhendor'lin-sandru, Phoenix Emperor and Last Emperor. Speaking the tongue of the Imperial Golden race, that no slave woman should know. If he should think that I . . .

And he stands, Santhendor'lin-sandru, a small, bright figure against the surrounding blackness. As I kneel at the foot of the dais, I see him raise his arms as if he can embrace that annihilation:

"O my sister, my lover, my self! Because she has entered the city, a great race shall come to corruption; because she has entered the city, a cancer eats at the living flesh of it, a plague that cannot be stopped nor stayed! Of chiruzeth that was living, it makes a death. Of life it makes a silence and a stillness and a light. . . . And from the cities it spreads out, irresistible; turns earth to crystal, and will not cease until all the earth is one sterile mirror, and only the wind moves, and blows silver dust across the face of it. . . . O Zilkezra, great is thy praise!"

Echoes die. For one moment I fear that power, fear that the old rituals can be reborn. An imminence is in the darkness. And yet the echoes of that ancient power are fading. . . . And Santhendor'lin-sandru again takes his place on that dark throne. He signals briefly to the dark slave male. The dark-maned male lifts his head:

"Hear the word of Santhendor'lin-sandru, Phoenix Emperor, in the great halls of Archonys. Hear his word! You are Our children, We created you from the beasts of this world. Now We go down into darkness, and you must follow. Now We go into darkness too bright for mortal sight; a brilliance that swallows up cities and earth and sea."

He bows his head to the floor, this Voice of the Emperor; and then raises himself again:

"Hear the word of Santhendor'lin-sandru, you who have hidden yourselves

326

away in corners of the world, seeking to end this. That ancient light dawns now upon the world. Once begun, it cannot be ended. Once created, it cannot be cured. Hear his word!"

Fear pulses through me, blinds me so that I cannot see, can only sprawl prostrate on that icy floor. Echoes whisper in the abyss of darkness above. I have thought it was my eyes that watched him, this Emperor of a dying world; and can it be that he knows what we have sought to do?

And suddenly there is a sound, a voice like the wind in dead leaves. It is he, the Last Emperor, speaking that tongue the Witchbreed do not deign to speak: the language of slaves:

"Do you think We do not know you? You who skulk in corners, call yourself Master, passing your feeble memories from life to life . . . thinking that because We do not exterminate you like vermin, We do not know you. . . . "

I look up, past the prostrate and terrified form of the Voice of the Emperor. Santhendor'lin-sandru smiles: that hawk-face brilliant and cruel. That rusty voice whispers on:

"Run, little animal, We will let you go. Run, hide. Seek out some lair in the south, in the Rasrhe-y-Meluur or the Elansiir. Use Our works, as you have done for uncounted ages, to pass on your little lives, one Master to another. . . . This age is ending, and Our works will not outlive that ancient light. Your age-long life is at an end, little animal."

Some lair in the south. I am shaking too hard with fear to stand, or to speak. Does he know? Can he know what we are making, in terrible haste, in the south; a last attempt to kill the cancer that has been set in the flesh of this world –

And Santhendor'lin-sandru gazes down from the mausoleum-throne. Black chiruzeth gleams in that light the colour of lilac and lightning. I can do nothing but look up at that face. His eyes are yellow, yellow as sunlight, as the eternal noon and infinite summer of Golden rule. . . .

"Try, little animal. Try to kill that living light. You may even halt it for a time, We will allow that. But you cannot hold it back forever. It cannot be killed. And soon, a few heartbeats or millennia, and you will join Us."

Far to the south is that structure later ages will call the Tower. Far to the south, we strive to hold back the devastation that eats away at this world. . . .

"Run, little animal. Run."

Now the dark male rises from the floor, gathering his sunrise-robes about him, and steps down from the dais. In his hand there is a flash of brilliance: a ritual knife:

"Hear the word of Santhendor'lin-sandru, Phoenix Emperor, in the great halls of Archonys. Hear his word! You are to carry Our speech to your companions in the southern lands – but you are not to return to them unmarked. . . ."

★

327

"Christie. Christie *S'aranth*."

The vast dome of the sky arches over me, webbed with light, flowing with the brilliance of Orthe's summer stars. The scent of *kazsis*-nightflower and *arniac* are chokingly strong. I can even look at my dirty human hands, and not lift them to wipe away the nightmares of blood hanging in my eyes. . . .

"*S'aranth*."

"Yes." A deep breath; some control. "You – I – the Hexenmeister should never have gone to him; too dangerous!"

Ruric Orhlandis grinned, as she squatted on her haunches by me. "So long as the body comes living, or newly-dead, to the Tower; the memory-transfer can be made. You *s'aranthi* would say we need 'living cells'. That isn't accurate, but it'll serve." She chuckled. "If I ever die outside, make sure my body gets back here! Wouldn't be the first time that's happened. Now it's too dangerous. I don't leave the Tower. Christie, are you all right?"

Her chatter anchored me in physical reality. The Tower garden, the cold *siir* in ceramic bowls; the night winds blowing from the city. And, distant, blotting out stars, the Rasrhe-y-Meluur.

"You'll have to tell me one thing," I said. "How you managed to destroy ancient light – "

And then I could only stare at her.

"That's right," Ruric said softly. "You know it. Ancient light can't *be* destroyed. Not once it's created. All we could do was hold it back. We are still holding it back. And, yes, that 'radiation' that so interferes with your technology isn't a result of war damage – it's all that holds ancient light at bay. If you like, call it . . ." she was plainly searching for Sino-Anglic terms ". . . a suppressor? Counter-radiation?"

I was abruptly conscious of the Tower, all the levels below me; created from Golden technology that no longer exists, and cannot now be reproduced. . . .

"It's housed here," I said.

Ruric stood up, stretching. She glanced down at me. "Here. Yes, here. And if that's all you know, that's all I'll tell you. But now you know why, above all else, the Tower must survive. And now you know why I'm afraid."

CHAPTER 27

Silence, Stillness, Light

Gravel scraped under my boots as I stood up. The night wind was warm against my face. *Arniac* rustled. I stumbled, unsteady, and the Orthean woman caught my arm. Above us the sky was a slow blaze of light; the Heart Stars, silver and crimson and blue; so thickly clustered that the edges of the Tower roof were a black silhouette against them. I looked up into that depth, that vastness . . . and had a sudden, almost physical comprehension of the thousands of years that have passed since the Empire fell.

"All of it," I said, "the *telestres*, the Coast families, the Rainbow Cities, the Barrens – all of it growing up in those years, whole civilizations, not knowing what's held back from them; that devastation. . . ."

Ruric let go of my arm, and brushed the black mane back from her face. There are some expressions unknown to those of us who live a single lifetime: hers was one. I felt isolated, alien.

I said, "What about their past lives? Ortheans wouldn't forget how Golden science works, and they wouldn't forget that ancient light isn't dead, only . . . quiescent."

The Orthean woman chuckled, and that was all Ruric, all Orhlandis. "Christie, my temper doesn't improve either, when *I'm* scared. . . . Very well, I'll give you an answer, but you know it: the Witchbreed themselves could barely comprehend the science the Eldest Empire bequeathed to them, and they never let the slave races have much comprehension of it. Though it may be that we understood it better than our masters. . . . And as for the other, they may have assumed that devastation had a natural limit, reached it, and so ceased."

Then, more soberly, she added, "It may be that they do know. I can't say. There has been nothing they can do about it, except bury it so deeply they never think of it. . . ."

Silence hung over the roof-garden. That gravelled space, filled with stone tubs and *arniac* and *kazsis*-nightflower, so very like the roofs of Morvren and Tathcaer: too mundane, almost, for such revelations. And no robed Master to speak of it, only this middle-aged and crippled Orthean woman, dressed in plain britches and shirt, one sleeve knotted up; and with the scar of an exile on her face.

329

A little whimsically, to gain time, I said, "And am I Hexenmeister now, or partly so?"

The woman broke into a laugh. It's the first thing I ever noticed about her, in that Residence eight years ago in Tathcaer: how her dark and sober face is illuminated by laughter, how those eyes almost physically glow.

"No, *S'aranth*. You've touched the edges of it. I have a dozen apprentices here like you. Except that, being alien, you may still have some different reactions from ours. . . . Still, you have the first stage. Not all."

Nearly 19.00; Douggie's contact would be due. I stood indecisive, watching the face of *amari* Ruric Orhlandis, Ruric Hexenmeister.

"All I have are memories, and memories aren't always reliable. Ruric, you're going to have to *show* me proof."

For all I've seen the satellite-images of devastation, the sterile wastelands of the Elansiir, the north Barrens, the Glittering Plain; for all that there *is* an atmospheric distortion that affects Earth technology – and for all that my memories of that crystalline death are so clear – still, I need proof. I will always need proof.

Ruric, quite cheerfully, said, "You always were a suspicious old . . . now let me see, I have an Anglic vocabulary, what *is* the word I want?"

"Er, I don't think we want to go into that too deeply. . . ." Is it possible to laugh and shiver simultaneously? Her knowledge of that language comes from my mind, eight years ago . . . and her use of it is nothing but a smokescreen.

"If you want my help, you have to show me proof."

"Christie, do you have any idea how hard it is for me to trust anyone?"

I hear echoes in her voice of that old man who was Hexenmeister eight years ago, echoes of the *T'An* Commander of the Hundred Thousand, and of phrases that I myself use. How many others, how many generations, live now in her memory? She watches me, this alien woman: that six-fingered and claw-nailed hand clenching, the starlight bright on sharp-edged ribs and dry-textured skin. I wish I could follow *telestre* custom, groom out that tangled mane where it roots down her spine, comfort her as one Orthean comforts another. But I have only human hands.

The Orthean woman fixed her eyes on my face. Then she nodded, once, and turned to walk back through the garden. I followed, almost taken by surprise. She said no word as we came to the Tower entrance. A brown-robed male ushered us down into the artificially-lit corridors, down into brown-walled chambers that I dimly remembered from my time here with Blaize and Rodion.

330

"Ruric – "

Without turning, she said, "This may be the most unwise thing I have ever done. Christie, I owe you a debt, eight years old. Prove I'm not as unwise in trusting you as you were in trusting me."

The Brown Tower is, like most things on the Coast, nine-tenths under the surface. I have myself been into levels that connect with the complex under the Rasrhe-y-Meluur. Now I expected us to go far below ground level, but instead the Orthean woman walked briskly through slick-walled corridors, past the library-room and its windows, to a chamber that would be perhaps one level below the city outside. A large chamber, low-roofed, with the same slick-textured brown walls; and I was about to comment, when I saw the brown-robe who stood at its entrance.

"Give you greeting," I said. "Tethmet Fenborn."

The artificial illumination struck highlights from his skin, green-gold, with its fine, waterproof texture. Stick-thin limbs, hands with hooked claws – he is one of the aboriginal night-hunters that still exist in the Great Fens. Membrane blinked down over those large, dark eyes. He glanced at Ruric.

"When you first brought her here, master, I warned you against her. . . ."

"Old friend, you don't let me forget it; and now I'm about to do a thing you will like even less. See that no one disturbs us."

Both spoke in the language of the Fens. I had a brief memory (my own) of fever, exhaustion; mudflats and reeds and fenborn hunters. Putting it aside, I followed Ruric into the windowless room.

Soft yellow light came from no discernible source. It illuminated stone benches, metal shelves, ridges of that wall-material that jutted out into platforms; blue-grey *chiruzeth* sarcophagi, like those in the 'Archives', many levels below. . . . All the flat surfaces were swamped with piles of books, parchments, half-finished artifacts of wire and metal and crystal, earth-trays with plants just beginning to shoot, *arniac* bowls with a scum of liquid drying in them, broken mirrors. . . .

"Camouflage," I said. "Like the library-room that you keep for visitors. Am I right?"

The dark woman grinned. "Only partially. I *have* been given to experimentation, over the years, but this is not where most of it was carried out." And then she became serious. "One thing I can show you, Christie. I was unwise enough, for a few generations after the fall of Empire, to experiment myself; see if there was not some way, still, of destroying ancient light. It had the result you might expect. I no longer experiment, because I no longer have the science to control what I create."

She walked between the piles of junk on the floor, to a *chiruzeth* tank not much smaller than those in the Archives.

"I've seen something like this before," I realized. The resemblance was strong – that octagonal hall in Rakviri *telestre*, where Barris Rakviri activated the growth of *chiruzeth*. About to join Ruric, I suddenly stopped.

She looked up. "What is it?"

"Something odd. If I were superstitious . . . No." Briefly, I explained what I meant; knowing she would remember similiar occurrences. "It's just that there were four of us present at – participating in – that vision. Only a few months ago. And out of those four, three are now dead. . . .

"Barris was killed, Jaharien committed suicide – and this morning, in Kel Harantish, I saw Molly Rachel dead. Murdered." I met Ruric's gaze, held it. "I *will* find out who's responsible. I can't let it pass." And thinking of that young woman, her body by now back on the orbiter in cryo-storage, makes coincidences trivial. I walked over to join Ruric at the tank.

She said, "The past is not always as dead as it should be. And I don't refer solely to 'ancient light' – that's the physical manifestation of . . . something quite other."

Black brilliant light. They fell in love with that bright shadow, Death –

She walked round to the other side of the tank, opposite me. The black mane fell across her forehead as she looked down. Lines of strain showed round her eyes, and membrane slid across that yellow gaze. I at last recognized that strained stillness for what it was: fear.

"I made this," she said bitterly. "It took me three generations, and was almost as foolhardy as showing it now to you, Christie *S'aranth*. Look."

The *chiruzeth* tank was half full of earth, and stunted shrub *arniac*, and withered *del'ri*. It was the pale earth of the Desert Coast, and that sourceless illumination cast a fuzzy shadow round each pebble and stick. A cluster of *kekri*-larvae squirmed beside a larger rock. A puddle of water glinted –

a mark, a lichen, a flower; chiruzeth is turning under his hand to dead crystal; spreading as swiftly as a crack in a shattering mirror

– no, not water, but light shining from a patch of stones and gravel that is clear now as glass; as crystalline, and as dead.

"See." The dark Orthean woman put her hand on the edge of the *chiruzeth* tank. The air in the interior shimmered. A wave of heat hit me

332

in the face; faster than the eye could follow came a flash of silver; I cried out – and all was still again.

Shrub *arniac*, *del'ri* stems; rock and pebble and stick . . . now they all gleamed. Silver-glass. I wiped my lip, that hurt; took away a hand marked with blood, where I had bitten down. Now, all the interiors of the *chiruzeth* sarcophagi shone, crystalline; and here splinters of light ran into the *chiruzeth* itself. . . .

Ruric Orhlandis reached down into the interior, and picked up what had been a living cluster of *kekri*-larvae. She held a handful of light, that crumbled away into dust, drifted on the air into annihilation. Her eyes were dazed. My palms ran with sweat; heart hammered; I thought I would be violently ill. She lifted her head. She was shaking. A line of white was visible round those yellow irises, in that face that had looked unmoved on the burning of Orhlandis *telestre*.

Unprompted, together, we moved to where we could hold each other in a necessary embrace.

An hour later. We stood in the parchment-odoured library; windows open to the night. A breeze rustled stacked papers, and brought a scent of the city beyond. The Heart Stars cast enough light.

"What do we do?" I said. Then: "Ruric, it would all have happened sooner or later. With PanOceania, or some other Company. We were called. . . . The Harantish planted Witchbreed artifacts where off-worlders would find them, knowing it was a bait we couldn't resist."

Ruric stood by the table. She slopped *del'ri*-spirit into bowls. "That wasn't the first time that happened, but my agents prevented the other artifacts from being found."

She handed me a bowl of *del'ri*, and sat down heavily on one of the couch-chairs.

"Kasabaarde has great and wide influence," she said, "but not total control. That's as it should be. I think so. Or perhaps I only hope that I think so."

I blinked at that. Then I sat on the couch-chair beside her. Starlight robbed the room of colour: all was black, silver, grey. I yawned and rubbed at my eyes.

"If I add it up, I've had about six hours' sleep in the last two days. . . . I can't even think, never mind come to terms with what I've seen here." I paused. "You're not telling me how the suppressor, the 'counter-radiation', how it functions."

"If you don't know, I don't have the right to tell you."

Through exhaustion I thought, If I had to guess, I'd say it was some property of the Tower's *chiruzeth* structure. Maybe it . . . I don't know

. . . modifies the radiation of Carrick's Star? And my 'guesses' are more accurate than I care to think about.

Chiruzeth; that, when it lived, the Witchbreed shaped by their will alone; that now can't be recreated, their secret being lost. . . .

I said, "*Is* all knowledge lost?"

Starlight gleamed on her black mane as she moved her head, drinking from the *del'ri* bowl.

"If there were any hint of Golden science left, the halfbreeds in Kel Harantish would have found and used it; or somewhere in the Barrens there would – "

She stopped and looked at me. Those yellow eyes were luminous, almost with their own intrinsic light.

"Christie, I have searched, for more ages than you can easily comprehend, for some way to undo the destruction that Witchbreed and Orthean together left living on this world. If there was a way, I would have found it!"

"And the Empress Calil? She questioned Rashid Akida, I'm certain of it; God knows what he found. And he's too ill to talk."

The Orthean woman said, "Goddess forbid that ancient light should again be used on this earth. I'm not at all sure it would be held back, as the Elansiir and the Glittering Plain and the north are leashed in, held in check – no, I'm not at all sure it wouldn't strain to breaking that restriction, and what then?"

That book-filled room was silent. The light of the Heart Stars shifted on the floor. I lifted the *del'ri* bowl to my lips, wincing at the bite of the spirit; fighting not only exhaustion, but the desire to use sleep as an escape. *I do not want to think about what I have just seen. A world of crystal mirrors, over which moves only the wind, and the silver dust of annihilation. . . . No, don't think. Or I will recall what I felt at Rakviri: that the bright shadow is so easy to look upon – and love.*

"And what now?"

"I have to ask you – " Ruric stopped and glanced up, to where a brown-robed Tower servant stood in the doorway. She beckoned. The male handed her a strip of parchment.

"I can use *rashaku*-relays and heliographs too," she said, with a smile of amusement. She read, and that sharp-planed face changed: I read amazement, and a kind of wry humour. "Well," she said. "Well . . ."

"What is it?"

"I have eyes and ears in the Hundred Thousand," Ruric Hexenmeister said. "Today was Midsummer; they've named a *T'An Suthai-Telestre*. You see how fast word can come to me."

I leaned over, reading the parchment strip that the long fingers of her single hand spread out on her knee. It was in the curling script of the Hundred Thousand. The name of the new *T'An Suthai-Telestre*, legible by starlight. . . .

"'Nelum Santhil Rimnith'. I don't believe a word of it!" And then I thought of him in the Wellhouse, with Bethan Ivris; how he had spoken of peace with the *hiyeks*.

Ruric threw her head back and laughed. "And after he was Portmaster in Ales-Kadareth, taking bribes from Kel Harantish – well, we do change. *How* we do change!"

I tapped a key on my wristlink. Well past 19.00 now, and though Douggie might expect communications to be unreliable, he would be concerned. I said, "If I can get through, I want to know if Nelum Santhil and Doug are down in Keverilde still, and what's happening about the *hiyeks* – if Sethri's still talking; if there's any fighting – "

"You won't be able to use that inside the Tower, I think." Ruric bent down and put her *del'ri* bowl on the floor, and then stood up briskly. "Rest, first. Christie, I have to talk to you again; there are things I must ask you. And you must leave the Tower soon. I'll have my people take you where you can sleep for a few hours."

And sleep was an escape; a welcome, dreamless dark. No need to think of this ancient Tower, eroded by the ages; the secrets of its creation and repair all lost. No need to think of the bleak devastation miles to the south; or how sunlight had gleamed upon the Glittering Plain. . . .

No need to think of that city, four hundred miles toward the sunrise, and a Empress throned on skulls; whose face is the face of the Golden. No need to think: *Is there the slightest chance that, after so many millennia, that weapon might be re-created?*

Sleep is an escape, a dreamless refuge; and a hand shook me out of it, shook me roughly awake: "We might not have as much time as I thought," Ruric Orhlandis said. "I've had word come down from the islands. The Coast ships in the Archipelago waters are beginning to move."

Dawn wiped the daystars from the sky. A midsummer day on the Coast: sky white as bone, and the wind a breath from an open furnace. I loosened the neck of my coverall, sweating; and swore in frustration as the wristlink showed me only static. I'd thought that on the roof-garden, outside the Tower structure, there might be less interference.

"It's no use." I thought: What's Cory doing, is she still on the orbiter? Where's Doug? I need to know what's happening in Kel Harantish; I'll ask Molly –

I stopped, taken by that surprise that is not (after all these years) unfamiliar. It takes time to know that someone's gone.

I walked back through the dusty garden to the domed roof-entrance. Ruric Hexenmeister was there. She looked as though she'd slept in shirt and britches, or else not slept at all; the early morning sun cruelly illuminating her shabbiness and exhaustion. She was pacing, bare high-arched and six-toed feet scuffing the gravel; and as I came up, stopped to pounce as a brown-robe brought a message. She exchanged words with him.

Amazing, I thought; still half asleep. Amazing how much there still is in her of *amari* Ruric Orhlandis. She is Ruric. And she is so many others as well. And while she's told me the truth about the Tower and ancient light, she will, if necessary, lie totally about what she's going to do about it. And we both know that.

The Orthean woman paced as if imprisoned; held by the claustrophobia of Tower walls. She stopped as I approached, and stood with her hand hooked in her belt. The dawn wind ruffled her mane.

"Is there any use my stopping on one of the Archipelago's islands?" I asked. "I could try to contact the *hiyeks* there."

"Christie, I doubt it. The rumours coming through are confused. Some say the *hiyek*-families are quarrelling now, that they can't agree on whether to sail back to the Coast, or finish what they've begun. I doubt you'd be able to do much."

A thousand *jath-rai*, scattered among all the Archipelago islands. . . . No, I thought. There isn't the time.

"As soon as I can contact Doug or Cory, I'll know what's happening. I *must* know what action Cory intends to take. She's terrified of hi-tech weapons in Orthean hands – "

Ruric grinned toothily. "So am I." Then she stabbed one claw-nailed finger in my direction: "All I hear from you is 'Cory' and 'Peace Force'. You're still in the Company, Christie. *You* restrain her."

"I don't have the rank!"

"I know," the Orthean woman said quietly. She took a step forward. "Try. Because of what you've told me – the Representative dead – there may be some way you can influence events. And yes, I know. I *know*, Christie. What business of the Tower's is a war between the Coast and the Hundred Thousand? None. None at all. My only concern is the Tower's survival, and that, at the moment, means watching Calil bel-Rioch. What happens to the Hundred Thousand is nothing to do with me, it's unsafe to interfere – "

She broke off and turned away, but I saw the pain on that dark face. How could I forget? A decade older than that woman who had been *T'An*

336

Commander, *T'An* Melkathi; but still the same Ruric, that I knew that long-ago summer. Accused, guilty: I still hear her voice saying, *All I've done, even to murder, I've done for the Hundred Thousand. As I love the land – I love it more than life – so I have tried to protect it.*

There is Blaize, and Haltern, and Cassirur; there is even Nelum Santhil. . . . I said, "You know I'll do what I can. And for the Coast, too; Anzhadi and the others."

She repeated, "It's no concern of mine. What I can do without risk, I'll do, but it won't be much. I would come with you, if I could; but I can't leave the Tower, can't take the risk of losing this. There are so few who can live with an aeon of memories, and it takes so long to find them. . . ."

The dawn breeze began to fail, and the temperature to rise. *Arniac* opened scarlet blossoms. Our shadows fell ink-black on the gravel. I glanced up, not sure if I caught a shimmer in the air, and wondered, *Tower defences?* But it stirred no recollection. There have (I know) been Hexenmeisters too alien, too early dead or driven into insanity, for the chain of knowledge not to have its weak links.

The Orthean woman turned back to me, linked her arm through mine; drawing me to walk between stone tubs of *kazsis*, away from the roof-entrance. "Christie, I said I'd ask you for help. . . ."

"Well?"

Ruric smiled; that quirk that is half humour, half self-mockery.

"Tell me I'm doing it again," she invited, as we walked in the early sun. "Tell me I can't be in a place without going against the law of it. . . . Listen: you must return here, and this is what we must most urgently discuss – you've said to me, you fear some synthesis of Earth's technology with Golden science? So do I. But I also think this: if such a synthesis were possible, might we not find from it some way to destroy ancient light? Not merely to hold it in abeyance, but to *destroy* that threat that hangs over us?"

"You . . ." The sun struck down like a blow; I wished I had eyeshields. The dry heat exhausted me. And for a minute, I didn't believe what I heard. "Ruric, you mean letting a research team inside the Tower?"

"They wouldn't come here?"

"Oh, they'd come here, all right! You wouldn't get rid of them. Isn't it an infinitesimal chance that we could understand Witchbreed science?"

Ruric inclined her head. Light glinted from skin and mane: the colour of flaked coal. "True. And if I were even to suggest such a thing to my people here – the Tower has always been inviolable; I confess I don't quite know what they'd do. If it's to happen, it will take very careful

337

handling." Membrane slid back from her sun-yellow eyes. "But it's a chance I can't ignore."

I drew my arm from hers and stopped, leaning against the edge of a stone tub. It was hot under my palms, and *kazsis*-vine writhed away from my touch. Ruric stood with that crook-shouldered balance, watching me.

"You wouldn't suggest it, if it weren't for the chance that Calil's got there before you?"

"No," she agreed equably, " I don't suppose I would."

"And that's down to us. The Company. We came here; we put a research team in Maherwa. . . . Christ, I wish I knew what was in Rashid's report!"

Ruric shrugged. "There are things even my agents haven't been able to find out. No one's infallible. Not even me." And she smiled, with that Orthean humour that has more than a little of the macabre about it.

"What we've spoken of – the Tower – I may have to go back to Earth. Talk to the top people in the Company home office and the government. It's not a decision to be made on-world . . . the security clearance must be something phenomenal." Almost a laugh; and I looked at her: "You can tell. It's too big; I'm afraid of it."

"So am I," Ruric said. "We do what we can."

By unspoken common consent, we turned and walked back towards the domed roof-entrance. The sky's brilliance dazzled me. Faintly visible against it was the first pylon of the Rashre-y-Meluur, and its suspended bridge-structure that vanished into sea haze, northward towards the next *chiruzeth* spire. . . .

"I'll send some of my people to escort you to your shuttle," the Orthean woman said. "If you need names of my people in the *telestres* and *hiyeks*, you can have them. You may need to get word to me."

"Not a prisoner, then?" I said.

That yellow gaze flicked up, humorous; met mine; and I thought, *Assassin's blade; ruesse; saryl-kabriz.* Perceiving that a threat is sometimes not an insult and not a betrayal.

"Weren't you marked for Her?" Ruric jibed; and then without any affectation or mockery added, "Christie, I trust you."

PART SIX

CHAPTER 28

Ashiel Wellhouse

Summer heat in the Hundred Thousand is mild, after the fierceness of the Desert Coast.

Still, we clung to shadows of *ziku*, the light of Carrick's Star streaming down through red foliage; and to the shadows cast by the walls of Ashiel Wellhouse, as the sun inched its way up to mid-morning. Warm air was full of *chirith-goyen* cloth-flies, dancing over the Wellhouse hives, specks of mica in the slanting beams of sunlight.

"Something's gone wrong." I stared eastwards, tense.

"You offworlders are impatient." The skeletally-thin fenborn male beside me smiled. "You and the *galeni*. Only we know how to wait."

Galeni is what the aboriginal fenborn call Ortheans. Tethmet Fenborn straightened, shaking the folds of his brown robe across that green-gold skin; and then stalked off towards one of the other groups of people waiting. *Has he seen someone who knows the Tower, someone who'll give him word to send to Ruric?*

The wind brought the scent of fertile earth. Beyond the *ziku* grove, I could see how daystars skeined a milky-blue sky. Carrick's Star shone down on dusty tracks that criss-crossed the hillside below Ashiel Well-house, running between banks of brown *saryl-kiez*, now just blossoming into blue flower. There were folds of the Ymirian hills in the north, and heathland to the south, fogged by a blue-white haze; and *there*, three or four *seri* distant, the black scar on the land where Keverilde had burned. . . .

"I don't see anything moving down there."

Doug Clifford appeared beside me. That round face showed strain; he was white round the mouth. He walked with none of his usual elasticity.

"You've been out of contact for forty-eight hours, I hope you realize. Lynne, I have to say, I didn't find that particularly helpful."

"I would have been here sooner. The shuttle was low on fuel. Cory's people sent a refueller out to Lone Isle; I met them there."

"Bringing him with you. . . ." Doug's gaze followed Tethmet, as the fenborn crossed the crowded yard.

On the shuttle I recorded and re-recorded coded message-blips, sending them through the orbiter to FTL-drones. Twelve days, I thought. Then PanOceania and the government will hear what I heard in

341

the Tower. Meanwhile: "I do have some new information," I said. "I'll be calling a meeting. Cory. Ravi; he's acting head of Research. You. I don't yet know if there should be any Orthean representation."

Douggie's head came up; he gave me a judgemental stare. With something of his old urbanity, he said, "I have the distinct impression that Commander Mendez assumes she's acting head of mission. When do you plan to tell her otherwise?"

I'm not telling her anything, let her find it out for herself. . . . Before I could phrase that tactfully, Douggie's attention was gone. He stared down the hillside towards Keverilde. Dust was rising, a mile or two distant. Others had seen it too, the crowd began to drift towards the gate-arch. I glanced back at the Wellhouse, to see if any of the *takshiriye* would come outside.

Scarlet mane and green robe flared in the darkness of the door: the Earthspeaker Cassirur stepped out into the dusty yard. A dark-maned male followed. He supported another male, swathed in a dark *becamil* cloak despite the heat, whose mane was a wispy white crest, and who spoke rapidly and quietly and continuously. Nelum Santhil, with Haltern. For a moment all three were framed against the Wellhouse: a sprawling complex, brick walls rising straight and then swelling into onion-domes; smothered with *kazsis*-vine and shaded by *ziku*.

As Douggie walked over to join them, and I was about to follow, a voice behind me said, "Representative Christie? Can you spare me a few moments?"

A young woman, with dark hair and slanting brows; she stood in the Merrum sunlight, sweating under the weight of WEBcorders. I know you, I thought; not correcting her assumption that I was the Company representative now. Or I've seen you, or –

"Roxana Visconti, Trismegistus WEB," she introduced herself. "Ms Christie, I wonder if you'd like to comment on the on-world situation here?"

Dust still rose from the distant track into the summer air. Closer now: possible to make out that it was a group of riders. The Wellhouse yard seethed with activity: Ortheans in priest's skirts bustling in and out of the Wellhouse itself, males and females with the gold crest of the Crown Guard checking winchbows and *harur*-blades, *ashiren* scrambling up on to the low outer wall to point and yell. There were Ortheans outside the outer wall, mostly wearing the thin robes of Melkathi; many with the faces of Keverilde or Rimnith *telestre*. Momentarily I wished I had some control over them.

"It'll have to wait – "

"Is it true that Commander Mendez is launching a full-scale investigation into the death of Representative Rachel? Will you yourself be returning to the Harantish settlement in the near future?"

I thought of Jamison, left to guard the T&A site at Kel Harantish; of Corazon Mendez up in the orbiter. Somehow none of it seems to have any relevance to who Molly was.

"This will have to wait. Look down there." I pointed towards Keverilde, the lace-silhouettes of charred *ziku* and *hanelys*, the black earth, the tumbled stones – visible even at this distance – of the *telestre*-house. Spirals of smoke went up into the air. Cooking-fires. "You can't see, but there are two or three thousand guerrilla fighters in that area. What we're trying to do here is talk. Defuse the situation. Ms Visconti, I *will* talk to Trismegistus, but not right now. Not when there's a representative of the Anzhadi about to arrive."

"What responsibility is the Company taking for this?"

Jesus Christ, I thought, now it's me that has to answer the awkward questions.

I said, "What does public opinion back home make of this?"

"The response is – unfavourable."

"Good."

When she looked sceptical, I added, "There should be an impartial group here. Look, Ms Visconti, if you want to keep me informed about how they react at home, I might be in a position to help Trismegistus here. How does that sound?"

She eased the strap of the WEBcorder on her shoulder. Patches of sweat showed under the arms of her coveralls. "I refuse to gloss over what PanOceania's doing to Carrick V, if that's what you mean."

"You tell it as you see it." I saw Douggie beckon. "Excuse me; I have to go."

Ashiel's outer wall is decorative, only a few feet high; and the gate-arch is a curving hoop of brickwork. Now, in early Merrum, young *rashaku* perched there, their scaled breasts glinting in the sun. Harsh metallic cries rang out: their warning. I walked to join the others at the gate, as the troop of riders came towards us.

"Let them through."

Nelum Santhil's voice was not loud, but it carried to the male and female Ortheans outside the yard. Some muttered; others stepped back a pace or two. Is it because he's Rimnith *telestre*? I thought. Because he's suffered? He wore plain shirt and britches; there was nothing to mark him out as *T'An Suthai-Telestre*.

Haltern Beth'ru-elen shifted his grip to my arm instead of Nelum Santhil's. Membrane flicked across his eyes; the skin round them crinkled. His grip wasn't strong. "Are they there, *S'aranth-te*?"

"I . . . yes, I can see four or five people from the Coast."

Marhaz walked delicately, lifting their split pads from the dusty track and replacing them with care. Their feather-fur pelts glinted bronze and white and black. Most of the riders wore green tunics with gold-crest badges, the mark of the *T'An Suthai-Telestre*'s Guard; and these were war-*marhaz*, both wickedly-sharp pairs of horns left uncropped. Almost lost in the mêlée were four riders in *meshabi*-robes.

After the *marhaz*, and now swinging wide round the group to draw up outside Ashiel, was a groundcar. A fair-haired Peace Force officer whom I recognized as Ottoway got out. He signalled to the foremost rider. I saw the scarred, dusty face of Blaize n'ri n'suth Meduenin, *T'An* Rimon.

The Earthspeaker Cassirur Almadhera said, "Bring them inside."

The four Coast Ortheans slid down from the high *marhaz* saddles with obvious relief. Blaize let his *marhaz* pace beside them as they walked to the gate; Ottoway and two officers fell in on the other side. As they approached, I saw one stout and bronze-maned Coast Orthean with a flask dangling from his belt: Jadur, is it? Jadur Anzhadi. And the white-maned female there is either Wyrrin-hael or Charazir-hael. . . . Both a head shorter than the *telestre*-Ortheans who pressed close in on them. A taller male, yellow-maned and white-skinned: no mistaking Sethri-safere. A female with him, with a dark mane and sallow skin – no, dark *hair*. In *meshabi*-robe, with a hook-knife at her belt –

"That's the Ishida girl!" Doug stared.

Arrest her on suspicion of hi-tech arms trading? It'll have to come, but: "Now isn't the time to do anything, Douggie."

The smell of *marhaz* dung was strong on the air; a complement to the heat. What can happen on such a day? But the tension is still there: stomach-wrenching; settling in the muscles between neck and shoulder.

"Doug, what say you're very understanding, very sympathetic. And then I'll hit them with the *jath-rai* in the islands. Yes?"

He nodded absently, still staring after Pramila Ishida. Nelum Santhil and Cassirur were closest to the *hiyek*-Ortheans, moving them towards the Wellhouse entrance; and the rest of the crowd followed: Doug with Haltern, Ottoway, the Visconti girl, Tethmet's tall, gaunt figure; males and females from Rimnith and Keverilde. Heat shimmered over Ashiel's low domes. Not a rich Wellhouse – no Wellhouse in Melkathi is – it still had a surprising number of young *ashiren* within its walls. They ran underfoot, under *marhaz*-pads; pointing at the Coast Ortheans and shrieking. No Earthspeaker rebuked them.

I tacked myself on to the end of the group, and then a *marhaz* brushed past my shoulder, and Blaize Meduenin dismounted beside me. In that dusty yard, amid shrieking children and the hum of *chirith-goyen* hives, I saw how the slanting sun illuminated that old scar masking half his face.

Foolish: all I could say was, "I thought you would be *T'An Suthai-Telestre*."

He gave the *marhaz* reins to an *ashiren*. "The Crown? Not me, I'm a fighter."

"Hal must be disappointed."

"Haltern Beth'ru-elen finds *T'An* Santhil – " Blaize paused. "I don't understand Haltern. Eight years ago Nelum Santhil took bribes from Kel Harantish; he betrayed the *T'an* Melkathi. Now he's Crown."

The stocky male beat dust from his clothing, and resettled *harur-nilgiri* and *harur-nazari*. I thought, Hal will find Nelum Santhil a kindred spirit; *that's* what you mean.

The last *telestre*-Ortheans were disappearing inside the Wellhouse. Groups still sat outside the walls, on the sparse mossgrass. All had *harur*-blades, most had winchbows. I turned to walk into the cool shadowed interior.

Blaize said, "I think about the Barrens. When we were there. Christie . . ."

"When there was none of this, no fighting, no factions; nothing but to be together and play *ochmir* and wonder if, after all, the Woman Who Walks Far had abandoned us, and we would die – oh yes," I said. "I think about it. Or isn't that what you wanted me to say?"

The hazy sun shone on angled ribs, visible through his sleeveless jacket; on paired nipples and skin with a fine reptilian grain. Membrane shuttered those whiteless blue eyes; claw-nailed hands clenched. It would be too easy to bury my hands in that silver-streaked mane where it roots down his spine.

"We have to get inside – "

"You make me envy the past," he said.

At last, from memory, came the face of that male in a far northern province; eight years ago and very distant now. Who had been, in the Orthean tongue, *arykei*, lover, bed-friend. "Do you mean Sethin Falkyr?"

"Him? No." He smiled: the scar twisted pain to mockery. "Christie, how can I be your *arykei* when you have no thought for any other *arykei* but *amari* Ruric Orhlandis? She's *dead*, Christie. Dead and gone to Her bright Realm. I've seen your face when someone speaks her name. You won't let her go."

And as he turned to enter the Wellhouse, he added, "And will you die here, hope to return when she returns, live when she lives? Take your chance, *S'aranth*. She was Golden-blooded. They don't return."

★

345

Ashiel Wellhouse has no corridors. Round-walled room opens into round-walled room: some are kitchens, some dormitories, some for storage. Slot-windows let in sunlight. It shone on white plaster walls, on the bright manes of *telestre*-Ortheans, picking them out from twilight. In the way of the Hundred Thousand, there was no central meeting, but a dozen or so groups talking at the top of their voices, and Jadur and Wyrrin-hael and Sethri each separately cornered.

I sat down at the edge of the group surrounding Sethri, on a bench beside Haltern Beth'ru-elen. The old male glanced at me. Then he looked again, milky membrane sliding back from those pale eyes.

"They tell me you have been to Kel Harantish, and to Kasabaarde. Christie, I have seen people who looked better for that journey."

I've long since given up wondering how Hal gets to know what he knows. I said, "I've just been told something, and I don't know whether it's suddenly crystallized a thought I've had, or whether it's completely wrong. . . ."

Sethri's voice came clearly from where he stood facing the Earth-speaker Cassirur Almadhera: "You give poor choices, *shan'tai-keretne*! Stay where we are, be attacked, driven out and killed. Or else enter your houses peacefully by ones and twos – and be killed. Where's the choice in that?"

He stood with a weary arrogance, speaking a thickly-accented Melkathi tongue.

"Kill all four of them!" called a young male, from the back of the room.

"That won't end this, Anzhadi-*hiyek* has more than we to sustain it."

Doug Clifford leaned forward, putting a restraining hand on Cassirur's shoulder. I saw how he deliberately avoided looking at Pramila Ishida, where the Pacifican girl sat beside Sethri Anzhadi. "*Shan'tai* Sethri, I assure you that we are fully cognizant of the problems you face. This is a precarious situation, we don't wish it to disintegrate further. If a way could be found for your people to make a tactical withdrawal from this area, then that might ease tensions on both sides."

Nice one, Douggie, I thought. The sunlight in that pale, domed room picked out crystal beads woven into black and brown and scarlet manes; it shone on the smooth-worn hilts of *harur*-blades, and on faces that now turned to stare at us. I pitched my voice to carry as far as Sethri-safere: "Before we discuss that, let's talk about the other *hiyeks*. Let's talk about the warships that are only days away from here in the Kasabaarde Archipelago – when they sail back to the Coast harbours, then's the time to talk about getting you out of here, *shan'tai* Sethri."

Mention of the *jath* ships in the islands made a babble of discussion break out among the *telestre*-Ortheans. Nelum Santhil left Wyrrin-hael to speak with Cassirur. Sethri-safere looked over their heads and smiled at me. That fox-face was thinner now, and the yellow mane straggling; still, he nodded an appreciation of intrigue.

My wristlink chimed softly. I hesitated, torn between priorities; but Doug was handling things well. With a quiet word to Hal, I left the room, looking for a chamber slightly less crowded, to speak in private. Privacy is not a *telestre* concept. I came at last to an archway leading into a larger domed room, where sunlight fell through a roof-slot on to white plaster walls. A black circular opening in the floor marked the Well of the Goddess. No Ortheans were there. I stepped inside.

"Christie here."

"Mendez." Corazon's image formed, small and clear. Behind her was one of the orbiter's control rooms. She looked at me, that sharp-planed face uncharacteristically wary. "I can meet you in two hours, I'm making planetfall again then. What's the purpose of this?"

"Not something I want to discuss on open-channel. Cory, will you do me a favour?" Always ask, when it isn't necessary to order. "Will you put the Kasabaarde settlement off-limits for the present? No landings, no overflights. Just surveillance. There is a reason. I'll discuss it with you when we meet. I'm at – " I gave the co-ordinates of the Ashiel Wellhouse.

"Yes." She linked bony fingers, and her thick silver rings caught the light. "Ottoway reports you're making progress."

"We've got a lever," I said. "The Anzhadi are isolated here, cut off. We're working on that one. A small group in hostile country. We might be able to lever the *jath* ships back to Reshebet and Nadrasiir and the other Coast ports."

In the interests of co-operation I didn't say: Their having few harbours to go back to doesn't make this any easier. . . .

"You may be all right," Corazon Mendez said, reaching out to cut the link. "Assuming your Coast Ortheans don't have much in the way of black-market hi-tech weaponry."

I stared at static: her image gone.

A small *ashiren* with black mane and brown skin padded in. *Ke* looked five or six seasons old. Black-bead eyes glanced up at me, and then the child crossed to the Wellmouth, and dipped a bowl into the water. *Ke* drank noisily.

"*Ashiren-te* – "

The child pushed its mane back from its face, with a six-fingered hand on which the claws were tiny and perfect. Dipping the bowl again into the Well, *ke* offered it to me. I walked across to take it, and drink; and

347

as I lifted the bowl, it came into the shaft of sunlight, blazed white: to drink was to drink liquid light, as cold as the stone from which it was drawn.

"*Ashiren-te*, will you go to your Earthspeaker for me? Ask him to bring the *t'an* Ishida here – the offworlder who is with the Coast people."

"Yes," the child said. Then: "I'll do it if it will make you *s'aranthi* leave this Wellhouse."

I stared after the child as it padded out on bare feet. *Ke* would not have been born when I was in Orthe before. Would have lived in that eternal circle of turn and return, year and year, land and sea. And now to find a world that we, or the rest of the universe, has made different. . . .

Feet scuffed the floor, startling me out of my thoughts.

"I don't have anything to say to you," Pramila Ishida said, as she walked across to stare down at the Well. Her image reflected in the black water: this young woman, with sallow skin now grimed with dust, brown hair roughly braided up; her *meshabi*-robe torn at the hem.

"I don't know what to say to *you*. . . ." It was intended to be disarming, it was (I discovered) true.

"Arrest me," she invited. "The Anzhadi will see it as provocation, of course. Or I could just stay here, in Wellhouse sanctuary." She grinned, maliciously.

"If the Company wants you, it will take you; and where you are or what you're doing won't matter. All I want to know from you is the extent of the arms trade that *you* allowed, and where those weapons are now." I let a pause occur, then finished: "Whatever loyalties you have now, some things override that. The prospect of a hi-tech war here is one of them."

Her head lifted. I saw again those startling green eyes, and that face that now showed what emotion – pity?

"I won't tell you a thing," the Pacifican woman said. "That should upset the great Lynne Christie legend. As for threatening me with the Company . . . I intend to see the *hiyeks* get a fair deal, all of them, and you can't do that by talk. At least I've got the courage to fight for what I believe." Pramila smiled. "Don't be jealous, Ms Christie. I've done what you always wanted to do, and never could – commit myself to Orthe. I'm with Sethri now. The *hiyeks* are my people. A lot of what I've had to do is wrong, but that's better than doing nothing at all."

"There might be some truth in that," I admitted. "As for what's wrong with it, I despair of explaining that to you – go on, get out of here. Get out of my sight."

The domed room was quiet when she'd gone. Voices beyond sounded

348

muffled. A scent drifted in: heat and *marhaz* and the lairs of *rashaku*. The sun's light shifted almost imperceptibly towards noon, when it could shine full on the Wellmouth: water blazing with light. . . .

I waited those few minutes. But it is only light and water.

Towards mid-afternoon, a groundcar jolted down one of the tracks from the west. Cory Mendez got out. I walked as far as the gate-arch, the air like warm water on my skin; and saw her give orders to her officers before heading in my direction.

"I've been in contact with Jamison, over at the Harantish settlement." She paused, letting her gaze sweep over the ever-growing number of Ortheans in the Wellhouse yard and the *ziku* groves. Her mental shrug of dismissal was almost visible. She went on, "I wanted Jamison to inform the local leaders that I plan a full investigation into Representative Rachel's death. Unfortunately, neither that self-styled 'Empress' nor her 'Voice' appears to be available." She clasped her ringed hands behind her back. "I've brought ten F90s down on Kumiel Island."

"That's two-thirds of your Force."

"That's right," she acknowledged.

"If we overreact . . ."

"I can't take risks. This is a highly unstable situation." She glanced back at the groundcar. A man whom I had taken to be Peace Force climbed out, and I saw that it was the acting head of the research team, Ravi Singh.

Corazon turned back to me: "Why call this meeting so urgently, and why insist on in-person, not holo-contact?"

Chirith-goyen swarmed noisily round our heads, glinting among the *kazsis*-vine that here swamped the crumbling brickwork of the outer wall.

"It has to be secure," I said.

Blaise Meduenin stepped out of one of the further outbuildings, talking with an older *ashiren*. Too far off to hear what he said; but I saw the *ashiren* fix a message-scroll to the *rashaku*'s hind claw and let it soar free. They stood gazing after it, until it circled round and flew off westwards toward Tathcaer. I thought, What I know and what I can't say puts a distance now between us, between me and Hal and Nelum Santhil and Cassirur. . . . I could find it in me to hate the Hexenmeister for that.

Assaulted on all sides by the Hundred Thousand, how can I remember that cool interior of the Brown Tower? With violence on a hair trigger here, how can I think of that other, sleeping devastation?

Ravi Singh joined us, blinking myopically. "Lynne, I have some interesting findings."

"Any news on Rashid or David?"

He blinked again, taken aback, and then said, "Bad, I'm afraid. They need cryo-travel to Thierry's World. The orbiter doesn't have the medical facilities they need."

"I'll authorize it." I looked at Cory. "Thierry's World can contact us, when either of them can talk."

Oblivious to all interruption, Ravi said, "Those new findings I mentioned . . . we have established fairly conclusively that 'interference' with comlink and other hi-tech systems here is inversely proportional to their distance from the areas of war damage; that is, taking into account the seasonal tilt of the planet, sunspot activity, and – "

"My navigators and comlink people have been using that as a rule of thumb for the past two months," Corazon said dismissively. "Lynne, about this meeting."

"I want Envoy Clifford present as well," I said. "Come inside."

Making our way through the crowded inner rooms, we at last came on Doug Clifford sitting with Nelum Santhil in a small chamber. The Orthean male glanced up.

"Ah." He inclined his head to Corazon and Ravi. "Christie, give you greeting."

I pondered tactfully getting rid of the *T'An Suthai-Telestre*, or else removing Doug from his company. At that moment the door-arch was blocked, and two more Ortheans entered behind us: Haltern clinging determinedly to the shoulder of Blaize Meduenin. The stocky male eased Hal down on to a couch-chair, by the round window that was choked with the foliage of *ziku* outside. Hal wheezed painfully, and then looked up at me with bright eyes.

"You will be interested to know," Haltern said unhurriedly, "that Tethmet Fenborn has made it his business to speak with me – and I with the *T'An* Rimon here, and the *T'An Suthai-Telestre*. He gave me word from the Tower. He said, the *S'aranth* will speak of a past time and a present danger. He also said, the Hexenmeister is unwilling all the Hundred Thousand should go in ignorance of this. . . ."

A shadow darkened the entrance. The gaunt figure of the fenborn male, blocking the door-arch. I looked questioningly at him, and he blinked green-gold eyes and silently inclined his head in assent.

Nelum Santhil, dark eyes somehow remote, said, "We have memories of a past time. Speak, *S'aranth*."

But how can I . . . ? A kind of relief went through me then, simply to have them there: Hal's sly smile, Blaize standing with half-scarred face in shadow, Nelum Santhil's quiet, corrupt confidence. While I still hesitated, Ravi seated himself on the other couch-chair; and Corazon Mendez and Blaize Meduenin took up identical stances either side of the door.

Yes, I thought, watching Orthean faces. Yes, you have a right to know; if only because, when that great Empire fell, you were not innocent bystanders.

"Normally I wouldn't call this meeting now," I said. "We've got all the crises we can handle. Invaders who may have illegal hi-tech weapons; a hostile fleet of *hiyek* ships in the islands. Normally, I'd say why call a meeting about something else, when we could be in for a bad enough time here?"

It was automatic to fall into the Ymirian dialect that serves for common language in Tathcaer; to repeat in Sino-Anglic what Corazon and Ravi didn't understand. I leaned both hands on the back of Ravi's couch-chair.

"Despite what I'm going to say, I have to tell you: I wouldn't discuss this at all now if it weren't for Kel Harantish."

"We heard of the *t'an* Rachel's death," Nelum Santhil acknowledged. "I know the Harantish well, or better, than any person here; and they may now be yours, *S'aranth*, but they're not our enemies. The *hiyeks* are our enemy."

"Kel Harantish. . . ." I paused. "I'd feel better saying this if there were any proof. There isn't. It may be an unjustified fear; I hope to God it is. If it isn't, Kel Harantish is a threat to you, and to the *hiyeks*, and to the Storm Coast and the Rainbow Cities, and the tribes that live over the Wall of the World. That's no exaggeration. That woman who calls herself Empress – "

Haltern interrupted in a thin voice. "We have still to rid ourselves of *this* war. Speak."

Now let me tell you, in this warm and summer land, under this clear sky, how to the north and west and south there is a living destruction, an ancient light. Let me tell you what I have seen in the Elansiir, the Barrens, and on the Glittering Plain. Now let me tell you of the legacy of the past – that is living still.

CHAPTER 29

The Last Nineteenth-Century War

Weather and truce together held: the long Orthean twenty-seven-hour day ticking away, always on the edge of violence, never quite crossing the line. Five more Coast Ortheans came out of the burned heathland under escort, these from *hiyek*-Aruan. And *telestre*-Ortheans arrived, by *marhaz* and by *jath-rai*, as word went out to Tathcaer and south Melkathi and the Ymirian hills – hundreds coming to look out over land that had been Rimnith and Keverilde and now lay occupied. . . .

Peace Force 'thopters harried the sky through that long day, scanning. Orbital satellites gave erratic images of the Archipelago, far to the west.

I found Cory Mendez in one of the outhouses that Ashiel no longer used, setting up a temporary comlink-base; she and her officers swearing over the data they processed.

"I'd ban all shipping from the area," Corazon said. "Any of these craft could be carrying communications for either side. If there was a way to enforce the ban – "

She pushed a hand through her silver hair, disordering its sleekness. For the first time, she looked as though she carried her fifty years with an effort.

"Don't do what you did on the Coast," I warned. "I won't authorize that kind of action."

Corazon Mendez sighed, and as she turned back to the field holo-tank, said, "I don't do it for the fun of it, Lynne, whatever you may think. It's a job. I won't do anything, until and unless I'm forced."

On the fourth day after that, a thick sea mist rolled over the land: hiding heath and shallow rises topped by *ziku* and heat-stunted *hanelys*. I sat with Doug Clifford in a Wellhouse chamber that opened on to the *ziku* grove. Unglazed windows let in humid heat, and vapour droplets, and the smell of cooking-fires. Bethan *T'An* Kyre sat with us, her *zilmei*-hide clothes and *harur*-blades making her look more like a mercenary than the governor of a province; Nelum Santhil leaned back against the white plaster walls, where he sat on a couch-chair beside her. And Sethri-safere faced us.

"We can't continue with this stalemate," I said.

Doug pursed his lips. On cue, he said, "I do have one suggestion we perhaps haven't given due consideration. In view of the PanOceania multicorporate's resources, is there a remote chance of Aid resettlement? That is, resettlement on another world like Carrick V – "

Bethan Ivris spluttered. I caught a very sly look from Nelum Santhil.

"*Shan'tai* Christie." Sethri shook his head. For all that there was dirt ingrained in that pale skin, and his yellow mane fell matted and filthy, he still by some compulsion could take the room's attention. He smiled ruefully. "We don't live in *telestres*, *shan'tai*. All the same, take us from this world and we die. . . . Offworld-born *ashiren* might live. Still, they'd have no *hiyek*, no family; they'd be Orthean in nothing but body."

"I know. It's a bad solution to this – but you're not leaving me any good ones." I could have left it at that and hoped, but I felt uncomfortable with the manipulation. "Really, I'm giving impossible suggestions in the hope it'll force us into something feasible. . . . You can very well say it isn't the Company's concern. We don't have the right to interfere. On the other hand, I *know* the Company has to bear some responsibility for how this came about. And I want to see it ended without bloodshed – screw PanOceania," I said, "*I* want it!"

Nelum Santhil snorted, black eyes gleaming with that Orthean humour that surfaces at the most serious moments. I felt Doug Clifford wince; he put in hastily: "Assuming we can reach a compromise here, it should be possible to have Carrick V declared a Protected world. This would mean a slower influx of technology, an assessment of what repercussions there would be from the Aid Programme – "

Nelum Santhil leaned forward, resting his arms on his knees. He glanced at Sethri. The *hiyek*-Orthean stood with his back to the window.

"We won't 'share' land," the *T'An Suthai-Telestre* said. "It isn't ours to give or yours to take. But as *T'An* Bethan here has told you, there's land north and west of The Kyre that has never been *telestre* land." And then, aside to the dark-maned female: "Haltern Beth'ru-elen *T'An* Morvren reminds me, that is how Peir-Dadeni came about. And hasn't the Andrethe of Peir-Dadeni been a friend to us?"

Bethan looked at Sethri. Disgust showed on her blunt features. "We would be well rid of *you*. Until I saw Keverilde, I didn't know . . . Your *ashiren*'s *ashiren* may shake off the taint of land-waster. But if there were an easy way to do it I would send you all to Her."

Nelum Santhil repeated, "Land north and west of The Kyre."

Sethri's face showed exhaustion, but no loss of control.

"Wasteland," he said.

"Wilderness," Bethan Ivris corrected. "There are few of us in The Kyre, and we content with mountains; we never needed to move out into the Northern Wilderness."

Watery sunlight shone in at the window. The *hiyek* male's eyes widened, membrane fully retracted; and I thought of seeing him at the *siiran*, under the Coast's incandescent light. The Anzhadi and Aruan and what other *hiyeks* concealed themselves in that heath to the east of us wouldn't own you as a leader – but they'll listen to you, I thought. The others that have come here will carry their own word; but it's Sethri-safere who'll sway them.

"Free passage," the *hiyek* male said. "For *jath-rai*, north up the river. And then passage across the mountains. Can you do that, *shan'tai?*" He jerked his head at the window. "They won't let us go easily. Can you make them?"

Nelum Santhil looked down at hands that were clenched into fists; relaxed them, and thoughtfully studied the sixfold imprint of nails in his palms. "When I was Portmaster down at Ales-Kadareth, I found nothing readier to quarrel with a *hiyek* than another *hiyek*. How long will it take you to get word to the *jath-rai* in the islands? And will they listen to that word when it's sent?"

I was conscious of Doug beside me; caught a glimpse of his face that, for all he controlled his expression, told me how hard he was trying not to hope. In case this is one more false breakthrough.

In case this is nothing at all. . . .

Sethri-safere said, "You had better find me an escort, *T'An Suthai-Telestre*, or clothes such as your people wear. I must go back and speak with Anzhadi. Your people outside these walls will kill me if they see me."

Doug Clifford looked up. "*Shan'tai*, I'll go with you."

"Cory's people can escort you," I said.

And are we there? I wondered, leaving them and making my way towards the temporary comlink-base outside. *We're moving, but are we there?*

Corazon Mendez grunted assent when I found her, detailing Ottoway as an escort. She herself remained seated at the field-holotank, studying images that were bright in the gloom of the round-roofed building. She seemed oblivious of the stink of old *rashaku* lairs.

"What is it?"

"Corpse. One of the 'thopters got it, over on the eastern boundary. Local, by his clothes. Being in the hostile area, I wasn't going to authorize a recovery." She remained bent over the holo-image. I didn't look; could only wonder, Was he Keverilde or Rimnith, could he not stay away from the *telestre* even after the burning?

"I wish I had a clearer image," Corazon said. "You can see, here,

354

that's a winchbow-bolt. Probable cause of death. What I'm looking for are wounds that might have been made with a hi-tech weapon."

Sea mist shifted as the noon hour passed, dissolved on a west wind, leaving Ashiel to swelter under the summer heat of Carrick's Star. I stood in a *ziku*'s shadow, staring into blue distance. Thinking: In Tathcaer now, what are they doing, Khassiye Andrethe, Howice *T'An* Roehmonde, Geren *T'An* Ymir? In Morvren Freeport are they waiting to sight *jath-rai* sails on the horizon?

Satellite-images show only quiet islands, under the sea-spanning shadow of the Rasrhe-y-Meluur.

Below me, all the slope that fell away from Ashiel was covered with temporary shelters of *marhaz*-hide, set up between clumps of the brown and blue *saryl-kiez*. Ortheans walked among them. Some wore the thin robes of Melkathi, others the slit-backed shirts of Ymir and Rimon. The sun glittered on *harur-nilgiri*, *harur-nazari*. Only the youngest *ashiren* played oblivious in the dust. Older children ran from group to group, acting (I thought) as messengers.

"Ms Christie . . ."

Not Trismegistus, I realized as I turned, seeing a man in combat-coverall, WEBcorder slung on his back. A tall, black man, with straight hair drawn back and tied in a horse-tail; with long slanting eyes and a challenging grin.

"Ariadne WEB," he announced. "My name's Mehmet Lutaya; I wonder if you want to comment on the absence of the government envoy at this time? Does this have any bearings on PanOceania's actions here?"

There is a certain glaze they have in their eyes. It means they see 'Representative' or 'Envoy' or 'Commander'; not the person. Down in that haze there, somewhere on the heath, Doug Clifford is with Ortheans who are a continent away from safety; nothing to keep him safe but words and luck – and I can't say that to you, I thought. Although I have to say *something*.

"I'll be holding a conference for all WEB representatives in about an hour," I said. The comlink-centre would be suitably private. Or as private as possible, in the Hundred Thousand.

"When do you anticipate developments?" he persisted. "I know some of the other WEBs have sent people to the other port settlement – Morvren, is it? Is that where – "

"I hope they know better than to land. Land's taboo," I said. With an effort, I held back from tongue-lashing this Mehmet Lutaya. No point in taking tension out on him.

"Representative, wouldn't you call that irrelevant now? The invading

355

force here is using groundcar transport, I've got verifiable holos of that. These people have Earth tech on their territory whether they want it or not."

There was no easy answer to that. "I'll see you in an hour," I repeated.

Having no greater desire than to be out of his way, I turned and walked back inside the Wellhouse. Picking a way through the crowds wasn't easy. Some *hiyek*-Ortheans were present in the inner rooms – Jadur Anzhadi lifted a cup in a friendly salute as I passed through one chamber, and I thought, That's not going to make the *S'aranth* popular. . . .

Tension twisted in my stomach, so acute it was painful. I felt as if one touch would make me ring like a wine glass, like a violin string tuned up to some unbearable pitch. Worst-case scenarios: Doug used as hostage, murdered out of hand. Desperately seeking consolation, I thought: He's professional, he's done this before, he knows the risks – ah, so do we all. And it doesn't help.

At the entrance to the Well-room I stopped. A male and a female stood together under that dome, by the Wellmouth; she with an untidy scarlet mane, and a green slit-backed robe falling to her high-arched feet; he thin and tall, the brown robe wrapped round his hips not concealing his seamed belly: the pouch of an oviparous species. Cassirur Almadhera and Tethmet Fenborn, talking together. Suddenly I felt very alien.

And why? Because Commander Mendez isn't stupid; she's manoeuvring me towards a position where I take responsibility for PanOceania, but have no authority over it. And that puts a distance between me and Ortheans.

"Give you greeting," I said, stepping inside the Well-room. "What news?"

She smiled sympathetically. "We wait. *S'aranth*, I could almost wish we had acted as the *hiyeks*, and taken your devices for communication – it would be swifter."

Tethmet Fenborn said nothing. Silence with him seemed, not a lack, but a natural quality.

"Kasabaarde has some spiritual authority on the Coast," Cassirur Almadhera went on, "if no temporal authority. Help me convince the *t'an* Fenborn that the Tower should make its disapproval known, influence the other *hiyeks* against Anzhadi."

I said, "I understand the Hexenmeister to remain neutral in these matters." And had a sudden image of that city to the west of us, of Tathcaer, white under the summer sun; and how eight years ago it sent into exile *amari* Ruric Orhlandis. For all her memories, she is Ruric still.

"Did the Hexenmeister say nothing to you about this?" I asked the Fenborn.

Tethmet's green-gold eyes blurred with membrane. If I didn't know his loyalty to the Tower, I'd have taken it for disapproval. "The word of the Hexenmeister has gone out to the *siiran*, to dissuade the *hiyeks* from war."

"May She make that not too late."

Cassirur's inflection made it 'Goddess', but I started; hearing it as plain 'she' – the Hexenmeister in the Tower. I was almost relieved when my wristlink chimed, and signalled a private communication I'd have to take on one of the larger holotanks in the comlink-centre.

"I'll speak with you later," I said. As I left, I glanced back. Orthean female and aboriginal male: one red-maned and middle-aged and untidy, the other sleek and dark and thin. Memory tells me the one is the child of the other – that, for all we speak with *telestres* and Coast *hiyeks*, it is Tethmet's people who have the prior claim to Orthe. The light from the roof-slot shone whitely down on both of them.

As I crossed the courtyard to the Wellhouse outbuildings, my mind ran half on the necessity for setting up the WEBcasters' conference, half on what this comlink message might be – Douggie calling in? Carrick's Star shone down through *ziku*, and *chirith-goyen* hung in brightness, suspended in spirals of flight. Voices came clearly through the warm air, from the temporary camp outside the wall. Slanting beams of sunlight fell on the trodden earth, on red spore cases fallen in the dust, and I thought of autumn: of the seasons Stathern and Torvern. Strange to think of that in high summer. . . .

In a moment of perception, I felt how I stood here: flat heathland stretching out to the east; the sea a few miles south, invisible in haze; the interlocking pattern of *telestres*. Ales-Kadareth far to the east, Tathcaer to the west . . . and, high above, invisible among white daystars, the orbital station and its daisy chain of observing satellites. *Carrick V a Protected world? The inferior is protected from the superior, surely; but here's a world not hi-tech but not inferior either. Orthe has outlived our kind of civilization. How can we aid them?*

And thinking that, I thought also: to the south, there is the Coast, the *siirans*, hunger and disease. . . . We created the conditions for this civil war, but how could we not interfere with poverty? Ah, but that's not the whole story. If Calil has rediscovered that ancient weapon, it's only because we came here.

If she can synthesize Earth and Golden science to create that, then we must synthesize our cultures, Carrick V and Earth; survive a little changed, maybe, but survive.

"Christie," a voice said, as I was about to enter the round-roofed outbuilding that housed the makeshift comlinks. It was Blaize Meduenin. Still in mercenary's gear, nothing to mark him out as *T'An* Rimon.

"Your *t'an* Commander Mendez was just taken up in one of the 'thopters." His Sino-Anglic was accented, heavy with the inflections of the Peace Force. He grinned, scarred flesh twisting. "Travelling west. She's had word. So have we – on the heliograph-relay. There are *jath-rai* sighted off Morvren Freeport."

The third hour past noon, Merrum Firstweek Sixday; and all I could think was, *We're not going to get away with this as easily as I hoped.*

"Blaize, there's always shipping off the Freeport, what makes you sure these are *hiyek* ships?"

He scratched at his blond mane. At last identifiable: the smile was not pleasure, but relief at being able to take action; any kind of action. He said, "We're not sure. That's why I'm going down there. A *jath* could do it in a day, but I don't have a day in hand. I want one of your ships on Kumiel to fly me there."

He stood with his chin slightly raised, daring me to challenge that; and I looked at that alien face. Jaw too narrow, forehead too wide; membraned eyes bright in ruined flesh. Old scars. The silver-blond mane definitely needed cutting, and he had braided a twist of it back into the shaggy mass. As he shifted his stance, *harur*-blade harness jingled softly.

"On condition that you report directly back to me, as well as to the *takshiriye* here. I could get word from Hal – but as you say, I don't have the time in hand."

Blaize laughed. "I'll do it. If you tell me what your *T'An* Mendez does."

Ochmir is not the only game Ortheans play to perfection. I agreed, and went on into the outhouse. Two or three Peace Force officers were dividing their time between banks of consoles and field-holotanks, in a round room ill-lit by sunlight. Dried mossgrass crackled on the floor as I walked over to a 'tank, wincing at the stench of *rashaku* that still lingered.

I keyed in for Secure communication, and Cory Mendez's face appeared. Backdraught from the 'thopter whipped her short white hair across her face, and she had to shout to be heard above the engine: ". . . images. Satellites are showing ship-movement in – " she gave a string of co-ordinates, and then added, " – the northern Archipelago islands. I'm ordering an overflight. Four F90s will leave Kumiel Island shortly."

"I want a report half-hourly," I said. "When your people are in the area, I want a report every fifteen minutes."

The older woman's expression was odd. I sensed how she wanted to handle this herself, on grounds of experience. What restrained her – and

358

would have done more so, had I been Molly Rachel, or officially had Molly's position – is that her people are only, to be blunt about it, the strong arm of the Company's commercial division. How long can I count on that restraint? I wondered.

"Have someone monitor my transmissions continuously." She signed off.

I called one of the officers over, and as I got up from the 'tank, shadows darkened the door. Haltern Beth'ru-elen walked with the aid of a cane, pulling *becamil* blankets round his thin shoulders; and a pace behind him came Nelum Santhil Rimnith.

"Good," I said, "I'd been thinking of inviting you to speak with the WEBcasters, and I'm about to hold a conference here."

"We have already spoken with them." Haltern eased himself down on to one of the console seats, and clasped six-fingered hands over the top of his cane. He smiled. "Most persistent, your young *s'aranthi*."

Long ago I learned that, though Orthean languages don't have the word for it, you nevertheless don't have to tell Haltern Beth'ru-elen anything about public relations.

Nelum Santhil paced round the block of holotanks, peering with interest at aerial overviews of this part of Melkathi. He seemed preoccupied. His short dark mane was slicked up by the heat, and there was a thin line of white visible round his eyes. Pinned roughly to his slit-backed shirt was a crest badge, such as the Crown Guard wear; and this was all now that marked him out as *T'an Suthai-Telestre*. The *telestres* love ceremony, they also know when to abandon it.

"Your *t'an* Clifford – no word?"

"Nothing yet."

Nelum Santhil rested one stubby six-fingered hand on the edge of a holotank. "The *hiyeks* have means to far-speak, by use of your devices; and I hear also that they have groundcars, to travel. How many?"

No point in concealment. "Eight, possibly nine," I said.

"Then the *hiyeks* will know what is happening in the Freeport. Call your *t'an* Clifford," the *T'An Suthai-Telestre* said. "Warn him."

Haltern, who sat resting his chin on his clasped hands, shot me a glance full of amusement. I could guess what he was thinking. *This is the man whom I brought to the Citadel one night, eight years gone; not only a traitor, but a betrayer of other traitors – and now he is Crown. Perhaps the one qualifies him for the other?*

I asked another of the Peace Force officers to make the contact. As I did so, a group of seven or eight young men and women arrived outside the building; and began to come in, talking, and setting down the more bulky pieces of WEB equipment. Lutaya and Visconti were there. As

359

well as Ariadne and Trismegistus, I recognized the sigils of four other WEBs: two of them Pacifican-based (so they would be funded by multicorporates), one offworld from the Heart Stars, and a homeworld crew who – after some thought – I realized must come from the USSA. With Ariadne from the European Enclaves, and Trismegistus based in the Home Worlds generally, that meant a fair spread of opinion.

The Peace Force officer approached. He said quietly, "I can't make contact with the envoy, Representative Christie. Shall I keep trying?"

Ironic – that I know what's happening eight hundred miles distant in Morvren Freeport, but nothing of what might be eight miles away, in what used to be Keverilde. . . .

Not conscious of a hiatus (but by the officer's face there must have been one), I said, "Keep trying." Thinking, What's the connection between here, and the *hiyek*-Ortheans sailing towards the Freeport? What's happened here? Sethri – *Doug* –

"Sorry, people," I said. "I'm going to have to put this off for a few hours. I could give you the usual keep-'em-quiet rubbish, but I don't think there's any need to mess you around. I will let you know as soon as I can authorize a news release for the WEBs."

One of the two Anansi WEBbers raised his voice. "My colleague in the western coastal settlement says there's a lot of new activity there. Is that connected with this?"

Dissemination of news might hurt the Company, I thought. Can it hurt Orthe? And noted in passing, as one does, how I was now thinking: what order of priorities. It was Nelum Santhil whose eye I caught, where he stood unnoticed behind the group of WEBcasters. When Dalzielle Kerys-Andrethe was Crown, she would have dominated such a group without effort; he, with an equal lack of effort, faded into the background, waiting his moment to move. His black eyes were bright with humour. *How can you?* I thought. And then realized it was personally directed at me. Here I stand where Nelum Santhil stood before: on both sides of the fight. . . .

I glanced round the outhouse.

"If you want to know what's developing, I should stay around here," I said. "I'll arrange a linkup to the orbiter, but I'll want replay facilities for my staff. That applies also to what your colleagues in Morvren send. In return, you can have unrestricted access to Company transmissions."

At least, I thought, as the group broke into excited discussions, *you can while I'm acting Representative. Cory Mendez will create hell, but by then it'll be too late. And things are moving too fast now. If I can hang on and get us through this crisis – that's all I ask.*

★

Reports came back from the F90s at thirty- and then at fifteen-minute intervals. I stayed in the comlink-centre. Once during the afternoon, two *ashiren* brought in food for those of us there – the WEBcasters, Nelum Santhil, Haltern, Cassirur; and Geren *T'An* Ymir who'd ridden in from Tathcaer. The small room was full. I became aware that the Ortheans outside had begun to drift into the Wellhouse yard. The hum of their talk was a constant background to the hiss and crackle of comlink transmissions, blurred by Morvren's closeness to the Glittering Plain.

All through those hours, with the *jath-rai* drawing nearer to Morvren Freeport, satellite-images showed no movement at all on the heathland of Keverilde. At one point I took over from the Peace Force officer and tried contacting Douggie myself. It made no difference. There was no answer. I left it, contacted the orbiter: checked on the condition of David Osaka and Rashid Akida, now on Thierry's World; and had words with the acting heads of PanOceania's commercial and research divisions evacuated from Kel Harantish. And then I left the comlink officer to continue trying to contact Doug Clifford, and slept briefly, and woke to find nothing changed.

Dawn was a white blaze in the east: Merrum Firstweek Sevenday. The population of the comlink-centre changed, some of the WEBcasters now (I saw) going off to snatch sleep; Cassirur and another Earthspeaker being joined by Tethmet Fenborn. I pushed the chair back from the 'tank and walked over towards him, thinking, *Word could have come from Kasabaarde*, but the youngest Peace Force officer intercepted me.

"I've got something here," she said. "Commander Mendez told me to notify her too. It's a sat-pic of a body down on the heath; it shows evidence of CAS weaponry being used."

I bent over the holotank beside her. "What evidence – visual? That's not usual – "

I stopped, breath cut off short.

The image was small and clear. He lay with the side of his face pushed into the earth, black blood run and congealed from his ears and eyes. CAS weaponry, yes; but it wasn't that that made my heartbeat stutter. The *meshabi*-robe marked him out for a *hiyek*-Orthean; and I knew him. As still as if he slept, Sethri-safere of *hiyek*-Anzhadi lay in a hollow of the earth, dew wet on his skin.

"Get me a heat-sensor reading."

"He's dead," the Pacifican woman said. "Been dead for six or seven hours, by medicomputer estimate. Do you want it picked up?"

"*Yes* – have whoever goes in be extremely careful."

For a long moment I stood looking at that image, made of clear light.

Wild *becamil* had woven thin webs between mane and shoulder and the earth. No movement of ribcage, no flicker of that eye half shut by membrane. . . . And once he sat down beside me in the heat and glare of Maherwa and said, *I will be a friend to you, Lynne Christie.* Jesus Christ! I raged internally, senselessly; some *friend*, how could you let this happen now? And my eyes stung.

"*S'aranth,*" Haltern Beth'ru-elen said urgently, at the same moment as the Peace Force officer began to hurry back through the crowd towards me.

"Hal, take a look at this. . . . What?"

"There is someone down on Keverilde – " The old male stopped short, recognizing the image of the dead Orthean.

"Sensors are picking up movement," the officer said. "A small number of people, at 908-657-867. Estimate two or three, no more; they're not making much progress, but they're heading for this place."

"Can you identify?"

She said cautiously, "One of them might be the government envoy. It's difficult to get a visual fix; there's a fog rising."

"If you – never mind," I said. "I'll do it. Find me a driver, armed. What's the distance involved?"

"Six miles. Representative – "

I pushed through the crowd, ignoring urgent questions from the WEBcasters, sidestepped Lutaya; and as I left the outhouse, found the Earthspeaker Cassirur beside me. Cold air hit me, made me shiver. Dawn was drowned in mist that the sun would burn away; that hid the onion-domes of the Wellhouse.

"They may be my people, and if one is hurt, you'll need me," the red-maned woman said. She signalled to an *ashiren*, who ran into the Wellhouse, and returned almost instantly with a satchel of *marhaz*-hide.

"I – yes, I'm not thinking. I'll take one of the Force medics with us."

It must have taken only minutes to walk down the hillslope to where the Company groundcars were, but time stretched out; the ground underfoot jolted me, the wet fog dampened hair and coverall, tension snarled into a knot in my gut. I noted that Cassirur now wore at her belt a *harur-nilgiri* blade. Using the comlink, I called a medic; he and the driver were ready to go when I reached the 'car. And then it seemed only seconds while the 'car crept down the dirt tracks below Ashiel, visibility nil, relying on heat-sensors to move at all. Six miles.

"There."

Cassirur stood, gripping the edge of the groundcar seat. She pointed ahead. Faint light was beginning to leak through the mist. We moved in a shifting circle of visibility some ten yards across; and shadowy figures appeared now at the edge of it. The 'car rolled to a halt. Two people – It *is* Douggie, I thought; knowing him without even having to see his face.

While the 'car driver stood guard, CAS-VIII at the alert, I got down; Cassirur and the medic with me. The fog muffled sound, but I heard one of the two men breathing harshly; and as I walked forward thought there was something familiar about the other – not human, but Orthean – and then I stopped.

Doug Clifford's arm was across the shoulders of the other male, who held him upright. His coverall was darkly stained. One foot was bare and bleeding. His head was hanging down, but as I stepped forward he raised it; cocking his head sideways as if listening. His lips moved soundlessly. A strip of rag was bound round his head, covering his eyes; rag that was soaked red.

"*Douggie –* "

The Company medic pushed past me, reaching for his kit; and the Orthean male released Doug Clifford's arm with a grunt of pain. I could only stare, until the medic began to remove the blood-soaked rag; I saw a mess of blood and matted flesh –

An Orthean male in black robes, muddy and ripped. Brown-skinned and black-maned. I fixed my eyes on him because I couldn't look at Doug; spoke to cover the sound he was making. "Who – ?" And then recognized him.

Pathrey Shanataru wiped his six-fingered hands on his torn robe. He glanced at the envoy.

"Who did that to him?" the Harantish male said. His voice shook; there was a line of white showing round his eyes. "It was Calil bel-Rioch. The Empress Calil."

CHAPTER 30

Turncoat

"If you have any sense of survival," Pathrey Shanataru added, "leave here. *Shan'tai*, she may send people after us."

"'Us'?"

"Take that for good faith," he said, with a nod of his head at the envoy; and then more urgently: "I must speak with you, with all *s'aranthi*. To come here, I've risked everything; I've lost everything; you *must* listen to me."

The medic looked up from where he knelt beside Doug Clifford, who was down on one knee in the dirt. "This man's in shock. I need to get him to Kumiel, those are the nearest facilities."

"Drive back to Ashiel." I stepped forward and took Doug's arm. His head turned towards me, blind behind plastiflesh bandages. My head was full of calculations: how long before the fog lifts? How long before a 'thopter can get him to Kumiel – or an F90 to the orbiter?

"Sethri's dead." Doug choked: I guessed at the effort of withstanding pain. His other hand came to grip my arm. He said again, "Sethri Anzhadi's dead. I saw . . . *saw* Calil bel-Rioch have him killed."

"We know. The sats spotted it. Doug, come on; we'll get you back – for God's sake be careful – that's it . . ."

Doug Clifford stopped. The muscles of his back were hard under my hand. Empathy and revulsion tore me in different directions; I stifled both under professionalism. There will be time to take this in later.

With a studied precision, Doug said, "You will need to be in reach of orbital communications, therefore Kumiel; take *me* to Kumiel and use the medic facilities there; on the trip, I'll impart some extremely necessary information. *Shan'tai* Pathrey is correct, you must listen to him. What he has to say is important – "

He sagged back against me. "Painkiller," the medic said, as he and I manoeuvred Doug into the groundcar, and I sat with him half-supported against me as the driver swung us round in a curve and back up the track towards Ashiel Wellhouse. Cassirur bent forward to speak to Pathrey Shanataru in the front seat, but the dark Harantish male only shook his head.

Minutes ticked past. The fog didn't clear, but it thinned a little overhead; was white, then pearl, then blue, and specked with white

364

daystars. We passed clumps of *saryl-kiez*, grey with *becamil* webs. Pathrey glanced round at the unfamiliar landscape. Only then did it hit me: *the Empress Calil here? But Harantish isn't concerned with this, this is hiyek business.* . . . The groundcar jolted. Doug moaned, hardly loud enough to hear; and I put my arms around him and tried to hold him still.

"Doug, listen. . . . Can you hear me? You're going to be okay. I'll have you on Kumiel within the hour." I paused, reluctant, and then forced myself to go on. "You're telling me to come to Kumiel. What about the peace talks here? What about the other Anzhadi who support – supported – Sethri? Doug?"

His first words were unintelligible. I thought, I shouldn't ask questions. His weight against me seemed so slight; as if he had crumpled into the dirty coverall. There were long scratches on his hands as well as on his bare foot; the one made by *kiez* spines, the other, I think, by hooked claw-nails.

Slurring his words, but still with that precision of language, he said, "The opportunity for peace talks is over. The *hiyek*-Ortheans no longer follow Sethri, obviously, nor does *hiyek*-Anzhadi have influence now that he is dead. If I put it in plain terms, I would say Calil bel-Rioch and her Harantish Ortheans are now controlling the invasion of the Hundred Thousand – " He caught his breath, found my hand by touch alone, and gripped it hard. "Lynne, did that make sense? I have to tell – did I – ?"

The groundcar's hum rose to a whine, cresting the hill. Ashiel's wall appeared through the fog. It muffled the voices, half hid the bright robes of Ortheans crowding round: Cassirur stood up in the 'car and ordered them to clear a path.

As I was about to move, my wristlink chimed. The face of a Peace Force officer appeared. I said, "Can't this wait?"

His voice was tinny in the open air. "You may want to take this contact in Secure, Representative."

"If it's that urgent, give it to me now; and for God's sake get a move on – " I moved my wrist and hand away from Douggie, and he slumped back against my shoulder. The miniature holo-image changed: the face of Cory Mendez appeared. Noise and vibration meant she must still be in a 'thopter or small shuttle.

Cory looked at me with a grim satisfaction.

"You wanted updates regularly," she said. "Take a look at this. It's live-transmission. The ships in the islands have moved as far north as Morvren Freeport. Now they're attacking the settlement."

The image was a blur, too small to focus on. In a tone that I hoped didn't show panic, I said, "Cory, I'm coming down there. Take no action, no independent action, do you understand what I'm saying?"

From blur to vision: the holo-image was clear as some painted miniature. That far west, dawn is just breaking, the sea is milk-pale. It laps the filigree-coast of a harbour island – viewpoint too high to make out people, but there is a *jath-rai*, and another, metal sails flashing in the light; *there* a thread of black smoke blooming. . . .

Corazon Mendez said, "Company regulations say I have to observe, under such circumstances. I'm observing, but I give you fair warning, Lynne; if a situation comes up where I have to take action, I won't hesitate." She paused, then added: "If I see signs of hi-tech warfare, I'll have no option but to send my people in to force a cease-fire."

Eight hundred miles to the west, Morvren Freeport burns.

Do we go by groundcar now, I wondered; risk rough travelling and fog? Or reckon that the fog will lift soon, and take a 'thopter? 'Thopter, yes.

I entered the makeshift comlink-centre, and found Ottoway in charge. He glanced up as I came in, and brushed fair hair out of his eyes. The holotank he watched carried images of Morvren.

"I need transport to Kumiel," I said. "Has Cory told you to stay here? Good. I want the closest surveillance of this area, if anyone leaves, either take them or follow them; use your discretion." *And where is Calil now?* "As far as you can, keep a cordon of neutral ground around Keverilde and Rimnith."

He grunted. "Yes, Representative. . . . Ms Christie, there are times when I curse Company regulations. If we could bring new tech stuff down to the planet's surface, half a dozen officers could enforce a peace. But they give us equipment that's twenty years old, and tell us it's to avoid cultural contamination – and *look* at that." He slammed a fist down on the edge of the holotank.

Is that orthodox opinion in the Force? I wondered. Could be; and does PanOceania know or care?

"You're to continue to allow the *takshiriye* – the local authorities – and the WEBbers free access to all communications," I shot back over my shoulder at him as I left. I didn't hold out too much hope of it happening that way.

Outside, fog had turned to ground haze. The air was warm and silky-smooth, beaten by the blades of a large 'thopter that rested on mossgrass beyond Ashiel walls; and as I came up to it, I found the tall medic had been joined by another, and both were helping Doug into the cabin. A little distance off, Pathrey Shanataru stood irresolute. He now wore a light *chirith-goyen* cloak, the hood drawn up over his head; he could, in this light, have been from a *telestre*. And down among the *marhaz*-hide shelters there was movement, and I guessed news was being passed round.

"Get in, *shan'tai*," I said. "We'll talk as we go."

The 'thopter swung in the air as if suspended from some sky hook. Ashiel, that had seemed so large, lost itself in brown heath and haze. Cold air blew through the plastiglas cabin; the thrum of the blades was deadened. Now I could smell the sea.

One of the medics sat forward with the pilot, the other stared absently out into void. Beside her, Doug sat with his hands flat on his thighs, and I realized: For the past three-quarters of an hour I have not allowed myself to think the word *blind*.

"I'll tell you what I can," he said. His face turned vaguely towards me, where I sat with Pathrey. The plastiflesh masked his eyes; left only that prim mouth to be read for expression. We sat cramped so close together that I hardly had to lean forward to take his hand.

"There are small groups of Coast Ortheans scattered all across that heath." Douggie raised his voice slightly, over the beat of the 'thopter blades. "Lynne, I don't know if we were as near a truce as I imagined . . . that's irrelevant, now. I knew something was going badly wrong when I saw Harantish men and women with the *hiyek*-Ortheans, and I suspect Sethri Anzhadi did, but we continued to go from group to group, putting forward the *T'An Suthai-Telestre*'s proposals. I think we saw several hundred people; I know there were more there."

Beside me, Pathrey Shanataru nodded. I gripped Douggie's hand. "What else?"

"I imagine some of the *jath* that Commander Mendez saw were carrying Harantish Ortheans. Has *shan'tai* Pathrey told you that Calil – that the Empress-in-Exile is there?" His scratched hands tensed. "Lynne, you don't dispose of Kel Harantish's grip on the Coast in just a few months. They're going to follow her. Obviously she had got rid of Sethri's main supporters while he was with us. She no sooner had him than she ordered he be executed – "

"With CAS weaponry?"

He loosed one hand, moving the fingers to touch the bandage over his eyes; and I saw how his mouth was a hard line. Quite clinically, and irrelevantly, he said, "She did this herself, with her own hands; I had still thought there might be a chance of talking so I allowed myself to be disarmed, that was a bad mistake – she has other CAS and hi-tech armoury, yes; but that was mine, Lynne. I'm sorry. I'm talking too much. It's true what they say about shock."

Does he know about Morvren? suddenly occurred to me. Was he able to hear what Cory transmitted to me?

367

The 'thopter dipped, straightened. Carrick's Star blazed off the surface of the sea, too bright to be looked at; and the coast of the Hundred Thousand was only blue haze.

"She's quite mad," Doug Clifford said. "I know Ortheans, by now. There's no rationality – "

"I know," I said, at the same moment that Pathrey Shanataru said, "She's ill, *shan'tai*."

I glanced at the time, reckoned close on twenty minutes before the 'thopter made Kumiel. And then a shuttle down to Morvren; how many hours . . . ?

"Can you add anything to what Doug's said?" I asked Pathrey.

He looked down at his hands, dark fingers bare of the rings he had worn. His hands perceptibly shook. At the one moment I thought of question and answer: *he fears flying more than other Ortheans, why?* and, *the Harantish have Golden blood, and so no past-memories of this when the Empire was here.* And wondered how I had come to take for granted that I think as Ortheans do about the matter – as with most things of Orthe, it all comes back to the Tower.

"I can add much," Pathrey Shanataru said. He kept his eyes averted from the plastiglas cabin walls.

"I . . . when I last saw you in Kel Harantish, I didn't expect to see you again here."

"We sailed within hours of you *s'aranthi* leaving."

Words came from him with great effort. I let silence prompt him now. He raised his head, and I saw there was a bruise on his temple, half covered by the rooting black mane. Membrane slid back from dark eyes. Alien, that expression; and then with surprise I read it for what it was: an aching sadness.

"I shouldn't be here. I should be with her still. After so many years . . ." Pathrey hesitated. "Is she mad? You *s'aranthi* tell me; I no longer know. After what I have seen her do in Harantish these past weeks, I no longer know. I fear for her, *shan'tai*."

It was Doug who broke the silence that followed. With a surprising gentleness he said, "Tell the Representative what you've told me, *shan'tai* Pathrey."

The dark Orthean male spoke in a more formal inflection. "The ambition of Calil bel-Rioch is to be Empress, *shan'tai*, and Empress as it was in the days long past. She would raise up that Golden Empire again, and make this land here a part of it, and all the land that the *hiyeks* have – " He broke off. When he resumed, it was in plain speech. "You saw her. She would be Santhendor'lin-sandru come again. She has your *s'aranthi* weapons, and now she has those weapons that the Coast has. *Is* she mad?

368

You live as a Harantish woman, *shan'tai* Christie; live shunned and feared and kept penned up in that barren pesthole, and you tell me! All I know is, half Harantish thinks as she does."

"Is that true? Literally true?"

"Oh yes," he said. "There are Harantish now with the *hiyeks* in the Archipelago."

"Since when?"

"Two days ago. Perhaps three."

Is he telling the truth, is he lying? Either way, what does he really know; he's one man, and how trustworthy is he? I thought of using the wristlink to contact Corazon Mendez, but hesitated. She would have this man who was Voice of the Empress-in-Exile debriefed, that would take time; nor would it happen soon, with the crisis going on in Morvren. . . .

"They do have hi-tech weapons," Douggie said.

The 'thopter tilted, dipping down towards hazy land that must be Kumiel. Sea glittered; and to the north I glimpsed what might be white *telestre*-houses in morning sunlight. Tathcaer.

"You must stop her, but not harm her," Pathrey said; his plump face wore an incongruously stubborn expression. "Nor should you put the blame on her alone, there are many in the city who thought as she did, and who help her now. If it were not she, it would be some other. *Shan'tai*, you must believe me."

I had no time to analyse that oddly wistful defiance. Doug's hand gripped mine tightly. He said, "Say what else you said to me, Pathrey."

The Harantish male blinked, translucent membrane and then eyelids; and reached out to grip a wall-hold as the 'thopter settled towards the earth. "What else. . . . You must understand, *shan'tai*, she speaks with no one now, not even I. Still, there is something more. When that great Empire fell, there was a weapon used, or so tales tell. Now if you talk with my people from Harantish, you will find that they believe that weapon can be used again – that she has discovered the use of it. I have never heard word of this before. I think therefore that *she* puts this rumour among us."

He opened his eyes. "*Shan'tai*, I have lived these many years. I have some power of reason. I do not believe the ancient weapons of the Golden have been rediscovered, but *she* may believe it. If she does, all Harantish does; all the *hiyeks* will. And that belief in itself may prove as destructive a weapon."

Now the 'thopter settled down towards the earth. Below us, ranked F90s lined rocky Kumiel; growing as the ground rushed up to meet us. I felt split in two: half of me thinking, *never underestimate ideology; charismatic insanity is not to be ignored*, and the other half, without the solace of black humour, thinking, *but if Pathrey's wrong and she does have Golden science?* The 'thopter touched down on blue-grey mossgrass, between shuttles, with never a jolt.

"I'll have to ask you to stay here," I said. "Cory's people will look after you, *shan'tai* Pathrey."

As he climbed shakily down from the 'thopter he looked back at me and with only the slightest irony, said, "Call it 'protective imprisonment'."

I slid down from the 'thopter, on to Kumiel's sparse blue mossgrass. The air was warm, shimmering over the island's pitted rocks; the white dolphin-backed ranks of F90 shuttles wavered with heat distortion. As the first medic followed me, I drew her aside.

"How is he?"

She glanced back up at the 'thopter cabin. "We can probably save the sight of one eye if we get him to the orbiter's tissue-regeneration facilities now."

"I'll authorize it."

Doug appeared in the cabin door, and I reached up as he put a tentative foot towards invisible ground; seeing how he turned his head in bewilderment. His hand caught mine with so hard a grip it made me wince. Then as I helped him down, I held him, feeling his heartbeat, his warmth; and what I'd meant to say went unsaid, choked in grief and anger.

"I ought . . ." His hands shook. "I ought to be in the Freeport."

"I'll handle the government side of things, till you get back. Christ, I ought to know the job," I said, "I did it for long enough."

He opened his mouth to speak, paused; my throat tightened in sympathy. I let the medic take his arm to lead him towards the shuttles, knowing how precariously he was holding himself together. And for a moment I stood there on the springy mossgrass, wanting to do nothing else but go with him up to the orbiter, not trusting others to care for him. *And you'll come back before you should*, I thought, watching that small figure limping towards the towering hull of an F90 shuttle. Not until then able to realize, *Calil, with her own hands –*

I walked briskly across the island towards their comlink-centre, tasting bile; all but sick with revulsion.

Eight hundred miles to the west. . . . I slept for as much of the two-hour shuttle flight as I could, not knowing when I'd get the chance again. Waking, the holotank-images showed bright morning. Shadows of clouds glided across the surface of the Rasrhe-y-Melvur, as we flew past the side of that great *chiruzeth* spire; coming in from the seaward side to overfly the estuary of the Ai River.

The shuttle-pilot said, "I'm fitting us into the holding-pattern, Representative."

At fifteen hundred feet, the island-filled estuary lay like a topographic map. Black specks crossed and recrossed airspace above it, and as the shuttle went into hover-mode I identified 'thopters and other shuttles. Sun flashed from the white hulls of F90s – Cory's in one of those, I thought, and reached out to key in a contact. Before I could do it, an incoming message appeared in the holotank.

"Christie here – "

And then I keyed that image to an insert, staring at the main tank. The surface of the sea glittered, pale blue and azure and indigo in the depths. Sparks of light came from the metal sails of *jath-rai*: ten, a dozen, twenty. . . . *There were more in the Archipelago, where are they now?* The island nearest the Rasrhe-y-Meluur was as clear as a miniature model; harbour and Watchtower and Wellhouse dome, a movement that might have been *marhaz*-riders – all obscured now, as black smoke plumed up from the *telestre*-houses nearest the docks. Unclear from this height: is that fighting, are those small specks of colour people? – and then the shuttle was over the island, past it; hovering over the channel between that and a larger Freeport island.

"*S'aranth?*" The face of Blaize Meduenin appeared in the holo-insert. "Sunmother! Will you tell this *t'an* Mendez of yours to land this ship? I must get into the city."

"Who's there?"

He frowned. "The river-*telestre s'ans*. *T'An* Khassiye Reihalyn, if the winds favoured him; he sailed from Tathcaer two days ago. But he's Andrethe, not *T'An* Seamarshal; Freeporters won't heed him."

Knowing Freeporters, they won't take notice of anyone . . . *T'An* Rimon or Company representative, I thought with grim amusement.

"Let me speak to Cory," I said; and when Corazon Mendez appeared, said, "Land the *T'An* Rimon on the island nearest to the mainland, will you? I'm going in, too. I intend to speak with the local leaders."

The white-haired woman blinked, raised an eyebrow. She said, "How far does your policy of non-interference stretch, Lynne? Just out of interest, you understand. When you yell for a 'thopter to get you out of that mess down there, you want me to send my troops into Orthean territory?"

"Cory, just *do* it, yes?" I keyed out.

In the shuttle's cool, green-lit interior, nothing was audible but the hum of the engines. Hard to believe that outside there is real air, stained with the smoke of burning. My guts ached, my hands sweated: I thought, Is this stupid or is this *stupid*? This is not a thing to get involved in, and it's much too late to stop it now it's started. For God's sake go back to Kumiel and wait. . . .

But then, there's no way to know what's really going on without going down there.

River gravel crunched under my boots as I sprang down from the shuttle-ramp. Downdraught from the F90's hover-mode blinded me for a moment in the swirl of grit. I ran for the cover of the quayside buildings. Blaize Meduenin waited under a warehouse archway.

"I'm getting . . ." I leaned up against the pale plaster wall, " . . . getting too old for this sort of thing. And what the fuck I think I'm going to do here, *I* don't know."

The Meduenin grinned. Wind off the harbour whipped his yellow mane across his scarred face, and brought the rank smell of *dekany*-weed and overripe *siir*-vine. Standing here, at sea level, there was no view in any direction. A windvane towered over this part of the quay, vanes slowly turning; I glanced up and down the dock – warehouses and companion-houses and no Freeporters at all. So quiet you could hear the waves slap at the harbour wall . . . and hear, in the far distance, voices loudly shouting.

"They've reopened the Seamarshal's palace," Blaize Meduenin said. I remembered seeing it boarded-up, half a year ago. He drew *harur-nilgiri*, holding it in his left hand; and membrane slid down over those pale blue, whiteless eyes. "Look: there."

Confused, I glanced round. Then, as he pointed, I saw the hoop-mast of a *jath-rai* not three hundred yards away in the channel between this island and the next. *Meshabi*-robed Ortheans crowded the deck. Morning sun flashed from the metal sail and chains. It was automatic to step back into the shadow of the warehouse-arch, and I thought *Lynne don't be ridiculous* and a chip of mud-brick stung my cheek. After a second, my eyes focused on the head of a winchbow-bolt, buried deep in a split in the brickwork.

"Think they'll be lucky, don't they?" Blaize touched my arm. "Christie – this way; come."

The sun was hot on my head as we crossed the quay again, slipping into an alley that led away from the harbour. Darkness flicked across the dusty earth and biscuit-coloured walls: the shadow of a 'thopter. I tried to push all thought aside. My stomach churned; I was aware of a sideways glance from Blaize.

The alley opened into a square, crowded with Freeport Ortheans. Over their heads I glimpsed the round-arched doors of the Seamarshal's palace. A crowd in constant movement, men and women arriving and leaving: in the far corner a bronze *marhaz* threw up its head and bugled loudly. I swiftly searched for faces I might know, in that confusion of dark and fair manes; Ortheans in Morvren's slit-backed robes, and the leathers of *marhaz*-riders from the north; there a thin, tall woman whose green-gold skin could only belong to a fenborn; there an *ashiren* no more than twelve seasons old, bearing *harur*-blades. . . .

"Khassiye will be in the palace, if he's here," Blaize observed. With that scar-crooked grin, he added, "When there's fighting, our *T'An* Andrethe will be well out of it!"

Loud voices rang in our ears; Ortheans calling and shouting. Morning sun shone back from pale walls. Two- and three-storey buildings surrounded this square, windowless but for slots on the top floor. As we pushed through the crowds, I searched for words; at last protested: "Blaize, this isn't a *game*."

His eyes looking at me were alien. He doesn't fear death here, how could he, remembering other deaths and other rebirths – but it is not a reality for me. Reality is the sickness, the weakness, the disablement of fear. I can call the 'thopter; I can call it *now* –

"There's Khassiye Reihalyn," I pointed to the low stepped terrace that ran along beside the Seamarshal's palace. The tall fair-maned male stood with three or four other men and women; his gold-studded fingers flashed as he gestured, giving orders. He frowned, seeing us.

"*T'an S'aranth*, we have enough Earth devices here without your setting down ships-of-the-air on *telestre* land."

"Unavoidable necessity, *T'An* Andrethe. But do you mean there are hi-tech weapons being used here? Have the *hiyek*-Ortheans – "

"Communicating devices," Khassiye Andrethe said. He squinted up in the sunlight as a shuttle glided overhead, casting its shadow down on the crowded square. "It must be so, *S'aranth*; they act together, though their *jath-rai* are beyond sight of each other. The attack came simultaneously upon our several different islands here."

Blaize put in, "This isn't their whole force. What word of the rest?"

A black-maned male in Freeport robes said, "Still in the islands, *t'an*. Doubtless they will come."

"And the attack?"

"There's fighting on Southernmost and Little Morvren and round Spire Gate. The fires on Little Morvren are beyond control." The black-maned Orthean turned to me. "Do you bring us help, *s'aranthi*, or only fair words?"

"We won't interfere in Morvren – on either side."

One of the Orthean females chuckled. She had her mane drawn up into a plume on the crown of her head, and braided down her spine; one of Peir-Dadeni's northern riders. With some derision, she said, "Trust *s'aranthi*? *T'an*, you'll interfere when it suits you."

A shout echoed. I looked up, and saw an Orthean male on the roof above, leaning over the low wall. He called again, pointing; and I didn't catch the words, but his urgency made me go cold.

"Caveth! Zilthar!" Khassiye Andrethe called two of the Seamarshal's guard to him, and gave a string of rapid orders.

"Call your people," Blaize Meduenin said to me. The square emptied rapidly now, Ortheans filing out into the broad avenues of that island. The windvane creaked as it turned, not far away; and under the sound I heard a confused shouting. Coming nearer? The sea wind whipped sound away: impossible to tell.

"Blaize – "

"There's nothing to be done," the scarred male said. "Go and speak with the *hiyeks* if you think there is. Go tell your *T'An* Mendez to fire on *jath-rai*. *S'aranth*, if you can't do that, all you can do is leave us to fight."

"That isn't fair!" I recovered some control. "I can't – I *won't* – order Peace Force intervention. I will try and make contact with the *hiyek*-Ortheans on those ships, though I don't hold out much hope – "

"Sunmother!" He swore. Then he moved down the palace steps, staring towards the avenues; and the morning sun shone brightly on that dusty silver-yellow mane where it tangled down his spine. *Harur*-blade harness made a soft metallic sound. Without looking back at me, he said, "Call your people. Leave. And when you leave, let me take that far-speaking device of yours. I need to know if the *jath-rai* in the islands sail."

I thumbed the recall key, and walked down to stand beside him.

"You're staying here? I suppose this is what I could never imagine – you as mercenary commander. And yet I've been in this position on other worlds, there've been outbreaks of fighting; low-tech weapons . . ."

Straining my ears, listening for the beat of a 'thopter's approach: all I could hear was shouting. Orthean voices; now there was no mistaking it, they were coming closer. Blaize rested his hand on my shoulder and I jumped. And then laughed, shakily; and realized how I looked all the time at the entrances to this square, the alleys and avenues; now empty, but all potential threat. Hot morning sun, and quietness, and distant sounds that must be fighting. . . . Deep inside, I went cold.

"Will you go?" Blaize said. There was something in his tone besides exasperation. "Christie, you were always stubborn. There's nothing you can do here. And you're terrified – I know; I've seen enough raw young fighters."

"'Young'?" That made me smile, for a second. A distant beat resolved itself into the throb of a low-flying 'thopter, and I thumbed the recall-key on the wristlink again, to give a location-fix. The roar of the engines drowned all other sound, and suddenly the sun gleamed on its plastiglas body as the 'thopter seemed to rise up over the roof of the Seamarshal's palace.

"They don't need you here – " I had to shout to make myself heard over the noise. He held out one six-fingered hand, gesturing at my wristlink. I unfastened it. He took it, and I thought, There's so much I want to say. How can I persuade you out of this – ?

The 'thopter grounded in a storm of dust and gravel. At the end of one avenue, a hundred yards away, there was confused movement: the momentary brightness of metal. Blaize Meduenin strapped on the wristlink and drew *harur-nazari*, almost in one smooth movement; as if it were choreographed, we ran; he for the shelter of the wall, me for the open port of the 'thopter. I ducked down, running under the rotors; hit arm and knee as I scrambled up into the cabin, realized *I can't leave* and shouted to the pilot to put down. He either didn't hear or chose to ignore me. The 'thopter lurched up a dozen feet into the air and I grabbed the strut by the open port, stomach convulsing. There were ten people in the alley now, more pouring in, bright-maned Order in dusty robes; all of them running together, mouths moving but I could hear nothing over the beat of the rotors.

Hanging there, on a level with the roofs, I looked dizzily down at Blaize Meduenin. The fair-maned male stood in the shadow of the wall. For a heartbeat I thought, *They'll all pass him*; and all did, except for one male who hesitated after the others had gone, running in a strung-out line towards the quay. My throat rasped sore; I hadn't realized I was shouting. The *hiyek* male stopped, shading his eyes with his hand as he looked up, attention taken by the 'thopter twenty feet above him; his gaze locked with mine. Thin-faced, middle-aged. His mouth moved as if he shouted, and he gestured with the hook-bladed knife he carried in his right hand. A flick of movement caught my eye and then Blaize Meduenin ran between us, one arm outstretched, hardly seeming to brush the *hiyek* male across the midriff; metal gleamed, the male folded over and fell to his knees, and slid down on the earth. The 'thopter lurched again and then rose like an elevator. Fifty feet straight up, swinging round in a curve; I vomited and then spat bile through the open port.

When I scrambled forward and fell into the seat beside the pilot, and got him to swing the craft round and double back over the island, there was no way to spot one fair-maned Orthean male amongst the running

crowds. I reached out to key the wristlink contact and then hesitated:
Don't distract him –

" . . . shuttle?" the pilot mouthed, sparing me a brief glance.
"Observation and . . ."

"Take us down as low as you can!" I had to shout to make myself
heard.

The 'thopter dipped and suddenly shot off towards the harbour,
skimming the surface, then rising to fifty or so feet above the waves; and
the smell of *dekany*-weed mixed with evaporating fuel. An island to either
side of us: it disorientated me – had our landing been there, or there, or
over there? Looking down on water that is jade green, blinded by the
morning sun as the 'thopter swings round again; and I managed to key
in an open channel and grabbed for the headphones, hoping to hear the
rest of Cory's ships:

" *– no, repeat negative, no usage of anything above level five technology –* "

" *– movement of local ships on the river on the increase. Request permission
to extend my flight further up-country; we don't want any nasty surprises from
that direction –* "

" *– estimated local casualties –* "

" *– make contact with the Company representative, and ascertain present
location –* "

The pilot glanced at me and I nodded, and he began to transmit co-
ordinates.

"Cory?" I yelled into the pick-up. "What's the fuel situation; how long
can you keep an observation-pattern going?"

" *– position you over the southernmost of these islands,* " Cory's voice
rasped. All transmissions had that intermittent failure that must be due
to what lay several hundred miles north: the Glittering Plain.

Now the 'thopter circled a small island, and I looked down on tiny
telestre-houses, roof-gardens thick with scurrying figures; down on alleys
in which the shadows were shortening – it must be late morning, close
on midday – and on a dock and a harbour arm. The masts of *jath* were
foreshortened from this height. One ship shimmered, quivering in the
warm air; small figures ran from invisible flames, plunging over the side
into cerulean water. My hands were flat against the plastiglas: a wall
between me and the world, *not real*, I thought; then the rotors feathered
the sea into flattened ripples, spreading out from us; one bright-maned
head dipped under the water, and never reappeared. The 'thopter
swooped up again, high over the island.

" *– attempt to force a cease-fire –* "

"What attempt?" I shouted. The comlink crackled, and I swore in
frustration; and then Corazon Mendez came through with total clarity.

" – I've made attempts at contacting the attacking ships with broadcasts from a low-level flight, Lynne. No, repeat negative, no response. I want your authorization to fire a warning shot. Simply a threat; no loss of life involved. I'll use mid-tech explosive projectiles. These natives can understand that. The threat of force – "

Interference washed out her voice. The 'thopter hung high over Southernmost, and the sun half-blinded me as we turned. Sea and earth and daystarred sky; and the long level line of the horizon. . . .

Cory's transmission faded back in:

" – the threat alone will have the required effect: but I want it entered on Company records, Lynne, that I have your authorization for this."

CHAPTER 31

The Viper and Her Brood

I didn't answer. As the 'thopter steadied, I touched the pilot's shoulder and pointed north. We swung away from the Rasrhe-y-Meluur, that great pillar of *chiruzeth* whose shadow fell on the waves below us. The port was still retracted: cool air blustered in, bringing a smell of ocean, making me shiver – but that was with more than cold. At two thousand feet now, the depths of the estuary made a pattern of deep green and shallow jade below us.

Voices intersected on the comlink-circuit. I ignored them. The thrum of the rotors drowned thought; I felt in suspension at some God-like point of overview – we passed over a *jath-rai*, its white trail fading; decks lined with *hiyek*-Ortheans.

"Cory, I'm considering what you say." I took a breath, hoping to rid myself of a sick dizziness that was nothing to do with flight. The docks of Southernmost flashed past beneath. Now the flames had a hold: black smoke rolled up from *jath* and dockside companion-houses.

"Yes, I'll give you your authorization," I said. "Listen to me – Commander. I'm not trying to teach you your business. I have a contact on Northfast, repeat, a contact on Northfast; that's the city-island nearest the mainland. Co-ordinate it so that he can attempt to pull some of his people back. That might just do it. We might just have our cease-fire."

"Affirmative. Lynne, put your comlink on-circuit; I'll have my officers co-ordinate the strike – "

I automatically followed her order. When I glanced up from the comlink console, seconds later, the 'thopter was again in the channel between Little Morvren and Northfast. Billows of black smoke swirled in from the west, and the pilot pulled us up another five or six hundred feet. Looking down on the smoke was like looking down on a coral reef or tree tops: the same shape, but this lived and moved. A spark burned below. How great a conflagration?

" . . . have to take us out of their air-space," the pilot called.

I leaned half out of the port as we flew north. *Telestre*-houses, windvanes, wide avenues. . . . People lay in the avenues; six, ten, a dozen; arms outflung, or legs twisted. Nothing to be seen but their stillness; they look as if they might at any moment get up and run. Suddenly my heart lurched: *that* is the Residence, *that* is the house of

378

Cassirur Almadhera, *that*, burning fierce as phosphorus, is the Sea-marshal's palace – square, flat-roofed buildings; the dry *kazsis*-vine sprouting into flame. Now there were people running, some in small groups, some alone, no crowds; running in the immemorial jerky patterns of street-fighting. It's wrong to look at this, I thought, wrong to be a spectator; and then my stomach and lungs clenched with fear: I might still be down there, no spectator at all.

The 'thopter, running low, no more than a thousand feet, passed over the docks. A shadow flicked us: the bulk of an F90 hung in hover-mode over the harbour arm. Part of its shadow fell on *hiyek* ships there, part on Ortheans running across the quay. I had to lean out of the port and look up to see the sun on that white whale-backed craft; it dazzled me. Then we were past.

"*Strike co-ordinate at twelve hundred –* "
" *– contact made with land forces –* "
" *– strike at 057.253.746; repeat, 057.253.746 –* "

Suddenly we were no longer over the sea, but skimming the mainland; the flat and dusty banks of the Ai River. Ferry-shacks were scattered along it; dense crowds gathered round them. *Marhaz*-riders raised dust-trails. Small boats bobbed like wood-chips in the mouth of the estuary, their yellow and white sails bright against the muddy water.

A grinding, bass explosion ripped the air. I felt it rather than heard it; felt it in the chest and stomach and bones; couldn't help glancing up at the clear sky – such a phenomenon must be thunder, too fearful to be manmade – and then turned in my seat to stare back. A dust-cloud ballooned up over Northfast, blocking out light and turning the sun sepia. A curious line seemed to be running from the island across the sea towards the mainland – simultaneous to realization, the 'thopter swung into the shockwave and was for long seconds buffeted and pushed sideways. My hands clenched on the siderail, knuckles white. Somewhere below a tidal wave must be hitting the estuary. I clung, eyes shut.

" *– made successfully at twelve-oh-two –* "
" *– no damage sustained by shuttle –* "
" *– I'm getting visual damage-estimate; wait –* "

Carrick's Star blinded me. I rubbed at my watering eyes, tried to focus. A thousand feet below, a river-boat lay on its side in the water. Tiny figures splashed, swimming; no larger than insects. No sooner seen than passed.

"Jesus!" the pilot whistled softly, in admiration. "Made a mess of them didn't we – sorry, Representative Christie."

After the fear, the exultation: I tried to repress both. No point now in thinking, *Was that the right decision, should I have waited, what else could*

379

I have done? And wrong to feel that joy that comes with the use of power, any power, for any reason. I leaned forward as we skimmed the side of that rising mass of dust and grit and rubble turning lazily end over end in the air, only now just beginning to fall. . . .

At first I saw nothing. Then I registered that Northfast no longer has a harbour arm. That long mass of masonry gone, and only shattered fragments at the quay end to prove it ever existed.

Smoke and dust clouded the dockside. Metal shone: a *jath-rai* driven up – up the steps that led to the Portmaster's office; it looked ridiculous there. Men and women clambered free of the fallen hoop-mast, staggering; one fell from no cause and didn't rise, and it was whole minutes later before I thought (as the 'thopter crossed the channel between islands) *winchbow-bolt*. I reached out to key in a contact with my wristlink, and found I had to use the console; the world not yet come together again in my head. *Did we really do that?* And: *yes, we did: we really did.*

The 'thopter ports closed, the air-purifiers hummed; dust from the explosion being filtered out of the interior of the craft. That cloud drifted south, dimming the daystars. It hid the pattern of F90s and YV9s, shuttling back and forth across this few miles of coast. How far inland did they hear that? I wondered. What's being said now in the river-*telestres*? How long will it take word to get as far as the nearer Archipelago islands?

" – do we have contact? Lynne?"

"I'm here," I said. "Give me your co-ordinates, and have your pilot here rendezvous with your shuttle. I'm coming aboard."

"Affirmative."

I closed my eyes, concentrating on the voices on the comlink circuit, knowing better than to interrupt with anything inessential. There was no voice yet speaking Rimon, or Sino-Anglic with a Rimon accent.

The F90 hovered squarely over Northfast, holotank showing a direct live-transmission of the island beneath. Corazon Mendez was standing by the holotank when her junior officer ushered me into the craft's comlink-centre; she glanced up briefly, but continued to talk without pause: " – the extent of damage for Company records. I want a full holographic record, Lieutenant." She keyed in a different contact. "Marston, has there been any resumption of hostilities?"

"Some sporadic firing, Commander Mendez. The sea-craft are still keeping their distance. Estimate them fifteen minutes away from any contact with land."

"Good." She keyed the channel shut, and straightened. Her hair was sleek, the Peace Force coverall neat. Nothing betrayed tension but that characteristic twisting of her silver rings, of which she seemed unaware.

"The *hiyek* ships have backed off?"

"For the moment," Cory said. "The next few hours will be quiet. If we pass the eight-hour mark, I may begin to think we've forced the cease-fire we were hoping for. If not, we're back where we started."

My legs not only ached, they were trembling. I walked across and sat down in one of the bucket seats. I was suddenly unaccountably thirsty. I said, "Not entirely back where we started. The Company's used force twice now on Orthe; that's as far as it's going to go. Or were you thinking that, if this hasn't worked, you can do here what you did at Reshebet?"

"That strike was effective," Cory said mildly. "May I remind you, Lynne, you're unofficially acting as Company representative. If anything, we share the responsibility."

Never argue on ground that uncertain. I said nothing in direct reply.

"Is there any news from the orbiter on Doug Clifford?"

"What kind of news?" She was bewildered.

Only a few hours, and communications are confused – I shook my head. One becomes resigned to this sort of thing in the field. "He was hurt in Melkathi. The Harantish – but you won't know about that either? No. Jesus Christ! Well, so long as you hear about it now. . . . You may want to call your senior officers in on this briefing."

The cool green lighting of the F90's cabin soothed me (as it is intended to do); I became aware of the power-hum, of a low chatter of communication; of other Peace Force officers through in different command-centres.

"Cory, I also want the *T'An* Rimon in on this one. He has local information you could find useful; he's fought here, and on the Coast." I thought, And for the *hiyeks* and against them – but what will Blaize Meduenin say when he knows that Kel Harantish has entered this war?

"I'll have my people contact him."

We spoke of other things. I kept up a façade of competence; what I said, I don't know. At last, with no warning, an insert in the holotank resolved into the scarred face of Blaize Meduenin, standing in the sunlight on Northfast; and he spoke with one of Cory's junior officers, in a voice hoarse with exhaustion. Relief of tension made my eyes prickle with tears, but I held them back.

I made no move to speak with him. The resolution of the image was poor, but clear enough to see the stains of black blood on the *harur-nilgiri* held in his right hand. Strain and exhaustion on his face, corrupted by the pull of scar tissue; lines deeply incised near the pale membrane-covered eyes – by being on Northfast for those two hours, he had gone

381

into a place where I could not follow; that place in him I have never more than partly understood.

Eight hours passed with excruciating slowness. I ate, slept; spoke with the Peace Force officers of the death of Sethri-safere in Melkathi, and what that might now mean. F90s and YV9s left to re-power; returned. Carrick's Star beat down unrelentingly, and a heat haze veiled the estuary: heat-sensors patterned the movements of people below, on the mainland, on islands, in the *jath-rai* that lay becalmed off Spire Gate.

Long effort at last got me a clear contact with Melkathi, with the acting head of Company Research, Ravi Singh. His image in the holotank blinked, bewildered: no, nothing was happening at Ashiel Wellhouse; no, nor anywhere in Rimnith and Keverilde.

"I shall move to our base on Kumiel Island," he announced. "I don't see any reason to stay here. All the evidence here points to the use of native low-tech, with perhaps some illegal Earth mid-tech weaponry; I see no signs of anything else. If you authorize me to return to the orbiter, I *do* have a research programme I could be getting on with."

I said something, fortunately in one of the Orthean languages; and cut the contact. What does it take to get through the cotton wool round you? I thought. But I made the authorization. And made another call to the orbiter.

"The government envoy is still in tissue-regeneration." This medic, Kennaway, an elderly black woman, smiled when she recognized me. "Ms Christie – I'll let you know, personally, as soon as there's any news."

I sat at the holotank for some minutes after that contact. Would it help now, to speak with Nelum Santhil, or Haltern or Cassirur? Is what they see at ground level different from satellite-images; is there something to be sensed, there, that can't be detected except through that contact born of the earth?

The small cabin intercom chimed, disrupting my thoughts. When I keyed in, a young Pacifican woman's face appeared: one of Cory's senior officers.

"Commander Mendez wishes to see you urgently," she said.

Outside the shuttle, Corazon Mendez stood with a group of Peace Force officers. Heat haze faded, though the air was still humid; my coverall clung stickily to me. The smell of burning hung strongly in the air with no wind to shift it, and the island across this narrow channel was invisible in a sepia twilight: Little Morvren blazing without hope of control. Some of the boats used for its exodus still lay beached on the shore below us.

As I walked across to join the group, I saw Ortheans there. Blaize

Meduenin's stocky figure, and an elegantly thin male, Khassiye Andrethe, and five or six others in Freeport dress . . . no one in the *meshabi*-robe of the *hiyeks*.

"This is your business, not mine," Corazon said without preamble. "I don't discuss compensation."

"Compensation?"

A Freeport male, older than the others in the group, said ironically, "There is the matter of Northfast harbour, *t'an*; or rather, the harbour that we had before your Company came lately to the Freeport."

"I think it may be premature to discuss rebuilding at this stage," I said. The old male's eyes veiled and cleared. Is that equal appreciation of irony, I thought; or anger, or sadness, or all three?

"You misunderstand me, *t'an S'aranth* – "

A younger shaven-maned male interrupted "Not only the harbour! You have put your ships to earth here, and on the banks of the Ai River; you desecrate *telestre* land with the touch of them! What possible 'compensation' can you offer for that?"

Heat made me sweat. The back of my neck prickled with what my empathy detected in Cory and her officers: the thought *native superstition* so strong that for a moment I saw the two Freeporters through her eyes – dark reptilian skin, pale manes rooting down their spines; gold and red robes belted with *harur*-blade harness, barbaric splendour.

"I am sorry for the necessity of it," I said. "*T'an* Earthspeaker, it would not have been done if there had been any other way. Ask the *T'An* Rimon." The young male's expression altered fractionally, realizing I'd recognized him as a priest of the Goddess.

Blaize moved a few steps over the dry earth and came to stand beside me. It effectively divided us into two groups: Orthean and Peace Force officers – and where am I? Between the two, I thought. Where else?

"I gave my word for the destruction on Northfast." Blaize spoke leisurely.

"And what else will you give your word for, while there is war in Morvren?"

The younger male's hostility was plain. On the other Orthean faces, I saw at best neutrality, at worst hatred. Now that the haze was almost gone, they stood against a background of sea and smoke; the flat horizon and low islands, and coiling pillars of ash that were spreading to form a ceiling, blotting out daystars and summer clouds. The only movement was a brief sighting of some YV9 or cruising 'thopter.

"We have the use of *s'aranthi* eyes," Blaize said, with a laconic jerk of his head at the aircraft. "It's always said Freeporters know a bargain.

That for this – " with a gesture that took in the ranked F90s, Mendez's officers, Corazon herself.

I said, "Would it please you to come aboard and see that the *hiyek* ships have retreated south past Spire Gate?"

"Witchbreed trickery!" the Earthspeaker muttered; but the older male gave me a considering look, and bent to listen to a whispered comment from the black-maned female beside him. I've more chance of persuading that Earthspeaker than I have of talking Cory into this one, I thought; and stepped back so that the Freeporters could speak comfortably together.

"Corazon said this is a critical time. What do you think?" I spoke quietly. Blaize shrugged.

"When I fought on the Coast, the *hiyeks* favoured night attack. *S'aranth*, I don't know. If I did know, I don't know what I would do." And then he smiled, mouth tugged askew by the blue-and-red mottled scar of an earlier burning. "Two questions. What will the ships hiding in the islands do? What will your people do? Can you tell me the answers?"

Oddly enough, it was her memory that came back to me; that exiled woman, Ruric Orhlandis. Who must soon be hearing in the Tower of what happened here – who must feel very much as I do, I thought.

"I can't answer for the *hiyek* ships. As far as the Company goes – you're on your own. We have to stay neutral. It isn't purely law or policy." It was instinctive to take his arm, and I felt how that alien musculature tensed; felt the infinitesimal but constant tremor of exhaustion. This the hand and arm of which *harur*-blades seem so much a part. . . . "Don't tell me I can't understand what happened on Northfast. I can't; I wasn't there. If I had been, I'd have run. But Blaize, you didn't see her in Kel Harantish – see Calil – you didn't see Douggie's face this morning; not his injury, but the *fear*. I've felt it. I saw her butchery in Kel Harantish."

The pale blue eyes veiled, cleared. He said, "She makes you incoherent."

"She – I – yes, she does. And I believe Pathrey when he says there are others like her. Listen, this is a low-tech war here. Don't tell me people are just as dead – I know it's a false classification. But if it escalates, if Calil bel-Rioch *does* have the weapons of the Golden Empire; if she uses them . . ."

Blaize rested one broad hand on the hilt of *harur-nazari*. The westering sun put his shadow on the eroded earth, falling too on the edge of the shuttle-ramp. I remember how in the Barrens I first learned, from Blaize n'ri n'suth Meduenin, how Ortheans carry their dead lives with them:

does he now remember how it was in the long and brilliant summer of Golden rule?

"The Freeporters could defend the city well enough," he said, irresolutely. "Should I be in Melkathi? You say she's there, this would-be Empress. If this isn't your battle, why are there Company ships here?" Some humour barely showed in his face. "I should have stayed; I'd at least have *t'an* Haltern to tell me what to do. I don't know, Christie."

I wanted to hold him, to take away that pain – and what do I know of those two hours on Northfast; what could I say? – but we stood among others: Freeporters in vociferous discussion; Cory Mendez speaking into her wristlink.

"Well, we must keep Witchbreed weapons from use," Blaize said; blackly humorous. "I want my part in the battle of Morvren Freeport remembered in past-lives; for that, there must be time enough to turn this into history."

"I'd like to make the history books myself," I observed.

"*T'An* Meduenin." It was the armed Earthspeaker who called. Blaize inclined his head to me, and walked across to the group of Freeporters.

Is it all over but the shouting? No, I thought. Not that easily. This is a lull, how can we take advantage of it? The essential thing is, somehow, to make contact with the Coast Ortheans in the *jath-rai* – how? We've come very close to showing ourselves on the same side as the Hundred Thousand, here. If the Company's lost its neutral status . . .

The sun lay just above the western horizon, flooding the flat estuary with pale gold light. Soon second twilight and the starlit night would come. For now, it made a deceptive peace; filigreed the edges of waves, outlined in gold the low slopes of this spit of mainland earth. I looked south, eyes drawn to that massive tapering pillar of *chiruzeth*; limned with light on its western side. Though it dominates the landscape, the eye refuses the sight of it; can't comprehend it. I kicked the mossgrass underfoot – if I dig down, will I find one of the Old Roads, leading south to the Rasrhe-y-Meluur? And south over all the Archipelago islands to that distant continent, to the garden that was the Elansiir, to that unimaginable creation: the City Over The Inland Sea? All that contained in the sight of this blue-grey spire, whose peak is lost in evening haze: so glassy that it reflects the clouds that pass across its surface. . . .

Dead, now, and hollow. They made of the Elansiir, a desert. They made of the City Over The Inland Sea, a desolation seen in mist and silver. They made, of that great Empire, a child-woman in Kel Harantish; throned above the bloody abattoir she has made of her enemies. And if she looses from her hand that ancient light, will it free the devastation that is barely held in check in the Barrens, the Elansiir, the Glittering Plain?

385

The evening light shines on Morvren Freeport. Each island is clear as glass, walls and *telestre*-houses and docks. Beyond them, the blur of the mainland: the northern continent. And what moves now in the *telestres*, in Shiriya-Shenin that lies nine hundred miles up the Ai River; what in Medued-in-Rimon, and those forested hills? Over the horizon, those blue hills; *telestres* and Wellhouses and Orthean cities – what word goes out by heliograph and *rashaku*-messenger? And far to the east lies the white city, Tathcaer, the heartland of the Hundred Thousand. . . . I thought for a moment that memories would overwhelm me, but I didn't know whether they would be of my time there, eight years ago, or memories of others who had come from this land, in centuries past, come at last to the Brown Tower.

It was some while before the thought crept into my mind: If we are not neutral, then the Tower is. And the desperately impractical question: Could Ruric Hexenmeister speak with the Ortheans on the *hiyek* ships?

Lynne, you're crazy; the Hexenmeister can't leave the Tower, Ruric Orhlandis can't leave the Tower –

No, but can she?

The Freeporters were still arguing, gesturing up at the hull of the F90 shuttle. I saw Blaize Meduenin settle back on his heels, speaking with a grim determination; and one of Mendez's officers walked over to join them, bewilderment on every line of her face. Cory had vanished. I walked up the shuttle-ramp and into the cool interior, making my way to the comlink-centre.

The WEBcasters will still be at Ashiel Wellhouse; Cassirur will be there . . . What about Tethmet Fenborn? And is this something I can talk about over open-channel?

I sat down at one of the smaller holotanks, not yet making a contact. It was automatic to key in surveillance, and while I sat thinking, I stared at the holo-image of the estuary: the setting sun, the smoke that at last began to dissipate.

Abruptly, I reached forward and keyed Cory's wristlink.

"Mendez here." Her image frowned. "What is it?"

"The *jath-rai* down past Spire Gate are moving," I said; simultaneously one of her officers cut into the transmission with "Commander, movement of hostiles at 475.930.756; estimate their present course local-south."

In the holotank, the images of *jath-rai* raised their thin metal sails in the twilight, catching the wind that springs up at sunset. Cory Mendez came into the cabin as I got up and moved to the larger holotank, leaning over the back of the comlink officer's seat.

"They're moving away from the Freeport," I said.

She reached down and keyed for satellite-image. After several seconds of interference, the image formed: visual, with heat-sensor overlay. The Morvren coast, the estuary – now enlarging to include all the northern islands of the Archipelago.

"Damn!" Cory pointed. "That's what I was afraid of."

The indicators marking *jath-rai* clustered round the islands near Spire Gate. Movement was just visible at this scale of image. As I watched, other indicators detached themselves from islands to the south – a handful, then a dozen, a score; and then like a flood the flecks of light marking *jath-rai* positions began to sift out from among the concealment of island settlements.

I gripped the side of the 'tank, willing the ships to sail faster. "Cory, the time to be afraid is when we know where the fleet's headed. It could just be that they'll set a course back to the Desert Coast. . . ."

The Peace Force Commander bent down to speak through comlink to a YV9 surveillance-craft, ordering it to fly south. Her hand, by her side, was clenched tight enough to drive the silver rings into her tanned flesh.

"You'd better get rid of the locals, Lynne. I don't want any complications." She glanced up, pale blue eyes brilliant with tension. "You know your job best; keep them happy, but keep them out of our way. Until we know what's happening here, this could be dangerous."

Hours crept by. My eyes began to ache with staring into the holotanks aboard the F90. Satellite-images alternated with images sent back from shuttles overflying the islands, fifty or a hundred miles south of where we were grounded. Interference made reception difficult. The satellites gave heat-sensor images – no usage of hi-tech tracked down, only the clusters of body-heat that are the crews of *jath-rai* and *jath* – many *jath*, those deep-sea vessels that can carry three or four hundred aboard. And the shuttles sent back night-images: leaf-shaped silhouettes of blackness on a sea made silver by the blaze of the Heart Stars. . . .

"Latest estimate is between seven hundred and seven-ten vessels," Corazon Mendez said, four hours after the movement of the ships had begun. "Lynne, does that seem feasible, from your local knowledge? Given the carrying power of the large and the coastal ships, that's about thirty thousand natives on board."

The *siirans* must be empty. No, more: the islanders must be joining the *hiyeks*. . . . I said, "If you want local knowledge, I'd advise you to bring the *T'An* Meduenin in on this. Cory, you may as well. He still has my wristlink, and I'd be very surprised if he hasn't been following this."

The older woman opened her mouth as if to speak, checked, and then shook her head. She laughed shortly. "Yes."

One of the officers put a call through. There was a hiatus, the shift changing in the comlink-centre; and I took advantage of that to stand and stretch, to wonder if I couldn't find something to drink. The F90's cabin felt changeless: green-tinted illumination, the brightness reflecting up from holotanks on to young, intent faces; the subliminal hum of communications between other Force vessels. This will be the same whether it's night or day outside, whether the Freeport is still standing in the morning, or whether these ships turn for the north to sail and burn it to the ground.

As the new officers settled in, I looked at those young Pacifican faces and wished for some way to move them beyond these holo-images. And then I thought: But what did I really see of Morvren, myself? A few minutes on Northfast, an hour above ground in a 'thopter; the rest by image in shuttles. . . . How can we *feel* what's happening here – and if we can't, how can we judge the right actions to take?

Blaize Meduenin came in, inclining his head to Cory. His slit-backed shirt and his britches were ash-stained; and the clash of *harur*-blades was loud in that quiet cabin as he slumped wearily down in the seat next to me.

"Where are they now?"

"Here. Most of them aren't far from land, still. By 'land' I mean the islands."

He leaned forward. The holotank light shone on his matted and filthy mane, and membrane slid down to shield his eyes.

"The different coloured dots represent vessels of different carrying power," a dark Pacifican officer said. He was hardly more than a boy; nineteen or twenty. "These figures are local wind-speed and – "

"I'm familiar with the Webster-representation," Blaize cut him off, Sino-Anglic accented but understandable. "Some years ago I was briefly on Aleph-Nine and Parmiter's Moon. Christie, have you made any contact with the *hiyeks*?"

Hiding a smile, I said, "No. It's been distance-contact, so far." And then I shrugged. "Cory sent 'thopters down earlier, to try loudhailer-contact. No response."

"No. . . ." The membrane blinked back from his eyes: a flash of sardonic humour. He raised his head, looking across the tank at Corazon Mendez. "They would probably kill anyone you sent in to talk with them in person."

Cory attempted a passable formal Ymirian: "*T'an* Meduenin, can you predict what action this fleet will take?"

I saw him register her attempt at courtesy. He had an expression I couldn't place, when he looked at her; and I thought, That's from Northfast. That is the look of one who was there, to one who – quite literally – stayed above the battle.

Blaize Meduenin stared down into the holotank, at dots that moved with infinitesimal slowness. Hard to translate that into the riveted metal hulls of *jath-rai*, cutting the water; thin metal sails spread to catch the falling wind; *jath* loaded to the rails with men and women of the Desert *hiyeks*. . . .

"They might attack the Freeport again, if your work on Northfast fails to make them fear." His eyes veiled. "They may attack the Morvren and Rimon coast, the *telestres* there."

"Is there any chance they've been scared into abandoning this, going back to the Desert Coast?" I suggested.

"Chance? *S'aranth*, there are always chances." He turned that scarred profile towards me. "You'll know – we'll know, well before morning."

The night passed. Cory Mendez grew more quiet, withdrawing into her self; and I could appreciate how she felt. All the Company's hi-tech sensors, transport, communications; all of it waiting on the result of *jath-rai* and *jath* and a south-westerly wind. Her officers plainly suffered the same tension.

I made brief communication with the WEBcasters, still at Ashiel Wellhouse; and with the shuttles on Kumiel Island. If it amounted to a news blackout, that is only because, acting representative or not, I didn't know yet how I wanted this handled.

The summer night passed. Before the ten hours were up, a pattern became clear. *Jath* and *jath-rai* drew out from the Archipelago into the Inner Sea, a score here, fifty there; setting courses that would eventually intersect. Plotted, they crossed two hundred miles north-west of Lone Isle. An easterly course that might, if they didn't turn north to the Rimon coast, bring them in a few days within sight of Melkathi.

"I don't care if you can't pick up transmissions," I said to Corazon Mendez, "those two groups are in contact with each other!"

Blaize sat, *harur-nilgiri* blade resting its point on the cabin floor, resting his chin on his hands that were clasped over the hilt. He leaned back in the padded seat when I spoke, and said wearily, "You told me of Harantish soldiers come to the Archipelago, and of the Empress Calil in Melkathi? Then that's where they're sailing, Christie. To Rimnith and to Keverilde, to break the siege."

I looked down into the holotank, at that firefly-scatter of dots on the Inner Sea.

"I think I should talk with Pathrey Shanataru again."

CHAPTER 32

The Woman Who Walks on the Sky

The YV9 shuttle, flying east at well below two thousand feet, passed over specks on the sea; some of which must (I thought) be the normal trading ships of summer, others – strung out in line, in many small convoys – Coast *jath* travelling towards their projected rendezvous.

Disembarking on Kumiel Island at about noon, I thought, Given they travel no faster than the slowest coastal *jath-rai*, given they have to raid shipping and the *telestres* for food – or did the Archipelago islanders provision them, willingly or unwillingly? – and then, given good weather . . .

The *hiyek* fleet will reach Melkathi no later than six days from now. Call it Merrum Secondweek Threeday or Fourday. That is a very narrow margin for us to take action in. But it'll have to do.

Daystars glittered round the horizon, pinpricks of light; and Carrick's Star blazed down on the island's rock and sparse mossgrass. North, towards the mainland, sea fog rolled whitely; I couldn't see the coastline, or the roofs of Tathcaer. Temporary Company domes now clustered round the ranked shuttles, I saw. Most stood on the lee of ridges, partly concealed from the city; and I smiled, thinking, *Tact and diplomacy from PanOceania? Wonders will never cease*, and someone behind me put a hand on my shoulder.

"I was about to contact you. Hello, Lynne."

"*Douggie* – "

He smiled, almost apologetically. That small, round face was pale; there were hard lines around his mouth. A grey pad covered his right eye. The left eye, bloodshot but clear, could obviously see.

"Looks like they've treated you well – Jesus, Douggie, you shouldn't be back here yet!"

"I find it preferable to have something with which to occupy my thoughts."

His grizzled red hair was neatly trimmed. I saw they'd given him new coveralls on the orbiter, with the PanOceania logo. That neatness somehow made him seem desperately fragile.

He kept his hand on my shoulder. "I won't have much depth perception until this heals. Lynne, I've a reason for returning prematurely. I have Pathrey Shanataru at the moment under the aegis of the

390

government, rather than of the Company; forgive me if I would rather it stayed that way. . . ."

It was automatic to move with him as we walked across the island. He moved uncertainly, stumbling; as if the dry earth and clumps of mossgrass were dubious territory. Now I saw him in profile, there were white shadows of scars in the socket of his eye. In time it will be just something that happened, long ago, on another world; I sensed that he was not yet free of the shock of it.

"You've been down long?" I nodded at the low dome that housed the comlink-centre; dwarfed by the subwave transmitter bulking beside it. "You know what's happening at the Freeport?"

Doug frowned. "There's no guarantee Morvren Freeport won't be subject to another attack. Certainly if I were Commander Mendez, I would expect some *jath-rai* to remain behind in the islands, and cause the greatest possible disruption."

"Yes. Blaize said that, too – " I broke off, recognizing the pony-tailed black man outside the comlink-dome. Mehmet Lutaya of the Ariadne WEB. Doug's palm was damp where it rested on the shoulder of my coverall, and I thought, I don't want to leave you, I want to talk to you; oh Jesus, I want to tell you about Northfast.

"Envoy," Lutaya said, striding over towards us. "Representative."

Northwards the sea fog was beginning to shift, and Rimon's white headlands gleamed, six or seven miles distant across the straits. Wind ruffled Lutaya's hair and clothing. He had that look that WEBcasters have, a curiosity both avid and totally detached.

"I don't have much time right now," I said, not breaking stride.

He shrugged. "Thought I might be doing you both a favour. We're beginning to get feedback through from the Home Worlds."

Doug Clifford hesitated, letting his hand fall from my shoulder, and queried, "Feedback on what, precisely?"

"On Carrick V. On the fighting, and how PanOceania's handling the affair." Lutaya looked at me. "Nothing's been released here – well, there's no public WEB, is there? Thought I might try to be helpful. Maybe get information in exchange for information? Worth a try."

Vibration thrummed through the earth as one of the F90s lifted, hovered, and then ripped the air apart as it flew west. Its white bulk faded against the daystarred sky. That'll be on Cory's orders, I thought. If I can find anything that'll help me curb the Peace Force, I shall be a great deal happier.

"Send records," I said, "we'll be – ?" and I glanced at Doug.

"In the government Residence, in the city," Doug supplied. "On the mainland."

391

No, really? But I wasn't about to ask why, not in front of a WEBcaster.

Lutaya nodded. "I'll bring a full record across. Want to discuss access to information, and to certain areas on this world – that means with Company *and* government, yes? Thought so. About two hours?"

I agreed, and watched him walk away. Doug chuckled. When I glanced at him, he had some shadow of that prim humour in his face; that urbane mask that he loves to wear.

"I imagine he won't be the sole representative of the Earth WEBs to come knocking on the Residence's door," Doug observed. "For my part, I must confess, I'm not being over-scrupulous about the rules on data-restriction. . . ."

"Who's in Tathcaer?"

The question didn't surprise him.

"In the Residence? As you might have supposed, Pathrey Shanataru. I put him there with Haltern Beth'ru-elen, on his return from Ashiel Wellhouse; and in the care of the *t'an* Cassirur." Now he had the remnants of that old, sharp gaze; head cocked bird-like and alert, for all the shock still in his system. "Morvren frightens me, Lynne. Now things have disintegrated this far, I begin to think that we have to take action with some speed. I intend to consult the *takshiriye* now."

"I'll come with you."

The summer sun reflected back from the rocks. At my feet, dusty mossgrass was turning brown; and thin stems bobbed waist-high, weighed down by crimson spore cases. Heat made me sweat; the sky was a vast arched dome; and for a second I was back on the Eastern Isles, eight years gone, my first step on to the surface of Orthe. . . .

"I'll give you something to think about while we're travelling over there," I said. "Douggie, the people we have to talk to aren't the *takshiriye*. We must get in contact with the Desert Coast Ortheans, either the fleet, or the people in Rimnith and Keverilde; *that's* who we have to convince."

"Impossible." He rubbed a sheen of moisture from his forehead, and looked away. "Impossible. Those people are led by fanatics now."

And what are the chances of making contact with the Harantish Witchbreed?

Mid-morning bells rang a sharp carillon. The shadows of *rashaku-bazur* flicked across the inner courtyard of Westhill-Ahrentine, and their harsh hooting cries echoed; and I came through the gate-arch from the alley outside, and found a game of *ochmir* in progress. Sun shone on the thin white mane of Haltern n'ri n'suth Beth'ru-elen as he raised his head from the board and smiled. A skeletally-thin male Orthean seated at the opposite side of the table also looked up, and I recognized Tethmet Fenborn.

"Give you greeting, *t'ans*," Haltern said mildly. His pale blue eyes moved to the upper-storey windows, an involuntary movement, soon concealed.

Doug Clifford nodded acknowledgement and didn't break stride. As he went up the outside steps to the upper storey, a young dark-maned *l'ri-an* pulled the bead curtain aside, and he spoke to *kir* as he went inside. I moved across to stand under the *ziku* that shaded the table.

"Do they play *ochmir* on the Coast, *shan'tai* Tethmet? I didn't know."

"The *t'an* Tethmet learns swiftly," Haltern said. I thought he sounded a little rueful: when I glanced down at the position of the triangular counters on the hexagonal board, I could see why. The old male went on: "Christie, this is perhaps the right moment to say to you, you may wish to see the *t'an* Earthspeaker Cassirur."

"Why is now the right moment, Hal?"

One thin six-fingered hand reached out to place a *leremoc* counter on the *ochmir* board. "Because the *t'an* Clifford is now absent. . . . Cassirur has one of your Company people in the Wellhouse, up at the Square."

That Orthean obliqueness. Sometimes I'm plain human and impatient. "Hal, *who* does she have, and why?"

"The Earthspeaker brought her back from Ashiel," Haltern said, not to be hurried. "I believe that her name is Pramila Ishida."

Now it was my turn to glance up at the top storey of the *telestre*-house. Doug is there, he'll be talking with Pathrey Shanataru, should I be there? But Pramila Ishida will know what the *hiyeks* in Rimnith and Keverilde are doing – *if* she'll tell me. She may even have information about the Harantish Ortheans. . . .

"Why did she – how – " I stopped. "Never mind. I'll go up there now. Hal, is the woman injured, is that why Cassirur has her up at the Wellhouse?"

Sun through *ziku* spines dappled the low table, and the *ochmir* board. Tethmet reached down to put in a *thurin* counter that completed a hexagon in his colour: the reverberations of that, in the overlapping hexagons, spread right out to the edges of the board.

"She's unharmed," Haltern said.

Membrane slid down over the fenborn's dark eyes, and Tethmet said, "She is not whole."

That's what you get for asking questions of Ortheans. I nodded, and as I turned to leave the courtyard, said, "Tell Douggie I'll be back before noon. *Shan'tai* Tethmet, please wait; I want to ask you to do something for me. Hal – "

393

"You will not see the *takshiriye* here; they are largely to be found in Melkathi still. Go. I have said to Cassirur that you will come."

"Yes, I thought you might. . . ."

My footsteps echoed under the arched tunnel-entrance, and I came out from that cool shadow into Tathcaer's hot sun. From outside Westhill-Ahrentine I looked down at the harbour, crowded with *jath-rai*; the sun flickered on the water, and on Ortheans who poled small boats between the shipping, or stood arguing at the quayside booths. Voices came faintly up the hill. And this could almost be any day in the summer trading season – I wanted to walk along the quay and overhear what Ortheans were saying, but instead I hailed a *skurrai-jasin* that was rattling down the slope.

All the way up to the Square, I leaned back in the small wooden carriage and tried to detect some difference in the city's atmosphere. The winding alleys were crowded, Ortheans standing in groups. As we passed *telestre*-houses, I began to see how many had barred and bolted their doors.

"What's your *telestre*, *t'an*?"

The *jasin* driver tugged at the thong attached to the *skurrai*'s nose-ring before he answered. The carriage swung a tight corner, uphill, and clattered out on to Crown Way; now we were under the shadow of *lapuur* that line it.

"I'm from Temethu."

"That's – north Roehmonde?" Upwards of eight hundred miles north of Tathcaer, on the way to the Wall of the World.

He turned halfway round in the *jasin* seat. A male, with wideset dark eyes, and an intricately-braided brown mane; if I'd known Roehmonde well enough, I could have told his *telestre* without asking, from the pattern of those braids.

He said, "Don't misunderstand me, *t'an s'aranthi*, I don't even like the Melkathi *telestres*, and I most surely don't trust Freeporters – if they trade with outlanders, what do they expect? – but since you *s'aranthi* brought land-wasters here, what else can I do but be here?"

The *skurrai* shook its long-skulled head, feather-pelt glinting bronze; all four split pads searching for purchase. Then, as the *jasin* crested the slope into the Square, the brown-maned male turned back to guide us through the crowds that thronged the great open space.

Getting down from the carriage at the Wellhouse steps, I overheard comments about *s'aranthi*. Anger, resentment . . . and more than that: a kind of massive dismissal. The stones of this city so old, that Citadel that crowns the crag there standing for two millennia; and the lives of these people built and rebuilt, like *telestre*-houses, structures of memory. No wonder offworlders seem so transient to them.

Cassirur appeared as soon as I entered the Wellhouse gates. She led me past courtyard and fountains, away from the main dome, to an onion-domed building. I pushed through the bead-curtain, blinking at interior shadows.

"She came to Ashiel at midday on the day that you left here," the red-maned Orthean woman said, walking through into inner rooms. Her green slit-backed robe was rumpled, travel-stained. At another curtained door, she stopped for a word with one of her *ashiren*.

"Is she hurt? I can't get any sense out of Hal."

The Earthspeaker Cassirur paused. Her eyes cleared, the bright pale green of sun on *lapuur*-fronds; she was a flame of colour against the brown brickwork of walls and ceiling and floor.

"If you were from a *telestre* I would say to you: the Goddess gave you your twin in her, and she hers in you."

I stepped through into the small room. Light seeped in through a slot-window; the air was hot. There was a low couch-bed pushed up against the wall, and the Pacifican girl sat up as I entered, and put her feet down on the floor. They were lacerated, bloody; there were deep scratches on her bare arms and legs. She still wore a *meshabi*-robe, and her brown hair was braided in an approximation of the *hiyek* manner.

"Where is he?" she demanded.

"Where's who?" And then I realized. I sat down on the edge of the couch-bed beside her. "You mean Sethri-safere?"

"I mean his body."

"They took it up to the orbiter, I believe." It seemed crass to state that it was for an autopsy.

"I want to see it."

"Pramila, I can understand that. I'll arrange it, if I can. I'll have to make other arrangements, too; you realize that? The Company will take disciplinary action – "

"I don't care about that."

She put her head in her hands, pushing her fingers through her filthy hair. So much tension in the line of her back: she was holding herself together by willpower alone. In that dim light I couldn't see if she wept. When she straightened, her expression was stunned, despairing.

"I don't think I even care about what happens to Jadur and Charazir and Wyrrin-hael, and he would call that despicable. . . . As for the Company, I – " She gripped my arm. Her nails were bitten down bloody. "We're always warned not to get involved. Aren't we? Ms Christie, I'm involved. His people are my people, it doesn't matter what I said just now. That's why I'm here."

"Can you take me to someone who can talk for the *hiyeks*?" I asked. I would have bruises where her fingers tightened on my arm.

"I don't know. I'll try. I – it wasn't easy to get away. There are things you ought to know." She blinked in the twilight. The heat was making her sweat; when she rubbed her face, it smeared the dust into pale streaks on her sallow skin.

"Cassirur's right. You were right, too," I admitted. "I could have done what you have. Perhaps I should have done."

"Yes." Not an ounce of regret in her voice. She let go of my arm, and wiped her hands across her face. "One thing the Company ought to know is the extent of the arms trade. We were able to bring in material from Thierry's World too. I'll give you details. Ms Christie, I'll give you whatever you need to know. His people are my people, and I don't care what I do, I'll stop Kel Harantish and that woman – "

"Calil?"

She stood up. Her balance was erratic, she swayed; and I stood up and took her elbow. She shook herself free. A young woman, barely able to stay on her feet; and she looked up at me with a face that blazed hatred.

"She and those like her. Sethri may have made me part of his *raiku*, but that's one thing I don't have: that ingrained obedience to the Harantish Witchbreed!" And the use of his name visibly hit her, she swallowed; all the Company's training in detachment coming into play.

"Will I find any group I can talk with at Rimnith or Keverilde?"

Waiting for an answer, I felt an empathy almost painful. This young woman, exhausted and filthy and determined, pushing herself to go on, crippled by loss – I might be her, I thought. If I'd ever had the guts to follow my instincts. And I might suffer a loss like that. Still, for all that, is what I feel something like envy?

"Stay away from Melkathi," she said at last. "Where are the other ships? If you can find them, there are some Anzhadi *raiku* there."

Blaize said, *They would probably kill anyone you sent to talk with them in person.* (And is he any safer, in the Freeport?)

"Can you keep going for a while longer?" I asked. "I'd intended to try contacting the *hiyek* ships myself, but there might be some chance of success if you're there, and they know you. If you can come with me, it'll count favourably on the Company report."

Pramila Ishida said, "Shit on the Company, and on all the Companies, and on all of us too. Yes, I'll come with you."

As we left the small room, the Earthspeaker Cassirur halted me for a moment. She pushed a young black-maned *ashiren* forward. "Send the child with your messages, *t'an* Christie. I'll be in the Citadel. The *s'ans* are coming to us now – we have to think of defence; of Melkathi, as well as Morvren Freeport."

That chilled me. I nodded and left her, following the young Pacifican woman out into the courtyards. She moved like an automaton through the morning sunlight, with Cassirur's *ashiren* scurrying at her heels; and heads in the Square turning to stare as we came down the Wellhouse steps. Nothing to do but go back to Westhill-Ahrentine now. There were no *skurrai-jasin* to be seen; rather than attract a crowd, I shepherded Pramila and the child towards the nearest alley-entrance. We could walk down into the city.

Sun reflected back from the upper storeys of *telestre*-houses, shadows shrinking down into the alleys as noon approached; for the moment I was cool. Above, a ribbon of sky was thick with a snowfall of daystars. Ortheans sat on steps, talking, or in the tunnel-entrances to inner courtyards. A hush made me tread quietly, footsteps in any case muffled by the dust; listening to the sounds of the city. The creaking axle of a *skurrai*-wagon, the soft pad of *marhaz* and rider . . . Cities are quiet on Orthe, so quiet you can hear people's voices. And is it because I expect to hear it, but is there a new tone, a new edge, an urgency there?

"I don't mean quantity alone," Pramila Ishida said suddenly. "What we brought in – not just CAS handweapons. It's all good Company equipment, seconded from Thierry and Parmiter. I – to tell you the truth, I'm not sure what we did bring in. Not all of it."

Does it surprise me to hear that? I thought. Knowing the multicorporates – no. Nothing wrong with some semi-official arms trading, so long as you don't get caught; and so long as you by no means allow your on-world staff to know what the fuck you're doing –

I swallowed down anger. "Give me what information you can."

"Yes."

It was the last word she said between there and Westhill-Ahrentine: an hour's hot walking, and the last mile or two by *skurrai-jasin*. Cassirur's *ashiren*, whom I thought to be six or seven, got over its shyness, and chattered solemnly as it walked beside me, pointing out barred entrances and the names of *telestre*-houses. Orthean young seem hardly humanoid, all spider-fingers and curling mane. *No, we are not like them; no, they are not like us: Pramila, how could you think it?*

But I know how.

The courtyard of Westhill-Ahrentine still held table and couch-chairs and *ochmir* board, but no Haltern. I sent Pramila Ishida and the child on up the steps to the upper rooms. And then I walked over to the scrub-

ziku, beneath which Tethmet Fenborn still sat: gold-green skin shining as if he had just come out of water.

"Has there been word from the Tower?"

That sleek dark head came up, and he fixed me with lustrous dark eyes. What on Ortheans are claw-nails are, on fenborn, indisputable claws: he pushed *ochmir* counters at random across the board.

"Word goes back to Kasabaarde," he said.

Irritated, I said, "In that case, you can pass on a message from me. Tell Ruric – " and then I hesitated.

"She is not the Orhlandis," Tethmet said.

"I know. . . . Tell her, if she has any influence over the Desert Coast Ortheans, she must use it. And if she has any influence over Kel Harantish, we need that even more. This has to stop before it goes too far."

At last, grudgingly, he inclined his head in agreement.

"Lynne!"

I looked up, and saw Doug Clifford at the upper-storey window. A shadow beside him resolved into a black Pacifican: Lutaya.

"Okay," I called; and then spoke to the fenborn again. "You can tell her something else. Tell her the Company's compromised. Tell her it's difficult for us to act as neutral arbitrators now, though we will. Tell her, the Tower may be the nearest Orthe has to its own neutral arbitrator."

"Yes," Tethmet said.

Tathcaer's white sunlight shone down in dapples through the *ziku*, falling on his sleek black shaven mane, and on green-gold skin that shimmered into invisibility. The *ochmir* board lay abandoned, two-thirds of the minor hexagons covered with white counters: *ferrorn*, *thurin*, *leremoc*. How does a fenborn male come to know enough of this *telestre* game to beat Haltern n'ri n'suth Beth'ru-elen? The fenborn live long. . . .

"*Shan'tai*, will you stay, please?" I asked. "I have something to ask of you. Not of the Hexenmeister, of you yourself."

He said, "I will stay."

The steps up to the first floor were steep, and the sun on my head was hot. I paused once, looking back at the fenborn male; and found him watching me. Then I went inside.

Ravi Singh and Chandra Hainzell stood by the holotank in the first room, he looking bewildered, she deep in conversation with the WEBcaster Lutaya, and both turned towards me as I entered.

"I'll be with you in a minute," I said; and pushed the bead-curtain of the second room's arch aside. The place still had its air of abandoned decay, print-outs and microcorders scattered across the low tables.

Haltern glanced up from a couch-chair by the open window. Pathrey Shanataru stood there, staring out over the harbour, and didn't turn as I came in.

And Doug was staring at Pramila Ishida with an expression so complex I despaired of interpretation.

"Lynne. Are you calling Company Security, or shall I exercise my authority as envoy, and have this woman confined and deported?"

"Now hold on just a minute – "

The Pacifican girl put out a hand to the back of the couch-chair, steadying herself. I realized she was on the point of collapse. I gripped her elbow, pushing her over to the other couch-chair, and made her sit down. Then I took Doug a pace or two aside.

"Yes, I'm notifying Security; no, she isn't being deported – not until we know exactly what she authorized in the way of weapons trade. And I may need her for something else."

"She has to face what she's done." Doug sighed, shook his head very slightly. "Lynne, I don't understand you. Regulations aside, what that girl has done on Orthe – the damage caused through her actions – makes *me* furious. You, I imagined, I would have to restrain from being homicidal."

The small room was hot, close. Harsh bells began to ring outside in the city, the deliberate strokes of midday; drowning out the clatter of *skurrai-jasin* and the high voices of *ashiren*.

"What's she done is more than criminal . . . Douggie, *I* could have done it, in her position." I went on quickly: "What I want to do now is get an analysis of satellite-images of the fleet. Somewhere on those ships there are Anzhadi *hiyek*-Ortheans. And then I'm going to take the Ishida girl with me, and fly in, and try to make a contact."

When he said nothing, I snarled, "*Somebody* has to try it."

He turned his head momentarily, so that I saw his blind profile, looking over at Pathrey Shanataru; and then his gaze returned from the dark Orthean male to me.

"It may be of little use to speak to the Desert Coast Ortheans. It's the Harantish Witchbreed who have the influence now, and if you plan to make contact with any of them, I imagine you'll find it worse than useless. Lynne, there is a point at which the danger outweighs the possible advantages."

"We've got maybe four days before that fleet can reach the Melkathi coast, and then we've got a full-scale invasion on our hands!" I became aware of voices silenced in the outer room, and added more quietly, "I'm also planning to ask Tethmet to come with me, if he'll consent to go. He

399

is the Hexenmeister's advisor, and that may just sow some doubt in Harantish minds."

"You must talk with Pathrey – " Doug broke off as Mehmet Lutaya came through from the outer room.

"I've got the records set up, Representative. Not just Ariadne. Some from Trismegistus, and Anansi." Lutaya blinked long eyes, waiting.

"We'll come through."

Haltern rose unsteadily from the couch-chair by the window. He rested almost all of his weight on the silver-topped *hanelys* cane as he walked to stand beside me. The hooded reptilian eyes blinked, lazily; and he smiled that old, sly smile.

"Don't deny an old man the chance of seeing this, *S'aranth-te*. To know how these otherworlds of yours see us, that would be fascinating." He paused, directing his thin voice at the WEBcaster. "To know if they see us as requiring a – what is your term for it? A 'Protected Status'. That, also, will be fascinating."

And if they don't see it that way, you'll be only too pleased to say whatever's necessary to *make* them see it – Hal, you don't change. For which small mercy, I suppose we must be grateful.

We crowded round the holotank in the next room. Pathrey Shanataru followed us, and Pramila Ishida also, looking as though she could barely stand up. Is this wise? I wondered. Douggie gave me a very quizzical glance. But if there's government and Company here, I thought, aware of Ravi and Chandra and the rest of the Commercial staff; if there's *takshiriye* and Harantish Witchbreed and WEBcasters, what difference can one more make? If I had my way, I'd have *hiyek*-Ortheans here too.

"This is one of mine," Lutaya said, activating the holotank; and for a moment there was an expression of diffidence on that self-confident face: not so oblivious to comment as I'd assumed. "For Home Worlds consumption. Summary-update."

The holotank filled with darkness. In the depths, star-fields took shape and gleamed; and the viewpoint shifted smoothly to a crescent of white and blue:

'Carrick V, called by its intelligent hominid species "Orthe", might have remained merely another backwater world on the borders between the Heart Stars and the Home Stars, if not for one thing – its past. Orthe is littered with the ruins of a vast and ancient alien hi-technology civilization, and with the devastation left by the war that destroyed that civilization, two millennia before humankind achieved space-flight.'

Beside me, Douggie said softly, "Oh dear. . . ."

"It's a matter of presentation," I said, wincing.

The holo-image dissolved into an aerial view of the Desert Coast canal system, that in turn faded to a long-distance shot of mesa-like white walls – Kel Harantish.

'Six months ago, Orthe became more than a backwater planet of interest only to anthropologists and academics. Six months ago, relics of Witchbreed technology were discovered – artifacts that are still functional. The Pan-Oceania multicorporate moved in a commerce-and-research team.'

The Desert Coast city was abruptly replaced by another image: a wide, island-studded estuary, sky dimmed by smoke, the buildings on the nearest island furiously burning. A metal-sailed *jath-rai* tacked across the channel, image clear enough to see the rails lined with armed men and women.

'Six months later, this is the result.'

"I protest," Pramila Ishida said. She was leaning both hands on the rim of the holotank, supporting herself; and then she caught my gaze, and frowned as if she puzzled herself. "That is . . . I don't hold a brief for the Company, not any more, but it isn't that simple."

"It's a summary. Other 'casts have gone out," Lutaya said, as his own image appeared in the 'tank. In shot with him, against a background of the Freeport estuary and the distant Rasrhe-y-Meluur, stood Cory Mendez.

'Commander Mendez, you're in charge of the Security force that Pan-Oceania has brought here to Orthe. Can you comment on this second use of armed force against the local population – the second use of force within three weeks?'

'In both cases, a small use of force was authorized, not against the local population, but in terms of a warning, against property. Harbour structures, in the main.'

Try to look at it as an outsider, I thought; seeing Cory's lined, capable face. Is she plausible? Is she right?

'Commander Mendez, the most reliable estimates for casualty figures on the southern continent are: 6 dead at Reshebet, 3 dead at Nadrasiir, 24 dead at Pazramir – '

'Those figures are open to other interpretations. The essential thing is that, by causing some unavoidable suffering, which the Company deeply regrets, we have put an end to the possibility of an all-out native civil war.'

Doug Clifford shook his head. "Not clever."

"Sometimes they sink themselves," the WEBcaster said; and his holo-image went on smoothly:

'I understand there is a native force of some seven hundred ships now on a course for the northern continent. Commander, isn't this that "all-out civil war" you've been trying to avoid?'

'*I have no comment to make at this stage; I suggest that you contact the acting Company representative.*'

"Thank you, Cory," I muttered. As the image dissolved into an interior shot, whose curved brown walls I recognized as Ashiel Wellhouse, I glanced up at Lutaya. "This is a 'cast I've seen and approved?"

"The tidied-up version."

No Mehmet Lutaya in this shot, only the image of a woman: fair-haired, approaching forty, in coveralls with the PanOceania logo – *that's never me*, I thought. As I always think. She sits on one of the Wellhouse's couch-chairs, face too seriously intent; there are lines of age on that face that I never see in my mirror.

'*Ms Christie, you're the acting representative of the PanOceania multicorporate on this world, following the murder of Representative Molly Rachel. Can you tell me what Company policy is in the current war situation?*'

'*Firstly, I would like to make it clear that this isn't a war situation – we have had some hostile incidents, which our policy is to contain wherever possible.*'

Doug raised his head from the tank. "Now who's simplifying issues? Not to mention a degree of obfuscation. . . ."

"I have to get this stuff past the Security staff on the orbiter, you know."

Now the holotank image showed Lutaya, sitting across from me as I remembered:

'*In your view, Ms Christie, what caused these "incidents"?*'

'*In my view – purely and simply: poverty. This is a world of people living in the margins. Living in the few areas that weren't reduced to sterile bedrock, thousands of years ago. There have never been many areas of Orthe that could support communities – and in some that have done, in the past, it's just not possible now. The land is exhausted. Particularly on the southern continent, which is where the fleet you mentioned originates.*'

"Could have done with better editing there," Lutaya said dispassionately.

'*And yet there was no war until PanOceania started its operations on Orthe.*'

'*Earth technology upset the social system – triggered off what would have happened eventually, as more and more communities reached the poverty line. Yes, that's true. It's also true that Earth technology can put this right – with a properly-funded Aid Programme to the starving areas.*'

'*Is that possible now?*'

"You could hardly ask for a better cue," Douggie observed.

I watched that image of myself pause, and had time to think, Too pompous, too ingenuous. And hope that what I said carried enough overt support of the Company to pass through intact the covert criticism.

'It's possible, if we can halt the fighting. . . . Orthe's social balance is so delicate, so artificial – after all, there are very few post-holocaust societies in existence – that it can take hardly any outside contact. We're considering this very carefully. By "we", I mean the British government, my Company, any other multicorporates in this sector, and of course the Ortheans themselves –'

"Of course," said Haltern, silkily.

' – and it may be that some restrictions may have to be made. Carrick V may need a Protected World Status. PanOceania doesn't wish to be responsible for inflicting severe culture shock on an alien hominid civilization.'

Too busy thinking, Why didn't I just tell them we've done terrible damage, and we're desperately trying to put it right; I didn't register the image-change until I heard Pathrey Shanataru's sharp intake of breath – he, and Haltern n'ri n'suth Beth'ru-elen. The 'tank snowed with interference, that only cleared slightly, but it was enough to show this for a satellite-image of the wasteland to the west of the Ai River. The silver gleam of sterilized bedrock: the Glittering Plain. Lutaya's voice spoke over the image:

'Serious as the situation may seem, it isn't the whole story. The Orthean situation began with the discovery of Witchbreed Old Technology. This is one of the continent-wide areas of submolecular devastation, left by the use of unimaginable alien weapons, millennia ago. I asked a senior member of the research team, Ravi Singh, about the possibility that this technology also exists in a functional state.'

"Did you clear this one through me? I don't remember it."

Mehmet Lutaya shrugged, not looking away from the holotank image. Ravi's dark features appeared, against what I took to be the comlink-dome on Kumiel Island.

'Professor Singh, isn't it possible, as other examples of working alien technology have been found on Orthe, that the technology to create this destruction also exists?'

One look at Ravi's face made me wince. Why not pick Chandra, I thought; or any other member of the Company team? Why pick the most conservative man in PanOceania?

'I'm afraid you have more than one misconception there, as is not uncommon with WEBcasts. A technology cannot exist without its hinterland – without the society that trains its members, so that they can create the industries – mining, manufacturing – that in turn can create the actual technological devices. All of that is gone, on Carrick V.'

There was a grin from the aquiline-featured Chandra, on my left, who murmured, "Once a lecturer, always a lecturer. . . ."

Lutaya's image persisted:

'*Your research team has found artifacts in working condition, that date from approximately two and a half thousand years ago. Why shouldn't weapons have survived?*'

'*Even if that were possible, which I strongly doubt, the knowledge to use such technology is lost.*'

'*Professor Singh, the southern continent has a functioning canal and water-purification system, dating from at least two thousand years ago, which the local population seem to have no difficulty in operating.*'

'*That was never proven.*'

Ravi's expression shifted from irritation to a kind of smug regret:

'*Unfortunately, with the tragic attack on Dr Rashid Akida, Company research records have been lost. However, I can assure you, no evidence was discovered to prove that the canal-system isn't operated purely by rote, handed down in that oral culture.*'

The image changed from Ravi to Lutaya, the WEBcaster standing on Kumiel, a blue and daystarred sky behind him.

'*That's how the situation stands today, with the –* '

"*T'an* Christie."

I looked up from the holotank, half-dazzled by its bright images; and at first couldn't make out who had interrupted me. Then I glanced down, and saw the black-maned *ashiren* standing in the doorway: Cassirur's child. *Ke* gazed up at the group of us with a remarkable self-possession.

"What is it, *ashiren-te?*"

"There is a messenger to see you, *t'an*." The child looked round at the others who stood in that sunlit, dusty room; the Ortheans and the humans. "It's the *t'an S'aranth* that the message is for."

"I'll come down."

"I've got on-the-spot 'casts from the Morvren Freeport settlement." Lutaya keyed the 'tank on hold. "I've also got some of the Home World WEBs' reactions."

"That's what I want to see – I'll be back in a few minutes. Douggie, if you'll excuse me. . . ."

He smiled, and inclined his head; and I heard their voices start up as the bead-curtain slid back into place behind me, and I followed the *ashiren* down the interior steps of Westhill-Ahrentine to the ground-floor rooms.

CHAPTER 33

Mutable Shadows

Intrigue in the *telestres* is second nature so I gave no thought to this request for a private meeting, except to run through the names of those *T'Ans* that might wish to gain some advantage from PanOceania's representative – which was all of them. The *ashiren* darted down the steps and through the bead-curtain that led into the ground-floor kitchen. These rooms are slate-floored, cool even in Tathcaer's summer; and I walked through into the main one, past *l'ri-an* busy with preparations for the midday meal. The bead-curtain of the outer door was tied back. Tendrils of *kazsis*-nightflower curled round the wooden frame.

And a woman with skin as black as jet leaned up against the larger table, and reached across it to pick up a sweetmeat which she passed to the child: "Thank you, *ashiren-te*. Give you greeting, Christie."

One of Kasabaarde's soft leather masks covered her face. She fumbled at the strings with her single hand, and then pulled free; shaking her head and that cropped black mane. She grinned. Eyes as yellow as sunlight . . . Now she stood, and *harur-nilgiri* and *harur-nazari* clashed; both slung at her shoulder for left-hand draw. She wore a plain shirt and britches, that could have been any mercenary's gear. Her feet were bare and calloused.

"Are you out of your mind?" I said.

"Tethmet just asked me that." Ruric reached across the table again, picking up a handful of *kiez*-fruit and stuffing them in her mouth. She said indistinctly, "Let's go outside. We're less liable to be interrupted."

'You *are* out of your mind.'

"Which one?" And she grinned again. "Let's say, a lot of my past-memories are of your opinion. I think differently. We shall see."

About to follow her out into the courtyard, I suddenly stopped. "But Tathcaer – you can't be seen in Tathcaer."

She stopped in the doorway, turning her head; and the sun outside made her a silhouette of brilliant blackness. Her face was shadowed. Those ten years lay heavily on her: she is not the *T'An* Commander now, or the *T'an* Melkathi who was named in the great Square below the Citadel, here in the white city, Tathcaer.

"I don't plan to be here long. And I've spoken with the *T'An Suthai-Telestre*. With Nelum Santhil Rimnith. . . ." She chuckled. There was a

405

kind of amazement in it. As she turned to go out of the door, she indicated a tray of *siir*-wine and ceramic bowls. "Bring those, will you? I need a drink, if you don't."

"But . . ."

By the time I carried the tray out to the table in the courtyard, the dark Orthean woman had seated herself there in the *ziku*'s shadow, and was taking no apparent notice of the fenborn male who stood before her.

" – have a responsibility; you should *never* leave the Tower! What if you're killed?"

"I have apprentices in the Tower still." Ruric Hexenmeister glanced up, staring at the upper-storey windows, and at the daystarred sky; and membrane slid down lazily over those yellow eyes. She leaned back against the *ziku*'s trunk. Her mane, that had grown a little longer, fell back from her forehead, and I saw the puckered scar of the exile's brand. As if she felt my gaze, she smiled; and her eyes cleared.

"You think I'm mad to come here? The young *ashiren* and *l'ri-an* won't know me, and I wear the mask in the city. Your *s'aranthi*, of course, won't care who I am." She gestured with that single hand, and I sat down opposite her. "Is there anyone here in the Residence I have to worry about?"

Thinking aloud, I said, "The Harantish, Pathrey Shanataru, he's never met you – or heard you, I suppose. Then – Ruric, Hal's here, Haltern Beth'ru-elen."

The fenborn male looked at her with as plain an 'I told you so' as I've ever seen on an Orthean face. He turned his back on us, staring at the arched courtyard entrance; disapproval in every line of that skeletal body. Ruric began to pour *siir*-wine. Her face had changed. She said softly, "I'll see Haltern before I go."

"Ruric – "

"No," the Orthean female said. "If I were Ruric, I wouldn't be here. It's because I'm Hexenmeister, and because, for years immemorial, the Hexenmeister has had some influence over the *hiyek*-families – and even, it may be, influence over the Kel Harantish Witchbreed."

Sitting here, the noise of the city came plainly to me; and the voices of the young Ortheans in the kitchens, and someone in the distance singing one of the atonal Dadeni songs. Hot, dusty; and I thought how much hotter and barren it is to the east, where Calil's fighters and the *hiyek* guerrillas wait in Melkathi – wait for the ships that sail on a south-west wind.

"When did you leave the Tower?"

"A week past – no, eight days," she corrected herself. "My people brought me word of *hiyek* ships in the Archipelago, and rumours that

Morvren would be attacked. That I thought might come. Then I had word from Annekt, in Kel Harantish. He said: the city is deserted, the bloodlines are gone, crept out in Coast *jath* in the hours of darkness; Calil bel-Rioch, who would be Santhendor 'lin-sandru, is gone from Kel Harantish. . . ."

She lifted the *siir*-bowl and drank, put it down, and wiped her mouth on her wrist. There was a sardonic humour on that dark face.

"I've left the Tower to come and argue with the Harantish Witchbreed – which is the act of a fool, I don't doubt, but what else can I do? I am Hexenmeister. All the weapons I have are words. What weapons Calil bel-Rioch might have – *that* is what frightens me. I suspect she has none, but can I take the chance?"

Something dawned on me at that point. I waited until I caught her gaze, and said, "*I'm* not going to tell you you acted wisely in coming back to Tathcaer. Particularly when four-fifths of the reason isn't that at all, but because the Hundred Thousand's being attacked – am I right?"

That pointed chin came up, and she stared at me with the arrogance of the Hundred Thousand; the look that Dalzielle Kerys-Andrethe used to wear as *T'An Suthai-Telestre*. All humour gone, she said, "What makes you think you should tell me anything?"

"I don't know. I never could tell you much. Not that you'd listen to, anyway."

Her mouth, drawn into a tight line, twitched unwillingly; she deliberately looked away, staring at the upper windows, and then she snorted; threw her head back with a bark of laughter, and swore. "*Amari S'aranth!* Of all the Motherless offworlders – "

"You're being too reckless. Taking too much of a risk."

"No more than anyone else." The dark Orthean woman sat, shade-dappled: points of light brilliant on the hilts of *harur*-blades. She glanced at Tethmet's stubborn back. He gazed across the small, dusty courtyard, oblivious. She smiled. 'There are others who can take my place."

"*No.*"

Her gaze fell. Those yellow eyes clouded; cleared; and she shot me a look that made me think, What did she hear me say? And wonder, myself. In the moment's silence that followed, I took a sip of *siir*-wine. Its acrid taste dragged me into the present, out of memories that are eight years gone.

"I'm undecided . . . whether to go back to Rimnith and Keverilde, or to try to contact the *hiyek* fleet. They should be south of the Medued estuary now. What do you think?"

She reached up with long dark fingers, knotting her empty sleeve more securely. That six-fingered hand paused to rub, as if amputated flesh still pained her after all these years; and the white sunlight wiped all the lines of age from her face.

"Speak with the families sailing *jath* and *jath-rai*. I'll come. I'll want to see your *s'aranthi* records first." She smiled. "*S'aranth-te*, yes. I would like you to tell me: this is the right action for the Hexenmeister."

Then the smile slipped, and it was a solemn child's face that for a moment I saw: the *amari* child run off from its *telestre* and come to the white city, thirty years ago. She looked up, yellow eyes under dark brows. On a shaky, indrawn breath, she said, "Tell me you think it's right, Christie. You might help convince me. There – we – I couldn't *not* come."

And at that moment, when she should have been most Ruric, I found myself tongue-tied because of those other, ancient memories; the other lives of the Hexenmeister, that I sensed in her. I opened my mouth; could think of nothing to say.

"Master," the fenborn warned quietly.

Movement disturbed the empty courtyard: the bead-curtain at the top of the outer stairs was pushed aside. The dark figure of Pathrey Shanataru appeared; and with him, Haltern, leaning on his *hanelys* cane, and peering myopically out into the sunlight.

"Is that the Empress's Voice?" Ruric asked. I nodded. She stood, pushing back the couch-chair, that scraped across the paving-stones. Her one hand looped the soft leather mask over her head, hiding yellow eyes behind dark eyeshields. All her attention was on that old Beth'ru-elen male: sleek, stooped, the white wisp of mane. I wished that I could see her face now.

"Talk with the Voice of the Empress," she said, standing with that crook-shouldered fighter's balance; and at her voice, even kept low, I saw Haltern's head come up. She for a moment rested her hand on my shoulder, and then she walked across the courtyard and up the steps.

Pathrey moved aside. I saw Hal frown, half reach out a hand and then let it fall back; deep lines of bewilderment on that bland face. Ruric reached the top of the steps. They stood for a full minute in Tathcaer's white sunlight. Then, together, they went inside.

Argument with Cory Mendez occupied me for the better part of an hour, through a snatched meal; interrupted by discussion with Douggie, and with Pathrey Shanataru. The comlink-contact with the Freeport proved fuzzy. All I could get from Cory were protests about Company Security.

"It isn't merely hazardous, it's foolhardy," she said. Her holo-image flickered: a rumpled, white-haired woman in the cabin of an F90 shuttle. "You'll end up dead, or held hostage; and Company policy with a hostage situation is to refuse any co-operation. Lynne, this is a local situation. It is not one in which the Company should interfere."

"It's a situation that the Company created."

Her gaze dropped. Part of the mulish stubbornness faded. She said reluctantly, "My people will complete an image-analysis for you. Lynne, I wish you'd reconsider."

"I think it's something we're under an obligation to try. . . . I'll take one of the YV9s," I said, "there'll be several other passengers."

I keyed out contact, cutting off her questions. Using the Residence's holotank made my back ache: couch-chairs aren't designed the right height. I stood, rubbing at the small of my back; hearing Douggie in urbane conversation with Chandra and one of the other Company people. Warm wind blew in through the open windows, rustling the bead-curtains. It isn't having too little to do that produces that stasis, but having too much: not knowing where to start.

Mehmet Lutaya walked through from the next room, carrying a bowl of half-burned *kuru* meat. Through a mouthful, he said, "Tune into the WEB frequency, Representative. Be good to see what's going on."

"I can tell you what's going on and it isn't good," I said, Cory's update in mind. I keyed into the channel the WEBcasts would be on, going up to Security on the orbiter; and stopped when I saw a face I recognized:

'I'm speaking to you from Northfast, the largest island of the Freeport settlement on the northern continent.'

The Visconti woman stood by a curving wall, shadowed by windvanes; Ortheans hurried past her, some in brown Wellhouse robes. She had that hunched look that comes from watching the sky; but she spoke clearly:

'The situation here has deteriorated badly in the last two hours. Hostile jath-rai ships, remaining behind after the main fleet, cruise the channels between these islands. My attempts to establish contact with the attacking forces have failed. I have personally seen low-tech shots exchanged. This is a winchbow-bolt –'

She held out her hand. A metal dart lay on her palm, the point fluted: a black iron bolt.

' – and this is the wound that it makes.'

The holo-image showed her stepping back, moving along the wall to where three or four Ortheans lay in its shelter. She squatted down by a fair-maned male. His back was towards the camera, splashed with blood like black paint. What I at first took to be torn flesh was the fletching of the bolt, buried deep a handsbreadth from his spine.

"Nice shot," Lutaya said. He absently offered me the bowl of *kuru*. For some reason, I wasn't hungry.

'Approximately seventy miles to the east of where I am now, the main body

of the Desert Coast fleet is coming together. Presumably, this is the preliminary to an attack; at worst to a full-scale invasion – '

"That isn't telling us anything we don't know." I scanned the other transmissions.

"Reckon to put something through every two hours," he said. "We're not just sending FTL-blips back to the Home Worlds. Most of us are getting stuff out direct to the WEBs on Thierry and Parmiter and Aleph-Nine."

And you think it's worth your while hanging round the Company representative, and the government envoy. . . . Well, who knows? I thought. You might be right. The next three or four hours are crucial.

Lutaya left, and I got through to Kumiel to make sure a YV9 shuttle was powered-up and ready. After I keyed out, I stood in that small, hot room – half human culture, and half Orthean: print-outs pinned up on the walls together with old ribbon-banners in the colours of Ahrentine *telestre* – and shook with cold; with a fear that made my hands icy and my stomach churn. Eight years ago, on Orthe, I rushed into things that make my heart stop now; rushed in with no perception of how final catastrophe can be. *Max*, I thought; suddenly guilty that he'd been absent from my mind for so long. *Some things you don't recover from.* And then realized that I had had to reach for that feeling, was not overwhelmed by it, as before. . . .

Not caring to analyse that too closely, I walked through into the other room, meaning to speak with Douggie, and Pathrey Shanataru, and, of course, Ruric.

"I admire your *telestre* fighters," Pathrey said smoothly. I found him sitting with Douggie and Hal in the courtyard – it is, simply, where one is least likely to be overheard. The dark, sleek Harantish male, mane falling in untrimmed curls; the frail bird-like figure of Haltern Beth'ru-elen, with a *becamil* rug over his knees; and Douggie's urbane poise – almost brothers, I thought. Different origins, but some unmistakable kinship between them.

"Were this an equal fight, I think *telestre* numbers would have it . . ." Pathrey paused and then added, ". . . eventually. There being a goodly number of us aboard the *jath* fleet."

As I sat down beside him, Hal eyed the Harantish male with polite dislike. Old loyalties die hard: Pathrey is still born of Kel Harantish. . . .

"There is one thing more. We have *s'aranthi* weapons." Pathrey put both hands on the table before him, linking fingers, and stared down at them. His bravado vanished. "Perhaps more than *s'aranthi* weapons. I've spoken of this before. You gloat that we of Harantish have no past-memories, being Witchbreed-blooded. I do not envy you remembering the use of that weapon, that ancient light."

"Calil has this?" Douggie pressed.

"Sometimes I believe she does. Sometimes I believe nothing of it!"

"You must have some belief," I said, "or you wouldn't be here now."

The edges of roofs and walls blurred with a faint sea mist, that through the arched entrance could be seen blotting out the harbour. It muffled the sounds of the city. Humid: sweat ran in patches. I watched the plump Orthean male, and saw on his face an aching regret.

"I shouldn't have left her. Half the bloodlines are vying for her ear now, all with dreams of Kel Harantish the new heart of Empire – but that's not what she plans. I know her. No one knows her as I do."

Douggie, letting him ramble self-pityingly, steered him back with the prompt: "What's her intention?"

"To strengthen her foothold in Rimnith and Keverilde, I imagine. And before many days," Pathrey Shanataru said, "she will say: I have that ancient weapon, that brought the fall of the Golden Empire. And if proof's required, she'll try to prove it – and that may prove the end of us all; if she does have our ancestor's science, that doesn't mean she can control it. But if she can, she will then say: You are again under the rule of the Golden Empire . . . or else you are a land where nothing moves but silver dust and the cold wind. . . ."

I said, "Is it a bluff?"

"*Shan'tai, all* of it may be a bluff. There is something about her now, I hardly know her, I – if she by some mischance has the weapon that Santhendor'lin-sandru used, well, he used it, and she is as he was."

A young *l'ri-an* came out from the kitchens with *siir*-wine and bread, and the conversation paused. As I helped set out the bowls, I thought, Do I trust Pathrey? Do I even trust him to be a traitor? He was closest of all to Calil bel-Rioch . . . and this could be nothing more than propaganda to scare us.

"Insanity, to hold that threat over our heads," Hal protested.

"I've known other worlds that existed under just such a balance." Douggie's unspoken addition was: *if not for very long.* He glanced at me. "At that point, Earth would intervene, and on such a scale – "

"And with what results?"

Hal cupped his hands, raising the bowl of *siir* to his lips; and when he had drunk, wiped his neat, puckered mouth, and said, "Calil bel-Rioch cannot live forever."

Pathrey's protest came too quickly. "Others have lived her life, in our city. Others have had centuries of shunned persecution, of revilement; have dreamed of the past and the Empire and," he concluded, with undeniable truth, "there are others like her. This could not have happened if it were just my Calil alone."

Knowing the Hundred Thousand (knowing Hal), there have been assassination attempts thought of. I filed that for future thought. My wristlink chimed, signalling the shuttle on Kumiel Island was ready.

"*Shan'tai* Pathrey, if you'd like to come back to Kumiel with me now . . ." Far safer to have him in Peace Force protective custody than left with *telestre*-Ortheans. I stood up, wondering where I'd find Pramila Ishida. "Douggie, what are you doing about this?"

"I think it is imperative that one of us stay here to co-ordinate government and Company affairs; it could, of course, be you," he said, steepling his fingers, and looking up at me.

"No, I'll go. If it looks too dangerous, I won't make the contact. There'll be other opportunities. The fleet has at least three days' sailing before it gets near Melkathi."

Hal turned his face to the misty sky. "I could wish for the weather to change. If She were kind, a summer tempest might solve this for us." He blinked, small eyes bright, and inclined his head in Pathrey's direction. "No ill will to your people personally, *t'an*, you understand."

"I understand perfectly."

Douggie's amusement was visible only to someone who knew him. He stepped in smoothly and took Pathrey Shanataru's arm, steering him towards the courtyard entrance, and a *l'ri-an* who stood waiting with a *skurrai*-carriage. As well as avoiding hostility, it would give the government envoy a last chance to speak to the Empress's Voice – I smiled, thinking, Too many years on Orthe, Douggie; it's taught you never to miss an advantage.

Haltern got to his feet. He shook out the folds of his *becamil* over-robe, that was stitched with green and gold thread; and gripped the *hanelys* cane in a thin, six-fingered hand. Droplets of sea mist swirled in the air. The honey-coloured stone of that courtyard seemed almost to glow, taking warmth from the hidden sun.

"You have had knowledge of the Hexenmeister since when?" he asked. "Since you and the *t'an* Clifford were in the Tower, these two months gone?"

"I couldn't tell you about her, Hal, I'm sorry."

That round, bland face creased into a smile. Since he'd spoken with Ruric, a few hours ago, some indefinable tension had been released in him; and now he chuckled, and said, "*S'aranth*, we will have you in the *takshiriye* yet! The T'An Suthai-Telestre is most impressed. . . . But I think it wiser none other knows that the exiled Orhlandis has returned. Or that she lives, and is Hexenmeister. Does she leave with you now?"

"Yes – " I answered before I properly thought; which is what one tends to do, prompted by Haltern n'ri n'suth Beth'ru-elen.

"Be eloquent with the *hiyeks*," he said. "*S'aranth*, I am too old for such travelling, or I would come with you; and too old for travelling at all, therefore I shan't return to Rimnith and Keverilde – but I shall stay here in the city, and do what I can."

I grinned, knowing what webs of intrigue among *T'Ans* and *s'ans* are known to the Beth'ru-elen. "Modesty doesn't become you, Hal."

He signalled to a pale-maned *l'ri-an*, who ran out to the alley for another *skurrai-jasin*.

"You'll find me in the Citadel, when you return." And then he fixed watery blue eyes on me, the whiteless eyes of Ortheans; almost spoke, changed his mind, and at last said, "Christie, I don't know why, after all these years, I should worry about you," and was across the courtyard and through the archway before I could think of a reply.

Sea fog hides the harbour, and the crowds at docked *jath*-ships; hides the upper slopes of Westhill, and its fortress that I have seen from this courtyard. Tathcaer, clustered full of blank-walled *telestre*-houses . . . still with the overgrown traces of eight years' neglect: *siir* and *ziku* and *kazsis*-vine; and this is not the same city that I came to as envoy, and that old man is not the same Haltern Beth'ru-elen. All that remains constant is the bond still existing between us.

I went back upstairs, to find Pramila Ishida sleeping the sleep of the exhausted, and roused her; Kumiel station called in again to say a YV9 was in readiness for flight. Then I looked for Ruric Hexenmeister and was for frantic minutes convinced she'd gone as secretly as she'd arrived – until a masked woman slipped back through the *telestre*-house entrance from the city outside: *amari* Ruric Orhlandis come back from her city, Tathcaer; unrecognized, unknown.

The first *jath-rai* starred the sea four hundred *seri* to the west of Tathcaer. The Company officers crewing the YV9 shuttle regarded me with disapproval, but that didn't bother me. At the moment I'm acting Company representative, I thought. While that lasts, I've got the authority to do this – if it lasts long enough, we're home. . . .

"Take us down to eight hundred feet," I directed.

The coastline to the north of us was invisible in haze. We crossed the *jath-rai*'s wake, coming down low enough to see *hiyek* males and females rush to the ship's metal rails and point up at us.

Pramila Ishida said, 'That's one of the mid-Coast *hiyeks*. Quarth area. Get the data-net on image analysis."

The young male officer she addressed frowned, glancing away from the shabbily-dressed Pacifican girl; and I nodded, authorizing it. I don't think Pramila noticed that rumours of her part in affairs were obviously circulating among Company staff – and you're past caring about it, I realized.

Ruric leaned down, studying the image in the holotank. The light reflected back from her yellow eyes. When she spoke, it was in the language of the Tower, that she and I alone would comprehend: "The *hiyek*-families are not the most important thing now, *S'aranth*. Don't forget: we must speak with Harantish Witchbreed."

Outriders of the main fleet came into scan. Tall-masted *jath*, made of riveted sheets of metal, their steel sails at once too fragile and too heavy-seeming. . . . First one *jath*, cutting a white line across the ocean; then another, then two more, then a dozen strung out in a wavering line – and *there*, the main fleet. I let the voices of the crew fade into the background, hearing them talk with Kumiel base and with Cory's people at the Freeport; all of that gone, all I could see was the fleet of the *hiyeks* of the Coast.

Jath and *jath-rai*, all sizes of ship; some loaded down so that they wallowed in the swell. Sails set to catch the strong, steady wind . . . small boats tacking across the fleet's main course. Sails bowing, rails crowded, males and females pointing and staring; and Carrick's Star a sunburst on the water. *Jath* wakes crossing, fringes of foam on a jade-green sea. . . .

The YV9's power-discharge ruffled the sea as we came down lower. One *jath-rai* passed below us, its sails with patches riveted on, and the deck littered with bundles, with stoves, with sleeping *ashiren*, with covered objects twice the height of an Orthean. I spared a glance for instruments: no heat readings. Yet. And then the shuttle's speed dropped again as we paralleled the fleet's course, going down past them. Easy for Cory to say, 'estimated seven hundred ships'. Now we passed small convoys and groups of ships, still flying west, still seeing no end to them; ships in groups that seemed to dot the sea out to northern and southern horizons – and we at last came on the trailing end of it. Two *jath-rai* wallowing without sail, furious repairs going on; one *jath* left abandoned; and on the western horizon, still the occasional speck of a following ship. . . .

Ruric said, "Not an invasion. A migration."

I straightened, rubbing the small of my back. "The data-net will have processed the images in a few seconds. Then we'll have a contact." I turned to the pilot. "Take us back, please."

Pramila Ishida had slumped down into one of the bucket seats. Now she leaned both filthy arms on the edge of the holotank and stared at the

414

images of *jath* and *jath-rai*, as the YV9 swung round and flew back across the fleet. She smiled. It was an odd expression, one could speculate uneasily about what she'd had to go through, to feel that way.

"A Company representative shouldn't put herself in jeopardy," she remarked.

"When I put a voicecast on narrowbeam, I'm going to make it clear we're armed, and we'll fire if necessary." And after Reshebet, I thought, they'll believe me. Ironic, if what Cory did there proves a protection to me.

The YV9 shuttle switched to hover-mode, some five hundred feet above the sea. Holo-images showed a daystarred sky, streaked with high cloud, and a summer haze still shadowing the horizon. A vast circle of ocean, with innumerable small ships dotting it; white wakes all curving like an arrow's flight to the east. . . . Blue and gold; and I could almost feel the cool wind, taste the salt.

I switched to data-mode, letting the analysis of the holo-images appear in the tank; and while it presented alternatives, set up an outside voicecast on a narrowly directional soundbeam.

"There are Anzhadi on at least three *jath*," Pramila said.

The cabin's soft green illumination shone on the worn seats, the rim of the holotank; the faces of the Company crew – all four of them barely into their twenties, and not knowing which to regard with greater suspicion: the alien woman, the renegade Pacifican, or the lunatic Company representative. I grinned. When I turned back to the data-images, Ruric spoke from the shadows of the cabin:

"Not Anzhadi, Christie. I'll tell you what I've seen, and that's Harantish Golden on every *jath* and *jath-rai* – a bare handful to a vessel, but is that all *K'ai* Calil needs?" The dark Orthean woman stepped closer to the 'tank. Her long-fingered hand massaged the stump of her right arm, that after so many years still pained her. "We must speak with – "

The rim of the holotank hit me hard under the ribs, and I gasped for breath. A klaxon split the air. Darkness: either the illumination cut out, or I blacked out for a second. There was a sensation of plummeting, and then I heard urgent controlled voices: the shuttle soared upwards. The klaxon ceased: interior illumination returned.

" – report fired on by hi-tech weaponry at 764.069.546; repeat 764.069.546. Damage report follows." The dark-haired young officer leaned back from the voice-record, grinned at me, and said, "We're still flying, Representative. They're not that good!"

"Get me an image rerun. *Now*."

Ruric's hand was under my elbow, shoving me into one of the bucket seats. Her fingers probed the base of my ribs and I winced.

415

"Bruised," she said. "You *s'aranthi* hurt easily."

Adrenalin still pumped with every heartbeat, and I let it carry me forward: fear is a good fuel. The holotank showed a rerun image: from one *jath* below us bursts a star of light, analysed as a microbeam-pulse weapon. And there, on the deck, a battered GHD4.

"Put us on an evasion-pattern. I want voicecast-contact with that *jath*-ship. Give me a close-in image." I bent over the holotank, one hand tight against my ribs, wincing. "I thought I'd seen that before. . . . Pramila, that's one of the ships with Anzhadi-*hiyek* on board. You come here. I want you on voicecast. You tell them, we want a truce, we want a meeting, and if we don't get it – if they fire again – "

"Yes?" And she smiled.

"Then we'll try another ship." Breath was coming back to me, and a degree of calmness. " I think it'll be easier, however, to make contact where you and I are known. Even if that isn't essential."

She hesitantly came to sit down in the seat I vacated, and took the comlink now on narrowcast. There was an expression almost of disappointment on her round face. As if it would have pleased her to have the Company threaten violence against Coast *hiyeks* – to have her worst fears realized?

"Kethrial-shamaz shan'tai Anzhadi – "

Her voice, magnified, quite clearly reached the deck of the *jath* below us. I saw how pale-maned Ortheans looked up at the hovering shuttle; the image in real-time, and clear enough to show expressions on faces: fear, confusion, hope.

" *– I was of Anzhadi's Ninth raiku, and the shan'tai Christie has been received in siiran. We would speak with you, without the firing of weapons. If you knew Sethri-safere of Ninth raiku, then listen; it would have been his will – "*

She keyed out the narrowcast, and sat for a moment without speaking. There were bright streaks on her face, hardly visible in the dim green light, and yet she smiled: an Orthean expression on a human face.

As the YV9's equipment picked up and sorted voices from below, filtering out the noise of the shuttle's power-hum, the wind and the waves, Ruric again reached over to touch my arm and indicate the holo-image of the *jath*'s deck.

"Those two? They're Anzhadi, yes, I know them."

"Not them. There: the Harantish Witchbreed," Ruric said. "You must remember, I have had my people in the port of Harantish, and on the canals. That is a face you will not know, but I do, though we have never met. That is Oreys, of the science bloodline Kethalu."

*

The pod opened, after what seemed like an hour of darkness and buffeting, and I stepped on to the swaying deck of the *jath*, Pramila Ishida close behind me, and, behind her, the robed and masked figure of the Hexenmeister. Bright sun blinded me. I took a quick squint into the brilliant sky, seeing the shuttle's bulk hovering overhead; and then through dazzles saw *hiyek*-Ortheans on the deck. The *jath* dipped, rose; and I staggered, catching my balance.

A cool voice said, "Give you greeting, *shan'tai* Christie." The sound was pitched to carry over the slap of waves on the metal hull, and the chattering of *ashiren* who now flocked towards the pod. They scattered as it rose, drawn back aboard the YV9.

"Give you greeting – " I spoke to the two *hiyek*-Ortheans I recognized: a stocky female, and, leaning on her shoulder, a thin and weary male " – *shan'tai* Feriksushar, *shan'tai* Hildrindi."

Pramila came up beside me, and said softly, "Greeting to Anzhadi, and to all *hiyeks* here."

Ortheans crowded the upper and the inner deck, some in the rigging; dozens of faces all turned in this direction. Their manes were white or yellow, they were small of stature, and thin; and I thought, How can we stop them? This is crazy. For diplomacy to work, it has to work *before* we've got to this stage –

But that won't stop me trying.

Feriksushar said bluntly, "What do you want, *shan'tai* Ishida?"

The Pacifican girl glanced at me, and then back at the older Orthean female. She let her gaze travel across the lines of Ortheans, and said, "Sethri-safere of Ninth *raiku* is dead. It was a Harantish woman who killed him. You have Harantish here. Let him speak with us."

The wind whipped hair into my eyes. I began to get the feel of balance, on that sun-heated metal deck. All the faces that I saw had a stolid impassivity, but I thought there was some reaction at the mention of Harantish Witchbreed, and I said to the thin male, "*Shan'tai* Hildrindi, has the Company now to negotiate with the people of Kel Harantish, about the affairs of the *hiyek*-families?"

His hand was clenched on Feriksushar's shoulder, bunching the thin material of her *meshabi*-robe. The bright sun on his face showed deep lines, and blue shadows about his mouth; and it came to me how few months it must be since I'd spoken with him in Maherwa, and how far his illness had progressed.

"You think to anger us," he said, smiling. "Anger speaks unwisely. We took your present approach for an attack on us: that was unwise. Or was it only premature?"

I should know better than to fence with you, I thought. Hildrindi-

keretne, like Feriksushar, carried a hook-bladed knife at his belt; she had a winchbow slung across her back. It was when I looked over their heads, to the GHD4 beampulser now shrouded in patched cloth, that I saw the Harantish male.

"Give you greeting," I called, "*Shan'tai* Oreys Kethalu. Come down and speak with *s'aranthi*, since you command this ship – "

The crowd parted and let him through. He was tall, loose-limbed, with a feline agility to catch points of balance as the deck dipped and swayed beneath him; and he came lightly down the steps from the upper deck to stand beside Hildrindi. He was pale-skinned, dressed in the brown scale-mail of Harantish; and at first I thought him white-maned, but as he came closer, I saw the roots of it were black. The eyes in his narrow-chinned face weren't golden, but brown.

"These are allies." Oreys Kethalu's voice was harsh, speaking the common *hiyek* slang. "Not servants, allies. Allies of the city Kel Harantish, and the Empress Calil – "

"Calil killed Sethri-safere!"

The young Pacifican woman stumbled on the metal deck as she stepped forward, face contorted. I half reached out a hand to stop her; then thought better of it. Anger speaks unwisely, as Hildrindi says; and provokes unwise speech in others.

Her human tongue stumbled with the formal speech of the *siirans*: "Listen, *raiku* of Anzhadi-*hiyek*! How many centuries have the families been slaves to the Harantish Witchbreed? This was your chance to win free – there's land on the north continent that you can have, that isn't *telestre* land; land that doesn't need canals, doesn't need *siiran*. The price is peace, that's all; and you could have it, but what do you do? You invite the Witchbreed to command you again!"

Feriksushar snorted, and over the shouted comments of the surrounding Ortheans said, "Sethri said he could free us from the desert so we followed him. If the Empress-in-Exile can win us land here, we'll follow her. And if you could win it for us, *shan'tai s'aranthi*, we'd follow you. Hunger's hard on principles."

Oreys Kethalu held up a blunt-fingered hand for silence. "We've been shut up in that pestilent city for more ages than you *s'aranthi* can easily count. If the *hiyek*-families were our servants, so were *we* servants to them. Now both our peoples have a free alliance."

Membrane slid across his eyes as he met my gaze, and then slid back. More quietly, he added, "Yes, we had from them food and water, that we could not get ourselves. And yes, they had from us our knowledge to keep canals and *siiran* alive. Who was then the slave, *shan'tai*?"

His unexpected honesty stopped me. A moment of stillness in all that

418

movement: the rocking ocean, the wind, the clash of sails, the deep thrum of the hovering YV9. Something brushed my arm then, and it was a robe of coarse brown cloth. The dark Orthean woman stepped forward: Ruric Hexenmeister.

"It's an old quarrel, that between Kel Harantish and the Hundred Thousand. Centuries have not seen the end of it. Now you enter that quarrel and call it an alliance, a hope of gaining freedom – *shan'tai* Feriksushar, do you think you will have freedom, under Calil bel-Rioch's rule?"

The stocky *hiyek* female shrugged. "The Hundred Thousand doesn't need canals to keep it fertile, so the Witchbreed – your pardon, *shan'tai* Kethalu – have no hold over us."

Salt was bitter on my lips, stiff in my hair. I suddenly had to clasp my hands together, behind my back, so that no one would see how they were shaking. Delayed, the shock of that attack on the shuttle hit all the harder. I let the fear again fuel action:

"You've got *s'aranthi* weapons, *shan'tai*, we know that. We'd know it even if Pramila hadn't told us – " I registered Hildrindi's ironic amusement " – and that's a matter for concern. Despite all that's happened, the Company's very reluctant to get involved in fighting a war. But now I'll ask you something – has the *shan'tai* Kethalu told you how Calil plans to subdue the Hundred Thousand? Has he told you what weapon she'll hold over their heads?"

Another Anzhadi stepped forward to talk urgently with Hildrindi-*keretne*. The babble of voices drowned all other conversation, all the *hiyek* males and females seemingly shouting at once; and the younger *ashiren* took refuge in the deck-tents.

"*There was –* " Feriksushar's drill-sergeant shout rose over other voices; she added more quietly, "there was some talk of weaponry, *shan'tai s'aranthi*. What of it?"

Beside me, Ruric reached up to put back the hood of her robe. That tangled black mane rooted down her spine, silvered a little with age; and her narrow, masked face turned, surveying all the *hiyek*-Ortheans. When she spoke, her voice was pitched so that they must strain to hear it over wind and waves: an old orator's trick.

"Let me tell you," she said. "You have memories. There are *keretne* among you. Let me recall to you a weapon of the Golden Witchbreed, that made the Elansiir and the Glittering Plain, and that Twilight Shore that lies in the arctic north of the Barrens. There is a weapon that ate like a cancer at the face of the world. There is a weapon that, when the Empire was at its height, when it was of such magnificence that even its slaves must be amazed at such a grandeur of tyranny – a weapon that, in that moment, brought the Empire to its fall. And that is the weapon Calil bel-Rioch claims to have."

The rhythms of the Coast's semi-formal language lulled them, as much as her Tower robes caught their attention. It was a deliberate piece of theatre, that must now be built upon to reach something real.

Oreys Kethalu, almost shamefaced, said, "It's a threat, no more."

With all the Hexenmeister's authority, sensed without their knowing who she was, Ruric said, "I have seen cities of crystal, dead, and turning to slow dust. That is the threat, *shan'tai* Hildrindi, *shan'tai* Feriksushar. *Hiyek*-Anzhadi, if the Empress-in-Exile has that, it is a threat to the Hundred Thousand, and a threat to you too."

Feriksushar glanced at Oreys Kethalu with something very like contempt. "The Harantish are few. We are many."

I said, "The Hundred Thousand are many, now, and you *hiyeks* are few. If you can hold a threat over them, the Harantish Witchbreed can hold that threat over you. But this isn't a very fruitful discussion, *shan'tai*. If we could talk of the land to the north of the Hundred Thousand – "

Overhead, the shuttle's hum deepened. The white hull flashed in the sun as it rose, circling slowly to the north; and I was about to make comlink-contact when I realized it was cruising between this *jath* and another that approached us. The second *jath* veered slowly away. I licked my lips, salt-bitter, thinking, *If they'd offer us hospitality we'd be halfway to a discussion, but we're talking ourselves out of time and patience here.*

Oreys Kethalu stared at the brown-robed Hexenmeister. "You are from the Tower, *shan'tai*? The Tower is no friend to Kel Harantish."

Feriksushar said, "Nor to the *hiyeks*. No friend to the *hiyeks* was ever found in the Brown Tower."

Ruric chuckled, startling both of them, and said, "You fired on us just now, and yet the *shan'tai* Christie didn't retaliate. That's one friend you have, and she has the closest connections with the Tower."

Kethalu, irritated, said, "That isn't what I meant."

She sees him as the key, I thought. The Harantish, not the *hiyeks*. And she's keeping him off balance very nicely.

Ruric, in a practical tone, went on: "Just now, I said that we were slaves to the Empire, and that was true. Neither you, *shan'tai* Kethalu, nor the *hiyek* people here, are slaves. The Coast was *not* slavery and tyranny, but a pattern of survival that you were locked into; the only way you could live in a land that, by all rights, shouldn't support life. And believe me if I tell you, all the Tower has ever done is correct that balance when either of your peoples forgot it."

Bodies brushed my elbows and my back, and I realized that the *hiyek*-

Ortheans had crowded in close. Only minimum sail kept the *jath* into the wind: all other attention was on us. Pramila, myself, Ruric: the Witch-breed male, and the Anzhadi. There was the dirt and musk scent of the *siiran* in that close contact.

Hildrindi-*keretne*, still leaning on Feriksushar's arm, said, "And now?"

Ruric's face was invisible behind the mask. I sensed them straining to guess her intentions.

She said, "Now, even you and the Harantish Golden can't make that desolation support life for many more decades. *Shan'tai*, go to the Northern Wilderness. The *telestre* land isn't yours to take, nor theirs to give up. The *T'An Suthai-Telestre* has said he will give you free passage north, to the empty lands."

"On whose authority?" Feriksushar grunted.

"On his own."

Oreys Kethalu again put up a hand for silence. Metal sails creaked; heavy water hit and echoed against the hull of the *jath*.

"And on the Tower's authority?" he asked.

"Yes, *shan'tai*."

"Well, I do not believe you," he said, and his brown eyes gleamed. "You are the Tower's messenger, you claim, but *I* do not believe the Tower would loose us from its grip. Not our city Kel Harantish; not the *hiyeks* that serve it. No, *shan'tai*."

The Orthean woman reached up, pulling at the strings and removing her mask. The light of Carrick's Star was harsh white on her fine-grained skin. She smiled to feel the air on her face; and I could see, as she looked around, her knowledge that no one could recognize the exile's scar on her forehead, no one could name her as Hexenmeister. Only this nameless woman, without authority, to persuade the *hiyeks* and the Witchbreed . . . and yet she has authority, I realized. You cannot carry the Hexenmeister's many lives, and seem unchanged.

"There have been those to whom the Tower deferred," she said mildly. "You will have heard of Beth'ru-elen *Ashirenin*, who came to Kasa-baarde's inner city, and who founded the province of Peir-Dadeni – and who made our religion of the Goddess real."

Oreys Kethalu blinked, two layers of membrane sliding down, inner and outer lids.

"The *keretne* here will know what I say is true. Your link with Her is blood and water. In the north, the link is the earth itself, and the wells of Her water; and if you make that link, you are the Goddess and She is you, and you can no more harm the earth than you can cut out your own heart. And the Tower will not go against that." Ruric paused.

"You were from a *telestre* before you reached the Tower," the

421

Witchbreed male said contemptuously, speaking under cover of the *hiyek*-families' loud reaction to what she said.

Then Ruric reached out, gripping his shoulder with her single hand. Before he could react, she said, "Look at me – *look*. Yes. I'm what you are, half Golden-blooded. *Yes*. If the truth were made clear, my Coast mother may have come from Kel Harantish itself. I have no past-memories. All I have is what the Tower tells me."

Hammerblows of shock opened his eyes: for a second defenceless, he stared at her. "I don't understand – "

"We're not like them," Ruric said. "We have no *keretne*, no past-memory. If the past isn't with us, we're not controlled by it. I've lived in *this* world, not in the days of the Empire. If Santhendor'lin-sandru could love death enough to give it to half a world, that doesn't mean *I* must, or that you can or will do the same."

He shook his head in bewilderment, this loose-limbed male in brown armour; and his dyed-white mane whipped in the sea wind. I shot a glance at Ruric: saw the wide-set yellow eyes glowing in that dark face.

"Be free of it," she said. "What you're doing isn't the only way. If the Tower can change, then so can the Hundred Thousand, and so can the Harantish Golden."

Almost sulkily, Oreys Kethalu said, "But I know nothing of northern lands, this 'Northern Wilderness' the *T'An Suthai-Telestre* speaks of. It may be no better than the Coast – "

Hildrindi leaned forward and with deliberate irony said, "*Shan'tai*, it could hardly be worse!"

Kethalu rounded on him, dragging him aside and speaking in a furious undertone. Both of them glanced at us from time to time. When I looked to see Pramila, she was amongst a group of other Anzhadi; then I realized our tight little grouping had broken up, was dispersing among the crowd of *hiyek*-Ortheans. The shrouded bulk of the beampulser stood abandoned on the upper deck.

"And if they can change," the dark Orthean woman said, "so can *s'aranthi*. Christie, I've got Oreys Kethalu to the point where he'll admit the possibility of change, if nothing more. Can I get you to that point?"

"Me?" I shrugged, then. "The Company doesn't change."

Ruric nodded at Pramila Ishida, where the Pacifican woman stood with Feriksushar and the rest of Twenty-Eighth *raiku*. "What of her? And does your Corazon Mendez think as she once did, now that she's seen the burning of Morvren Freeport? And you, Christie, you're Company. Admit a possibility that things can be different?"

The *jath* dipped, metal prow cutting the ocean and sending up a rainbow-fan of spray. Other ships glided on courses parallel, cutting the

422

bright sea; and the wind came clean from the west. The hull of the shuttle caught the light of Carrick's Star. I kept my footing on the swaying deck, and felt for a second the same sense of release that Oreys Kethalu must have felt. It was nothing that dared to be optimism, and yet – things can be different.

"I admit the possibility," I said, and saw her grin, and couldn't help but return it. "This is only one ship, Oreys Kethalu is only one man. It's a possibility, not a probability. Still, I think . . . we've got too much hard work and too little time: I'll tell you what I think in a few hours."

Ruric Hexenmeister stood with bare feet slightly apart, on that hot metal deck; standing with the old crook-shouldered balance. She looked at the Anzhadi, at Kethalu; and her smile remained. She said, "It isn't over until it's over. And that hasn't happened yet."

CHAPTER 34

Waiting for the Morning

"It doesn't happen that easily," Corazon Mendez said.

She made a shuttle-to-shuttle transfer on the morning of the following day, letting her F90 go on to Kumiel Island to repower. I'd had my YV9 repowered twice now by air-to-air contact. Thirty hours is about the limit for how often that can be done, and the crew were exhausted.

"There's still fighting at the Freeport," she added.

"I know. There's fighting here. We've been fired on twice." I didn't look up from the holotank. "Out of a possible seventeen contacts, we've made six successfully – ah, there; see?"

She leaned over my shoulder. Her black coveralls were crumpled, rank with sweat, as mine were; and there was an unhealthy whiteness to the skin round her eyes. She squinted at the visual image. A multitude of *jath* and *jath-rai*, their shadows cast long on the shifting waters by the rising sun, and here a pinprick of light, and there another, answering: the dot-signals of heliograph messages passing from ship to ship of the fleet.

"And I know it doesn't happen that easily," I said. "Nothing's happened yet. Pramila and the Hexenmeister and I have spoken to, what, a dozen people directly, and maybe ten times that many indirectly. Nothing's happened yet. But it still may."

"Jamison said you had to threaten force to get off one *jath* ship."

Jamison has no damn business to be monitoring our transmissions, I thought. My temper was short; I'd only managed to snatch a few hours' sleep. The time when I could do that and still remain sunnily enthusiastic is long gone.

Cory pinched the bridge of her nose, blinked, and refocused on the holotank images. "You've split up, then?"

"It's safe enough, I think; we're each going in with an armed officer from here. Pramila's on that *jath-rai* – " I keyed an inset that showed the broad-built ship wallowing in a deep swell, some three-quarters of a mile to our rear. "The Hexenmeister is on the larger *jath*, with a group of the Harantish Witchbreed."

Cory shrugged. "Gets to the point where it's all names to me, Lynne. All I want to know is, what preparations are you making for when these ships get to the Melkathi coast? I estimate we've got about sixty hours

424

before we're forced into a decision – do we let these natives fight a hi-tech war without interference?"

"It may not come to that."

She paused, and I looked across at her. Whatever she had been going to say, she visibly changed her mind. "I'd advise you to go back to Kumiel for a few hours, Lynne, you look half dead. *You* have to be in a condition to make decisions."

That green-shadowed cabin had begun to make me feel nausea. From shuttle to *jath*, and from *jath-rai* to shuttle – just how disorientated am I? And Cory's right. I can't be at less than peak efficiency. Not now that we have this final chance. . . .

"Doug Clifford will travel out to meet you," I said, "if you've no objection to working with the government envoy? I've already spoken to him about this."

"You don't seem to have left me much choice."

"Molly Rachel used to tell me I could never trust people to do things as well as I can do them myself – even when I can't do them at all! Cory, we've known each other for six years, I've *never* approved of what you do – do you wonder that I'm concerned, now, after Reshebet?"

The white-haired woman tapped her finger twice on my shoulder: a peremptory gesture.

"Lynne, I'll take that from you when you come up with a better idea of how to handle this."

"Right now this is thistledown, a breath could send it either way."

She frowned. It wasn't disapproval but consideration. I could see the figures and positions ticking up behind her eyes: so many ships on Kumiel, so many at the Freeport, so many in reserve at the orbital station. This many personnel here, that many in the northern continent, that many on the southern continent. . . .

"Lynne, I've been on worlds where the Company's failed. I don't mean a short conflict, deaths, I mean a real failure: the kind of bloody war that drags on for years, for generations, that keeps going by the momentum of its own atrocities, long after all involved have forgotten the original cause. I've always been afraid that I would be responsible, somehow, for one of those catastrophes. The only way I know to avoid it is to stop it before it starts."

Cory eased herself down into the bucket seat, motioning the crew to continue their duties, with a kind of unconscious arrogance. She added thoughtfully, "Having said that, I can't know all the factors involved here. Nor can you, nor can the government envoy. We take decisions blindly and that scares the shit out of me."

Not what she said so much as the weariness in her voice; I thought how Ruric said, *Does your Corazon Mendez think as she did?* I don't have the right to judge.

"I must know what hi-tech fire power these people have. Lynne, Security must have the Ishida girl for debriefing *now*."

"All right," I conceded. Could I do it if I had her in front of me now, dirty and exhausted and still punishing herself for Sethri's death? Well, if she's after suffering, Security will cure her of that. And no need to wonder what I'd do, when really I have no choice. It isn't the *hiyeks* that are important now, I thought, it's Calil's Witchbreed, and Pramila isn't a factor there. . . . . "When the pod picks her up from the *jath-rai*, have a couple of your officers take her up to the orbiter. And keep me informed, Cory, okay?"

Cory leaned over to the comlink: "I'll have one of the F90s pick you up here, en route to Kumiel."

Early morning, and it would still be early when I got to Kumiel. Flight-time between the *hiyek* fleet and the island diminished each time I made the journey. Now it was close on ninety minutes.

"Data-processing facilities are there, Representative," the F90's lieu-tenant said as she left my cabin, indicating a small data-tank set into the wall. I nodded; and after she'd gone, stood for a moment rubbing my forehead. The vibration of the F90's power-hum found a correspondence in the tremor of my hands; eyes and head ached. Metal warrens, these shuttles, and they bring out all my claustrophobic tendencies.

I sat, and keyed in the data that Mehmet Lutaya had passed on to me. WEBcasts from Orthe didn't much interest me – but I want to know how they're reacting at home, I thought.

When I tell the Company home office that Carrick V needs Protected Status, I want *some* idea of what public response on Earth will be.

' *– Ariadne WEB news update, sixteen hundred hours Pacific Standard Time. This is Evan Kodály on 'cast from the main chamber of the House of Delegates in Tokyo –* '

The image in the wall-tank was small, not well-focused. Twelve days, I thought. To get an FTL-drone from Earth to Carrick V. A lot can happen in twelve days. . . .

' *– interview with NuAsia Company's Commercial Delegate, and I asked him his reaction to the escalating sequence of events on Carrick V.*

'*Delegate Chen, you've been making strong protests to the PanOceania delegation here.*'

Squinting into the small 'tank, I made out the overly-familiar features of Wu Chen; a round, baggy face rarely out of the WEBcasts.

'*You have only to look at the evidence of commercial exploitation! The*

PanOceania multicorporate has caused cultural disruption on Carrock V to the degree that a major war is now in progress – a war that their Company has done nothing either to prevent or to stop – '

'Isn't it also true that on Carrick V – ' Kodály's slight stress corrected Chen, and I smiled to myself. *' – on Carrick V, PanOceania has also invested in a substantial Aid Programme?'*

'That's merely camouflage, to disguise thinly the blatant exploitation of an alien culture. In the NuAsia multicorporate, our policy has always been to involve the local population at all levels, to provide a guiding hand, as it were – '

I skipped forward, knowing Wu Chen's 'guiding hand' far too well to want to hear the routine again.

' – news on Trismegistus WEB, Eurotime twelve-midday. Reports are still coming in of casualties in the fighting on the Heart Stars sector world, Carrick V. Nominally, the world is under the authority of the British government, and I spoke to a representative of that government about the actions of the PanOceania multicorporate there.'

' – I cannot stress too strongly our condemnation of the use of active military force – '

Jesus! I thought, and sat up, and keyed back the image. Blond, bearded, and standing against a backdrop of the Department's offices – Stephen Perrault. What the hell are *you* doing as WEBcast representative for the government, I wondered. I'd have to go through his reports when I got back to Kumiel.

' – condemnation of the use of active military force; however, reports have confirmed that the local population has access to hi-tech military equipment themselves. PanOceania have therefore been forced into taking action.'

'Representative Perrault, may I ask whether it's known how the natives of Carrick V got their military equipment?'

'I regret to say that there is evidence that it was illegally supplied to them, by members of the PanOceania multicorporate themselves. I need hardly add that this was not sanctioned by PanOceania's governing board, and I have no doubt that steps have been taken to remedy this. However, my government feels that the damage has already been done.'

'Is your government raising the matter of compensation?'

'Undoubtedly. We also must respond to the public demand for some kind of protected or isolated status for alien cultures, like Carrick V's, that are so susceptible to outside interference.'

"Nice one, Stephen," I muttered. "When it comes to PanOceania, sink 'em with a smile. . . ."

Few of the 'casts added anything to that. I was on the point of skimming through to the end, when one caught my attention. I keyed back and ran it in real-time:

' – *WEB-Taliessin. Public scandal continues to grow in the matter of PanOceania's involvement on the Heart Stars world, Carrick V. This evening, we bring you comment on the multicorporate's military strike on the harbours of the southern continent of that world –* '

Faces flicked past in rapid succession. Public-access hour on the WEBs is usually crowded; but now I sat up and stared at the sheer number of calls coming in. And this is only Taliessin, I thought; Taliessin's not the most extensive WEB – I *must* have a rerun of WEB-Marduk and WEB-Tz'u-hsi. . . .

'*It's terrible. Just terrible. I don't know how we're supposed to accept this –* '
A middle-aged man, with flat brown features that for a heart-stopping moment brought back Molly Rachel; he stared bewildered into the imager, ' – *there are people dead on that world, and we killed them; I don't know how the Company expect us to support them now –* '

Background images stayed the same: some street in a southern-hemisphere city. A group of young men and women crowded round the imager:

'*We want to protest –* '
'*What right do we have to do this?*'
' – *nothing more than a private army! No Company has the right to that. First it's some little world out in the Heart Stars; next it'll be us, you'll see, it'll be us, here –* '

All of them wore multicorporate insignia on their coveralls; I judged them part of some Zealand Company. Looking at those young sallow faces, I felt something that might have been regret: for outrage and indignation that I can't feel that strongly now.

' – *I saw the live 'casts, there were bodies lying in the rubble. What are our people doing there? Why didn't somebody stop them? And it's just going to go on getting worse, more killing –* '

Frozen image: a shabbily-dressed man on some Pacifican city street. For a second I stared at him with hatred, this nameless man; thought, *Suppose you try it, before you criticize?* and then keyed out the recorded WEBcast.

The F90 thrummed, jolted with air turbulence, and I sat back in the bucket seat; aware of the small cabin, of the empty space outside, of the orbiter miles above the surface of the world, of the vast distance between here and Thierry's World; of the light years between me and home – a distance incomprehensible. If Orthe's sun were visible now in Earth's sky, it would shine with the light that shone upon the Golden Empire in the height of its power, five thousand years ago. . . .

Things can be different. The last thing I said to her, before we split up to contact *jath* separately, was, "Is it wise to tell the *hiyeks* they haven't been slaves to Kel Harantish? It's all very well you talking about 'locked into a pattern of survival', but there was nothing involuntary about the Harantish Witchbreed's grip on the canal system."

She grinned, membrane veiling those yellow eyes in amusement.

"Lie in a good cause," she advised. "If I've learned one thing as Hexenmeister, it's that history is what you remember it to be. Right now I'd like Calil's people to remember the peaceful days of the Golden Empire – and if I had a choice," Ruric Hexenmeister said, "I'd wish them to forget Calil bel-Rioch. But we may manage that yet."

The F90 shuttle began its descent to Kumiel Island.

Doug Clifford met me on the makeshift landing field. We walked briskly across the island, on tracks that had not existed until the Company began to use this land; and Carrick's Star rose higher in the east, a white and silver glare. Already hot: the day promised a heatwave.

"You've left the estimable Corazon Mendez overflying the *hiyek* fleet? Isn't that a trifle . . . how shall I put it? Rash?"

Glancing at him, I thought his urbane manner was a mask over exhaustion. "I'd have said it was unavoidable. If it worries you, console yourself with the thought that you'll be on the spot – I've committed you without asking you, Douggie, but I couldn't contact you."

He shot me a sour look. As we were walking, he pointed to the white hull of a government shuttle, grounded near the comlink-centre.

"I've been in Melkathi, and having a problem of contact myself – I know there are upwards of two thousand *hiyek*-Ortheans in Rimnith and Keverilde, but can I speak with any of them? No. I know that there are Harantish in the area, and the same applies. Ride into the burnt area, and it appears deserted."

"And Calil?"

He halted at a crossroads in the trodden earth tracks. Wind from the mainland hardly ruffled that grizzled red hair, silver over the ears; and he paused and surveyed the blue-grey mossgrass and the granite rock, so different from one foggy morning on a heathland *telestre*. . . . One hand strayed up to touch his bandaged eye.

"Who knows where the Harantish Witchbreed go? There are ships moving along the coast all the time. And there's been sporadic fighting between them and ships of the Hundred Thousand." Doug pursed his mouth. "I had hoped to cool that situation down, but it seems unlikely now."

The exhaustion that had attacked me on the F90 was stronger now; I could have fallen asleep standing up. Carrick's Star shone warm on my face. Distantly I heard the sea on the rocks round Kumiel, and the metallic cries of *rashaku-bazur*.

"Will you go out to the fleet? You ought to talk to Ruric, Douggie."

"Seven hundred ships," he said. "Thirty thousand people. Much as I admire Ruric Hexenmeister, I can hardly conceive of her having an effect on them at this late date. Those people are committed. Having said that, of course, I would find it repugnant in the extreme to contemplate leaving any avenue of action unexplored."

"Does that mean you're going?"

To my surprise, he chuckled. "Yes." And then, more soberly: "The government shuttle is powered-up for approximately six hours. I'll do what I can in that time. When can we expect your return?"

Stephen Perrault's reports want looking at; I've had no reports from Thierry about David Osaka and Rashid Akida; I must speak with the *telestre*-Ortheans and find out what they plan to do when the *hiyek* fleet reaches Melkathi. . . . Merrum Firstweek Nineday: we have no more than three days before they do.

And if I continue to rely on stimulants, I'll sleep for six days, not six hours.

"I'll be out with you before noon," I promised; and he nodded curtly, and began to walk towards the government shuttle. I blinked against the white light of that alien sun, and called after him, "Douggie, be careful. I hate to say it, but – go armed."

The next few hours passed in an eyeblink: sleep, a session with the data-tank, and a snatched meal. I conferred with Chandra about evacuating the remaining Commercial personnel up to the orbiter. And I ordered notification, every thirty minutes, of the position of the *hiyek* fleet, and of any change in the local or continental weather patterns.

There were no changes in the hours before noon: the daystarred sky remaining clear, and the wind blowing strongly and steadily out of the south-western quarter of the compass. As Haltern n'ri n'suth Beth'ru-elen said, one summer tempest could end all our problems. . . .

I've been in storms at sea. Less sanguinary than Hal, I can't wish that terror on anyone. But (I thought) I could wish for a force of nature to take this decision out of our hands.

The Desert Coast Ortheans have hi-tech weapons, they have at least one GHD4 beampulser. When they reach the coast of Rimnith and Keverilde, are Cory's ships to fire on them? Or are we to watch *telestre*-Ortheans fight hi-tech with *harur*-blades? Christ! I thought, it's ridiculous, the very idea is both ludicrous and tragic. What can we *do*?

Noon came: I found a pilot for a repowered YV9, and flew westwards across the Inner Sea.

"There," Ruric Hexenmeister said. She indicated the image of the Rimon and Ymirian coastline, bright in the holotank. "To come to Melkathi anywhere north of the Melkathi Sandflats, they must either change course and sail round the Sisters Islands, or else they must risk sailing in amongst them – Ahrentine and Valerah and Perniesse and the rest. Those are dangerous waters, if not known."

"They won't risk it, surely?"

This F90 thrummed, flying the decreasing distance back to Kumiel Island to repower. Somewhere in the night outside, Merrum Firstweek Nineday was turning to Merrum Secondweek Firstday: time ticking on. Coded images in the holotank showed the long scatter of *hiyek* ships, hugging the shelter of the Rimon coast.

"All the Inner Sea is dangerous, if not known," Ruric added. "They'll have *jath* shipmasters who know that, even in summer, to stay this long on open sea is to risk storms. Turn it about: the Sisters Islands are some shelter from that."

My eyes blurred, and I sat back, rubbing at them. Fourteen hours, and this Orthean summer day not yet over; a day spent airborne above *jath* and *jath-rai*. Of a possible nine contacts, seven successful. I thought: I can't judge, any longer, what 'success' might be. . . .

Ruric Hexenmeister leaned back from the holotank, one bare black foot coming up to rest on its rim: high-arched and claw-nailed, and worn with much walking. Her single hand went back to scratch among the roots of her mane.

"I've read their heliograph signals," she mused. "Plain enough. They're using the canal trade-codes. I read dissension between *hiyek* and *hiyek*, dissension between the families and the Harantish Witchbreed. If not," she said, with a crooked smile, "it isn't for lack of trying! Whatever else we're doing, we're giving them something to talk about."

I keyed in figures. "According to this – and I'm not sure I trust it for calculating sailing-ship navigation – the first *jath* will reach that turning point early tomorrow morning. If they *do* go in among the islands – "

"There is Ahrentine *telestre*, and Valerah *telestre*, and the *telestre* Perniesse."

The comlink chimed. I ignored it for the moment: it was likely to be Doug or Cory, on their way back to Kumiel now night was falling.

"We should talk with Nelum Santhil," I said. "With Hal and Cassirur and Bethan, and the rest of the *takshiriye* in Tathcaer."

She raised her head. In that narrow Orlandis face, her yellow eyes glowed; and membrane slid down to cover them, hide some unreadable emotion. With a clinical rationality that was all Hexenmeister, she said, "The Hundred Thousand will not wait long before they send these land-wasters to the Goddess. If the *hiyeks* attack the islands, the islanders will fight. I think it will not matter to them that the Desert Coast brings with it more than winchbows, more than blades – they'll fight. And so we may not have to wait until the *hiyeks* reach Melkathi to see what offworlder weapons your Company gave them."

"Ruric –"

She overrode my protest: "If it's shelter the ships need, then we should hold off. Give the *hiyek* quarrels time to spread. You must tell Nelum Santhil that waiting may do our work for us, and he must tell the island *s'ans*."

"'Our' work?"

She rubbed a hand across her forehead, where the old scar of the exile's brand still puckered that dark flesh.

"Christie, it may be well that I can't be known again in Tathcaer. If I could, I'd be all Orhlandis instead of only a part, all *telestre*, instead of only a part. . . ." Her eyes flicked up to meet mine. "Tethmet will be there when we land, telling me I should go back to Kasabaarde, stay inside the Tower. I believe I'm more use here. I can talk to the *hiyek*-families. But, do you know, even if that were not so, I'd find it hard to stay away from the Hundred Thousand now."

"Will you come into Tathcaer?"

The pale green illumination of the F90's cabin gave her flesh a sickly cast. An ageing Orthean woman, in shirt and britches, the slung *harur*-blades replaced now by a CAS-IV in a belt-holster; still she is more exiled mercenary in her appearance than she is Hexenmeister – even I see that, who share her memories in part. And it is safer, oddly enough, to be recognizably the exiled Ruric Orhlandis than to be recognizably the Hexenmeister of Kasabaarde.

She turned her attention back to the holotank:

"We have a few hours before we know what they'll do. Time to go into Tathcaer, while we're waiting for the morning."

Orthe's summer stars blazed, white and blue and red and gold. That light is brighter than Earth's moonlight, and it shone now on the windowless towers of the Citadel, and the rock of Citadel crag, and the many-coloured mossgrasses that grow in the Stone Garden. Dew pools glimmered. Ornamental waterfalls flashed in the starlight, and the noise of running water was a constant background to the talk. A white *rashaku-bazur* clung with all four claws to a rock spire, beating wide pinions and

432

crying harshly. There was the scent of mossgrass, as the sun's heat faded from the rocks.

"Give you greeting, *t'an*." A male Orthean in Ymirian dress stood as I came down the carved steps beside the waterfall. "What news? Have you used *s'aranthi* weapons?"

At that moment I saw the *T'An Suthai-Telestre*, and so muttered something conciliatory and uninformative, and walked across the garden to Nelum Santhil's table. Here there was a crowd, mostly *s'ans telestre*. Small children scuttled underfoot, and the older *ashiren* brought herb-tea and *kiez*-fruit. When I glanced round to say something to Ruric, I found that she and Tethmet Fenborn had lost themselves in the press of bodies.

"Give you greeting, *t'an* Christie. What news?"

Before I could answer Nelum Santhil, Cassirur looked up from where she sat beside him and said: "The Wellhouse *rashaku* bring word, that the *hiyek* ships lie some forty *seri* west of Perniesse."

Beside the scarlet-maned female sat a hunched male, and he blinked bird-bright eyes and said, "My people tell me they have *s'aranthi* weapons aboard those ships, and that you have felt the use of them."

I took the seat beside Haltern. "Why ask *me* what news? You know as much as I do!"

The remaining person at this table, the stocky female Bethan *T'An* Kyre, grinned broadly at me. "We are not fools, *s'aranthi*."

An *ashiren* put down a bowl of herb-tea on the table before me. These tables are carved from granite slabs. All the Stone Garden is dotted with them, set into hollows, or on slopes, or – as this one – tucked into an alcove under an arch. And all the granite is coated with a thin film of soil, in which grows blue and scarlet and yellow and viridian mossgrass; and which now was hardly visible at all, for the number of Orthean males and females crowded into this small area. Across dark-maned heads, I glimpsed a black coverall: saw it to be Jamison, and guessed, *Cory isn't far away*. Then I saw her, sitting with Doug Clifford at another table, surrounded by *s'ans* who wore Rimon dress.

Nelum Santhil linked six-fingered hands, leaning back from the table. His dark mane was slicked down and his eyes showed a thin rim of white around the black iris: signs of exhaustion. Still, he wore the *T'An Suthai-Telestre*'s authority easier now.

"Have you nothing to add to that, *t'an* Christie?"

"Only questions, *T'An* Santhil. In a few hours the *hiyek* ships will be in the Sisters Islands – or else they'll turn aside, and in a few more hours be within sight of the Melkathi coast. What are you going to do when that happens?"

His dark head turned towards the Ortheans, gathered in voluble groups in that garden.

"You know the Hundred Thousand, *t'an* Christie. It isn't wholly for me, or my *takshiriye*, to say."

Cassirur put down her bowl of herb-tea. "Fight, or wait to kill secretly, that's what I'd say; if not for – no, *t'an* Haltern, I will speak – if not for rumours that go about the city, saying that it is Witchbreed weapons that come with the fleet."

"That may be true, or it may not."

"I've questioned the *t'an* Pathrey Shanataru," Haltern said. His voice was level; it was none the less chilling.

"You haven't – "

"Shanataru is in the Wellhouse," the Earthspeaker Cassirur said, moving that scarlet-maned head briefly to indicate the city below the crag.

Nelum Santhil said, "The truth of it is that we have no one mind among us, to be agreed on what we'll do. Christie, that's been our strength, that if any attack us they face not one enemy but one hundred thousand. Now the *s'ans* and the *takshiriye* quarrel, every *telestre* quarrels with its *s'an*; Morvren Freeport is becoming deserted under attack, but the Melkathi coast has riders travelling towards Rimnith and Keverilde from all over the Hundred Thousand."

I tasted the sour herb-tea. A cool wind began to blow, bringing the sound of the Oranon River, a hundred or so feet below at the foot of Citadel crag. A priest-robed male came to speak with Cassirur, and she got up from the table and moved aside.

I said, "I may have to withdraw Company forces from this area entirely. It's possible the fleet would attack Kumiel Island – "

Nelum Santhil raised a brow. "Even with *s'aranthi* weapons in their hands, *t'an* Christie, I think you overestimate the danger to yourselves."

"Don't be a fool, Santhil." Haltern straightened, glaring at the *T'An Suthai-Telestre* as if he were the same Portmaster of Ales-Kadareth still, caught out in intrigue and stupidity; and I saw amusement on Nelum Santhil's face.

"Foolish, am I?"

"She means to withdraw before provocation can occur. Am I right, *S'aranth*?"

"It would avoid the danger of retaliation, yes."

"And leaves us *harur*-blades to stand against your technology," Bethan remarked sourly.

"Will you fight?"

Direct questions are not much admired in *takshiriye*. All I got in

434

answer was Nelum Santhil's casual wave at the assembled *s'ans*, and his comment: "Some may fight. Some may not. You must ask them. Ask each *s'an* of the *telestres* nearest the fleet, and each man and woman of those *telestres*, and then you might know. If they know."

A female wearing the gold circlet of a *s'an* dropped into Cassirur's vacant seat, six or eight other Rimon-dressed Ortheans with her. She began to harangue Nelum Santhil in thickly-accented Ymirian. Bethan *T'An* Kyre leaned across to join in the argument.

"Walk with me," Haltern Beth'ru-elen invited.

I hesitated. A glance showed me Douggie had been abandoned by the group of Ortheans at his table. He was speaking in a low tone to Corazon Mendez, who frowned. I thought: We've got no real part in these talks now, these are for the Hundred Thousand. . . . And I stood, and took Hal's arm, and followed his lead across a tiny stone bridge, and up mossgrass-covered steps, until we had come almost within the shadow of the Citadel itself.

Small oil lanterns were strung on wires, illuminating what the starlight left shadowed. A tall, thin figure stood up from the nearest table: I recognized the brown robe and sleek black shaven mane of Tethmet Fenborn.

"Where is she?" Hal demanded. I frowned, then realized there was only one *she* he could mean.

The thin Orthean male shrugged. "She could not wait, *shan'tai*. One of the brown-robes here told her that the Empress's Voice is held prisoner in the Wellhouse, and she went to speak with him if she could. She told me to wait, and tell you this."

The old male leaned more heavily on my arm. He nodded, smiling ruefully; and when he did, the old sly Haltern Beth'ru-elen was plain on his face. "*S'aranth*, I had thought you should speak with Pathrey Shanataru again, it seems I am anticipated. Go down. My *l'ri-an* will take you. I'd go myself, but I weary easily."

"Is there any use in my talking to him, Hal?"

"Who knows?" Hal said. "It's this, *S'aranth*, if it's nothing else – it's a way to pass the hours until the *hiyek* ships reach Perniesse. Go now, *S'aranth-te*."

He signalled, and a young fair-maned *ashiren* in Peir-Dadeni robes ran up the steps to us. The child had plump features, and something of the Beth'ru-elen face. I followed it, Tethmet Fenborn walked beside me; and I looked back once to see Hal on that lamp-lit terrace. The elderly male was looking down on the tables in the Stone Garden. I remember thinking, eight years ago, that a night spent studying the configurations of talk among the *takshiriye* on such occasions could teach a lifetime of *telestre* politics. Can it tell him what will happen tomorrow?

The low-roofed chambers of the Citadel were as crowded as the Stone Garden, and Hal's *ashiren* led us through a press of bodies. Warren-like, the Citadel, and all its rooms and galleries were full of *s'ans*, and of males and females from the city, and from the country Wellhouses, and from the ships that had come into Tathcaer harbour from everywhere in the Hundred Thousand. Ortheans in Roehmonder furs jostled me, and stared with fear at Tethmet – they have reason to fear the aboriginals of the Great Fens. I blinked in the oil-lamp light that was reflected back from crystal beads braided down spines, and from jewelled *harur*-blades. Dadeni *marhaz*-riders, shipmasters from Ales-Kadareth, farmers from Rimon and upriver Ymir. . . . The jostling was rough, and deliberate, and I ignored it. No *s'aranthi* will be popular now.

At last we came out into the grounds again, passing *lapuur* with their fronds curled tight against the night air; walking down the zigzag Crown Steps to the Square below. All the city below was invisible, but for a sprinkling of lights – companion-houses, I thought – and ghost-grey images visible in starlight. Voices came distantly on the wind. The midnight bell had long since sounded, but there was still a smell of cooking-fires: Tathcaer more crowded than at Midsummer, even, and sleepless. . . .

"Wait."

I stood still, at the foot of Crown Steps, and checked my wristlink. The holo-image showed easily-read symbols that were heat-sensor readings. Difficult, standing there on cold flagstones, in the heart of the city, to translate those symbols into *jath* and *jath-rai* on the open sea.

"Any change?"

"Negative, Representative. ETA still 09.00 local time."

"Keep me informed." I keyed out. Tethmet's face was expressionless, but the young *l'ri-an* looked up with something that might have been concern or disgust. *Ke* turned, and led us across the Square to the gate of the Wellhouse's courtyard. Those great *ziku*-wood gates were shut.

A hundred and fifty miles to the east, there are Desert Coast Ortheans. On Rimnith and Keverilde. And there are Harantish Witchbreed, and their 'Empress'. . . . *Is Calil there?*

When the view-slot in the great gates opened, I said, "Tell your Earthspeaker I want to interview the *shan'tai* Pathrey Shanataru. He may have information about the murder of the Representative Molly Rachel."

The slot shut again. I had time to feel the cold – Tathcaer's rivers mean the city has that night chill – and to squint up at the massy stars, and to yawn; and then the great gates soundlessly opened, and Cassirur Almadhera appeared.

436

"Give you greeting, *t'an*. You keep odd company."

I glanced over my shoulder at Tethmet, but he didn't speak. "You could say, it keeps me."

"Well, we have another of the Tower's friends with the *shan'tai* Pathrey," the Earthspeaker said. A voice called inside the courtyard, and she glanced back to make a reply, and then said, "I must attend to the *rashaku* messages. The other *telestres* of the Hundred Thousand wish to know what happens here. Come in if you must, *S'aranth*, but don't hinder us."

Once in the courtyard, the great dome of the Wellhouse and the lesser outbuildings blotted out starlight. Tethmet walked without stumbling, but I don't have his night vision: it was some minutes before I recognized the small domed building that Hal's *ashiren* led us to. And are you a prisoner, Pathrey? I was a prisoner here myself, Blaize and Rodion and I; and that other one of our party, the woman Havoth-jair. . . .

"I know the way," I said, entering.

The main, locked room is small. Lamplight now illuminated the dome of brown brick, and the low tables and benches; and shone too on the shabby, plump figure of Pathrey seated at one of the tables, and on the cloaked woman who leaned up against the wall, speaking to him. She glanced up as we were let in, and her mouth below her mask smiled.

"Give you joy of him. *S'aranth*, I can get nothing useful at all." Ruric nodded a greeting to Tethmet.

Rooms without doors. That is what I first thought, in Kel Harantish; and now there is this room, with one arched doorway, and no windows at all. . . . I pulled a bench across and sat down by Pathrey.

"I want to know how Molly Rachel came to be murdered," I said. "*Shan'tai* Pathrey, you were the Empress's Voice; if you didn't actually see it happen, I'm damn sure you know how and why it did. I want to know."

I was conscious that Tethmet had moved aside to speak to the Hexenmeister. The yellow light was oily on the Harantish male's dark skin. He wound his fingers together nervously, and under the sleeve of his robe I saw the edge of a cloth dressing. Hal's people would have questioned him more brutally than I wanted to think about.

"I don't . . . there was no . . ." His head came up. The brown eyes were bright, and it startled me to realize that was anger. "What must I do to convince you of good faith? I rescued your *s'aranthi* envoy Clifford, I told you all I know of *K'Ai* Calil's plans. I expected to be a prisoner, for a time, but the questions never end! First them, and now you."

"*Shan'tai* Pathrey – "

His hand slammed flat on the table. "All I want is to rest!"

I studied him, thinking, *How good a liar are you?* This small, dark male, still in dirty Harantish robes that had gemmed embroidery visible under the mud; sitting now with his head bowed, lank mane falling about his face.

"You brought us into Kel Harantish," I said. "Molly and I; that first day we came to you. Now she's dead and I want to know how it happened. I have to make a report, but that doesn't matter. *I* want to know."

Without looking up, he muttered, "Ask *K'Ai* Calil."

"If I could, I would. Believe me."

At that, he raised his head. There was nothing sleek or mannered about his expression.

"Yes, I'll tell you. *Shan'tai*, I will. She and your other *s'aranthi* were in the city when the Emperor Dannor bel-Kurick was overthrown, and I put them where it seemed best to me, that is, safe out of the fighting. And then, when Dannor had been butchered, and his head hacked off and made the first of many at the foot of the Phoenix throne – then *K'Ai* Calil went to speak with your *shan'tai* Akida and your *shan'tai* Osaka in their captivity, where I had them safe. And then she went on ninth level, where I had put *shan'tai* Rachel, and she spoke with *shan'tai* Rachel."

He stopped, half gasping, and the expression on his face was pure malice.

"I'll tell you. *K'Ai* Calil learned something from the first two that she spoke of with the third of my prisoners. And when I went into the *shan'tai* Rachel's room, the *shan'tai* Rachel was dead. It had been done with a small blade, such as the city's beggar brats carry. I think you were lucky not to find *s'aranthi* dead in the throne room, *shan'tai* Christie."

Calil bel-Rioch, enthroned: little and dirty and brilliant and bad, with the face of a mad child – and yet she's a woman of the Golden, I thought; and whatever she is, the Harantish Witchbreed follow her.

"Why the hell would she do that!"

"You will think that I know," Pathrey Shanataru said, "but I don't. All I can tell you is that I believe it was *K'Ai* Calil who murdered your friend, although I didn't see it done. But I know her."

I went to stand at the door. A breath of cold wind from outside reached me. After a time, I became aware of Ruric beside me.

"Are you all right?" she asked.

"Some of what I saw in Kel Harantish . . . it makes me feel sick to remember it."

The walls muffled sound. Only the pad of bare feet outside, where Earthspeakers were on guard, came to my ears. Did Molly find out from Akida about research at Maherwa – and if she did, *what* did she discover?

And is killing the best way to silence someone? Or was that the psychopath, the woman responsible for the butchery I saw –

"It doesn't get me much further," I said quietly to Ruric. "It doesn't give me proof of anything. I do begin to have an idea, though."

"What?"

"That if I can, at any time, get proof of the person responsible, then I'll have them. If it's Calil herself. Someone'll answer for it."

The dark woman said nothing, and I was grateful; even if such threats are merely bluster, voicing them is a kind of comfort. She stayed beside me, masked and anonymous, while the brown-robe Tethmet put a few desultory questions to Pathrey Shanataru, and got only the briefest answers. My wristlink signalled an hour past midnight. I checked the sensor readings, but there was nothing there I didn't expect to see – *jath* drawing closer to the mainland. And still no change in the weather.

"You might do well to stay away from the *K'Ai* Calil," Ruric Hexenmeister said quietly. "From what you've told me of your experiences at Rakviri *telestre*, you're susceptible."

It's called empathy, I thought sourly. Mention of Rakviri again brought Molly to mind, and I thought of that odd coincidence again: she and Barris and Jaharien dead, and of all of us in that vision, or whatever that experience was, only me left to tell of it. I glanced at Pathrey, seeing even in him (though I couldn't have told you how) some touch of Golden blood.

"I understand them," I said. "And so do you."

Now that I accept them into myself, the Tower's memories don't torment me – and yet, they're still there. Yes, I thought, I understand them: Santhendor'lin-sandru and Zilkezra and the Golden. . . . They fed on death, grew fat on death, glutted on death. Knowing that hour of extinction must come, they felt that knowledge spread back and poison all the hours and years before it, until all life was coloured with this shining darkness. Because extinction is a miracle, they worshipped it. And this is what I have within me now, have had since I came here: visions of that brilliant blackness. Until I can almost see, as Calil sees, how beautiful are all the colours of corruption.

Sleep caught me in the government Residence at Westhill-Ahrentine, an hour before dawn. When I woke, it was to find Douggie bent over the holotank in the centre of the room, intently studying the images. Bleary-eyed, I got off the couch-chair and staggered over to the comlink.

"Nothing of any great import has occurred."

"What? Oh." The light, now that first twilight was passing, shone in at the windows and hurt my eyes. I waited until the first disorientation faded. "Anything from the Citadel? I thought I'd better contact the orbiter through the comlink-booster, so I left the *takshiriye* to it. . . ."

"People are still coming in." He straightened, walked over to the inner door, and called down to the kitchens for herb-tea. On his way back, he added, "The *T'An Suthai-Telestre* wishes to have messengers present here, at the comlinks, so that news of what happens to the fleet will be passed back to him without any loss of time."

"You agreed?"

Douggie brushed ineffectually at his hair. Like me, he'd obviously slept in his clothes.

"I've also notified the WEBcasters on Kumiel Island," he said. "I imagine they'll be linked in to the communications."

The first bowl of herb-tea tasted more sour even than usual, but it sufficed to wake me. The *l'ri-an* in the kitchen would be more interested in news from the Sisters Islands than in cooking, I thought. I went down to tell them they could return to their *telestre*-houses in the city if they wished, and on the way back up met Haltern n'ri n'suth Beth'ru-elen coming in. He leaned part of his weight on his silver-topped *hanelys* cane, and the rest on the arm of Ruric Orhlandis.

"Give you greeting," he said, "from the *T'An Suthai-Telestre*. I have messengers ready to go to the Citadel."

By the time we'd settled him in a couch-chair near the holotank, the dawn bells were ringing across the city. Ruric let her cloak fall, and then pulled off the soft leather mask; and turned her face to the open windows. The early sun shone in upon us.

"We passed the harbour, coming here. All the companion-houses are packed, waiting for news; and there are people all the way up to the signal towers on Westhill-Crown." She abruptly swung round, and gazed into the holotank. Visual image overlaid with heat-sensor readings – I saw her comprehension.

"The leading *jath* and *jath-rai* are here, off Perniesse," Douggie said, with a touch of pedant in his manner; and the hand that indicated the image trembled slightly.

"Soon, then."

"It won't happen all in a minute," I said. I crossed to the comlink, establishing contact with the shuttles overflying the *hiyek* fleet, and spoke with Jamison, who was on an F90. Cory Mendez, whom I'd half expected to find with him, answered my contact from the Kumiel Island base.

Haltern Beth'ru-elen, watching the images as intently as a child does, suddenly exclaimed, "See! They're turning."

I pushed between him and Ruric to get a look at the 'tank. Visual image showed the sea, pearl and grey and pink in the early morning, cut

440

with the hundreds of thread-thin wakes of *jath* and *jath-rai*. An inset-image appeared, and in it would be any ship that had made a significant course change, and *there!* I thought; seeing a metal-hulled *jath* tack across, course slowly changing. . . .

"North?" Ruric said. "Sunmother! not Melkathi, then. Or not now – "

"Look."

Whatever shuttle was sending back this image was flying parallel to the ships, all the strung-out groups and convoys in that great fleet, and now as it approached the leading edge of the fleet I saw one *jath* after another begin to curve away from their previous course. . . .

"It may just be one *hiyek*." Ruric spoke as if she warned herself. "Quarrelled with the other families, perhaps."

"No, look." And I keyed in a closer image, and now the faint blue line in the east became Perniesse; and the *jath* of another group began to move gradually northwards. . . . *Changing course as soon as there's light to see. But what are they going to do?*

To speak of 'the Sisters Islands' puts them in a close group, really they are several dozen miles apart – Ahrentine not even visible in the image that showed the headlands of Perniesse – and surrounded by rocks and shoals, as well as wide and sheltered channels.

A noise broke my concentration. At first I thought it something quiet and close at hand. Then I realized. Through the open window of this *telestre*-house, I was hearing the noise of the crowds up at the top of Westhill, where the heliograph station stood.

Ruric looked up from the images, a fierce grin on her face. "They don't attack."

"They've hardly changed course, never mind got to any island," I said testily.

Minutes ticked past. Four of us with heads bent over the holotank, oblivious of the sun climbing the eastern sky. I spoke quietly with the shuttles, ordering overflights at a higher altitude – almost as if they could scare off this possibility, I thought, amused; and then thought, Possibility of what?

Wind and tide cannot be hurried. Hal shifted on his couch-chair, easing old bones, and muttered, and sent word to one *ashiren* in the courtyard to go to the Citadel, and then returned to staring at the bright miniature ships. I saw Douggie speak into his wristlink, and realized he was talking to one of the WEBcasters on Kumiel. Figures ticked up, inset into the 'tank: thirty per cent of the *hiyek* fleet now committed to a course taking them into the islands. . . .

Ruric Hexenmeister said, "Can you show Perniesse?"

I keyed in a message to a YV9 – and saw the chronometer and blinked:

441

two hours into the morning of Merrum Secondweek Twoday, and it seemed like only minutes. The shuttle acknowledged.

On Perniesse's blue-grey hills, nothing moved but the herds of *marhaz*. Then the data-net detected readings, the image zoomed in; and we had a shaky picture of slate-roofed *telestre* buildings, and Ortheans who ran purposefully. Too distant and too distorted to see what they carried, but I knew it would be *harur*-blades.

Sixty per cent of the *hiyek* fleet now committed to the course, or already passing into the sea that lies between Perniesse and the mainland of the Hundred Thousand. . . .

"They'll never find the islands more unprepared than they are now," Ruric said, "and if they mean to attack, they won't give the island *telestres* time to gather their forces."

In the holotank, the image of a *jath-rai* was momentarily as clear as life. Metal hull, scarred with corrosion; spreading metal sails – and on its crowded decks, *meshabi*-robed Ortheans; some running, some crowding the rails – and then the shuttle's overflight lost the image. In memory I taste salt-bitter lips, feel the swell. The *jath-rai*'s image returned. That's strange, I thought, it looks almost crumpled. . . . And then I realized that the metal sails were sheathing, folding into themselves, and the ship itself sliding to anchor in what must be a shallow, sheltered channel.

Not one of the four of us spoke, as we watched ship after ship fold up its sails and anchor in the lee of Perniesse, and other *jath* sail on to shelter near Ahrentine; no vessel close to shore. Even when the noise from the city outside was at its loudest, none of us spoke. Frightened, in case this should be a chimera, and speaking of it break the spell.

At last, when it seemed that all but the stragglers were moored in the sheltered waters of the Sisters Islands, and messengers had begun to come from the Citadel down to the Residence asking urgently for confirmation, Hal raised his head and looked at Ruric Hexenmeister. She nodded once.

"Not an attack. Not *yet*," she amended hastily. And then grinned at her own caution.

Douggie put his arm tightly round my shoulder. I wiped my face, my hand came away wet. Hal bustled to the window to shout down at his messengers in the courtyard below. The WEBnet blocked, overloaded with transmissions.

That afternoon, as if to mock our fear, a storm blew up from the west, but passed safely south of the Sisters Islands.

PART SEVEN

CHAPTER 35

The Passing of Fire

"The longer it lasts, the longer it *will* last," Haltern n'ri n'suth Beth'ru-elen observed. "If I were *T'An Suthai-Telestre*, however, I confess I should wait some hours before sending an envoy to the islands. . . ."

Nelum Santhil raised his head from a pile of thin parchment scrolls: *rashaku*-carried messages.

"You're not *T'An Suthai-Telestre*," he said cheerfully, "and I choose to send the *T'An* Commander today. If the *T'An* Meduenin is willing to go."

This morning of Merrum Secondweek Threeday was overcast, humid, and a watery sunlight slanted through the slot-windows. The room, like all in the Citadel, had windows facing on to one of the myriad inner courtyards; and I sat on the narrow ledge, impatiently fidgeting. Hal and Nelum Santhil sat among heaps of reports, half of which they consigned to the iron braziers, the other half of which they let clutter the low couch-chairs they sat on. The stone walls made the room chilly.

"Are you willing?" Nelum Santhil persisted.

Blaize Meduenin turned from the room's other window to face the *T'An Suthai-Telestre*. I hadn't known he was back from Morvren Freeport, and I wasn't certain, now, whether I was glad or not. "The fighting in the Freeport has stopped. In the main, because the Free-porters have abandoned Little Morvren and Southernmost to be looted. There's little more I can do there. Yes, I'll go to the islands."

He wore a drab cloak over Rimon shirt and britches, and the fair mane straggled down his spine. *Harur-nilgiri* and *harur-nazari* hung at his belt. Difficult as that scarred face is to read, I thought something was troubling him; and Nelum Santhil paused as if to let him voice it, but the stocky Orthean male remained silent.

"And you, Representative?"

"I want to know what you're going to do about – " I abruptly remembered, *He's Rimnith telestre* and changed what I'd been going to say " – about Melkathi, and the *hiyek* people there."

Hal tutted, and tucked his thin six-fingered hands into his sleeves; and then had to give up his irritation to speak with a young *ashiren* messenger who entered the room. Nelum Santhil shrugged.

"When the Desert Coast fighters have gone, the land may be healed – "

445

"Yes, *when*. It's possible the Empress-in-Exile is there still. I want to know what you're planning."

Nelum Santhil sat back on the low couch-chair, and looked up at me gravely. "May I ask, *t'an* Christie, what business that is of the Company representative?"

To me, he is still the Portmaster of Ales-Kadareth who betrayed SuBannasen and Orhlandis, and both of them in a remarkably inept manner; but years pass and people change, I thought, and he *is* the *T'An Suthai-Telestre*. . . .

"It's our business so long as there are hi-tech weapons in *hiyek* hands, which I suspect there are, in Melkathi. That's all, *T'An* Santhil. Ideally, I want them recovered, or disabled. Failing that, PanOceania will want some reassurance that they're not about to be used."

He nodded thoughtfully. "That must be considered, yes. I'll talk with you later today, *t'an S'aranth*."

As I stood up, plainly dismissed, Blaize Meduenin said, "I'll walk down to the city with you."

There was no opportunity for speech in the crowded grey-stone galleries of the Citadel. Once outside, it was a matter of pushing through the *s'ans* and *t'ans* ascending Crown Steps; and I didn't pause to draw breath until I reached the Square, and looked round for a *skurrai-jasin*.

Here in the shadow of the cliff-wall, that was covered in blue-grey vines, we stood momentarily out of the crowd. A hand grabbed my elbow – as I wrenched free, I realized it was Blaize n'ri n'suth Meduenin, pulling me round to face him; and I left a sharp retort unsaid, seeing the bitterness on that scarred face.

"No word," he said. "Nothing! You can trust Haltern and Nelum Santhil and half your Company, but not *me* – "

"I don't know what – "

He put one claw-nailed finger on my shoulder; it rested heavily there. "I've *seen* her."

Her? And then it made sense.

"For years I've thought that she was dead, that Haltern was her murderer – however indirectly – and now, without warning – "

I shook him off, turning away; seeing nothing but the Square and the crowds and the wall of the Wellhouse courtyard, and not that accusing face. When I was ready, I turned back.

"It's nothing to do with trust. You were in Morvren, it isn't something I could tell you over a comlink."

"No?"

"No! Listen, Meduenin, with all that's been going on here these last few days, you think I've had time to worry about your – your pride?"

The wind blew his fair mane across his scarred face, and he looked away, head momentarily bowed. "If you call it that . . . I suppose . . ."

I have put him on the defensive and done it too easily, *Blaize you're no politician!* It isn't fair to take advantage of honesty: "No, it isn't pride. . . . Anyway, she isn't Ruric now. Or, not only Ruric."

One hand moved to *harur-nazari* hilt, clawed thumb stroking the sweat-stained guard. His blue eyes veiled, cleared, and then he broke into a loud laugh.

"What's *funny*, for God's sake?"

"You, if you think it isn't obvious she has the mark of the Tower on her now. *S'aranth* . . ." Bewilderment replaced humour. "She is the Orhlandis, and she is not. I've spoken with her. . . . If Hal's people didn't kill *amari* Ruric, then I think that, in its own way, the Tower did. That saddens me. But do you remember what I once said to you, *S'aranth*? Now, the Orhlandis is not my rival."

"Rival?"

His eyes deliberately sought mine; blurred with nictitating membrane.

"I won't wait any longer," he said. "You've delayed and delayed, *arykei*, and I have thought the cause Ruric, alive or dead, or one of your Company men; and now I've done with waiting, and will have an answer."

Only one day since the *jath* and *jath-rai* came to anchorage in the Sisters Islands: it seems like a year. If I weren't so tired, I thought, if I weren't so shattered, would I know what to say?

"I wish you'd been here," I said. "When the fleet got to the islands, I wished you were here with me."

The white-mottled scar tissue pulled back as he smiled, and his eyes veiled. Again, he rested his hand on my arm. Easy to feel that swordfighter's strength of his.

"Don't you think this is a mistake?" I asked.

"No, *S'aranth*, I don't."

"I think . . . I think it would be well if they could have been *arykei*: the Blaize Meduenin who was a mercenary assassin, and the Christie who was Christie *S'aranth*. We're not who we were then."

His eyes, level with mine, cleared; and he grinned like a boy. "Delay, delay." And then with Orthean reasonableness, said, "You've known since Morvren. Since Kasabaarde."

Out of all that I could have said, I chose: "You know where in this city to find me."

A bronze *skurrai* drew up a few yards away, and the driver on the *jasin* leaned down to hear my directions. Watery sun shone through sea mist that blurred *telestre*-houses, and made Blaize's pale mane gleam. Easy to

447

give impulse free rein, to touch that shaggy mane, run hands down the line of jaw and chin and shoulder. . . . I stepped back, out of his grasp, and climbed into the *skurrai-jasin*; my hands tingling with that movement.

"Take care," I called. And then had to smile at myself: Blaize is a fighter of forty years' experience, such men are careful. Before the *skurrai-jasin* had crossed the Square, I looked back to see him conferring with two males who wore the crest of the Crown Guard.

The *skurrai*-carriage jolted down narrow passageways. The sky between *telestre*-houses was a ribbon of haze, and damp heat beat back from the pale walls. Through open arches, I saw crowded interior courtyards; and it occurred to me to lean forward and direct the driver to go by way of Guild-Ring, where I could listen to market rumour. A limp exhaustion, together with the heat, made me heavy-eyed. The humidity kept the city's smells trapped: food and herb-tea and the dung of *skurrai* and *marhaz*. And this is where I began my journey, eight years ago; going north into cold Roehmonde, followed all unknown by SuBannasen's assassin. . . . And would she smile to see him *T'An* Commander? Would Rodion have wished it? Rodion Halfgold, who once asked me, *Is he a good arykei?* Yes: but that's not the answer to my own question –

"Christie!"

I started awake, and signalled the driver to halt. We had passed the Guild-Ring's market stalls, and now stood outside one of the companion-houses near the docks. A woman in the mask and brown cloak of Kasabaarde crossed the alley.

"I've heard news from the island *telestres*," Ruric Hexenmeister said. "Are you going back to the Residence? I'll tell you on the way there. Is there profit in talking with Nelum Santhil now? – although if there is," she interrupted herself, scrambling up into the *jasin*, "it'll be the first time in my acquaintance with him!"

"Don't underestimate Nelum. He's got Hal with him, remember."

"I don't forget."

She leaned back into the corner of the *jasin* as it rocked over the unpaved alley. *Ashiren* scattered out of the beast's way. Wisps of sea fog glimmered round the *telestre*-houses' flat roofs, and there was a faint moisture clinging to her black cropped mane. The mask was disturbing in its blankness: the lines of her mouth gave nothing away.

As we came out on to the docks, and the smell of *dekany*-weed and harbour rubbish hit me, she said, "There are times when I like to play that I am only Orhlandis."

The cloak's hood framed that corded neck and lean shoulders; fell down in folds that hid the knotted empty sleeve of her shirt; and I wanted to comfort her – but she is not Orhlandis – or reach her: but the mask is her protection. Still, I wish I could see those yellow eyes.

"What's the *telestre* news?"

"That the Hundred Thousand are safe so long as the *hiyeks* quarrel. Which, they say in the city here, means safe forever." Her smile faded. "I hear rumours of offworld weapons – not used, you understand, but shown, when the island *telestres* have sailed out to parley with the Desert Coast ships. So: and we know there are offworld weapons in Rimnith and Keverilde. . . ."

"It isn't over until it's over."

"It isn't over yet. Christie, I've seen – I remember – too much. It makes me fearful. Are we really going to get out of it this easily?"

"There's Calil's people yet."

The *skurrai*'s pads squished on mud, where fishing boats had spilled their catch that dawn. Wind blew more strongly now, shifting the sea fog. Light danced on the estuary waters. *Rashaku-bazur* wheeled and cried: that cry that is like metal tearing. All the quayside here was lined with *jath* and *jath-rai*, and Ortheans crowded the warehouses and companion-houses and food-booths.

"I want to talk to Douggie and Cory Mendez about this," I said. And then I looked at Ruric: that dark profile, the sharp lines of her alien face. "I'm not sure I'm capable of judging a matter when Calil bel-Rioch is involved. Because of Rakviri, because of Maherwa . . . let's say, because of what I 'remember'. I'd be happier if there was another Company representative here."

"Frightened?"

"Terrified. Ruric, I'll do it because I have to. It's just that . . . do you remember what you said, once? You called offworlders 'Witchbreed'."

The dark face stayed staring ahead. "I remember. It was in the Citadel, when I was made exile."

"Because of what we are, because we're human, I think we understand the Golden Witchbreed better than any Orthean can. And you must know that, because you're Hexenmeister, and you know what I know." I gripped the *jasin*'s rail as we swung away from the harbour, turning up into the alleys of Westhill. "Even Nelum Santhil thinks this is a war for land, that it's because the *hiyek*-families have lived in poverty and now won't live that way any more. The Harantish Witchbreed know different. What am I supposed to say, Ruric? That even if Calil loses the support of the *hiyek*-families, she's still in Melkathi, and she still has her people with her, and she may – she *may* have a weapon that brought about the fall of the Golden Empire."

449

"She may, and she may not. She is not the sanest ruler the Harantish ever had," the Hexenmeister said, and her lips under the mask curved in a smile.

No, I thought. I can't judge Calil. I remember the City Over The Inland Sea, and that was a vision in a dry and dusty land; and I remember what I saw at Rakviri *telestre*, and how those others who saw it are dead, and – all I know is that fear is irrational, and I am irrationally afraid.

Westhill's *telestre*-houses passed by, and the *skurrai* slowed as the hill became steeper. Sunlight gleamed on its shaggy bronze featherpelt, and on the two pairs of cropped and capped horns.

"And even the *hiyeks* are not satisfied," Ruric said, "not yet; that requires negotiation. This is a temporary truce, at best. Christie, I *need* there to be peace here. All else aside, I need to speak with you of what we said before: if offworld science might, given what I have in the Tower, find out some way to cure this world of devastation – to destroy what Calil calls 'ancient light'."

"You've no guarantee that our species can analyse Golden science."

The *skurrai-jasin* drew up outside Westhill-Ahrentine. Through the archway, I saw Doug Clifford in the inner courtyard; he beckoned. As Ruric got down from the carriage, she said, "I want to speak with him, and with you – and, if it can be contrived, with Nelum Santhil, and with some of the *raiku* on the Anzhadi ships."

I have thought it over, and this is only a lull; I have thought it ended, and this is only the beginning of that.

"Perhaps the *shan'tai* Pathrey Shanataru tells the truth," the Orthean woman said. She reached up to pull off her mask as we entered Westhill-Ahrentine, and those yellow eyes in that dark face were bright and exhausted and full of dread. "Perhaps all that *K'Ai* Calil and her people have is a memory of ancient light, and a bluff. If we've ended the fighting here, that's good, but perhaps the real war is only beginning."

Towards noon of the same day, I went out to Kumiel and spoke in person with the WEBcasters there. That kept me busy for several hours. I'd barely finished when Cory Mendez came into the communications-dome, and slumped down in a seat beside me.

"Give me strength!" she said. "Lynne, your idea of a surveillance operation is – extensive, to say the least. Well, we did it. Now I want to know what Security precautions you want from now on, regarding the situation here."

I leaned forward as Ottoway pushed past behind my chair. There was no sign of Chandra Hainzell. Must mean they've been evacuated to the

450

orbiter, I realized. Does that mean the only Company personnel on-world are Security? I guess it does. . . .

"I want to keep a low profile," I said, and then as Ottoway came back and hovered, I glanced up at him. "Yes?"

"There's a real-time contact, Representative. For you, from Thierry's World."

Cory raised a brow; I excused myself, and went to the furthest of the line of holotank comlinks in that temporary dome.

"Christie here."

The image in the tank snowed, cleared. Startled, I was about to speak, but I remembered the thirty-second real-time gap in transmissions from Thierry's World. Plenty of time to recognize that sallow, Pacifican face; the rough blond hair, and the young face now white with illness. David Osaka: the shape of a skull sharply visible in his face.

"Lynne? Am I through? I insisted on notifying you myself. He wouldn't listen to me or the medics – Rashid Akida, that is. He said he had to report in person. I'm sorry I'm not making much sense. I've been under sedation."

"Why is Rashid coming back? Is he fit to travel?"

David stared blankly into the imager: then I saw my words reach him.

"No. The medics say not. It's about the research team's report on Maherwa. He insisted nothing be said on comlink channels."

"David, can you tell me anything?"

Again that pause, then:

"No. I had no clearance for those records. Lynne, I don't know why he's certain it's important. I thought you ought to know he's on his way."

Being used to PanOceania, I translated that without difficulty as: Do nothing until you hear what he has to say. And what is it you won't say on open-channel? I wondered.

"Okay, I have the message. You – no, hold contact, David, please. I want you to report to Security while you're on-line."

In the half-minute before the words reached him, I stood up and called Ottoway over to the holotank.

"David Osaka on Thierry. You wanted a statement about what he saw in Kel Harantish; if he knows anything about Representative Rachel's death. Here."

Calculating when a ship might arrive from Thierry's World occupied my attention, and so Douggie had to call twice before I saw him walking up the track towards the comlink-dome. The daystarred sky behind him was milky blue, blending with the mossgrass of the island; and the wind brought the scent of humid vegetation.

"Are you going back to the city?"

I shrugged. "Came outside for some air, that's all. Douggie, to tell the truth, I don't know *what* to do."

"There may be a valid reason for that," he said, absently dusting his sleeve and glancing back at the mainland. Tathcaer was clearly visible: white *telestre*-houses on the rising slopes. "That reason may be that there's very little any *s'aranthi* – I beg your pardon, any offworlder – can do at this precise moment. Might I suggest we wait until there is?"

"There ought to be a neutral arbitrator between the Desert Coast Ortheans and the Hundred Thousand."

"I believe," he said carefully, "that the fenborn Tethmet and the other person from the Tower are quite capable of fulfilling that role. At least, I understand them to have gone to Perniesse some hours ago with that intention."

Douggie's care was not for what I might hear, I noted with amusement, but for the comlink officers, who were Cory's people. A figure of six hours came into my mind: as well as I could judge real-time elapsing during FTL travel, the earliest at which a ship from Thierry's World could arrive. And that will be about sunset tonight, I thought. Resolutely refusing to speculate. It may be that there's nothing useful at all in the research team's report. . . .

"I intend to put another report through to home office," Doug added. "Lynne, if the situation stabilizes here, I plan to go to Earth in person – yes, I know what you're going to say: it takes time. However, if I'm on the spot, and able to use what connections I do have, I think I have a respectable chance of getting Orthe Protected Status."

"You're telling a Company representative?"

Humour lifted the corner of that precise mouth. He clasped his hands behind his back. There was a confidence about him now, that had been missing (I thought) since Ashiel Wellhouse and Sethri's death.

He said, "I'm telling *you*, Lynne. You've seen public opinion on the WEBcasts. I'm going to push from the government side. You're going to push the Company the same way."

"Am I?" I looked at him. "I'll rephrase that: I am."

His attention focused on some object behind me, and I turned in time to see the WEBcasters Lutaya and Visconti approaching. I felt a hand on my arm.

"If I might offer an unsolicited opinion, I suggest that you take a rest before you fall over, Lynne. We're none of us as young as we were, and speaking for myself, I'm ageing by the minute. I don't like to see you looking so strained."

"I will rest," I agreed. "I've got my own report to make out for home office in Pacifica."

Six hours. And what else will have happened here by then, I thought. We're still so finely balanced I'm half afraid to breathe. . . . And why is nothing happening in Melkathi?

Quite irrelevantly, then, as often happens, I thought of both of them: Douggie . . . and Blaize. I *know* Douggie. I know there is a great deal of the poseur about him, and that the small frightened person we all keep inside ourselves is, in Doug's case, not so frightened at all. And what I don't know I can guess, from common shared backgrounds: country, world, species. What do I really know about the humanoid alien Meduenin?

I know that I feel oddly maternal towards this stocky, scarred man; who has fought thirty years as a mercenary and is in need of no one's protection. Who said feeling follows understanding? The heart moves and we, rationalizing, follow after. I know that Blaize has all of Douggie's self-mocking humour and more, and I know that I see myself through his eyes better than I am.

I was preparing to shuttle up to the orbiter and meet Rashid Akida as he arrived, when my wristlink chimed and summoned me out of the F90. As I walked down the ramp to the earth of the makeshift landing field, a darkness blotted out the sky that was pearly with second twilight, and an orbital shuttle sank down with hardly a whisper of noise. I felt the vibration of its grounding through the soles of my feet. It settled on to Kumiel, towering over the smaller craft.

A beam of light broke from it as the port slid up, yellow against the blue twilight. By the time I'd crossed the hundred yards between me and the shuttle, a small figure had left the ramp and was looking round in disorientation.

"Dr Akida?" *Is* it? I wondered. This gaunt Sino-Indian didn't look like the man I'd seen in Morvren. His coverall hung off him, and there were deep lines in his face. His eyes met mine; I saw him sway.

"Ms Christie? Are you the representative now? It's urgent that I talk with you – under Secure conditions, please. I must insist."

Anywhere on Kumiel, we're recorded; and anywhere in Tathcaer, we're spied on. I almost laughed aloud. You forget what you take for granted. Old training came back to me, and I indicated the track leading down to the shore, half-invisible now in the long twilight.

453

"We'll cross to the city, the government Residence; tell me as we go. Can you walk that far?"

"Of course I . . . if we could go slowly, Ms Christie, yes I can."

Now, with twilight, the blue-grey mossgrass released a fragrance as we trod on the fronds. Rock outcrops caught the last light of Carrick's Star, silver in the west, and the slanting light caught Akida's face, and he looked nearer sixty than forty – *If he collapses, what will you do?* I asked myself, and slowed my pace, and quietly checked my wristlink for a rapid medicall.

At last, when he didn't speak, I said, "Molly Rachel left a message, in Kel Harantish, before she died. She said she found it necessary to destroy all Company records of research in Maherwa. Why is that?"

"To prevent the inhabitants of that settlement somehow hearing of what I'd – what we'd done." He stopped, on a small rise, and gazed down the track to the sea. The waters shifted, restless; the air was just on the borderline between warm and cool. He turned his head, and his gaze was direct:

"Briefly, I and my team established no analysis of the ancient civilization's science. I couldn't begin to hypothesize about the basis of it – something so far in advance of our own Paradox Physics that it makes us seem like children. What we *did* discover is the rate of decay of the area's canal system."

"Decay?"

"To summarize, while the pump and purification systems have been maintained, to a degree, there have been no actual *repairs* to the system for, I would estimate, several hundred years. Estimates are difficult, of course. The *chiruzeth* substance is not at all rewarding to analyse. However, bearing in mind that it is an estimate – "

"You mean the system's running down." Even as I said it, I didn't believe it; that is too shocking a thing to be told, on a summer evening and under a clear sky. The Sino-Indian nodded sharply; and began to walk down the path.

"Molly – the late Representative Rachel needed a good deal of convincing. I wish I had my records, but I assure you: given access to the canal system, the research can be duplicated. She felt it might be dangerous for this to become generally known among the native population."

"But I don't . . ." *believe it,* I thought. I remember how long the Harantish Witchbreed have maintained the canals.

I remember that the Golden Empire did not build only for a day or a year or a century, but for millennia.

454

"Assuming this to be accurate, Dr Akida, what is the rate of decay? How long will the canals continue to function?"

He was quiet, and I could hear the noise of our feet on the earth, and the hiss of the surf. He put lank black hair back from his forehead, wiping away sweat. In pain, I realized; Christ, girl, don't bait him when he's doing this to bring the news personally!

"You push me for definite answers, Ms Christie, and I have only hypothetical estimates. Given that my assumptions are correct, I would say between five hundred and eight hundred years, Earth standard."

A cool wind blew off the sea, and flared the pitch torches being lit by the ferry, down on the shingle. It brought the sound of voices. Across the water, lights still showed on the island-city; and a *rashaku-bazur* glided silently within a yard of us, and I started violently at that white apparition. Rashid Akida put out a hand and muttered something profane.

"I'm not completely divorced from the world," he said suddenly. "Molly Rachel knew how much social and cultural shock something like this can cause, and *I* know, and I've no desire to cause it, believe me. That's why I insist on Security. Do you seriously think that, if I didn't appreciate that fully, I would have allowed Ms Rachel to destroy *all trace* of five months' research?"

"I – no, I'm sorry; I didn't see that."

"That's five months of my career, of my life. From what I hear, the chances of a research team getting back to that continent are negligible. No, I don't take this lightly."

Chastened, I put out a hand to help him over the shingle. We came down to the edge of the sea, and a *jath-rai* drawn up to the tiny dock. And then the implications hit me, and I stopped dead. Akida looked back at me with irritation.

"The old civilization, their science – you *can't* analyse it?"

He wiped his forehead again. When he felt in his belt-pouch for painkillers, I could see that his fingers were shaking. He said, "Negatives are impossible to prove. All I can say is, that with the full resources of Earth's data-net at our disposal, we've failed to comprehend any of it on more than a basic cause and effect level – no, not even that. I don't understand what the cause might be of any given effect. I know the *chiruzeth* canal system somehow circulates pure water, but I don't know *how*. I have artifacts that perform actions, but what their *function* is – "
He stopped for breath.

It was as if some knot untied inside me: all I could do was stand on that twilight beach, half deafened by waves, tasting the alien salts of that alien sea on my lips, and think: *A synthesis of Earth and Golden technology, is it? Calil, you're bluffing. You don't have the knowledge, there's been nowhere to get it from!*

"We'll cross to the city," I said, and hailed the ferry crew. When I recognized one of the younger Ortheans as Beth'ru-elen *telestre*, I realized I had a messenger. "Dr Akida, there are people we have to see."

All exhaustion vanished: I could have raised the *jath-rai* ferry's sails myself. Akida slumped down on a bench, but I walked up and down on the swaying deck, going to the rail to look first at Tathcaer harbour as we approached, then at Kumiel, vanishing into blue darkness. Brilliant clusters of stars began to come out in the high dome of the sky. I used my wristlink for what calls I could, spoke with the Beth'ru-elen *ashiren* to send *kir* to the Citadel; and then returned to gripping the polished *ziku* rail, feeling the seaspray cold on my face.

Momentarily, I thought *artifacts that perform functions* and my heart stopped: who knows what relics might survive in Kel Harantish, that treasure-junkheap of the world? Then relief rushed over me. If a weapon was found, I thought, it would have been used before now. The only reason we believe the claim was that possibility that Earth science might restore that lost knowledge. And that possibility's gone. If they can't restore the canal system, I'm damned if I believe they can have Witchbreed weapons!

The *jath-rai* dipped, meeting the turbulence of sunset tide in the Oranon's estuary. Cold seawater soaked my arm. I stood back from the rail as we tacked across the expanse of water that becomes Tathcaer's harbour, gazing up at the dark shadows of Westhill and Easthill against the starry sky.

Rashid Akida's voice came from behind me: "I'm afraid, if the situation remains thus, that this world is of correspondingly less value to the Company."

"Is it likely to change – is a breakthrough still possible?"

His voice sounded weary. "Breakthroughs in understanding are always possible. I should like to compare data on Golden science with that on other Heart Stars and Home Stars worlds. That would mean a five or ten years' research project, and I doubt the Company will fund that now."

I turned to watch us dock, so that he shouldn't see me smile. Of less value to the Company. Dear me, I thought, what a pity. And yet if I do pity anyone, it's Rashid Akida.

The Beth'ru-elen child scuttled off through the crowd on the quay, heading for the Citadel. It was an easy walk up to Westhill-Ahrentine, but none the less I hired a *skurrai-jasin*; and came to the *telestre*-house shortly after full night. The sky cleared, the stars blazed. *L'ri-an* opened the barred tunnel-entrance to us, and I helped Akida up the steps and

456

into the upper-storey rooms; meeting the stares of first Tethmet Fenborn, then Blaize n'ri n'suth Meduenin, and then – I was equally startled – the *shan'tai* Hildrindi of *hiyek*-Anzhadi.

"I've tried to get in touch with Ruric, and Hal, and the *T'An Suthai-Telestre*," I said. "Douggie and Commander Mendez will be here as soon as they can – it's all right, Blaize, it isn't as dramatic as it looks; Rashid, I've also requested a medic. . . ." I relinquished Akida's weight on to Blaize, as the Orthean male helped him to a couch-chair.

Tethmet blinked dark eyes. "She is at the Wellhouse, with the Witchbreed."

I mentally translated that as *Ruric* and *Pathrey Shanataru* respectively. I crossed the room, checking holotank and comlink; and then became aware that the pale-maned Desert Coast male was watching me with a wry amusement. Hildrindi-*keretne* said, "I will go, if you wish, *shan'tai* Christie, but I am curious."

"I'll let you know if you should go in a minute, *shan'tai*."

Blaize stood up from bending over Rashid Akida. *Harur*-blades rang a dissonance. The Meduenin was still in clothes soaked to the knee with seawater, and I wondered how matters had gone in the *hiyek* fleet. He pushed back yellow mane from his scarred cheek, and looked at me, puzzled.

"All the technology of the Company, and you bring your business in person? Or is that necessary? Christie, what in Her name – ?"

I took his hands in mine. They were dry, warm; with that temperature just subtly different from the human.

"I'll tell you," I said. "If what I've heard just now is true, we're safe."

CHAPTER 36

That Bright Shadow

Westhill-Ahrentine's crowded upper chambers grew hot, and smelled – or stank – of *kazsis*-vine, and herb-tea, and human sweat.

"I'll tell you what makes it credible," Corazon Mendez said, leaning her hip back against the edge of the comlink console. "My people have been certain Rachel and Osaka and Akida were attacked for the same reason. Now it makes sense. To keep news of the technology fraud from getting out of the Kel Harantish settlement."

Oh, it 'makes sense', does it; Molly's death and their pain? Christ, I'm glad of that!

"Cory, you – " But the comlink's chime interrupted me. "Yes. Christie here."

"Kumiel base, Representative. Lieutenant Ottoway wants to know if you want day and night surveillance kept up over the Rimnith–Keverilde area."

"Yes, I do – "

Cory leaned down to the pick-up: "Downgrade it one level. Tell Ottoway he'll need the YV9s to keep up surveillance over the sea fleet. There'll be considerable movement there over the next four days: I want it watched."

"Acknowledged; will do, Commander Mendez."

No, I thought. No. This is not the time to quarrel with Cory Mendez. Or anyone else, for that matter.

A thin ceramic bowl of *siir*-wine stood on the console-top, and I reached for it; sipping the viridian liquid and welcoming its bite. Corazon Mendez pushed herself upright, weight on her wrist. The thick silver rings on her fingers clicked against the console.

And what *are* we going to do about Rimnith and Keverilde, and the guerrilla fighters in Melkathi?

This small chamber was crowded: Rashid on one of the couch-chairs, with Kennaway, the black medic I'd last seen up on the orbiter; Doug Clifford in deep conversation with the Visconti woman from WEB-Trismegistus – all of them seeming gross and clumsy beside the frail figure of Haltern Beth'ru-elen, and the two delicate *ashiren* who ran his errands. Through the bead-curtain, in the other room, I could see the *shan'tai* Hildrindi talking to Bethan *T'An* Kyre; and both of them being

458

watched by the silent Nelum Santhil. *How did this place come to be neutral ground?* And then I thought of the comlink under my elbow, the data-tank; and realized *speed of communication*.

The bead-curtain on the outer door clashed back, pushed aside by a fair-maned male and a dark female, both in the shabbiest of Orthean dress; who were, respectively, *T'An* Commander of the Hundred Thousand and Hexenmeister of the Brown Tower. . . . Sunlight shone in: this morning far advanced. Blaize nodded a brief acknowledgement, on his way through.

"I've spoken to the Peir-Dadeni *s'ans*, they'll let the fleet travel up the Ai River, but it must be done in small groups – " His voice became muffled as he came up with Nelum Santhil, and spoke to the *T'An Suthai-Telestre* in that familiar accented Rimon.

Ruric, bowing with a studied formality, said to Cory Mendez, "Forgive me, I must take the Representative from you for a short time."

I took the hint instantly, and followed Ruric back outside. A table in the inner courtyard had been set with a meal, and we walked down the steps and seated ourselves there. The morning sun was warm, shining on the red *ziku* and the pale sandstone. Haze put a faint bloom on the morning: soft blue.

"I can't spare long," I said. To be truthful, I could have sat on that wooden bench and gone off to sleep. Avoiding that, I took a drink of the herb-tea on the table; and leaned back and studied the dark Orthean female. "Not masked?"

She chuckled. Lines showed in the fine-grained black skin round her eyes. "Officially, I'm not here. Unofficially, there are still those who know me – having been up at the Citadel, that's unavoidable. Khassiye Reihalyn, I beg his pardon, Khassiye n'ri n'suth Andrethe – you remember him? – was appalled. But there seem to be people from Melkathi who still have a kindness towards me." She shook her head; smiled. "Strange."

"No, not really. What about . . ." I looked at the scar on her forehead.

"Truly, yes, I should find myself in the Citadel's prison. Or else the lesser penalty, death. Maybe it's that much is forgiven someone wearing the robes of the Brown Tower. And that," she said, "is what I'd speak with you for, *S'aranth*. My Tethmet reminds me constantly that I shouldn't be outside Kasabaarde, and I begin to think I should not; so I've come to beg a favour of you, and that's a journey in one of your shuttlecraft."

"Of course."

She turned her head to look across the courtyard, through the entrance archway to the alley outside. The shadow of *ziku* dappled her dark face.

Light fell on that narrow jaw, the fine line of her mouth and chin; left her eyes in shadow, citrine-bright.

"When will you leave?"

She smiled. There was nothing of Orhlandis in it; it was an expression I have seen before, in a far southern city, on the face of an old male Orthean, in the Brown Tower. *I hardly recognize her*, I thought. *No, no need for Ruric Hexenmeister to go masked in Tathcaer; who would know her?*

"A day or so," she said. "Christie, I dare not stay longer than that. If I did, I couldn't leave."

Humid heat brought out sweat on my face, under my arms; and I leaned back, thinking *why is there always an ache somewhere?* and *thirty-eight isn't old.* The haze of the morning was creeping down to blur the flat white roofs of *telestre*-houses, and hide the distant view of the harbour at the bottom of Westhill.

And Molly was, what, not quite thirty?

I looked up at the upper-storey windows, hearing voices, but not able to see faces. Doug Clifford, and the Akida: both mauled by this world. And Molly Rachel not going home at all, unless it's in coldfreeze; and that (as we used to call it in the Service) is the short way home to Earth, shipped back faster than living tissue can stand.

Flagstones gritted dusty underfoot, and I leaned forward to reach the jug of herb-tea, and was suddenly conscious of how far, how very far, this hazy courtyard is from the acid heat of the Desert Coast. . . . *Have we really done that? Started a war and then stopped it? No: we were only the pebble that triggered an avalanche, and avalanches can be diverted, but – at a cost?*

That's not for me to judge; if there was a price, it wasn't me who paid it. And we will never know, I thought, all that has happened on Orthe in this last half-year. How many lives have changed, on the canals, in the *siiran*. What hurt it is, when you are Rimnith or Keverilde, and smoke darkens the sky. . . . What deaths have happened, in cities without walls, in rooms without doors.

"One more thing." Ruric's voice broke into my thoughts. "Pathrey Shanataru comes back with me to the Tower. He being closest to the bel-Rioch child, I wish to know what he knows. You're aware I can discover more than you offworlders."

I met her gaze, thinking, *Havoth-jair.*

"Last time you asked me that, I consented. You *are* Hexenmeister, aren't you?"

Her long fingers rubbed at the stump of her amputated arm as if it pained her.

"Christie, I said then and I say now: the Tower *must* stand. Any danger to it is a danger to Orthe. I want to know if Calil bel-Rioch heard somehow of that devastation she calls 'ancient light', and if she knows that it isn't ended but only held back. . . ." She blinked fine membrane down over honey-yellow eyes. "And if she heard it, I must know where, and stop it being heard again. Or if she remembers, I want to know how it is that a Golden-blood has past memories. You *know* I have to do this. For our own safety."

"Will the Wellhouse let you take him? Sorry, no. That's stupid of me. When did the Wellhouses ever refuse the Brown Tower?"

The bells for mid-morning rang across Westhill, muffled a little by the sea mist. Small *rashaku* soared up from the flat roof of the *telestre*-house. When the bells ceased, they gave way to a silence in which only the humming of *kekri*-flies could be heard.

"I'll let you have the transport," I said.

Such a reward for betrayal, I thought. To leave Calil bel-Rioch, to bring valuable information here, to be imprisoned in the Wellhouse; and now to be taken south and have one's mind and memories ripped open. . . . Pathrey, Pathrey – and I can't stop the Hexenmeister doing it, because I, also, remember; and know that it's necessary.

And then I sipped herb-tea, and with an Orthean black humour thought: You wanted to help us, Pathrey; you'll be more help than you intended. And who was it told me there's no justice? *Nobody* gets what they deserve, not you, and not Molly Rachel, that's for sure.

Ruric leaned back, cupping a bowl of herb-tea in her single hand. Though she still looked towards the archway, her gaze seemed turned inward. She said, "A day, or two. Nelum Santhil doesn't fully trust the *hiyeks*, I think, and the past has given him good reason not to, but still, we can't falter at this last stage. It should end well for the Coast, as well as the Hundred Thousand. If there's a way it can be done, I'd have it end well for Kel Harantish."

I said, "And for Earth?"

She grinned at me then, raising her bowl in a mocking salute. "And for Earth, too."

The comlink dragged me up from a heavy sleep in the early hours of Merrum Secondweek Fourday, the following day.

I pushed back the *chirith-goyen* sleeping-cloths and sat up, half-dazed. Westhill-Ahrentine's rooms are lit at night with *kiez*-oil lanterns, and the yellow light shone on rumpled clothes and my discarded coverall, and on the half-uncovered back of Blaize Meduenin beside me: that line of naked shoulder and hip and thigh, made subtly different by alien

461

musculature, and the tangled roots of a yellow mane. His body warm, dry, against my skin – and then he rolled over, coming awake with less than a mercenary fighter's swiftness.

"Sunmother! what – ?"

"Jesus, it's an *alert*."

I staggered through to the next room, pulling on my coverall, and slapped the acknowledge key on the comlink console. Blaize, behind me, grunted as he banged against the edge of the holotank; and I saw that instinct had made him, all oblivious, catch up *harur-nilgiri* before all else. *Who's here?* I wondered: a reasonable question considering the activity in Westhill-Ahrentine the last two days, *Nelum and Hal at the Citadel; where's Douggie?* –

The wail of the alert cut out. Ottoway's image appeared in the comlink 'tank.

"What the fuck is going on?"

Ottoway vanished, abruptly replaced by Corazon Mendez: "Lynne, get back here – I'll send a 'thopter in now to pick you up."

"What's happening?"

The white-haired woman turned her head away, speaking to someone out of comlink range; then turned back: "Is Doug Clifford with you?"

"No, he's with the *takshiriye* in the Citadel. Cory, what the hell – "

"We're getting sensor readings from the sea vessels in the islands, your *hiyek*-ships, Lynne; they're moving."

The bead curtain rattled, and Blaize came back dressed and pulling on *harur*-blade harness. He went to the head of the inner stairs, calling, and a wide-eyed *ashiren* came up from the kitchens.

"Send word to the Citadel, *arykei-te*?" he said. "The child can find Clifford. What message?"

"I don't know, I don't understand – Cory, those ships are going to move. They've got to find safe moorings, reprovision before they can go north. What's the problem?"

"They've been moving for twenty minutes now, and we're getting readings consistent with weapons power-up. Whatever they've got on those tubs, Lynne, they're ready to use it; and goddammit, you ought to be here, there has to be a decision taken about what action we'll take!"

"What course – never mind: I've got it."

Some moments are frozen, out of time, quite separate from life. Now in this lamp-lit room, among heaped parchments and print-outs, night pressing against the windows; *now* is one of those moments. Blaize with one warm hand resting on my shoulder as he leans over the holotank, its light harsh on his intent, scarred face. And the child-messenger, ten or eleven years old, with great dark eyes in a triangular face; padding across the *ziku*-wood floor to peer into the holotank, claw-nailed hands gripping the edge, scarlet mane rooting down its spine. . . .

In the holotank, bright images: the firefly-specks that are heat-sensor readings of *jath* ships sailing out from the shelter of the Sisters Islands. Blue lines that are projected course estimates, and more than two hundred and thirty vessels are moving, and the course estimates are east: all of them east, towards the sunrise and Melkathi.

" 'Power-up'?"

"There," I said. "Satellites wouldn't pick up CAS weaponry, but those are beampulsers; see, there. . . . Christ Jesus, what are they *doing*? Cory's panicking – no, no she's not – " I keyed repeat on the comlink. "Where the hell is Doug, why doesn't he answer?"

Blaize's calloused hand tightened, released. "How long will it be until your craft comes from Kumiel?"

"A 'thopter? Ten minutes or so – no, wait. Cory," I turned back to the comlink, "I'll want the 'thopter for local transport here. I'll keep in real-time contact with you, but we need to know what the response *here* will be. As soon as the 'thopter gets here, I'm going up to the Citadel. We can't take a decision until we see what's happening."

"Acknowledge."

The contact snapped to relay, and I keyed it into my wristlink.

"Christie."

The *ziku*-wood floor was hard under my bare feet. I blinked, still sick with the suddenness of that waking; and reached out to Blaize. The child gazed at us with silent curiosity, *s'aranthi* and Orthean not often seen together. After a few seconds Blaize broke away, and said, "Go to the Citadel. I'll go up to Westhill-fort; I must see the Crown Guard."

"Come to the Citadel first."

He hesitated, and then nodded; and went through into the further room, and came back with two cloaks, and with my boots, and with the CAS-IV stungun in its holster. I belted it on with fingers that shook.

"*T'an*," said the child, puzzled (and I realized we had been speaking Sino-Anglic, both of us), "what's happening? What shall we do?"

Blaize said, "Wake the house, and warn them that a ship-of-the-air will come, and that they should wake other *telestre*-houses here; it may be nothing, but it is better to be ready."

The child's running footsteps faded, clattering down the inner stairs. I looked at Blaize, that scarred face that was now blank with calculation. As at Northfast, I thought, You've gone where I can't go – where I hope never to be.

"Mother of the Wells," he said; and then the membrane slid back from those pale blue, whiteless eyes. "They're fools if they do this."

463

A muffled roar grew in volume, rattling the windows in their sockets. The door's bead-curtain lashed inward. The room was filled with the intermittent flash of the 'thopter's landing-lights; descending down into the inner courtyard. The noise was too loud to shout over. I gestured, and with Blaize behind me, ran down into the courtyard and scrambled up into the hovering 'thopter, half-blind with dust raised by its blades.

As he fell into the seat, pressed against me by upward acceleration, I put my mouth close to his ear. "If they do what? Fools if they do what?"

Blaize Meduenin said, "If they attack Tathcaer."

So much confusion on Citadel crag: I didn't think even the landing of an ornithopter could get the guards' attention. Cory's pilot put the machine down near the top of Crown Steps, on a mossgrass lawn between night-curled *lapuur*. While Blaize scrambled out, I keyed an automatic acknowledgement back to Kumiel, and then followed him: staring up at the multi-towered Citadel, hearing shouts, seeing messengers rushing to and fro between buildings; and then – as we came to one of the main entrances – a voice hailed me in Anglic:

"Lynne! Have you contacted your people? I can't get through to the Residence."

"There's no one there now. Yes; Douggie, we've got to talk."

I saw a frown on Doug's face, that lasted for only a second. *Blaize*, I realized. Then Doug glanced past both of us at the 'thopter, idling now; raised his eyebrows, and said, "The *T'An Suthai-Telestre* has messengers going out for you, and for the *T'An* Commander. We'd better find him."

It's those ships out there we have to contact, I thought. The Desert Coast families . . .

How?

As if he read my mind, Douggie stopped under the archway-entrance to the Citadel. "I believe some kind of observation may be in order. Lynne, if I could borrow your 'thopter for half an hour: I want to get to my shuttle on Kumiel."

"You're not thinking of overflying those ships – "

"One might make a voicecast contact."

Two Orthean males in Crown Guard uniform pushed between us, and Blaize called them back; stepping to one side to speak with them urgently and concisely. Doug's gaze followed him. That prim mouth quirked a little, and he looked at me, but said nothing. Two *s'aranthi* among so many Ortheans . . . Doug checked his own wristlink again, and his face cleared.

"Kumiel are answering. Lynne, I'll tell the pilot to come back here, as soon as he's flown me to the island."

"If you overfly, stay out of range. The *hiyek* ships fired on us before."
I shivered. The wind began to blow cold, and though the east was still
dark that meant first twilight wasn't far away. Starlight was dimming.
Voices of messengers and guards rang in the Citadel's cold stone walls.

"I imagine I'll be back here within two hours or so," Doug said.
"Convey my apologies to the *T'An Suthai-Telestre*."

He turned and walked hurriedly away from the arch, across the dew-
soaked mossgrass, and I saw him duck under the 'thopter's idling blades
and speak with the pilot, and then climb up into the cabin. A siren-blast
split the night air. Two or three Ortheans close by moved rapidly back,
and the 'thopter lifted, curving away off Citadel crag and out over the
city.

Blaize appeared beside me. "I'll be with you as soon as I've put this
troop in order. Tell *T'An* Santhil I'm setting up heliograph-links between
here and the forts on Easthill and Westhill. Riders aren't fast enough.
Send word if you need me, *arykei-te*."

I touched the comlink fastened to his broad wrist. "Send word if you
hear anything before I do."

Hardly minutes that we stood there: still, a dull grey light was growing
round us. First twilight passing into dawn. We parted, and I went into
the Citadel's low-roofed interlocking rooms. The press of the crowd was
even greater here. I caught sight of a male in Wellhouse robes, and began
to push through towards him. Then, bright against the pale plaster walls,
there was the scarlet mane of Cassirur Almadhera; and I forced my way
through to the Earthspeaker's side.

"Where are the *takshiriye*? Who's here?"

She held a thin strip of paper in those brown, six-fingered hands. A
rashaku message? When she looked up from reading it, her face was
grave. "Give you greeting, Christie. The *T'An Suthai-Telestre* is in the
north tower. I'll accompany you there. I fear . . ."

Cassirur said no more, but drew her slit-backed green robe closely
about her, and pushed hurriedly between a group of *s'ans* in Roehmonde
dress. I followed. She went unerringly to lesser-used rooms, and then
out into a courtyard surrounded on all five sides by high walls, and
crossed to a flight of outside steps. I felt the cold wind. The arch of the
sky was grey, paling to white; the highest pinnacles of this Citadel just
touched with a yellow light.

I lifted my wrist, about to key in a contact to the Kumiel Island base.
Before I could do that, the wristlink suddenly emitted a high-pitched
squeal.

"*S'aranth*, what – ?" Cassirur stopped with her foot on the bottom
step.

465

"I don't know. I – *Jesus Christ!*" I ripped the wristlink off, dropping it on the stone; and the sound rose to a pitch and then shattered: the casing split with a sharp crack. That gunshot-sound echoed back from high walls. Cassirur Almadhera frowned. I knew then what it was: for a minute the implications silenced me. Then: "Warn the people here. Cassirur, let's move; that means – "

She said, "I don't understand. You can't speak with your people?"

Blaize, I thought. And then: What's happening to Doug, now? And Kumiel – Christ, what are they doing on Kumiel; what will Cory do!

Cassirur's urgent questions went by me unheeded, I could only stand there, in that deserted courtyard, watching the light of the unseen rising sun gild the high walls; watching and waiting, and – *there*. A sound in the distance, a hollow noise. So very small, for what it is. Another followed, and another; and the red-maned Orthean female turned her head, listening.

I bent down and picked up the useless wristlink and put it in my belt-pouch.

"Pulseblocker," I said, not caring that she wouldn't understand. "Oh, damn Pramila Ishida. Her and Sethri and all the others. . . . They've got a transmission-blocker on one of those ships. A CAS-II. That's done us, that's finished us. . . ." I looked at Cassirur. "That's *all* communications out. Ship-to-ship. Ship-to-base. Base-to-orbiter. We're isolated. I can't talk with Cory's people – hell, they can't talk with the shuttles that are already on surveillance – Christ, what a mess!"

That hollow noise came again. Small and soft: only frightening because of how distant it must be, and so how devastating at its source. . . .

Cassirur Almadhera pushed the red mane back from her face, intently listening. Then she turned back to the steps. "Come. I'll hear by *rashaku*. By heliograph, when it's light. We're not in ignorance, *S'aranth*. Come."

The attack's begun, but where? What's happening? Is it a few ships, is it all of them, is it only here, is it – *what's happening?* We should have guessed they'd have transmission-blockers; if I didn't, Cory should have; what we could have done – what could we have done? What can we do *now?*

Across the six-mile distance between the Citadel and the harbour comes, faintly, the sounds of beampulser and projectile fire.

A white fog clung to the land. It shrouded the river on the city's eastern side, blurring the line of the Ymirian hills, far to the sunrise. And it hung in the alleyways, between the *telestre*-houses, so that I could see only a glimpse of flat roofs below. That and the gilded dome of the

Wellhouse, and running figures in the Square. . . . Almost dawn: river fog turning from grey to white to gold.

"'. . . attack on harbour'." Nelum Santhil Rimnith turned away as the heliograph-spark ceased to flash. "Christie? Give you greeting; I've no time for *s'aranthi* now, unless you've news?"

The lookout post was no more than a flat stretch of the Citadel crag's rock. A low wall had been built on the edge, so that no one could fall down the cliff that went sheer, vine-covered, down to the Square. A handful of Ortheans stood on this pale rock, gazing south over the city towards Easthill, on which the heliograph lately ceased; tall and braided-maned and richly robed – the *T'Ans* of the Hundred Thousand.

"Only that our communications are cut," I said.

He nodded once, and his eyes veiled. Without another word, he gestured a young male to him; and as I watched them speaking I thought, *Yes, you know what it means.*

I put both hands on the low wall to steady myself. The pale stone felt cold. Across the fog-shrouded city, the two hills were faint grey lines on the horizon. A brief flash of light there drew my gaze. Two more followed: the *crack* echoed up to us minutes later. I squinted, the sun in my eyes – and realized, that warmth on my cheek, that the sun was rising above the fog: Carrick's Star burning silver, acid-white. And saw also that pale specks caught the light high above. Peace Force shuttles. Not in cruise-patterns, but criss-crossing the area at random. *What will they do when they see –*

See the attack?

Something wrong with the silhouette of Easthill, Easthill where I once had my envoy's Residence – and then I made out that the line of the hilltop was jagged, not smooth. The whine of CAS-weapon leakage reached my ears, and I thought, *At this distance?* and *I should do something* and *What?*

"*S'aranth*, you shouldn't be here," a worried voice said; and Haltern n'ri n'suth Beth'ru-elen came to stand at the wall beside me, leaning heavily on his *hanelys* cane. "You can be of no use; go."

"Hal – "

"Why are they doing this?" He gripped my arm, little strength in that thin six-fingered hand. "Christie, I never thought I should see this!" He raised his head. "What will your people do now?"

One of the *s'ans* a few yards further along the cliff cried out. As he pointed down into the city, a Wellhouse male came up with a *rashaku* message; and I leaned out from the wall and stared into the distance – and there: firing to the west side of the city, flashes of light, and now a plume of dust going up into the morning sunlight.

Haltern said, "Ferries. Ferries and bridges. They will send their *jath-rai* upriver to destroy the bridges!"

An answering flare and *crack!* drowned out his words. Down in the fog, still blotting out the eastern-side river, red and yellow flame billowed up: a black pall rising. Sun glinted on metal sails. *Jath-rai. Jath-rai* and the sunrise tide, I thought stupidly, and: why are they blasting the bridges?

The *T'An Suthai-Telestre* Nelum Santhil strode away, back towards the walls and arches of the Citadel, half the Ortheans going with him. I turned, would have spoken, thought: What can I say? A male in Wellhouse robes padded across the pale rock towards us.

"*T'an S'aranth. T'an* Beth'ru-elen. Will you come? We are to get all who may leave away from the city, while that can still be done." His eyes veiled, as the sound came of distant explosions. "If you will come, come now."

"Hal . . ."

He looked up at me, the morning light sharp on his lined face and wisp of white mane. Those harassed blue eyes had the clarity of a child's. The city lay below and beyond him, mist rising as the sun burned it off, and, rising with it, the smoke-palls of explosions. The air shook. Fear cramped in my stomach, as I knew then: this is happening, this cannot be stopped, they are attacking.

If I can get somewhere I can signal to a shuttle. . . .

Such a feeling of isolation gripped me that I clenched my fists, nails biting into my palms.

"There are Beth'ru-elen in the city," Haltern protested.

People are here that I have known and worked with for the last half-year; some that I've known for far longer – and I didn't, even to myself, think: Where is she? Citadel or Wellhouse or down in the city?

"We're coming," I said, putting my arm round Haltern's shoulders and urging him towards the Citadel walls. The Wellhouse male nodded and set off in front of us. "Didn't you always tell me to leave a losing game?"

"This isn't *ochmir, S'aranth.*"

Footsteps eat up so small a distance, compared with what we have to cross: the mossgrass lawns, black with dew; the rooms of the Citadel, the city's alleys, the ferries or the bridge. . . .

"Hal, I'm scared, and I'm taking you out of here. What do you think will happen when CAS weapons and beampulsers attack people who have *harur*-blades and winchbows? For God's sake, Hal!" And then, seeing his face, I was ashamed of that brutality: "Please come. There isn't time to argue now."

Explosions sounded nearer. A *crack!* sounded almost at my side, and I jumped, and then saw how – quarter of a mile away – one of the eastside bridges cleared the mist. Two stone pilings jutted out into the water: beyond that, heaps of fallen stone smoked in the air, and the river-water rose swiftly to choke the makeshift new dam. At this distance, figures no larger than ants ran with ants' seeming purposelessness. The cold east wind made my eyes sting. I had a sudden flashback to another place and time – *what world was that?* – and then realized: Not my Service career, but when I was a child, thirty years ago, caught when they put down the Food Riots in the European Enclaves. The child's fear now bitter as copper in my mouth.

"Hal, come on – "

One hand under his elbow: I hustled him into the shadow of the Citadel's walls, and then – since I must let him rest – called the Wellhouse male back. Two Ortheans in Peir-Dadeni dress left the crowd, and Hal raised his head to speak breathlessly with them. I stared east. The edge of the crag hid the city, and the sky was silver-bright. A deep grinding roar sounded, so that I felt it rather than heard it: the very rock vibrating. A dark speck crossed the arch of the sky. A shuttle – and I'm *here*, I raged inwardly. How can I signal, how can I let them know?

What is Cory Mendez doing now?

I turned to the Wellhouse male. "Are there *rashaku* on Kumiel Island? Or a heliograph? Is there any way to get a message there?"

He shrugged, alien musculature moving lightly under the brown robe. I wanted to hit him. His fair mane was shaven down to fur, and his eyes were veiled with membrane; and he had the calmness of an Earthspeaker. I thought of Cassirur's *many will go to the Goddess* and I wanted to cry.

"*Is* there?"

"If there is, *t'an*, you would have to go to the forts on Easthill or Westhill, or the great Wellhouse here, and I think that impossible now. The forts – "

"I'll go to the Wellhouse."

The sun is not yet clear of the dawn mist, it isn't ten minutes since the 'thopter landed me here. Ten minutes, I thought. I walked across to Haltern Beth'ru-elen, and said, "I'll join you as soon as I can. I'm going to try and get word to Mendez."

The old male looked up. "What will you tell her to do?"

"I – don't know. Don't wait for me; I'll find you."

My shadow was long in front of me, slanting into the west. I ran towards the Citadel, found a path that seemed to skirt it, and followed that; breath sawing in my throat. Few people blocked my path. Stopping for breath, I thought, *Where?* and then heard the shouting of a crowd,

469

and as I came round one buttress of that great sprawling complex of buildings, saw Crown Steps thick with Ortheans. Brown-robed priests kept the cliff-path from being a bottleneck. Evacuation, I realized; bent double, trying to catch my breath, and in that unguarded second thought *Blaize* and then *Ruric* and then straightened up, throat tight, and ran on.

Flagstones jarred under my feet. A blast of sound rocked me and I staggered, slipping to one knee. The stone was wet under my hands with dew. Roar of sound: a bass rumble that caught in the throat and chest, and *crack!* and I stood up, shaking, and leaned against the wall.

Dust drifted between me and the sky. A spatter of grit stung my cheek, so that I spun round and put my hand up and brought it away bloody: realized that I had the smooth grip of the CAS-IV stungun in that fist and thought *What the fuck use is that?* and squatted down, back to the wall. Cold stone. The noise went on and on.

Dust, pale in the golden air. It caught in my throat and I coughed and spat, was for one second certain I would vomit; then leaned back again. Sound hit like a hammerblow: I flinched. *I must get up and move fifty yards along this wall and there are the Wellhouse gates. Move!*

The dust-cloud billowed across the Square, that wide open expanse of space. There was sunlight shining on the blue vines that cloaked the cliff, and no one to be seen; jagged beams rising out of rubble that had been *telestre*-houses, those white façades that line the Square, and no living thing moving: only *there* – and I looked down at the flagstones between my feet, and not at the sprawled bodies. *Come on, Lynne, move!* I hauled myself up, the muscles of my legs shaking.

A high-pitched whine pierced the air, making me grunt with pain. Something down the far end of the Square moved, the flagstones shook, and a cloud of stone-dust rolled like a wave between buildings: the surf of it spattered against the Wellhouse wall, fifty yards down from where I stood. *Why can't I see them? Why can't I see who's doing this?*

Easier to run than walk. I kept close to the wall, bruised my shoulder when I knocked against it running; and the air began to clear, blue and gold above me, and the fine dust sifted down and whitened my coveralls, showed the tracks of my feet; there was a silence so abrupt that I heard my own ragged gasps for breath, and then I was through the gates and into the Wellhouse courtyard.

"Cassirur!"

Panicked, I thought *They've gone* and then I saw Ortheans in the arched doorway of the great dome, and slowed my steps as I came up to them. An exhilaration born out of fear began to grip me, and I grinned at the young female Earthspeaker who pulled me into the arch's shelter.

"Where's Cassirur Almadhera? No, anyone will do, anyone who can help me get a message across to Kumiel Island."

"There isn't time!" She stared out, up at the sky; and flinched back. I shut my eyes in time: the laser-flare was scarlet against closed lids. When I could see through streaming tears, I said: "What about messages coming in? What's happening?"

"*I don't know.* There is one bridge still, at Eastwall. Go while you can." She put up claw-nailed fingers before her face, membrane flicking to clear vision; and at last focused. Without another word she strode back into the Wellhouse.

Still on the crest of that exhilaration, I thought, *Where else can I go?* and moved a few steps into the courtyard. Two Earthspeakers passed without noticing a *s'aranthi*; a third, running, shouting words I couldn't catch. Through the open gates in the high wall, I saw a flash of colour, realized it to be riders on *marhaz*, and ran on suddenly aching legs towards them. By the time I reached the Square they had passed, vanishing into dust and haze.

Weariness caught me. My fingers ached, gripping the butt of the CAS-IV, and I absently put the stungun back into its holster. What is useful for personal protection is no use when – and I lost the train of thought: *crack!* and again, and again; and I pressed back against the high wall. They must be firing from the ships still, and that's the noise down at the harbour. And here? If they've destroyed the bridges, they're turning their weapons on the city.

I wiped my mouth. Dust was gritty in my teeth; thirst an unacknowledged pain. The wind brought the smell of burning. The sun caught the pinnacles of the crag above the Square, and I stood in cold morning shadow, and then without any sense of decision began to walk out into the open. *One bridge still, at Eastwall.* And so to reach the end of this wall and go down into the alleys, down the hill, would take me towards Eastwall (towards the noise of firing), would take me towards a bridge (away from the smoke of burning buildings; how fast does fire spread in a dry summer?) and out of the city.

Blaize, I thought. Ruric.

I stopped, now almost at the far end of the Square, still beside the wall surrounding the Wellhouse. Baked clay bricks cold with this early hour: I reached out a hand for support. Not a hundred yards away, *telestre*-houses made a wasteland of rubble and beams and dust rising into the sunlight; and the sky cleared milky blue, skeined across with bright pinpricks that are daystars, the signs of a hot, clear day. *Is it possible to get back into the Citadel?* The distant cliff-walk stood deserted. *Is there any point?* A few figures, tiny at this distance, could just be seen on the crag's edge.

Ruric, I thought. Blaize.

The ground shuddered. I stumbled away from the high wall. Its shadow was long, blocking out sunlight. Broken bricks littered the flagstones, had in their fall ripped up a tangle of *kazsis*-vine, that wept a clear sap. I stood and stared up, tipping my head back so far that it made me dizzy. *Will the 'thopter come back? That was hours ago. No, not hours; not half an hour* – The daystarred sky blurred. Sound battered my ears: came from behind me, from the banks of the river; came from the distance, down by the harbour; came from everywhere at once. The stink of burning grew stronger, and I coughed.

Quickly, keeping some yards out from the wall, I walked to the end of the Square. I skirted rubble. And then, when I came to the end of the wall, stopped: a few yards downhill, more rubble blocked the alley.

If I stop, I won't move again; I'll be too afraid, I thought, and so I turned without breaking stride and began to walk out across the Square, heading out across that expanse of flagstones, towards the *telestre*-houses on the far side. The white, windowless façades gleamed in the sunlight – untouched? But smoke rose from somewhere.

Another silence: in it, far away, a voice screamed in animal pain – my palms sweated; I was almost glad when a sharp explosion blotted out the sound. *Don't think: move!* A great tiredness weighed on me, and I stopped, and stared round.

Nothing moving but the drifting dust, and the plumes of black smoke that rise over the roof-tops. . . . The sun cut through in shafts, slanting from the east; and I walked a step, and looked back, and stopped again. *That* is unchanged – the brown dome of the Wellhouse and, there, the cliff-walk and the pinnacles of the Citadel, high in the morning air, and the blue sky beyond – and I stand here, feet like lead, panting, dazed: *What do I do now?*

Sound blotted out the noise of burning, a roar so deep that I only felt it. It took the breath out of my lungs. I blinked against the flash of the explosion, and felt air hot on my face, and then opened my eyes again and found myself staring up at the grey stone walls of the Citadel. *Something is wrong,* I thought idly, and the rock and masonry began to peel apart like an opening flower and fall into the air, and part of the cliff began ponderously to slide down towards the Square and I turned to run.

472

CHAPTER 37

Dust and Sunlight

Vomit tasted sour in my mouth. Something hard dug into my back and I flinched away, blacked out again – again? – for a second; and then I was leaning with my back against something, sitting up, and a thin bile down the front of my coverall. I moved: nausea swamped me, it was some time before I recognized it as pain.

What – ?

The blurred light came into focus. I stared up at golden air. Dust hung in suspension, gently drifting . . . blurred again: tears pouring down my face. With my right hand I fumbled for my belt-pouch, got it open, and crammed two painkiller tabs in my mouth: too dry to swallow and so I chewed, bitter froth at last letting me choke them down. Dust moving in the early sun, hazing in gold the heaps of rubble, broken masonry, spilled furniture, smashed glass. . . . And my back was pressed up against a great slab of granite. Stone splinters littered the ground. To move – and I yelled: pain sickened me. *But you're not even marked.* Pain settled: my right leg. Coverall torn slightly at the knee and I thought *How the hell – ?* and tried to push myself more upright and screamed.

The sound echoed. All else, silence.

You should be dead, I realized.

Tears poured down my face, and every breath made me gasp. I felt the instant the painkillers began to hit, and opened my eyes (when did I shut them?) and felt sun warm on my wet face. My heart hammered. Even that movement made me feel sick.

I couldn't turn my head. I saw, a few yards to either side, tumbled grey rock like some river ravine, but the sides freshly splintered open; and further off the beginning of demolished *telestre*-houses, and there, beyond a fallen wall, the roofs of the buildings built on the lower slopes of Easthill and *I shouldn't be able to see that from here.* Still breathing as hard as if I'd been running, I looked down, careful not to move; one leg untouched, the other – the right leg – with only the smallest cut in the beige cloth. Pain burned, centred in the knee. It was a reflex action to try and bend – *no*, I thought, *Jesus Christ, don't!*

Cautiously, I reached down. There was a tightness, flesh swelling under the cloth. Already? And then I thought: But how long was I blacked-out for? Not more than minutes? I worked my fingers into the rip in the cloth and, centimetre by centimetre, widened the tear. The flesh was puffy. Dare I touch it – and bit back another scream. I bruise easily: a bruise yellowed all the right side of my knee, and it was grazed and weeping blood, and how can that hurt this much? I thought. And knew: the kneecap's broken. I rested my head back against the granite that supported me and swore aloud: my knee throbbed as if a hammer hit it. With shaking fingers I got out the pain-tabs from the belt-pouch. Two taken: six remaining. Without much thought I put one in my mouth and chewed. It made no difference.

Five or ten minutes passed? Fluid thickened my leg so that the knee was hardly visible, and the pain of it brought the sweat out all over me. *How long have I been here?* and then *I ought to move, it isn't safe here!*

"Help!" The effort made me gasp. Mouth too dry: how can I be heard? I gathered strength, shouted in two or three Orthean languages. There was no answer. Nothing moved but the dust and smoke . . . and the faint sound of explosions. No, not faint; Christ, I thought, I can't hear properly! That's close – is it? I can't stay here.

If you try to put weight on that knee, you'll be unconscious, some pedantic part of my mind informed me. Think: you've had Service training. What to do? *Think. Do* something.

There is wood in that rubble and wood is splints, is something you can use, can tie round; nothing to tie it with – the belt, that's it. If I can get there, it isn't far –

I put both palms flat on the flagstones and lifted myself, moving sideways. Pain hit me. The nausea faded slowly, and I slumped back; *not* the way to do it. . . . A cool breeze blew out of the east, bringing the smell of the river and the alleys; and the acrid taste of smoke. I bent forward and got my hands one under my thigh, one under my calf, lifted; moved the leg inches before pain made me hiss out a breath and rest; and then lifted myself another few inches sideways, to the limit of tension on my knee, and then bent forward and *lift* again. . . . Inching sideways, sight blinded with tears; crying out because what does it matter who hears me? I want to be heard. Conscious of cold flagstones under my palms, of grit and rock-splinters; conscious that the stone was now warm, that I must be in the sun, and that I must rest.

A shadow crossed the ruins: a shuttle cruising low, and I looked up so sharply that the pain made me swear. Sun gleamed on the white hull and then it was gone.

"Bastards!" No more than a whisper: drowned out by the muffled *crack!* of an explosion. Is that near? I thought. No, I'm sure it's not. It's down at the harbour. It is.

The painkillers began really to bite. Is it so short a time? I thought. I won't have much respite, I'd better do what I can now. I rested for a moment, licking my palms where I'd cut them; eyeing the nearest heap of bricks and timber. Too precarious even for someone who could walk. . . . I leaned forward, getting my hands round the nearest piece of wood; and then stopped and with some effort tore both sleeves off my coverall at the shoulder-seams. Wrapping them round my hands gave me some protection against splinters. Every tug on a plank or brick jolted my knee; and I doubled up, noises wrenched out of me.

By the time I'd cleared three flimsy slats from the edge of the heap, my hearing was coming back. Every distant explosion made me wince. The sun was hot, even though it was early; and *kekri*-flies buzzed round me in the heat. At last I could turn my head far enough to see the Citadel – and stared: the morning sun shone now on a titanic stump of rock, a few layers of masonry clinging to it here and there. The northern sky seemed bright, seemed *empty*: I have always been used to seeing the Citadel there, and now . . .

I got two hands to my leg and lifted it, laying it down on the stoutest wooden slat – and that's not so strong, I thought; not at all – and rested. Two other slats at the side. And take off the belt, and rip up cloth sleeves, and remember Service training – *no!* I rested. The dust made my lips dry. *If you don't do it now you won't do it at all.* I pushed one end of the belt under the slat, looped it round the two side slats, took a breath, and pulled it tight round mid-thigh. *Where are my blackouts when I need them?* It almost made me laugh: true hysteria. I knotted the first torn sleeve round the splints below my knee, feeling the support bite; chewed another pain-tab; tried to tie cloth *over* the knee and fluid swelling, and screamed. Tied it also below the knee.

You ought to be dead; you're lucky you're alive. Hold on to that thought.

Whatever caught me a glancing blow could have killed me, I thought; and it's done more than break that knee, it's smashed it, I'm sure of it. Jesus Christ, what am I going to do!

Move.

For minutes I stayed still, lying back on the ground, staring up into the depths of the pale blue sky, watching daystars. Not even an hour past sunrise. The light still comes strong and level from the east. Every splintered beam, every brick, every uprooted vine casts a precise shadow. Haze and dust blur the edges of vision, the air still golden with dust that sifted down, and I could taste the smoke of something burning; strain as I might, I couldn't *hear* fire. Not close, then. No, but how close does it have to be, when all I can do is crawl?

I'm not sure I can even do that.

My hands smarted as I eased myself up into a sitting position. You'll be worse cut yet, I thought, staring at the only clear way between sprawls of collapsed walls and buildings. And how *far* is it clear?

Doesn't matter.

I tightened my belt, although it made my thigh throb. Anything to immobilize the joint – and yes, I can ease forward; can drag the leg, and it hurts, but I can do it, I can. *God!* Ah, stop squalling, you little fucker; *move*. That's it: move.

Feeling dwarfed between fallen stone and rubble, I put my hands down and pushed; eased back a foot or so, grunting with pain; and if I had any humour, I thought, I'd laugh at me dragging myself along backwards, can't see where I'm going, but no, I don't feel like laughing. And there have to be people *somewhere*.

The wooden slats scraped on the stone as I pushed myself across the ground, bending double, lifting; trying to ease my leg. The sun was hot on my back. A feeling of sickness swept over me, and I halted; then began again to drag myself slowly across the littered flagstones. The horizon became a shattered wall, jutting up into a blue sky. As I inched on, more came into view – the house split open, exposed to the air; there a first-floor inner window, part of a ceiling. . . . Suddenly I looked down, concentrating on my hands. Better not to see some things. Better not to see a crushed arm covered with masonry, a gold stud still set into the skin between each slender claw-nailed finger. Better to look down and see the flagstones, brace a heel and *push* and *lift*. . . .

The rumble of fire grew so constant that I ignored it. Only when a shuttlecraft roared overhead did I look up, helpless, and shout and wave; but nothing happened, and I went back to that slow progress. Every few seconds I looked over my shoulder. Tumbled stone blocked one way, and here two or three buildings had fallen together – several bodies lay in the rubble, not moving. And part of a fallen wall.

When I turned my head back, and rested, and checked the splints, my hands left bloody prints on the cloth of my coveralls. Splinters of glass and stone. . . . Frightened into effort, I hauled myself forward. The weakened cloth bandages parted. When I could see, through tears of pain, I picked up the lengths of cloth and knotted them together again, tied them, thinking *How long will this last?* The sun now made flagstones and rubble hot. When I twisted round preparatory to moving, I saw there was no way between the heaps of rubble. No way at all.

I'd like to see this from the air. Cory will report it as 'a simultaneous strike on the harbour and the Citadel' – Jesus, they've flattened every-thing round here. *How far?*

I leaned forward, resting, breathing heavily. My coveralls were filthy.

What I could see of my knee through the torn cloth was a pallid white, swollen with fluid; the bruises turning from yellow to black, and I thought *How can it look like nothing and hurt like this?* If I could see how far this extends, I'd know what to do: go back, go forward, stay here – no, I can't stay here. Wreckage burns. Well then. . . .

Carefully, I lifted myself on to the edge of the heap of fallen brickwork. A house-wall had come down all of a piece here, and bracing my heel I pushed myself up on to it; and then I lifted again and shifted a few inches further up the slope, and felt broken brick under me, cutting sharply. A splinter drove up under the nail of my forefinger. I swore, sucked at it. *Push* and *lift*. Brace heel. Now I was a few yards above ground level, I could see how the Square was devastated – buried under the rock-slide of the collapsing cliff. If I can see where I'm going, I thought, and twisted, moving one hand –

Came down on empty air. Bricks shifted, a kaleidoscope of sky, walls, roofs blinded me; there was a horrible grinding noise and I fell. Plunged backwards and down and *rolled*, throat ripped open with screaming, felt the wooden splints on my leg give – and hit sharp edges with outstretched hands, not able to stop that sickening slide; bricks falling with me, and I hit something that knocked me breathless. Pain convulsed me; I vomited. I was still, but sprawled backwards across the foot of a wall, and splints and belt gone, and leg crooked at an angle. I blacked out.

The pain brought me back to consciousness.

When I felt for pain-tabs, two were gone. A bitterness remained in my mouth. Did I take them? I wondered. And realized that I must have. The white sun dazzled me and I moved my head. The world swung. Nausea made me shut my eyes; when I opened them, I saw my hand lying on the earth in front of me, and realized I must be on my back. Earth, not stone. I raised my head. The rubble-slide had left me on earth, and I lifted myself a little further, seeing that my right leg was still crooked; bruised and swollen.

Reached down to touch my hip, that seemed all hot fire. My leg, lying still partly on broken brick, and the foot and calf turned in at an angle – I shut my eyes, sick; every gasp made pain flare through me, made me sob on every harsh indrawn breath. Which hurts more, the pain or the fear? Fear: I daren't look at my leg, the torn cloth covering swollen flesh, now torn and ripped, and seeping blood and a pale fluid. The sun was hot on my head and the earth warm under my back and I couldn't tell what hurt, myself or the earth; pain too large to be contained in blood and flesh and bone.

★

Time passing: minute and slow minute. *Dear God let me black out.* Each minute carrying its full weight of hot sun – still just past dawn – and thundering noise. Each explosion made me sob, shake; I shifted, and screamed, and the pain choked me off: voiceless, blinded with tears.

Minute by minute in the hot morning, lips cracking and dusty. *If this doesn't stop I'll die.* And the realization, quite cold and apart, *Yes, I will die.* Not of the injury, not even of shock and pain, but if the fighting comes this way, or the wreckage burns, or this goes on through days and nights without water and food.

Somewhere in those minutes – twenty of them, or half an hour, no more – I put the last pain-tabs into my mouth, and chewed a bitter dust.

The painkillers cut the edge of it, and I lay for a minute and panted, thinking *Pain exhausts* and blinking against the sunlight above me. Now I could turn my head to the side, away from the slope of fallen masonry that loomed on my left hand, and strain to focus . . . into distance.

I lay on broken earth above a slope. A *telestre*-house wall, hit by projectile fire, had dragged part of the hillside when it fell: landsliding down on the alleys and buildings below. Broken earth began three yards from where I lay. I looked down on earth and uprooted *kazsis* and a scatter of kitchen implements and two dark-maned Ortheans. One was buried except for a head and arm. The other – an elderly female – lay face down and motionless. I looked away.

The slope of the hill below me shone in the eastern sun. Pale-walled *telestre*-houses, untouched. Figures ran on flat roofs, scurrying from cover to cover. Beyond that – squinting into the rising sun – the river gleamed. It tumbled and rushed over a fallen bridge. The metal sails of *jath-rai* shone too bright to look at. Faintly through the air came the whine of CAS weaponry, like the hum of *kekri*-flies at this distance. There were people down by the bridges and that cold part of my mind observed *Anyone I can see must be dead; the living will be under cover from the firing* and I turned my head away: pain hammering behind my eyes.

No wooden slats now, nothing within arm's reach or even close, to use as splint or support. . . . I caught my breath, eased back – and slumped down: seconds before my vision cleared, and *no there's no point in moving, where can I go?* Better to conserve strength.

I heard voices, close at hand, and without any pause to consider, shouted – voice a dry croak, and taking a breath was agony, but I shouted:

"Help! Over *here* – "

A head rose over the top of the heap of fallen masonry, and I looked up at a brown-maned and brown-skinned Orthean male, hardly more than *ashiren*; and his eyes widened, and he called down behind him, *"S'aranthi!"* and then scrambled over and down – I threw my arms across my face. Grunted with pain – but no slide of fallen bricks came down with him; he stepped lightfootedly down beside me, and squatted down, and glanced first at my leg, and then at this exposed position and the town below.

"Can you walk?" he said in a soft Ymirian accent.

"No I – " And what's he to know about it? "No, I can't move; my leg's smashed."

"Don't worry." He flinched as a *crack!* sounded, and on the hillside below, smoke boiled up from a *telestre*-house. "Hey, Sulis; down here! Quick!"

An older female appeared, so like him that they must be of one *telestre*, and I lightheadedly thought, *I should tell you to get out, it isn't safe here!* and knew I wouldn't. She scrambled down the heap of bricks and masonry and timber, cat-cautious, her gaze on the river below; and without preamble said to the boy, "We'll have to carry her out", and to me, "This will hurt."

She grabbed me under the arms, signalling to the boy. Strong hands gripped my good leg; I felt myself lifted – and screamed: no help for it, screamed and swore at them to put me down for Chrissakes I'm in fucking agony; and the blue sky and the sunlight ran together, and I passed half-in, half-out of consciousness.

And then I lay on the flagstones thinking *back where I started* with hysterical amusement; this isn't an hour since I stood in the Citadel and talked with Douggie and Blaize and Hal; and I saw the rubble and realized *they must have carried me; how in hell – ?* The woman and the boy stood over me, talking urgently. Then she lifted her brown hand, signalling.

"Thank you – "

The boy squatted down beside me. He put one six-fingered hand up to brush back his mane, and his eyes were on the ruins we were in and not on me. "Wouldn't have stopped if you hadn't called out, *t'an*. This is our last time through. You're lucky. You – I'm coming, Sulis. Here!"

Wood hit flagstones with a crash; hands lifted me so swiftly that I had hardly time to cry out; and then there was wood under me, something soft jammed into my side; the tail of the *jasin* was fastened up again by the woman, and with a jolt we moved. I raised my head, sick; vomited bile, and then retched. I wiped at the front of my coverall, and the stink made me close my eyes. When I opened them, seconds later, the *jasin* was passing under a grey stone arch, in cold shadow, and out on to a windswept quay, and I thought *Where?* and *we can't have come so far in moments.*

What lay soft against me was an Orthean female, unconscious and moaning; and I twisted to look back over my shoulder, and saw two more Ortheans in the carriage – one stared at me; her arm was soaked black with blood – and a *skurrai* with the brown-maned boy at its head, and beyond the beast a number of other carts and carriages, and wounded men and women lying on blankets spread on quaystones, and the wind whipped crests on to the river – no, the estuary.

The wide sky was clear, and bright, and the wind brought a fine spray – lips tasting that sweet-salt alien water – and far out, almost to the other side of the water, a ferry tacked in to land on the mainland. I shut my eyes, shivered; was hot and then cold; found that I couldn't stop shivering. *They're going to move me, going to lift me off this cart; going to move me again, Christ Jesus!* I opened gummy eyes and stared blankly, and managed to focus on my leg. Swollen flesh: pressing hard against the ripped cloth. The cloth now stained a bright pink. Other leg crooked up, braced against the *jasin* tailboard, *how did I have the sense to do that?*

" – she's an offworlder!"

"I don't care, she goes with the rest. I'm leaving no one here that we can move!"

They came into my field of vision, silhouetted against the estuary, and the morning sun off the water momentarily blinded me. The female, Sulis, and another woman.

"Sunmother, no, I won't take her! Let her stay here and rot."

"I haven't got time for this!" The dark-maned female swung round, walking away, and threw back over her shoulder: "Ask the *T'An* – don't bother me – leave her, then!"

I got a hand on the edge of the *jasin* and pulled myself up an inch or two. A small quayside area, a steep hill above; and the sun coming from *there* and so this must be one of the west-river ferries.

Muzzily, I called out, but the Orthean woman was no longer there. The air was full of noise: explosions in the distance, CAS fire much nearer; the crackle of wood on fire, voices shouting, and voices in pain; screams, so that I sank back and gasped and sweated.

A hand touched my hot forehead: the fingers like ice.

"Don't – " And then I focused. *Delirium*, I thought, quite certain of it; so certain that I didn't speak; and someone called, "*T'An*, there's another boat to load, which lot do we take next?" and Ruric raised her head and called, "By the steps – there."

She looked down at me and said, "What can I do? Think and tell me, Christie. What can we do that will help you, not hurt you?"

"What are you doing here?" Then I thought how urgent it was to move. "I had a splint, to keep the bone from grating – Ruric, for God's sake! What are you doing?"

She stayed leaning against the side of the cart. The sun shone on her black mane, thick now with dust; and on the sharp lines of her face; and her gaze went to the estuary, watching the half-dozen small ships rocking on the water. "Getting people out. You should have seen the Wellhouses! They must have moved hundreds in the first hour – anyone who can walk has gone, or if they haven't, they're fools – " She broke off to shout an order down the quay. " – and now it's casualties. The harbour . . ."

"What time is it?"

"About an hour before midday." She grinned, and the lines in her face deepened. Membrane veiled yellow eyes against the dust. "That's my *S'aranth!*" And she turned away, giving orders to another Orthean.

The noise deafened me. Vision swam: I was aware that I was fever-hot. Then a sharp pain convulsed me, I sat upright; cried out. There were makeshift splints bound round my right leg with strips of a torn cloak, and in confusion I thought *When did that happen?* and Ruric Orhlandis said "Better?"

"I – uh; yeah, better."

"Liar." She raised her head. The wind blew her cropped mane back from her face. The sky above her seemed hazy, and I realized it was high cloud; daystars barely visible in the milky blue. No shuttles, I thought. The Orthean woman said, "You'll be on the next boat across."

The splints felt tight. My knee throbbed; but now at least every breath didn't move it. The *skurrai*-cart being needed, I was lifted off and laid down on the quayside with a dozen other Ortheans. The flagstones were sun-warmed. Intermittently my sight blacked out, and the pain began to bite as the painkillers wore off; I thought, *How can I get to a shuttle? to Kumiel? no medics here –*

An Earthspeaker who tended the other wounded crossed the quay and examined my leg; but didn't touch it. Glad or sorry? I wondered. Human anatomy is not Orthean: I'd sooner they didn't meddle. Christ, somebody do something!

People still came down on to the quay from the alleys. As the sun rose to midday, the noise of firing increased. A cold sweat came out on my face and neck and back: I thought, No. This is enough. Too much. Not again. All I could see was smoke and dust that hung in the air at the top of the hill. Towards the sea, downriver, black smoke rose and fires raged; and it was a long time before I thought, *That's Westhill* and heard the sharp *crack!* of a beampulser.

481

I looked down, across the water, fearing to see the metal sails of *jath-rai*.

" – and come back across."

Ruric's voice, speaking to a dark-maned male in Rimon dress. As he moved off, she came to squat down beside me; where I lay propped up against the wall of the quay steps. The noon sun dazzled on the water. One of the Ortheans with me – the female with the wounded arm – muttered something under her breath; a male grunted and looked at Ruric and spat: "Orhlandis!"

Ruric ignored him. Her hand moved to rub at the stump of her arm with long dark fingers; and I saw that her shirt was filthy and her britches dust-stained; and she carried a CAS-handgun at her belt. The smooth butt had no Company logo stamped on it. And so it must have come from the *hiyeks*, I realized; and in what riot and confusion – does it matter?

"We'll have to move," she said quietly, "they're moving upriver from Westhill. *S'aranth*, crossing over is risky, but so is staying here."

Her eyes followed the Rimon male she'd spoken to. I saw him supervising the loading of stretchers on to a small boat, shouting at the *ashiren* that was all his crew. The boat lifted and fell: tide flowing down towards the estuary. Ruric lifted her head, looking at the hillside and the *telestre*-houses above us: "There's more need bringing out."

"What's happening?"

She shook her head, and was silent. A roar sounded over the noise of explosions and the whine of CAS weaponry, and a shuttle soared high across the city and vanished over to the east. Another explosion rocked the quay: loud and sudden and there was blood where I bit my lip; Ruric stood and gazed east, listening, but the roar died smoothly away. She sank back down. Now I could smell burning again, over the stink of sea and fear.

"Sunmother!" she whispered, "I'll make them bring the boats back across here." She threw me a quick glance, and rested her hand on my shoulder. "Christie, don't worry."

"The *Citadel* – "

She said nothing, but the membrane slid back from her yellow eyes, fever-bright in her dark face, and she looked up at the city from under dark brows; and my pulse stuttered, a stab of adrenalin cold as ice. Her fingers locked on my shoulder.

"You don't ask what keeps the fighting to the harbour and the rivers."

Pain making me stupid, I muttered, "Keeps it?"

"They're fighting offworld technology with winchbows and *harur-*

blades. As a diversion." Her mouth moved in something that might be a smile: ancient and sardonic; and then it was Ruric Orhlandis again, her face sharp with pain, who said, "Christie, who do you think? The *T'An* Commander, the guard; a handful of mercenaries. They're down there *now*."

She stood up, shouting across to Ortheans bringing two more loaded *skurrai*-carts out of the alley-entrance; brown-robed Earthspeakers ran to the wounded, and I tried to shut my ears to the noises, the pain. *Blaize.* Confusion muddled me; childlike, I thought *T'An Commander, that's Blaize Meduenin* and then *no, he can't be back there, I don't believe it!* and sobbed on an indrawn breath: *yes, he's there; Jesus Christ* –

"Get him out. Ruric, get a message; get him here!"

"What about the rest of them here? If we don't get people out of the city – " She swung round: "Get them on board! There isn't time for that; carry them if you have to!"

I don't give a fuck about anybody else; get Blaize out; and where's Hal, did he get out early? And Cassirur and Nelum; this is . . .

The raw pain and the fever reached a balance: I thought, with utter certainty, *This is a nightmare.* It cleared my head. The sun made my eyes water. The sea-wall was hard against my back; and three of us lay propped up against it: a pale-maned female with an arm roughly bandaged and stained bloody; a young male; an older male who cradled a hand smashed and wet. The sound he was making tore at my gut. Sunlight, white and harsh, shattered on the surface of the river; and the wind off the water made me shiver. I hugged my arms across my chest, feeling the sting of cut palms.

Every crash, every loud explosion, made me shake.

Blank-walled *telestre*-houses on the hillside above the quay were quiet, pale in the sun; and I strained to see figures on roof-tops – nothing. *For how long?* The sun blinded me. Ahead, where the river curved, must be Westhill; clouds of smoke rolled down now to the water's edge, hiding the city there. I dropped my gaze and looked along the quay, it was a confusion of people rushing about; makeshift stretchers manhandled down on to the deck of the small boat; one of the Earthspeakers glanced down at a male on the quayside and shook his head; Ruric – *when did she go?* – came back at a run with two males, pointed at the group of us; and they went to the pale-maned female and lifted her, carrying her towards the boat.

"Look." I pointed. Ruric knelt down beside me, veiled her eyes, and stared downriver against the sunlit water. I saw how my hand shook. Dirt and blood. Then the dark Orthean woman drew in her breath as if she'd been hit.

"I see it." She straightened up.

A glint of light on metal . . . and then it turned with the wind and was clearly in view: a *jath-rai*, metal sail gleaming, emerging from the smoke that hid the side of Westhill. Staring across a hundred yards of open water, I saw small white-robed figures on the deck. A thunder of explosions made me wince: I shrank back, realized *that wasn't this side of the city* and got my hands to the top of the wall, and hauled myself upright, weight on my good leg.

Another ship appeared from the smoke. The two *jath-rai* caught the wind, prows curving slowly as they came round. For a split second I thought *they're going back* and then sails shifted, figures ran about the decks, both ships began to head upriver towards us.

"Get them under cover!" Ruric gestured violently; turned to look at the *jath-rai*, then back at the wounded littering the quay. The small boat rocked, was abruptly a yard out from the quay steps and raising its own sails; I saw a spray of water catch the sun. Ruric groaned under her breath; again shouted: "Under *cover*, get back! Get them out of sight!" Her voice was drowned out by a sharp *crack!*

She turned abruptly, seized my arm and pulled it across her thin shoulders, said, "Hold on!" and began to half carry me across the quay, towards the shelter of the abandoned companion-houses there. Each step jolted agony through my leg; my vision blurred with tears, the low-roofed buildings becoming only a dazzle; but I got a grip on her shoulder tight enough to make her wince, braced against her: walked; and then as the noise rose to a deafening level, began to half limp, half run, in red agony; and collapse in shadow; she against me; and look out from under a doorway at the quay and the river and the hull of an F90 shuttle as it roared downriver, a bare five hundred feet above.

" – Mendez!" But I couldn't even hear myself over the rattle of explosive fire; a thunder that went on and on.

We lay on the earthen floor just inside the low building. That earth vibrated now, a shaking roar that I thought must be the dockside collapsing into the river; the walls shivered. A hollow *boom!* echoed up from downriver.

"Wait. Don't move." Ruric knelt up, got to her feet; and shaded her eyes with her single hand, staring out across the water. She stood in the doorway for a moment, then ducked outside. Smoke drifted acridly across what I could see of the dock, there were moans and screams; I glimpsed her and another male and an Earthspeaker, each dragged a stretcher towards the shelter of the dockside *telestre*-houses.

As if there were all the time in the world, I thought, *Cory is firing on the Desert Coast ships*. I caught hold of the door-jamb, levered myself up

484

on my good leg; and smoke made me cough, eyes streaming. Men and women were dragging themselves away from the quayside in panic; those who were still must be too hurt to move; I caught my breath and then realized, *I can hear them screaming; the firing's stopped.*

Smoke began to thin, from black to sepia to gold. Sun shone down on the quay, on the bricks and timber – I never heard that hit; what did they get? – of a *telestre*-house fired on by the *jath-rai*. One *jath-rai* still remained. It drifted, fifty yards away; the river current beginning to turn it around.

Sharp explosions still crackled in the distance, and there were flashes like summer lightning, and I slid down to the earth, resting my back against the doorframe. It was involuntary. I wanted to move, wanted to get out on to the quay, no matter the ship or the firing; but it wasn't pain that swept through me, it was a weakness as if every tendon had been cut. And then pain made tears run, and I could do nothing but sit and blink and breathe in rasping coughs; and the hard jamb of the door cut into my spine.

A minute later and a shadow fell across my closed eyes: "Haven't you sense enough to be inside?"

I opened my eyes and saw sun on the water and rolling smoke, and Ruric Orhlandis. The dark Orthean woman stumbled through the doorway. She glanced back over her shoulder, winced as a volley of explosions rocked the air; and knelt down, her hand and arm tight across her lower ribs. Her shirt, torn down the back, exposed the wiry roots of her black mane; and as she raised her head the alien musculature shifted under her skin.

"Christie, for Her sake, get in – "

My arms gave under me as I tried to push myself up; I could only lean back against the inner doorjamb. She stayed for a moment, ribs heaving, and then half fell beside me; and the membrane drew back from her eyes, a white line appearing round the yellow iris.

"Hurt – you're hurt?"

She looked dazedly at the interior of this empty companion-house. A tiny white-walled room, with couch-chairs and tables overturned in the panic of flight; dust and sunlight drifting in through the slot-windows.

"Might as well – stay here." She shook her head as if to clear it. "Sunmother! Something hit me here – " The arm across her ribs tightened.

"Are you bleeding?"

"No; bruised, I think." Her mouth twisted. "It's tight; that's all."

Pain and weakness went together now: again, it felt as if they balanced.

485

Clear-headed and feverish, all at the same time. I rubbed my hands down my coveralls, then wiped my mouth; tasted grit. Cold wind blew in off the river.

"How bad is it?" I met her gaze. *Can't get your breath and it's a chest-wound* – And I was suddenly cold, mind clear; looking at that narrow face, and the pain. "Is it bad enough to be a broken bone?"

"Could be." She twisted, sitting down next to me; let out a grunt of pain; and then coughed and cut it off halfway.

Outside, concussion split the air; somewhere close there was a crash. Someone screamed. Thunder rolled: pounded at the walls of the tiny room. *Has to be a shuttle coming in low,* I thought; but black smoke swirled across the quay, and I could see nothing. And she sat with her back to the wall, this alien woman; head thrown back and gasping; and the sun faintly shone copper on her black mane and on her shoulders, on the six-fingered hand that clenched on her high-arched ribs. *Humanoid is not human* I thought coldly, and then *but a rib can pierce a lung, all the same.*

"What's happening out there?"

She caught her breath, that rasped in her throat. "I can't – there's no telling; you can't see. I saw *s'aranthi* ships over Westhill. I think they were firing." And she looked at me, and shook her head. "We're pinned down here."

She makes too much sense to be injured. I looked up past the edge of the door, and saw the billows of smoke clearing again, and the blue sky beyond, and a glint of light that must be another shuttle.

"You said – said they were coming this way. From Westhill and down that way," I said.

Her head moved slightly: a nod of agreement. Without opening her eyes, she said, "An hour. Maybe less. Then they'll be here."

And what happens to us then – *no,* you don't think about that. And I wondered if, in a few minutes, I could seriously think of how we might move (and go where?); but for the minute just to sit and not cry out with the pain was effort. I reached over, and could only brush my hand against her shoulder.

"We can – "

Her breath caught in her throat again, and her head went back; corded neck stretched in pain. Her arm fell to her side. Abruptly she bent forward, coughing. The harsh sound cut off midway, became liquid; and she put her hand up to her mouth, brought it away black, and spat out a mouthful of blood.

"*Jesus Christ, no –* "

The light from the window shone down on her. A dark woman,

486

cropped mane falling over her forehead; and the lines of pain and age cut deep in her face. Her white shirt was caked with dust. That six-fingered hand pressed on the stone floor, leaving a dark smear; and then she caught hold of my hand in a painful grip. Her eyes opened, amazed; looking at me.

"Where were you hit? Show me." I kept her hand tight in mine, and she pulled it free; dragged the shirt away from her lower ribs on her left side. The flesh had a pulpy look to it. She let the cloth fall.

"Don't move; don't talk. Stay still."

What I said was drowned in the roar of falling masonry. Something hit the flat roof above us with a crash. Light flashed on the far wall of the companion-house room: leakage of laser-fire; and I blinked back after-images.

Between gasps, the Orthean woman said, "Tethmet was right. He said I shouldn't – leave the Tower. Right." And she made a grimace, trying to smile.

"Don't talk, you'll aggravate it. Stay still."

She nodded, once, and rested her head back against the wall. I watched her chest rise and fall. Tight, jagged movements. Wondered what it was that hit her and then thought, It wouldn't help to know. Christ, don't let it be bad; don't let it be what it looks like!

Long minutes passed. My mouth was dry with thirst and fear; and it was a fight not to slip into unconsciousness. The noise didn't abate. But in this tiny, pale room, it passed unnoticed. She opened her eyes, frowning slightly. *What can I do?* Nothing but keep her still. If she's got a pierced lung, *if* she has, then the medics will have to get here fast –

She bent forward, spasms wracking at her; and I dragged myself a few inches closer and, half out from the pain, held her shoulders while she coughed, while her head came back; and blood haemorrhaged, ran down her mouth and neck and soaked her shirt.

" – Christie?"

It was a minute before I realized where I was: still leaning against her and against the wall, and acrid smoke seeped into the small room and stung my eyes. My leg and hip were liquid fire. I wiped sweat off my face and couldn't feel it on my hand.

"Christie?"

"I'm here."

"Stupid," she said. "This is – a stupid thing to happen – *ah!*"

"Don't," I begged, and felt tears on my cheeks; cursed weakness. She gasped, dragging air into her lungs, and it was a wet, frothy sound. I managed to get my arm all the way round her narrow shoulders, supporting her against my left side; her body was heavy, fever-hot, and she coughed again, thickly.

"*Don't* move. Oh, Jesus, *why* didn't you get out on the first boat? Of all the fucking stupid things to do – "

Glass imploded, scattering the floor. I flinched, and then cried out at the pain of the movement. Either the firing was further off or I couldn't hear properly; one loud *crack!* was followed by an almost-silence.

The smoke thinned, and the light of the sun came in through the shattered window, and made an oblong on the stone floor. It shone on her legs, stretched out before her. I grabbed hold of the doorjamb and pulled myself forward, so that I could see through the door; and Ruric slumped against me. I leaned back. The firing started again, closer now.

Coughing shook her; deep spasms, that brought up blood. I wiped at her mouth with my hand.

And this is your Tathcaer, your city, how could you leave it? Oh, Jesus, why didn't you go?

Gently, I leaned her head back against my shoulder. Her weight on my uninjured leg was almost a dead weight. I gripped her shoulders, leaning her back a little on me. Her mane was rough against my arm. I saw her hand in her lap clench, those slender claw-nailed fingers digging into her palm; felt how she tried to hold back the coughing, hold herself still. *This cannot be happening, I don't believe it can happen like this.*

"Stay still," I whispered. Her skin felt hot, and her pulse hammered.

The light was cruel now, showing her age; showing the skin stretched tight over high cheekbones. Her head moved the smallest fraction. She opened her eyes; and the skin round them crinkled, her mouth moved – the faintest echo of that smile I saw once, in this city, eight years ago.

I said, "They'll get to us. Don't move; you won't do any more damage. They'll get to us soon."

So quiet that I hardly heard her over the noise of the firing outside, she said, "It doesn't matter if I talk. I want to say some things." And then, all on out-breaths, and with a ghost of asperity: "I do know – about lung wounds."

"So do I."

Now the wind off the river brought the stench of dead weed and garbage, and cordite; and raised chills on my skin. It came to me as a simultaneous perception: all the years that I have spent away from Orthe, all the time between then and now – and all that happened to me then, here in this city: how in the Citadel Dalzielle Kerys-Andrethe sent me out to the *telestres* in this woman's company, and all the long journeying that brought us at last to a room in the Citadel again, she going into her exile and I into mine. It's no use to regret. And she is not *amari* Ruric

Orhlandis now, not *T'An* Commander and *T'An* Melkathi; she is Ruric Hexenmeister – ah, but still: how could she stay away?

"Get me back to the Tower – " Her breath caught.

"They – can they heal you there?"

"Take me there anyway." She coughed, and it was tight; coughed until she bent forward and I held her, and she brought up dark blood, and spat, and coughed again; fighting for air.

She leaned back against me. "Do you know – in the Citadel? When you came there?" It was obvious she meant her exile. "I would – ask. Would have asked you to come with me. I don't know why I didn't."

Eight years ago it wouldn't have been true, I thought, but now it is. And I said, "If you'd asked, I would have gone."

She did smile at that, yellow eyes wide and with that intrinsic glow they have in shadow; and the sunlight from the window fell on her hand and hip, and outside the whine of CAS weapons was louder. The minutes passed. She gasped for breath.

My knee and leg and hip throbbed, pain keeping me conscious. Everything in that tiny room stood out with preternatural clarity: the overturned tables, the dust on the floor, the splintered glass. Dust billowed along the quay outside. The sun grew hot. Noise was a constant, no longer noticed. I am thirty-eight years old, she is older; I am holding her here in this empty room and I cannot move.

A few minutes later she coughed again, and this time she didn't stop. I held her while she shook with it, crying out with pain; and my hands were wet with her haemorrhaged blood. Her weight rested against me, heavy and warm; and her black mane was rough against my cheek; her spasms jolted me so that I had to bite on my lower lip to keep from screaming.

A little after noon, her breathing became shallow, and then stertorous. She rested against me, this Orthean woman with satin-black skin and mane; head resting in the hollow of my shoulder, and all my clothing soaked with her blood. The lungs fill and they drown, drown in their own blood; human is not humanoid – but sometimes it is. I looked down at that narrow face.

I held her in my arms until she grew cold.

CHAPTER 38

Past-Memory

"One more here!"

I managed to focus against the light blazing in at the doorway. The voice added something unintelligible, shouting to be heard over the thunder of a shuttle's flight; and then a young Orthean in a priest's robe knelt beside me.

"Just wait, *t'an*, we'll have you safe soon."

Pain and fever and memory hold me: looking down at my lap, I can see that the patch of sunlight has moved only inches, shines on my human hands that are black with blood and *not more than an hour's passed*, I thought, *why weren't you here an hour ago – ?*

A deep roar sounded, split into distinct successive explosions. The young male's head came up and he flinched, pale eyes veiled; that face narrow at the jaw and wide at the forehead, quick with life. Past him, I saw the river. Light shattered off the water, off the metal sails of a *jathrai*; and suddenly a great plume of water shot up beside the ship, a shadow darkened the air and passed overhead – and then the roar of the shuttle's passing: I put my hands over my ears.

" – wait, and we'll get you out with the others!"

I found myself alone. I sat propped against the wall, legs out before me; the pain made me gasp with every breath.

An hour is long enough to come to a decision, I thought. And as long as I've decided, I'm okay; I can do it. If it's cowardly . . . that doesn't matter now.

Deliberately and with effort I moved my hand, getting the fingers round her long-boned, cold wrist; and locked them, and thought *They won't separate us* and began to laugh – caught my breath in pain: laughed so that I shook, and the tears ran down my face.

"Here. Lift her. Help me." The young male Earthspeaker ducked into the doorway, followed by an older male; and then as he bent over me, hesitated, and then reached down to pry loose my fingers.

"You don't leave her – "

He put a dark-skinned hand on her throat, where she lay against me still with her head thrown back. Momentary irritation gripped me: *do you think I don't know how to find breath or a heart-beat?*

"She's dead, we can't help her."

490

I tightened my grip on her wrist. Tears ran down my face and in blind panic I repeated, "You don't leave her here! She comes with me!"

"*T'an*, she's *dead* – " He turned, as the older male whispered something. They stood up, talking in the doorway; and it was irresistibly funny, I thought, *To have to drag a lump of dead, cold meat along with me* and the pain in my smashed knee flared so that I couldn't help but claw at it; and then scream again when that hurt. I bent double. The body slid down on to the stone floor beside me.

The sun was warm on her face, that sharp high-boned face wiped clean of haemorrhaged blood, but when I put my hand on her, her face was cold and soft. Her mouth hung a little open, and her eyes were closed. The lines in that fine-grained black skin made her seem old, and she will not be old, not now.

I reached for her hand again, where it lay fallen on her breast, and held those long amber-nailed fingers, and again felt laughter tight in my lungs. I screwed my eyes up against the light through the doorway, looking at the distant daystarred sky. *A good joke.* When she should be buried now – and a sharp *crack!* shook the companion-house.

"Bring it, we haven't time to argue," the Earthspeaker said urgently, "we can't leave this one even if it is *s'aranthi*; get to the boat!"

He caught my arm and pulled it across his shoulders and I came up on to one leg that twisted and wouldn't hold me. The other male gripped her body under the arms and dragged it out on to the quayside and even with the pain lancing through me, I saw her heels jolt comically over the stones, and laughed on a soundless breath, and retched: part from the pain, and part from the realization, O God, that there should be a *use* even for the dead.

The flat-hulled ferry dipped sickeningly. A rush of spray soaked me, brought me to a semi-conscious state. White wake trailed downriver, a solid wall of sound struck me; and the person next to me screamed, and thrashed, and a hand caught me across the face. I blinked away tears. High overhead the F90 swung into a curve. The sun slid like a silver bead down the length of its hull.

Current turned the boat. Between the gap of deck and rail, Westhill came into view: the slopes hidden now by rolling black smoke. Smashed buildings blocked the lower end of the harbour. A few boats bobbed helplessly in the swell. Dark specks ran on the quay. Dots in the water: the heads of swimmers. A pall of smoke blotted the sky, split by the F90 shuttle's passing; a *jath-rai* listed in the water and men and women jumped from its sides.

The ferry stank of blood and excrement. Cries and screams were loud, over the noise of firing. An Earthspeaker crossed the deck, stepping between bodies laid out on the wood; that rolled as the boat rolled. When I turned my head, I saw that the Orthean beside me was white-maned and white-skinned and wearing a dirt-stained *meshabi*-robe.

The early evening sky. . . .

Pale blue and filled with clarity, as a glass is filled with water or light. To lie and look up is to fall into the sky. And no, not quite evening, not more than the end of afternoon, in the long Orthean day.

She rises to her feet in one swift movement, all the old swordfighter's grace still there. She stands in the sunlight, in the Tower garden. This lean, ageing woman, skin like flaked coal; with bare feet, and mane straggling out of a half-crop. That narrow, merry face.

Makeshift tents of *becamil*-cloth are drab against the sky. Ortheans walk between them on hurried errands, walking on dry earth trodden bare of mossgrass. . . . I moved slightly, lifting my head; and saw, between the tents that shelter the injured, the wide grasslands that run down to the Oranon River. Acres of flat mossgrass. In the far distance, people trek away from the city against the skyline. Haze blurs distance, the land trembles in this summer day's heat.

She speaks as one remembering more than her own memories. Like the sun on the surface of a river: one minute all brilliance, all Ruric; and then the light shifts, and under that surface are depths. . . .

I heard faint, desultory cracks: the distant sound of projectile fire. The noises here drowned it out. Not far off, someone screamed, another voice sobbed with pain; and I rolled my head to one side and saw an Orthean male bent over one of the wounded, feeding him a liquid – *ataile*, to ease pain? – and moved restless to look the other way, and saw a human face. A black Pacifican, hair pulled back into a horse-tail; squatting on his haunches beside me, his gaze fixed on the distant city, and it seemed an hour before I could remember his name.

"Lutaya?"

He glanced at me, then over his shoulder at the camp, and then back at me. "The medic's here somewhere – don't worry: you're going to be all right. Lie still."

WEBcast equipment cluttered his back, on a knotted makeshift strap. There were dark stains on the knees of his coveralls. Sunlight on his face showed it strained, eyes with a bruised look to them; and though he tried to sound reassuring, his tone was flat.

Painkillers. I recognize the feeling: that time has slowed or stopped completely. . . . My mouth had a sour taste in it. Without thought, I hitched myself up on to my elbows; dizziness blacked out vision and I thought *It should have been painful* and realized I could feel nothing of my right side: numb from shoulder to hip to ankle. . . . The leg of my coverall was cut away. A grey plastiflesh covering encased me from thigh to foot; and I reached down and touched the rigid, warm surface. What damage – *no, that's not important now.*

"I found you." Lutaya's voice had a touch of child-like pride. "Didn't know there were any of us caught in the settlement. Thought it was all local wounded here. Came down. Took some good shots. You're a bonus."

He grabbed my arm as I attempted to sit up, and managed it, and all but retched with a sudden nausea, and he was no more troublesome, no more importunate, than one of the *kekri*-flies that swarmed round. Blue and green and black: *kekri*-flies clustering on wounds, and on bodies that lay motionless a little way off.

"For God's sake!" he protested, shocked. Then: "Kennaway – over here! She's hysterical – "

I smothered laughter with a dirty hand, rocking back and forwards. *Someone listened to me,* I thought. The *becamil* blanket that I lay on was large, and its further edge lapped over a still shape: a body of which I could see only one foot and ankle. . . .

"This – is – *grotesque* – " And the sun was hot, nauseatingly hot; my face ran with sweat; and all I could do now was roll over, dragging my numb leg with me like dead wood, and reach over to pull the drab *becamil*-cloth. Then it was nothing grotesque, only her face, and her dark body in filthy shirt and britches, and a darker bruise on the skin over those arched ribs. And that face, sunken in repose. The skin indented down round her eyes, so that the shape of the bone is plain. . . .

"Broken rib through the lung," the WEBcaster said, without much interest. "Is there a story for the WEB in it, do you think, Representative?"

Quite calmly, I thought: You're piqued because I don't thank you for fetching a medic. Puppet-like, I mouthed suitable words. Now I was sitting up I could see the extent of this temporary refugee-camp. *Becamil*-cloth draped over sticks, small fires, huddled people; it surrounded me, and desultory groups trailed off towards the Rimon hills, and I had been staring for several moments before I saw that a good half of them wore the *meshabi*-robes of the Desert Coast, and mixed with the others unharmed, almost unnoticed.

"What . . . ?"

Lutaya stood up, staring across the valley towards the city. His tone was hard. "I've sent my reports through, Representative. That's all that concerns me. If your Company chooses to fire on that settlement, if – "

493

he broke off. More quietly, he added, "The locals don't seem much bothered now about who's who. They *all* ran. Don't make much difference when you're under fire, I guess. Here's Kennaway."

A woman in Company coveralls approached. I recognized the black medic I'd spoken to on the orbiter, when I'd called about Douggie. The woman smiled, and said briskly, "We'll have transport here in a minute. How do you feel now?"

Now? But the painkillers wouldn't let me feel. I tried to swallow, and she knelt down and held a flask to my lips:

"A sip – that's enough."

The water tasted tepid, antiseptic, wonderful.

The late afternoon sky. . . .

Clear and blue and daystarred: and Carrick's Star an incandescent white light over my right shoulder. Pain pulsed once in my head. I got my left heel and my hands – when did they get bandaged? – braced on the ground, and tried to stand: caught Kennaway and held on to her and stood, while she swore at me: "Don't put weight on that, you'll damage it even more than it already is! I didn't go to all this trouble to have you mess it up again – "

"Are communications back?"

"*Sit down.*" She lowered me back to the ground. The knee wasn't painful. No more mine than a block of wood: why should I be careful of damaging it?

The earth was warm under my bandaged hands: I could feel it through my fingertips. Only the slightest warm breeze blew. It raised the hairs on my bare arms. A stand of *kiez* scrub blocked off the nearer shelters, and its brown foliage was already spotted with pale blue fruit: summer turning into harvest, into cold days, into the bitter frosts of winter. . . . I stared round at all the nameless faces. Where are my friends who were in the city? Where are the people I know? I can't ask at every campfire, at every shelter, at every pile of bodies waiting for the funeral burning – ah God I can't stand never to know! But sheer numbers and time defeat me now.

"Do something for me," I asked. "I want to – I need them to bring something from Kumiel Island. Is Kumiel still . . . it doesn't matter. Tell them I'm bringing – a body back for burial. I want . . ."

Some way for her to go home with dignity. Kennaway's face showed incomprehension, impatience, and with a touch of that same macabre humour I thought, *I daresay they're busy at the moment.*

Manoeuvring my stiff, numb leg so that it didn't get in my way, I eased myself over to where I could wrap the drab *becamil* blanket around

494

her cold body, and sit beside her, and wait for them to come.

Not long now, I promised. And then I can put my decision into action.

'Now that I'm Hexenmeister,' Ruric said, 'I have the memory of your coming here, eight years ago. And I have the memories the then Hexenmeister took from you. . . . I've been Lynne de Lisle Christie. . . . I'd been four years in exile from the Hundred Thousand, Orhlandis was broken up, Rodion dead, Suthafiori dead. And because you were here before you went back to Tathcaer, and found out what I'd done, I saw myself through your eyes, as you saw me: a friend.'

Friend, is it? I put the brightly-coloured memory away; and with a gruesome humour, thought: Last time I was in the Hundred Thousand I thought travelling with a child slowed me down, that's nothing to travelling with a corpse. . . .

"I'll give you a shot." Kennaway reached for her medic-pak.

"I don't need anything." You can take laughter for hysteria, for battle fatigue, for whatever you like to think of it as: I see it, simply, as fact. She is dead and she is a damn nuisance –

Kennaway's voice reached me, muffled: "That's better. You'll do better to cry; best treatment I know."

Clouds cast their shadows on the sea, and on the hills below, and Carrick's Star shone white on these cumulus, gliding east away from the sun. The waves soughed: a constant hiss on the shingle. Light caught their green crests as they rolled over and exploded into surf. The rock jolted my leg as I was lowered down from the 'thopter. Pain stabbed my hip: the knee had no sensation at all. Kennaway gripped my arm, signalling to the 'thopter pilot, and the craft soared up again, rotors raising dust from the dry earth of Kumiel Island. I heard a distant sound like sheet metal being shaken. The crags of the island blocked my view of the mainland, across the straits to the city. . . . I stared up at the evening sky: pitch-black with rising smoke. No wind blew to bring the smell of burning.

"Representative, I'd better get you to the shuttle."

I glanced at Kennaway, tightened my grip on the metal strut that, tucked under one armpit, made a makeshift crutch, and then realized that two of the young officers who'd travelled in the 'thopter were going ahead now. They carried a heavy, cloth-shrouded bundle between them; treading carefully on the earth tracks of this rocky islet. The sun sent their shadows long and dark before them.

I dug the strut into the earth with every step, swinging my immobilized leg; and the pain in that hip began to sicken me. The setting sun brought

495

sweat out on my forehead. I reached the top of the slight rise.

Two F90 shuttles stood on the landing field, their crews clustered round the ramps; and I looked past their sunlit hulls to the dome of the comlink-centre, saw a distant figure which must be Lutaya rushing to put out another 'cast – the Company representative found – and then two or three more people came out of the dome, and one pointed in my direction. Even at this distance, I knew him. I was conscious of no joy. I could only think, *I've nothing to say to you now.*

I stood still, waiting, as they crossed the hundred yards between us.

"Shuttle?"

Kennaway said, "Most base personnel have already been evacuated up to the orbiter. Excuse me, Representative; I'm just going to contact the medic team up there." She turned and strode towards the dome, calling a few words as she passed those approaching.

A fair-haired Peace Force officer: Ottoway. Another officer that I didn't know, who broke step to speak with the body-carriers, and looked across at me with a frown on his face. Behind them, Douglas Clifford.

"Oh, my dear." He put his arms round me, and I felt him shake. Then he stood back, and the level sun caught his face, and showed exhaustion on those prim features: there was dirt on his grizzled hair, and the plastiflesh dressing on his eye. His gaze went past me to the shrouded body. "Who – ?"

Douggie, is there any part of you that for one moment thinks – hopes – it's Blaize? But that's not important now. I dug the strut firmly into the trodden-down earth of the landing field.

"Put her in the shuttle," I ordered. "Keep it powered up; and I want a pilot."

"Lynne, for God's sake, who is it?"

"Ruric," I said, and saw the beginning of a stupefied shock on his face; turned my head and watched them carry her across the field so that I wouldn't have to see Douggie. What can I say to you? Nothing, I thought.

The pain gave me energy now. I said sharply, "Where's Commander Mendez?"

A slow flush spread under Ottoway's fair skin. The stocky man opened his mouth to speak, shut it again, and then burst out: "What else could we do? It was *three hours* before we knocked that transmission-blocker out! We had to fire on them before they got in with the friendly forces or else it would have been indiscriminate massacre – !"

Indiscriminate. I felt a laugh catch in my throat "'Friendly' forces! Did you hear that Ortheans fired on that 'thopter when it picked me up – oh yes, only winchbows in the camp, but they fired!"

"*We* didn't attack first – "

I shifted, and a stab of pain made me gasp. Doug, with a concerned expression on his face, moved to take my arm; I waved him away. He stared intently at me. Nothing to hear now but the distant surf, the distant roar of engines; the sun is warm on my cheek.

"I don't want to know about it," I said. "Where's Cory?"

Ottoway shrugged. "The Rimnith–Keverilde area."

"*Melkathi?* What – " Incredulous, I turned to Doug.

It was a second before he answered, that intent gaze still on me, and when he did, it was to say absently, "There's been fighting in several areas, not just Tathcaer. I believe it's still going on." He stepped to the right, pointing; and I limped across and stared out to sea, following his gaze. "And there's that. . . ."

The still blue surface of the sea was darker on the horizon, as if it had soaked up ink. Specks reflected back the light of the setting sun, where they cruised far out to sea; and they were metal-sailed, and though I couldn't see properly at this distance I knew them for *jath* and *jath-rai*.

"Are they waiting?"

"Scared to come in – and too badly provisioned to go home," Doug guessed.

All along that panorama of the sea: dozens of the tiny craft. . . . I turned my back on them. *That, also, is not now my concern.* It hit me again: that face of hers, forgotten for whole minutes at a time, so clear in my mind's eye: Ruric Hexenmeister.

"Representative?" Ottoway said cautiously. I looked at him; his expectancy, and shook my head. Did I want to ask you questions? I thought. Did I really? Why?

"See to the shuttle for the Representative," Doug ordered; and Ottoway shrugged at the dismissal, and walked away across the landing field; and I watched him go without really seeing him.

"I think you're in shock."

"No," I said.

"Of course, you realize that this has finished Corazon Mendez's career. The WEBcasters are cutting her to pieces. In twelve days there won't be a Pacifican on Earth who doesn't know her name and revile it." He watched me narrowly.

"And my name?" That made me smile.

"Yours too, yes, but please don't be concerned. Lynne, I'm certain that it can be put right." He waited. Then he sighed. "You haven't the slightest interest in that now, have you? It's hardly surprising. Lynne, you must rest for a short time; even if it's only a few minutes – please."

A dizzy inconsequentiality touched me. What does it matter what I do now? In a short time – a very short time – it won't matter at all.

"Where do you want me to go, Douggie?"

He frowned, and looked me up and down in the sunlight.

I must present a figure like some WEBcast refugee; hair thick with dirt, coveralls ripped, leg bound rigid in plastiflesh-cast; hands bandaged, and a crutch to walk with. . . . And suddenly there was a pulse of pain; the world snapped into focus.

"Christ, yes, let me sit down!"

"Sit down before you fall down," he advised, the humour no more than reflex; and hovered beside me as I limped across towards the comlink-dome. It towered white in the sunlight. I was almost at the port when I registered torn cables, shattered plastiglas; and realized I was staring at a twelve-foot hole in the side of it. *They did attack Kumiel, then. I thought the hiyeks wouldn't pass us by.* I entered, and faces turned towards me, and I eased down into the nearest seat, leg jutting out in front of me.

"Representative, what – ?" One of the young officers stood up.

"The Representative needs medical care," Doug interposed.

I leaned back, shutting my eyes and letting it pass me by.

The vast dome of the sky arches over me, webbed with light, flowering with the brilliance of Orthe's summer stars. In this Tower garden the scent of kazsis-nightflower and arniac are chokingly strong. . . .

Doug's hands were warm around mine; he clasped them very lightly through the bandages. I opened my eyes. He sat leaning towards me, all the urbanity gone from his manner; and I could see (as one rarely sees with friends) how he comes to be a government envoy.

"I must be sure I have this right. Lynne, you're telling me Ruric is dead? The Hexenmeister? That was her body they were carrying to the shuttle?"

"Yes."

The Tower garden, the cold siir in ceramic bowls; the night winds blowing from the city, Kasabaarde. And, distant, blotting out stars, the first chiruzeth spire of the Rasrhe-y-Meluur. . . .

'You know it,' Ruric said softly. 'Ancient light can't be destroyed. Not once it's created. All we could do was hold it back. We are still holding it back.'

Douggie swore: his hands tightened on mine so that I winced.

"Lynne, I'm sorry, I didn't mean – " His voice was too quiet to be heard at the half-dismantled line of holotanks and comlink consoles; still, he leaned closer to me. "I never knew her as you did. All I can think is, all that knowledge lost – the Tower Archives must be priceless; and with her gone, who can understand them?"

"It isn't quite like that, Douggie."

498

The sun leaked whitely in through the breach in the dome, and shone on his sparse, tightly-curled hair; and cast a shadow down over one injured and one bright eye. His head came up, he nodded once, sharply, to himself: "I thought there must be more. Good God, what have we done when we came here?"

And Ruric Orhlandis grins, in that Tower garden; speaking with a macabre humour that is part her, part that old man who was Hexenmeister, and partly a hundred generations of others:

'Wouldn't be the first time that's happened! . . . So long as the body comes living, or newly-dead, to the Tower, the memory-transfer can be made. You s'aranthi would say we need 'living cells'. That isn't accurate, but it'll serve.'

And I thought of her voice not six hours ago saying, *Take me there anyway.*

"I can't stay here long. I'm taking her body back to the Tower." Now I drew my hands away from his, but only so that I could take a grip on his fingers; try to pass through that touch some idea of how critical this is; and I said, "Douggie, I want to tell you. . . . I – she and I – we owe you some explanation. And what does it matter what you know now?"

Analgesics kill pain but not weakness. Knowing even the smell of food would sicken me, I choked down protein-supplements; buoyed up on the impatience of waiting for the shuttle to power up. Two more F90s came in during that time. I couldn't stand to listen to comlink-nets, but when I limped outside and listened, I could hear distant engines, but no explosions. No firing.

Carrick's Star hung on the rim of the sea.

All the clouds in the vast dome of the sky glowed lilac, and ash-white. I turned my face up to the sky. The line of light is invisible, except where it strikes the upper limits of the pall of black smoke, drifting infinitely slowly to the east; glowing amber in the upper sunlit atmosphere.

I wish that I could see her face. There was a discarded crate on this edge of the landing field, and I eased myself down on to it, leg sticking out straight; and rested the strut on the sparse mossgrass. The F90 shuttle rested on the earth fifty yards away. *I wish that I could talk to you again.*

There is grit on the earth at my feet. Each pebble has its own precise shadow. There are things I would sooner think of than the way you died: choking, in agony, without dignity, without hope. You will have seen such deaths before, being a soldier. And that's no comfort. Something broke in me when you died; and if I hadn't turned my back on this world, I should always have known that it would.

499

Take me there anyway.

I raised my head and looked past the shuttle, past the edge of the rocks and out to sea. Lines of currents curve to the estuary here; but my back is turned on that devastated city, on the *telestres*, on whatever fighting there still may be. Out there, sea meets sky. And beyond that, far to the south, is a desert coast and a desert city, and a Tower that has stood these five thousand years.

And the Elansiir and the Barrens and the Glittering Plain. Because there was a city seen in mist and mirror-light . . .

And the sea is quiet.

"You should rest," Doug's voice said from behind me. He walked to where I could see him.

"I have to go to Kasabaarde."

The sea took his gaze. After a moment he put his hands behind his back, absently tapping his fingers together; and I couldn't help but smile: *that's Doug.* As he turned he saw my expression, and frowned.

"I'd feel easier – " He hesitated. The sun was at his back and I couldn't see his face, and squinting was painful. He repeated, "I'd feel easier . . . Lynne, you ought to grieve." That said all in a rush: then he added, "God knows this is a disaster, but if you go as well, I don't think I – well, it doesn't matter. I know you well enough to know this isn't shock or grief, and I don't like it."

Blinking into the light, I said, "I can hold it together – just – because I've got this that I have to do; and then I've taken a decision."

He came and squatted down on his haunches beside me, this middle-aged man in envoy's uniform; and the sunset put his long shadow on to the crate and the mossgrass. Sparks danced in the air: a handful of *kekri*-flies.

"Lynne, I didn't persuade a Company 'thopter to land out at that refugee camp and fetch you, just to have you commit suicide on me."

His tone was rallying, serious enough to let me know he thought it a real possibility, and I looked at that round face; no humour at all in it now, and thought how she would have laughed, and said *too serious to be solemn about.* And so it is, I thought, so it is. . . .

"In a way, yes. Just that."

Shock spread over his face. He protested inarticulately.

"Don't, Douggie. I shan't die – but I shan't go back to Earth, either."

It was an effort to get up unaided, even with the stick, but I made it, and stood sweating for a moment; grinning at the pain. Pain is sometimes the only sensation you can bear. Now I could see him without having to look up at him: Doug Clifford, envoy. And see (however he tries to hide it, out of respect for grief) how much he disapproves.

"You'll stay on Orthe."

"Yes."

And once you said to me, *There are so few who can live with an aeon of memories*. But I can. He made me apprentice, that old man the Hexenmeister, though he never intended it for this. Would your Tethmet Fenborn approve, if he still lives? I think he wouldn't. But I *know* I can live with the Tower's memories, I have done just that for the past eight years – if not (and I hear how you would laugh) if not very well.

To Doug, I said, "It's the only way that I can handle this. Please. Understand that."

A change to something unimaginable. . . . Is that what it means: to be named for Her, for Orthe, to become all of Orthe? And if, when, I take her memories, will I have Ruric with me again? Can I bear it, to see me as she saw me!

I thought, But I know one thing. If I go into the Tower again, I shall not be Christie after that happens; not Lynne Christie, and certainly not Christie *S'aranth*.

CHAPTER 39

The Child of Santhendor'lin-sandru

A low hum filled the air. One YV9 shuttle came over the northern edge of the island, hovered, and then sank down on to the landing field; another followed; and then an F90, settling to earth almost silently, and I felt the ground vibrate underfoot. The sunset shone on the white hulls, now stained with smoke and soot. As I watched, the ramps extruded and the crews came out on to the field.

Doug Clifford said, "There's an hour or so of light left. I'm going to take a 'thopter out to the Oranon River valley. . . ." He sighed heavily. "If the *T'An Suthai-Telestre* is alive – or the Earthspeaker Cassirur – or any of the *takshiriye* . . ."

"How will you find them?"

That urbane self-mockery returned for just a moment. He said, "Lynne, I shan't, but it eases me to *look*."

The powering-up must be almost complete, I thought, keeping my gaze fixed on the further shuttle. Pain made a nagging ache in my hip. I clasped both hands on the metal strut and leaned it on the earth between my feet.

"You won't find any of them."

Cassirur and Nelum Santhil, Bethan *T'An* Kyre, Khassiye Reihalyn . . . Romare Kerys-Andrethe and Hildrindi *hiyek*-Anzhadi . . . the names bring faces to me: they are suddenly real. *If Hal is still alive* – and I left you by the wall of the Citadel in the early morning light; left you there. It comes to me now that I won't see you again.

Douggie gave me a concerned look: the one name between us is *Meduenin*.

"I'll go," I said.

"It's several hours across the Inner Sea; the pilots are most unwilling to fly at night without a navigation-WEB – " He broke off, glancing over his shoulder.

Ottoway came out of the comlink-dome, squinting at the level light. It shone on his florid face. Aware only of irritation, I waited until he strode up to us, and said:

"Is the shuttle powered?"

"I'm sorry, Representative. Commander Mendez won't authorize the flight."

502

I laughed. Looked at this man in Peace Force uniform and laughed, and then said, "But I'm going anyway, you know that."

"Commander Mendez won't authorize it yet." He shot a glance at Doug that was almost an appeal for help. Run ragged, I thought. It's all fallen apart and even *you* know that. I said nothing.

Ottoway said, "She's in the Rimnith–Keverilde area. When we reported you'd been found alive, she – Representative, she wants you there, wants you with her; she says a matter of the utmost urgency – "

"Commander Mendez isn't in a position to give orders now."

Curious, to stand here arguing. This is trivial. . . . The warm air soothes my skin, and back-blasts of heat come from more shuttlecraft as they land; and it is easy to look across the earth to the shuttle where her body lies. *I won't be long about it; we'll be gone soon. Tomorrow –*

How do I know that I have a day's grace to get her to the Tower? And then I thought: Listen to the memories. I already know a little of what she knew. That means I know what to do.

" – Representative!"

Ottoway stepped into my field of vision, blocking out the shuttle and the sea beyond. I brought my gaze back from the horizon, that line that is unique in nature, being straight; and stared at the man.

"Commander Mendez has a prisoner," he repeated. "She told me to give you the name of *Calil bel-Rioch* – "

That name, stumbled over by this man, spoken with a Sino-Anglic accent – he doesn't know what he's saying, I thought; and Douggie's hand closed on my good shoulder, and I felt his tension.

"She's alive?" he demanded; then shook his head. "It doesn't matter. I don't want to know. Lynne, I'll see you before you leave." He let go of my shoulder and abruptly walked off.

A precipitate flight . . . he vanished into the entrance of the comlink-dome; a small, neat figure. And Ashiel Wellhouse will always be with him, I thought; and Sethri's death, and a cold heathland *telestre*, and the blindness and the fear.

"I can speak more openly, Representative, now that the government envoy isn't here. Commander Mendez wishes your help in interrogating the prisoner," Ottoway said, with a kind of self-satisfied pleasure in this remnant of Security routine.

"She doesn't need *me*. The shuttle – "

"Commander Mendez won't pass a message in clear, except that she needs your specialized knowledge. It concerns the discussions you had here two days ago; and the research-report made by Dr Rashid Akida."

I clenched both hands on the metal crutch; and suddenly realized how fragile a balance I held between control and collapse and I can't take this: Ruric, what do I do?

The sky is blue and daystarred, but I have been where Orthe's sky is acid-white. Where a city stands without walls, where there are rooms without doors; and I remember the Voice of the Emperor Dannor, and how we stood together in Kel Harantish, Calil and I, and called up a vision of the past aeons; and I remember her face in the throne-room saying *Your Molly Rachel is dead.*

Doesn't she know her bluff's been called? I thought caustically. Doesn't she know there's no weapon she can threaten us with now?

Lost, momentarily; I have no grip on the Tower's memories. I was conscious of being worn to the edge of exhaustion. The noise of shuttles landing battered at my ears; on the earth and sparse mossgrass, under a sky still shrouded with the smoke of burning.

"Get the shuttle ready," I said. As Ottoway protested, I added, "Contact Cory. Tell her I'll be landing in Melkathi inside the hour – and that I'll be leaving again immediately afterwards."

In the few minutes before the shuttle was readied for flight, I limped up the slope to where I could look out across Kumiel Island to the north. And I could see across the straits and the estuary, to Tathcaer.

A summer wind began to blow, now that the sun was setting. The stink of burning grew strong enough to catch in the throat, and in eyes; is it possible, across six miles, to hear the crackle and roar of burning?

The silhouettes of the hills were ragged, no forts visible; and on Westhill, Westhill-Ahrentine would be *there* – no, too distant to make out one *telestre*-house. I strained my eyes, seeing alleys choked with rubble, smashed-open courtyards and buildings; half-sunk *jath* in the harbour. . . . Smoke rolled down Easthill, obscuring the view. From here you can't see people, can't see the long trails of refugees. The blue hills are quiet, the river valley peaceful, even the pall of smoke hangs still and delicate in the golden air . . . pain and misery invisible now, and I thought *Blaize.*

How could I explain to him what I'm doing and why? I couldn't bear to see the look on his face – *I never want to see you again but I want to know you're living!*

And some caustic inner voice, that is no one else's but mine, observed, *You'll find that out eventually, the Tower has its agents and ways of knowing. You will discover, in the months to come, who has lived and who has died: all of them.*

And by then, maybe I won't care.

A voice hailed me from the field, and I went back, slow and awkward, to the ramp of the F90 shuttle; and went aboard.

Second twilight darkened to night over Melkathi's heathland. I walked from the shuttle to Ashiel Wellhouse, feeling the cold night breeze; and paused on that hill slope to look down to the east – the land was dark. Some things it is better not to want to see. The Peace Force officer fussing at my elbow came back, waiting impatiently; and I rubbed at my hip, at the top of the plastiflesh casing, and took a pain-tab from my belt-pouch. Chewing the bitter analgesic, I gripped my stick and limped across the courtyard – the domed building loud with lights and voices and then I saw why: Earthspeakers went between groups of wounded, lying out on the warm earth; gave *ataile*-juice for sleep; and when *s'aranthi* passed, ignored us as if we had no existence. A child sobbed, over by the low wall, and *They'll hate us more for the wounded than for the dead; death is the lesser penalty*, I thought. And then, ironically, *And when did* we *become the enemy?* One young, still face I didn't recognize until I had passed by; and then thought of a Freeport quayside and Rakviri food-ships – Pellin Asshe Kadareth, all threats silenced now.

"Commander, the Representative is here."

Corazon Mendez stepped from the entrance of the Wellhouse, out into the torch-lit courtyard. Flickering yellow light shone on her rumpled uniform, on that sleek short-cut white hair; and I saw a CAS-IV holstered at her belt, a comlink held in the hand that now seemed suddenly thin; silver rings loose on those liver-spotted fingers.

"No one else on the shuttle?" Her voice was sharp.

"No, Commander," the young officer said hastily.

"I'll have no WEBcasters travel on Service ships; I want none of them out here – Lynne, will you come inside."

As I limped past her, I glanced into her face. It had a vague, almost blurred look; in sharp contrast to her speech. The pupils of her blue eyes were pinpoints; and she shut her eyes and squeezed the lids together, and casually dismissed the young officer.

"Glad to see you made it, Lynne."

The bathos of that made me stop, in the curved inner room, and stare back at her; my hip ached and my leg was numb and I held self-control on a very fragile thread: "Is that all you can say!"

"I don't want any of that nonsense."

She walked past me, heading towards the inner rooms. They looked, through the round-arched entrance, to be deserted; I wondered why, and then saw the armed Peace Force officers there. *In a Wellhouse* – but there are worse things, now, than that.

"I'll see Calil bel-Rioch and then go," I said.

"I thought . . . she's threatening us with Witchbreed Technology; nothing in it, of course, but one has to cover every eventuality. Seems to know a lot about it. God alone knows how much black-market arms trading the Ishida girl did; don't have to worry about *alien* technology . . ."

Corazon Mendez hesitated. A torch in a wall-cresset flickered, and her shadow shifted on the brickwork; and the wind brought the smell of many people crowded into close quarters: musk and sweat and dirt and sickness, and I tasted pain, metallic in my own mouth. Cory still stood as if she listened for something. Almost inconsequentially she said, "There's still fighting going on. There'll have to be mop-up operations."

Not with you, I thought. Anyone involved in this will be crucified at home, because PanOceania will have to make themselves look good; and so there have to be villains to pillory. You, and me if I were here, and *That also is not my concern*; in a way what I'm doing is cowardice.

As I followed Mendez through into the next room, I was suddenly hit by a memory – I have thought of Wellhouses, and of what I once said: to be marked for Her is not a privilege but a responsibility. Not *all* cowardice; I am going where the responsibility calls me. And if there are other apprentices in the Tower better suited, then I'll come back to Earth and take that responsibility there.

But I think I will not leave Orthe again.

"See if you can get anything out of the woman," Cory Mendez stood back from a door-arch for me to go through. "I don't – haven't the time."

As she turned away I realized, *She's given up*. A kind of sadness touched me briefly; and vanished. I know very well that when the shock passes, she will have justifications that even she will believe, for what's happened here – for what we have done.

I stepped through the arch, into the main Wellhouse dome; and without knowing how I thought or sensed it, realized *Danger* and then *is Mendez right; is there nothing to be concerned about?* and a sudden fear twisted in my stomach: *it isn't over until it's over. And it isn't over yet.*

One of the Peace Force guards took my CAS-IV as I went in. The stone floor was hard underfoot, and the metal strut I used as a crutch skidded slightly; I put my weight down on my cased leg, and hissed as pain shot through my hip. I crossed the floor of the inner dome in a few limping steps, and lowered myself down to sit on the raised rim of the Wellmouth.

Light filled the room. Starlight shone in through the roof-slot, and an iron candlestand dripped under the weight of *becamil*-wax candles; that

506

familiar sweet scent. Apart from that the room was bare. Yellow light, and moving shadows. No tables or couch-chairs and I thought, *Cory may not know or care what this place is, but why has the Wellkeeper let her use it to keep a prisoner in?* The Goddess's Well defiled by a Harantish Witchbreed in the inner sanctuary – and then I saw her and I knew. . . .

"*Kethrial-shamaz shan'tai*," said the Harantish Orthean woman, as she walked across the uneven brick floor. She carried a metal jug in one hand, and was chewing; and as I looked up she swallowed and wiped her mouth, and put the jug down on the rim of the Well beside me.

Small, no more than five feet high; and thin – her pale grained skin caught lamp and starlight, almost luminous; and her mane was a white fire drifting round that narrow face; and I sat gazing up at her for a long minute, silent, and realized that this woman was barefoot, and wearing a *meshabi*-robe yellow and brown with dirt; girdled with a verdigris-copper chain; and that she was ash-stained and bleeding from one foot, and none of it mattered – *she is Golden; is Santhendor'lin-sandru's heir, who was Phoenix Emperor and Last Emperor* – and I reached for my stick to try and stand up: pain jabbed hip and thigh as I tried to rise; and it cleared my head.

She is only one Orthean woman; a woman of the city Kel Harantish. And that's all she is, I thought; sinking back down, and reaching forward to shift my leg and try to ease it:

"*Kethrial-shamaz shan'tai* Calil."

Never underestimate charismatic insanity – but she's a prisoner now. And more than that: the Tower has put memories in my mind – when she lies, I'll know, I thought; *and I'll know when, and if, she tells the truth.*

The young Orthean woman put a dirty, high-arched foot on the rim surrounding the Well. Starlight shone down into the Wellmouth, gleaming on black water that lay only a few inches down from the rim. There is never a smell of stagnant water in Wellhouses; I don't know why. She looked down at the glittering blackness, and her profile was sharp and unhuman. White mane rooted down her spine, fell forward over high cheek-bones; and she turned her head to gaze at me, nictitating membrane sliding back from sunny yellow eyes.

Why her and not you – ?

"So you're living still," the Orthean woman remarked cheerfully. As if she were perfectly at home, she sat down on the rim of the Wellmouth, rested her foot on the stone, and cupped Well water in her hand to bathe blood from her cuts; adding, "I want to talk to you. These *s'aranthi* here are fools."

Disgust filled me. *I could rehearse what she's done, these past few* months; but what use. I said, "You're not important, Calil. Can you grasp that? You're not important; I've a few minutes here; if you've got anything to say, then say it. But you haven't, have you?"

Becamil-wax candles hissed in the silence, and burned tall and smoky. The pale plaster roof above them was becoming soot-blackened. The young Harantish woman leaned forward, resting her arms on her raised knee; so close to me that I could smell the musk of her skin. She smiled.

"No, I'm not important, *shan'tai* Christie. I always told you that. You would have it that no one in my city wanted this except myself – well, no matter; my Harantish bloodlines are still out there – " a thin, six-fingered hand gestured to the door; and the land beyond – "in the hills, or on *jath* and *jath-rai*. . . . I tell you truthfully, whatever *I* would do if I were there now, there are a hundred Harantish who will do the same. And so no, I don't matter at all."

Listening to her, I almost believe that she wants to be here. That the Peace Force guards just beyond the arch are unnecessary. That this is, as it was in that *chiruzeth* hall in Kel Harantish, an audience with the Empress-in-Exile. . . . *What a farce*, I thought, half-amused, half-disgusted.

These are the people who would have occupied Tathcaer. And then this Calil bel-Rioch would have threatened the use of a weapon she doesn't have; would have threatened to make the Hundred Thousand into what the Elansiir and the Glittering Plain already are: sterile crystalline devastation. . . .

"What do you want to say?"

Instead of answering, she put her arms down from her knee, and lowered the leg to the floor, and began to wipe at the mudstains on her *meshabi*-robe. The tiny hook-nails on her fingers were bitten ragged, and they caught in the cloth; and the skin of her six-fingered hands had in it a gold-dust sheen. She raised her head quickly, as if a sound startled her.

Why, yes – and I couldn't, for a moment, breathe; the realization choked me. That pale hawk-face is younger than hers, but similarities go deeper than the eyes: that high-boned face is so like . . . Ruric, didn't you say to me once, *My Desert Coast mother may have come from Kel Harantish?* And so she may, I thought. Is it coincidence, or some distant kinship of a bloodline?

Ah, but it doesn't matter to you now.

Calil bel-Rioch said, "What have you done with my Pathrey Shanataru, *shan'tai?*"

"Done with – " I bit back amusement, thought, *What have we done with him?* Ah, that's a question. He could be halfway to Kasabaarde and the Tower now – and at that, cut off all thought; I can't stand to remember yet what we said and did, Ruric and I, before this day.

"The *shan'tai* Pathrey was very useful in bringing us some information." And let her remember *that*, I thought; and repeated, "What do you want?"

"I was not mistaken," the Orthean woman said.

She rose lightly to her feet. My head swam when I looked up: the room lurched. Exhaustion – I don't have time to waste here, I thought. The shuttle . . .

Candles burned steadily, and then dipped; a night wind blowing in through the roof-slot, where the clustered stars blaze. Her elongated shadow danced on the pale, curving wall. She stood with her cut foot resting on claw-nailed toes; poised, as if she could run. Her robe was torn, and the smell of ash and soot hung in it. And as she turned to look down at where I sat, there was a line of head and shoulder and leg that was all grace, all strength; and the light shone on her floating white mane.

She said, "I was not mistaken. You have the look of the Tower about you. . . . *Shan'tai* Christie . . . have you travelled there, and learned, and learned well? I thought once that *I* would have to come to Kasabaarde. What I know, I do not know from them. *Shan'tai* Christie, have you learned well, and learned of what the Elansiir is?" Those lips curved; the nictitating membrane blinked down to veil her eyes.

"I've learned from the offworlders who were in Maherwa and the canals," I said bluntly. I got both hands to the metal strut and levered myself upright, resting no weight on my right hip.

As the pain abated, I said, "I don't know what it is you do. I don't care how close your people think you are to being Golden-blooded; I'm not even sure of what that means. You're threatening with something you don't have, your people don't have, no one has had on this world for thousands of years – and it's immaterial now. If I get one thing out of this, I'll get Cory to make certain you suffer for Molly's death. That girl . . ."

I see her in my mind's eye. Not the woman in PanOceanian uniform, but something I found in her Company record when I made the report on her death – an early image-cube. Against hot sunlight, an aborigine girl standing barefoot and in an old cotton dress; somewhere in her Pacifican homeland. That is Molly Rachel; that's all that's left.

"Her? That was not I; that was my Pathrey. He is something of a liar," the young Harantish woman said; but her gaze shifted away from mine.

I want to hurt you – if exhaustion and pain weren't confusing me, I thought, I would know what to say; I would damage you so that you *care*. That it's a pinprick, compared to what is happening now on this world, I know and I don't care; and that there are others doing what you've done . . . Rage faded with the realization that quite probably any of the Harantish would have acted as she did.

Calil bel-Rioch turned, walking away from me. She carried one foot lame. When she stopped, it was on the far side of the Wellmouth. Candles gleamed on the black water. Her reflection shone – mirror-perfect: pale mane, gold-dust skin, and that hawk-face with the unveiled yellow eyes. . . .

"They make their religion of this," she said thoughtfully, staring down at the Well water. "We gave them this, too. When we bred them from animals, bred memory into their bone. . . . *Shan'tai* Christie, what did you learn in the Tower?"

To look down into that dark water is to sense the aeons of time past, the millennia that are gone; my eyes dazzled with the darkness. I have forgotten (or chosen to forget) that the past is not dead in me. That memory lives. I shivered, hands gripping tight on my stick; drugs and fever making me light-headed. I looked round at the Wellhouse walls, the pale plaster, and rough brick floor.

"I learned that what is made just for expediency's sake can become genuine."

"Can it so?" She smiled, shook her head; and then reached down to dip her hand in the Well water, and straightened up again, and put her fingers in her mouth. And it was that simple movement that brought memory back in a rush: the Golden Empire and the dead who are gone, and this half-blooded Harantish woman wears the face that is Santhendor'lin-sandru's.

All I could say was "*Why?*" Blood doesn't compel; the past is not the present, surely?

She stood quite still. There were smears of black ash on her hands. Her robe was dirty. She stood: that whitefire mane taking the colours of candle-flame and starlight. Her eyes met mine, and I saw her exhaustion, her fear; and only then wondered how she had been hunted, captured, this young Orthean woman who now looks at me as if it is me she sees – not the Representative, not the *S'aranth*, but me.

"It's true that I wanted the Hundred Thousand for my people," she said, "and that certain things – to be Empress – I have wanted very badly. But that wanting, that desire, wouldn't be assuaged now by the having of it. Wanting things like that somehow awakens the real desire, the *real* longing, of which that is only a shadow or a memory."

The water of the Well is ruffled, and the night wind is cold. Her soft voice continues:

"I *want* . . . something I had, or saw, or heard of, long ago. And if you ask what it is that I desire, I don't know. I have sensed it sometimes in the way light and haze and shadow fall – they remind me, I do not know how, that somehow and long ago I was disinherited; *we . . . were disinherited, robbed, sent into exile;* and we will always desire something to put in place of what we lost, and there is nothing to match that desire."

Do the candles flicker, does the starlight fail? Between pain and fever and blindness; I want to call out, there are guards just outside this room. But the dome is thick with shadow. *You have cause to be afraid. We have all cause to be afraid!*

Tower-memories are mine, and at my control. Now, as she walks towards me, reaches up to brush my cheek with her long-fingered hand, I feel how it is to have memory *imposed* upon the mind: recall how eight years ago in the Tower I felt this pain that, if it lasted longer than an instant, would be intolerable agony; but this is not the Tower –

high walls thick with shadow

– Calil bel-Rioch's yellow eyes; and vision:

The Golden have lit fires upon which they cast bone and bread, in the secret places of the city; and speak over them words that should not be spoken; and go willing where – soon or late – the dawn of that ancient brilliance will take them. The thin tang of smoke and the charnel-house stench of the butchery in the lower city comes on the cool air to me now. . . .

"Hear the word of Santhendor'lin-sandru! Hear the word of the Golden Empire. In the heart and centre of this city, in Archonys of the Six Lakes, this is Night's Festival!"

The half-blood who is the Emperor's Voice stands beside the Emperor's throne. And his words are hidden now in a great roar of sound, a multitude of voices; for this is the city's last festival, and this is the Empire's last festival, and this is the last that earth will know of us and we of earth.

"Hear the word of Santhendor'lin-sandru of the Golden! He has created in darkness a light that does not die. He has set in the flesh of this world a plague and a canker and a disease of all that is mortal. Now is the last ritual!"

On the vast chiruzeth floor, we raise our voices. Our robes are coloured grey and ash and black; and I stand, moving with my brethren of the Golden – they walk on high-arched feet, whitefire manes electric in the dark air. Our faces are this night hidden behind fantastic masks, painted blue and gold and silver; masks and robes reflecting in the mirror-black chiruzeth floor.

Now music sounds: the only music we will have, and that is our voices, raised in high paean: now one voice and now another, joining, changing, harsh, atonal – the echoes ring back from cyclopean galleries. We sing together, who are the Golden of Archonys.

Here on this timeless night, I have no name. I move alone.

And night comes.

Our hands lift, to scatter handfuls of light-dust upon the night air. Dust that swirls and drifts and glows the colour of frozen lightning. Arms sweep up, long-fingered hands open: light is cast upon the air, reflects in golden eyes, on sharp high cheekbones, drifts to catch in tangling manes. . . .

One leads us, in a robe that is black and silver, and he cradles in the crook of one slender arm a globe and ragged staff. He comes to where we are, taking in his cold hand another's hand, leading us out to dance – no choice now but to join the dance – and he takes another's hand, and the chain begins to form. Led away, each of us: Golden and slave, great lords of the Witchbreed made equal now with the beast-born race; all equal in the Dance that ends all pride, levels all ambition –

I hear our voices soar up frail into the dark. Chiruzeth is cold under my feet: time breathes from its substance, darkening the air with the chill of aeons. A slender hand reaches out: I take it and move to the ritual measure.

" – Stop!"

Beyond the pillars I see out into the night, into the city. The walls go up into an infinite dark, that shrouds cornice and pinnacle and balcony and terrace. And in avenues like canyons between palaces and mausoleums, they are holding masquerade and festival –

"Cease!"

Dancers halt: a frieze of shock. Santhendor'lin-sandru on his high throne looks down and sees a slight figure, one of the slave race. It is one of our failures, a child that has remained child although adult: the beast race call it ashirenin. There are a number of them every year, their lives are short.

Ke raises kir head, gazing with membraned eyes at the Emperor Santhendor'lin-sandru on his throne. Kir skin is a rich, burnt-earth brown, and kir mane is gold, flowing down the spine, braided round kir sharp face.

"O did I not say – "

Kir rich, sexless voice; halfway between speech and song.

" – say, your time would come to you, as it came to the Eldest Empire before you – "

Slowly, we gather round. Ke is barefoot on the black chiruzeth floor, and ke stands and gazes, ignoring watchers; kir eyes only on Santhendor'lin-sandru.

" – that your time would come, and you would pass away from the earth!"

Ke laughs. There are small flowers braided in kir mane, and ke puts that mane back from kir lined face, with hands calloused by long years of labour. Somewhere far up in the galleries a flute is being played, up in the tenebrous arches.

Santhendor'lin-sandru stands. His white metalmesh robe trails after him, its collar frames his hawk-face: *that face that is all angles; cruel mouth and sun-gold eyes. Behind him are swathes of crepuscular light.*

Wearily, he says, "Take that and kill it."

"No, you who were called Emperor!"

And he says, "Why not? You are Ours, We created you, bred you up from the night-hunter beasts of the fens to be Our servants – "

"As you were bred by others." *Ke smiles, head high, alone.* "Emperor of the Golden, we were all created, and what is that to you or me?"

There are knives in the hands of us who crowd close to kir, but ke ignores them. Seems small and dirty beside the pale grandeur of Santhendor'lin-sandru, that white and gold.

And in softest voice Santhendor'lin-sandru asks, "What comfort have you for Us, who now pass from this earth?"

The ashirenin says, "None."

Silence in these halls, so deep that one feels the pressure of it: a sea-bed silence.

The ashirenin looks at him with clear eyes.

"I have no comfort for you, Last Emperor. You have cut yourself off from all comfort. What consolation there is, is ours. Is that of the beast-made, the slave races, the followers in dark cities of a light that does not die – of a light that returns dawn by dawn, and fails sunset by sunset, only to return again.

"We have the comfort of Her face, that brings life from the earth, and quickens death to life again. We have the comfort of that turn and return of the solid world; for we shall come again and walk upon the earth, for we have our knowledge of Her – we meet, and part, and meet again, and do not forget."

And, sardonic and amused, the Emperor says, "You have Our permission to believe that. When We made you, We bred that memory into your bone, into the motes of your flesh, so that you recall your mother's lives, and your mother's mother's; but do not ever take it for more than that. We allow you your delusion, little animal, but We mock that belief, for We know whence it came."

Black chiruzeth reflects them, white and gold shadows in the depths of night; they are dwarfed by the pillars, and by the catafalque-throne, but all our eyes are on them, those two bright figures.

The ashirenin stands, a scatter of light-dust about kir feet, sphere-lights above kir in the tenebrous air:

"This will be remembered, and forgotten, and remembered again, in the ages that are to come – hear me, Santhendor'lin-sandru! We may come to joy by way of an evil act. We may come to truth by way of a lie. Could She not use you, as you have used us? If you made us as we are, still, She made all as it is.

513

"O hear me, you in the city, you in the darkness! Hear me!"

The ashirenin turns now to face us, to the tens of thousands that watch kir; and ke stands, mane woven with flowers, tunic ragged and earth-stained. Kir eyes are clear as spring water.

"Hear me," ke says, "for I have been marked for Her, in the secret places of the earth, and I have drunk from the Wells of Her wisdom, and I see, I know – for our love of Her, we have only this reward: to carry the burden of Her preservation, and that burden we may not set down. You have loosed a death upon the world, but it will not ravage all. I see, I know –"

It is the last word of the ashirenin. Our bodies surge forward and overwhelm kir, we cry out as ke falls, and then there is a sound of bone wrenched from bone and flesh . . . A stain upon the chiruzeth, spilled blood; no other sign remaining.

And Santhendor'lin-sandru looks down upon us from his high place, and speaks:

"Let the Dance again begin!"

The stars move in their ritual patterns, and this earth turns towards the dawn.

Pain breaks it.

I felt the metal strut slip on the uneven floor; then my cased leg slid out from under me and I fell, twisting sideways; the leg without any sensation at all – but the red agony that ripped through my side and hip! I struggled, got one leg under me; felt my grazed hands on the floor. And then two hands gripped my shoulders, and I froze: aware of the candlelight flickering on the walls, shimmering on the surface of the Well. And saw, as she knelt down by the low wall, the face of Santhendor'lin-sandru's child.

I opened my mouth to cry out and she said gently, in that language that only the Imperial bloodline have ever spoken:

"___ __ _____"

Be silent, now.

My voice dried in my throat.

The brick floor was painful under me. Her face, close to mine, shone with a light that seemed to come from beneath her own skin. *Santhendor'lin-sandru. Zilkezra of the Golden.* And I have seen through those eyes –

Incredulous, I thought, *That's no Tower-memory; how did she – ?* and remembered a shared vision, outside Kel Harantish.

"This is Our city's festival," she said, "and this is the last night. That ancient light will dawn upon us, in an hour and an hour and an hour. And you have seen that great city; and you have seen the fall of the Golden Empire."

Her yellow eyes unveiled, clear as water; held me in some fascination or some moment out of Time. Pain throbbed, my mouth was dry; and I saw her simultaneously, Calil bel-Rioch of some dirtwater settlement in a desert, and Calil bel-Rioch who is the last of that ancient race, the Golden Witchbreed.

And why should she not be answered? Ruric left me a legacy of the past, of the Tower; I can answer her now.

"No – " Speech an effort: I forced myself. "If that's a true memory, what does it matter now? The world didn't end with the passing of the Empire."

I have the memory in me of those who have been Hexenmeister. With those intent eyes on me, I spoke at last with the full knowledge of that. As if I exist on two levels: this human body, dirty and pain-ridden and weary with grief, that will one day be only another's memory; and the mind that sees, in her face, the past-memories of the Golden. . . .

"The secret of its making is lost," I said, "and you cannot recover it. If *I* could not, in all my lives in the Tower, then you in your handful of years cannot expect to search out the secret heart of it, no more than Rashid Akida could. You do not have that weapon to threaten us with, Calil bel-Rioch. No matter that your memory of it is clear after three thousand years."

She said, "Do you think that We do not know what you do, what you hope?"

Her thin hands knot in the cloth of my coverall; bitten claw-nails scratch the skin. There is a sour stink of dirt about her; her copper belt stains her robe green. And all of this exists with that hawk-gold face, those shining eyes.

"'You may even stave it off for a time, you in the south, with your Tower, and your memories that are of the mind and not of the blood. . . .'" Calil speaking words that are not hers. "'But you cannot prevent it forever. We can wait the millennia that are only moments. It will come.'"

Now she stood, and I could no longer see her face; and it was Calil's own voice that went on:

"There is a Bright Realm that they speak of in the Wellhouse here. The Goddess's fire, that is the sun's fire; and do they know, I wonder, that you built a Tower that holds the sun in its grip; that it is only the sun's radiance holds back the disease of earth, holds back ancient light from their cities and their fields. . . . Do they know, or do they choose to forget, or did they never know? Tell me, *S'aranth*."

The only movement I can make is to shake my head.

"Do they know," says Calil bel-Rioch, Empress-in-Exile, in that Wellhouse room that is cold with night and silence, "that their only protection, for millennia, has been the Tower? And do they know that when the Tower falls, all else falls?"

And she says, "Call a festival, for this is the last night of my people – "

But the Dance is ended.

Dawn comes through the great arches, and I walk towards them. These have been windows opening into depths and darkness, the view from a height, and now – dawn. Warmth falls on my face as I approach, leaving the shadows. The cool of chiruzeth halls is replaced by fragile heat. The sun glows azure and aquamarine in the edges of the chiruzeth arch, a great open archway, and beyond it –

It is early morning. Pale haze is fading with the sun's rise. I look down, down on terraces of chiruzeth that fall away below me like cliffs. And all the terraces are crowded with my people.

Their skins like milk in the morning light, their manes like clouds; and they stand at balustrades carved with vines, all their faces turned towards the east, the east where the sun rises through the mist into a pale blue sky skeined with daystars.

They look. O they look, my people, and there is no space in that intense gaze for speech. I see how we stand together, arms interlinked, hands clasped, in embrace.

And as I watch, that pale yellow sunlight is tinged on far eastern hills, with a harsh silver –

Archonys of the Six Lakes, great beyond all cities, your towers in the morning sun, your great halls, your ziggurats and terraces – !

Now all eastern-facing walls are crowded with the city's people, come out to see this last dawn. Come out to stand in warm air that smells of leaves and city dust, come out to stretch in the heat of the morning sun; their faces turning up like flowers towards the light –

On eastern hills: a line of light that is silver, older than Time, bright and deadly.

I walk out on to the terrace, chiruzeth cool under my bare feet. I hear the soft clash of the metalmesh robe as I lift it from me and let it fall: stand naked to the gold eye of the sun.

And from here to the eastern hills, all is Archonys; is that great city. And on terraces that face the east, they stand, my people.

Casting aside their metalmesh robes, and raising long-fingered hands to tear their manes, to scratch their cheeks and lacerate their eyes, to raise up their voices in lamentation, to stand naked to the morning that is the last morning that this great city will ever see –

Crying their agony, the long agony of regret, for night passed that will not pass again, for day come that must soon die; for all the years that now will not come to aKirrik and Simmerath, to the City Over The Inland Sea; agony for this heart of empire that beats no more, for Archonys that is fallen, fallen; and for all the days and years and centuries that now we shall not have –

Do I weep the tears of the Golden, the world vanishing in splintered light? Do I see those sunwarmed terraces transmute to silver-crystal death?

Ah, there is no time: no time for regret that pierces sharp as a sword. We have loved the darkness and the light; and now the face of the Sun is turned from us, She has left us, earth's children, now we fade into a dream of ancient time, into a past that holds greater Empires than ours, but no greater death –

"_____ __ _____"

"____ _____"

"_____ __ _____"

Give praise, O praise us; and weep for us who loved that bright shadow, and wept too late; and will not see again sunlight and noon –

'_____ _____'

Weep for Us, and praise the light!

" – Do they know," Calil bel-Rioch says, "that when the Tower falls, all else falls?"

Her face is weary and exalted and incandescent; as if she has found at last something that will assuage that desire. The shadow of Santhendor'lin-sandru's joy (and, yes, his grief) is in her eyes. And in that ancient tongue she says:

"Did your people tell you, it cannot be created now? Ah, that's true; but it is already there and waiting. And we made our plans long ago for this, and now the Tower falls, and all barriers with it. I could not halt it now, even if that were my desire – "

A moment's aching regret, and then her voice continues:

" – all barriers fall. And we have loosed that ancient light, to dawn upon the world."

CHAPTER 40

Carrick V

Whatever I would do, she said, *there are a hundred Harantish who will do the same.*

I got to my feet somehow. At the arched doorway, I stopped; one of Cory's officers glanced at me with concern, and looked past me into the Wellhouse room.

"Do you want her moved, Representative, or kept here?"

That small figure is seated on the stone rim of the well, looking down into black water; and one thin hand holds a metal jug with which she scoops up water and pours it out again, in an endless repeating cycle . . . starlight lays a mist of silver above the Well; and her whitefire mane falls down on to her filthy robe; and that hawk-face looks down into the Goddess's Well.

And now the Tower falls.

What I said to the officer I don't know. The Wellhouse's claustrophobic domed rooms passed by in a dream; I limped, and pushed my way between Ortheans clad in priests' robes, and the wounded who lay blanket-wrapped on the floor.

And then the world came back into focus.

"*Cory –* "

Two or three young officers already occupied the room where she was; clustered round a field-comlink. Their voices had a note of hopeless urgency. Ignoring the thin crackle of reports coming in from the F90 and YV9 shuttles overflying the *telestres*, I braced my stick on the floor and limped across to where Corazon Mendez sat.

She sprawled on a couch-chair, legs stretched out before her. That sleek hair was now slicked to her forehead, pale against her liver-spotted skin; and she stared up at me with blurred eyes, and a face looking ten years older.

"You've heard what she says, then? Brought her in an hour ago, and then suddenly she claims . . ."

"What have you done?"

Cory Mendez swung her feet down, and stood up; her silver-ringed hands brushing at her coveralls, and with a touch of her old sharpness, said, "What do you take me for, Lynne? I've had round-the-clock satellite surveillance on that place, since we were informed how vital it is. There hasn't been a minute in the last few days when I haven't had a sensor reading of the Kasabaarde settlement available."

And I completely forgot to . . . But relief was swallowed up by apprehension: "Have you got any shuttles there now?"

"No." The Pacifican woman's face relapsed into lines of age. "With what's been happening here? I ordered two F90s out an hour ago, from Kumiel, but they have to repower. . . . The Kasabaarde settlement's quiet; nothing's happening!"

"What are we worrying about? She can't destroy the Tower." But a dread was growing in me. I thought: No matter how long ago it was thought of . . . what arms; what technology . . . *but didn't someone say to me once: Anything can be a weapon?*

Corazon Mendez said, "There's enough dangerous equipment on that continent to destroy a dozen settlements. It isn't the arms trading I'm thinking of. Representative Rachel had Trade&Aid programmes under-way. If you check the records you'll see earth-blasters, automatic deep-mine construction equipment – which T&A trains the local population to use. And that could have been moved. If this has been a long-term plan – "

Outside, the heathland is dark under the Heart Stars' radiance; and a few miles to the south, the sea laps on the Melkathi sandflats; and over the ocean, south and west, lies a desert shore: there is Kasabaarde, there is the broken and deserted inner city, that home of violence and vision; there is the Tower. If will could move me, I would stand there *now*.

"I'm taking the shuttle," I said. "You?"

The woman looked over at the young officers round the field-comlink. Her face was blank with bereavement. Stripped momentarily of her role as Security Officer, Company officer; she now turned her face to me, and we both stood in silence. *If we had only known* becomes *too late* in the tick of a clock. She smiled vaguely, painfully; said, "Yes. I should be there."

As she left with me, she turned back and ordered one of her junior officers: "See that government envoy Clifford is informed about where we've gone. I'll contact him from the shuttle. Tell him it's a matter of – " Corazon paused, expression fully conscious of irony. How to make words encompass *this*? She said bitterly, " – a matter of the utmost urgency."

The hull of the F90 shuttle curved against the stars, the light bright enough to show the fire-stains on it; and as I limped awkwardly up the ramp, I smelled in the night air the scent of crushed mossgrass. Cool dew fell. I looked back once at the domes of the Wellhouse, and the flickering yellow lights. A *rashaku* cried, invisible in the night air, disturbed by the noise the wounded made. Hill and heathland stretched silver-grey under starlight, and far to the east there were pinpricks of orange light that might be fire.

The shuttle thrummed into life, and I let the port close, and leaned heavily on my stick as I walked down the cabin and sat by the holotank. Soft green light illuminated the consoles. The pilot, a Pacifican man in his forties, looked queryingly at Corazon Mendez: she leaned over his shoulder to key in a course.

I reached down, lifting my plastiflesh-cased leg and trying to ease it into a comfortable position. Pain throbbed, held back by tabs; and, light-headed, I thought, *Here am I in a shuttlecraft of the PanOceania multicorporate Company, on telestre land in Melkathi* – And not far inland of us now is the place where Orhlandis *telestre* burned, one summer, eight years ago.

If you had seen this then, *amari* Ruric, what would you have done?

The cabin floor vibrated as the shuttle rose. I reached to key in a holotank image. The comlink crackled with transmissions from other shuttles – refuelled at Kumiel, and gone out again? – flying surveillance over the Hundred Thousand: Melkathi and Rimon and Ymir, the city Tathcaer and the Oranon River valley. . . .

Land is burning, now. The white city is burning, its pale plaster-walled buildings smashed open; and Citadel crag is smashed; and what dead lie in the wreckage, and what hurt and unrescued – ? *If we had generations, it might heal.*

Corazon Mendez leaned over to key out the volume of the comlink transmission, and I said, "Leave it."

Comprehension came. She didn't speak, and the pilot was silent as he swung the big craft round and set a course to the south-west; and the quiet of the cabin was broken only by the comlink's crackle and hiss: thick with interference.

Don't let it clear.

If that goes, it will be the first intimation that the Tower no longer functions; and that the barriers against the spread of ancient light have been broken down.

And the hours of the night pass, this ship racing above the ocean, as the dawn line races at our heels. The stars move in their ritual patterns, and this earth turns towards the morning –

I sat at the holotank, watching the images of night and the bitter sea.

Nothing has happened, nothing is happening –

The seat was uncomfortable, the cabin hot. Cory Mendez sat by the pilot, saying nothing. I leaned back from the holotank, rubbing at my hip.

Half a year. . . . Impossible, I thought. Six months ago I stepped on to Orthean soil, outside that city without walls; and Molly with me; what did we think we were going to do? Aid the starving and win profits for the Company? Ah, it seems incredible. How could we have guessed, then, that it would lead to this?

My mouth was sour and dry. I manoeuvred myself up to get a pain-tab and a drink from the console, pausing to listen to the comlink. No words distinguishable now, only the hiss and spark of a radiant interference: *counter-radiation, a suppressor. . . .*

I didn't go to the cabin at the rear of the shuttlecraft, where her body lies.

As I sat down, staring into a holotank that showed only blackness, I thought, *But it was inevitable.*

Once such destructive power is created, it will be used. No matter that years pass, and millennia; that is only a hiatus. The universe is older than comprehension and time is infinite. In time, it has been only a tick of the clock since that great Empire fell: this was implicit from the beginning. . . .

I thought of Calil's face, drained of all vision. *I want something I had, or saw, or heard of, long ago. . . . I have sensed it sometimes in the way light and haze and shadow fall.* And then: *That desire wouldn't be assuaged now by the having of it . . . it awakens the real desire, of which that is only a shadow and a memory.*

And my head is full of visions, hers and mine and history's: the face of Santhendor'lin-sandru, and that great city, and the slave race that gave into their hands the power to destroy a world, and which came first? The power to consume all earth in annihilation, or the desire for that bright shadow?

For a moment I believe that I felt it, that same triumph that Calil bel-Rioch dreams in one of the Goddess's houses, a continent away to the north; and then I had a sudden memory of how, all one long afternoon, we had played *ochmir* in the great square under the Citadel, Haltern and Blaize and I; how Ruric and her child Rodion waited with us, waiting to hear, at Midsummer-Tenyear, the name of the new Crown of the Hundred Thousand – *which will never happen again.* That is true, whatever happens now. And –

After so much, to lose by so little, when we thought we'd won.

Night passed, clouds blocked the stars and then cleared as we flew southwards; cased in that small craft that sped on, five miles above the surface of the ocean. A speck inching across the face of the world: drawing steadily away from the northern continent, the *telestres*, the outbreaks of fighting; coming closer all the while to a desert coast and deserted canals, and a city that lies in the shadow of the Rasrhe-y-Meluur.

Corazon Mendez moved between the comlink console and the holotank, studying the heat-sensor images that the satellites transmitted from orbit.

"Nothing yet. . . ." The black-uniformed woman slumped down into a seat beside me. She rubbed at her eyes. "I can't raise Kumiel, but I imagine Clifford is following us. The troops in the F90s should arrive at least an hour before we do; I'll have them turn that settlement inside out."

"If there's anything there, they'll find it." I checked the course in the data-tank. "Estimate we'll get there inside two hours from now."

I looked round the narrow, cramped cabin. The thrum of power vibrated through the metal walls; and figures changed constantly in the 'tank, feeding in navigation-details, bright in the dim light. Tension made a hard knot in my chest, and I thought *Do we dare hope?* Oh yes: in the face of all the evidence!

And I turned my head briefly to look down at the door of that closed cabin, behind which lies the body of *amari* Ruric Orhlandis, Ruric Hexenmeister. *When I am in the Tower, when I inherit her memories with the memories of others who were Hexenmeister, then I'll know – if she ever forgave me for coming here: s'aranthi, offworlder, human.* Is that a petty consideration, in this clash of worlds? Yes: but I can't comprehend worlds, only her.

Silence.

Cory's head came up, I had time to think, *What's missing?* and realize that the hiss of comlink interference no longer filled this cabin; and the transmission broke through clearly –

" *– massive power-discharge! All craft out of the area; repeat, out of the area –* "

Alarms blared. The satellite-image in the holotank cut out for a split second. It refocused: the pattern of heat-sensor readings leaping wildly. And then all in a minute became still.

Corazon Mendez looked in blank disbelief at the hologram-images.

Lights flashed on the comlink console, and transmissions blared, frantic voices overriding each other with questions, and each voice sounded with no distortion: clear and complete, in the silence.

*

522

Earth turns, faster than we travel.

The dawn line raced across the sea, passing us, leaving in its wake fire and foam, and the morning white and gold. The Company shuttle flew low now, at ten thousand feet. The images in the holotank showed storm clouds massing along the southern horizon.

And over that horizon, in the heart of the southern continent that the Witchbreed called Elansiir, weather-patterns are shifting out of constrictions they have endured for millennia, and now endure no longer.

Is it hours or seconds that pass?

The shuttle's cabin grew hot; loud with the transmissions coming from other shuttles, from the base nine hundred miles away on Kumiel Island, from the Company station in its earth-circling orbit. Corazon Mendez left her seat and took the pilot's place; the routine of flight needing all her concentration now; and the officer came to stand beside me where I stared down into the holotank. Visual images: clear and precise.

Flying south, to the Desert Coast.

We came in over the sea, casting a moving shadow on the blue water. The wide dome of the sky was azure, and thick with white daystars; and on the southern horizon clouds began to rise up into the stratosphere.

Some things are too big to be seen: I had been staring for whole minutes before I saw that here there was no skylined *chiruzeth* spire. The blue-grey of the Rasrhe-y-Meluur gone – and then the shuttle dipped low, and we passed over titanic ruins: the deep ocean itself not sufficient to cover them. Deep green water washed over *chiruzeth* that is splintered, tumbled like an avalanche into the sea covering the continental shelf.

A very few minutes after that, the shuttle reached land.

Walls breached, buildings shattered: the floodwater of those vast tidal waves still washes through the harbour of Kasabaarde. We are too high to see more than moving specks, high above panic and terror and destruction. I thought dreamily, *Earthquake waves*, awed by the magnitude of such destruction; a destruction whose epicentre lay a little to the south. Dust still hung in the stratosphere, dispersing slowly. And below –

Now there is no trade-quarter, those ramshackle buildings are gone, and the *jath* ships driven on to rocks or into deep water. Now there is no inner city, those white domes turned to powder.

And where the Tower stood is a crater, quarter of a mile across and eight hundred feet deep; sensors in this ship perceiving through a haze of pulverized rock no life, no recognizable structure, no stone upon stone left standing.

Because we have entered the city, a wasteland will grow here. Because we have entered the city, great ones will go to corruption. We are the bringers of death. Go you and cry: we are dead and come to corruption, in this resurgence of that ancient light.

By noon, a raw wind was blowing. The sky cleared, bright and daystarred, and the wind blew in gusts that tugged at the grounded shuttlecraft, and shook it where it rested on the rocky earth.

The dome of the sky shone clear above me, and Carrick's Star dazzled from other shuttles a little way off. Dust skirled. The diggers in Company uniforms rested on the haft of the machine, swore, and then manoeuvred it back to carving a slit trench in the ground.

I rested, leaning on my stick, and the wind tugged at me. All around stretches the barren rock and earth of the Desert Coast, a glint of sea there between low hills; and there, in the west, the sky that should hold the *chiruzeth* pinnacle of the Rasrhe-y-Meluur, and that sky is empty now. And at my feet, shrouded for a burial which is not the custom of her people, lies *amari* Ruric Orhlandis, Ruric Hexenmeister. And the wind blows.

No, I thought fiercely, not *your* failure. If this hadn't happened in your lifetime it would have been in someone else's; no one should have to take decisions like these! There *are* no all-knowing, infallible authorities – not my people, and not Ortheans; and no, not even in the Tower.

Southward, the low hills of the Elansiir stand out distinctly, as if they stand out against a raw light.

The Company men backed the excavator out of the grave in a flurry of dust; and as they did so, I saw other people approaching from the shuttles. Corazon Mendez walked ahead of the others, carrying herself stiffly, and at her shoulder came Doug Clifford, speaking in a furious undertone that as he halted burst into speech: "If not for your ships firing, your provocation, this would never have happened!"

The Peace Force commander swung round on him, her face drawn, and said incredulously, "*Provocation!* I couldn't let Company personnel be fired on and do nothing. Your business is to keep the situation from getting to that stage, *envoy*; why didn't you?"

"Don't – " It isn't right that we should argue over a grave as if it were offal we're burying!

They fell silent. Closer to the shuttles there were guards, and I squinted against the sun, and saw a dark Orthean male amongst them; realized then that Pathrey Shanataru must still have been on Kumiel, and would have been brought here by Doug, and *what does it matter, now?* If we learn the names of whatever Harantish Ortheans brought Trade technology into the city of Kasabaarde; and exactly what kind of equipment it was; does it matter?

524

Another Orthean walked past the guards, crossing the stretch of rocky earth between the shuttles and this makeshift grave. Walking in the raw air, eyes veiled against noon: a male with a yellow mane, in mercenary's gear, and with *harur*-blades, and with a face half masked by the scar of an old burn. . . . Blaize Meduenin stopped, and glanced down at her shrouded body.

"You should give her the passing of fire," he said, "it's the custom of the Hundred Thousand."

Noon shadow pooled blackly at his feet. I reached out a hand but he stepped back. That scarred face turns to the sky, as if he can see past daystars to inhabited worlds, to the worlds of the Heart Stars and the Home Stars, to Earth. As if he can feel urgent voices on WEBcasts, recriminations already beginning. . . .

"You can leave worlds behind you," he said. "Where can we go, who can't leave this earth and live?" His face twisted with disgust.

Doug Clifford interrupted: "You're as much to blame for this as any of us, *T'An*; you fought the *hiyeks*!"

The light on the horizon is silver: older than Time.

"No, don't – please – "

The noon sun of Carrick V shines down with a radiance that is fragile and bright and powerless; shines down on Ortheans, Envoy, Representative, Commander; who stand as if this is a ritual that we must conclude.

Our quarrelling voices rise over this barren land, and the unfilled grave where scavengers already gather.

THE END

APPENDICES AND MAPS

APPENDIX 1

Glossary

Ai-Telestre – literally the Hundred Thousand, traditionally all the *telestres* existing between the Wall of the World in the north, the Inner Sea to the south, the Eastern Sea, and the Glittering Plain to the west. Unified by Kerys Founder after the fall of the Golden Empire.

amari – 'born of no mother; motherless'. A term used in the Hundred Thousand, referring to a child born of a non-*telestre* mother (and usually a *telestre* father; but possibly adopted *n'ri n'suth*). The child is motherless in the sense that it is not of the earth of the Hundred Thousand; thus the *amari* are always slightly feared or shunned, since a different inflection can make this mean 'without the (mother) Goddess'. It has both a descriptive and a condemnatory use.

arniac – a small shrub that grows in the infertile soil of the Desert Coast. Broad red leaves, black berries, growing to a height of half a metre. The leaf when dried is used to make herb-tea, and the berries are a cure for headaches and fevers.

arykei – literally 'bed-friend', lover, pair-bond (in some rarer cases, a triple or quadruple bond occurs). Given that the care of children in the *telestre* is communal, the *arykei* relationship is not child-based, but depends on mutual temporary or long-term attraction.

ashiren – a child, nominally under fourteen; literally one who has not yet attained adult gender. Diminutive: *ashiren-te.*

ashirenin – one permanently *ashiren*, one who does not change to adult gender at age 13–15 but remains neuter. Change then occurs between the ages of 30 and 35, and invariably results in death. The *ashirenin* are rare, said to have strange qualities for good or ill. Most famous of the *ashirenin* is Beth'ru-elen.

ataile – tough-leafed herb growing mostly in Melkathi and the Rimon and Ymirian hills. When chewed, the leaves produce a mildly narcotic effect, and are addictive.

becamil – the webweaver-beetle, giving its name to the tough multi-coloured waterproof fabric spun from its web. Hives are kept commercially all over the Hundred Thousand.

Beth'ru-elen – called Beth'ru-elen *Ashirenin*, a latent Orthean who died at 35 during late change to female. Reformer and revolutionary. During exile from Morvren Freeport spent time in Kasabaarde's inner city, formulated the philosophical and religious insights that led to the reformation of the church of the Goddess. Later became *s'an* of one of the six founding *telestres* of Peir-Dadeni: the *n'ri n'suth* line is still in existence.

brennior – large quadruped used as draught-beast in the Desert regions. Sand-coloured, thick hide, tri-padded foot, tailless. Short flexible snout. Poor sight, good hearing. Omnivore.

Brown Tower – home of the Hexenmeister in Kasabaarde's inner city. Founded some ten thousand years ago on the ruins of an Eldest Empire settlement, for the preservation of knowledge. Most of the underground installations are defunct, though it is still said to have connections with the Rasrhe-y-Meluur and the ruins under the Elansiir. One of the two sole remaining instances of viable Golden technology.

chirith-goyen – or clothworm, the fibre-spinning larvae of the *chirith-goyen* fly. The fibre is woven into a light fabric throughout the Hundred Thousand, and is easily dyed.

chiruzeth – a substance created either by the Golden Witchbreed, or by their predecessors. It has been described as a semi-sentient crystal, manipulated by mental energy; and as a substance in some way analagous to human DNA/RNA. Techniques for altering it from its present inert form have been lost.

dekany – tuberous weed found in shallow waters of the Inner Sea; useful for rope-fibre but not for much else.

del'ri – staple crop of the Desert Coast, a bamboo-like plant with edible seeds in the knobbed stems. Pale green, growing to a height of 2–2½ metres. Harvested twice a year.

Desert Coast – general name given to that part of the southern continent that borders on the Inner Sea, and to the various ports and city-states there. Cut off from the wastelands of the interior by the Elansiir mountain range.

Earthspeaker – sometimes called the Landless. An office held by the members of the church of the Goddess after their training at the theocratic houses. They travel the Hundred Thousand, giving up their own *telestres*, and acting in a multitude of roles which may include priest, agrarian advisor, psychologist, healer, etc. The extent of their authority is impossible to define.

Emperor-in-Exile – hereditary ruler of Kel Harantish, chosen from the lineal half-breed descendants of Santhendor'lin-sandru's imperial dynasty. A tyrant with absolute authority in Harantish's highly-structured society. Claims the ancient right of ruling both northern and southern continents as the Golden Empire did.

fenborn – aboriginal race of Carrick V, now reduced in number and confined mainly to settlements in the Greater and Lesser Fens. Oviparous night-hunters living in a stone-age culture. In the past carried out raids of considerable ferocity on north Rimon and Roehmonde, but have remained within the fen-borders since Galen Honeymouth's treaty with them some two hundred years ago.

Fens – the Greater and Lesser Fens: marsh and fenland covering some two thousand square miles, paralleling the Wall of the World and separating the provinces of Roehmonde (to which it is comparable in size) and Peir-Dadeni. Not least among the dangerous fauna are the fenborn.

ferrorn – see *ochmir* appendix.

galeni – a term used by the aboriginal Orthean species, the fenborn, to refer to

530

that humanoid race now more generally regarded as 'Ortheans' (who are the product of genetic engineering, cross-breeding fenborn and the Golden Witchbreed). *Galeni* derives from the first *T'An Suthai-Telestre* to ensure the Greater and Lesser Fens were regarded as fenborn territory, the *T'An* Galen Kerys-Andrethe, called Galen Honeymouth.

Goddess – sometimes referred to as the Mother or the Sunmother, or occasionally the Wellmother. A sun and earth deity. The church was designed and set up by Kerys Founder as an anti-technology device after the fall of the Witchbreed. It was later transformed by Beth'ru-elen *Ashirenin* into a genuine religious movement. Now more of a philosophical discipline including a reverence for all life, and a recognition of reincarnation. They hold that their spirits pass through many bodies, reuniting in death with the fire of the Goddess ('fire' and 'spirit' have the same root-word in most Orthean languages); the main heresy holds that this is merely genetically inherited memory – possibly why the Hexenmeister is regarded with such deep distrust.

Golden Empire – the five-thousand-year rule of the Witchbreed race, under whose autocratic rule the two continents enjoyed peace, prosperity, and total slavery. Ended by Thel Siawn's infertility virus, which gave rise to a war that devastated most of the southern continent, left the cities and land north of the Wall of the World in ruins, and is still visible in the transformation of Eriel to the Glittering Plain.

hanelys – commonly called tanglebush, a plant propagating itself by runners; 2–3 metres high, stems very hard black fibre with long thorns, yellow leaves during Hanys and Merrum, and small orange fruit in Stathern.

harur-nilgiri, harur-nazari – traditional paired blades, the former a kind of short rapier, the latter a kind of long knife. Used ambidextrously. Common throughout the Hundred Thousand.

Hexenmeister – ruler of Kasabaarde, guardian of stored knowledge, and a sequentially immortal personality. Head of an information-gathering network that spans two continents.

hiyannek – term of endearment on the Desert Coast, 'best blood', that is, best-descended.

hiyek – translates literally as 'bloodline', in the sense of family or lineage. The *hiyek* is the matrilineal-descent family upon which Desert Coast society is structured; and given their dependence on the canal system, it is perhaps not surprising that the root-word can also be translated as 'water'. Blood is understood to be the carrier of past-memories within individual bloodlines. Whether this means that Coast Ortheans assume themselves reborn within the same bloodline, or only allow themselves memories that reinforce this concept, is unclear. A drug used to access these memories, *keret-nen-hiyek*, can thus be translated either as 'Blood of Memory' or 'Water of Truth'.

hura – species of hard-shelled water clam found in rivers throughout the Hundred Thousand.

jath – double-masted, ocean-going vessel, usually with lateen sails; design originating in Morvren Freeport.

jath-rai – single-masted small coaster or fishing boat.

K'Ai Kezrian-kezriakor – a Harantish term translating as 'Emperor/Empress-in-Exile', applied to the descendants (or supposed descendants) of Santhendor'lin-sandru, the Last Emperor of the Golden Witchbreed. The *K'Ai Kezrian-kezriakor* rules the settlement Kel Harantish, and the canal system upon which the *hiyek*-families depend for their survival. The 'exile' referred to is from the territory covered by the Golden Empire: the northern and southern continental land-masses. Abbreviation: *K'Ai*, Empress/Emperor.

Kasabaarde – a Desert Coast city with curious philosophies and influences. Sited at the point between the southern continent and the Kasabaarde Archipelago, gaining wealth from trade and tolls. Divided into trade-quarter and inner city, the latter run by the Order houses; both under the authority of the Hexenmeister.

kazsis – usually called *kazsis*-nightflower, a vine native to Ymir and Rimon. Bronze leaves, dark red blooms, the scent is particularly noticeable after dark.

ke, kir – neutral pronoun used for the young of the Orthean species, and sometimes for the Goddess.

kekri-fly – an insect with a short segmented body and triple paired wings; coloured blue, green, or black, with reflecting wing-surfaces. Fond of sewage.

Kel Harantish – once a garrison outpost of the Golden Empire, now one of the smaller Desert Coast city-states. Completely dependent on imports for survival. Home of the last surviving descendants of the Golden Witchbreed, and the Emperor-in-Exile.

keretne – translates as 'eldest blood', 'truthful memory', and refers to those Coast Ortheans, not necessarily old in a physiological sense, who have by gift and training a close access to their past-memories. The *hiyeks*, being mobile, have little use for literacy and records; they therefore rely on this oral culture-store.

Kerys Founder – credited with spreading the *telestre* system that arose after the fall of the Golden Empire, of unifying the Hundred Thousand and founding the Kerys *telestre* at Tathcaer. Led the first crusade against Kel Harantish, and began the Hundred Thousand's long association with the Brown Tower. Set up the church of the Goddess to prevent the rise of another industrial society.

Kirriach – ruined city over the Wall of the World, once known as aKirrik. Part of the Golden Empire's middle province, now called the Barrens, along with Simmerath, Hinkuumiel, Mirane, etc.

lapuur – the feathery-leaved tree of south Ymir, Rimon, and Melkathi; pale green trailing foliage, main trunk growing to a height of 3–4 metres.

leremoc – see *ochmir* appendix.

l'ri-an – one who is learning a trade or performing a paid service; usually a young adult or *ashiren*. Literally: apprentice.

makre – a form of double-lobed grain flourishing in temperate areas of the Hundred Thousand; particularly north Ymir, Rimon, and parts of southern Roehmonde.

marhaz – the common *telestre* riderbeast, referred to as *marhaz*-mare, *marhaz-*

stallion, *marhaz*-gelding; of reptilian ancestry like the *skurrai*. Cleft hooves, and a double pair of horns. The thick shaggy pelt is composed of feather-structured fibres. Enduring rather than speedy.

marshflower – skin blemish: a dappled pattern sometimes said to resemble the marshfern, and to be more common in those *telestres* that border the Great Fens.

Melkathi – that province distinguished by the Melkath language, comprising the Melkathi peninsula and the Kadareth Islands, the *T'An* Melkathi being resident in Ales-Kadareth. The most infertile *telestres* of all the Hundred Thousand, the most reluctant to accept Crown rule. Mostly comprised of heathland, bog, marshes, and sand-flats. Ales-Kadareth has the name of being an old Witchbreed city, pirate port, and home of strange sciences. Famous for atheists, malcontents, heresy, and rebellion.

meshabi – robe worn by Coast Ortheans, consisting of a length of *del'ri*-cloth belted at the hip; a superfluous fold of which can be brought up to hood the head and back.

Morvren – small cluster of *telestres* holding land round the mouth of the Ai River; the Seamarshal is resident in the Freeport itself. Freeport has links with the Rasrhe-y-Meluur, Kasabaarde, and the Desert Coast; its language is a south-Dadeni dialect. A great maritime trading centre famous for voyages to strange places, river-craft, false coins, sharp practice, odd visitors, bureaucracy, and general moral irresponsibility. Rumoured to trade with Kel Harantish.

mossgrass – staple vegetation of the Hundred Thousand, a stringy-fronded species of lichen that roots shallowly in topsoil. Seasonal changes in colour.

n'ri n'suth – 'adopted into the *telestre* of': literally translates as brother-sister. A *telestre* child bears its mother's name, its own name, and the *telestre*'s name.

ochmir – see Appendix 2.

Peir-Dadeni – the newest province, founded five hundred years ago by a group of rebels from Morvren Freeport. Follows the Ai River, bounded on the west by the Glittering Plain, and on the east, stretches from Morvren and Rimon up past Dadeni Heath to the Fens, and the Wall of the World. Keeps the pass at Broken Stair guarded. One founder was the reformer Beth'ru-elen, another the assassin Lori L'Ku, and another was Andrethe, from whom the ruling *telestre* takes its name. Famous for river-craft, trade, dubious frontiers, legends of Berani and the Eriel Frostdrakes; for the Heath's *skurrai*, the river-port of Shiriya-Shenin, and for mad riders. Swears alliance with, rather than allegiance to, the *T'An Suthai-Telestre*.

raiku – the basic unit of the *hiyek*: a group-marriage. The *ashiren* of the Desert Coast families will spend a year alone in the cities of the Coast, forming small groups of four, five, or six, that will become their *raiku*: a lifelong bond of emotional and physical interdependence. This will often include members of the same birth, and stay within one bloodline; though exogamy is not frowned on. *Raiku* are numbered according to the groups formed within one year. *Kei-raiku*: one who is outside the *raiku*, either by not yet having joined, or by losing one's group by the deaths of the other members, or – very rarely – by expulsion.

Rainbow Cities – general name given to the settlements in the tropical regions of the southern continent, of which only Saberon and Cuthanc are large enough to be properly called cities.

rashaku – generic term for the lizardbird having the appearance of a small archeopteryx. Feathered wings, scaled breast and body. Four clawed feet, the front pair greatly atrophied; gold eyes with nictitating membrane. Distinctive metallic call. Size and plumage colour vary according to habitat: from the white of the *rashaku-bazur* (sea) to the black and brown of the *rashaku-dya* (hill country). Other varieties include the *rashaku-nai* (fens) and *kur-rashaku* (mountains).

rashaku-relay – the Wellkeepers train a species of *rashaku*-lizardbird in the carrying of messages between Wellhouses. The *rashaku-dya*, with its acute colour-vision, is most often used; they are trained to respond and fly to different destinations when shown different colour-codes.

Rasrhe-y-Meluur – commonly called Bridge Alley, a remnant of Golden Empire engineering; being a suspended tunnel-structure built on pylons from Morvren Freeport down the Kasabaarde Archipelago to Kasabaarde itself. Still passable, though inhabited.

Rimon – central province, bordering the Inner Sea between Morvren and Tathcaer, sharing the Oranon River border with Ymir. Downland country, lightly wooded, having one main river, the Meduin. Famous for *marhaz*, grain, vines, wine, and border-river disputes with Ymir. The *T'An* Rimon is resident in Medued.

Roehmonde – northern province bounded by Ymir, the Lesser Fens, the Wall of the World, and the Eastern Sea. Hilly forested country, famous for mining, metal-working, charcoal-burning and hunting. The *T'An* Roehmonde is resident in Corbek, a city that never wholly accepted Beth'ru-elen's reformation of the church. There are few large ports on the inhospitable eastern coast. Roehmonde is one of the largest and most sparsely inhabited provinces, a country of insular *telestres*. They guard one of the great passes down from the Barrens, the Path of Skulls.

ruesse – a substance, derived by a method which is unclear, from certain glands of the *brennior*-packbeast. Ingested, it causes paralysis of the respiratory system in Ortheans, death following rapidly. Its effects on humans are similar but much less severe. To humans, also, it has a characteristic scent, reminiscent of roses; this is undetectable by Ortheans.

rukshi – land arthropods, small and segmented with patterned shells and two pairs of claws. Now rare.

s'an telestre – landholder, elected to office by the adult members of the *telestre*, and having unspecified authority. More of an administrator than ruler, having more responsibility than power. The *telestre* is held in trust for the Goddess.

s'aranthi – a human, or humanoid offworlder. This derives from *S'aranth*, a name given to the first contact envoy in the Hundred Thousand, and translates literally as 'one who does not carry *harur*-blades', one who is weaponless. It is ironic that this should come to be applied to hi-tech offworlders as a general term.

saryl-kabriz – an organic poison, fatal to Orthean life, distilled from the bark of the *saryl-kabriz* bush. Has a characteristic sharp scent, difficult to mask. Not to be confused with

saryl-kiez – a similar shrub, brown with blue berries. The sap, unlike that of the *saryl-kabriz*, is not a poison. It can be used as lamp oil; the scent is pungent.

seri – unit of distance, equal to one and one-fifth miles on the standard Earth scale.

shan'tai – 'one outside the *hiyek*, or bloodline', a stranger. This term of address on the Desert Coast can, according to inflection, have varying implicit degrees of welcome or rejection. The respectful greeting *kethrial-shamaz shan'tai* is an invitation to share water/blood/hospitality on a temporary basis.

siir – a thick-boled vine or creeper, fungoid, growing to a height of several metres, and spreading to cover wide areas of ground. In the Hundred Thousand it is allowed to spore; the yellow spore cases are then gathered and fermented into a green wine-like liquid. The effect on a human is slightly hallucinogenic. The name *siir* derives from a Witchbreed term meaning 'fertile'. The plant was possibly created through their bio-engineering as an all-purpose food crop. A further derivation leads to the *Elansiir*, the 'garden' or 'harvest-field', a name applied to the central region of the southern continent, now made barren by war damage.

siiran – 'shelter'; one of the underground chambers of the Desert Coast canal system, used as habitations, and also used to grow crops in uninhabitable areas. The term suggests a link with the Witchbreed food-crop *siir*, and possibly the canal system was constructed to raise these plants. Climatological changes following on war damage in the central Elansiir means that *siir* itself rarely flourishes on the Coast now.

skurrai – the *telestre* packbeast, referred to as *skurrai*-mare, *skurrai*-stallion, *skurrai*-gelding; double-horned and reptilian; basically a smaller stockier version of the *marhaz*.

skurrai-jasin – the *skurrai*-drawn carriage common in Tathcaer.

Sunmother – see **Goddess**.

takshiriye – the court or government attached to the *T'An Suthai-Telestre*, resident in Tathcaer (and Shiriya-Shenin during the winter season).

T'An – the administrator of a province: *t'an*, general polite term for strangers and visitors. Derives from 'guest'.

T'An Suthai-Telestre – in the informal inflection, the Crown of the Hundred Thousand. Self-chosen from the *T'Ans* of all the provinces, re-elected on every tenth midsummer solstice. The unifier of church and *telestres*.

Tathcaer – capital of the Hundred Thousand, an island-city solely under Crown law, sometimes called the eighth province. Home of every *T'An Suthai-Telestre* since Kerys Founder. The Hundred Thousand have each a *telestre*-house in the city; also there are the Guild-*telestres*.

telestre – the basic unit of Hundred Thousand society, a community of any number between fifty and five hundred Ortheans living on an area of land. This unit is self-supporting, including agriculture, arts, and crafts. The *telestre* system rose spontaneously out of the chaos that followed the fall of the Golden Empire. Given the natural Orthean tendency to form groups, and their talent for making the earth yield, the *telestre* is their natural habitat.

tha'adur – a Peir-Dadeni term for the Andrethe's court and governing officials resident in the city Shiriya-Shenin.

The Kyre – a province of remote *telestres* in the mountains that lie south of the Wall of the World and north of the Glittering Plain. Very insular in character, occasionally trading with Peir-Dadeni. Mostly they subsist on hunting. The province is very sparsely populated; the *T'An* Kyre is resident in Ivris, a market *telestre*. Famous for milk, cheese, wood-carving, mountain-craft, and lack of humour, popularly supposed to be a result of the appalling weather.

thousandflower – mosslike plant growing in woodlands over most of the Hundred Thousand, forms a thick carpet 10–15 cms deep, and varies in colour from light to dark blue.

thurin – see *ochmir* appendix.

tukinna – evergreen tree, thin-boled with black bark, twisted limbs, growing to a height of 10 metres. Foliage concentrated at the crown: scroll-like leaves, small black inedible seeds. Prefers northern climates (like Roehmonde forests).

Wall of the World – gigantic geological slip-fault that has split the northern continent in a northeast–southwest division; being now a range of mountains in which there are only two known passes from the Barrens to the Hundred Thousand: Broken Stair and the Path of Skulls. The barren land north of the Wall is occupied by barbarian tribes living in the ruined cities of the Golden Witchbreed.

Wellkeeper – title given to those members of the church who give up their own *telestre* to run the Wellhouses, sometimes called theocratic houses. These may be places of worship, of philosophy and refuge; working communes for adults or *ashiren*; universities or other places of learning; weapons training houses; or craft workshops.

Witchbreed – sometimes known as the Golden. Originally the humanoid race brought to Carrick V as servitors to the Eldest Empire – this being an apocryphal name given to the alien settlers who first landed some twenty thousand years ago, but died out soon after that. Nothing is known of the 'Eldest Empire', but it left its mark in the genetic structure of both the Witchbreed and the native race of Orthe. The Witchbreed had great talent for using and developing the technology that was left to them, and made use of both the physical and sociological sciences. They fell to a sterility virus. Sporadic instances of interbreeding took place between Witchbreed and Ortheans, but in general the two species are not inter-fertile.

Ymir – the oldest province, with the most archaic form of language; occupying the land east of the Oranon that lies between Melkathi and Roehmonde. Good grazing on the Downs, good soil in the lowlands, and the many tributaries of the Oranon make this one of the richest provinces, famous for good harvests. The *T'An* Ymir is resident in Tathcaer. The *telestres* close to the city are famed for ship-building. Ymir is known for its theocratic houses, traders and merchants, beast-tamers, eccentricities of all kinds, and the most convoluted argumentative minds outside of Kasabaarde.

ziku – broad-leaved deciduous tree with edible fruit, grows to a height of 7 metres. Bronze-red foliage, dusty-blue fruit. Common in Ymir and Peir-Dadeni, preferring to grow near water. Hybrid form grown in Rimon with larger and more plentiful fruit, harvested in Stathern.

zilmei – found in north Roehmonde and Peir-Dadeni forests. Black and grey pelts, wedge-shaped skulls, and retractable claws. A bad-tempered carnivore. Distinctive hooting cry.

APPENDIX 2

Ochmir

A game played in the Hundred Thousand, originating in the cities but popular everywhere. It is played on a hexagonal board divided into 216 triangular grid-spaces. The 216 counters are double-sided, the ideogram-characters traditionally blue-on-white and white-on-blue; and are divided into *ferrorn*, which must remain stationary when placed on the board; *thurin*, which may move one space (across a line, not an angle); and *leremoc*, which have complete freedom of movement. The object of the game is to have all the pieces on the board showing one's chosen colour.

This is accomplished by forcing a reversal of the opposition's counters, by gaining a majority of colour in a minor hexagon. The 6-triangle minor hexagons form a shifting, overlapping framework.

The distribution of characters means that a counter may or may not have a duplicate value on its reverse side; it is thus necessary to remember when placing a counter what is on the obverse.

A 'hand' of counters is drawn, sight unseen, from the *ochmir* bag on every sixth turn (a hand on Orthe is six). Only one move or placement can be made per turn, unless this results in a majority in a minor hexagon, in which case all the counter reversals are carried out. Since majorities are retrospective, the turning of one hexagon to one colour will affect the hexagon-frames overlapping it.

There are no restrictions on where on the board a game may begin, and it is usual for two or three separate pattern-conflicts to be set up. It is the *ferrorn* that determines the area of conflict.

Ochmir can also be played with three players (blue-white-brown), in which case the number of spaces that need be occupied for a majority in the minor hexagons decreases from 5 or 4 to 3. In this case there is also the shifting balance of alliances between players; and the game ends when one player gains the 144-counter majority of one colour.

A player may not turn own-colour counters to reverse. In the case of a 3–3 split in a minor hexagon it is left until the shifting framework divides it up amongst other hexagons. The game can be played with retrospective reversals even when all 216 counters are on the board. *Ochmir* is not only about gaining control, but about keeping it afterwards.

The game is based on manipulation, not territory; and on mobility rather than on rank. The value of the counters shift with the game; a player's own counters are also those of the opposition. These themes of interdependence, mobility, manipulation, and control have led some authorities to see a connection between *ochmir* and *Ai-Telestre*, and even to equate *ferrorn*, *thurin*, and *leremoc* with *s'an telestre*, *T'An*, and *T'An Suthai-Telestre*.

538

APPENDIX 3

The Calendar of the Hundred Thousand

WINTER SOLSTICE: New year festival.

ORVENTA: the longest season, 11 weeks. Winter. Favourite season for the custom of keeping *telezu*. No trade, travel, planting, etc., due to bad weather. One of the two main periods of activity for *takshiriye* and *tha'adur* in residence in Shiriya-Shenin. Practice of arts, music, sciences, etc. Usually the First Thaw festival occurs around Tenthweek.

SPRING SOLSTICE: festival of the Wells.

HANYS: 3 weeks. Spring ploughing and planting: busy time for the *telestres*. Prevailing westerly winds. Floods. Inner Sea liable to sudden storms.

DURESTHA: Early summer, 8 weeks. Long spells of hot weather. Travel possible, roads repaired. Guild ships leave for Desert Coast and Rainbow Cities.

SUMMER SOLSTICE: Naming day and midyear festival.

MERRUM: 9 weeks, high summer. Period of great administrative activity in the *takshiriye*, resident in Tathcaer. Favourite season for travel, trade, sea voyages, etc.

STATHERN: 2 weeks. Everything stops for the harvest. Culminates in

AUTUMN SOLSTICE: harvest festivals.

TORVERN: 4 weeks, early autumn hunting season; also the time for fairs and markets. The last season for travel before winter weather makes the Inner Sea impassable.

RIARDH: 7 weeks. Hunting season. The beginning of winter, preparation of provisions, storing food, weaving, etc. Some late autumn sowing. Usually includes First Snow Festival.

Note: the week consists of nine days, of which every Firstday is a feast-day, every Fiveday a holiday, and every Nineday a fast-day. The day has a length of 27 standard hours. With a 400-day year, this means that in practice the Orthean year is 85 days (12 weeks) longer than the Earth standard year.

ORTHE

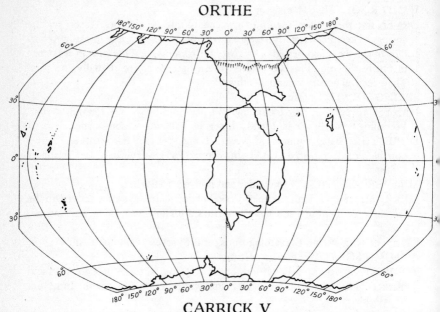

CARRICK V
from PanOceania Company Records

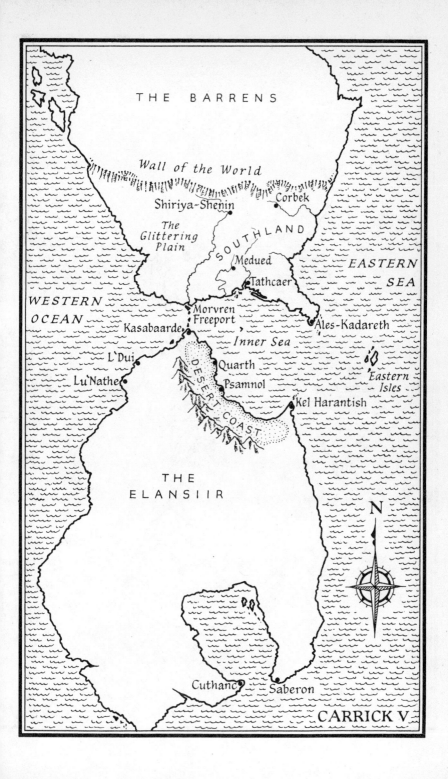